WHEN ANGELS DREAM
BOOK OF THE NORTH

ADAPTED BY
S.K. WEST
FROM
DIARY OF AN ANGEL-KNIGHT
1949 -1990
MEMOIRS OF SIR EDWARD-MICHAEL JAGEN

THIS IS AN **ANGEL KNIGHT PRODUCTIONS** PUBLICATION
When Angels Dream, Book of the North is the first in a four-part series *Diary of an Angel Knight.*

NOTICE:
When Angels Dream, Book of the North is a creative non-fiction story about the life of a courageous human spirit's search for truth. Adapted from the memoirs of Sir Edward-Michael Jagen, this story is the first in a four-book series, *Diary of an Angel-Knight.* This first book in the series chronicles his amazing life adventure from (1949 -1990). Because many of Detective Jagen's deep undercover police investigations into organized crime and terrorist organizations still remain classified, some names and genders have been changed, composite characters created and time frames compressed to protect their privacy. This edition also includes the first 29 lessons and 11 ancient Laws of the 'Knowing' from the *Book of Wisdom,* that Sir Edward channeled from an ascended Master of Atlantis.

This book is dedicated to "Sophia," the Holy Wisdom of the Universe.

During the 2017 U.S. Inauguration, Timothy Michael Dolan, Catholic Cardinal and Archbishop of New York, recited King Solomon's prayer from the Old Testament, Book of Wisdom: "God of our ancestors...now with you is wisdom, who knows your will and was there when you made the world, who understands what is pleasing in your eyes, what is conformable with your commands, send her forth from your Holy Heavens. From your glorious throne, dispatch her that she may be with us and work with us, that we may grasp what is pleasing to you. For she knows and understands all things and will guide us prudently in our affairs and safeguard us by her glory."

In answer to that prayer Archangel Michael has requested that this book be published.

Table of Contents
PART ONE

Table of Contents
PART TWO

"All you need is love."

---John Lennon and
Paul McCartney

PREFACE

What is this book's purpose?

Before you go any further, you need to close your eyes, take a deep breath, search your soul and ask yourself the following two questions:

"Could I be one of the 144,000 Light Bearers of Ancient Legend?"
and
"Am I willing to participate in changing the human consciousness and saving our planet from the darkness that threatens to destroy it?"

If you answered "yes" to these questions, then this book was written for YOU! However, first you must set aside all that you think you know and open your mind to a deeper meaning of that knowledge! For only then will you find the wisdom in it.

'*The Path*' described in this book is not the only path. There are many ways to reach enlightenment. This is but one. If it does not suit you, find another, or none at all. God gave us the free will to choose."

'The Path' is best described as full immersion spirituality. You are either in, or you're not. If you have heard the call, it becomes your life, your breath, and your being. You become very aware that every thought you have truly echoes through eternity and affects the collective consciousness. To accept this divine quest is both an honor and a burden because in every moment the most important thing is to do your very best. Many will hear the call; few will be strong enough to stay the course. The knowledge in this book is only seeking a "few" of the over 7 billion humans on the planet right now to align with a "Knowing" that will change your life forever. The number it seeks is 144,000 to be exact. We all may never meet, but it is said, "When we are apart we are together and when we are together we are a part."

One great channeled literary work with the purpose of helping humans to wake up is *The Course in Miracles*. It emphasizes, "… application rather than theory, and experience rather than theology." It furthermore states, "… that a universal theology is impossible, but a universal experience is not only possible, but it's necessary."

But is there is a missing link in that statement? It isn't that a universal theology is impossible. It is that it doesn't exist, because the real universal goal we are aiming for is a universal *doctrine*, or Universal Truth. Theology is the study of religion. Religion is a belief system, typically accompanied by a set of rules. The rules have been given to humans, by way of channeled messages and visions from prophets. Innocent and pure in their original form, many dogmas have been bent and twisted, in order to control the minds of man and gain power.

The purpose of this book is to speak to 144,000 Light Bearers, currently dwelling on this planet. Their awakening will raise the consciousness of humanity and make the leap necessary for the universal truth to manifest. It is crucial for the future of humanity that this alignment happens. Once it occurs, the Greater Understanding will be engaged and the True Universal Doctrine will be revealed.

The Light Bearers were born into a life's purpose, of which they may or may not be aware. The text and lessons in this book could very well "awaken them" and also guide others on a path to find their true purpose in life. They will feel the homing signal and simply "Know."

This text is the first of four books that chronicle the life of one man, Sir Edward-Michael Jagen; noble and true, and his dream of a lifetime. He surrendered his personal life to a divine purpose. There is no human understanding that can fully grasp the true depth of the vow he took. As it stands today that understanding exponentially increases with every breath he takes. He channeled ancient, lost lessons that are interlaced in Part Two of this book. And they are elaborated in the Appendix for easy reference. These lessons comprise 'The Book of Wisdom.' They are what those in power don't want you to know because they free the mind, while exposing the lies and misinformation we have been led to believe as truth.

The story is adapted from Sir Edward's memoirs, *Dairy of an Angel-Knight,* so you will learn how he attained the "Knowing." You'll also learn how he applied it to keep catastrophic events from occurring, and how he shed light upon the dark places where evil dwells. It is his hope that you do the same.

Because some of the events and police intelligence investigations covered in this story still remain classified, some names and locations have been changed, composite characters created and time frames compressed to protect the privacy of those involved.

May Sir Edward's life's story and words resonate within you, sparking your own personal awakening. God speed!

Foreword

By Lady Sophia Key West

Angels. What are they? Who are they? How do I connect to one?

There are as many answers to each of those questions as there are people on the planet. That is because as Universal Mother Sophia Pistis said, "Upon each I put a unique star, a great light from the heavens. And in that starlight, is encoded a special message that will be made known only to the bearer as the awakening begins."

Everyone and everything has a time of its own. When you are ready and if it is your path, your channel will open and you will connect to the Divine in the unique way that is yours. Many are similar, but like fingerprints, no two are exactly alike--even though we are all connecting to the same universal energy. It is like being a thread in a tapestry. We all make up the tapestry because each of us has a unique color combination that brings a piece to the whole. Part of your journey to enlightenment is to find how you connect and be open to know when it is *your* time. For some, it happens at a very young age. For others, it's after trauma. And for some, it may be spontaneous. And for others, it may be on their deathbed.

The Diary of an Angel Knight book series chronicles the life and times of Sir Edward-Michael Jagen. The books recount the tale of a mystical dream he had after a near death experience. Sir Edward, for lack of a better description, is an enigma and has led quite a fascinating life.

I met Sir Edward shortly after his 52th birthday. I was 39 and nearing the end of a 14-year career in ophthalmology and on the cusp of my holistic health career. I had been volunteering with the Good Knight Child Empowerment Network for seven years, but had never met the elusive "Blue Knight." During one of my volunteer gigs with the Network, I heard the "Castle" was holding a festival for alternative medicine and new age concepts. "SpiritFest" it was called. They had spaces available for the healing arts, Reiki, Seated Massage, etc. So I asked a group of my fellow massage therapy classmates to split the two-day fee for the booth. Their response was a resounding YES… so we were all set to participate.

It was an unseasonably chilly May Saturday morning when we set up. Our assigned location was underneath a crop of tall trees next to the famed life-sized "Sword in the Stone" puzzle. Being in the shade of those tall trees did not help the chill factor of the day. Our location and lack of notoriety had us twiddling our thumbs from boredom. It was like we were invisible or cloaked. No patrons came to our booth. Our egos took a hit, but our spirits soared, due to the booth's location overlooking the Labyrinth of Miracles. It was beyond peaceful.

I sat there, enjoying the energy of the Castle, and did some people watching.

The festival was well under way that Saturday when I saw **him**. At first glance, I knew there was something unexplainable about him. A *presence*. And oddly enough, a presence I was familiar with, but could not quite put my finger on the "where" or "how" of my knowing. I just "knew."

That day was truly the first day of the rest of my life. It led to my resignation from a very nice career in ophthalmology. I took a leap of faith into full-time volunteering, with a side job in holistic health, to try to just get by. From the day I heard "the call," money didn't matter to me anymore. It never really did to begin with, but through my life, I was programmed to believe money is more important than it really is.

Over the years of working side by side, with Sir Edward-Michael, I have seen many miracles… simple things like controlling the weather, diverting someone's attention (like "these are not the droids you are looking for…"), to a woman who died in my arms and was brought back to life. And oh, by the way, this also includes him bringing me back from the dead!

It happened one morning. Several of us were working on the final draft of a grant. All of a sudden, I felt a weird swoosh in my head. The phone rang. I saw myself in slow motion answer it, but I had a hard time speaking. I felt this weird pressure on my chest, as if someone was pushing me down. I said to Sir Edward, "I feel odd, like I am going to pass out. Something is wrong." I panicked and grabbed at his shirt, as I fell to the floor. I was pleading, "I don't want to leave yet. Don't let me go. Please don't let me go!" I could hear my heart beat slowing. It beat, beat, beeeaat, beeeeeaat, beeeeeeaaat…then silence. It stopped beating completely. But I was still in my body. How could that be, I thought? I was looking out at a black tunnel-like opening similar to looking into the wide top of a tornado. There were gray clouds swirling around the opening. Then Sir Edward used his body to shield me from the opening. He became larger than life. Like a huge bear hug hovering over me, but yet not. He was talking to me, and I was answering him, but neither of us was speaking out loud. He held me down from floating into the tunnel and all of a sudden I breathed a huge breath and heard my heart start beating again.

It took several hours for me to regain control over my body and speech. I was talking to him and the others around me, but they said I was speaking gibberish. In my head, it was perfectly clear.

He saved me.

During those moments, I pledged my life once again to 'The Path,' which in some energetic way, then opened an even clearer channel for me to the Divine.

Like I said before, Edward's story is amazing and unique, as is mine--but so is yours! You will come to realize that, as you read the story. His time to connect to his life's purpose started when he drowned and came back to life. Even though Edward saving me opened a greater channel, it was not the beginning of my connection.

This was the beginning of my time…

As young as 3 years old, I can clearly remember my conversations with God. I had a great awareness of 'The All' and the presence of my guardian angel, who I later found out was Archangel Michael.

I vividly remember seeing Angel Michael standing in the corner of my room at night. Watching. Just watching. It scared me at first. *His presence.* Just standing there in the corner so tall, wearing a black hat and what looked like a cloak. Hovering over his head, I noticed a beautiful crystal blue bubble. The first time I saw him, I thought he was there to "get me." But almost immediately after the thought arose in my mind, the blue bubble floated in the air toward me. It came right up to my heart and then disappeared into my body. I felt this warm comforting feeling swirling in my heart and stomach "telling" me I was being protected and all would be okay.

I didn't know it back then, but I was born as an empath. My processing center, my stomach, always seized up when danger was afoot... or a calming sensation would come over me and almost speak "it's okay" when all was well.

Little did I know when "Tall Man" (that's what I called him) showed up, that the real threat in my life was just days away from beginning and would come from within my very own home. "Tall Man" was simply sent to watch over me. He was there night after night to comfort me after the beginning of the "troubling time."

"The troubling time!" Ha! At least that is what my mom called it anyway. It made me feel like *I* was the trouble.

Everyone in the family thought something was wrong with me. I was afraid to sleep alone. No one knew why, except for me. I knew why, but was told I couldn't tell, or else!

I would look to "Tall Man" night after night when going through the pain. As long as he was there watching, the pain just went away. One night, after the pain started, his cloak dissolved right before my eyes and the most beautiful golden wings emerged from behind him. I was so mesmerized by his wings that it was many moments after we were in the air that I realized we were flying. From that night on, when the "troubling time" started, he would pick me up... and we would fly away.

During the day, I could tell from the feeling in my tummy whether or not "Tall Man" would be there when I went to bed. As much as I wanted to see him and fly again, I wasn't afraid to go to sleep on nights that I knew he wouldn't be there because on those nights, the troubling time wouldn't happen. I remember thinking he was somehow sending me messages, through my belly, to let me know it was okay to go to sleep that night. It was like he knew beforehand what was going to happen or not happen!

I learned at a young age to listen. No, more importantly, I learned to *feel* the guidance of my angel.

Throughout my teenage years I called it "listening to my gut." I must've heard that saying from an adult, because I haven't a clue why I called it that. However, it really was like my gut was talking to me; just not with words, but with sensations. My mother liked to describe me as someone who always had stomach issues. Unbeknownst to all of us it was a gift, not an illness.

As I grew into adulthood, I started to process the messages given to me in more ways than just my gut. I would see lights and energy moving. A scent would be in the air and a chill would run up my leg or down my arm. I would "feel" someone or *something* in the room. I would be drawn to pick up a book and open it to a page that had important words for me. All my senses became fine-tuned to allow me to receive messages through impressions.

The amazing thing happening over the years was the honing of my ability to analyze energy and sense someone else's experiences as well. The older I got, the stronger my gift became and the broader my abilities. Honestly though, it wasn't until my early 30's that I actually tried to work with my skills. Until then, I always thought, "Hey, this is who I am. Doesn't everyone feel this way?"

The answer to that is, "No!" Everyone is different. Not everyone has the heightened ability, inclination or desire to manifest a greater sense and use of their gifts. And even if they do, each of us has a unique set of gifts that we have the free will to develop or ignore. Everyone's time to connect comes exactly when it is supposed to and is uniquely different from everyone else's.

Before you embark on Sir Edward's journey, I thought it important to share the above experiences I had with my angel(s), as a way to share how communication can happen in a variety of ways. You don't have to experience it like we have, in order for it to be "right."

And by the way, in case you were wondering, I am a Christian. I was raised Catholic and, furthermore, pursued Catholicism as an adult by choice. Above all, I believe God is Love and there is no stronger force in the Universe than Love. Love is positive, so all who live by a belief system that is also positive are at least on the right track, I feel. I also feel everyone has the right to their own beliefs because God gave us free will to choose. Who are we to take that away?

There are many great religions of man. All have common threads, which are quite fascinating to me. How is that possible? When did the breaks take place, if they all came from one source? If they all did originate from one source, is it possible for them to re-unite, under the Doctrine of Love, of God's true purpose for us?

I believe it is possible. I also believe that His Eminence Pope Francis plays a big role in bringing us back together. I don't believe this because I am Catholic and he is the leader of the church. I believe this because he personifies unconditional love. I see the stars in his eyes, placed there by our Mother and our Father. All signs point to him knowing more than the box he lives in will allow him to say. Mark my words and watch it all unfold, as the events in this story come to life for you.

This book is one man's dream of life, not just with an angel, but as the legs for an angel. A truly gifted, clear channel, not just because he died and came back. But because he accepted the call and became a truly devoted servant of God. His story is different from mine in the way we "obtained" our connection with the Divine. Your focal point, when reading, shouldn't be how either of us connected. It should be the *possibility* of the connection. It isn't when, what or how you receive or use your gift or call, it is simply that you do. In the doing, your understanding will expand and all will be made known when your waiting is full.

Throughout Sir Edward's *Diary of an Angel Knight* series, there are many references when St. Michael or another angel "spoke" to him, like *"...Michael said, ... "*Please do not confuse those words with the notion of hearing voices in his head. There is no human word to *best* describe what happens when receiving a message from an Angel. Again, it is unique to the receiver, coming in impressions that best suit the one interpreting the message.

The lessons he channeled that are included in this series will play an integral role in the development of your gifts. I suggest you review them each more than once and practice often.

You will read that Angels can't be human and humans can't be angels, not even in death. But, every 500 years in order to give human consciousness the best opportunity possible to evolve, we are given a chance to merge together and play on the "same team" so to speak.

We can answer the call and be one of the 144,000 Light Bearers to allow our bodies to be the vessels for great divine energies. This will help propel the human condition forward and away from annihilation.

Will you be one that answers the call?

Introduction

By Sir Edward Jagen

Ephesians 6: 11-12

"Put on the whole Armor of God so that you may be able to stand against the wiles of the Devil. For we wrestle not against flesh and blood, but against principalities, against powers, against the rulers of the darkness of this world and against spiritual wickedness in high places."

Special Note:

The intent of this book is not to have you question your religion or to highlight any one religion in general, but to offer you the possibility of a greater awareness and perception of our Creator.

Humans have so much untapped potential. If they could just set aside what they think they know and absorb the unseen that is all around, many secrets would be unlocked for them. With this book, I have offered you the key.

Archangel Michael

Do you believe in angels? A poll conducted by CBS News in 2011 claims that eight out of ten Americans believe in angels and that many people have had close encounters with them. I am one of those people, but I had to have a near death experience at eight years old to make the connection with one. One thing that became perfectly clear to me, from that experience, was that our existence does not end when our physical body dies.

I was shown there are many dimensions all around us that we must negotiate our mental being through. The physical dimension, in which we exist now, limits the level of understanding about our expanded existence. We are energy and energy cannot be destroyed. It only transfigures into another form of energy. I also learned that humans can't be angels and angels can't be human. But there are rare occasions when the energies of the two can fuse together as one. I was offered one of those occasions, but there was a great understanding I had to gain first. I have been asked to share all that I gained with those, who seek to stand within the Shadow of the Spirit of Truth.

The angel said to me, "When we are apart we stand together. And when we are together, we are a part of the All." He then shared this oath.

Oath of the Archangels

"When goodness grows weak and when evil increases, we will return to earth seeking the mighty 144,000 Light-Bearers of Oneness. Together, we will deliver the holy and shine our Light upon the Great Lie of the Deceiver, as we re-establish the divine Order of Righteousness on Earth as it is in Heaven."

What is an angel and how do we know if one is around? For me he was a "voice" in the back of my mind that I know was not my thoughts. I couldn't hear him with my ears or see him with my eyes. He spoke to me through impressions and showed me visions in my mind's eye. I never saw him physically, but I "knew" he was always wearing blue and gold armor. Other times he would appear to me as a blue orb of light.

The angel was here on earth during this age of man because he had a very serious mission to complete that was started way back during the time of Atlantis. He needed to groom a human body and mind in our time in an attempt to complete that mission.

I was given a second chance at life in order to be that body. However, first I had many years of working alongside the angel before my understanding would reach a point where I had the ability to learn the ancient wisdoms and gain a "Knowing" that was lost to mankind long ago.

The angel now wants that wisdom shared with a very special group of humans that are scattered across the globe. There are 144,000, and you could very well be one of them. This is their time to shine. The 144,000 will come from all beliefs of the modern world.

The angel told me "The first religious views came from the belief Atlantis held of the Creator. But that belief in God quickly turned into 'Knowing God' once they were able to comprehend the knowledge found in the Book of Wisdom."

During my life, the angel guided me through a most traumatizing childhood that set the stage for an incredible police career. We helped protect and save many lives to include a well know Native American Indian activist/actor, as well as Ronald Reagan, the 40th President of the United States.

From 1985 to present, over thirty years, we have mounted a quest to elevate the consciousness of over 20 million children to the negativity that preys upon their innocence. We built an amazing castle museum complex in the suburbs of Washington, D.C. It was designed for families to have an interactive adventure quest, while absorbing lifesaving safety messages to keep the darkness at bay.

The angel left me in 2013. He said, "Our work together was complete." He raised a very special Sword and Stone from the abyss, and we presented it to a little girl for safekeeping. I retired and was instructed to write down all that I had learned, so the 144,000 Light-Bearers could easily gain the "Knowing" needed to prevail. Walking away from everything was the hardest thing I have ever done, but I honored the angel's request.

On Friday, November 13th, 2015 the angel returned to me after the attacks on the innocent civilians in Paris, by the terror network, Isis.

"We have work to do. It is time to dispel the negativity that lingers throughout the world," he said. "It is driven by an evil presence within humans that makes them need to dominate and enslave the mind, body and spirit of their fellow man. The evil presence perverts that which is good within some religions to justify their murderous hatred for others that don't follow their strict doctrine."

He finished by saying, "The presence and the Sons of Darkness will not rest, until their mindset rules the earth again. During the 2016 Presidential election, America will be left with a choice between someone that represents everything that's wrong within world politics or someone that represents everything that is wrong within world business. Egos will be out-of-control egos. The most transparent candidate will win the election."

That's when the angel gave me a vision of the future.

As expansive as this vision was, it came and went in an instant, but embedded deeply on my psyche.

The Vision

The vision began with President Reagan, giving a grievous warning from the grave to remember his words: "Freedom is never more than one generation away from extinction. We don't pass it to our children in the bloodstream. It must be fought for, protected, and handed on to them to do the same or one day we will spend our sunset years telling our children and our children's children what it was once like in the United States where men were free."

I was not given a year or location, but I was transported in time and shown that over a billion people on earth are dead or seriously injured after six thermonuclear devices were detonated. The group taking credit called themselves the Sons of Darkness. They warn the rest of the world, "If you do not convert immediately to the will of the one true God, you will be the next to die. This is the countdown to Armageddon."

The angel said to me, "The Sons of Darkness once again want to control the collective consciousness and enslave humanity to their manifestation of God. Remember as it always has been and always will be, if you choose to believe in 'a God' you must bow down in worship. But if you choose to believe in the Creator, simply open your heart and receive a loving embrace. The Almighty only wants his creation to enjoy all that has been given."

I questioned, "Why does man choose to manifest a God that needs to be worshipped?"

The angel answered, "The Creator manifested man, with an incredible God-like imagination to create. But through the ages, some power-hungry humans have used that imagination to create a God to fit man's image of prideful, superior domination. Religions and belief systems don't start off with mal intent to the worshipper, but sometimes when the darkness distorts the hearts of those in power, religions become perfect control tools for humans."

The vision was so vivid and real. In a moment, it was over, and I broke into a cold sweat. I was forlorn to know that something must've shifted in order for the angel to return. I also knew from past experiences, with the battle between light and dark, that the Paris attacks meant more than the human atrocities the world witnessed.

Regardless of why he returned, the angel in blue armor was back after a long absence. It was good to have him, by my side again. He had been with me ever since 1957, when I drowned off the coast of Jupiter Beach, Florida and was given a chance to return to life.

He guided me through a turbulent childhood, several years in the military and then through a career on the Washington D.C. Police Department. The angel wanted me to learn what drove humans to abuse, mistreat and murder one another. During that period of time, as a deep undercover investigator, I infiltrated many organized crime and terrorist organizations. I witnessed things that will haunt me forever.

I found that most people are driven by the urges of anger, greed, lust, envy, laziness, gluttony and mostly egotistical pride. From myths of old, I learned it was those seven demons that Zeus sent to earth in a jar we call, Pandora's box. The angel came, with a plan to help the "Children of Tomorrow" maintain their virtue and drive those demon vices back into the box... from whence they came.

Of my 65 years of life, it was the last thirty years that were the most eye opening. On August 8th, 1988, the angel guided me to the spirit of an ascended Master of Atlantis. Over a four-year period, the Master passed on one lesson a month. If I mastered the lesson, on the eighth day of the next month, I would receive the next lesson. The angel wanted me to solve the riddle of why in the Pandora's box myth did HOPE remain when everything else escaped. After receiving the fifty-third lesson, it became obvious. It wasn't the virtue of "Hope." It was an acronym. I learned the only way to get the seven demons that haunt humanity back into the box is to H-help, O-open, P-people's, E-eyes to the evil that comes when we allow negative spirits to control us.

The fifty-three lessons became Seeds of Wisdom for me. Once I gained the "Knowing" from the lessons, it kept growing until my personal powers and abilities gave me the understanding of why humanity was on the brink of destruction.

I was told that at the root of the destruction there existed a fissure in our society, caused by Greed. Humans are forced to live the great lies of the power hungry. From those lies, fear is bred and people are then easily controlled by their fears.

I asked the angel once, "When does a lie become the truth?"
He answered. "When enough people choose to believe it."

In order to expose the truth and set humanity free from the great lies, the angel asked me to publish a series of books about our adventures together called, *Diary of an Angel-Knight*. Originally, he said within the next twenty years the fifty-three lessons from the Book of Wisdom would awaken 144,000 Light-Bearers. These would carry the "Knowing" into the collective consciousness, during the End of Days. This "Knowing" will defeat the Sons of Darkness and humanity will take its rightful place within the cosmos.

However, since the angel has returned, the timeline moved forward, and the countdown has begun fifteen years earlier than forecasted. I was told that I must publish the lessons immediately, if we are going to find the 144,000 Light-Bearers in time to STOP the slaughter of so many innocent men, woman and children.

This book is not for most of the seven billion people on planet earth. It is meant only to awaken a dormant spark of light, within 144,000 Sons and Daughters of Light, that prophecy says will be needed to repel the darkness, during the End of Days. If by that time, they have gained the ancient wisdom and can maintain the Willpower to project the "Knowing," the collective consciousness of humanity will take a quantum leap forward.

I don't wish to bore you with my life story, but the angel said I should share it, so you can see how the "Knowing" came to me. Remember we are all different parts to the whole. Our timing and methods can vary, but when our "parts" come together we are complete. I hope my story helps illuminate your path and make sense of the incomprehensible.

Good luck my friend! I hope your light shines bright in the sea of darkness that lays ahead. Remember to listen with your ears, eyes and heart. The impressions you receive should guide you to goodness. If it guides you anyway else, you are going down the wrong path.

Chapter One

Entering the Dream of an Angel

When I got far enough away that I felt safe from Billy, I started riding the waves on my big yellow banana. Totally focused on the fun, I was unaware the current was taking me further and further out past the breakers. I was having a ball until I got knocked off the float by a huge wave. I swallowed a lot of water. I was flailing around as the banana drifted away from me. I was screaming for help, but no one could hear me.

The people on the beach looked like the size of ants. The waves crashing on the beach were too loud for anyone to hear my screams for help. I was getting tired and couldn't stay afloat any longer. I went under, held my breath and started fighting my way back to the surface. When I came up I saw the lighthouse but went under again and again, gasping for air each time I came up. This happened several times until I couldn't fight anymore and just started sinking. My lungs felt like they were going to burst from the pressure. The further I sank, the darker it got. I had to let the air out, but I knew if I did, all I would take back in was water and I would drown.

My ears started buzzing just as I exhaled. I stopped sinking. I felt like I had been kicked in the chest and then I felt nothing, but the darkness all around me. My eyes were closed, but I could see a speck of golden light coming toward me. I opened my eyes to see what it was. The light was getting bigger. A feeling of comfort came over me. The closer the light came, the better I felt. As it approached me, I could see that it was a beautiful golden haired lady.

I remember thinking, "Is this the Lady of the Lake that Frankie was talking about?"

The lady grabbed my arm, and we floated down a long dark tunnel toward a bright shining white light. She stopped half way down, looked at me and smiled. A feeling of comfort came over me. I had never felt that way before.

She spoke to me through her mind never moving her mouth. In my mind, I asked, "What's your name?"

She said she was nameless, but I could call her the Constant Walker, or "Connie" for short.

When we reached the end of the tunnel she spoke again, "This is your time. Everyone has a time that is uniquely theirs."

I looked at her when she spoke and could feel my brows crinkle.

"I don't understand," I said.

"It is time for you to die and cross over to the other side, but I don't want you to leave life just yet," she uttered so sweetly. "I have a very good reason for you to continue to live, if you choose to do so."

She went on to say, "You can stay with Us now for eternity or go back into life and become the legs for my great Angel-Knight champion. There is something he must do, and he can't do it alone. He must return to earth every five hundred years, seeking a special Sword and Stone. If he finds the Sword and the Stone, he will need you to help him deliver them to a very special little girl, who will safeguard them for the Children of Tomorrow."

I then proclaimed, "If going back serves you, I will go back."

Connie then took me into a cavern where I saw a huge angel fast asleep next to a large boulder. He was wearing blue and gold armor, holding a sleeping baby in his arms. There was a glowing sword by his side.

I did a double take.

The sword looked like the one my father had carved me!

Connie said that the angel's name was Michael, and he was dreaming about the life I could have and the things that could be accomplished, if I returned to life.

She told me, "Go. Lay next to Michael. Fall asleep and you will see his dreams. In those dreams your destiny will be revealed."

I climbed to Angel Michael and the little baby.

Staring at the two of them, I asked, "Who is this sweet special baby?"

Connie replied, "She is nameless, but I call her MV. If you decide to return, you and Michael will search for her. When you find her, you will know God's True Love."

Chapter Two

A Chicago Toilet

My story actually begins in 1944, five years before I was born. My father, William Jagen, was in the war, fighting his way through North Africa (see Image 1) into Europe and across Italy, France then finally into Germany when he and his best friend, Mike Sparrow, were taken prisoners by the Nazis. They were tortured for several weeks for information. My father told me many years later that the pain would stop when he focused his thought on a statue of the Archangel Michael that stood above the door of the church he went to as a boy on the south side of Chicago.

William and Mike made a promise that if they survived the war and made it back to the states, they would become the godfather of each other's first-born sons.

"We're in this together Billy. All the way," said Mike. "I can't wait to see your little Mikey playing with my son, Billy. They are going to be best friends."

Their friendship carried them through the darkest moments as they constantly looked out for one another. It was a true partnership. My dad would say to me, "Our friendship is what saved us, but we looked out for each other not just for the sake of the other person, but because neither of us wanted to be alone there."

Late one night, after everyone else was asleep, Mike whispered, "Billy. Bill, you awake?"

"Yeah. What's up," my dad asked.

Mike, who spoke German, said, "I overheard one of the SS officers talking about sending us to Dachau Concentration Camp in a few days. That place is deep inside Germany. We are done for if we go there. Rumor has it that they're killing the Catholic POWS along with the Jews."

Both men fell silent after that and didn't discuss it again.

That night my father told me he prayed hard, asking Archangel Michael to help them escape. While he was praying, he promised St. Michael that if he would save him, he would devote his life, and the lives of any children he might have, to Michael's service and mission on Earth.

Funny how when faced with death and in painful moments, we make pledges without fully knowing the ramifications of our words.

The next day in the early morning hours, dad said he heard a knocking but didn't know where it was coming from. He heard it again.

"I must be dreaming," he said out loud.

Then he heard a sweet female voice saying, "It was me knocking on your soul. It's time to wake up. Follow the blue orb to safety."

When my father opened his eyes, there was a blue ball of light hovering above his chest. Then it moved to the door. He woke Mike up and whispered to him of the dream, then pointed at the blue orb. Mike couldn't see it, but he believed Dad when all of a sudden the door unlocked by itself and opened. Dad saw the orb move though the doorway and down the hall.

Dad said he felt invisible as they moved past the guards, unseen or heard. More than once he thought he was still dreaming. As soon as they were outside, they got down on their bellies and started low crawling to the barbed wire fences that surrounded the compound. He didn't remember how they got through the barbed wire. All my dad remembered was crawling for hours following the blue orb through the forest, until they felt comfortable enough to start walking upright.

When the sun came up the blue orb disappeared never to be seen by my father again. Two days later a U.S. Army battalion picked them up and several weeks later, they were with one of the units that liberated Dachau Concentration Camp.

My dad said, "It was one of the most horrific sights I have ever seen. Train boxcars were stacked from floor to ceiling, with dead emaciated bodies. The smell of death was everywhere. Some of the G.I.'s talked about killing all the German POW's, but we were warned if we did, we'd be arrested and charged with murder. Somehow a group of the prisoners we liberated got a hold of machine guns and took their revenge on the Nazi soldiers we had corralled in a large fenced-in area. Everything went crazy for a while."

I could tell that those visions would haunt my dad as long as he lived.

Image 1 –William Jagen in North Africa 1944 WWII.

After the war, Mike Sparrow went back to Chicago. Mike's brother Joe was part of the Capone crime family, so he had work. But with all the G.I.'s coming home, my dad couldn't find work as a carpenter. He heard that there was plenty of work in Washington D.C., so he moved there.

It was a good thing because he met my mother, Kathryn, there and were married. Within a year, my brother Billy was born, and my mother's brother became his godfather. My father felt guilty about not keeping his promise to Mike.

As fate would have it, Mike had also married, and they were expecting their first child. Mike called my dad, asking him to be godfather, as in the pact they made. While he had my dad on the phone Mike told him that he was working for Sears Tower. His company had a three-year renovation project, and they were looking for carpenters. The job was paying twice as much as Dad was making in D.C. Mike said he could get my father the job, if he wanted it.

A few weeks later, my family moved to Chicago. As my mother tells the story she loved Mike, but his brother, Joseph, was a total egomaniac. He was a know it all who always had an opinion. Her favorite saying was, "Opinions are like assholes and every asshole has one! Especially Joe!"

The following year, my mother was pregnant with her second child – me! Mike, of course, was overjoyed because the promise the two men made during the war would finally be fulfilled. If it were a boy, his name would be Michael. And if the baby were a girl, her name would be Michaela.

When Mike's brother, Joe, found out the baby's due date was mid-July, Joe's birth month, he would tease Mike. Joe stood up and declared, "If this baby is a boy born on my birthday, July 22nd, then his name would be Joseph and I will be the godfather!" Joe was very proud of his birthday. He shared the date with his idol John Dillinger the infamous American gangster. Dillinger was gunned down on July 22, 1934 the same day that Joe turned 21 and became a member in Al Capone's Chicago Outfit. My mother would cringe when he proclaimed that--and he said it often during her pregnancy!

Mike would just say, "Dream on brother." Mike was a good guy and pampered my mother for nine months. Mom told me it made her feel very special.

Every Friday night my father would play poker with the Sparrow brothers. It was loud, according to my mom, and there were always good-natured arguments. Except when it came to Joe. Being in the mob gave him this air of 'untouchable.' Mom would tell us that she thought everyone was a little afraid of Joe. Not her, she hated him.

A few weeks before I was born, Mike had been drinking a little too much on poker night. He was dead sure he was going to win the pot. It came down to him and Joe. Right in the middle of the hand, Mike ran out of money. He wanted to borrow money from my dad.

Joe said, "No loans brother, but you could cover the bet with the right to be the baby's godfather."

Sitting there holding four kings, Mike felt it was a no brainer. He wrote "Godfather" on a slip of paper and threw it on top of the pot.

Joe laid down a spade straight flush.

Mike was devastated.

Dad told me later, "It was as if you could watch all the color drain from Mike's face. The one thing he wanted more than anything else was to be your Godfather, and he lost it."

Mike's heart was broken, while Joe was happy as a lark. He danced around the room and over to my mother. He patted her belly and said, "Can't wait to meet you Big Joseph, my little gangster!" It appeared Joe had big plans for my future.

My mother said Mike stopped coming around after that, but Joe was there all the time watching her like a hawk and checking the days off the calendar.

On the evening of July 21, 1949 Joe, his wife Dorothy, and her sister, Anna, showed up at our door. "We are taking you two to see *The Great Gatsby* movie," piped Joe. "You need to have a night on the town before the baby comes. Anna will watch little Billy."

Mom said Joe pictured himself like the Gatsby character, very flamboyant. He threw money around when it was his idea, but God help you, if you asked for a loan. Little did my parents know, Joe had an ulterior motive. He wasn't letting my mother out of his sight that night because the next day was his birthday. He wanted to make sure that if I arrived, my name would be Joseph!

After the movie, everyone went back to our apartment to play a few hands of cards to pass the time. Joe planned on camping out there. My mother said she was craving sweets and wanted some butter-brickle ice cream. So Joe gave my father some money and sent him off to the store.

My father said later, "I thought Joe was up to something when he gave me the money." Joe was always such a cheapskate. He never offered to pay for anything unless it benefited him. It was around 10:45 p.m. when my father left.

A few minutes later, my mom got up to go into the kitchen. As she stood up she bent over in pain and screamed, "Oh my Lord! The baby is moving." Right after that her water broke, and she went into strong labor. Dorothy gently guided mom into the bedroom and got her to lie down.

In what Anna said seemed like seconds after they were in the bedroom, Dorothy came out screaming, "We must get Kathryn to the hospital the baby's coming."

Joe said, "I'll drive her to the hospital and you two should wait in the apartment for Bill." He then barked the orders, "Dorothy, you come to the hospital with Bill. And Anna, you stay and watch little Billy."

When Joe got my mother down to his car, as the story goes, he took off his bootlaces and tied my mother's knees together. He told her it would help ease the pain of the contractions. Little did she know, he was tying her legs together to keep me from coming out.

With my mother screaming from the pain in the back seat, good ole' Uncle Joe went for joy ride around Lakeshore Drive. It was a little before midnight when he pulled up in front of the hospital. My father, Dorothy, Anna and brother Billy were all waiting at the emergency room entrance, very upset.

Joe took out his knife and cut the bootlaces as my mother was yelling, "The baby's coming. Hurry quick the baby's coming now."

The nurse checked my mother's condition. Feeling she hadn't dilated enough the nurse said, "You must just need to go to the restroom." She ushered mom into the bathroom in the emergency room waiting area.

At 12:01 a.m. I fell from the warmth of a loving mother into the cold waters of a Chicago hospital toilet.

"Uncle" Joe was so proud of himself; not giving any thought to the safety of an unborn child and its mother. All he could focus on was that the baby was born on his birthday and the date John Dillinger died!

As soon as he found out I was a boy he yelled, "Yes! It's decided then. His name is going to be Joseph Jagen. Right?" he asked with a "you better or else" energy attached.

My mother had a very strong will, but throughout her pregnancy she just usually sat back, watched and listened to everyone. Humoring dad, Mike and Joe with their antics about my name. Little did everyone know, Mom had promised her father that she would name her second son after one of his World War I buddies, Eddie Rickenbacher.

When it came time to fill out the birth certificate information, my mother told dad, "We are naming our son Edward, after my father's war buddy. And we should give him Michael as his middle name to honor your vow with Mike, not his asshole brother."

When she told me the story, she said that my father seemed to be afraid of Joe and didn't want to cross him.

Dad snapped back, "Joseph must be part of name."

Reluctantly she filled out the birth certificate form, Edward Joseph.

In later years when telling the story of my strange toilet birth she told me that she only allowed me to carry the name Joseph to remind me not to be selfish like my godfather.

In defending his actions, Joe would say, "I had everything under control."

"That's your opinion Joe." She said, "Opinions are like assholes and every asshole has one." My mother's words of wisdom still ring true in my ears when I listen to the delusional crap some people try to get others to believe.

A few years later, my sister Kathy was born. She was as cute as can be. Quite a contrast from brother Billy, who seemed to think I was put on this planet to be his personal punching bag. My brother's nickname for me was "Little Turd" for the obvious reason of my birth in the toilet situation. My nickname for him was "Bully" Jagen. He was always angry and had a mean streak that went deep and wide. I tried to stay out of his way, but that's hard to do when I had to share a bed with him. His favorite thing to do was hold me down and fart on my head.

For the first five years of my life, I thought Billy was Satan, and I was Jesus Christ. My mother was always screaming, "Billy you devil! Leave your brother alone. And Jesus Christ Eddie, just stay away from your brother before he kills you."

That was easier said than done. Billy was like a dark cloud that followed me around. I was always praying that one day someone would come along and torture him.

When I was five and a half, my wish came true. My Aunt June and Uncle Benny from New York City came to visit with their son, Damian. They stayed with us for two weeks, while Uncle Benny looked for work. He and my godfather, Joe, became very good friends.

That was the week my prayers were answered. Damian was a tough street kid, three years older than Billy. The two didn't like each other from the start. One day, the three of us were playing cowboys and Indians. I was always the cowboy, with a wooden gun. Billy had a real bow and real arrows that he would shoot at me. I could tell he was doing it to look cool for Damian. Damian wasn't really into the game though, but played along. I got pretty good at dodging arrows, which made Billy mad. His plan to impress Damian, by using me as a target didn't work. So after I dodged the arrows, he would chase me, catch me and push me down on the ground. Once he had me under control, he would sit on my head, squeeze out a very loud stinky fart and then start laughing.

He would look up to Damian to see if he was laughing too. Unfortunately for him, Damian didn't think it was funny at all.

7

After the fourth-time Billy farted on my head, Damian knocked him off of me with a full-on tackle. He stood up, grabbed Billy by the collar of his shirt with one hand and curled his other hand up in a fist, then said, "If I ever see you do that again, I will kick your scrawny, loser ass."

The look on Billy's face was priceless. That was the first time anyone came to my rescue. For the rest of the week, Billy stayed away from us.

Uncle Benny did get a job working for Joe's company. Benny became his representative in New York City, so the family moved back. I hated to see Damian leave because I knew my brother would start on me again. However, I knew this time it would be even worse. I remember thinking, "I wish Damian was my older brother."

Image 2 – The Jagen Family (left to right): Eddie, Bill, Kathy and Kathryn.

Chapter Three

If Wishes were Fishes

When I was six, my family moved again to a sixth-floor apartment building on the south side of Chicago, across the street from the stockyards. It was a very smelly place to live. I remember at times the gutters would run red, with the blood from the cattle that had been butchered.

We were very poor and there was never much food in the house. We would often go to bed hungry or with only a peanut butter and butter sandwich for dinner. I would fall asleep at night, wishing to have a nice juicy steak. Then I'd hear the mooing from the cows, crying across the street, and I would change the wish to a big fish to eat.

My father was a union carpenter, out of work most of the time, only finding a job a few weeks a month. Not having much in the way of clothes and toys I would go around, wishing for stuff all the time. I would wish for this and wish for that. But most of the time, I would wish that my brother would stop beating on me.

We didn't have a lot of trees and grass in our neighborhood, so when we'd visit my Grandma Jagen in Edmonton, it was like a trip to the country. I remember during one visit to Grandma's house, I was walking around wishing for a bunch of stuff. She would always say, "If wishes were fishes, beggars would eat for free." But this time with her thick Irish accent she said, "What are you wishing for now, Eddie me boy?"

I stopped everything and said, "I can't really remember. Lots of stuff I guess." I was so focused on making wishes that I forgot what I was wishing for most of the time.

She said, "Exactly!"

While giving me a stern Irish look and a shake of her head, the gray bun of hair on top of her head would wobble. I couldn't help but stare at the bun instead of completely listening to her words. She broke me out of my trance by saying, "How do you know if your wish comes true, if you can't remember what you wished for? Wishes can only come true one wish at a time. Wishing for more than one thing is selfish!"

Grandma Jagen then told me that she would show me a special way to help make my wishes come true. She said, "Go into the backyard, Laddie. Find a four-leaf clover and bring it back to me."

I searched every patch of clover in her yard for what seemed like hours, but I could not find one with four leaves. I even tried to fool her, by taking a three-leaf clover, and a leaf from another clover, to make four. I ran up to her with it, and she said, "Nice try small fry. Keep looking."

Finally, I gave up. "THERE ARE NO FOUR-LEAF CLOVERS OUT HERE," I yelled from the backyard.

A few seconds later she came out and started looking at the ground. Would you believe that within a few minutes, she found one with four leaves? I was so very happy, jumping up and down, until she said it was hers.

"You have to find your own," she said.

"But what if that was the ONLY one?" I yelled with tears of frustration in my eyes.

Grandma Jagen told me that my problem was that I couldn't see the forest for the trees.

I told her, half sobbing, "I'm not looking for a forest. I was looking for clovers like you said to do." She didn't think that was funny. She showed me how to search for the elusive four-leaf clover.

"You start with patience, clear your mind and let your eyes become like a bumble bee looking for something different from everything else you see," she said.

I tried to clear my mind. Do you know how hard that is for a little kid? The more I tried, the more I thought about everything. Clearing my mind was impossible. Finally, I decided to make a buzzing noise in my head like a bee, looking for the four-leaf clover to land on. "Buzzzzzzz. Buzzzzzzz. Buzzzzzz." I couldn't believe my eyes… I found one within a few minutes. I ran back inside and told her that I couldn't clear my mind, but I filled it with buzzing and that led me to the clover. I gave her the clover, and she said, "Aye, this is a grand one, Eddie me boy. Extra special I see."

Using some kite string she tied four knots around the stem of the clover, then tied the string around my left wrist. She said, "Now, think hard about something you really want. Touch the clover and by the time the string breaks your wish will come true, **if** you are deserving."

I made a lot of wishes in my short life, but the one thing I wanted more than anything right then and there was a set of Fanner Fifty, ivory handled, silver six shooters. I loved westerns on TV, and my favorite hero was the Lone Ranger. The guns I wanted were just like his--and I had to have them. So that was my wish.

A couple of weeks passed and the string still hadn't broken. I was beginning to think it was just a joke my grandma was playing on me, but I wasn't going to give up. Then my left wrist started hurting and swelled up where I had the string. My mother wanted to cut the string off, but I told her no. I wanted my wish to come true, and I had already invested a lot of time and energy, wearing that string. The four-leaf clover had dried up and fallen off that first day, and grandma said that the wish passed to the string.

A few days later my wrist became so swollen it broke the string. A large lump started to form under the skin on the back of my wrist.

My dad said, "It's a carbuncle. We need to take care of that before the kid loses his hand."

My godfather, Uncle Joe, heard about my problem and came over to help. I remember him to be a nice guy as long as you did what he said, but he was very nasty, if you didn't. I remember one day seeing him punch a guy in the nose for telling a joke he didn't like. Blood went all over me. So, I always tried to make him laugh in other ways than telling jokes.

As a side note - My godfather was known as the Gum-Ball King. All the grown-ups said Joe was connected to the mob because he ran the vending machine operation for them on south side of Chicago. He did have a gun in the glove compartment of his car. All I knew was we kids loved to visit his house because his basement and garage were full of wooden barrels of gumballs, toys, magic tricks and prizes. We would go home, with bulging pockets. For Christmas and birthdays, most of our presents came out of his garage. My mother would wrap some of the toys up, but I knew where they came from. She always gave me the magic tricks because she loved when I'd put on magic shows for the family and friends. Unfortunately, Billy would always spoil the show by telling everyone how I did the trick.

While Uncle Joe showed me some cool things from his gumball machine, to distract me, my mother boiled an empty coke bottle in a pot of water. I was sorting through all the gumball toys. And then the next thing I knew, Mom tried to put the hot bottle's mouth hole over the bump. I let out a God-awful scream from the pain.

"It's burning me!" I yelled.

She said, "Hold on Eddie. You have to sit still. I know the bottle is hot, but it will draw the poison out of the bump."

I didn't care what it would do. I wasn't letting anyone touch me with that hot bottle again. My hand hurt bad enough as it was. I might have been a little kid, but I wasn't stupid.

My dad distracted me this time, and then all I remember was when my mother put that hot Coke Cola bottle on my bump, and I let out another scream that would wake the dead.

Dad yelled, "Joe hold him down!"

I broke free and ran from the kitchen, looking for a good hiding place. I knew right where to go. I used it all the time to hide from Billy.

I slid between the back of the couch and the wall. I then waited for them to forget about me. A short time later, Uncle Joe entered the living room and sat on the couch. I held my breath.

He said in a calm voice. "Eddie you know, if you don't get that poison out of your wrist, your hand will rot and fall off, right?"

Uncle Joe was always telling Billy and me that something was going to fall off. If I picked my nose, my nose would fall off. If I played with my belly button, my butt would fall off. Billy was always pulling on his wiener. Uncle Joe told Billy if he kept it up, his wiener would fall off. I was prepared to lose a hand rather than have that hot bottle on my bump. But then I thought about it and decided that I'd look pretty silly, with two guns and one hand.

He then said, "If you let your father get the poison out of the bump, I will buy you anything you want."

Hmmmm, anything? A light bulb went off in my head.

I agreed and ten minutes later after the hot bottle drew everything to the surface, my father cut the top of the bump and squeezed.

I let out another spine tingling scream. Some of the nastiest stuff you'd ever want to see came out of that bump. My mother cleaned and bandaged my wrist. My father grabbed two beers from the icebox and gave one to Joe.

"Thanks Joe," he said. Uncle Joe just nodded, opened his beer and plopped on the couch.

I got my jacket and cowboy hat and said to Uncle Joe, "Well let's go."

He said, "Go where?"

I walked up, took his hand and said, "To the toy store down the street before they sell my Lone Ranger gun set. You promised to buy me anything."

My mother let out the biggest belly laugh and said, "You're lucky he didn't ask for a white horse named Silver, Joe."

That night, I fell asleep wearing a new set of silver six shooters, with ivory handles.

Grandma was right. My wish came true!

My father explained the next day that good luck came into play when Uncle Joe came over unexpected. If he hadn't, I wouldn't have the pistols. I shared the four-leaf clover bracelet secret, with some of my friends, and it worked for them too. I didn't know how it worked, but I didn't know a lot of stuff in those days. And quite frankly, I didn't care how it worked. I had my guns, and that is all that mattered to me.

Chapter Four

When Things went Wrong

I didn't like one of my dad's friends. His name was Fredrick, and whenever he came over to our house, he was always trying to touch and kiss my mother when my father was out of the room. The man gave me the creeps.

On my seventh birthday, my dad was working. I was sad because I wanted to be with him that day. Fred, who was also my dad's supervisor, knew he was working and said he came over with a present to cheer me up.

"I'm gonna' pay for all you kids to go see a movie for Eddie's birthday," he said. Billy and Kathy were excited, but when we left, I had an awful feeling that something was not right.

We went to see, *Lady and the Tramp*. As I sat there eating my popcorn, I started getting sick, so I ran to the rest room. When I returned, I told Billy and Kathy I wanted to go home, because I was sick.

Billy refused to leave. As usual he never did anything he didn't want to do.

"But Mom said we HAD to stay together," I said. "Come on Billy, my tummy hurts, and I think I'm gonna' puke."

Kathy said, "It's okay Eddie. Don't worry 'bout him. I will walk you home."

Kathy and I headed home. I threw up three times along the way.

When we got inside the apartment I went in my mother's bedroom to tell her I was sick. When I opened the door, Fred wasn't wearing any clothes, and he was doing something weird to my mother. I didn't know what it was, but I certainly didn't like it.

My mother started to cry and Fred ordered me out of the room. A few minutes later, they came out of the bedroom and sat me down at the kitchen table.

Fred said, "Your mother was helping to heal an old war wound I suffered in the Navy. I had to take my clothes off, so she could see it."

He then pulled up his shirt and showed me a scar he had on his back. She put some iodine on a bandage and covered the scar. It didn't make much sense to me, but what did I know. I felt confused.

Fred then said, "Listen kid, don't scrunch your eyes at me like you don't understand. You are a smart boy. You know what will happen, if your father finds out. It would just start a big fight, and you'd be to blame. Anyways," he said, "I'm moving to Florida next week, and I was just saying good-bye to your mother."

That was the best news I had for my birthday! I felt like that was more of a present than the movie tickets. Just to be safe and not get into any trouble, I never did say a thing to my father or anybody else for that matter.

Shortly after my birthday I could hear my mother and father fighting all the time. She wasn't happy anymore like she used to be. I tried to do more stuff to help her, but she was still always sad and moody. No one wanted to get on her bad side.

At school, I prayed and prayed for her to be happy again. We went to St. Mary of the Angels, a Catholic school in our neighborhood. Billy was always getting in trouble with the nuns. Today was no different. It was just before Christmas that year when Billy and I had returned home from school. He threatened me not to say anything because not only would he beat me to a pulp, he was also gonna' tell Santa I was a snitch. Billy wanted to get "his side" of the story out and lay the pouty faced ground work with mom, before the letter from the nuns arrived. When we walked in the house, my mother was in her bedroom, with the door closed. Billy peeked through the keyhole, before knocking, because he wanted to make sure he wasn't going to wake her up. That would've been extra trouble.

"She's wrapping presents Eddie," he whispered. "Looks like you are getting some really great toys this year. Come on, look for yourself."

We tip-toed to the door, and I bent over to look. I couldn't see anything. Billy grabbed me by the shirt, opened the door then wedged my body half in the room and half out. I was trapped! Billy was pulling the door closed on me, and I was stuck.

My mother yelled, "Jesus Christ shut that door!" I was freaking out because I couldn't move. My body was lodged between the side of the door and the doorjamb. Billy wouldn't let go of the knob. I could see her face grow red as a beet because I wasn't listening. She had a pair of long silver scissors in her hand. When I didn't move to back out of the room, in a fit of rage she drew back her arm and let them fly. The scissors lodged in the top of my head. Billy let go of the doorknob and ran, as I hit the floor.

My mother was afraid to take me to the hospital. She knew there would be questions. She pulled the scissors out and lucky for me a nurse lived upstairs. Ms. Angela was her name, and she was about 111 years old. Well not really, but she sure looked like 111 to a little kid. Mom had Billy went up to get her.

Ms. Angela came down to treat the wound and told my mom, "I cleaned the wound out best I could. He has a pretty good lump under that cut. His skull could be fractured. A doctor should see the boy."

But that never happened.

Mom told my father when he got home, "Billy is going to be the death of Eddie someday." She didn't give Dad all the details, but just enough that Billy got in trouble. He may have skated on the school issue, but he paid the price anyway.

That Christmas was really nice, even though we didn't have much money. Most of our gifts came out of Uncle Joe's basement and the toys in cereal boxes that my parents collected during the year. They also wrapped up hand-me-down toys that my father got from the church. It didn't matter to us. At least we got something. My parents always tried their best to make Christmas special.

We all woke up early and ran downstairs to open our presents. Dad cooked breakfast. Mom had a bad headache. She got up to watch us open our presents, but then went back to bed. She still seemed very sad. As I watched her go back upstairs, I got that same bad feeling again, like the day of my birthday when Fred sent us to the movies. The feeling quickly left me though because it was Christmas morning. My dad gave me a very special gift. He had carved a sword out of a piece of wood and painted it silver and gold. It was almost as big as me.

King Arthur and the Lone Ranger were my two favorite role models and Dad knew how much I loved swords. That night when I went to bed, I was happy. I had my guns that Uncle Joe bought me and my father's sword. Little did I know, my whole world was soon going to be turned upside down.

The next morning, after my father left for work, my mother woke us up and said we were going to Washington D.C. to visit our grandparents. She said to pick one toy to take with us for the train ride. I wanted to take the pistols, but Billy was being his usual jerk self and hid them, so I took the sword. I was so glad I did.

While we were on the train, something didn't seem right. My mom was excited. She looked bubbly even. I never saw my mother so happy to visit her parents. I really knew something was wrong when I started seeing palm trees out of the train windows.

My heart sank. I was no dummy. I knew right away we were going to Florida. The next day, we got off the train and there he was, my father's old buddy Fredrick.

My mother told us that my father didn't love us anymore, and we had to leave Chicago, so he could start another family. I knew it was a lie, but what could I do?

Billy hated the cold weather, so he loved Florida and Kathy was too young to understand any of it. I was at a loss.

Fred rented a house in West Palm Beach. The house backed up to a huge swamp. Not only was the house infested with rats and scorpions, we were warned that the swamp was full of poisonous snakes and alligators. Lovely. And me without my pistols!

We had to put the legs of the beds in coffee cans filled with water to keep the scorpions from crawling in bed with us. Unfortunately, that didn't stop them from dropping down on me from the ceiling.

I did have a room by myself. That was a plus. I'd lie in bed at night, counting the bugs on the walls and listening to the bull alligators, calling for a mate. I'd always fall asleep, wondering what my father was doing and hoping that he would rescue us from the hell we were living in.

Chapter Five

The Sunshine State

1956 was not a good time to live in Florida if you were Negro or had a German last name. There were lots of rules to remember. The first thing mom said was, "When you say your last name, make it sound American!" The next thing we learned from a neighbor was, "Don't you play with the 'colored' kids. They don't belong on this street."

Me being me, I had to ask, "Why?"

The answer was always, just mind your own business, and do as you are told!"

It was so strange for me, since several of my friends in Chicago were what they called "colored." I never understood what colored meant. Living in the Midwest, my friends were black, brown, yellow, red and white. We all got along with each other back home no matter what our skin looked like. With my freckled Irish complexion, if I stayed in the sun more than 10 minutes I'd turn bright red. So really, what was all the hubbub about skin color? I remember thinking back then that we are all the same underneath the skin. We are all God's children. At least that is what I learned at St. Mary of the Angels School.

Anyways, there were a lot of Ku Klux Klan families living around the swamp. Their kids were all mean and hot tempered. As far as I could see, they were the ones I needed to stay away from.

Now Billy might have been the brat in the family, but I guess you could say I was the obstinate one. Especially if you couldn't give me a good reasonable explanation for why I shouldn't do something. Never one to be told not to do something, I made friends with a six-year-old boy everybody called "Black Frankie." I must admit he did have the blackest skin I ever did see. I felt weird calling him "Black Frankie," but he insisted. He said his father gave him that nickname, and he was proud of it. I still just called him Frankie when we were together, but "Black Frankie" when I talked to other people about him. Everybody in that section of town knew him. Frankie was one sweet kid.

It was funny how we met. I loved to fish, but didn't have a fishing pole. Being a problem solver, I tied a piece of fishing line and a hook to the sword my father made me and headed to the lake. I cut up a frog and used the leg meat for bait. Almost immediately, I caught a bass. It was hard to work with the sword to get the fish on shore, so I decided to put the string on a long stick. I waited for what seemed like forever, but I didn't catch a fish. When I transferred the string back to the sword, I caught another fish right away. It was weird.

I remember saying out loud, "Wow, this sword must have magical powers." I kept using it from then on.

One day while fishing, this little kid passed by me and stopped. He wanted to know why I was using the sword Excalibur to catch fish.

He said, "You know that sword has magic powers?"

I looked at him when he said that and I think if someone had taken a picture of me they would've seen my eyeballs bug out. I was like, "Wow! How did you know that? It does have magical powers!"

I told him the story of when I started fishing here and tried with a stick, but didn't catch anything. Then every time I tied the line to the sword, I would catch a fish.

He just smiled the biggest brightest smile I ever did see. He was a cute little kid. He said, "My name's Frankie Jackson and I'm six years old. What's your name?"

"Eddie Jagen," I said swallowing the last syllable so that it didn't sound too German.

Then he told me, "Excalibur once belonged to the Lady of the Lake, and it's probably the Lady, putting those fish on your line."

For being only six years old, Frankie sure knew a lot about King Arthur and the Knights of the Round Table. After he told me some more about the legend of the Lady of the Lake, he started to walk away, pulling a wagon loaded down with wood behind him.

He stopped again and said, "Hey, I'm building a castle in the woods down yonder. Wanna' help me?

"A Castle? That's my dream," I told him.

When we got to the spot, it didn't look much like any castle I'd ever seen in books. It looked more like the three little pigs house made of sticks.

I laughed and said, "This is a castle?" I could see right away I made Frankie feel bad. I told him, "I will help you build a better castle!"

Back in Chicago, when I had gone to work with my father when he built houses, I always loved to get on the roof. I remembered watching him use large sheets of plywood for roofing, so I told Frankie that we needed to find some plywood for our castle. That way, it would be as easy as building a house of cards.

That, too, was a game I used to play with my dad. The goal was to set the cards up like little square rooms. Then you put cards on top of those rooms, so we could build the next floor. The winner was the first to use all fifty-two cards before the building fell down. It was funny how everything I did made me think of my dad and the times I spent with him.

About a half mile away was Roger's Junk Yard and Emporium. I asked Mr. Rogers, if he had any old wood that I could use to build a fort. He was a grumpy old man and told me to get lost. On my way out, I spotted a trash truck dumping wood and debris in a pile. I asked Mr. Rogers how much money would it cost to buy that pile of trash?

He replied, "I'll let you pick through it for ten dollars."

I said, "You have a deal. Can I have a week to get you the money?"

He said, "Sure, now scram and don't come back until you have ten bucks."

17

As I ran out of the yard, I looked at that pile. It was like finding a lost treasure. I couldn't wait to get the money! I saw an old broken flatbed cart that could be fixed and used to haul all the supplies to our castle site

I asked my mother and Fred if I could do chores around the house to earn the ten dollars, but Fred said I should be doing chores for free, since I wasn't paying rent to live in his house.

My mother said, "Why don't you go around the streets and collect soda bottles? There is a 8two-cent deposit that you could collect on each bottle, if you turn them in at the Piggly Wiggly and A & P food stores."

"Wow!" I said. "I know where there are lots of bottles!"

We were in business. Frankie would take his wagon and go in one direction, and I'd go in the other, searching for the soda bottles. It was amazing how much money there was in trash.

The deal I made with Mr. Rogers was that I'd pay him ten dollars every two weeks to be able to search the trash pile for things we needed to build our castle. It was weird though, because he'd ask me what I needed and the next time I'd visit, exactly what I needed was right on the pile. Sometimes I thought Mr. Rogers wasn't really grumpy. I think he acted that way so people wouldn't bother him.

While looking for bottles on the street one day, I passed Burdine's Department Store. There was a team of artists in the window, building a large castle for a window display. I was mesmerized by what they were doing. They were making plain wood look like stone. It was so interesting. I sat down on the sidewalk and watched for hours, as they layered three different colors of paint and used brushes and sea sponges to make texture. When they were finished, I could hardly believe my eyes. I couldn't wait to try it.

Once Frankie and I finished building our plywood Castle, we stood back and looked at it. "Wow, we did it!" Frankie said. "Now all we need to do is paint it."

I said, "I know exactly what to do. I'll meet you back here tomorrow."

Remembering what I saw the artists doing in the Burdine's Department Store window display, I ran down to the Mary Carter Paint Store to see if there was any free paint leftover I could get.

When I asked the cashier about paint for my castle, she sent me to a guy with a white beard and long hair pulled back into a ponytail. He asked, "Can I help you with something, son?"

The name tag he was wearing read "Benjamin T. Wizard, Manager".

I pointed to the Burdine's window display across the street and asked, "Do you have any paint left over from that display over there that we could have cheap or for free?"

"We? Who's we?" he asked.

"Oh, my friend, Frankie, and I are building a castle sort of like the one in the window across the street. I saw the people getting the paint from your store," I said.

He looked down and saw my father's sword lying on the cart and asked, "May I see that?"

When he held it, a huge smile came across his face. He looked like a little kid again. I actually saw something come over him. I was thinking that sword really did have magical powers.

Mr. Wizard asked, "Where did you get such a powerful sword?"

I told him, "My father carved the sword and gave it to me for Christmas. It was the last time I saw him. Then the next day my mother brought us to Florida, without my father knowing, just so she could be with another man."

Tears came to the old man's eyes, as I talked. When I finished, the man gave me all the paint I wanted for free. I didn't need much, just two gallons each of black, white and brown. Thanks to his display artists, I knew exactly what to do with it.

When I went to leave the store, Mr. Wizard picked my sword up once again and touched it to my shoulder, as he said, "Little Sir Edward, never stop dreaming and never let yourself grow older than nine. I will teach you something very important. It's Wizard math. How old are you?" he asked.

I said, "Seven."

He continued, "When you reach ten years old, drop the zero and become one again. But know this time, you will do one better because you're not in diapers. On your eleventh birthday, add the two numbers together. One and one are two. You are two again, but better this time. Always add the two numbers of your age together until your age reduces down to just one number. This way you will have the heart of a wizard, and you will never grow old. Don't do what I did. I gave up on my dream and aged."

I never forgot Benjamin and wizard math. He was right, I did have the heart of a wizard and sixty-five years into my life's adventure, I can proudly say I'm two again.

When I got to the castle the next day, I couldn't wait to show Frankie the six gallons of free paint, brushes, paint roller and sea sponges I got. I knew he would be so excited! I pulled the wagon up to the drawbridge, only to see Frankie sitting there on an old log in front looking very sad.

"What's wrong?" I said.

"Today is one year since my dad died," Frankie said.

I remembered over hearing the man next door, telling Fred about it right after we moved in, "Right over yonder was where they hung Black Jack Jackson. He was a local gambler they claimed and was cheating at the cards. Done paid a heavy price, he did, for gambling with Klan members. He was found hanging from that there tree out in the swamp as a reminder."

"I'm sorry Frankie," I said, while patting him on his back.

Frankie told me, "My momma said the Klan killed him, but no one was ever arrested for it. Today on my way here, some of the Klan kids in the neighborhood were teasing me. They wanted to know how I felt about my 'Dead Niggra' father. Why are they so mean?"

While he was fighting back the tears, Frankie went on to tell me before they let him go, Tim Irving, the leader of the gang knocked Frankie down and pissed on his back. I could smell it.

I walked Frankie home. And when we got there, Frankie's mother saw the streaks the tears made in the dust when they ran down his face.

She asked Frankie what happened. When he told her, she said, "I told you not to be a playing with those white kids. That's why they come after you, boy." She slapped him upside the head, then looked at me and yelled, "You stay away from my Frankie. Go play with your own kind and leave my son alone. We have enough trouble."

19

She was really upset and even as young as I was, I could understand her worries. I didn't understand the racial issue back then, but I could certainly feel the tension.

Even though we weren't supposed to play with each other anymore, I was bound and determined to finish Frankie's castle. We both lost our fathers, but his was gone forever and mine was out there somewhere. I felt it made us blood brothers no matter what our skin looked like.

The next day when I got back to the castle, I mixed the black and white paint to make gray and painted everything. I worked as hard as I could to get over the hate I felt for Tim Irving and his gang peeing on Frankie. They are the bullies in my school. They have picked fights with my brother, Billy, before. They called him a Nazi Hitlerite. I didn't know what that meant. I just knew I had to stay away from those guys. All my effort paid off. I worked so hard painting that I forgot about them and could think of nothing, but going home to sleep.

I came back the next day, and the paint had dried, so I started making the stone-look pattern I saw the artists creating in the department store window display. I dipped the sea sponge in brown paint, then pressed it onto the gray walls, floors, ceiling and crowning. It made a nice contrast. I then did the same thing with the white paint until the whole building looked like stone inside and out. I then took a small brush and, with black paint, I cut in mortar lines making all the surfaces look like stone blocks.

Mr. Rogers gave me a large round table top that I nailed to three orange crates and painted it brown. Walaa! I had King Arthur's Round Table of Peace. I was so excited. However, I could only get six chairs around the table.

I cut shields out of plywood and made swords out of old fence pickets. After painting and decorating, I nailed them to the walls. I even brought in old cinder blocks and made a fireplace. It didn't have a chimney, so we couldn't have a fire but it looked good. Over the entrance, I painted "Good Knight Castle, only the GOOD may enter." The castle looked great. I wished Frankie was there to see it.

I hadn't seen Frankie for weeks. I really missed him. I felt that I had to at least let him know that his Good Knight Castle was finished. He could have it to play in, with his friends, if he wanted. I didn't want to cause him any more trouble. He was a good kid and needed a place to get away to feel good about himself. I only had one brother beating on me. He had six mean cousins and his mother's boyfriend that was mistreating him. Plus, having to worry about the Klan all the time.

I walked over to his house. On the way, I ran into his little sister, Rita. I was glad because I was a little afraid his mom would yell at me again. I told Rita to tell Frankie that the castle was finished and he could have it for his friends. I didn't need to be part of it anymore. I just wanted to help him finish it. Rita said she would tell him.

That night I felt good about finishing the castle for Frankie. As I lay in bed, listening to an alligator off in the distance, I thought about my dad. It was great being able to use some of the skills I had learned from watching him build houses. In a way, it helped me feel close to him again when I built things. I was hoping if he saw what I did, he would be proud of me and want me back again.

The sound of the alligator was getting closer and closer and jogged my mind out of the thoughts about my dad. Our house sat on cinder blocks to keep water out of the house when the swamp rose during storms. It was mating season and they were so loud. That bull gator must have been following a female because the two crawled up under the house and started rolling around. I heard a thump, thump, BOOM. The next thing I knew my bedroom sank about two feet in one corner and I rolled out of bed. They must've knocked into the cinder blocks on the corner of the house. I ran into my mother's room and told Fred that an alligator was trying to get into the house. When he went outside with a flashlight, he found that the house had fallen and squished that gator.

The next morning, I couldn't wait to go outside to see what had happened. It reminded me of *The Wizard of Oz* when Dorothy's house fell on the wicked witch. There was one good thing that came out of the alligator, attacking my bedroom. Fred said we were getting a dog to scare the gators away. I always wanted a dog.

That afternoon when I came home from school, I changed clothes and ran back to the castle one last time to get my father's sword. When I arrived, Frankie was there. He was scared when he first saw me.

He said "My momma will beat the tar outta' me if she knew I be seeing you again. Rita told me you gave me the castle and you don't want it."

I didn't like the way he was looking at me. Fear was all over his face.

"I just came back to get my sword. I forgot it," I said. "Yes, I just wanted you to have it. It's yours."

He seemed to relax when I said that, and he began looking at everything I had done. He was amazed at the detail.

He said, "It doesn't look like the little pig's house made of sticks anymore."

I said, "No, it looks like a castle built for Sir Frankie the Good Knight, Son of Black Jack." Frankie beamed a huge smile.

I guess we pushed our luck a little too far and I should've just got my sword and left. But Frankie was my friend, and we were the legendary Good Knights that needed to do knightly deeds.

We were sitting at the round table when it happened.

From outside, there was a voice, "Black Frankie are you in there with that Nazi nigger lover?"

It was Tim Irving and his gang. They were all about thirteen years old and for some reason, because my last name is Jagen, they claim I am related to Hitler. The six boys kicked down the door and grabbed us. They then tied us to palm trees and began knocking down our castle. When they were finished, Tim accused us of stealing all the wood from Roger's Junk Yard. One of the boys in the gang was Paul Rogers, the owner's son.

Paul said, "That's right Jagen, I saw you sneaking around my Dad's yard putting things on your cart."

I said back, "I paid for those things fair and square."

But of course, they didn't believe me.

One of the other boys in the gang found the left-over cans of paint and accused us of stealing them too.

When Tim saw the cans he laughed and said, "Hey, let's paint the nigger white, since he likes playing with white boys. And we can paint the Nazi black, since he's a nigger lover."

Frankie started crying, so Paul stuck the paintbrush in his mouth. I refused to cry or open my mouth.

Tim Irving said, "Look guys we have two toilets--one for Whites and one for the Niggers. I think it's time to take a piss."

As we were being drenched, I could tell that Paul Rogers realized that it wasn't funny anymore and Frankie started yelling like he was crazy. He was wiggling and screaming for them to get him out of the ropes that held him to the tree.

Paul said, "Come on guys, let's go."

They zipped up their pants and started to walk away. As Tim passed my sword lying on the ground, he picked it up.

Frankie yelled, "That's Excalibur. It belongs to Sir Edward, leave it alone."

Tim turned, looked at me, smiled and said, "Who the hell is Sir Edward? All I see is a piss-ant." He then broke the blade in two over his knee and tossed the pieces into briar bushes.

My heart sank. I couldn't believe how happy I was a few minutes earlier and now I was painted, pissed on and totally humiliated.

Frankie was the first to wiggle free of his ropes. He was dazed and just started to walk away.

I yelled, "Frankie, aren't you going to untie me?"

With tears streaming down his face he screamed, "This is all your fault! My momma told you not to come near me anymore!"

Our eyes locked, and it was like we could read each other's minds. No, it wasn't my fault. It wasn't Frankie's fault. It was just plain ole' sad. In our hearts, we knew we were best friends that lived in a world where it wasn't allowed. As Frankie dropped his head and started to walk back over to me, my heart felt a pang knowing we had to accept the fact that this was how it had to be. He untied me.

"Thanks," I said, as I picked up my broken sword from the bushes.

Then I walked Frankie home. We never spoke, and I knew that would be the last time I'd see him and wanted to make sure he got home okay.

When I got home, my mother wanted to know what happened. I told her everything.

I said, "I want to call the police and have those boys arrested."

"Are you crazy? Jesus Christ! That would cause even more trouble," she yelled. "You know who that Tim Irving's father is, don't you? He's Klan. They are very vengeful people."

I started to cry. As mad as she was, I thought she was going to beat me, but instead she came over and sat next to me and pulled me into her arms. She held me so tight I thought I was going to pop! I knew then it wasn't really me she was mad at. She was just scared. So was I.

After the hug, she held me at arm's length, smiled and said, "Cheer up! I have two surprises for you. My boss is going to take us all to Jupiter Beach on Saturday for a family picnic. I think a trip to the beach is going to make all these bad feelings wash away."

"What's the other surprise?" I asked.

"Well," she said, "that has to remain a surprise for now."

I smiled back for her sake, but inside all I thought was, "She's wrong. Nothing is going to make this day go away. It will be etched in my memory forever." All I wanted to do at that point was get even with Tim Irving for what he had done to us.

That evening the second surprise was revealed. Fred came home with a doghouse and a black German Shepherd. He was told that barking dogs keep alligators from coming around.

I didn't care what the reason was that he got the dog. I was just so happy about having a dog, I could hardly stand it.

"Can he sleep in my room, since that is where the alligator tried to get into?" I asked.

My mom said, "I don't see why not…"

Interrupting her, the landlord who was there with some guys to jack up the corner of the house and put it back on the cinder blocks, said, "No, you need the dog outside to scare the gators away. Won't do you no good living on the inside."

If my looks could kill, he would've been dead. I felt like saying, "Why don't you mind your own business and let my mom answer me?" But I kept my mouth shut, since this had been a pretty bad day already.

After they jacked the house up, they took the dead gator and threw it in the swamp. One of the guys gave me a tooth from the gator as a souvenir.

All of a sudden I was starting to feel better. I made a necklace for my tooth then played fetch the stick with the dog. I named him "Poochie the Gator Eater." And I stayed outside until supper, playing with that dog. I soooo wanted him to sleep in my room.

At the dinner table that night I asked again, "Can he please sleep in my room?"

Fred said, "He can't keep the gators away if he is inside, Eddie. But you can go out and sleep in the doghouse with him, if you'd like."

Everyone started laughing and Billy piped up, "Yeah Eddie, go ahead sleep outside, so it's easier for the gators to drag you away."

Under the table my fists were all balled up. "Boy I would like to knock his block off," I thought.

That night, as I lay in bed watching a scorpion catch and eat a cockroach, I was thinking about all the buttheads in my life. Billy, Tim Irving, Paul Rogers, Fred. Wow, what a list. I felt so helpless against them. I prayed to God to help me. I just wanted to have a way to not get pushed around so much.

Right after I said, "Amen," I saw a beautiful blue light flickering on the ceiling right about where the scorpion was a few minutes ago. It moved over to the windowsill. I got out of bed and went to get a closer look.

As I got to the window, I heard the loud bellow of a bull alligator out in the swamp calling for a mate. It startled me, and I lost sight of the blue light.

Soon I heard good ole' Poochie barking. The gator stopped his call. A few moments later the gator started again and from the window, I could see the dog running around barking. The gator's booming call stopped again. I guess it worked. They were right. Poochie needed to be outside.

The next day before Billy and I left for school the neighbor came over and told my mom that we had to clean up her yard. Poochie had gotten into her trashcans and garbage was all over her yard.

She told Fred, "You keep that dog on a chain or I'm going to call the police."

We cleaned up the trash, but didn't find the dog. The woman had hit Poochie with a broom to get him away from the trash and he ran off. I was worried he ran away into the swamp and got snake bit or worse.

Billy said, "Come on, we're gonna' be late. We can't look for him now."
Sadly, we headed to school.

When we got there, some of my brother's friends had heard what happened the day before to Frankie and me. They laughed and said, "Do you smell that? Smells like piss to me."

My brother looked at me and said, "What are they talking about Eddie?"

I just walked away. I knew I'd pay for it later, but at least he wouldn't thump me in front of the teachers. I didn't tell my brother what happened on purpose. Now the whole thing was out, and the news was spreading fast through school. That was the longest day of my life.

When I got home, Poochie was chained to the doghouse. Fred found him. I looked at Poochie and could tell he didn't like being on the chain. He just laid there looking sad. It didn't feel right.

That night, as I lay in bed exhausted from a day of humiliation and teasing, the bull alligators started calling for mates again. I was drifting off to sleep, as the dog started barking. I half heard it, as I slipped into a deep sleep.

The next morning when I went out to feed Poochie, he was gone, doghouse and all. There were drag marks in the dirt that lead right into the swamp. My heart sank, thinking what probably happened to my dog.

A few days later the doghouse was found, floating up against a cypress tree, by a neighbor driving a swamp buggy. That's a vehicle with huge tractor tires, used by hunters in the swamp.

The hunter said, "Sorry son it looks like the alligators ate your dog. You should never chain a dog up in gator country. It's like leaving out a snack if the dog can't get away."

I was devastated. When I went back inside the house Fred and my mother were fighting because she had put on her shoe and forgot to check it for scorpions.

You ALWAYS have to check your shoes for scorpions where we lived.

Mom had gotten stung, but luckily it was a small one.

She yelled at Fred, "I'm tired of living in a bug and gator infested swamp. I want to move."

I piped in, "Mom why don't we go back to Chicago? Dad's still there!"

"Shut up Eddie!" Mom yelled through the tears.

After a lot of yelling and things being thrown back and forth across the room, Fred announced that night he was leaving.

When I woke up in the morning, Fred was gone.

That had to be the worst week of my life. I remember thinking, "My castle, well Frankie's castle, was destroyed. The sword dad made me was broken in two. I was tied up, painted black, pissed on AND the alligators ate my Poochie! Now mom was crying in her room. What else could possibly go wrong?"

24

Chapter Six

Jupiter Beach

My mother worked as a waitress at the Sail Inn Restaurant. Her boss was a really nice guy. His name was John Wayne, just like the movie star. He was rich, wore a white cowboy hat and drove a big, gold Cadillac convertible with steer longhorns on the front. He also had a big sailboat.

Fred was always jealous of John because he brought us something each time he came to visit. John was shorter than mom, a little round and told funny jokes all the time. Mom told us to call him "Uncle John."

When Uncle John showed up to take us on the picnic, he brought each of us something extra special. He knew we had been through a lot that week and that Fred had left.

He gave Kathy a doll and Billy a nice fishing rod. He gave me a big, inflatable, yellow banana to float on in the water. He knew I couldn't swim very well, so he thought this would help me feel more comfortable.

We drove to Jupiter Beach for a picnic and day of swimming. I loved going to the beach.

After we ate lunch, I blew up the banana float to go swimming, but mom told me to help Kathy build a sand castle. When we were finished my brother, Billy, tied his towel around his neck and started acting like superman flying around.

He circled the sand castle a few times, then jumped right in the middle of the castle saying, "Yes and I am able to squish small buildings in a single bound." Kathy started crying.

Then Billy started threatening to pop my banana float to prove his super human strength. Mom yelled at Billy to knock it off, but he never listened to anyone. So just to make sure, I grabbed the float and moved further down the beach to get away from him.

Mom was kissing Uncle John under the umbrella, as Kathy went off to play with her doll and another little girl at the water's edge.

I couldn't understand why everybody, but Billy, seemed happy. He was always so negative about everything. I prayed that one day he would be plagued by a bully worse than him. Someone that would make his life a living hell like he made everyone else's. I remembered when Damian came to visit us and how much peace I had for a week. I found myself wishing again that I had a brother like him, instead of the one I had.

When I got far enough away that I felt safe from Billy, I started riding the waves on my big yellow banana. I didn't know it, but I was going further and further out past the breakers. I was having a ball until I got knocked off the float, by a huge wave and swallowed a lot of water. The float drifted away from me. I was screaming for help, but no one could hear me.

The people on the beach looked the size of ants. The waves crashing on the beach were too loud for anyone to hear my screams for help. I was getting tired and couldn't stay afloat any longer. I went under, held my breath and started fighting my way back to the surface. When I came up, I saw the lighthouse but went under again. This happened several times, until I couldn't fight anymore and just started sinking. My lungs felt like they were going to burst from the pressure. The further I sank, the darker it got. I had to let the air out, but knew if I did, all I would take back in was water. And I would drown.

My ears started buzzing just as I exhaled. I stopped sinking. I felt like I had been kicked in the chest and then I felt nothing except the darkness all around me. My eyes were closed, but I could see a speck of golden light coming toward me. I opened my eyes to see what it was. The light was getting bigger. A feeling of comfort came over me. The closer the light came, the better I felt. As it approached me, I could see that it was a beautiful golden-haired lady.

I remember thinking, "Is this the Lady of the Lake that Frankie was talking about?"

The lady grabbed my arm, and we floated down a long dark tunnel toward a bright shining white light. She stopped half way down, looked at me and smiled. A feeling of comfort came over me. I had never felt that way before. All I know is her smile lit me up, inside and out. It's hard to describe how I felt. It's like there are no words adequate enough to do it justice. All I knew then was that I felt good and the pain in my lungs went away.

She spoke to me through her mind and never moved her mouth. In my mind, I asked, "What is your name?"

She said she was nameless, but I could call her the Constant Walker, or Connie for short.

When we reached the end of the tunnel she spoke again. "This is your time. Everyone has a time that is uniquely theirs."

I looked at her when she spoke and could feel my brows crinkle.

"I don't understand," I said.

"It is time for you to die and cross over to the other side, but I don't want you to leave life just yet," she uttered so sweetly. "I have a very good reason for you to continue to live, if you choose to do so."

She went on to say, "You can stay with Us now for eternity or go back into life and become the legs for my great Angel-Knight champion. There is something he must do, and he can't do it alone. He must return to earth every five hundred years, seeking a special Sword and Stone. If he finds the Sword and the Stone, he will need you to help him deliver them to a very special little girl, who will safeguard them for the Children of Tomorrow."

I was so caught up in her beauty and the way she made me feel loved. I replied, "I want to stay with you Connie. I want to feel like this forever."

As I stared into her eyes, I instantly knew that her love would be with me forever, no matter what. In that moment, I would've done whatever she wanted of me.

I then proclaimed, "If going back serves you, I will go back."

My life had turned to crap. I didn't really want to go back, but the thought of disappointing that beautiful vision was unbearable.

Connie then took me into a cavern, where I saw a huge angel fast asleep next to a large boulder. He was wearing blue and gold armor, holding a sleeping baby in his arms. There was a glowing sword by his side. I did a double take. The sword looked like the one my father had carved for me!

Connie said that the angel's name was Michael, and he was dreaming about the life I could have and the things that could be accomplished if I returned to life.

I asked, "Will I be able to build a castle that can't be torn down and protect people from villains, like Tim Irving?"

She said, "Tim is not a villain. He is a product of his environment. He thinks nobody loves him. That is why he acts that way. And yes," she continued with a giggle, "you will build lots and lots of castles, because that is what Edwards do!"

She then told me, "Go. Lay next to Michael. Fall asleep and you will see his dreams. In those dreams your destiny will be revealed."

I climbed to Angel Michael and the little baby.

Staring at the two of them, I asked, "Who is this sweet baby?"

Connie replied, "She is nameless, but I call her MV, Michael's Victory. If you decide to return, you and Michael will search for her. When you find her, you will know God's True Love."

My heart filled with something I had never felt before just by looking at that precious baby, lying there in the wings of the great angel. There was something about her. I had seen plenty of babies before, but this one, this one felt like she touched my heart just by being next to her.

I did as Connie told me to do. I laid down next to the angel and fell asleep, I was shown many things. I remember wearing blue and gold armor like the angel's. There was a huge machine made out of stone tubes that people walked through, a castle with towers, mirrors and lights, a large sword with a bright crystal, children, lots of children, and I was on a stage talking to them. I began knighting the children, with a flaming sword. I then saw a battle against evil demons. There was a great storm. The earth was shaking; people were running and people were dying. It was chaos.

Then I saw myself sitting at a great round table, with fellow knights. So many things were shown to me that my head was spinning. The last vision in the angel's dream that I remember seeing was a little girl in a super girl costume.

She looked straight at me and said, "Thank you, Ada, for coming back for me."

Her voice was enchanting like a melody that vibrated deep within my soul. All I felt at that moment was the need to find this child. The world needed her. I knew it. I knew they would all feel the same way about her as I did. She is the one that could help the Tim Irvings and Klan people of the world find their way into the light. She was pure love, and that is what was needed most.

With that realization, my soul vowed to go back.

The next thing I saw was my body floating in the ocean. I was hovering above it, as if I was flying. I saw a woman swimming out to get me. She grabbed me under my arms and pulled me to shore. When she got me on the sand, she started pushing on my chest and blowing into my mouth. Then she rolled me over and started slapping me on the back. I was still hovering over her, looking down. My body looked dead, but I felt very alive and free. I could tell the girl was getting tired and ready to give up.

She said, "Okay one last time. Please God wake this little boy up, please!" She slapped my back again and water shot out of my mouth. It was like something reached up and grabbed me. I went slamming back into my body. I saw a blinding white light and then felt pain in my chest. I started coughing and gagging.

I remember saying, "Where am I? What happened to me?"

The girl told me her name was Sophia, and she was jogging down the beach watching a manatee pushing something in the water. That something turned out to me. She was afraid I was dead. She then swam out to get me when the manatee swam away. She was tall, with long black curly hair and very pretty.

I told Sophia about the yellow banana float, Connie the beautiful woman, the baby MV and some of the things the angel showed me in his dream.

After I was finished, Sophia replied, "All I saw was an old sea cow pushing your body to shore. You might not want to tell anyone that because they will think you're crazy."

When I got back to where my mother and Uncle John were, I told them what had happened.

Sophia was right.

All my mom said was, "I think you've been out in the sun too long. Come, sit under the umbrella for a while and have something to eat."

I felt stupid and embarrassed, so I never brought it up again.

Chapter Seven

First Encounter with the Demon Lust

With Fred gone, Uncle John helped us find another house away from the swamp that happened to be right down the street from his restaurant on Lilac Court. On my birthday, Uncle John bought me another black dog because he knew how sad I was after the gators ate my first one. He dated my mother for a few months, but his wife, who had run off with another man, came back and wanted to work on their marriage.

Uncle John still came around, but mom started dating other guys that came into the restaurant. Some were good and some not so good.

One of those "not so nice guys" my mother dated was Big Jim Jones. She had been dating him for about three weeks when he started to sleep over. After a few nights with us, he started acting like he owned the house. One day when my mother was at work, Big Jim was lying on the couch, drinking beer and watching television. He had done it before when mom was home, so I didn't think anything about it. Billy had gone to the park with his friends. I went out in the backyard to play with my new mutt that I named, "Poochie Too." She was very protective of me. After throwing a stick a few times to Poochie, I started to feel buzzing in my ears.

I had the feeling something was telling me to go get my sister Kathy out of the house. When I walked into the living room, I saw Big Jim sitting on the couch with Kathy on his lap. He had his hand under her dress. He was pulling down her under pants. Kathy was only four and didn't know what he was doing, but I did. I ran up and grabbed Kathy off his lap. She fell on the floor and started to cry.

I said, "Run Kathy get away from him. He is trying to hurt you."

"No, he's not. He bought this new dress for me," she sobbed.

Big Jim got up. I could see he was drunk because he was wobbly and had trouble walking. He went for Kathy again, but I stepped in the way saying, "You get out of my house, or I'll tell my mother what you're trying to do to my sister."

Big Jim's eyes turned black with rage, as he gave me the back of his hand. That blow sent me flying across the room. I hit the wall with my head and shoulder. I was dazed, but I could hear the buzzing in my head grow louder. I never heard the voice, but words that were not mine came into my mind saying, "Little Sir Good Knight, let me in, he is going to hurt you, if you don't."

I remembered what Connie had said about her Angel-Knight champion needing legs. I knew the time had come. All I said was, "Yes, let's help Kathy."

The hair stood up on my arms and on the back of my neck. I felt electrified. I got up and ran into the kitchen. I grabbed a long butcher knife from the draw. When I came back into the living room, Big Jim had my sister in his arms again. I felt like I was ten-feet-tall, standing there with a huge broadsword in my hand.

My voice commanded, "Put her down demon!"

I thought, "Where did that come from? Demon? I never call people demon."

I began to advance toward Big Jim with such courage I had never felt before, slashing, darting and stabbing all the way. Something else was controlling my every move. And I **liked** it! I felt invincible!

Jim reached for the knife, and it sliced off his little finger. He recoiled in shock. I don't know what it was that Big Jim saw in my eyes that day, but it certainly wasn't a scrawny eight-year-old kid. Jim's faced filled with fear. He dropped Kathy, picked up his severed finger and ran out the back door. Once outside, he tripped over Poochie's chain and dropped the finger. Before he could grab it, the dog gobbled it up. Big Jim looked back and saw me running out of the house, still swinging the knife. He jumped the fence, never to be seen again.

When mom came home, I told her what happened. She asked Kathy if she was okay. Kathy said, "Big Jim gave me this new dress and doll." That's all she remembered. It was probably better she didn't know what he was about to do to her that day.

Word of what I had done to Big Jim spread around the neighborhood. One day a little old lady, who lived down the street, Mrs. Winslow the local busy body, called me into her yard. She said, "It's such a shame you kids are left at home all day with no one to watch over you."

In talking to her, I blurted out about Big Jim and the finger my dog ate. She wanted to know if we kids were getting enough to eat. I told her that I was very good at catching fish and the church helped out a lot, by giving us a food box every couple of weeks.

"You poor baby," she said. "Would you like a cookie before you go?"

Not one to turn down a cookie I said, "Yes please!" With my mouth full of cookie, I mumbled, "Thank you ma'am." As I skipped out of her yard, I was thinking what a nice sweet little old lady she was.

A few days later the police came to my house, while my mother was at work. I was fishing at the time. Billy was supposed to be watching Kathy, but decided to go across the street to play with his friends. Kathy was left watching the television home alone. When the police knocked, Kathy answered the door. The police wanted to know where our mother was and who was watching her?

Just when I got home, Mrs. Winslow, who knew the police were there, came over and told them that our mother worked up the street at the Sail Inn restaurant. One of the police officers drove to the restaurant and brought my mother back. They told her that someone in the neighborhood complained that she was leaving her children alone without proper supervision and if it continued the state of Florida would put us in foster care.

I whispered to my mother, "It was Mrs. Winslow, who complained." But I think she had figured that out on her own.

In front of the police, Mrs. Winslow said, "I know a very religious colored woman, named Edna May, who lives a few blocks away. She could baby sit and keep house for a fair price. She's done it before for others."

The police said that they would be checking back on us to make sure we were not left alone.

My mother contacted Edna May, and she agreed to watch us.

Mom loved Edna May and so did Billy. Kathy loved everybody. Me on the other hand, not so much. There was just something about her I didn't trust. I could tell she was saying everything my mother wanted to hear. Billy liked her because she let him go out to play in the neighborhood, with his friends all day, but she didn't like me. She was always making me sit on the floor, by her smelly feet, as she read the bible to me. For some unknown reason, she was convinced that I had the devil in me, and she felt it was her job to get him out. One day when I was playing with my dog in the bedroom, she came in and grabbed Poochie by the collar picking her off the ground.

The dog was choking, and I yelled, "Put my dog down, damn it!"

She got furious and threw the dog outside. Then she took me into the bathroom where she tried to wash my mouth out with soap. I fought back, trying to run away. "If you don't do what I tell you boy, I will come back tonight and hang that dog in the tree outside your bedroom window," Edna May said.

Being stubborn, ornery or maybe just a glutton for punishment I told her, "I swear I am going to tell my mother that you are being mean to me and my dog. She'll fire you!"

She said, "If you do, little devil boy, I will come over here one night and burn your house down, with you in it."

I was scared. What was I supposed to do? I asked the angel for help, but I didn't hear anything. I got the feeling he couldn't help me. I had to help myself. I was confused how the angel could help Kathy, but he couldn't help me. I thought, "Some guardian angel-knight champion I have." I relented and let the old woman put soap in my mouth, so she'd leave me alone.

She made me bite a chunk of the Ivory soap and chew it before I could spit it out. It was the worst tasting thing I've ever had to do. Then she pulled me by the ear and threw me up against the couch. Edna May then made me listen to her read her bible out loud. She stopped every once in a while, and said, "Lord, take the devil from this child, in Jesus' name. Praise the Lord, praise the Lord."

She would read on, then kick me when she got to certain parts when I was to say, "Praise Jesus and his loving disciple Edna May Johnson, Amen." She puffed up with pride when I would say it, but I felt bad because I knew I was talking about Jesus and the Devil in the same sentence.

Edna May was very slick. Before I could tell my mother what Edna May had done to me, she told her that I was smart mouthing her all day.

"The demon must'a took him over. He was cursing up a storm. I had to wash his sinful mouth out with soap and make him read the bible with me all afternoon."

With a puzzled look on her face, my mother said to Edna May, "That's not like Eddie." Mom turned and looked me in the eyes then said, "What has gotten into you boy? Miss Edna is a good Christian woman and you better do everything she says. We can't afford to lose her. Do you want the police to put you in a foster home?"

Edna said, "Don't you worry none Ms. Kathryn. He's got the devil in him, he does, but I'll get him out. Me and Eddie has come to an understanding. Didn't we boy?"

I thought, "Not a shot, you devil woman. We don't have anything close to an understanding."

As if she heard my thoughts, she looked at me with cold, dark eyes and then she gave my mother a smile of innocence.

Over the next several months, Edna May made my life a living hell. She knew Frankie's mother, and the two continued to blame me for what happened to him. Edna convinced her that I was a devil. Any shot I had at ever seeing Frankie again was all but lost.

Edna May only lived a few blocks away from my house, so she would show up outside my bedroom window at night peeking in to intimidate me.

"You better not be sleeping, with devil thoughts in your mind boy. You'll pay for it tomorrow," she said. "I know you touch yourself at night in unholy ways," she would whisper through the screen.

I didn't know what she was talking about. But I did know she was obsessed. Or maybe possessed was a better word. Her mistreatment got worse. She insisted on baptizing me once a week in the bathtub. She pinched my skin with cloth pins and tied fishing line around my genitals, pulling the line at times while she read certain passages in the bible that excited her. That's when I would have to say, "Praise Jesus and his loving disciple Edna May Johnson, Amen."

The pain was harsh and the angel would take my mind away to future events, far away from the pain of this crazy woman. My favorite place to go was a beautiful castle with water falls, ponds, gardens, rabbits, turtles, goats, birds, horses and children playing. I was all grown up and wore a blue and gold suit of armor, just like angel Michael's. The children would all sit around me, as I told them stories about how to stay safe from bad people that wanted to hurt them. Inside the castle was a large round table, with a fire in the center. Sitting around the table were, Sir and Lady knights all wearing different color suits of armor. It seemed so real at the time, but I knew it was just my imagination.

I always knew that time would pass and the pain would stop. My mother would come home and Edna would leave. Sometimes when I fought back the angel didn't come, and I was forced to endure the torment.

Edna May would say, "If you don't do as I say, your demon dog will suffer the consequences."

One day when I came home from school I found my dog Poochie dead in the back yard. Her tongue was hanging out and foam was coming out of her mouth. There were two sticks fashioned into a cross lying next to the dog.

The neighbor said, "Looks like the dog was poisoned."

I knew it was Edna May.

Finally, she had pushed me too far. I had enough of this woman's zealot craziness. I was more than done with it when she had me lay my naked body across her lap, as she spanked me with her bible calling on the "Lord of Lord's Jesus Christ" to free me from Satan's grip. I would rather be in a foster home than continue to live in fear of this nut job.

That night I was sobbing in bed. Why didn't the angel save my dog? Why is all this happening to me? Where was my dad? He'd kill this woman, if he knew she hurt me. It wasn't bad enough I lost him. Now I was being beaten and molested and lost not one but two dogs. I felt so broken and hopeless. I cried myself to sleep.

I had a dream that night that the angel in blue armor dug a hole outside my bedroom window. Filled it with snakes, then covered it over with sticks and leaves. In the dream when Edna May paid her usual visit at my window to taunt me, she fell into the hole breaking her leg, as the snakes bit her. That was a great dream!

Later that same night I was awakened, by Edna looking in the window whispering, "Want the same thing to happen to your mother that happened to that demon dog?" I pretended I was asleep and didn't answer her. This woman saw herself as a saint, but I knew she was a dark-spirited, crazy witch. I vowed that night would be the last night I would live in fear.

The next day after school, when Edna May wanted to have her perverted bible study class with me, I refused. I ran outside and hid in the bushes across the street, until my mother came home and Edna left for the day.

As she walked down the street she yelled, "Boy, I know you are out there watching. Don't think you are going to get away with this. Jesus will send his angels to strike you down tonight!"

After dinner, I began digging my snake pit. Kathy helped me lay out the sticks and palm leaves on top of the pit. I didn't have real snakes, but did have a rubber one I put in the hole. My trap was set. I laid awake in bed and waited. I was shaking inside. Not from fear, but from adrenaline. I waited for what seemed like an eternity. Then all of a sudden, I heard a loud thud outside my window and a high-pitched whimpering moan that would've woke the dead. I never got up to see what happened. I just lay there smiling.

Edna May called my mother the following day and told her that she couldn't work for us anymore. She had taken another job.

I saw Edna at the market a few weeks later. She didn't break her leg, but her arm was in a sling. I made sure she didn't see me. It was done.

A new lady took over watching us for my mother. Her name was Roberta, and she was an angel.

I told Roberta what Edna had done to me and she said, "That doesn't surprise me. That old woman is pure evil with all her talk of devils. She thinks she is an agent of the Lord himself. Someone is going to put an end to her foolishness one day."

A few months later, I heard Edna May got hit by a car and killed. All I could think was it might not have happened, if she was still watching us. I didn't like hearing what happened to her, but I also thought if she were still alive she could be hurting other kids somewhere. I was glad she wasn't.

Now the only terror in my life was my brother Billy. He still thought he was the Fart master sitting on my head when life bored him. I'd lie in bed at night wishing that Damian would visit and kick Billy's ass for a change. I remembered the four-leaf clover string bracelet my grandmother made me. It worked once, so I decided to make one again. Using the buzzing bee method, it didn't take long to find a four-leaf clover. Using some kite string I tied the clover to my right ankle and wished that Damian was my older brother. I asked that he come and beat off

Billy. Three days later the string broke in the middle of the night. I waited to hear the good news, but it didn't come. It looked like I was stuck with Billy forever.

A month had passed when the phone rang. It was my mother's sister from Washington D.C. She told mom that Uncle Benny and Aunt June were killed in a car crash in New York and my cousin Damian needed to be with other kids near his age. She wanted to know if Damian could live with us. My mother agreed, and two days later he arrived on the train. I was so happy. My wish had been granted again, but I felt guilty about my aunt and uncle dying.

My mother announced that Damian was no longer our cousin. He was our older brother. Billy didn't like that, but I loved it.

Damian started picking on Billy all the time. The farts on my head stopped.

I made the mistake of telling Damian about my wish. He immediately blamed me for killing his mother and father to get him to Florida. I told him that God doesn't work that way.

He asked, "What God? You asshole, you believe there's a God?"

I knew what the priest told us in Catholic school, but I had a hard time believing that God was a huge man living in heaven. I told Damian I believed that there is something mighty that we came from, and when I drowned I saw a very powerful Goddess-like woman and a huge angel in blue armor.

Damian told me that his god was Satan because Satan gives him everything he asks for.

Wow! Damian had really changed in the few years, since I had last seen him. He was thirteen now and no longer my protector. He started treating me worse than my brother ever did. After a few months, Damian and Billy became friends. I asked the angel why I had to live with two bullies now?

Communication with the angel wasn't very clear back then and most of the time my understanding of things came when I dreamed at night or during daydreams, when I was focused on something else. However, when I asked that question his answer was clear as a bell.

I heard, "Be careful what you wish for! You wanted another older brother, and you got him. People are in your life for a reason. Learn from them all."

I told the angel, "I wished for my dad to come for me every day, but that wish never came true. Why?"

The angel didn't answer me.

My mom was very fond of Damian. She enjoyed having him as a third son.

One of my favorite TV shows back then was "Leave it to Beaver." Damian reminded me of Eddie Haskell. Haskell was always a sweet angel around the Beaver's mom, but when he was around the other kids, he was a devil.

34

Chapter Eight

A New Daddy

I missed my dad a lot. I wished every day that he would find us, so things would be good again. But I knew he would never knew where to start looking for us.

My mother started dating a new guy, Frank. They married a few months later. I was glad for her because she seemed happy again. They had two more children a year apart, Maureen and Michael. Mom finally had her Michael. With Frank taking over the family and having his own kids, I felt like a second-class child. He worked at the local Safeway food store, stocking shelves at night. We kids had to be quiet in the house, so he could sleep during the day.

Frank signed Damian, Billy and me up for newspaper routes. He said that we needed to pay rent, if we were going to live in his house and eat his food. We would have to get up at 5:00 am to wrap two hundred newspapers and deliver them on foot before school each day. I told Daddy Frank that I wanted to save some money to buy a bicycle. He said, "No! They are too expensive, and I need all the money for the rent."

One day when I was collecting from my customers for the papers, Damian came riding down the street on a red bike. He had taken it out of my customer's garage. Damian took the bike home. He and Billy stripped the fenders off the bike then painted it blue, so no one would know it was stolen.

"What a couple of jerks!" I thought.

However, before they had finished painting the bike, the police showed up. The guy's wife saw Damian take the bike out of the garage. Frank was so mad and told the police to take us all to jail, just as the owner of the bicycle showed up. I told him, "I didn't have anything to do with it. I swear. I'm sorry my brothers took it and painted it blue."

Billy shoved me from the back and said, "Shut up or else!"

"Why?" I screamed, "I wanted to save my money for a bike, but Daddy Frank won't let me get one. He said all my money had to go toward the rent. Now you guys probably ruined it forever for me!" I watched Damian. He was just smiling and acting innocent.

I told the man, "Since they messed up your bike, I would like to buy it, if it's for sale. I have been wanting one for my paper route."

The owner of the bike looked at me. I could see in his eyes he felt sorry for me, being in this situation. Somehow I think he seemed to know that I was caught between two bullies. "I'll tell you what," he said. "Seeing that your brothers ruined my bike by taking it apart and painting it blue, I really don't want it anymore. I'll sell it to you for ten dollars."

Frank said, "No, he ain't spending ten dollars on a bike!"

"Well, in that case," said the owner, "you owe me fifty dollars, since your kids stole and vandalized my bike."

Frank grabbed me by the arm and said, "Pay that man the ten dollars you owe him and be done with it."

Daddy Frank was a bit of a jerk. I wondered why my mother ever left my father. Really? Could it have ever been as bad as this situation was?

I walked up and handed the man ten dollars out of my paper collection money. He winked, and I broke out in the biggest smile ever. I had my bike! Now delivering papers would be much easier.

After that, my brothers refused to deliver papers, so I inherited their routes as well. They'd sit at home while I did the work then they'd make me go buy them a basket of Fitz's French fries, or they'd kick my ass. There was no justice in that house. There was no one to complain to. There was nowhere to hide. Frank didn't want to hear anything, and my mother just said, "Eddie you have got to learn to get along with your brothers."

One early rainy morning, while I was folding newspapers under the awning of a used car dealership, Tim Irving showed up and yelled, "Hey Nazi boy. Got any money?"

When I said, "No," he kicked over my bike spilling the basket full of papers everywhere.

He said, "I don't believe you. Come here and let me search you."

I had about seventy dollars in my pocket that I had to give to my paper route manager after I delivered the papers that morning. My understanding about how the angel communicated with me was getting better by then. The impression I got was that Michael wanted me to run. I "heard" that Tim was going to hurt me bad, even if I gave him the money.

I took off running, with Tim right behind me.

I slid under a pickup truck and hid. I could see his feet running around, looking for me. When he got to the pickup I was under, he stopped. I closed my eyes and held my breath.

I thought, "Please Michael, don't let him look under this truck."

I heard him move away, so I slid out. But as I came to my feet, Tim came diving over the hood of a nearby car and grabbed me. I broke loose and ran again. I reached my bike and stood it up to make my escape. Just as Tim got close to me, he slipped on the folded newspapers. His body flew up in the air as his right arm came down on the chrome spiked hood ornament of a car. The cross-pointed spike went through his arm, and he couldn't get his arm loose. Blood was gushing out of his arm.

Tim begged, "Help me. I'm gonna' bleed to death. Don't leave. Don't leave me!"

All the memories of that day Tim beat, painted and pissed on Frankie and me came flooding back. I was never more humiliated then to have this boy pee on me and spit in my face. This was the perfect time to get my revenge. All I had to do was pick up my papers and leave. But he looked so helpless, hanging there on that spike. I sensed the angel was waiting to see what I was going to do.

I told Tim, "Hold on. I'll go for help."

He screamed, "You Nazi son of a bitch, you're not going for help. I wouldn't help you. I'd let you die, you piece of crap! Why would you help me?"

Without another word, I got on my bike and peddled away as fast as I could.

Tim cried, "Come back here, you bastard."

I couldn't believe I was helping this guy, who was still calling me names, but I was. It wasn't in me to leave him helpless and suffering. I knew he was telling me the truth when he said that he would leave me, if I was stuck on that spike. But I couldn't live with myself, if I didn't try to help. As I was peddling, Angel Michael gave me the vision of Fitz's, a local restaurant where a police car was parked out front.

It was amazing. When I got there, everything I saw in the vision was the same in real life. I ran inside yelling, "I need help! A boy is bleeding to death, and he needs help now." The two police officers at the counter were the same two that came to my house when my brothers stole the bike. I told them there was an accident, and a boy was pinned to the car hood at the used car lot a couple blocks down the street. They raced out to help. When I showed up with the police, Tim was unconscious. He had pulled his arm off the car hood spike and was lying on the ground in a pool of blood.

The ambulance arrived a short time later and took Tim to the hospital.

The police asked me "Were you having problems with that boy? He's a known trouble maker, but we never get any evidence on him." As one of them pointed at the ground, he remarked, "Looks like someone was being chased here."

They told me that Tim's father was a drunk, who used to beat him all the time and then lock him in a shed for days without food or water. "Probably why the boy is so mean," said the taller officer. "His father is in prison now, and it looks like Tim is following in his footsteps."

I told the officers, "He wanted my newspaper money and was chasing me to get it when he slipped. But I think having him arrested is just going to put him in with kids worse than him." I didn't know where the information was coming from, but I told them that Tim would be worse when he got out of jail than he was now.

One officer said, "If we lock him away, he won't be hurting anyone. But if he is allowed to stay on the street and hurts someone, it would be your fault for letting him off the hook this time."

I thought about that, but something inside was telling me not to make a report. So, I didn't.

A few days later, while I was folding my papers in the used car lot, Tim showed up with his arm bandaged and in a sling. There was something different about him. He had a glow around him that wasn't there before. He had changed.

"I wanted to tell you that I am sorry for what I did to you and Black Frankie," he said. "I also want to thank you for not reporting me and what you did for me. You saved my life."

Tim went on to say that the doctors told him in the hospital that it was a miracle he was still alive because he had lost so much blood, he should have died. I wanted to hug him, but boys didn't do that. It would be weird. Plus, thoughts of his mistreatment of me came flooding back into my mind. I think that will live with me forever. I realized that day what forgiving, but not forgetting really meant.

I could feel Michael coming into my mind. Then he spoke using my voice saying, "Tim you deserved a second chance at life. Your father was mistreated as a child by his father, so he mistreats you. That's all you know, so you have become like your father, bullying others, so the cycle continues. When you have a son, it is likely you will mistreat him. But, now you have been shown love and compassion. Remember that the next time you want to hurt someone. Perhaps you should start protecting kids from bullies. Break the cycle, it's far more rewarding." I felt a whoosh and then snapped back into myself. It was weird. I was there all the time listening, but yet not there.

Michael told me later that Tim's fall was the best thing that ever happened to him. He bled out his father's bad blood. That blood was replaced with the blood from people that cared, and my act of kindness will live with him forever. I don't know what happened. All I knew was Tim Irving was a different person when he got out of the hospital.

A couple months later, Roberta told me that Frankie was missing. He went out to play and never came home. When his mother called the police, they told her that he must have run away from home. I told Roberta that Frankie loved his mother and would never run away from home. No one was looking for him. I asked Roberta if she could get me a picture of Frankie. She said she would.

As soon as I got the photograph, I started walking the streets, showing the picture to people. I told them that I think he was kidnapped. Many people I showed the picture to knew Frankie, but they hadn't seen him lately. Even Tim Irving helped me search for Frankie. I asked him if he thought the Klan would have hurt him. He said if they had, he would have heard something. We searched everywhere. We even returned to the place we built the Good Knight Castle. Someone had set all the plywood on fire and there was little left but a memory.

One night in a dream, I saw Frankie walking down the street. A brown skin man walked up to him and said something. Then the man took Frankie's hand in his. They walked to a nearby car, got in and drove off. I woke up screaming, "No Frankie. It's a trick." I didn't know what was going on, but it didn't seem right. There was something about the man that I didn't like. He reminded me of Big Jim. The man who tried to hurt my sister.

All I could think about was what happened to Frankie? I wanted to know what someone could say to a little kid to make him want to get into a car, with a stranger. I asked the angel what it all meant, and he replied, "They can say many things, but there are only ten tricks, and one day you will share them with the world."

I wondered, "Was this the reason why the angel was sent back to earth, to help kids learn the tricks?"

He said, "All will be known when your waiting is full."

Feeling unsettled about Frankie, I became very depressed and quit my paper route. This pissed Daddy Frank off. Damian and Billy refused to work, but for some reason Frank picked me as the one that he demanded work. He told me he needed the money for bills, and I needed to find another job. He said it was my obligation to help support my mother. He had a way of making me feel guilty, but this time, I didn't want to hear it. I was too down. All I did was go to school, come home and stay in my room alone with the angel buzzing in my ear. I wasn't even answering that.

One day Damian and Billy were tormenting me to the point that I couldn't stand it anymore. I grabbed Frankie's picture and ran out the door. I found myself walking the street downtown where I ran into the manager from the Mary Carter Paint store.

Mr. Wizard saw the picture of Frankie I was carrying and said, "I heard that Black Frankie ran away from home. Is that why you seem sad?"

"Yes," I said. "I had a bad dream that a man in a car kidnapped Frankie."

Mr. Wizard said, "I'm going to get a banana split. Want to join me? My treat!" I was never one to turn down ice cream.

While we were eating, he asked, "Whatever happened to that castle you were building?"

I told him what Tim Irving and his gang did to the castle and us. And about Tim hooking his arm on the car, while trying to rob me one morning.

He said, "After what those boys did to you I'm surprised you still helped that boy. I knew from the first time I laid eyes on you that you're one of the good guys. Who are your favorite heroes?" he asked.

I said, "King Arthur and the Lone Ranger."

He smiled and nodded his head in agreement. He then asked, "Do you still have your father's magic sword?" The question hit me like a ton of bricks. I burst into tears, sobbing so loud that a woman came up to ask if I was okay.

Mr. Wizard told her that I was having a really bad day. He showed her the picture of Frankie and said, "This is Eddie's best friend. We believe he's been kidnapped."

The woman sat down and gave me a big hug and then dried my tears.

I said, "I'm sorry, big boys don't cry."

"But real men do!" She replied with a smile. Those words, for some unknown reason, touched me. They reminded me of something in my past, but I couldn't remember what. I just knew there was something to those words and soon I was feeling better.

As we were leaving the store Mr. Wizard asked me, if I wanted a job working for him in the store and helping deliver paint to homes. He said the job paid $25.00 a week. He also told me a job would take my mind off being depressed about Frankie. I was only making $40.00 a month on my paper route so making $100.00 a month would really help out at home.

When I told my mother that I got a job she was happy. Frank said that I could keep $25.00 a month for myself. He said any more than that I'd just get in trouble, anyway. When it came down to it, I really only got to keep about $7. Damian and Billy were great magicians when it came to making my savings disappear. Wherever I'd hide it, they'd find it.

I really liked working for Mr. Wizard. He was very philosophical. It was like listening to the thoughts Angel Michael put in my head. I didn't understand them, but I knew someday I would.

In the winter of 1958, I was still working for Mr. Wizard. He got a huge order that needed to be delivered to an estate on the oceanfront. It happened to be the Kennedy estate in Palm Beach. I had delivered there before during the summer, but there weren't many people around other than the grounds-keepers. They had a beautiful pool that I passed on my way to the gardener's shed. I can remember wanting to jump in. It was such a hot, humid Florida day, and that pool was calling my name. Luckily for me, I didn't answer it. I was a good kid and didn't want any trouble. EVER! This time when I passed by the pool, I saw a very sad looking man, sitting and talking on the telephone.

I didn't know how I knew he was sad; I just did. I think it was because he looked like he felt the same way I did, when I was sad about Frankie. I waved at him and he smiled.

After walking past the man with paint a few times, I got up the gumption to go over to him and ask, "Why are you so sad?"

He smiled. I really liked the way he smiled. Everything seemed to light up when he smiled. I noticed that he was playing with a coin in his hand.

"What makes you think I'm sad?" He answered.

I said, "Even when you smile I can see that you are sad about something."

I told him that I was sad for a long time because my best friend, Frankie, was kidnapped. But my boss, Mr. Wizard, at the paint store, told me that being sad wasn't going to help Frankie or me. So, I just remember the good times that I had with him."

The man said, "That is a wise way to look at the problem."

I could see that I wasn't helping the man.

Just then the grounds manager walked up and said, "Senator, is this delivery boy bothering you?"

He said, "No I think he has come to do the impossible. He's gonna try to cheer me up."

I thought, "Holy crap. What can I do that will make this man laugh?" Then I remembered a poem that Frankie taught me. I said, "When I'm sad and missing Frankie, I recite his favorite poem. He said that his daddy told him a President of the United States wrote it for a dinner party at the White House. I recited the poem in a talent show in school last year and had a funny skit to go along with it. I didn't win, but I had everybody in the audience cracking up. Wanna' hear it?"

The man said he'd love to.

I broke into a little dance, then flamboyantly threw my arms into the air and said, "For a beauty, I am not a star, there are others more perfect by far. But my face, I don't mind it, you see, it's because I'm behind it. It's the people in the front that I jar."

There was silence. The man and grounds manager just looked at me. I could see the man was holding back a laugh. The corners of his mouth were quivering. Then both men broke into laughter. The man said, "That was good. Here please take this. It's a good luck charm. I have carried it with me for years. I hope it brings you good luck now."

Then the man gave me the coin that he was playing with as a token of my concern for him. He said, "The inscription on the coin should remind you always to 'Mind Your Business'." The man went on to tell me that it was the Fugio Cent, designed by Benjamin Franklin, and the first coin minted in our newly formed nation in the 1700's. He told me that Ben Franklin was a wise man who hid meaning in symbols. He showed me on the back of the coin there was an interlocking chain of thirteen links circling the words, "We Are One." He said, "See this…" as he pointed to the engraving, "… it means a chain is only as strong as its weakest link." On the front of the coin was the sun shining down on a sundial that sits above the phrase, "Mind Your Business." He said, "It means, Time flies, so do your business." Then he patted me on the side of my face, winked and said, "*Your* business is helping people feel better." He gave me back the coin and said, "That's your gift. I hope you never lose it."

Normally, I would have welcomed the gift, but I knew it was a lucky coin that he kept sacred for a long time. I said, "This is your lucky coin, I can't take it."

The man said, "Nonsense. I insist. You made my heart happy. I have to go now, and you must be on your way as well."

"Thank you," I said. We both turned and walked away in opposite directions. I had no idea at the time how important the coin would become later in life.

Over the next year, I delivered paint many times to the Kennedy Estate, but I never saw the man again in person. However, in 1961 I saw him on television. He had just been elected President of the United States. He still had that smile that shined like the sun on my coin. I still felt guilty taking his lucky coin, but didn't know why. The angel told me some people live to change the world and some must die to change the world. Michael then gave me the vision of President Lincoln being shot in the head, with an Indian's arrow. I didn't know what that meant at the time, but I was sure it would make sense one day.

Image 3 – Kennedy's Fugio Coin given to little Eddie Jagen

Chapter Nine

The Move to Maryland

The following year in the fall of 1962, Daddy Frank's mother got really sick, so he moved the family to Palmer Park, Maryland to be closer to her.

She lived in Washington, D.C. and worked at the U.S. Capitol for a Congressman. After she got better, I loved going to visit her at work. The U.S. Capitol building was a really great place to explore.

I made friends with another kid. His name was Rudy, and his father was a U.S. Capitol Police Officer. We went down into some really scary places underneath the Capitol building. There was talk that it was haunted, but I never saw anything.

Michael was communicating regularly with me now. When I was in that old building, he was really active. He told me that there were a lot of human spirits still trapped on earth that haunt the Capitol and other areas of Washington.

I asked him why they were trapped.

He answered, "For many reasons. One day I hope that we can help free them."

I never really had to ask out loud when I had a question. I just thought it, and the answers would come.

During those years, my favorite female movie star was Marilyn Monroe. She looked and made me feel a lot like the Constant Walker did, when she asked if I would return to life to help her angel-knight champion. My favorite movie of hers was Niagara. I always dreamed that one day, when I was grown, I would take a ride on the "Maid of the Mist" boat and kiss Marilyn, under the mist of Niagara Falls.

What healthy American boy at the time didn't have such dreams?

I was not surprised to learn that she and President Kennedy were very good friends. I'm sure we shared that dream. I remember when Marilyn sang, "Happy birthday, Mr. President, on TV." What a birthday present that was!

I felt like my heart was ripped out of my chest a few months later, when I heard on the radio that she died from an overdose of sleeping pills. She was only thirty-six years old. That's only nine in wizard years and only five years older than me, since I was doing four again. All I knew at the time was the boyhood love of my thirteen years of life was gone.

Later that year, Daddy Frank and I were visiting my friend, Rudy, at the U.S. Capitol. And I saw President Kennedy, walking down the hall surrounded by reporters. I learned that he was speaking that day to the Congress about rockets that the Russians put in Cuba. I told Frank that I had to give the coin back to the president, but he said there was no getting that close to him. I just felt he needed his lucky coin back.

That night I had a dream that Indians shot several arrows, hitting President Lincoln and President Kennedy in the head. Everybody was sad and crying. I saw a black horse and on both sides of the saddle was a boot turned around backwards.

The following year my waiting was full. President Kennedy was assassinated. I knew then why I felt it was so important to return the coin. However, I was still confused about why I saw Indians shooting at Lincoln and Kennedy when it was white men that killed them both.

I hadn't been that sad since Frankie disappeared. It seemed like I was becoming a professional sad sack. I missed my Dad, Frankie, Marilyn and now President Kennedy. I noticed the angel was more active around me, when I was missing certain people. He told me that the way I missed people was a testament to the depths of my love. All I knew was it sucked. Why were these people being taken out of my life?

Life in the early sixties for me was not like *Happy Days*. Frank had rented a duplex house for us to live in, and it wasn't in the greatest neighborhood. Every subdivision had its gangs and Damian and Billy were quick to join one. They started carrying knives and chains because rival gangs would come to Palmer Park for monthly gang wars. Damian was definitely taking Billy down a wrong path. Kids my age had also started gangs. Michael kept giving me flashbacks of Tim Irving and his gang. Just the thought of those days sent a shiver down my spine.

I joined the Boy Scouts to stay out of trouble. I learned a lot from the scouts, and most of all that I could survive on my own if I had to. I didn't know if I would ever need to or not, but I thought it was cool that I could.

Even with Michael guiding me and with the scouts to keep me out of trouble, Prince Georges County was a rough area to live. A lot of street gangs were coming from Kentland, Bladensburg, Wheaton, College Park and other neighborhoods to rumble with the Palmer Park gangs.

My brother, Damian's, gang nickname was "Hot Stuff," like the little red devil in the comic books. Billy and Damian were all grown up now, with greasy hair, pegged pants, switchblades and all. By just looking at them anyone could tell they were headed for trouble.

My mother didn't know what to do with them. She knew that Damian was the one, pulling Billy into the negative life of a gang member. Then one day, she packed us all in the car and drove to Great Falls in Virginia. It was a beautiful place to watch the white-water rapids as we walked along the river. We picnicked at one of the overlooks. While we were there, a U.S. Park Police Officer came riding up on his huge brown horse. He got off and hugged my mom. She said his name was Bob Knight. He was the closest thing I had ever seen to the Lone Ranger. I was in awe. My mother wanted Captain Knight to talk to us about staying out of trouble and to stay away from gangs. He said that gangs will say anything to get you to join.

43

The gang members will claim to be the only ones that care about you, but once you are in, the only way out is death.

Brother Damian said, "That's a boat load of horse shit! Nobody gives a shit. That's why you have to take what you want and screw everybody else."

Captain Knight was shocked and said, "Do you kiss your mother with that dirty mouth son?"

Even I was surprised how he was acting. He always acted like an angel around Mom. He really was becoming a hardcore gangster.

The Captain grabbed Damian by the arm and said, "Come with me boy. We gotta' talk."

The rest of us stayed at the picnic table, while my Mom, Damian, the horse and the police officer walked away. When they came back fifteen minutes later, Damian was crying.

Captain Knight got on his horse, said goodbye and rode away.

On the ride back to our house, Kathy was sitting in the front seat with mom. I was in the back seat between my two brothers. No one was talking, so Billy started punching me out of boredom. Damian reached over and grabbed him by the neck. If looks could kill, Billy would be dead. I didn't know where this was all going, but I didn't like it. Me, stuck in the middle of *those* two. Even if I wasn't the one they wanted to punch, I'd be in the way of their punches on each other!

I sat there thinking about the day I drowned. I was wondering if I had made the right choice in coming back to life. I felt so good when I was with the Constant Walker, and I didn't see how I was help to the angel. In the car between those two lug heads, my decision to come back seemed like a bad one.

I never did find out what Captain Knight said or did to Damian, but I really didn't care either. Things quieted down only for a while. Teenage lives being what they are, there was always some drama in and out of the house.

During those years, I felt the pull to the negative side of life. It was hard to resist. When I discovered girls, I also discovered that they liked bad boys more than good boys. I watched all the girls go after Billy and brother Damian.

They had already both been arrested several times on assault and weapon charges and placed on probation. My mother was devastated. They both became even more brutal toward me. They loved to humiliate me in public.

I never knew what they were going to do to me next. While growing up with Billy, he pushed me out of a second-floor window, threw rocks at me, shot me in the ear with an arrow and slashed me with knives. Now Damian was out to get me too.

What scared me most was they started carrying guns. I was afraid that one day, in an attempt to scare me, I'd be shot and killed. Knowing my brothers and their thug friends, my body would never be found.

However, even Brother Damian got a taste of his own medicine one day when he went over to his gang's clubhouse for a meeting.

The club president said to Damian, "Hot Stuff, get some beers out of the fridge for us."

Damian opened the door and found the head of one of the members that had snitched to police on another member. They wanted to send a clear message to Damian about what happens if you turn against the gang.

That day changed Damian, and it wasn't for the better.

44

Being a badass must've been a magnet for girls. He was a tall, black haired, good-looking guy, with a girlfriend for everyday of the week. I was a little envious, I must admit. Even Billy only had one girl friend, Nancy.

I decided I needed a girlfriend too, but I could never forget the face of my golden hair first love, "Connie" the Constant Walker. I was always looking for her in the faces of other girls, but none of them measured up to Connie.

One day, when I walked into my new 7th grade classroom at Kent Jr. High, I saw her. It was Gayle Ball, the second love of my life. She was the closest thing to Connie I had ever seen. She was from a rich family. Mine was poor, with six kids and getting larger. No shot there, I thought. Her parents would take one look at me and never let her leave the house. It didn't stop me from thinking about her though … a lot!

At that very sensitive time in my life, we were living in a three-bedroom duplex Daddy Frank rented for us. It was crowded with Mom, Frank and six kids. I never had a private moment at home.

One day after dinner, Frank got up from the table and announced his ex-wife and their two daughters were moving in with us. I about choked on my meatloaf.

My mother, clearly, wasn't happy either saying, "There is no way you're bringing your kids AND ex-wife to live with us. I won't have it!"

"Deal with it." Frank said, bluntly.

He held true to his word and, by the weekend, they were all living with us.

Daddy Frank was living the good life sleeping with both women whenever he wanted. I couldn't believe my mother was putting up with that crap!

Damian and Billy were moved to the living room sleeper sofa. My brother Michael and I moved into the laundry room on a roll up mattress. Kathy, Maureen, and Frank's two girls got the one bedroom and his ex-wife, Betty, got our bedroom all for herself.

That was not the best of times. Let me tell ya'! Talk about feeling like the odd kid out. I spent more of my time out of the house than in it, during, those days. Billy stayed with his friends most of the time, so I hardly saw him; which was actually a good thing. Damian seemed to have a little thing going on with Betty.

After about three months, Frank got into a fight with his ex-wife. He caught Damian in bed with her one night when he snuck in for a quickie. All hell broke loose. Betty and the girls moved out the next day. I felt bad for the girls. They had no direction, moving from one place to another every few months. Besides that, their mother was a bitch.

My communication with Angel Michael was getting even clearer. I think the more time I spent away from the chaos at home helped me understand him better.

One day when I was walking home, I saw a prayer card in the gutter. It was like it was calling to me. I had to pick it up. When I looked at the picture of an angel on the front, I gasped! The angel looked exactly how I saw Michael the day I drowned. On the card, he didn't have wings, but was wearing the blue and gold armor. Under the image was the name George, he was a Catholic saint.

I heard Michael say in my head, "Humans have given me many names, through their cultures and spiritual beliefs, but angels don't belong to the religions of man. We are here to serve the Creator and the great awakening of His Divine children. I've been sent back in this age to raise a mighty sword and deliver it to the children of earth. With it the 'Children of Tomorrow' will bring peace. If my mission fails, all will perish in a great disaster."

He went on to tell me that humans can't be angels and angels can't be human, but once every five hundred years, they can fuse together to spark a huge leap in human consciousness and understanding.

At fourteen years of age, all that made no sense to me and, quite frankly, was a little scary. Michael knew I didn't understand him. He never pushed the issue either. I could tell he was just waiting for me to grow and mature. I could feel he just wanted me to be a kid, and I also knew he was actually enjoying being a kid with me.

When I started to go wrong, he was always there buzzing in my ear. Bringing me back on the path of goodness. My ears buzzed a lot in those days!

Billy started to stay over at his girlfriend's house more and more. He really got along with her parents. They were Italian and treated him like a king. I loved Nancy too. She was the sweetest girl. Billy started treating me better. He told me that he planned on marrying Nancy as soon as he turned sixteen. I thought it was a mistake, but if he lost her, he would turn back to the negative life he and Damian were living. I was happy for him. With Billy out of the house more, Damian started treating me worse.

In the coming months, Damian started running with an even more dangerous crowd. Now that we had our bedroom back, he was coming home drunk every night. Nobody in the house wanted to mess with him, not even Frank.

One night he woke me up, as he stumbled into the room. He fell over the foot of the bed and passed out as soon as his body hit. I wondered if he was dead. I crept over to the side of the bed, and he let out the biggest guttural snore. It scared the crap out of me! What was worse, though, I could see he now had several guns. They were all over his body. One was tucked in his belt, one in a holster behind his back and one in each boot. I got that buzzing again. No message came through, but I felt danger all over this.

Michael wanted me to keep my distance from Damian that was for certain.

The week after seeing all the guns, Damian came home and told me he was going into business for himself. I was afraid to ask what he was going to do.

"I'm going to be a tattoo artist," he proclaimed proudly.

Feeling the hair raise up on the back of my neck, I said, "Good luck with that" as I headed out the door as quickly as I could.

Damian starting to spend his days, using a needle, thread and Indian ink to practice on anything and anyone. It was giving me a bad feeling. I knew he was skipping school to tattoo guys in the park. He was making a lot of money, but it took a long time the way he was doing it. His customers slacked off because word got around that not only was it painful, but Damian's method was too slow.

That's when he had a stroke of genius. It was hard for me to give Damian credit for anything, but looking back, it was a really good idea he came up with.

He grabbed one of Daddy Frank's old electric razors, took the heads off and attached the needle to the vibrating arm of the razor. The needle vibrated up and down with speed. He tested it on cardboard, and it was amazing how fast and precise it was for a homemade device.

46

Now all he needed was someone to test it on. No one volunteered. Little did I know, he had someone in mind.

It was a beautiful spring day, and I was so excited because I had a half day off from school. I couldn't wait to get home. I knew Mom and Frank were working, Billy was living at Nancy's house full time and Damian spent his days in the park. The other kids were still in elementary school, which had a full day. My plan was to eat whatever I wanted out of the fridge and then actually have a peaceful nap, with the windows open in my bedroom.

Just when I was about to doze off, I heard the front door slam. Soon after, Damian and his best friend, Troy Pain, came storming into my bedroom. They held me down on the bed, pulled the covers over my head and started with a simple round of who could fart the most on my head.

They pulled the covers off and Troy sat on me while Damian tied my left arm to the side of the bed. Then the buzzing started. This time however, it wasn't Michael. It was Damian's homemade tattoo machine. It hurt like hell. Ink went flying everywhere. Blood dripped down my arm onto the sheets. When finished, I saw Damian had carved a cross on my upper left arm.

"There," he said, "you self-righteous bastard. You are mom's little angel boy. Now you can carry this cross with you forever."

His new tattooing device worked. A few days later, he had Troy carve the "Hot Stuff" devil on his arm. How á propos. He was back in business.

Word of Damian's antics spread rapidly. He had a bad reputation.

It was hard on me because I trailed Damian and Billy in school. My teachers, who had them a few years before me, automatically thought I was like them. It was assumed that I was a bad ass because they were.

I felt like I was going through school, with a giant target on my back. Not only did the teachers have a problem with me (because of Damian), but kids, who wanted to prove themselves, always picked a fight with me. They all wanted to be "the guy" that kicked Damian's brother's ass.

I was a peace-loving kid never looking for trouble, so everyone thought I would be a pushover target. I may have been freckle faced and scrawny, but I was never caught unaware though. Every time anyone attempted to ambush me, the buzzing would start in my ears.

"Okay Michael," I would think, "I hear you."

One day after school I avoided a major beat down, by listening to Michael. I felt so empowered. I was walking on air. Proud of myself that I listened.

The path I took home that day to avoid the trouble ran me right into Gayle. I was still flying high from outsmarting the thugs and even worked up enough nerve to ask Gayle if I could buy her an ice cream, carry her books and walk her home. I was shocked when she agreed.

When we got to the shopping center, I saw Damian, sitting on top of the big red, white and blue mailbox outside the High's Ice Cream store. He was surrounded by most of the local school bullies.

Trying to impress Damian they all had something to yell.

"Hey Ed-weirdo!"

"Loser!"

"Dumb Ass!"

And Damian's personal favorite, "Hey Fart Head."

Damian said, "Gayle why are you with my faggot brother?"

A boy who was in my class in school, Billy Moster, got up in my face and said, "Fight back, you wimpy faggot." Then he pushed me. His nickname was The Monster. It fit him to a tee.

I just said, "Leave us alone," as I took Gayle's arm and walked inside the ice cream store.

Monster was the class clown, who was always getting into trouble. He was a brute of a guy. He towered over me more than Damian did. At the time, I stood about 5'2" weighing 85 pounds. The Monster was a beast, standing 6' tall and weighing about 150 pounds. Everyone knew he could squash me like a bug.

"So why did he need to pick on me?" I thought.

When we came out with our ice cream, Damian said, "I told them to stop picking on you Eddie. Give me a bite."

He slid off the mailbox and walked over to us.

Monster yelled, "Do it Hot Stuff." He was always kissing my brother's ass trying to be cool, but he just looked like a jerk.

I knew something was up, but what? Snatching the cone from my hand my brother took a lick and said, "Hmmmm, butter brickle. I hate butter brickle." He then smashed the ice cream cone on my forehead, laughed and said, "Gayle are you walking your pet unicorn home from school?"

The insult was bad enough, but Gayle's laughing made it even worse.

To cover my humiliation, I started laughing and said, "I must admit, Damian, that was a good one."

I pulled the cone off my forehead and continued to eat the ice cream while acting like a unicorn.

I could see Gayle was embarrassed, so I wasn't surprised when she said, "I think it is best that I walk home alone."

Telling my mother on Damian was futile since all she did was yell at him. If I told, I'd wind up getting another ass whipping or wake up in the middle of the night to another round of head farts. Things like that had just become a way of life for me.

I learned to shut my mouth and pray. I prayed to not get beat up and prayed for someone to come into Damian's life and treat him the way he treated me.

My prayers did not get answered soon enough. All I could do was hope.

Everything came to a head in school a few weeks later when some of Damian's friends spread the rumor that I was running around saying, "The next time Billy Monster gets in my face, I'm going to kick his ass."

That afternoon, while walking home with a friend, we saw a crowd of kids gathering in the park behind Kent Jr. High. Gayle was there with her girlfriend, Joyce. I wanted to talk to her and apologize for the ice cream incident.

When we walked over to see what was happening the crowd formed a circle around me. It was a trap and Gayle was the bait.

The Monster stepped into the ring. "Okay, Ed Weirdo, I heard you're going to kick my ass." He said as he brought his fists up, into a fighting stance.

The buzzing in my ears told me Michael wasn't far away. I put my hands up to block any punches. This was my first fight. I really didn't know how to fight other than what I saw on TV. Monster threw his first punch. He hit me in the left side of the head, knocking me to the ground.

Seeing the blood come spurting out of my nose must've frightened Gayle.

She and her girlfriend yelled, "Stay down Eddie! He won't hit you again, if you stay on the ground."

Michael said for me to get up. I thought, "Okay then, a little help would be nice." I got up, and The Monster knocked me down again. Back up on my feet for the third time, I threw a punch. I missed and he knocked me down again. When I got up this time, I saw Gayle crying.

Kids in the crowd were yelling, "Monster leave him alone, he doesn't want to fight you."

Monster kicked me in the chest. I went flying through the ring of onlookers and hit the ground again. I landed next to a tree branch a few feet away from me on the ground.

Gayle yelled, "Run Eddie, run now."

Everyone was expecting me to run away, but I had enough of this bully crap. I thought, with or without Michael's help, it was time to make a stand here and now. I thought, "Billy Monster came for an ass whipping and that's what I'm gonna' give him. It's gonna' be the ass whipping I always wanted to give my asshole brothers." In my mind, I had all the incentive needed. I crossed myself and asked God for help.

Suddenly I could feel Michael's strength swelling within me. The pain in my face was gone. My heart stopped racing. I became cool, calm and collected, as the saying goes. I grabbed the limb and stood up, holding it like a staff.

Monster yelled, "That's not fair. Drop the stick faggot, before I make you eat it."

I moved in and just let Michael guide my every move. I twirled the stick-striking Monster on the arm. It had no effect. He kept charging.

I thought, "Holy crap I'm in trouble now."

My arm moved by itself with no control by me. I suddenly was holding the branch like a spear. Monster ran right into it, thrusting it into his abdomen. It didn't pierce the skin, but did knock the wind out of him. His legs buckled, and The Monster fell down for the first time. The crowd started laughing. He jumped up and tried to grab the stick, but I hit him on the neck, then quickly on the arm and finished with a sweep of his legs. The crowd cheered as Monster hit the ground. I hit him again on the ground when he tried to get up.

I said, "Stay down Billy, or I'll hit you again."

He tried to get up, so I knocked him down again.

Resting the end of the branch on his neck I said, "Billy is this over now for good!" Monster looked at Damian, who was laughing his ass off.

I raised the branch as if to strike him again when Billy said, "Yes it's over."

After that, Billy Monster and I became great friends. I earned his respect that day because I could have easily fought dirty and hurt him bad while he was down on the ground, and he knew it.

My confidence soared. I liked the way my body moved to protect myself and I felt safe. I wanted to learn more. Using my savings, I started taking Tae Kwon Do martial art classes. I'd go around breaking boards and sticks all the time. I like it so much that I would go to construction sites, asking carpenters for any scrap lumber they might have, so I could practice. My backyard and closet had stacks of broken 2" x and 12" x 10" boards piled high.

The slogan for my dojo at the time was, "Now nobody bothers me!" And they didn't. Word of the fight with Billy Moster and my Tae Kwon Do skills were spreading. I was suddenly not such an easy target. What I learned from my instructor, Jhoon Rhee, would save my life many times over in the years to come.

Jhoon Rhee also talked to us about King Arthur and the Code of Honor the Knights of the Round Table lived by. It made me think of Frankie and the castle we built together. Master Rhee impressed upon us that the skills we were learning were for the peaceful warrior. Not to be used for offense, but only for defense. One thing that left an indelible mark on my mind was when he said, "If you are under attack, there is no such thing as a fair fight. You will only have a few seconds to put the attacker down, with any means at your disposal."

Although Michael was always with me, my path taught me some hard lessons in which he couldn't intervene. He could only guide. He always told me, "Never pick a fight and always defend. Think, stay alert and never strike back, until you have an edge." Most of all, he said, "Plan your escape. Always make sure you can get yourself out of anything you get yourself into."

From all I've experienced, I believe every child should learn personal defense. Michael told me that the day would come, when I would be teaching kids my own style of martial arts. That was one of the reasons he had me learn everything I could. He showed me in a vision that I would be surrounded by kids. I was wearing a blue Karate gi. Around my waist was a black belt. The kids were wearing white uniforms. There was a little girl, wearing a blue Super Girl costume, standing next to me. The vision made me feel proud. I took a deep breath, sighed and thought, "I can't wait for that day!"

A bonus I earned from the day I stopped "The Monster" from hurting me, was a new level of respect from my brothers. It only lasted for a while, but I certainly enjoyed the reprieve.

A year later in the same park behind Kent Junior High School, I was sitting on a picnic table eating a Twinkie. I had a bad day at school and wasn't in the best of moods. I also wasn't paying too much attention to my surroundings and was caught off guard when Damian and Troy Pain came up from behind me. They sat on either side of me.

Troy snatched the other Twinkie in the package and shoved the whole thing in his mouth saying, "Don't be a selfish pig."

I said, "You're the pig." He pushed me against Damian, then my brother pushed me against Troy. When I tried to get up and run, they pulled me back down and the pushing game started all over again.

Troy said, "I feel a fart coming on. You don't have your stick Eddie boy. Now what are you going to do?"

I was scared and frustrated. I forgot to breathe and think things through.

I thought, "Why is this always happening to me?" I just wanted to be left alone. I just wanted peace.

Michael said to me, "Little Sir Edward, you must pick your fights and do what you can to live with the consequences."

I knew this shoving game was not going to end well for me.

After hearing Michael's message, I thought quickly, "Okay, I've got to live in the same house as Damian." He was sitting on my right.

"Troy's the one that's got to go."

I swung my right fist and caught Troy Pain in the right eye. It knocked him backward off the table, and he tumbled onto the grass dazed.

Damian jumped up but, instead of hitting me, he said, "Run Eddie, before Troy kicks the shit out of you."

I took off running.

When Troy revived all the way, he and Damian gave chase. I ran down into the creek that ran under the overpass tunnel. Not feeling safe, I looked for a better hiding place. There was a small storm drainage pipe in the wall. I climbed head first into the pipe that was just a little larger than my shoulders. It was a tight squeeze.

I remembered too late Michael's warning about planning my escape and not getting into something I couldn't get out of. Moments before I crawled into the drain I heard the buzzing telling me that wasn't a good idea and I should keep running. I was panicking and too scared to listen.

I heard the two thugs enter the tunnel. Fearing that they would see my tennis shoes in the smaller pipe on the sidewall, I wiggled further into the darkness. It was so tight, I didn't have enough room to look back, but I could feel them searching for me.

I could hear them talking about looking in the two side drainage pipes.

"Nah, they're too small even for that scrawny shit," said Troy.

"Yeah," said Damian, "he'd be too scared in here, and it's so small. I don't think he would fit."

I heard them move on with their search, as their voices were trailing off in the distance. It reminded me of when I was hiding from Tim Irving under the pickup truck. I got out too early, and he almost got me. I stayed quiet for a long while just to be safe.

When I felt they were no longer nearby, I tried to back out of the drainage pipe. Quickly I learned why Michael didn't want me to go head first into that tiny pipe. I was stuck! I couldn't get enough traction with my shoes to pull my body back out the way I came in.

So... this is why Michael told me to never get myself into anything I couldn't get myself out of.

"You could've made that a little clearer!" I yelled out loud. All my frustrated yelling did was hurt my ears, as the sound reverberated in the pipe.

Damn! I couldn't get out of that pipe.

"Holy crap," I thought, "what do I do now?"

I could see myself dying in that drainpipe and my body not being found, until a heavy rain flushed me out. I laughed out loud and then got mad at myself for laughing. Idiot!

I thought about the story of me being born in that hospital toilet and now I was stuck in a sewer pipe awaiting the big flush. I thought about my head being used as a toilet seat, receiving all those years of farts. My life was flashing before me just like they said in the movies.

I started sweating and getting really scared. I could feel some, multi-legged bugs crawling up my pant legs, in my hair and over my face. The whole pipe seemed to come alive with hungry bugs. I was ready to freak out.

Then Michael said, "Calm down. Take a breath. Getting upset will not help matters. Think. Think always. Place your hands flat and push back at the same time you pull your body back, with your toes."

51

"That is easier said the done," I yelled out loud, forgetting what that did to my ears the last time. "I'm really far up in this pipe. Do you know that?"

"Yes," he replied. "Breathe. Calmly breathe, Eddie."

Just communicating with the angel already started to calm me. I didn't feel so panicky and alone. I took a deep breath, and when I did, I felt a surge of energy flow into my body. Michael gave me a strength greater than my own.

I was moving. Only about an inch at a time, but the movement kept my mind off of the bugs and stinky wet muck that I was laying in. Inch by inch, I wiggled my way out. It took me over an hour, but I made it. Exhausted and bitten from head to toe, I started to walk home. I was out! I swore then that I would *never* be confined in a tight space like that again.

Once out of that damn drainpipe Michael asked, "What lessons have you learned today?"

I said, "To listen."

He said, "And never get yourself into any situation you can't get yourself out of. Always think seven steps ahead of everything you do and widen your range of perception, to include everything around you."

I asked, "How do I do that?"

He said, "A good start is to become a soldier. First a soldier for your country, and then a soldier for our Divine Creator."

Chapter Ten

In *Michael's Sacred Service*

My mother and father were never church going people. As a matter of fact, my mother never had any religious upbringing at all. The only reason we attended Catholic school when we lived in Chicago was because it made us members and eligible for the monthly food baskets. And, oh yeah… it was a tuition-free, awesome behavior modifier as well. No kid wanted to mess with Chicago nuns. Not even Billy.

My brother, sister and I had to attend church every Sunday because of school. It was a requirement. Although my parents didn't go to church, my father did have us baptized Catholic as infants, honoring an old pledge his great grandmother made in Ireland over a hundred years earlier.

As the story goes, my grandmother was born four weeks premature. Back then, babies usually did not survive premature births. Her family was from the O'Curry clan. They were Northern Irish Protestants. Her mother desperately prayed in their small church every day for the baby to be spared, but the baby was still getting weaker and near death.

One night in a dream, the Archangel Michael appeared, telling her if she would convert the family to Catholicism, the baby would be okay. They did as Michael instructed and the baby survived.

Great Grandma O'Curry went on to give birth to my grandmother, who passed the devotion and divine oath to my father. My grandmother would tell me that story all the time. She was emphatic about the vow they took and told dad that if he were ever in trouble, he needed to ask St. Michael to help and not to bother Jesus. She felt Jesus was too busy, helping God in Heaven.

"He will always show you the way, me' boy. Don't you ever, ever forget that," she insisted.

That's why, during the war when my father was about to be sent to the concentration camp, he called on Archangel Michael. The family's oath was a powerful devotion and sacred to them. It was that very oath, I believe, that landed me in Archangel Michael's Sacred Service. It took many years to weave itself into my life, but it was growing in intensity. I could feel its call to service. A call I answered.

Michael came to me one evening and told me he had to leave me. He called it a "return to the Father." He was going to be gone for a year or two. He warned me to stay out of trouble and not to give into my inner demons.

I didn't know what that meant.

No sooner had he left, I started hanging around with Monster and his friends. They were a wild bunch. We'd stay out late every night, getting into mischief.

One evening, a new friend, Paul Beetle showed up with two six-packs of beer that he had taken from his father's garage. We went to the park to party and drink. I stole a pack of Camel cigarettes from Daddy Frank's carton at home. With the beer, we felt like a gang of cool teenagers, drinking, smoking and feasting on life.

That became the big thing we did. We'd get someone to buy beer or slow gin for us, and we'd go to the park to drink. Most of us quit school. We thought there wasn't anything school could teach us that we didn't already know.

I got a job working at a salvage yard called Bladensburg Metals, with my brother, Billy. He married Nancy, and they had a son also named Billy. My job at the salvage yard was to sort out different types of metals from mountains of garbage. The metal was to be melted down and poured into ingots.

Some of the guys I hung out with from work started a gang called "The Hellions." They started carrying guns, knives and chains. At lunch break, they talked about going to other neighborhoods to fight rival gangs. They were trying to get me to join, but I was determined to resist. I knew where that life led. I kept my pledge to Michael. I didn't join the gangs although there was a lot of pressure to do so.

When Michael returned in 1965 he said, "I see you going down the same path as your brothers. Enlist in the Army. It will save your life."

I didn't see it that way. I had resisted the gangs. I kept my nose clean. I was a drop out; drinking and smoking, but at least I had a paying job. I felt I was just having some harmless fun. I certainly wasn't too keen on becoming a soldier. "Save my life? Was he crazy? Isn't it easier to die in the army than in my neighborhood?" I thought. Guys from Palmer Park had already gone off to war just to return in a body bag and nobody cared. I didn't want to end up that way. The last thing I wanted to do was go to Vietnam and get shot. While Michael was gone, I had started dating Gayle. She was my girlfriend now, and she liked "Fast Eddie," better than she did "Good Edward," who was boring.

When I told Michael that I wasn't going into the Army, I sensed he was hurt, but I didn't care. I was brazen and felt like I knew what I was doing and wasn't going to get in trouble. I did think it odd, though, that an Angel could get hurt feelings. I wondered about that for a while.

Then I asked him, "Are you upset with me for hurting your feelings?"

He said, "My feelings are not hurt. Your life is your own. When you declined my advice, I merely was given a vision of your future, and I was dismayed for you, not hurt."

"What did you see," I asked.

Then Michael shared the vision.

I had been arrested for something. The police put me in a jail cell with some older kids that beat me bloody. I was close to death, and with that death, the fate of humanity would lie in jeopardy.

I shrugged off what Michael showed me. I was at that age where no one could tell me anything. I was certain I could handle myself, and I'd never do anything to get arrested. I did enjoy drinking beer and smoking cigarettes with my friends, but that was where I drew the line. What he showed me would never happen! I turned a deaf ear to him.

Michael was disappointed in me and our connection was breaking down. I knew I was letting him down, but it was my life. I was only going to be a teenager once. I wanted to have my fun.

I really enjoyed taking Gayle to teen club on Friday nights. She taught me how to slow dance. I loved holding her in my arms and looking into her blue eyes. That decade was the time when girls teased their hair, so it poofed out all around their head. She looked like sweet blonde cotton candy. It brought back those feelings from the time I spent with the Constant Walker. I was in heaven.

All the boys, at the time, put grease on their hair. I used "My Knight" pomade (seems like there were signs of the future everywhere for me).

One night, after dancing cheek to cheek for a while, one side of Gayle's hair was poofy and the other side was flat as a pancake. The pomade in my hair flattened hers. Her girlfriend, Joyce, motioned to her, pointing at her own head and making a silly face. Gayle was so embarrassed. I tried to make a joke by saying, "At least no one stuck an ice cream cone on your forehead." Unfortunately, she didn't think I was funny. We had our first fight, and she called her mother to come pick her up. I felt like an inconsiderate jerk.

With Gayle gone, Monster and I were looking for something to do. One of our friends, Mike Hess, showed up with his cousin from out of town. He was 18-year-old Paul Bugs from Bayonne, New Jersey. He drove a brand-new midnight blue Chevy Impala Super Sport, with flames painted down the sides. The New Jersey license plate was the second thing I noticed. Damn that car looked fast.

They were going out cruising for chicks and wanted to know if Monster and I wanted to ride along.

"Hell yeah," we said, as we piled into the back seat.

They had two six packs of beer and a carton of cigarettes, so off we went for a night of cruising and carousing. We drove around for a while, but it was raining and there were no girls to be found.

Monster had just received his driver's license and asked to drive the car. Peter climbed into the back seat with me, after he dumped all the empty beer cans onto the street. Fifteen minutes later Monster ran a stop sign. I looked across the street just as we passed a police car, hiding in the shadows. The officer turned on his dome lights and gave chase.

About a mile up the road, Monster pulled over, while we all stuffed the remaining beer cans up under the front seat and shoved Double Mint chewing gum in our mouths.

As the cop started walking toward our car, Peter let us know that the trunk of the car was full of stolen clothes they had shoplifted from several department stores downtown. And, oh yeah, he also added another little tidbit of information that the car was stolen as well.

Hearing that, Monster's foot hit the gas pedal and off we went, leaving the officer in a spray of rainwater and exhaust.

To make a long story short, it started pouring down rain like I had never seen before. Monster drove like a maniac trying to lose that cop. The car must have been pretty fast because we were a good distance ahead of him. Then Monster slid off the road, trying to make a turn. The car flipped over into a shallow creek. We all crawled out of the car and started running into the woods. By the time the cop got to the car, we were all hidden. Several more police cars arrived with K-9 dogs searching for us.

Michael's vision was right on target.

"What a damned idiot I was! Why didn't I listen to Michael?" I thought. No one was going to believe that I didn't know that car and the trunk full of clothes were stolen. I was going to jail, sure as shit.

Peter Boggs had climbed a tree to hide from the barking dogs that were closing in on us. I was about twenty yards away from him, lying on the ground next to a fallen tree trunk. I tried to cover myself with sticks, brush and leaves. The K-9 dogs went right to Peter's tree and then started barking in my direction. Flashlights were shining everywhere. I called for Michael to help me, but he didn't respond.

I kept saying in my mind, "Michael if you get me out of this mess, I will enlist in the army on my seventeenth birthday and follow your guidance as long as there is breath in my body."

Still nothing. I must've really pissed him off this time. The regret came over me like a ton of bricks. It looked hopeless for me.

The police got Peter out of the tree and cuffed him. The K-9 officers started working the dogs closer to me. Off in the distance I could see more flashlights converging on my location. The dog barking was getting closer. About fifteen yards to my right, the dogs stopped at the base of another tree. They found Monster, who had climbed high within its branches. I knew I was next, but the cops stopped looking on the ground for us and started focusing up, in the surrounding trees. Several cops gathered around Monster's tree with guns drawn. They commanded him to climb down.

He refused saying, "Why don't you come up and get me, coppers." He was very dramatic and stupid that way. I thought at times that I hit him a little too hard on the head with that stick the day of our big fight.

I was scared and my body was freezing. I have never felt so cold. It must've been fear mixed with the rain and damp leaves where I was hiding. I asked Michael to help me, but I couldn't feel his presence. I knew he was pissed and leaving me to my own demise. Then I realized that Michael was right. I had let my demons take over, and they had led me down this path. My ego was played for a fool. I wanted to be seen as cool. I had become a true Hellion, without ever joining the gang. I didn't want to get arrested.

My brothers had been arrested several times, and it was killing our mother. I saw how sad it made her, when she and Frank had to go to court and hear the bad stuff that Damian and Billy had done. I didn't want to put her through that. Plus, I didn't do anything wrong. I was just riding around in a car. I didn't know it was stolen, and I didn't steal the clothes in the trunk of that car.

All these thoughts flooded through my mind, but deep down inside I knew that just being in the car made me guilty of the crimes.

A voice said, "Guilty by association."

I could hear the buzzing of Michael in my head. He was here! I quietly covered myself with more leaves and branches, as the dog moved in my direction. It started raining harder than I've ever seen before. I could feel a pressure of something laying over me. It was Michael trying to shield my trembling body.

He said, "What are you going to do now, little one?"

I said, "I better go in the army before I do something I will regret forever."

My heart was beating out of my chest, as the rain came down harder. Flashlight beams were dancing all over the leaves covering my face, but they couldn't see. The dogs were so close I could smell their wet fur, but they couldn't smell me.

I felt Michael lift off my body.

The dogs were startled and moved away to my right. The police officers followed. I knew Michael was orchestrating the diversion. Then Mike Hess jumped up and started to run. I heard one of the cops say, "That's the last of them. Let the dogs loose."

Once they were far away, I sat up. Out of the corner of my eye, I could see a blue orb. It was blinking in the opposite direction that Mike Hess and the police went. I knew it had to be Michael, showing me the way out.

I started crawling on my belly like a reptile. Elbow, elbow, knee, knee was the cadence. Around downed trees, rocks and sticker bushes, my low crawl moved me forward. Like in that drainpipe I methodically traveled, inch by inch. The whole time I was crawling I had the vision in my head of my father crawling away from the German soldiers the night he escaped and avoided the Nazi death camp.

Michael had me crawling for what felt like miles and miles. I know that seems a bit dramatic, but the fear and chill of the damp night was wearing on me. Long after I was well away from the police, I kept getting the message to stay down and crawl. I didn't know if he was trying to prove a point and this was some sort of penance or not. As soon as I had that thought, Michael projected the vision once again of what my father had to do to survive. If it weren't for my dad's midnight crawl, I wouldn't be here now to tell this tale or anything else for that matter.

My elbows and knees were raw and bloodied. I was cold, wet and muddy from head toe. After what felt like an hour, I came to a dirt road. The blue orb was gone, and I knew it was okay to get up.

I felt alone again. Guilt was my only companion. I was sure that Michael was pissed at me. My mind was flooded with thoughts of how I was screwing up Michael's plans for me and humanity. In that moment I had an epiphany! The day I drowned and laid next to Michael and the little baby on that rock, he wasn't dreaming. He was planning his return through me!

"Man!" I said out loud. "What a screw up, I am. This isn't how I wanted to turn out. I'm so sorry."

The silence was deafening. No buzzing. No pressure. No nothing.

I walked for about two miles down that old country road when it started thundering and lightning. I looked up to the sky, spread my arms and said, "I'm so sorry Connie. Truly I am. How can I make this right to you? Please help me. I know I don't deserve it, but please?"

The rain stopped immediately, after I uttered my last "please." Off in the nearby field, I saw a tobacco barn. I could feel the presence of my sweet Connie.

"Stay in the barn until morning. All is forgiven, my brave knight," her melodious voice trailed off toward the barn.

My heart was happy again.

I bounded toward the barn like a little kid, or a convict set free from a life sentence. I guess that last analogy was closer to the truth than I care to admit. I was definitely given a second chance. Once I got to the barn, I wasn't quite so happy. It was the creepiest place I had been in since, forever. Well, at least since the drainage pipe incident.

"Geez," I thought, "I sure do get myself into some weird situations, and I'm the GOOD son!" Every scary movie I had ever seen in my life haunted me that night. I received no comfort or sleep, but at least it was a dry place to be alone, with my thoughts. A small price to pay for not spending the night in jail.

"Thank you God for Michael," I exclaimed. I realized in that moment what real gratitude was. Up until then I always focused on the crap in my life. Looking back, I see how I was always being cared for.

Gratitude is of utmost importance.

The next morning, I started my long walk home. Michael still was not communicating with me. I felt like my egotistical, selfish craziness damaged God's mission and Michael's plans to complete it. Shame washed over me like a heavy coat of paint. "He only gets one chance every five hundred years," I said to myself, "and he, the mighty archangel, got stuck with me!"

I started to cry uncontrollably. Immediately I felt foolish and cried out in frustration "STOP IT!" Big boys don't cry."

But then I heard Connie's sweet voice say, "No, but real men do!" Her presence around me lifted the veil of shame and self-pity I was wallowing in.

When I arrived home, I crashed in my bed and passed out for the entire day. Stress has a way of wearing on ya, I guess.

The next morning, I woke up fresh and with a new resolve. I was committed to the new path of becoming a soldier in the United States Army. In retrospect, it was the best guidance Michael ever gave me. I started planning my escape from the crazy life I was living. I read everything I could get my hands on about the army. I started to prepare my body to get into physical condition.

The news always led with stories about "Vietnam heating up" and "President Johnson is sending more and more troops over to fight." None of that deterred my plans. I was laser focused, even when friends of my brothers were being drafted and many more were coming home injured or in body bags.

Damian was afraid of being drafted. Old '"Hot Stuff" and Troy Pain were talking about going to Canada to escape the draft. All of a sudden, my gangster brother who loved to fight, was talking about being a conscientious objector. That cracks me up every time I think about it. Bullies usually are cowards turned inside out.

Even though Damian and Troy tried to get me to run with them, I kept my promise to Connie and Michael. A year later on my seventeenth birthday, I enlisted in the U.S. Army. Michael still hadn't communicated with me, since the low crawl away from the cops. I felt like I was supposed to find my way on my own and use everything he had taught me up to that point.

I had basic training at Fort Bragg, North Carolina and A.I.T. (Advanced Infantry Training) at Fort Gordon, Georgia. I hated it when I first went in, but didn't want it to end when I was finished sixteen weeks later. At graduation, they told us that we were all being sent to 25th Infantry Division in Vietnam. I was fully prepared. I felt that, with every ounce of my being.

I was walking back to the barracks after company revelry on the morning we were scheduled to leave for Vietnam, when the Admin Corporal came up to me and handed me new orders.

"You've been reassigned, you lucky bastard," he disclosed. "You're being sent to the 24th Infantry Division in Germany. The personnel clerk made a typo on your original orders. Lucky for you, we caught it in time."

"I want to go with the rest of my friends," I answered.

"Not my problem," he said. "You can go check in with Personnel, but if I were you, I'd think about that first. Think long and hard. It's like you had some sort of divine intervention. I wouldn't mess with that if I were you."

It was like I didn't hear a word he said. Again, not being one to be told I couldn't do something, I headed straight over to Personnel. The Major happened to be on the way out, when I was walking in.

Major George P. Cotton was taller than Damian and a tad bit meaner-looking as well. He was in charge of the Personnel Division.

I handed him my papers and asked if I could be switched back to my original company.

He said, "Are you stupid or something? Have we been too hard on your head these past sixteen weeks? It's too late. You're damn lucky to get the assignment. Your guardian angel must be watching out for you. Be grateful."

GRATEFUL.

DIVINE INTERVENTION.

GUARDIAN ANGEL.

The words all flooded into my head at the same time. Chills went up my legs and spine. "Okay Michael," I mumbled low, "I get it. Thank you!"

"What did you say boy?" Shouted Major Cotton.

"Sir, I said thank you, Sir!" I quickly replied.

I made a mental note to self at that point, "Watch how and when you talk to your angel."

Later that day, sitting in the mess hall waiting for my transport, I overheard guys talking about the 25th Infantry Division. Come to find out the reason so many guys were being sent was to replace all the soldiers that had been killed in recent combat action. The 25th was in the thick of it over there. I knew then Michael had something to do with that typo. He may not have been in communication with me directly, but he was still watching over and guiding my life as best he could.

Once I arrived in Germany and went through processing, it was obvious that the angel was, indeed, guiding where they stationed me. What started off with me just being another infantry line rat on the Czechoslovakian border, turned out to be an assignment to the 24th Infantry Division's Headquarter in Augsburg on Sheridan Kaserne. That's when I met Tyrone Campbell a thirty-five-year-old barber, drafted from Detroit, Michigan.

While Tyrone and I were being processed into the division, a clerk told me of the hazing ritual headquarter command has. "Within the first forty-eight hours of a newbie's arrival, a team of veterans will capture you when you least expect it. They will hold you down, strip you naked and paint your groin area red, white and blue."

He added, "If the team can't catch you within forty-eight hours, you are home free."

I asked, "How many guys have avoided capture?"

While counting on his fingers for about ten seconds, he said, "To date ... none."

Wow! I thought, isn't this great? It was all just an ugly reminder of the day Tim Irving and his gang tied Frankie and me to those palm trees. I made up my mind right in that moment, I wasn't gonna' go through that again.

The clerk said, "You should just surrender, and let them get you. It's childish, but its tradition."

In my head, I said, "Screw tradition!"

The entire first day was spent in the processing center. We had checked in at Headquarters, and they couldn't find us a room. So the 48-hour clock was already ticking.

The next morning after chow, we reported back to headquarters and were assigned to a room. After putting my stuff away, I went outside to get a feel for the base. I noticed two guys following me. Everywhere I went, they were watching my every move. It was Sunday, so I went to church. I figured nobody would attack me in a church. The priest was holding Bible studies, so I sat in on all the classes to kill time. As a bonus, I learned a lot about the different ways people and religions viewed God. I was rapidly learning just how much I didn't know.

After the classes were over, I went to the mess hall again. While I was eating, the two guys sat down on either side of me. One of them said, "Well my newbie, have you found Jesus, yet? You sure spent a long time in church today."

The other one said, "There are two ways we can do this. There's the easy way, you just submit, and it will all be over in five minutes. Or there's the hard way. We pick your young ass up and carry you out back. One way or the other, your junk is going to look very patriotic in a few minutes."

I didn't know what to say or what to do!

Thinking fast, I said, "I'm not going to fight you guys. I heard it's tradition, and no one has ever escaped the ritual, so I surrender. You got me. Let me take my tray up, and let's get this thing over with."

I picked up my tray as they walked to the front door to wait for me. I looked through to the kitchen and saw a door open behind the mess hall. I dropped my tray and took off running through the kitchen and out the back door. I ran and ran until I couldn't run anymore.

I stopped in an alley across from a movie theater. *Doctor Zhivago* was playing, so I brought a ticket and set up camp for the rest of the day.

That is one movie I never want to see again. I stayed in that theater until it closed at 10:00 p.m.

I ate candy and popcorn for dinner, but at least I was still safe. The problem was I had to be back for bed check at 10:30 p.m. If I missed bed check, I'd be marked AWOL by the CQ. All this was going through my mind.

It looked like they had me.

When I got outside, it was cold and started to snow.

I made my way back to the headquarters building, where Tyrone and I shared a room with two other guys. Tyrone had just finished talking a shower. He said the hazing crew got him, as he was leaving the Mess Hall after dinner, and it was quite an ordeal. He said he still couldn't get all the paint off. He opened his towel to show me. That picture is forever burned into my mind.

It was now 10:15 pm, and I had another hour and forty-five minutes to go before I was safe. We were on the second floor, and my bunk was next to the window that faced the street. I opened the window and looked outside. There was no screen on the window, which was good in case I had to jump to get away. The other two guys assigned to my room came back for bed check. Then they were going back down the hall to play cards, with some other guys. I had stripped down to my underwear when the CQ came in. He marked us all present, then left. The next thing I knew, the door flew opened and three guys rushed in. Like a shot, I was out the window without even thinking.

What I didn't know was our company commander had pulled up in his red BMW and went into the building to get something. He left his girlfriend in the car, which was parked right under my window. I had never heard a woman scream so loud as when my half-naked body landed on the hood. I rolled off onto the snow, as one of the hazing crew came running out the front door to chase me down. I started rubbing my ankle and yelling that I broke my leg. The guy took one look at me, then another at the colonel's girlfriend, who was still screaming. He took off running.

I was freezing. I jumped to my feet and, as I passed the passenger side window, I yelled, "Sorry" to the woman. I ran as best I could with my new-found limp, back into the building and took the five flights of stairs to the attic. It was a cold, dark and spooky place. The only light coming in was from the streetlights outside. It reminded me of that old tobacco barn I stayed in the night of my big screw up. I sure could have used my guardian angel, but he wasn't answering me. I found an old very dusty tarp that I wrapped around me for warmth, while I waited until the church bells down the street rang midnight.

When I went back downstairs, I thought I was safe, but I ran into my roommates. They told me that the colonel wanted to see me in his office at 0800 hours in the morning, with a good explanation for scaring his girlfriend half to death. I was just glad to take a hot shower and slide into a warm bed.

The next morning, I reported to Colonel Sutton's office. While I was waiting, a big Asian-looking Master Sergeant sat down next to me. He was built like a Sumo wrestler. He smiled and said, "Congratulations private. You are the first ever to avoid capture, during the hazing hours."

I said, "Thank you Sir."

He said, "Don't call me sir and don't thank me yet. You're in a lot of trouble. I understand that the Colonel's girlfriend saw something last night she will never forget. And it appears the Colonel is going to make sure you're not going to forget it, either."

Just then Colonel Sutton yelled, "Private Jagen, front and center." I entered and saluted.

He said, "Sergeant Kiki, have a seat. Jagen you can continue to stand at attention." "Would you like to explain what made you polish the hood of my car with your naked ass last night, son? Your shenanigans ruined my plans for a romantic evening."

He was a grumpy old fellow, and if looks could kill, I'd be a dead man.

I replied, "Yes Sir." I went on to explain what happened to Frankie and me when I was seven. And when I heard that the division hazing tradition was being stripped naked, I just wasn't going down without a fight. It brought back some really bad memories for me. I ended with, "and they never got me, Sir."

Sgt. Kiki said, "He is the first newbie to beat the clock. That should be worth something more than a hand shake and a kick in the nuts."

The Colonel chuckled.

After hearing my story, the Colonel assigned me to a week on police duty, not with the MP's (Military Police,) it was KP (Kitchen Police). I peeled several mountains of potatoes, eight hours a day for seven days straight. I was then told to report to the Sgt. Kiki in Division Quartermaster Supply.

I got to know Sgt. Kiki very well, as a result of my shenanigans.

As a joke, Sgt. Kiki and his staff presented me with a black leather cord necklace. It had a weird silver thing, with wings hanging from it. After studying it, I saw it was a penis with wings. Sgt. Kiki said that Colonel Sutton wanted me to have the "Flying Cock and Balls Combat Award" for being the only recruit to avoid capture, during the division's hazing tradition. It was the first award I had ever received and, to this day, my most coveted. After my 'jumping out of the window stunt,' the hazing tradition was ended.

Sgt. Kiki was a very interesting man from Hawaii. He came from a long line of Hawaiian shaman. He really liked me. He said, "You have tenacity kid, but just not much common sense."

We would sit for hours, talking about the separation of the mind, body and spirit.

I didn't have a clue what he was talking about at first but, over the months, it all started to make sense. He said that he saw the electro-magnetic energy around people, called the "aura." He disclosed to me that mine could develop into the golden aura of a gifted shaman someday.

Sgt. Kiki said, "I feel that you have been sent to me from the Hawaiian Demi-God, Maui, for a reason."

I asked, "Who is Maui and what is a demi-god?"

He explained that he held a Doctorate in Theology from the University of Hawaii, and he had been studying the religions of humanity all his life.

"I was appointed as an apprentice to the Shaman in our village. When I was born, there was a sign in the sky. Mako-Mako, our village elder came to my parents telling them that the village Shaman, Kahuna Huna, must raise me. I stayed there with him, until I was eighteen. Then I asked Kahuna Huna those same questions you just asked of me, 'Who is Maui and what is a demi god?' That is when he told me it was time for me to go to the University and learn all the world's religions."

Sgt. Kiki went on to tell me that throughout time, shamans and spiritual leaders have always held that there was a main powerful god force and many lesser gods or demi-gods that dwell in the great beyond. That is called polytheism. When the old religions were replaced, by just the main "One God" principle, it's called Monotheism.

"But," he said, "the mind of man must still eventually reconcile to the universal truth of the cosmos. The lesser god energies have become the spirits of saints and angels. A demi-god is a person in mythology, who has some of the lesser powers of God, or could be described as a being, who is part god and part human.

Examples of a man-god are Hercules, the pharaohs, or even Jesus when he became the Christ."

I asked him, "What about Archangels? Where do you feel they fit into the God/Demi God thing?"

"Archangels? Anyone in particular?" he asked.

"Saint Michael," I said. "He seems to kind of always be around my family for some reason." I skirted the issue because I didn't want to reveal too much to him. I liked my assignment and didn't want him to ship me out to a mental ward.

He answered, "A powerful Archangel like Michael, who is God's commander, definitely has the same energy as the demi-god Maui. In the Judeo-Christian belief, he commands God's forces and his name means, "Liken to God."

As soon as Sgt. Kiki said that, I felt the buzzing in my ears again.

Michael had come back to my consciousness.

That night while I slept, the angel mapped out why and when he arranged to have me sent to Germany, and why I am now working under Sgt. Kiki.

It was to learn to be open and connect to the spirits of earth bound souls. The shamans of the world hold the wisdom of the ages and know how to tap into the many energies of the earth.

My training under Sgt. Kiki would allow me to help understand the troubled souls, bound by the past atrocities in Europe. Historically it was a brutal place over the ages. Michael wanted me to tour the castles of Europe and learn all that I could on how Adolf Hitler and the Nazi Party deceived the people to follow his mindset. I was also to get my G.E.D. and enroll in the University of Maryland, Augsburg Campus, to start my college education. He said it was imperative for me to study Psychology, Theology and Criminology, if we were to be successful in our mission.

"I have to focus on arranging things on seven levels or dimensions," he said.

Even though I understood the words, I didn't understand the meaning of what he was saying. He showed me a picture of seven chessboards stacked on top of one another. They had light and dark pieces sitting on light and dark squares. When a light piece moves on one board that allows a dark piece to be moved on another board. Michael told me, "When I am trying to help humanity move forward, I depend on the piece staying light. Remember the day when I reached for you and the light had all but gone dark?" he asked.

I got a sudden chill up my spine.

His message for me was loud and clear. I promised him that I would keep the mission in the forefront of everything I did from then on.

He disclosed, "Many innocent lives depend on you keeping that promise." The last thing Michael said to me was, "Don't date the woman, you need to stay focused."

"What woman?" I asked.

And he was gone.

Over the next two years, I absorbed every detail presented to me, from European architecture to Shamanism, from psychology to mythology and basically everything in between. My whole being felt like a sponge, as I soaked it all in. There was an understanding I was gaining with each fact I was taught. It was like I was both the student and the master at the same time. I never learned so easily before.

School was not my thing growing up, but now I was drawn in like a moth to the flame.

At the end of my second year in Germany and fourth semester of college, I hit a limit. I learned so much, I felt like my head was going to explode. I needed a break or a distraction for a while.

That thought was no sooner out of my mind when a distraction manifested right before me.

I was in psychology class one day, when I looked up to see the time on the clock. There she was, walking right in front of me. A beautiful German girl named Maria Bickler. She had long black hair and an hourglass body.

I shook my head and wondered, "Where did she come from?"

I assumed she was new, but later found out she not only was in my psych class, she was in my criminology classes two semesters in a row. I guess I was so focused on my studies the last two years, I wasn't really in touch with my surroundings.

Even though I knew I needed a mental break, I was determined not to derail.

No chick is worth messing up again. But one evening, while leaving class, I saw her being hassled by an Italian guy, trying to push her into his car. When I when over to see if I could help her, I found that the guy was drunk.

He pulled a knife out and was waving it toward me, slashing in thin air.

"Get the 'fug' back, Mr. Army man," he shouted in broken English.

Growing up with my brothers gave me a great education about knife attacks. They were always slashing at me, with knives, or throwing them at me. For a while, I thought I was a carnival act, it was so bad. Luckily for me I was very agile. I got really good at batting the blades away. With that skill under my belt and with my combat training still fresh in my mind, I was a lean, mean fighting machine.

I took his knife with one hand and, with the other, I palmed him under the nose. It knocked him out cold. I dragged him to his car, opened the door and plopped him in. I sat him up in the front seat and then closed the door.

I turned to Maria and said, "We should call the police."

She fearfully replied, "Oh no, no. Police don't like G.I.'s. They will arrest you for fighting, and I will be in trouble too." Her English was actually a lot better than I expected, but she did have a very heavy German accent.

Maria was terrified and too upset to catch the streetcar, so I borrowed a car from a friend and offered to drive her home.

"Can we go for coffee first? I don't want my parents to see me so shaky," she asked.

I was actually hungry and asked, "Feel like going for a bite to eat instead?"

"Sure," she replied.

After we ate, and she settled down, Maria told me that many Italian guys move to Germany, thinking that all German girls want to have sex with them.

"And they won't take no for an answer," she frustratingly proclaimed.

Tears welled up in her eyes and she banged her fist on the table.

"I was raped last year. A cute Italian guy asked me for directions and tricked me. He had a knife and held it to my throat. Then pulled me into an alley."

I felt bad for her. The two things I hate the most are child molesters and rapists.

I drove her home. Like me, she was 19 years old and lived at home with her parents. She asked me to come in and meet them. They were the sweetest couple. I wound up staying for three hours, talking to them.

I found out that her mother loved to cook and her father was a carpenter, just like mine. They didn't speak a word of English, and I didn't speak German, so Maria translated all night. I learned that her father was a soldier, during the war. He hated Hitler and the Nazi's.

Maria said, "We can't speak about them though. Too many people have mysteriously disappeared."

Over the next six months of visiting Maria's family and the countryside, I learned so much of how Hitler manipulated the minds of the German people. Maria became my interpreter. I was beginning to understand more German than I could speak. But from years of translating thoughts from the angel, I seemed to understand people's meanings just from their emotions. Sometimes it was like reading their minds.

Together, Maria and I toured most of the major castles in Germany, France and Austria. It's safe to say that we spent A LOT of time together.

On our last trip to explore the castles near Paris, I experienced my first horrific vision. I was looking at the center of town when, all of a sudden, I felt like I left my body.

I was transported to August of 1572. All around me, there was chaos in the town. People were being dragged from their homes and murdered in the street. I saw a knight wearing a white tunic, with a red cross on his chest, fighting to protect his pregnant wife. His sword broke while clashing with another knight. The townspeople subdued the couple, tied them to a post facing one another, and a priest lit a bonfire at their feet. I couldn't believe I was watching people being burned to death.

A blue orb descended from above them. It transfigured into an angel in blue armor. As the angel turned, I could see that he was holding the woman's baby in his arms. It was Archangel Michael. He smiled at me, nodded and disappeared.

I popped back into my body to find Maria shaking my arm. "Are you okay?" she asked. "You were staring into space and not answering me. I was scared."

"Yes. Yes, I am fine. I was just thinking about something," I replied.

Later that day, I learned that the town was one of the sites of the St. Bartholomew Day massacres. It was all starting to come together for me. The child must have been the one Michael was holding in the cavern when I drowned and first met the Constant Walker. The knight burned at the stake must have been the one the Archangel was working through five hundred years earlier.

Fear came over me, thinking that crazed religious, fanatics might seek to destroy me one day. Then I remembered the "good Christian" woman, who tortured me as a child. She was convinced she was doing God's work. It had already been made manifest in my life, so it was a very real possibility for the future as well.

The next day, we went to Bordeaux where I was guided to Saint Andre's Cathedral. That's where I had my second vision when I stood before a bronze statue. This time the vision was a brief glimpse of people running from machine gun fire.

As I looked up at the statue, I realized I had finally come face to face with my destiny. I dropped to my knee and wept at the base of this huge bronze of an Archangel in armor, lifting up the body of a man holding a broken sword. The statue is named Gloria Victis, "Glory to the Vanquished." I was never the same again after that.

A few weeks after our tour of the castles, I went to dinner at Maria's house. She was crying when I arrived. She had heard a rumor that the 24th Infantry Division was being deployed to Vietnam and the 25th Infantry Division was replacing us in Germany.

"Were you ever going to tell me, or were you just going to disappear like most G.I.'s that date German girls," she shouted at me.

It all hit me out of left field.

I was thinking, "What in the world is she talking about?"

I raised my voice back at her, "I haven't heard a thing about redeployment, and by the way... I didn't know we were even seriously dating!"

We had kissed a couple of times, but that was all. I was still a virgin and since she had been raped, I didn't think she was interested in sex. I never even thought about pursuing her. We were just friends. I knew that would get me in trouble with Michael's plans for the future.

Maria got mad and ran upstairs to her bedroom and slammed the door.

I didn't know what to do, so I said goodbye to her mother and started for the door.

She stopped me, then motioned with both arms flying up and down, "Gehen Sie bitte zu ihr," she said. And then pointed upstairs in the direction of Maria's room.

I heard enough German to know that meant, "Please go to her."

I climbed the stairs to Maria's room and knocked. All I heard was sobbing. I spoke through the door, "Maria. I'm sorry. I don't know a thing about leaving. Plus, I'm in Headquarters Company. I would be the first to know."

She opened the door, and we sat on the bed to talk.

From there, I can't tell you what the hell happened. My mind is a blank. One thing lead to another and this I know, we kissed. She touched my forbidden fruit and the next thing I know, I'm waking up in the morning a non-virgin.

When I returned to Sheridan Kaserne, the whole camp was turned upside down. The 25th Infantry Division was rotating to replace us, and we were going to replace them in Vietnam. Our entire division was given thirty days to inventory and store every piece of equipment.

As Sgt. Kiki said, "That's every tank, truck, tent and tooth pick."

We were going to be working twelve-hour days. We were being sent to Ft. Riley, Kansas for specialized training for three months, then on to Vietnam.

I called Maria and told her that she heard right and my division was leaving Germany in thirty days. Then I told her that I wouldn't be able to see her until the weekend because we were working twelve to sixteen hour days.

She broke down and started crying and pleading with me, "Don't leave me behind. I have never met such a caring man." She continued to turn the screws on my heart, "I'm in love with you! Please, please transfer to another unit so you can stay with me in Germany."

Argggggg! She was breaking my heart. I didn't know what to do. I wasn't really sure that I loved her. I certainly didn't have the same feeling for her that I had for Connie. However, I'm a sucker for a crying woman.

That afternoon I spoke to some of the guys about Maria. Everyone warned me that many German girls around the bases would say anything to marry G.I.'s just so they could get to the states. Then once they are in the good old U.S. of A. they would dump the G.I.'s for a variety of reasons.

Sgt. Kiki echoed the same advice, "Don't be tricked, my friend. It's a ploy."

Not being one to be told anything, I checked on transfers anyway. It was not an option. I called out for Michael to help. I got the feeling that he was watching to see what I was going to do.

That weekend when I had dinner at Maria's house, she had a bad fight with her father. I understood some of what was being said, but not all of it.

The long and the short of it was Maria's dad felt that I should go to Vietnam, with my division, because I had more important things to worry about than a young, foolish German girl. Her mother, on the other hand, let me know straight out that if I slept with her daughter, I should marry her. End of story.

No one spoke at dinner.

Her father kept smiling at me and moving his fingers across the table like a running man. He was telling me to leave and don't look back.

Where was Michael when I needed him most?

After dinner, we went for a walk. Maria was still very upset and begged me not to leave her. She wanted to be my wife and live with me for the rest of her life.

I was haunted by the angel, warning me about getting involved with the girls here. I wondered how much it would mess things up if I did? All I can say is my heart breaks when I'm in the presence of a woman in distress. Enough said.

My fate was sealed.

Two weeks later, Maria and I were married. All the guys wished me well, but they were taking bets on how many months the marriage would last once we got back to the states.

Chapter Eleven

Back in the U.S. of A.

When we arrived in Fort Riley, Kansas for training, before being sent to Vietnam, the closest house we could rent was forty miles away from the base in the old western town of Woodbine. The phone service was still a wooden crank telephone that connected to a switchboard party line system.

The old farmhouse sat in the middle of twenty-five acres of wheat. The house was mouse and grasshopper infested.

Maria was not a happy camper. She was expecting "America the Beautiful" to be much more. However, we soon found out that another German girl lived nearby, so she had a friend to keep her company when I was at work.

When the angel returned to my consciousness, he was not pleased that I didn't heed his warning about staying away from the girl, but he said he wasn't surprised given my past track record.

That made me feel like shit.

I was excited about going to Vietnam, but Michael said, "That is not going to happen." I didn't think anything more about what he said other than he must've been in bad mood, because I didn't listen to him about not getting married.

We finished the specialized infantry training so all the units started shipping out one by one. I was the only soldier in my company without orders. Then I was called into my company commander's office. Colonel Sutton told me that, since I only had six months left on my three-year enlistment, I needed to re-enlist or I would not be shipping out.

Angel Michael was against me re-enlisting. He had other plans for me. I was now a Specialist E-5. The Army promised to promote me to supply sergeant E-6 with a re-up bonus of seven thousand dollars, if I re-enlisted for three years. It was a tempting offer. Maria wanted me to re-up, but Michael said that deep down inside she was hoping I would be killed in action, so she could receive benefits and my life insurance. I was hoping he was wrong but, in my gut, I had a feeling Michael was right.

When I decided not to re-enlist, I was reassigned and my MOS was changed to Personnel Specialist. I basically typed orders and transfers for army personnel.

While doing all the monotonous typing during the day, Michael would give me visions of the plight of the American Indian past and present.

I asked, "Why now? Why are you showing me all of this?"

"You are sitting on sacred Indian land," he said. "You are a Light Bearer. And where you step, you illuminate the darkness and wake up trapped souls, within the earth."

He went on to show me visions of experiments he wanted to conduct, with the hope of releasing earth-locked Indian spirits that are affecting the living on the land. He said his objective is to protect humans from the negative influence of dark, hate-filled spirits from our past.

To get prepared, Michael wanted me to explore the western culture and the activities of the Native American people.

Maria was afraid of Indians, due to American cowboy and Indian films she saw back home, so she declined my offer to attend a Hopi sweat lodge ceremony with me. It was a good thing. She would have hated it.

The medicine man, conducting the ceremony, was about eighty-five years old. His name was Makya, which means, Eagle Hunter.

I have never been so hot as I was in that sweat lodge. I felt like my blood was boiling. Eagle Hunter stared at me through the whole ceremony. I thought maybe he was expecting me to pass out from the heat. I didn't, but I sure felt I was going to several times.

After the ceremony, Eagle Hunter came over to me, put his right hand on my left shoulder and his left hand on my right shoulder. Then he stared deep into my eyes, twisting his head back and forth, as if it helped him look deeper. I felt as if he was searching for something inside of me.

He spoke, "I see a Great Spirit around you. The Great Spirit told me I should give you a special gift you will need in the future. Come," he said, "look inside and chose your gift. Take what it is you need. He looked puzzled."

I felt bad for the old fella. He lived in a small, stone and mud pueblo hut no bigger than the 8'x8' castle Frankie and I built as kids. It had a dirt floor with a small bed, fireplace and one small window. Inside he had a drum, a spear, animal skulls, blankets, a bottle of Jack Daniels and little more.

How could I take anything from a man that had so little?

Looking around at his humble possessions I said, "Thank you, but I can't think of anything you have that would benefit me in the future."

Jokingly I said, "Maybe a shot of Jack Black."

He shook his head, no.

I tried to give him three ten-dollar bills, "Please take this. The knowledge you have given me is gift enough."

He threw the money into the fire and stared at me, with sad but stern eyes, saying, "Don't bullshit me grandson. You might not know what you are, but I know the Great Spirit has sent you to me for a reason."

Eagle Hunter then walked over to the blankets. Tossing a few of them to one side he picked up a roll of rock hard rawhide leather.

"This is what you will need. It is from a sacred bull buffalo I skinned. For months, it has been dried by Sun and blessed by Moonlight just for you," he disclosed. "You will wear it one day. It will see you through all the bullshit on the path you are to take. Go now and make ready for battle. I am tired. For it's a good day to die."

That old man literally burned my money, kicked me out of his house and then locked the door. How rude! And without a shot of Jack.

I was convinced Makya was crazy.

I asked Michael, "What did all of that mean?"

All he uttered was, "Giving you that rawhide blanket will be the last thing that he will do in this life, so honor it and him. All else will be made known when your waiting is full."

Michael wanted me to feel the suffering of the Native American people, so he had me visit Indian reservations in New Mexico, Oklahoma, Texas, Nebraska and North and South Dakota. All I saw was the appalling living conditions everywhere I went. I saw Indian children forced to live in terrible conditions. Whole families used broken down vans and station wagons, with all four tires missing, as a place to sleep. It was very difficult to see, and I couldn't help but wonder why and what all this had to do with saving humanity?

I had so many questions. Each time I thought of one, I got the same message, "All will be made known when your waiting is full."

I didn't know what he meant by that, but I *KNEW* it was right.

So I surrendered to the process, and on I went.

Michael had me meditate at Wounded Knee and Little Big Horn, the sites of two horrific massacres. I saw many visions, during those days, that turned my stomach and still haunt me to this day. I felt like I was caught in a nightmarish dream and couldn't wake up.

A question arose in the back of my mind, and it is still there today, "How can humans be so cruel to one another?" I remembered back to the vision in France where the knight and his lady were burned to death, by self-righteous zealots.

Michael says, "God is LOVE! When you serve a god that causes you to torture and murder others you are serving a god of human creation, not the God that created humanity."

Michael felt my sorrow and told me, "One day we might have an opportunity to stop another terrifying massacre from occurring to both sides on the same day. It won't erase the past but will help the future and could stop a cycle."

Being out west reminded me of when I was a kid, playing cowboys and Indians. The other kids were always teasing me because I refused to kill the Indians. I was always more of a Lone Ranger, peacemaker type of cowboy.

After completing all the journeys and having the experiences he guided me to, Michael then had me change direction. He wanted me to become a police officer. I actually liked that idea. It felt right to me deep down in my soul. Police recruiters were on base from Houston, Chicago and Washington D.C. I visited each booth to learn more about the departments. I wanted Houston, because the pay was higher and well, yes ... I *was* a cowboy at heart.

Michael said, "The choice is a no brainer. We can advance the mission faster in the seat of great power, Washington D.C., and you will need the help of a future president if we are to succeed."

I wasn't too keen about going home near Damian, Billy and thug central, but I took the D.C. Police test and passed, with flying colors.

The department sent me an invitation letter of acceptance. President Johnson was giving earlier outs to military personnel, who join police departments under part of his Omnibus Crime Bill, so I separated two months early... and off I went to join the Washington, D.C. Metropolitan Police Department.

70

Maria wasn't thrilled about the move. She had made friends on and off base that she didn't want to leave behind. As soon as we arrived in D.C., her attitude changed. She saw all the metropolitan life that was available. The party girl in her came alive.

My police career was intriguing to say the least. I could see that everything Michael had me experience was coming to the forefront. Understanding human behavior was crucial!

Under the G.I. Bill, I could go to college for free, so Michael guided me back to school to study psychology, criminology, theology and art at Georgetown and American University. Going to these schools would also fit into my undercover investigations in the coming years.

I tried to get Maria to enroll with me, as we had done in Germany, but she started hanging around with my brother's wife, Nancy, and friends. All she wanted to do was party with the girls. I didn't have a lot of time to try to convince her otherwise.

I was assigned to the 14th Precinct in uniform. It was a scary time to be white and a cop because it was only one year after Martin Luther King's murder and the D.C. riots that followed. Again, I never really understood the racial issues between men. I thought back to how quickly Frankie and I became friends, despite our color, and wondered why people held such hatred in their hearts for past events. I knew there were atrocities, but I also knew that when we hold onto those feelings, the atrocities live on inside of us whether they happened to us or not. The only thing that comes from not letting go of the past, is a festering rage that holds us back. It does nothing to the people that started the hurt. I guess that can be said of every bad situation in life. What you hold onto, only holds YOU back. I saw this in the case of the kids in the neighborhood on my beat. I felt bad for them. There wasn't much of a chance for most. They ran the streets most of the day and night. When I policed, I believed in the three-strike principle. I gave first, second and third chances before I would charge someone, with a petty crime. My thinking was, "Why ruin a kid's life before they had a chance to live it?" I also thought a lot about the night when Michael saved me from being arrested for something I didn't do.

This went totally against what most of my fellow officers were doing, some of whom would lock people up, if they looked at them cross ways.

In studying these kids, I saw that most of them only had what they took from somebody else. If anyone put something down for a second, someone else would take it. I realized that a lot of the parents didn't know what to teach their children because no one ever taught them.

One frigid early morning about 3:00 am, I found a two-year-old little boy walking down the street, alone and naked. I grabbed a tattered blanket from a nearby trash pile and wrapped the kid up.

I tried to find out where the child lived, but my investigation was quickly leading nowhere. The streets were all but empty that night.

Then came the buzzing in my ears. Michael was present. The blue orb started blinking ahead. I followed it for about four blocks where Michael guided me to an abandoned apartment building. It was filthy, reeking of urine and feces. My eyes were watering and the putrid air was making me nauseous. I had to take my handkerchief out and wrap it around my nose and mouth. I have a hair trigger gag reflex. It was all I could do not to puke.

Weaving my way into the building, through floors filled with dozens of sleeping bodies, I found a thirteen-year-old girl. The blue orb rested right on her chest and she woke up.

She was dazed. Her eyes were crossing, and she was slurring her words, "Anton. Why do you have my Anton?"

"I found him walking the streets alone, without any clothes on," I told her.

"He don't have no clothes," she slurred back.

"What's your name?" I asked.

"Maaarrry," she garbled.

Mary. Her name immediately gave me visions of the baby Jesus, born poor and homeless in a stable.

I thought, "Anton is a child of God." It boggled my mind when I saw such sad sights. How could God allow these things to happen to his children?

Immediately after that thought, I felt like I got hit by the palm of someone's hand right between my eyes. I saw sensations of God's love. Impressions flooded in my mind of how much God loves us, so much that he lets us live the life we choose, based on the choices we make.

Michael said only one phrase, "Free will."

I didn't know at the time, but Michael led me to experience these heart-breaking sights to elevate my awareness, and prepare me for the road ahead. He was here on an earthly mission to help the "Children of Tomorrow," as he put it.

I had to try to stay detached as much as possible, while absorbing all that was presented to me.

To lift my spirits, Michael would often show me a vision of a beautiful castle where kids were playing and swimming in a pond surrounded by fruit trees, gardens and a waterfall. The children were happy, shining like bright beings of light. Around the children were winged angel-knights, wearing white tunics with a red equilateral cross on their breastplates. I didn't know if it was a vision of heaven, or if it was of something yet to come on earth. I didn't know what it meant, but it made my heart happy to think such a place existed, even if it was only in my mind.

I wasn't making much money as a rookie, about $8,000 a year. It was barely enough money to cover the monthly bills, but I couldn't resist buying ice cream for some of the kids on my foot beat.

It broke my heart when the Good Humor truck jingled down the street to the sound of kids screaming, "Wait a minute ice cream man." The driver would pull over just to find that most of the kids in the line didn't have any money.

It hurt to see the disappointment in their sad faces, so I bought some ice cream for the kids, who didn't have money that day.

The next day there were three times as many kids, waiting for me when the ice cream truck turned the corner.

Michael told me, "Don't give ice cream away for free. The kids will not understand or appreciate the gesture. If you do this, you will see every kid in the precinct gathering around you, when the word gets out."

He said, "Make them earn the ice cream."

Michael was right, and I knew it. So from that day on, I challenged the kids to clean up the streets. They had to collect the trash, bottles and old tires. It worked! I saw the kids helping one another and caring for their neighborhood. Kids that were once fighting with each other were now working together. I saw promise and hope for some of the kid's futures. Still there were the negative kids, who didn't want to work for ice cream. If they didn't get it for free, they didn't want anyone to have it. They would lay in wait, out of my eyesight, to pummel the kids who got the ice cream.

Even some parents had a problem with my buying ice cream for their kids. One father ran up to me in a fit of rage, yelling, "Don't give my son ice cream to ease your honky ass guilty conscience." That was more about him than me. My "honky ass conscience" was clear. I had adults come up, blaming me for them being slaves for five hundred years.

I'd say, "I never owned a slave, and I bet you never picked an ounce of cotton. You don't look a day over thirty." Saying that stopped them in their tracks and usually made them scrunch up their face in confusion for about 30 seconds. Then they'd start yelling at me again. They didn't quite get it. I did believe what I said planted a seed and hoped one day in their future, they would see the wisdom. We all have to learn the lessons from the past, but we need to let the hurt and injustice go, in order to move forward as a society. It's our only hope to come together.

I knew they'd never get ahead until they broke out of the "poor me," victim mentality. I thought of Frankie, who was just glad to be alive. He never complained about anything, and most of the people, confronting me, were complaining about everything. I'd walk away, saying a prayer for their peace of mind.

After about a month of hard work in the neighborhood, the negative kids started bullying the positive kids so much that the clean-up stopped. And no one even showed up at the ice cream truck anymore. The trash built up again in the streets and things went back to the way they were. It was sad but I, for one, learned some great lessons.

After six months on my foot beat, I was assigned to a police patrol car, Scout #45. It was an old Ford Galaxy clunker, with a six-cylinder engine, that went from 0 to 30 mph's in about forty-five seconds.

Yes. It was slow. Molasses moved faster. I covered more ground, by walking, than driving. But Michael liked the car.

He said "It will be hard to kill yourself in that car."

It was a turbulent time in Washington D.C. Every month saw anti-war demonstrations downtown. It was very scary being out numbered two thousand to one. I saw some nightmarish things on some of those details. And I didn't always agree with the way the other police officers treated the demonstrators.

I didn't know how a peaceful demonstration could turn to chaos. But when it did, some police officers went crazy. It reminded me of the visions Michael gave me at Wounded Knee.

Chapter Twelve

The Urban Cowboy

One hot summer evening about 7:30 pm, I was operating as a one-man unit, when I received a radio run from the dispatcher. "Scout #45 respond to the McDonald's at 614 Division Avenue N.E. for a robbery in progress, two suspects, one displayed a handgun."

I replied, "Scout #45, 10-99."

I was two blocks away, driving in without red lights or siren, hoping to catch the two suspects in the act.

When I arrived, the store manager came running out of the restaurant and said the two black males that robbed his store just drove off in a yellow, two door late model Chevy, with a black racing stripe down the sides.

After getting a little more information on the suspects, I told the manager, "I will come back to take a full report, but first I want to try to locate the suspects and the car, while they're still in the area."

I broadcasted a lookout on the two suspects, as I began cruising nearby streets and alley ways, "Scout #45, I have a lookout."

There was a pause. Then the dispatcher said, "Go ahead Scout #45, with your lookout."

While driving with one hand on the steering wheel, holding the radio-microphone in the other hand, and looking side to side for the suspect's vehicle, I said, "Scout #45. Wanted for the robbery hold-up with a gun of the McDonald's at 614 Division Ave. N.E."

Taking a deep breath, I continued, "Be on the lookout for two male suspects. Suspect #1 a black male, mid 20's, 6', shaved head, wearing blue jean pants, a white Washington Redskins jersey, with the red number 34 on front and back. Suspect #2 is armed with a revolver. He's a black male 17 or 18 years old, 5' 6" large bush afro hair, wearing a blue t-shirt and dark shorts. Both suspects were last seen driving north on Division Avenue in a late model yellow, two door Chevy with a--"

I stopped the broadcast.

Midway through the lookout, I spotted the yellow Chevy making a left turn off of Division Avenue onto Grant Street N.E. The bald guy, wearing number 34 was driving.

About that same time, they spotted me and took off driving at a high rate of speed. They drove on sidewalks, through yards, alleys and vacant lots to escape.

I gave chase, clunking along at a lower rate of speed.

"Really?" I yelled out loud, as I banged the steering wheel. I didn't know if I did that out of frustration, or if I thought the banging would make the car go faster. I got a grip and notified the dispatcher that I was in "slow, but hot pursuit" of the yellow Chevy.

Just when I thought all was lost, they made a mistake. Unbeknownst to both of us, the street they turned down was a dead end.

I caught up! It was a good and a bad thing. Mr. #34 spun his car around and headed straight for me.

Just before our vehicles hit head on, I turned the wheel. We crashed head to passenger side and slid for 100 feet or so, until we both rammed the side of a building. Suspect #2 had a gun in his hand, but when our two cars hit the building, the gun went flying into the back seat. Finally, the cars came to rest, driver door to driver door. My passenger side was up against the building and my door was pinned against his driver door. Both suspects scrambled out of their passenger side door and started running down the nearby railroad tracks on foot. I climbed through their car and out the other side to give chase, but the two immediately split up when they saw me.

Suspect #2 jumped a fence and disappeared in some tall brush on a vacant lot, while Mr. #34 continued down the tracks, with me hot on his tail. You would have thought this guy was a professional football wingback as fast as he was running.

I was no slouch back in the day, either. As I started to gain on him and just a few feet behind him, I felt the strength in my legs giving way. I decided to try a tackle. Just as I leaped, Mr. #34 looked back and side stepped me. I came crashing down onto the blue stone in between the railroad ties.

Mr. #34 laughed as he continued to run away yelling, "I busted your balls, pig."

I was flipping furious. I climbed to my feet and continued the chase, but with a limp now. I could feel blood running down my left leg, from where I fell on my knee.

Mr. #34 ran into the basement of a vacant apartment building on the other side of Division Avenue, not far from where the chase started. My last sight of him was a vague shadow that disappeared down a dark stairwell.

I continued my pursuit down the stairs and entered a dark maze of rooms. I was without a flashlight or radio to call in my location for back up. I drew my revolver saying, "I know you're in here. This place is going to be crawling with police in a few minutes. Come out with your hands up."

That always worked in the movies.

Apparently, Mr. #34 never saw any movies. Unfortunately, that line didn't work here. I heard movement in one of the rooms down the hall. I stopped to make sure it wasn't the sound of my foot slushing around in my blood-filled boot.

It wasn't.

Then everything went silent. I stopped and listened for more movement. The only light in the basement was from the headlights of traffic, passing outside and flashing through the narrow casement windows.

The hair went up on the back of my neck, and I got a bad feeling. I called on Angel Michael to help me, as I had many times before in my life. It's hard to describe communicating with a being that comes from another dimension. The Angel never spoke like you or I do, but I knew what he was "saying." I never saw him, but I sensed where he was in his bright blue and gold armor. He communicated to me, with visions and emotions, and projected thought into my mind. I learned over the years to distinguish his messages from my own thoughts. It always came with the buzzing in my ears. That night, his communication came in the form of a vision. I felt myself leave my body.

I saw myself walking into a dark room with a pentagram painted in black on a red door. When I entered the room, Mr. #34 stepped out from the shadows and struck me in the back of the head with a 2" x 4" board that had several nails sticking out of the end. I saw my lifeless body, lying on the floor. Blood was on the floor all around my head.

Michael was warning me to get out of there, or I would not survive.

He then showed me a slow-motion vision of me chasing Mr. #34 on the railroad tracks, but this time I had stopped running and pulled out a set of bolas. After twirling them over my head for a while, I released them. They flew through the air, dropped to the ground, bounced once, and then wrapped around Mr. #34's ankles bringing him to the ground.

After the vision, I snapped back into my body and felt a surge of emotion in message form.

I clearly heard, "Discretion is the best part of valor. Sir Edward get out now."

That was the first time he referred to me as Sir Edward, and I felt that was odd. It was something Frankie had said to me many times. I didn't know what to think. Weakened from blood loss, I felt drained. I broke off my pursuit and left the building. Once outside, too weak to walk another step, I collapsed just as Scout #39 pulled up to assist me.

I was taken to D.C. General hospital, where emergency room doctors cleaned my cuts and stitched up the gash in my knee. While I was waiting to be released, I noticed there was a documentary on the television about South American cowboys, using bolas to bring down ostrich and cattle.

The words of Mr. #34 came back to me, "I busted your balls, pig."

I vowed never to chase another suspect again, if I could avoid it.

In order to recoup, I was put on two weeks of sick leave. I spent that time hand-making a set of bolas. I braided twine into three ropes. On the end of each rope, I tied a heavy lead fishing sinker. I then cut three leather squares, drew up the ends into a cup shape and dropped in the sinkers. I filled the leather pockets the rest of the way with sand. I wound fishing line around the top of the leather pockets and the rope, which created a heavy leather ball. I then braided the other ends of the three ropes together, into a six-inch long handle, that I could grip before throwing. They looked as good as any bolas I saw on TV. I used the rest of my leave, perfecting my throwing technique.

When I returned to work, I was on daylight shift. I decided to go back to the basement where I lost Mr. #34. I couldn't get the vision out of my mind that Michael showed me. Not that I doubted him or anything, I just felt the need to go. I retraced my steps back into the building and went room to room. While inspecting the crime scene, I did find a room with a black pentagram painted on a red door. Inside I found a 2"x4" with nails sticking out of the top just like in the vision Michael gave me. A cold chill went up my spine. I knew I was supposed to have died in that room, but I lived to fight another day... thanks to Michael.

My reputation for the safe apprehension of suspects, the bolas, was getting around. I was knocking down escaping purse snatchers, dope dealers and car thieves. If you ran, you went down.

The bolas were given the nickname "Flying Cock and Balls" (funny how that was the second time that nickname came into my life) When I threw them, two balls would spread out to the sides and the one in the middle would stay straight in the center position. The middle one was the one that would go through the suspect's legs, while the other two would wrap around the outside of the legs in a tangled mess. I painted a black rooster head on each ball to validate the name, *and* keep it clean when challenged.

One evening the precinct's Vice and Tactical Commander asked me to join in on the execution of a few narcotic search warrants. He wanted to see me use the bolas in action. During the briefing, I was shown a photograph of the man, William Thacker, wanted for selling heroin to an undercover officer. I was told that Thacker had escaped capture several times already, when they tried to apprehend him. He was a fast runner and always seemed to have a planned escape route.

I said, "If I get a clear shot at him, I guarantee he will go down."

When we arrived at 34th and Benning N.E. Road, the River Terrace Apartment complex, we learned that Thacker was in a laundry room, selling drugs. He had two guys with walkie-talkies at the front and rear of the building, watching for police and telling customers how to make their purchases. He was an enterprising young man.

If you wanted to buy heroin, coke or grass, you had to go to the outside laundry room window and place your order. Thacker would then pass a metal box welded to a long pipe out the window. The buyer would then put the money inside the box. Once Thacker had the money, he would pass the drugs back out the window and the transaction was complete. Thacker created this system, so no one could testify in court that they actually saw him sell the drugs.

The plan was to raid the laundry room and hopefully take Thacker down inside, without incident. If he were to escape from the building, no one would have a chance of catching him before he reached the wooded area at the shore of the Anacostia River. Once he reached the river he would be gone.

I positioned myself at the last apartment building nearest the river and watched as the raiding party entered the building where Thacker was dealing. The lookout at the front of the building radioed Thacker that the police were on their way in, and he should get out immediately.

About ten minutes passed and the raiding party came out, unsuccessful in locating Thacker. He had made good another escape.

Michael told me, "Hold your position."

Moments later, I noticed the lookout in the rear of the apartment building making an all-clear hand motion to someone. A few seconds later, a tall man wearing a dark, blue hoodie and sun glasses appeared and started walking in the direction of the river. Almost simultaneously, the vice squad lieutenant gave me the signal that they were packing up and leaving. I pointed at the man in the hoodie.

When the lieutenant looked in his direction, the guy took off running.

The runner hadn't noticed me, yet. I was the only cop in uniform, so I figured if he saw me, he'd change direction. I stayed put, waiting in the shadows.

Two of the vice-officers gave chase. Thacker was running straight for me. He was out running the other two officers. Boy, could he run. "He really should be in the Olympics," I thought. My plan at that time was just to step out when he got closer, pull my gun and tell him to freeze. It didn't look like the bolas would be needed.

He came charging my way. I stepped out and yelled, "Freeze," with my gun pointed at his center of mass.

I did surprise him, but he didn't freeze as commanded. He just changed direction and was now running away from me.

I holstered my weapon and grabbed the bolas.

I swung them over my head and yelled, "What's wrong Mr. Thacker don't you want to play ball?" When he was about twenty yards away, I released them. They flew through the air, tagged their target and brought Thacker crashing down onto the parking lot pavement.

The other two vice officers reached him first and made the arrest.

His backpack was full of narcotics, so along with the arrest warrant, he faced some pretty heavy charges.

Taking Thacker down was all the convincing the Vice Commander needed. He asked the precinct captain to transfer me out of uniform and into the Vice and Tactical Squad.

My undercover investigative career was about to begin.

Chapter Thirteen

The Phantom

The Mayor and Chief of Police of Washington DC reorganized the fourteen police precincts into six districts. Everything on the east side of the Anacostia River, precincts #11 and #14, became the Sixth District. I was transferred and promoted to detective in Sixth District Vice.

Game on.

My first assignment was to help a pair of narcotic detectives close out an undercover officer, who had been making narcotic buys from street dealers in several high crime areas around the Sixth District. That night, we had to serve nine "John Doe" arrest warrants.

The undercover officer had purchased drugs from street dealers, but he hadn't positively identified them yet, so the warrants were in the names of John or Jane Doe. He knew street names for the subjects, but not their true names, so we drove around the streets and hangouts where the suspects were known to frequent. We would have the undercover officer try to spot one or more of the suspects. He would point them out, and then we would form a takedown strategy, case by case.

This worked well for several weeks. It got to the point where all I had to do was swing the "Flying Cock and Balls" over my head and suspects would stop running from us.

No one wanted a mouth full of dirt or pavement.

One night, expecting trouble, our team leader Detective Tony Farrell had his partner, Detective Jesús Mendez, check out a shotgun from the armory.

Tony barked the order to me, "Go ask the captain, if our team could borrow his cruiser for the evening."

It was a brand-new sleek, 1970 black, four-door Ford Fury.

"Are you serious?" I asked back.

"Serious as a heart attack, Jagen," he said. "The Captain likes you. Don't worry."

Oh, I was worried all right. I might not have been an old timer on the force, but I was aware enough about how these guys respected property, especially if it wasn't theirs. I knew just enough to keep me worried all night.

When I asked the Captain, he said, "Okay Jagen, but next time I see my cruiser it better not have a single scratch or dent on it."

I got an instant sick feeling in my stomach when he said that, and a feeling of dread came over me.

I told Captain Light that I would be in the backseat with the Phantom, our undercover officer, and Detective Sergeant Farrell would be doing the driving.

He smiled a shifty smile saying, "I'm giving the keys to you, detective. You bring the keys and my cruiser back without a scratch. Understand?"

A lump formed in my throat, but I nodded saying, "Yes sir, I understand." Michael assured me that as long as I was driving the cruiser everything would be fine.

However, when I told Detective Farrell that Captain Light was holding me responsible for the safe return of his new cruiser, and I had to drive, he laughed. Detective Farrell quickly snatched the keys out of my hand and said, "My undercover officer, my investigation, my warrants and my night to drive, *rookie*." He did out rank me, and I had only been in the vice unit for three months. I didn't want to piss anyone off, so I didn't say another word.

The undercover officer picked up the street name of "The Phantom" because Detective Mendez dressed him up in all black, complete with black hood, stocking mask, with eyeholes, and black Halloween gloves, with long, extended, boney fingers. They were really creepy. He looked like the grim reaper. He would use the boney index finger to point at the suspects we had warrants for.

In the three short months I was with this squad, I quickly learned the routine. If the suspects we wanted were standing on the street or in a bar, with a crowd of people around them, we would pull up and announce, "Police with arrest warrants. Freeze." Detective Farrell would pump a shell into the chamber of the shotgun and I would start twirling the bolas, around and around over my head, ready to throw them at any one of the arrest warrant suspects, if they attempted to flee. Most of the time, if any of the people in the crowd were dirty or in possession of weapons, drugs, or other implements of crime... they would just drop the items on the ground rather than be caught with them, if they were searched. Farrell would yell out "If your buddy throws dope on the ground, and it lands by you, it's yours."

Nobody wanted to catch a beef for anyone else's stuff, so we heard a lot of, "That shit ain't mine mother fucker." There was also a lot of pushing and shoving amid the crowd at times; normally where contraband could be found. This was a good safe way to get a lot of guns and drugs off the street without having to arrest anyone.

Jesús would then bring forth the dark figure of the Phantom who, like the grim reaper, would raise his arm and point the finger of shame at the person we had papers on. The Phantom would then disappear while we made the arrests.

That night, it was business as usual, except we were all dressed in plain street clothes, so we could move about without standing out too much. I was wearing a brown wide brim leather cowboy hat. I would take it off at times when it was safe to bring the phantom in to make a positive identification of the suspects.

So far, everything was going pretty smooth. It was about 1:30 a.m. when the Phantom spotted someone that we had a warrant for. We were making a turn onto East Capitol Street and Benning Rd N.E., as our suspect entered the Shrimp Boat Restaurant and Carryout on the corner. Detective Farrell pulled into the lot and hurried into the front door of the restaurant, as I ran to the side door to cut off anyone who tried to escape. When the suspect saw the Phantom get out of the black cruiser, he bolted and ran out the side door.

I yelled, "Police! Freeze!"

The man replied, "Fuck you pig!" And kept on running.

I thought "Pig?" That voice sounded awfully familiar to me.

As I watched the man running away, I grabbed the bolas from my belt, held the ropes in the center and let the balls drop down to start twirling the bolas over my head.

I quietly said out loud, "Revenge is best served cold mother fucker." I gave the suspect a good long head start. When it appeared he thought he was going to get away, I released the ropes.

It was a beautiful sight.

Everything went into slow motion. Just like Michael had shown me in the vision. The three leather balls separated perfectly, as the ropes dropped behind him onto the sidewalk, then bounced up; sending one ball through the middle of his legs as the other two balls wrapped around his knees. He slid about five feet, got up, tried to run and then fell again.

Jesus ran up and handcuffed the suspect, as I approached.

While untying the bolas from the suspect's ankles he said, "You fucking pigs. You would never have caught me on foot."

With a smile, I looked the man square in the eyes, took a deep breath and said, "You're right. The last time you busted *my* balls. This time my balls busted you!"

It was Mr. #34 looking back at me, shocked. He shook his head, laughed and said, "Damn man. That ain't funny."

I actually thought it was quite funny. So did Jesus, who was laughing his ass off all the way to the patrol wagon, with Mr. #34.

After the patrol wagon took off, Detective Farrell said, "Before we head back in for the night, we should check out one more haunt at the top end of East Capitol Street near Eastern Avenue. The Phantom says it could be hot up there tonight."

Michael immediately sent me the message that it wasn't such a good idea, "There is danger in that direction."

I announced to the squad, "We shouldn't push our luck. Let's call it a night. We can end on a high note."

Farrell said, "No. One more and, if no one's there, we'll go home."

I didn't like it. A vision of flames flashed in my mind. I didn't know what it was. I just remember thinking I didn't like it.

We cruised by the spots where the Phantom had made his narcotic buys. There was no one on the street. It was about 2:45 a.m. and very foggy out. The streets were deserted and downright spooky! I got a chill up my spine.

Detective Farrell was cruising slowly through alleys, as not to alert anyone to us coming. I unbuckled my seat belt to move the bolas off my belt to the seat next to me, so it would be an easy grab, if I needed them. As we turned off 57th Street S.E. and onto East Capitol Street, something hit us from behind like a rocket.

My body was snapped up and back from the force. My head smashed through the back window. My leather hat folded up around my face protecting me from the glass. Thank God!

The wide brim of the hat shielded my face from being shredded by the glass, but I felt something snap in my lower back, just as a sharp pain shot down my left leg.

Our sleek, black cruiser was sliding sideways down the street, as I saw a dark blue Ford Mustang fly by us in flames.

Through the pain, all that came to mind was, "What the hell am I going to tell Captain Light?"

My side of the car was heading directly toward a telephone pole. We hit, and I was thrown against the door with great force. The undercover officer was on top of me. I smelled gasoline as Detective Farrell jumped out of the car.

Knowing the crash would draw a crowd he told the Phantom to "beat feet," in order to maintain his cover and identity. The Phantom's door was jammed, so he rolled down the window to escape, but first asked me, if I was ok. He quickly crawled out the window and ran, before I could answer him.

I could see Detective Farrell, running toward the Mustang. I then observed the driver, a young black male, climb out the window and run off into the projects.

I thought, "A car thief."

Jesús was holding the microphone in his hand, trying to call in the emergency, but he didn't notice the microphone cord was swinging free, having snapped off from the radio console in the crash.

I said, "Jesus Christ, get out Mendez. I smell gas."

He couldn't get out of the front passenger door because we hit the telephone pole right between our doors on the right side of the vehicle, so he crawled out of the driver's side and ran. I tried to open my door and jump out, but it only opened about a quarter of the way. I hurled my body through the opening, but stopped short. I tried to crawl free, but my feet were caught on something.

Looking back, I could see that the bolas had fallen to the floor. Somehow they had wrapped around my feet and the underside of the seat in front of me. I was wedged and locked in position, half in and half out of the car. I tried everything, but couldn't get free. I was half hanging out of the car and, as I looked under the cruiser, I could see gas, dripping from the fuel tank and forming a stream that was slowly moving toward the flames, down the street to the point of impact where the Mustang struck our cruiser.

It was beginning to look like a fuse in one of those Road Runner and Coyote cartoons, except I wasn't a cartoon character that could get back up after an explosion. This wasn't looking like it was going to end well for me.

I called on Michael to help, thinking, "Michael, please don't let it end this way. I don't want to burn to death."

I could feel Michael enter me. I felt bigger than life.

There was a blinding flash of light.

When I could see again, I was lying on the front lawn of the house across the street. When I stood up, I had a tremendous pain in my lower back. I hurt like I had never hurt before. Other than some cuts, bruises and a pain in my lower back, I was fine. I told Detective Farrell that I didn't need to go to the hospital, but he insisted. In the emergency room, I was cleaned up and told to see the police doctor in the morning.

When I went to the doctor for the pain, they put me on two weeks bed rest. I had cracked two vertebrae in my lower back and nothing could be done to fix it.

The doctor warned that I should put in for medical retirement now because the discs could start to deteriorate, if I continued to put stress on them.

I was young and knew that Michael was counting on me, so retirement at that age wasn't an option.

The doctor warned me that most likely in my late fifties I would need to have my lower spine fused together.

I thought, "How in the world could he know that? Was he a psychic or something?"

The good news was, I kept my word to Captain Light. He never saw a dent or scratches on his brand new black cruiser.

It was totaled that night, stripped of its police equipment and sent to the salvage yard, without him ever seeing it again.

Chapter Fourteen

Moving on with my Life

While I was recovering, Mendez would come over to my apartment and teach me how to play the guitar. He and Detective Farrell started a rock band, and they wanted me to sing with them in their group. Every once in a while, when we were on surveillance, I would burst into a James Taylor song. They said I really sounded a lot like him.

Mendez never liked my wife, Maria. He felt she wasn't trustworthy and was "a user of men." Maria didn't like him, either. I think she knew he saw right through her. Maria wasn't happy being married. She wanted to date other guys, but still live with me. It was time to divorce. Jesús was glad to hear she was returning to Germany, even if it was for only four months. While she was gone, he helped me find a good divorce attorney. We were, officially, starting our one-year separation.

One evening, Jesús wanted to know if I would double date with him and his wife, Scotty. They knew a young, attractive girl named Linda, whose husband had run off with a younger woman.

He said, "You two have a lot in common. Linda is an artist with an angelic spirit."

I took him up on the offer, and the four of us met for dinner and a movie. I had a great time. Linda was a gorgeous, little hippy chick, very happy on the outside, but I felt she had sadness down deep that she was covering up. Mendez was right. We did have a lot in common. We became great friends and started dating on a steady basis. Linda had a five-year-old daughter, Dawn, who was a real sweetheart. Linda's husband, Richard, was half Indian. *The half that shouldn't drink.* And he drank a lot. Michael showed me a vision that whenever Richard drank, his anger with life would come out and he would take it out on his 5' 2", 98 lbs. wife, Linda.

Yes, Richard was a wife beater. Michael said that Richard was going to be the death of Linda one day.

I asked, "What can I do to help her?"

He said, "Let her know she's got a friend, but you are just her friend. Do NOT marry this one; it could conflict with the mission. When you divorce Maria, stay single for the rest of your life." Michael was counting on me to be in the right place at the right time, so he could make strategic moves. He likened me to a knight on a chessboard that he needed to be able to move at any time. A wife could just get in the way of him having the freedom to move me where and when he needed.

He showed me again the vision of seven chessboards stacked on top of one another. Strings connected them all. He was playing all seven against dark forces at the same time. I understood a little more about the chessboards this time than I did the last time he showed me.

The Angel explained that relationships could compromise the mission and, if I could be controlled through my heart, it could be the ruin of all that we were working on together.

Michael said, "You are too sensitive to the feelings of women, and you must learn to think with your head, not your heart. The mission must come first over all else. Didn't you ever wonder why the Lone Ranger was called the 'Lone' Ranger?"

That would be easier said than done, but I swore to him I wouldn't let anyone stand between me and whatever our mission was at the time.

I asked Michael, "What exactly is our mission?"

He answered, "To do whatever it takes to help humankind make a positive leap in consciousness and the delivery of the God Sword to a very special child, with the initials M.V. If I tell you anymore at this time, it would just confuse you."

I understood as best I could at that point, but it still didn't make complete sense to me.

I would take Linda and Dawn out to dinner and movies, trying to help them over the hard times they were having. We kept it just friends. I could see that Linda was still very much in love with her husband. She was twenty-four, and he was thirty-two. I told her that as long as Richard was drinking, I felt her life was in danger. However, she felt that she could handle him.

Richard's 18-year-old girlfriend dumped him a few months later. He learned I was befriending his wife, and he wanted back in the house, but Linda refused. I backed away, but kept in touch as a safeguard.

Because of financial problems the year prior, Linda and Richard had moved in with Linda's mother, Hester. He wasn't able to keep a job more than a few months, for a variety of reasons. It hadn't taken long, living under the same roof, before Richard's negativity forced poor Hester to move into an apartment a few miles away.

Hester didn't know what to think of me, a longhaired, bearded hippie with a gun and a badge. She confided to me years later, "Anyone would be better than Richard." I took that as a back handed compliment, but a compliment nonetheless.

One day, I ran into Hester at the grocery store. She asked, "Could you help keep Richard from moving back in with Linda? I'm afraid he might harm her one day. Richard has started coming by more and more, wanting back in the house."

I said, "I'll do everything I can, but they are married, and she still loves him." Hester was scared for her daughter and granddaughter's safety. And so was I.

Over the next few weeks, I would be invited over for dinner and drinks. Sometime Linda would also invite Richard, so we could meet. She thought I could help him deal with his emotional issues. I must say, some of the stuff Michael had me quote was pretty profound at times. I said stuff that was really helping Richard. I would also tell him things about his past that no one else knew and even he had forgotten.

Richard asked me, "Are you a psychic or something?"

"No. It's more than that." I said. "I just have friends in high places feeding me helpful information." I could tell I scared him. He liked me, but didn't want to.

Richard was a big, good-looking fellow, standing about 6'-2" and weighing 220 pounds compared to my 6'-4" and 185 lbs.

I joked with him, "What I don't have in muscle, I make up for in bullets."

I could tell that if it weren't for me always carrying a gun, he would have tried to take a poke at me when he drank. He didn't want to chance being shot though. I could feel that he wanted to beat me at something, anything. His ego was on the line. If not a physical beating, maybe a mental beating would suffice.

Image 4– Edward Jagen's guitar lessons with Mendez

Chapter Fifteen

The Board is Set

One day, Richard challenged me to a game of chess. He considered himself a chess master. I told him that I had learned the basic chess moves back when I was a kid in the Boy Scouts, but I wasn't very good.

In a threatening tone he said, "Then you won't mind when I beat you. And if I beat you, you can't come around here anymore."

I countered, "But who would protect Linda, if I'm not here?"

Michael saw a chance and said through me, "I'll play you one game, and you'll be in checkmate within eight moves."

I thought, "Holy crap, how could anyone win in eight moves?" I could only hope that Michael knew what he was doing.

Richard seized the opportunity of saying, "You'd sooner have angels fly out of your ass than beat me in eight moves, Jagen."

Michael replied in a calm voice, "Brother, if I do beat you in eight moves or less, you must promise you'll never hit Linda again. If you do, you must leave her forever."

Richard's confident grin turned into a stiff jawed, black, stone-eyed stare.

I could tell there were things happening on many levels above and below me. I didn't want to screw things up for Michael. I could see that Richard didn't want me to know he beat Linda, and she didn't want me to know it either.

Michael said to Linda, "Agreed?"

She nodded her head. That wasn't good enough for Michael.

He said, "Say the word Linda."

She said, "Agreed."

He then said to Richard, "Say the word." I could see the anger festering inside his tormented mind.

Richard finally said, "Agreed."

The board was set, and the pieces needed to start moving.

Linda was truly enjoying herself. She had the man she loved, and the man that was protecting her from him in the same room, fighting over her. I don't think she understood that if I lost, it would be the last time she would ever see me. Then I thought this might be a trick that Michael was using to remove me from helping her anymore. There was nothing I could do, but play along.

When the chess game began, all I remember was, my king's white knight was Michael's first move, two spaces up and one to the right. On the seventh move his queen's white knight put the black king in checkmate.

It all happened in a matter of a few minutes.

A hush fell over the table.

Richard was furious. He jumped up and stormed from the room. He went onto the sun porch bar to fix a drink. He drank it down, then fixed another.

Linda looked at me, with eyes filled with fear.

I said, "Just relax you're the winner here because he promised. You also have friends in very high places that will hold him to that promise."

Richard came back into the living room with his drink and a bottle of beer in his other hand. He sat back down at the table, looked at the chessboard and said; "You said you'd beat me in eight moves. That was only seven. I win."

Michael looked him deep in the eyes. I could see the rage inside of him.

Richard asked, "What would you do, if I walked over there and stomped your ass?"

Michael took my hand, picked up the white knight and knocked over the black king then said, "Eight." Shaking my head, I answered Richard's question, "I'd probably have to shoot you, brother." I knew he was just rattling swords to satisfy his huge, male ego. I smiled a confident smile at him.

He smiled and passed me the beer.

Linda said, "I have to work tomorrow. Both of you guys should leave now."

Richard said, "No, I want my family back. I want to stay."

Linda said, "Richard you've been drinking too much. Go now. You have a lot to think about and a lot of changing to do before I take you back."

He didn't like what she said, but I could see it gave him hope.

I said, "Great, we can begin a positive future for her, by leaving together as friends."

I noticed Richard found a certain peace with that. I could only hope he would honor his promise to Linda.

A few days later, Linda told me that it was a miracle. Richard had changed back to the man she had married five years earlier, and he was moving back in with her and Dawn. I was sure Hester wasn't going to like that, but like I told her, Linda still loved Richard.

I told Linda, "I truly hope it works out this time."

I then moved on with my life.

Not too long after that, Maria came back from Germany and wanted to work things out with me. Michael told me that she couldn't be trusted and was just playing me. She didn't have anywhere to live, so I let her move back in.

It was understood that it was only until she found a job and a place to live. My attorney said that my one-year waiting period would start again once she leaves.

Maria found a job as a bartender at a nearby restaurant. She wanted to stay with me and promised to be faithful. I could see that something had happened in Germany that changed her.

One evening she didn't come home. She called and said that she was staying at her girlfriend's for the night.

I knew something was up.

I asked Michael what was going on.

He gave me a vision of Maria, living with a black guy when she returned to Germany. One morning when they woke up, she told him that she was pregnant with his child. There was an argument, and the man told her to leave because she was married to a guy in the states.

I didn't want to see any more, but the vision continued.

Maria wanted to have an abortion because she knew there was no way she could convince me that I was the father. She cut her trip to Germany short and returned to Maryland to arrange a secret abortion, through one of her girlfriends. In the vision it ended with me finding Maria dying.

I was working a midnight narcotics surveillance with Detective Mendez that night. We sent an informant into a house to purchase heroin. After the buy, we secured a search warrant and knocked the door down to find three people in the basement, cutting and bagging a half a kilo of heroin for distribution. It was a big seizure of drugs.

However, it was hard to focus on work after that vision of Maria still on my mind. Something wasn't right. This time I could *feel* something. It was like a cloud of doom hanging over me.

That morning we papered the case in court. Jesús wanted to go to breakfast, but I felt I needed to get home.

When I arrived, I found Maria on the bathroom floor lying in a pool of blood. The toilet was also covered in blood. A bloody pair of silver scissors was on the floor next to her. She had secretly started an abortion process earlier the day before with the help of her girlfriend. Someone had inserted a thin rubber tube inside of her. When her body rejected the tube, it did the same to the fetus. Apparently, she started hemorrhaging on the toilet, once she got home. Her skin was very pale. I felt for a pulse in her neck. It was faint. She was lucky I came home when I did.

I called an ambulance hoping it wasn't too late to save her life. I loved her, but she just wanted more than I had to offer. She was a product of her environment. Maria grew up, loving the attention from lonely GI's. I'm sure it was a thrill for her to be desired, and she was addicted to that thrill. One of her girlfriends had an open marriage, and I knew that's what she wanted from me.

That I couldn't give.

The EMT said, "She's lost a lot of blood, and it doesn't look good."

Looking at the cut umbilical cord and blood coming out of her, he asked, "Where is the fetus?"

I never gave that any thought. I was just worried about Maria.

I looked into the bloody toilet and just hung my head. I got an instant pang in my gut and nauseous from the sight. I thought of the story of my toilet birth was bad. At least I had a chance at life. This poor child never will.

I asked Michael to please help save Maria's life.

While she was still laying on the floor, I saw a bright ball of white light come down from the ceiling and cover her body. I didn't know what it meant, and I could tell the EMT's didn't see it, but her heartbeat immediately became stronger.

I spent the next two days at the hospital, holding her hand and praying that she would be all right. She thanked me for saving her life.

I confessed, "Angel Michael showed me a vision of you and the black guy in Germany." From the look on her face I knew it was true.

89

She said, "I want to have an open relationship with you. I have to see other guys."

I told her, "I think you are addicted to men and the attention they give you. Your ego feeds on their attention. I am not interested in that kind of relationship. I can't walk that path with you. You'll have to walk it alone, but I am sure you will find plenty of company along the way."

After her release from the hospital it wasn't long before Maria returned to her party girl lifestyle. I decided I was finished and told her I wanted to proceed with the divorce again.

She said, "If I had to be married you are the perfect husband, but I'm too young to be tied to one man." I agreed with that one! Then I quickly filed the papers for legal separation again.

A few days later, Farrell and Mendez's band was playing at a nightclub near Fort Washington. Jesús asked if I wanted to sit in and sing a couple of songs. I was pretty depressed and needed to focus on something. He said that his wife, Scotty, invited Linda and Richard to the club as well. I had been wondering how things were going with them, so I accepted his offer. It was a beautiful clear night. We were far enough away from the city lights that I could see billions of bright stars. As I was getting my guitar out of the trunk of my silver Vega, I noticed Richard pull up. He was arguing with Linda in the car. I watched for a short time then went inside. It didn't look like things were going well for them.

Inside the club the band had already played a set, and Jesús was sitting at the bar with his wife. I told them that Richard was outside, yelling at Linda, and I got the feeling he didn't want to come in. Farrell gave the signal that the break was over and Jesús returned to the stage. I remained at the bar. They had played a few songs when I noticed Richard and Linda come in. They didn't notice me and sat at a table in a dark corner. I could tell Richard was already drunk, but he was still ordering double bourbons. He was tossing them down like shots. Linda was drinking red wine. I could see she had been crying. That's probably why she took the table in the back, so no one would notice. Then Linda noticed me sitting at the bar. She smiled, and that's when Richard noticed me as well. I could see he was furious.

I got the feeling that Linda knew I'd be there, but he didn't. In an act to show me he was the winner, he grabbed Linda by the arm and dragged her to the dance floor. It was obvious she was embarrassed and didn't want to dance. It was all Richard could do to stand, let alone dance. When Linda tried to walk away, he pulled her back and raised his hand, as if to slap her. I jumped to my feet and headed to the dance floor. Richard stopped dancing. I could see he was preparing himself for the fight he'd been spoiling for.

When I got to the unhappy couple, I stuck out my hand and said, "Good to see you again, brother." It really was like I was speaking to one of my bully brothers. He was shocked at my words. He was expecting something else. I winked at Linda and said, "I'm on my way to the stage to sing a friendly, little song."

I told Farrell the song, picked up my guitar and approached the microphone stand. I said, "We have a request from an angel out there, who wants to let you know you are never alone. This is by your friend and mine, James Taylor."

The lights dimmed, and I started strumming and then sang, "When you're down and troubled, and you need a helping hand... and nothing, nothing is going right. Close your eyes and think of me, and soon I will be there... to brighten up, even your darkest night."

Richard stopped dancing and dragged Linda back to their table, as I continued, "You just call out my name, and you know wherever I am, I'll come running, oh yeah baby, to see you again." Richard glared at me.

"Winter, spring, summer or fall... all you've got to do is call... and I'll be there, 'cause you've got a friend..."

That was more than Richard's ego could handle. He grabbed Linda by the arm and headed to the door, as I finished the song. I knew that if I pursued, there would be a confrontation outside, so I turned to Jesús and asked if he would go out and check on Linda's safety.

A few minutes later he came back in and said all seemed well, and that they drove away.

Chapter Sixteen

The Angel of Death

Meanwhile, back at my mess of a life, I helped Maria find a furnished apartment. And on move-in day, I loaned her my car, so she and a girlfriend could move her stuff in.

What? Did you think I could leave her high and dry?

That day I rode to work with my partner, Detective Mendez. That evening about 11:30 p.m. when Mendez dropped me off at my apartment, I noticed my car wasn't in the parking lot. I called around looking for Maria, but couldn't locate her or my car.

I could feel Michael's energy was restless. I asked him, "What is going on?"

He said, "There has been a disturbance in the Ethers."

I felt it before he answered me.

"Is Maria all right?" I asked. I got an immediate impression that she was fine. However, I felt dread and didn't know where it was coming from, so I pressed him for an answer. "Something is major wrong, what is it?" I pleaded.

There were no words.

Then Michael showed me a vision of Jesús and I going to a funeral. When we walked up to the casket, it contained the body of Linda. In the vision, Hester came up to me sobbing, "You did this to her. You could have saved her, but didn't, why?"

I went into a feeling of panic and shouted, "What happened? Why didn't we stop it?"

Michael finally spoke, "Just leave it alone. She made her choice. She has to live or die with the choices she made."

Still to this day, I can feel how cold he sounded. He obviously knew my thoughts because he immediately reminded me, "Don't ever forget, one of my functions on Earth is an Angel of Death. Many people die because of their bad choices."

"Wait, she hasn't died yet?" I questioned.

"No, soon," came the chilly response.

When I found out that Linda hadn't died, I wanted to help her.

Michael said, "You asked me to save Maria, and now she is out of your life. If I help you save Linda, you will be bound to her for the remainder of her life."

I said, "I've saved others from death. Why is this one so different?"

He said, "Because this one is going to take her own life. She is to become a suicide. You would be saving her from herself. You will become responsible for her soul in the Eyes of the Creator. Do you want that? Would she want that? She will become your life long assignment to safeguard."

A sick feeling grew in my stomach. I didn't know what to do. Visions of Linda's daughter, Dawn, growing up without a mother. And her having to live with what her mother had done... all started swirling in my mind. Then I thought about her, growing up with an angry drunk for a father. "Would he start beating her? What chance would she have to grow up innocent?"

I thought about the child that Maria flushed down the toilet and the meaning behind my own birth in a Chicago toilet. It all seemed like one big puzzle I had to put together. I felt compelled to do something.

I called Linda. When she answered the phone, I was relieved.

"It hasn't happened yet," I thought. "Whew! Thank God."

Linda started to tell me about Richard. He started mistreating her again a week after he moved back in, but it really got bad, after the song in the nightclub.

She sounded somber and stopped after each sentence.

"Hold on, I need a drink of water," she said.

I found that strange, since Linda didn't like to drink water.

She went on to tell me, "Richard's girlfriend called today and asked Richard to move back in with her." She paused, and then said, "He moved out again a few hours ago."

She drank more water.

I said, "Where is Dawn?"

"I took Dawn over to Mom's apartment, until I wooaark thinnngs ooout," Linda started slurring her words.

At times, she would stop talking completely.

I asked, "Why are you drinking water? You hate water."

She replied, "Because I finished all the wine. Hold on..." as she drank even more water.

Linda had a phone in several rooms of the house. I was trying to pinpoint her location. A vision flashed in my mind. I saw her sitting in the dining room at the telephone desk near the back door. On the desk by the phone was a pill bottle. White pills were scattered all around the desktop. For confirmation of the vision I asked, "It's so late, are you in bed?"

She replied, "No, I'm sitting in the dining room."

I was hoping I was wrong, but realized everything Michael showed me would happen, if I didn't do something. I asked, "Linda, what are you doing?" She didn't answer.

I told her, "Richard leaving is a blessing. Now you can move on with your life." I could hear Linda start to cry and then drink some more water.

She said, "I don't want to talk about Richard anymore."

I didn't know what to say. She wanted to talk about fun stuff like the possibility of me taking her to a concert in a few weeks to see the band Chicago. We both loved their music.

There was a long silence. Her breath on the other side was the only sound I could hear.

I said again, "Linda what are you doing? Nothing stupid, I hope." I was afraid I tipped my hand and revealed that I knew what she was up to.

After another long pause, she replied, "Ed, I have to go. I'll call you right back." She hung up the phone.

I waited about five minutes and called her back. The line was busy. I thought, "Was she talking to Richard? Did he decide to get his head out of his ass and realize how fortunate he had it, with Linda?"

I could only hope.

I waited another ten minutes and called back again. The line was still busy. I knew Michael didn't want me to get involved any further, but it wouldn't be me, if I didn't do everything in my power to help this poor, mistreated woman. I loved her, and I wanted her to know it.

She was in love with a loser. Richard was one of those guys who is hell bent on destroying himself and everyone else around him. I had seen so many of these kinds of guys, both in the army and in the police department.

I said, "Michael, I'm going to do this thing, with or without your help!"

He didn't answer me.

I called the operator and identified myself as a D.C. Police detective. I said, "I have been trying to reach a number for the past hour, and it's been busy. Can you check for conversation on the line?" The operator advised me that the phone was off the hook. I sat down with my head in my hands. I tried to calm my mind and focus on Linda's house. I saw a vision of Linda dressed in a long white nightgown lying on the floor next to the back door, with the phone still in her right hand. Not what I wanted to see. I ran outside to get my car and drive over to Linda's, but remembered Maria still had my car.

"What to do? What to do? Think! Think!" I cried out loud!

I had five bucks in my pocket and lived a half hour from Linda. I couldn't even call a cab. Then the words, "Call on Jesus," flashed in my mind's eye.

I thought, "That's weird."

I then realized it was Michael, telling me to call my partner Jesús Mendez. He only lived about a mile away from Linda's house. I called Mendez and explained everything. He was used to my visions and, being half Indian, he was very familiar with how visions worked.

Mendez drove over to Linda's house and found her exactly as I had described. He forced the door open. She was unconscious, but still breathing. He told me later that he felt robotic as if something else was controlling his body movements, saying. "In one swift move, I picked her up in my arms, placed her in my car and drove like a bat out of Hell to the hospital," he recounted.

I announced, "More like a dove out of Heaven. Welcome to Michael's world."

In the emergency room, doctors pumped Linda's stomach out. After Linda was admitted for continued observation, Mendez picked me up and took me to Maria's new apartment, so I could get my car. I was angry that she was so selfish. I told her that not returning my car might cost a woman her life.

She didn't get it or care. Maria's only thoughts were of herself.

When I arrived at the hospital, Dr. John Steinberg, a friend of mine from high school, told me that if Linda had gotten to the emergency room ten minutes later, she would have been D.O.A. He went on to say that she had consumed a lethal cocktail of wine and sleeping pills.

I asked, "John, is there any way we could cut down on the pill count so it looked more like an overdose rather than a suicide attempt?"

He smiled and said, "What pills?"

I took a week of leave from the police department and made arrangements with the hospital to sit in Linda's room, as her personal security detail.

Michael said, "That's á propos, Linda is your assignment now. You are responsible for her soul as long as she lives." It would turn out to be the best assignment I ever had!

By the second night of my vigil, I was getting used to nurses coming in and out of her room. I would just open one eye when the door opened and then I'd go back to sleep. One exception to that was a middle of the night visit. I was half asleep when the door opened to Linda's hospital room. My watch read 1:44 a.m. A strange stillness came over the room. A tall man wearing a dark hat walked to the foot of Linda's bed. He put his hand on her foot, then looked at me and smiled. He turned and walked back out the door. It took me a moment to gather myself wondering who the fellow was. Then I jumped to my feet and ran out into the hall, but he was gone.

I asked a passing nurse, "Did you see the man wearing the hat? He just left Linda's room."

She looked quizzically at me and just shook her head "no".

The next morning, while Linda was eating her breakfast, I told her about the man. "You must've been dreaming," she offered.

About three weeks later, when I was having dinner at Hester's apartment, with Linda, Dawn and her mother, I noticed a black-and-white photo on the bookshelves of the man I saw in Linda's hospital room. He was wearing the same hat in the photo.

I asked Hester, "Who is that man?"

"That's Linda's father," she replied.

I turned to Linda and said, "I saw him, and he saw you! I feel he was so glad that you survived, and he doesn't want you to fall into such a state of despair again."

"I'm finished with Richard," she retorted.

But a month later, Richard's girlfriend dumped him again, and he was back on Linda's doorstep. He had showed up one night drunk and demanding to talk to her.

I was out of town on an undercover assignment in Miami, Florida.

The next day when I got home, I called Linda at work and was told she called in sick. I drove to her house. Richards's car was in the driveway. It was about noon when I knocked on the door.

Richard yelled, "Go away Jagen, she doesn't need your help anymore. Get off my property, before I call the police."

Michael flashed a vision of what had taken place the night before. Richard pushed his way into the house. He was in a drunken stupor and tried to seduce Linda. When she resisted, he said, "You are my wife and you will give me what I want. I'm moving back in." He smacked her around and then took her. I could see she had two black eyes, and a swollen lip. Some men think that a wife can't be raped because they own their wife's body, and it's theirs for the taking.

God, I hate dominate sex abusers, and this guy was the poster boy.

I wanted to put this sick dog out of his misery, but I knew everything was happening for a reason. I responded, "Richard I know what you did to Linda. Open this door now, before I call the police. You are going to have a hard time explaining the two black eyes you gave her. You can't beat on her anymore. It's time for you to go and never come back."

The door opened on its own. I entered the dining room and saw Richard standing in the kitchen with a butcher knife in his hand. Linda was nowhere to be seen.

The knife was not bloody. That was a good thing. I reached for my gun and called out Linda's name. She didn't answer. I wanted to ask him where Linda was, but Michael took over. I don't know what he said to Richard. All I know is he walked out of the house with the knife and never returned.

I found Linda upstairs. She had locked herself in the bathroom, so I couldn't see her swollen face. Michael told her that Richard would never bother her again.

A year later Linda learned that Richard had moved to Las Vegas and became a blackjack dealer at a casino. All I cared about was that he was out of Linda and Dawn's lives forever.

She filed for divorce and never heard from him again.

Chapter Seventeen

A Change of Direction

I was learning better how to work with Michael moving in and out of my body when he needed to. He told me that there were many lives that we were supposed to save and events we must try to change in the future. He wanted me to maneuver my way into the police department's most elite investigative unit, the Intelligence Division.

I knew that wasn't going to be easy, but Michael said "Leave that up to me. I have set things in motion."

I was going to miss working with Detective Jesús Mendez. He was the only partner I ever had that I trusted with my life.

As fate would have it, there was a large anti-war demonstration planned for the coming weekend on the National Mall that ran between the U.S. Capitol, the Washington Monument behind the White House, and further down to the Reflecting Pool at the Lincoln Memorial. One hundred thousand people were supposed to attend. Out of nowhere, I was chosen to be detailed to the Intelligence Division to work undercover. I was assigned to Detective Gary Bender, who wanted me to go into the crowd and monitor any dangerous actions or civil disobedience planned that could disrupt the public's safety.

On the day of the demonstration I remembered when, two years earlier, I was in uniform detailed from the 14th Precinct to the front line of an anti-war demonstration. I witnessed terrible things on both sides that day. I saw hotheads in the crowd, taunting police into throwing tear gas. When things went south and the tear gas was administered, some of the frustrated police officers started "busting heads," taking their frustrations out, indiscriminately, on innocent people.

I witnessed mild mannered cops, with good hearts, turn on a dime and go berserk in fits of blind rage. I think they did it out of fear of not being able to control people.

Human nature is truly unpredictable. It was like a war zone. Blood was everywhere. Families, with kids, were laying on the ground, moaning, beaten by police.

I remember seeing a CDU (civil disobedience unit) sergeant, with malicious intent, shoot a flight-rite CS Gas Rocket into the back of a student, as he ran away from harm.

If the kid had died, I don't think the cop would have cared less.

I saw mounted U.S. Park Police officers, riding through the crowd and beating demonstrators with long riot batons.

It was out of control.

Michael showed me several visions of General Custer and his 7th Calvary Division, riding into a Sioux Indian village, killing everything that moved. The bodies of men, woman and children were laying everywhere, bloodied. The vision was heart breaking and what I saw, with my own eyes on the streets of Washington D.C., was deeply disturbing as well.

Nothing had changed.

I was also reminded of WW-II scenes I'd seen of Nazi Storm Troopers, beating and murdering the innocent. Then there were the visuals I had seen on the television of police in Mississippi and Alabama, where they were beating black and white freedom demonstrators in the sixties. Now it was happening all around me in the Capitol of the United States, and I was helpless to stop it.

In remembering back to my first demonstration, that's when it happened. I got a taste of the emotion that created some of this brutality.

I was wearing my gas mask. Along came a scraggly-haired, bearded white guy, wearing a U.S. Army field jacket. He was in the peaceful part of the crowd that I was holding back. He up and threw a brick that hit me in the face, ripping the left side of the gas mask and knocking me to the ground. Then hordes of frightened demonstrators moved forward, trampling me.

I felt anger rise inside me, but just as quickly as it reared its ugly head, it subsided. Suddenly, I realized the guy didn't know me from Adam. I couldn't take what he did personally. It had absolutely nothing to do with me and had everything to do with his frustration with the situation.

Perspective. It's all about perspective.

These experiences changed the way I viewed my life from then on. I guess that is the whole idea behind experience. It gives us a foundation from which to examine or judge all other facets and situations that come into our existence.

Michael gave me some hard lessons to learn then, and I was now seeing things from all aspects of the spectrum. I was thankful that he was giving me a chance in this anti-war demonstration, so we could keep violence from occurring as much as possible. My life walking the beat in the ghetto was looking very peaceful at that moment, and I couldn't wait to get back there. Although, the Vice Squad Commander had other ideas for me. I was staying put for a while. I was good at what they had me doing and they knew it.

After the protest violence the night before, Detective Bender called me into his office. "Jagen," he barked. His voice went right through me. I quickly reviewed the night before, trying to think of something I could've done wrong. I thought for sure I was up a creek, by the tone of his voice. My worried thoughts were erased and in their place, I heard, "Calm yourself. He's got something going on at home. It's about him, not you."

"Hmmm, okay," I sat back in my chair and then just listened to Bender.

"I want you to identify the troublemakers. We're taking a lot of heat from the City Council, because some cops can't control themselves. I want you to infiltrate and get names."

I had my assignment. Now, where to start?

The first thought that came to mind was locating that jackass that hit me in the face with the brick. I had a visual on him. His looks were easy to spot.

Michael conveyed, "The best way to catch a snake in the grass, and to avoid detection, is to dress like the snake you seek."

By then, I had grown shoulder length, light brown hair and a full beard. I wore my army field jacket with Sergeant stripes and 24th Infantry Division insignia, bell-bottom jeans and cowboy boots. I kept my gun and badge in one boot and a small police radio in the other. Of course, I wore my lucky brown leather cowboy hat and my guitar slung over my shoulder. I fit in perfectly. I must admit, I was quite a hippie, dippy sight to see.

"Now go out and mingle in the grass with the snakes," Michael instructed.

As soon as I got out on the street, I felt robotic. Every step I took seemed to be directed. I realized after a while, it was Michael. He was moving me around that day, like a knight on a chessboard. I felt like I was hovering above my body, just observing it moving around. I trusted Michael's lead, because I felt lost in a scary sea of humanity. Walking with this group and talking with that group. I had no idea where I was in the great scheme of things.

Out of nowhere, I felt like I came slamming back into my body.

That's when I spotted him, the bearded hippie in the army jacket that hit me with the brick. I followed him through the crowd to a place under a long white banner with large red letters that read "V.V.A.W." He disappeared into a mass of O.D. green army jackets. It looked like a Z. Z. Top convention. Everybody was bearded and looked like me. I certainly fit right in. I felt like this was a good place to start.

Most of the guys in Vietnam Veterans Against the War were just ex-GI's, who were sick of Nixon's escalated war. Some of them had been wounded and all of them lost friends. They had been in the hot, steamy jungles taking one hill, while watching their buddies get shot up, just to move on and have that same hill fall back into North Vietnam's control the next day.

There were a few "military wannabes" in the crowd, but most of them were just kids who their country turned into killers and then brought them back home. They were dumped on the street to go on with their lives, as if nothing had ever happened.

However, something did happen to them, and it was driving them crazy. They didn't have anything else to do with their lives other than to oppose that mindless war on a people, who just wanted to rule their own destiny. I felt bad for most of the guys. Trauma like that changes a person. They were men society just brushed aside. Those who never served were callous when they viewed veterans and never thanked us for our service. We were spit on and called baby killers.

Most of the vets in V.V.A.W. just wanted the war in Vietnam to end before another body bag was sent home. In general, they were peaceful guys, who I felt proud to call brother. These were the guys I was fighting for, on my mission to keep the peace, but I knew that if they suspected I was a cop, they'd feel betrayed and hurt me really bad. If not flat out kill me.

The V.V.A.W. was one of many anti-war groups that I joined to maintain my cover. More than anything, I wanted to keep those guys safe from further harm. There was a wide range of beliefs and ideals all along the spectrum, supporting each segment of the protests; peaceful to downright deadly. One example was the more radical anti-war faction, Youth Against War and Fascism. A lot of the veterans were also drawn to that group. These guys were totally cynical of everybody and everything.

What Michael showed me about cynics was they believe people are only motivated by self-interest, rather than acting for honorable or unselfish intent.

What I observed on my own about every cynical person I'd ever met was they were all motivated by self-gratification, had little or no honor and were extremely selfish people. They just wanted to control every situation, with their view of things. They desired to be right, even if they are dead wrong and knew it.

These radicals didn't even like each other. They were cynical against one another, the anti-war movement and the U.S. Government. Most of all, they hated the police.

As a side note, it is important for you to know about cynics, so you know how I had to work amongst them. They find their way into your mind and convince you their view is the only way. Most of them fall under the definition of "zealot." History has seen examples of their mind control. The whole world saw Adolf Hitler do it, with his many speeches to the German people. He'd start off saying nothing, only looking at the crowd. Then he would speak slow and steady, saying what the people wanted to hear. Once he had the crowd's attention, he'd start ramping it up, until he was screaming. The crowd would feed on Hitler's electrifying dark energy, until they were under his deceptive spell, seeing him as the new messiah.

When I was in Germany, I went to a magic show where the magician was also a hypnotist. I was amazed at how easy it was to change a person's reality. He pulled off his black belt and threw it on the floor, telling ten people it was a black snake. They all saw it as a real snake, even though the rest of the audience could plainly see it was just a belt. They were terrified but, in reality, had nothing to fear.

The human mind is very susceptible to suggestions. Self-serving zealots will turn lies into the truth. Such was the case in these radical anti-war factions.

I watched, as some of the members of the more radical anti-war groups were manipulating the minds of youth. They were using basic, brain washing techniques to win trust, while converting those individuals into a more dissident personality that would provoke police into a violent confrontation when instructed to so.

I labeled them "inciters" because they were inciting, with the purpose of causing a riot. Once they started a problem within the crowd and provoked the police into a violent attack, the inciters would run away leaving the peaceful demonstrators to be beaten or tear gassed.

As I infiltrated each group, I played stupid and let them suck me into their madness. Their main tactics were to form a wall of five to ten people who linked arms while pushing the innocent people in front of them to overrun the police line. This action would be viewed as an attack on police, who were holding 36" riot batons, and the "head busting" would begin.

The inciters would also wear shoulder slings and pouches filled with rocks, bricks and bottles. Nonchalantly, they would move into the middle of a crowd of demonstrators, pick a few police officer targets and start throwing. Then like invisible ninjas, they would move on to another crowd, where they would do the same thing.

I identified several of the members of these violent groups as actually being Soviet KGB operatives.

When I would learn the areas these inciters intended to disrupt, I'd steal away to my car where I felt safe, in order to radio Detective Bender and report what I had discovered. Typically, he would tell me to go back to the group and keep monitoring their activities. He wanted to know where and when they would strike. That was hard to learn, since they were random acts of violence.

Man, cell phones and texting would have been a great tool in those days!

One night, Michael informed me, "Leave the gun, badge and radio in the car. Things are going to get ugly." He showed me being kicked into a fire, by a police officer. The cop then shot me when my gun fell out of my boot, as I hit the ground.

I thought "Holy crap! I gotta' do everything I can to avoid that from happening." I followed the Angel's advice and left everything in the car.

When I returned to the group of radical inciters that I had joined, the leader, a tall western European guy named Serkan, probed, "Where did you go?"

I replied, "To get something to eat. Why?"

He said "You're not a cop are you, my friend?"

I said, "You're joking, right?"

He said, "I never joke, my friend."

"Am I your friend?" I asked.

"Search him Sven," he commanded.

I was then grabbed by two guys and searched by a third. Their search was very professional. They didn't miss a spot. *Ahem…*

These guys were also not Americans, and they knew what they were doing.

I pulled away and got defiant saying, "Hey what the fuck do you think you're doing? I don't need this shit."

Serkan went through my wallet and found my artist business cards and a couple of dummy joints filled with oregano and other leafy green material that I'd light up, if everyone started smoking dope. He smiled at me when he gave me back my stuff saying,

"No, I guess you're not a cop," he announced.

My cover was still intact, thanks to Michael.

The demonstration that day went down without any real mishaps. Detective Bender had teams of specially briefed, uniform police officers, assigned to the areas I told them would be targeted for disruption. They were looking for guys with shoulder pouches and backpacks. If they searched and found rocks and bottles they arrested the inciters for possession of implements of a crime before they could set in motion their criminal mischief.

I felt really good about what Michael had me doing. Again, there were many lessons to be learned at every corner that day. I was happy that Michael and my communication level was improving.

The sun had set, and it was getting cold, as I walked through the National Mall near the Smithsonian Museum of National History. A group of demonstrators were standing around a large campfire where people had thrown the cardboard signs and wooden sticks they were carrying in the demonstration. I stopped to get warm and try to gather more information that might be useful before moving on to radio Bender.

The demonstration was over and people were leaving. As people passed by, they tossed their signs on top of the pile, a plume of sparks and smoke would go skyward. It was like fireworks.

None of us noticed the U.S. Park Police motorcycle officer, driving up behind us until it was too late. As he passed me, he stuck his foot out.

I yelled, "Watch it asshole!" It was too late. The nudge threw me off balance and right into the fire. I could see how that fall would have dislodged a gun if it were still in my boot. This guy would have shot me dead for any excuse.

Two of the people quickly helped pull me out of the fire and brush off the burning cinders, as he rode around the circle of people.

The cop stopped his motorcycle, set the kickstand and jumped off the bike like an outraged mad man. He was big, black, and I could tell he did not like white long-haired hippies. He ran toward me, like a dark storm cloud ready to bring thunder and lightning down upon me.

I was taken back to when my brothers and their friends would crash into me like that. I couldn't fight back then, and I definitely couldn't protect myself now. Defending myself against an aggressive police attack would be viewed as an assault on a Federal Police Officer and resisting arrest; both are felonies. All those things ran through my mind, as he slammed into me. I was knocked back into the fire.

He said, "What did you call me, you hippie freak?"

Not wanting to be shot as in Michael's vision, I kept my mouth shut and passively looked down. Whenever confronted by a wild animal, you never make eye contact, and this razorback was out of control.

I heard, "It's important not to make eye contact with the beast when he has the advantage, Ed," said Michael.

I was thinking, even if I didn't have my gun on me, he did have one and I didn't want to get shot by this madman.

While watching me crawl out of the fire for a second time, a larger crowd of people began to form. The cop realized he had to do something, so he said, "Okay, you are all under arrest for disorderly conduct, arson and destruction of federal property." Pointing at the newcomers he continued, "If you don't want to be arrested too, you had better move on." And move on they did, quickly. No one wanted trouble with this guy.

One of the girls standing next to me asked, "What …" I raised my hand to stop her from talking, since I knew there is no talking sense to stupid, but she continued anyway. This guy had a burr up his ass and was going to take it out on us because he had the power to do so. "… Federal property did we destroy?" she wanted to know.

The angry cop said, "You set fire to the grass, and the grass is owned by the federal government. That's arson, destruction of federal property and you are gathering without a permit. That's disorderly conduct."

All I could think was, "What a Dick!" I couldn't believe it. One of the last things Bender told me was, "Don't get arrested."

Here I was, not only arrested, but also charged with two felonies and a misdemeanor.

When we were transported to the D.C. Police Central Cellblock, I was fingerprinted, photographed and charged. The motorman told the jailers that I was a smart-ass police hater, who needed to be put in with the nicest fellows they could find. I didn't like the sound of that. He certainly wasn't telling them to do me any favors.

When he left, he said, "Sweetheart, have a nice evening." I thought, "This was a great day's work on my new assignment. I saved people from getting hurt on both sides, and I get locked up." I couldn't wait for my one phone call. I was going to call Detective Bender and have that asshole cop's badge.

What a filthy place the cellblock was. Thrown in with twenty-five thugs, who didn't like any part of this tall skinny white boy. Well, there was one part of me I knew they liked when two of them referred to me as "honey." But that's a story for a different day.

I was just hoping I didn't run across anyone I had arrested in the past. Cops don't fare too well in jail when inmates find out who you really are. My mind kept going back to wanting to burn that cop's ass, but Michael had other ideas.

He told me, "Go after that cop, and you'll blow your cover and all our hard work would be for nothing."

I thought, "*Our* hard work? I'm the one who wound up in the fire. Twice!" In fact, to this day I think Michael had a lot to do with how that cop saw me.

I told him, "I could have been killed."

Michael simply said, "No, I wouldn't let you die. You might suffer a little bit, but suffering is good for the soul." He went on to say, "People don't need a reason to hate us. We're like a mirror, reflecting their shortcomings. So sometimes all they see is the one thing they hate - themselves."

While waiting for my one phone call, Michael told me to call Bender, but said, "Don't have him get you out of jail." He projected a vision to me of that girl at the fire; apparently, she was a big wig in a large anti-war organization. He wanted what he had set in motion to play out.

When I did get my phone call, I told Bender that I wanted to stay in jail.

He said, "That's gutsy. Are you sure?" Bender agreed with me, since it was my undercover investigation. As I hung up, I knew he would monitor the situation, regardless.

True to what I felt, Bender did have me moved into a safer part of the central cellblock, with people less threating to my ethnic persuasion. I was glad. A couple of my former cellmates were already talking about what a pretty mouth I had and how they needed a long-haired, bearded girlfriend for the night.

The next morning, the U.S. Attorney dropped the case on us because the Park Police Officer couldn't prove we started the fire. All they could prove was that we were just bystanders getting warm.

Once on the street outside the jail, I saw the girl and some of the other guys, who had been arrested with me. I found out the girl's name was Gwen, and that she worked for the National Peace Action Coalition, a large anti-war organization, with offices on DuPont Circle.

Gwen came over to me and asked, "What do you do for a living?"

I shrugged my shoulders and replied, "Well I'm a thriving, but sometimes starving, artist."

She told me the Washington branch (WPAC) of her organization was helping to plan some big peace rallies for D.C., and I should consider volunteering sometime for the movement. It was the perfect cover for me. I'd setup my art displays in DuPont Circle to make a little money on the side by day and work in the WPAC's office at night. I could keep tabs on things for Detective Bender, while finding out information on all the subversive organizations in the area.

I joined Abby Hoffman's Yippies, Rennie Davis' S.D.S. and Anti-War Union, V.V.A.W, Red Army, Weathermen, Baader Meinhof Gang, Irish Republican Army and just about every subversive group that passed through the nation's capital. I was invited to every demonstration and had a ringside seat to the inside intelligence of any threats from other groups that wanted to disrupt the peaceful demonstrations. WPAC didn't know it, but I was working behind the scenes to keep their demonstrations peaceful. I wasn't there to spy on them. I liked most of them. I was after the dark-spirited people, who wanted to incite riots and destroy the peace.

The intelligence I gathered helped uncover many negative plots of civil disobedience, bombings, kidnappings and murder.

When you are undercover on the scale I was, you are working 24/7 – 365. You have to live your assignments. Since Linda was also my assignment, I took her along as part of my cover. Having a girlfriend, cut down on the possibility of compromising my investigation, by being hit on by other women. It was the early 1970's and free love was all around. Linda was officially listed with the police department as confidential informant "L-1." We made quite a team. I could send her in to get information from guys that wouldn't even talk to me. It got a little dicey a few times, though, because there was some conflict with her conscience and the task at hand.

One evening, Detective Bender wanted me to cover a gathering, in Georgetown, of Native American Indians... about an upcoming march on Washington. I brought Linda, so my Irish German presence didn't look so conspicuous.

Linda is one third Cherokee. As a team, we looked like we belonged there.

Unfortunately for me, she was very saddened, by the way the Native people have been treated. During the event, a number of Indians got up to speak, condemning the white man for their plight. Linda started nodding her head and pumping her fist in the air. She turned and looked straight at me, like I was one of the white devils they were talking about. Needless to say, I couldn't remind her right then and there of our purpose. I was there, ultimately, to keep the peace. I didn't want anyone to get hurt on either side of the issue.

You know... "Blessed are the peace makers."

Just to be on the safe side, I didn't bring Linda with me anymore when Indians were involved.

Chapter Eighteen

Where White Men Fear to Tread

When the American Indian Movement's Trail of Broken Treaties caravan came to Washington, I got a call at the WPAC office from Detective Bender. For him to take a chance on breaking my cover, I knew this was huge. He wanted me to respond to the Bureau of Indians Affairs building at 19th and Constitution Avenue N.W.

Bender said, "The Indians took over the building, were breaking up furniture and barricading doors. It was yet unknown, if they had taken any hostages."

I whispered, "Okay, I'll work it into my cover story and try to have WPAC send me down, as an assignment."

I spoke to my friend, Jerry Gordon, the head of WPAC. He was a very impressive speaker. I agreed with most everything he believed in. I announced, "I just heard Indians took over the BIA building, and they are planning to hold the building and hostages until their grievances are met."

Jerry said, "AIM (the American Indian Movement) is dangerous and this could turn into another Wounded Knee massacre."

I said, "I think we should go down there to show solidarity for the Indians' plight." The inner actor in me came out, and I became very animated. I rattled off some of the atrocities against the Indians, past and present. "I have friends on several reservations in the Midwest, and the way the Indians are treated by the Bureau of Indians Affairs is inhuman!" I yelled.

He said, "Okay, okay!" responding to my emotional state. "I'll see what we can do."

I had donated several of my paintings to WPAC for fundraisers, so to pacify me, he made a few phone calls to other members.

When finished, he called me into his office, "Okay you go over and cover it."

I said, "We should take up a collection, so I can buy the Indians some food. They're going to get hungry."

Another fellow in his office said, "We take up collections for WPAC. You show them solidarity. If you want to give them food, you pay for it."

Michael warned me that this would be a very dangerous assignment, but if we played it right, great good would come out of it. He also informed me, "One of the leaders of the movement carries the Spirit of Crazy Horse around him and he's bat shit unpredictable." The angel didn't say "bat shit," but that was the impression that came through.

Michael showed me a vision.

I was sitting on a hill in the warm sun, eating something. As I looked up at the building in front of me, I saw a white man jump out of a second-floor window. When the man hit the ground, he was tackled outside the building by Indians and held spread eagle over a bolder. The white man had a thunderbird on the back of his shirt. After a search of his person, a very tall Indian found the man was carrying a gun and badge in his boot. I couldn't see the white man's face and wondered if it was me, since I carry my gun and badge in my boot.

Just then I saw an Indian chief. He had a crazed look, white lightning bolts painted on his cheeks and a buffalo horned headdress. He was riding a painted horse and, after dismounting, the chief was given the man's pistol. He looked at the gun and then, without giving the white man a second thought, shot him in the back of the head. The chief had the white man's body thrown over the horse and he rode away.

Night fell.

The Chief on the painted horse rode out onto the steps of the great building and said, "It is a good day to die."

He dropped the dead man's body to the ground and raised his rifle to the night sky. A shot rang out, and the great chief fell, dead from his horse.

Then soldiers and police advanced toward the building. A peace fell over the land, as the troops moved inside. There was a loud clap of thunder, and a woman screamed, then a fiery explosion. People were dying inside. I heard gun shots and screams as police, soldiers and Indians came running out of the building with their clothes on fire.

It was like watching the Hindenburg burn on old newsreels.

I heard the words, "Oh the humanity." A great sadness fell over the land and the people who survived, lived out the rest of their lives in shame.

My heart was hurting after that. I had a lump in my throat. I asked Angel Michael, "Am I that man?"

He said, "No, but you will know him when you see him."

"We have to stop that awful thing from happening," I pleaded.

He casually replied back, "Then you need to go shopping and find a way inside the building."

"Easy for you to say," I said under my breath. It never mattered whether I whispered, spoke out loud or thought something--I knew Michael "heard" what I said. That was always a good thing to keep in mind when he pissed me off.

I called Detective Bender and asked if could I get some money from the division's investigation fund to buy some food for the Indians. "It might help me get inside the building, so I could look around and see what the Indians are planning," I tried to convey in the most convincing voice possible.

Bender said, "Nixon is outraged about the takeover of one of *his* buildings and wants the Indians out tonight. He feels it's an embarrassment to have these radicals take over a federal building just a few blocks from the White House." He went on to disclose, "I've been told the Government wants to starve them out, so there is no way the department will spring for a bunch of food. Sorry."

I drove down to the BIA building to scout it out. There was very little police presence and an awful lot of Indians running around, with no direction. I got the feeling they were surprised that the police hadn't responded to their action. I climbed the stairs to the front doors and tried to enter, as if I was part of the takeover, but was stopped by an older Indian. I heard someone call him Ten Bears.

With arms crossed, Ten Bears informed me, "No non-Indians allowed to enter the building."

"I don't want to go in. I was sent down from the offices of the Washington Peace Action Collation to show solidarity for your cause. I wanted to offer food and legal assistance, in case any arrests take place."

In the moments I had to look inside, Michael took my attention to the face of one Indian standing alone just inside the building's lobby. I had seen that face before in the vision. It was the chief on horseback that got shot.

Ten Bears walked over to the man and told him of my offer. The Chief shook his head no, then glared at me.

I yelled, "Can I bring you anything... food, water..."

The Chief looked very angry. He interrupted me and said, "Bring me guns, because it's a good day to die."

Shaking my head from side to side, I said, "I'll bring you some food. Think about it." I started to leave, but paused and turned around. I proclaimed out of nowhere, "It's a better day to live, Crazy Horse."

The man looked puzzled. His mean countenance turned to a slight smile.

I turned and walked away.

As soon as I got out of eyesight, I reported back to Bender, "I made contact with the radicals. The Indians seem very disorganized right now. I talked with one of the leaders, who said that since I was sent from WPAC, I could bring in food."

Okay, so I had to stretch the truth a little to keep my investigation going.

Bender asked, "Who was the Indian leader you spoke to?"

I said, "I don't know. You don't ask names in those situations. It makes people paranoid. I just called him Crazy Horse. He seemed to like that nickname."

"Alright, meet me in 30 minutes at checkpoint Charlie. I want to show you some photographs of the A.I.M. leadership," he ordered.

I asked, "Can you try to get me some money for food, so I can take back to the BIA building? I think we can make the best of a bad situation this way, but without food, I don't stand a chance of ever getting inside the building." On my way to meet up with Bender, Michael assured me that the quickest way to get inside that building was to act like I didn't want to get in, and bringing the Indians food would be the key to get me in.

Bender showed me a number of photographs. I only identified one man, the one I called Crazy Horse. Bender said, "That's Russell Means, and you pegged him well. Means is one of the American Indian Movements founders, and he is a hot head. Watch out for him. Means is *mean* and is suspected of shooting several people who didn't agree with him on the reservation. One of them was an undercover U.S. Marshal."

I brought up money for food, "Were you able to get any money, so I could buy some food?"

Bender responded, "Lt. Erwin Grape said, 'Tell Jagen to use his own money and if his plan works, he can submit a reimbursement voucher. If it doesn't, he's on his own. Sorry." There was a reason the detectives in the Intelligence Division nicknamed him "Goofy Grape."

I borrowed fifty dollars from Detective Bender and then drove to Linda's office at 20th and L St. N.W., where I got seventy-five more. Adding in the twenty-three dollars I had, I was then on my way to the Safeway food store! A little money bought a lot back then.

I had purchased lots of bread, candy, cans of tuna fish and vegetables, large jars of peanut butter and jelly, snack cakes, bags of potato chips, fruit and cases of Pepsi, Root Beer, Dr. Pepper and more. I packed my silver Chevy Vega so full I couldn't close the hatchback.

As I passed a McDonald's, I got a strong transmission from Michael, "STOP!"

I slammed on the brakes and the adrenaline was rushing. All the food came forward into the front seat.

I thought, "What? What the hell?"

"Turn around," he roared. "Go buy a sack of McDonald's hamburgers and fries for Russell Means. Crazy Horse will enjoy the beef."

"You scared the living crap out of me," I exclaimed out loud.

I was in a zone trying to plan my entrance into the BIA building. Didn't he know that, I wondered. Wasn't there a better way he could have stopped me? These were the times I thought Michael was up there somewhere laughing his ass off (if he had one) because he liked messing with me.

I did get the burgers and went on my way again.

When I arrived back at the BIA building that afternoon, things had changed. The Indians had become very organized. Police barricades weren't letting anyone into the compound and anyone, who tried to leave would be arrested.

That was great.

I thought, "How am I going to get inside that building now?"

I parked about a block away in the rear of another government building parking lot. I badged the GSA security guard and asked him to watch my car until I came back for it.

The guard was reluctant until I said, "You don't want those Indians to take over your building too, do you? We don't know what the Indians did with the GSA guards at the BIA building."

Apparently, that appealed to his good sense. He agreed to watch my car.

I left my gun, badge and radio in the car and grabbed the bag of burgers. I went to find a safe way to get the food to the Indians, without being arrested *and* blowing my cover.

I walked the outer perimeter of the building to get as close as I could, without coming into contact with the police. If I was seen, talking to the cops for any reason, I was dead. My cover would be blown in the eyes of the Indians, not to mention I never knew if I would run into another cop who knew me, *as a cop.* That was always a worry for me.

Unlike most undercover officers who are chosen right out of the academy before anyone has a chance to know them, I had already been around for three years in uniform and as a detective in vice. Plus, there were the many hours spent in court papering and testifying in cases. I didn't only have to worry about cops, knowing who I really was, but there was that questionable group of people in my past known as defense attorneys. A lot of them were very sensitive to the anti-war movement and would snitch on my true identity in a heartbeat to get me back for cases lost.

From my position, I saw the back of the B.I.A. building had a parking lot that could be entered from the side of the building. Michael showed me that I could drive in over the grass to avoid detection.

I walked down a short hill, into the parking lot where two Indians, standing guard, stopped me.

I explained, "I spoke with two of your officials, Ten Bears and Russell Means about smuggling in food to feed your group. All entrances are blocked by cops, but I could drive my car in over that hill into the parking lot without being seen."

They were hungry, so I started giving out hamburgers.

"Here's the sack. Make sure Russell gets a few burgers, since he ordered them," I stated.

I didn't wait for their approval. As I took off toward my car, I yelled back, "I'll be back in a about ten minutes. Try to have some help here to unload the food from my car. I don't want to be seen carrying anything in."

When I returned to my car, that I had nicknamed the "Silver Bullet," I found that several other GSA guards were standing around. I didn't want to get arrested as one of the demonstrators. I told them they had nothing to fear because the Indians were contained at the BIA. I thanked the guards, and they wished me luck.

I radioed Detective Bender to let him know that I was ready to make my move, and the Indians were ready to receive the food.

"If all goes well, I'll be able to get inside to see what the conditions are and what they were planning," I relayed.

"Well, act as quickly as possible. The government task force is planning to activate the D.C. National Guard to move the demonstrators out of the building at ten o'clock tonight." He ended by saying, "Oh, and Ed, please don't get locked up again. It will look bad on your resume."

He laughed, but I didn't.

I drove directly from the parking lot to the back of the BIA building almost on autopilot. I knew Michael was doing the driving.

A Park Police vehicle pulled in behind me. I'm sure I looked suspicious with a car full of food. The car's emergency lights turned on just as I was ready to jump the curb. I pulled over, but the police car sped past me, like he didn't even see me. I felt cloaked, with some sort of invisibility, like in Star Wars when Obi Wan said to the storm troopers, "These are not the droids you are looking for." I jumped the curb and continued on my way down the hill. I went right into the parking lot and the waiting arms of the hungry Indians.

I was accepted, as if I was part of their group. It may have been because of the way I was dressed. I'm also sure Michael had something to do with the way they perceived me. Everyone grabbed something out of the Silver Bullet and started carrying the boxes and bags of food into the building.

109

As soon as I entered, I could smell gasoline. We passed rooms that were totally ransacked, desks upside down, chairs broken, file cabinets open and papers everywhere. I snuck into one room where someone wrote on the wall, "Custer died for your sins." I had the overwhelming feeling that the Indians were planning for their last stand. I also found out they had drained all the cars in the parking lot, and now they were pouring the gas into bottles making what they called "fire bombs". It seemed like everyone had a weapon, from knifes and pistols to machetes and some spears, made up of broken scissors on the end of mop handles.

After dropping off the last bag of food inside, I started to head for the door and my waiting car. My head was full of ideas. I got in. I gave them the food. I saw what looked like a planned offensive and/or suicide mission. Now what?

Out of the blue the tallest Indian I've ever seen stepped in front of me. He had to stand seven-foot-tall. I found out later they called him "Cody," and he was somehow related to the well-known Native American actor/activist Iron Eyes Cody. He was the famous crying Indian in the anti-pollution commercials that appeared on TV in the sixties.

Cody loomed over me and asked, "What are you doing in the building? I was told you are with a national peace group sent to bring food to us, in support of our occupation. I was also told you said Russell Means had okayed it. Is that true?"

"Of course. And I was just leaving," I responded..

"No. You aren't. Not yet anyway," Cody growled, as he sent for Russell Means.

I was told to sit in a chair, until I was cleared.

When Means arrived, he was mad as a hornet. I knew I had stretched the truth a bit and thought that's why things were getting tense. Michael always told me to use comedy to break tension, so I quipped, "It's a good day to eat, eh Crazy Horse? Did you get the hamburgers I brought you?"

In my life, I've seen a lot of deadly looks from people, but man if the "looks could kill" phrase had a contest for poster boy, this guy was the winner. I could see, however, deep down inside, he had a good and caring heart. A slight smile crept to the corners of his mouth.

He responded, "Mr. Good Night, I see you are still feeding the Indians your bull."

I laughed and asked, "Who is Mr. Good Night?"

He said, "Charlie Good Night. He was a good friend to my ancestors long ago."

I was confused and asked, "What did he do?"

Means' reply stunned me, "He was a white man, a Texas Ranger and cattleman, who cared about my people. Go to your library and look him up. I feel his spirit around you."

Russell Means turned his back and walked away saying; "Now get out of here before someone removes the hair from the top of your thick head."

I was escorted back to the parking lot where my car was and told I was banned from going back inside the building. I retorted with, "If you remember, I didn't want to go inside the building right from the start."

The looks on their faces and the way they nodded their heads told me they remembered. I could feel that fact, immediately lessened their suspicion of me. I did have to let them know, however, that I couldn't simply drive out the way I came in because of the roadblocks. I would have to wait in the parking lot for a more opportune time to leave. One of them shrugged his shoulders and then the two of them walked back into the building. I guess they didn't care one way or another, as long as I kept my behind out of that building. They were hungry and wanted to eat.

I was in a bit of a pickle now. I couldn't leave even on foot to give my report to Bender because the Indians were watching my every move.

So, I sat and waited.

About one hour later, while I was eating a Hostess Twinkie and listening to my car radio, I heard screaming from inside the building. I looked up at a second-floor window and saw a familiar face. It was Detective Roger Day dressed like an Indian perched in the window.

"Get him!" I heard from inside.

Detective Day jumped to the ground and began running across the parking lot, chased by Cody and two other Indians. He was tackled and went down hard. From my vantage point, I could see blood coming from his mouth and nose. He must've hit hard. Then Cody grabbed him and threw Robert across the trunk of a car spread eagle. I noticed a thunderbird painted on the back of his blue denim jacket.

"Oh shit!" I thought. "This was the same vision Michael had given me before. I just pictured it a little differently."

It was happening.

I was shaking my head. Damn! I thought what I did would've stopped this. What went wrong? I felt Robert Day was about to die at the hands of Russell Means.

Cody found Day's badge and snub nose S&W 38cal revolver, just as Russell Means was walking out of the building. Cody handed the gun to Means just like in the vision. I reached under my seat and grabbed my pistol and slid it into my boot. Then I slowly moved to the hood of my car to watch what would come next. I thought, "I can't let Means shoot Roger, but if I shoot Means, the Indians would tear *me* apart. Crap, I don't have *that* many bullets. I guess it isn't a good day for Detective Day ."

Russell Means pointed the gun at Detective. Day I started to draw my gun out of my boot.

Michael yelled through me, "It's a better day to live, Crazy Horse, especially since you haven't found what you came for."

I could see something *or someone* came over Means. It was like a light switch was flipped. He wasn't angry for the first time in decades. He slid the Smith and Wesson into the middle of his back, as if he keeps one there often.

Then Means pulled Detective Day off the car and said, "Cody, take him inside."

I could tell Russell was stunned. As he entered the building, he turned and looked back at me, nodding and shaking his head. Like I could read his thoughts, an overwhelming impression came over me that he had no idea what to make of me. I think I spooked him a bit.

Hell, I've spooked myself at times.

As soon as they disappeared into the building, a sense of urgency came over me. Michael revealed, "If you don't find a way to immediately pass this intelligence you just gathered, all hell is going to break loose. Especially since the Indians now have a D.C. Police Detective as a prisoner."

I had to do something fast. There was no time to lose. I started the Silver Bullet and drove to the exit of the parking lot. I stopped. A uniform police sergeant got out of his cruiser and started to walk toward me. I saw the chance, so I drove over the grass, sidewalk and onto the street, hoping not to get shot. Another police vehicle gave chase. I carefully drove through several red lights, before I felt far enough away from the Indians to pull over. The two front doors of the police cruiser flew open with the uniform officers perched behind them with guns trained on my car.

"Put your hands out the window," one officer commanded on the scout car's loudspeaker.

I put both hands out of the driver's window. My left hand was holding my badge and ID folder. I yelled, "I'm working, can I get out? I'll keep my hands in the air." I exited the Silver Bullet, with my hands high and badge gleaming.

When I reached their vehicle, I gave them my identification and told them that I was with the D.C. Police Intelligence Division. I was undercover and had infiltrated the BIA building to investigate the Indians' vulnerability. I politely asked, "When you clear the stop on my vehicle, can you advise the dispatcher on a landline phone, so it won't blow my cover? It's possible the Indians have a police scanner and are monitoring our dispatchers?"

They cleared me, and I took off. I met with Detective Bender, who was on his way to a federal task force meeting about the takeover situation. "Russell Means just took Detective Roger Day captive, after they saw him trying to escape from the building," I reported. "I don't know why he was trying to get out unless something else tipped his hand. He jumped out of a second-floor window and got beat up pretty bad, before they found his gun and badge."

I went on to reveal, "Bender, make no mistake, the Indians intend to die for the cause, and they will take as many government agents and soldiers out with them as they can. They want to become martyrs and create an international incident. I saw what they had inside. They're making gas bombs. Their plan is to lure the police and National Guard troops into the building and then start throwing the bombs at their feet, setting them ablaze. For the glory, they will go out fighting hand to hand."

"The task force will want to step up the time frame for the offensive in this case," he shared.

"I don't think that's a good idea. Their mantra is 'It's a good day to die,' and they are prepared. The safest action for all is just to get Detective Day back and wait the Indians out," I said. "If I'm right, they will just end up, walking away in a few days. But there is more. You need to tell the task force what I learned about why this all went down in the first place," I pleaded.

I began recounting to Bender what I learned from Ten Bears and some others inside the building. "Apparently, that day started off very peaceful, with the Indians just walking into the building, wanting to talk to the Secretary of the Interior. The group was ushered into a small presentation room to wait, and the door was *locked* behind them. They felt like prisoners. After about an hour, an old Indian woman asked if she could go to the bathroom, holding herself, jumping from one foot to the other. When the GSA Guards finally opened the door, the Indians all ran out from their captivity. It was not a planned takeover, it just happened. Nevertheless, that's when the Indians all began walking the halls of the building looking for the Secretary of the Interior. The government employees inside, fearing it was a building takeover, got scared and ran out of the building, leaving only the Indians inside. That was about the time you called me, and I went over and first met with Russell Means. He and the other leaders were scratching their heads over what to do next. Remember I told you they were very disorganized at the time? Now it has escalated to assaulting a police officer and kidnapping. We can't let another atrocity take place, knowing these people just wanted a peaceful meeting," I cried out, getting a little animated.

I hate when the underdog and vulnerable are taken advantage of.

He said, "No, of course not."

There was one particular item I didn't disclose to Bender. I knew Means and the other Indian leaders inside the building had a search going on for files showing that the U.S. Government knowingly violated the treaties over the Black Hills, because gold was found on Indian lands. The American Indian Movement wanted to sue the U.S. Government to reclaim the Black Hills. They also wanted reimbursement for all the gold that was taken off their lands.

Michael told me all of this, but I didn't have physical or visual proof in order to share it with Bender. If I told him "my angel told me," well then, I'd be the next one locked up... and not in a jail. I'd be a new resident of St. Elizabeth's Mental Institution.

I also did not mention that to Bender because I was sure there were people in government, who didn't want those facts coming to light as a dark spot on our American History. I learned early on that there are many sides to every story.

Detective Bender concluded by saying, "Good intelligence Ed. Now go home. We can handle it from here. It's too dangerous for you to return now, since someone may have seen you run the roadblock."

I took off in the opposite direction to get something to eat and then found my way back to the BIA and camped out in the front of the building. I sat under a tree playing my guitar singing "Bye, Bye, Miss American Pie." It was the first song Detective Mendez taught me to play way back when.

A short time later, I saw Detective Bender, walking toward me in a roundabout manner. He was trying not to call attention to himself or blow my cover. I thought he was going to call me out for going back to the building. He eventually came up behind me with his camera, taking photographs of the crime scene and the onlookers that had gathered.

Not looking at me, but talking directly to me he said, "The Indians have agreed to release Detective Day in an hour. By the way, what the hell are you doing back here?"

I answered, "I had to see this through!"

True to their word, Russell Means and his Indian "security" staff brought their police captive out of the occupied Bureau of Indian Affairs building and released him, without any further incident.

The tension was off.

After reviewing the intelligence information that I, and other sources, had gathered earlier about the conditions inside the building, and of the Indians' plans to make this "a good day to die," the Federal Government Task Force decided to follow wise logic and take a wait and see attitude.

The Indians must have found what evidence they were looking for in the bureau's files, because they all vanished from the B.I.A. building in the middle of the night a few days later.

One interesting fact, the Indians did not return Detective Day's S&W 38 Caliber snub-nose revolver and badge, when they surrendered him. I heard the gun was recovered in an armed robbery on the Pine Ridge reservation the following year. The badge was never recovered.

After the dust had all settled, Michael told me, "We have not seen the last of the spirit of "Crazy Horse" and Russell Means. The day will come in the far-off future that "Crazy Horse" will be asked to accept an apology from you, on behalf of all the wrongs done to the Indian people, by the white man and the United States Government."

I said, "He'd never accept my apology. He's so proud. And, why would he?"

Michael answered, "Because salvation for the spirit can only be found in forgiveness, and he will accept the apology from the spirit of Charlie Goodnight who Russell sees around you. So before you two meet again, you need to become the next best thing to Charlie... a Good Knight."

I had no idea what Michael meant, but back in those days, I didn't understand the meaning of most the things he said or asked me to do. I just tried to follow his lead and prayed I'd come out alive on the other end.

Whenever I asked Michael to explain anything I didn't fully understand, all he would say was, "All will be known when your waiting is full."

Try getting that for an answer and not letting yourself get irritated. That was my biggest challenge at the time.

In the fall of 1973, I was assigned to cover an anti-war demonstration, even though the war in Vietnam was all but over.

The rally point was at the Kennedy Center, near the Watergate Complex in Southwest Washington. It was a nice, brisk, sunny day, and I was looking forward to the march. I had just reported to Detective Bender that, for the most part, it didn't look like any group was planning any civil disobedience.

As I returned to my position within the main body of the demonstration, a tall, skinny, white man approached me. "I know you. You're a cop," he said. I recognized the man right away. He was a defense attorney, who'd represented a drug dealer I had arrested several years earlier, while in vice.

Unfortunately, there was no hiding it. I still looked and dressed the same now, as I did then. I told the fellow that he was crazy and to get out of my face. He left and went over to talk to a couple of known KGB operatives I had spotted in the crowd earlier. The agents, immediately, went to some thugs in one of the more radical organizations, and told them that I was a spy and possibly a police provocateur.

I didn't want to tangle with these guys. They were well known to put a hurt on people, who got in their way, so I could only imagine what they'd do, if they got their hands on me.

The march had just kicked off, so I jumped in at the head of the crowd. I could see the four thugs break up and move in different directions, within the march. Michael suggested that I should break away from the main body of the march at the next turn.

When the opening came, the march went left, and I kept going straight. I breathed a sigh of relief.

Just when I thought I had skirted danger, I felt a pain on the left side of my neck and shoulder blade. I turned to see one of the KGB agents. He had struck me, with a blackjack. Speaking something in German, he mumbled something about "....toter hund." I didn't speak much German, but I did understand he was saying something about a "Dead Dog."

Without even thinking, I swung around and caught him in the throat, with a lucky punch. As he grabbed his throat, I side kicked him in the chest, knocking him to the pavement. A woman started screaming for the police. I thought, "I am the police, lady, but I dared not identify myself. It would blow my cover."

The KGB agent grabbed a radio out of his back pocket and tried to call his buddies, but he was having a hard time talking because of the pain in his throat. I snatched the radio from his hand. They were trying to coordinate their locations with one another, but couldn't raise someone called, "Helmet." I could see one of them half a block away, still looking for me.

I answered the radio saying, "Helmet can't answer the radio right now, friend. He has a frog in his throat."

On the other end, one of them said, "Who is 'dis?'"

I answered, "Der Frosch."

"Who?" someone on the other end asked.

I responded in English this time, "The frog, bitch!"

I picked up the blackjack from the ground as a souvenir and disappeared, down a nearby ally.

Image 5 - Undercover Detective Edward Jagen and the "Silver Bullet"

Chapter Nineteen

It's Time for a Change

Little did I know when I turned away from the March that day, I would actually be turning away from much more.

During a meeting that evening with Detective Bender and our Inspector, it was deemed too dangerous for me to continue my undercover investigations, within the anti-war community. Surprisingly, it wasn't at all due to Mr. Helmet and KGB and his buddies. Detective Bender passed me a surveillance photograph, taken of me by the U.S. Secret Service at a demonstration.

He said, "The Feds want to know who you are. They feel you have ties to the Weather Underground."

I said, "Well, it's getting a little hot out there on the streets. It's time for a new direction." I had to change my appearance, if I was going to continue, so I cut my hair and shaved off my beard. I traded my army field jacket and jeans for three piece suits and a tie.

My alter ego emerged.

Michael told me he had to leave and "return to the Father, for a while." I thought it was good timing, since I would be off the streets and, hopefully, not needing him to get me out of any jams for a while.

Linda and I had been dating for some time, now, and she wanted to take our relationship to the next level. She had become much more than "my assignment," as Michael always put it. I just didn't want to do anything that would jeopardize what Michael was planning. Also, the last thing I wanted to do was marry anyone, with the possibility of making her a widow somewhere down the road.

Linda was a strong force. We had already been dating three years, and she gave me the ultimatum that if I wasn't ready to marry her by the end of five years, she would end the relationship.

I said, "But we could still be friends, right?"

She said, "No. Once lovers, never friends."

I said, "That's bullshit, and you know it. If you can kiss me off that fast, I guess your feelings don't run as deep as you think."

I wondered, "Where was this headstrong chick when Richard was beating on her?"

Her stance definitely put me between a rock and a hard place. I loved her deeply but didn't want to screw things up again, as I did when I married Maria. Michael said I was responsible for Linda for the rest of her life, but also told me never to marry. Michael wasn't back yet, so I played out every scenario with Linda in my head. There was only one that could be the answer.

I remembered Michael saying a long time ago, "In the future, you must locate a very special child with the initials M.V. The child will be a girl that will become the caretaker of the Sword of God, that we are to raise and deliver to the Children of Tomorrow," he would always remind me.

I knew I couldn't have children, so the child couldn't come from Linda and me. *But* I thought it could come from Dawn, if she married the right man! I saw a way to make it work.

Ignoring Michael's guidance, I decided to ask Linda to marry me and adopt Dawn as my own. I didn't formally ask her yet, but threw out some clues, here and there, to make sure she wouldn't bolt. Linda and I discussed not having children.

Just as I made my decision, Michael came back, none too happy. He warned me that there is a chance the nameless child with the initials M.V. may never come into existence, if I took this course of action.

I felt like I got sucker punched in the stomach.

When I heard the word "nameless," I had a flashback to the Constant Walker in the cave the day I drowned--and was given the chance to become part of the angel's dream. One of the first things Connie said to me was, "Although I am nameless..." My heart filled with love, and all fear vanished just at the thought the M.V. child could fulfill me, as Connie did.

Michel said, "If you find the child, you will know her by the way your heart fills with love."

Chapter Twenty

Me, dad? My Daddy!

Michael said, "Since you have decided to start a family, the time has come for you to find your father."

I was taken aback by this announcement. I knew there was more happening on Michael's chess boards than me getting married and finding my father, but again I just learned to go with the flow in Michael's Sacred Service.

I borrowed some money from the Police Credit Union and picked out a nice set of rings. They represented the constellation of Orion. The wedding band held three small diamonds in a row that represented the Belt of Orion, and the engagement ring was a larger diamond that represented the sword in Orion's belt. Michael told me that, in our galaxy, Earth is located in the Orion Spur... more on that later.

I told Linda the time had come for me to find my father. She wholeheartedly agreed.

Before searching for Dad, I booked passage for two on an Old Spanish Galleon in Annapolis. We dined on the largest lobster tails I'd ever seen, and during dessert of flaming Spanish coffees, I had the Spanish hostess deliver the rings, saying, "From the old world to the new…"

I dropped to one knee and said, "Linda, I don't always know where I'm going, but if you marry me, we can get there together."

Her eyes sparkled with delight, and she said, "Yes, I'd love to marry you," as she burst into tears.

The next morning, I called my mother and told her I was marrying Linda. My mother loved Linda and couldn't stand Maria, so she was very happy for me. I went on to tell her that I was leaving later that day to try to find my father.

I asked, "Do you have any clues, as to where he might be?"

She said, "Last I heard he had married a woman named Ruth, one of our old friends, and moved to Houston, Texas. It'll be like finding a needle in a haystack, since the Jagens *never* had a listed phone number."

"Well," I said, "I've taken a week off from work. I'm going to start my search in Chicago, just in case my grandparents still live there. Then I will work my way down to Texas."

Then she said, "But again, he might be living in Miami, Florida now because Ruth's parents lived there, and she was very close to her mother."

"I guess it will be a true test of my investigative skills," I declared.

Of course, all along I was secretly hoping that Michael would help guide me.

I called my sister, Kathy, and told her that I was marrying Linda and setting out to find our father. She wished me good luck on both counts.

My father always said that he had three offspring, two biological and one diabolical. Never did that hit home until I called my brother, Billy, and told him I was getting married and was going to search for our dad.

He started off with, "That fucking bum. He never cared about us."

Well, you get the gist of his mood.

Billy had many unresolved issues. I prayed that someday he would find somebody, who would help turn his life around. This was a far cry from when I was little and just prayed for a bully to treat him the way he treated me. At this point in my life, though, I felt bad for him. He always seemed lost. He and Nancy had two sons now, but were divorcing, and he became even more bitter. I had gotten over the past and prayed that someday he would find happiness.

I never considered Damian as my real brother, so I didn't tell him I was leaving to find my father. To keep my mother happy, I called him "Brother Damian." While I was in the Army, he had moved to Canada to avoid the draft and married an Asian girl, named Jinx. She was a born-again zealot, and now Jesus had become Damian's Lord and Savior. I was happy for them, but all they talked about was their religious beliefs, trying to get everyone to believe as they did. They would say "Jesus is God. Accept him or be damned."

I made the mistake of asking Jinx once, "What happened to the God that Jesus believed in? You know, his Father?"

She replied, "Jesus is God, and there is no other God than Jesus!"

"Okay," I thought. "There is no arguing, with that line of thinking." She was one of those toxic zealots in the world that I seemed to rub me the wrong way. I decided to try to stay away from them as much as I could.

With all the leads I had jotted on the front of a 3" x 5" card, I was now off, down the yellow brick road... to find my long lost father. I was sure Michael would guide me.

As I drove into Chicago, I was in awe at the size of the city. I stopped at the first pay phone I could find and started looking through the phone books for my father's name. My mother was right. No Jagen was found.

That's when Michael piped up, "Look up your godfather's name."

But I could not find Uncle Joe's name either.

Then Michael said, "No, silly, your *real* Godfather, Michael Sparrow."

I looked and found several.

Michael directed, "Call the seventh one down."

I did, and a man answered. I said, "Hi, I'm trying to locate the Mike Sparrow, who was in the war with Bill Jagen. I am his son, Eddie, and I'm in Chicago, trying to locate my father." Nervously, I continued, "I'm getting married and want to invite him to be my best man."

The man on the other end piped up, "Eddie this is your lucky day. Your father was just over here last night, playing cards, and he was still raving about his kids that he hasn't seen in over twenty years."

Mike gave me my father's phone number.

"Thank you. Thank you so much!" I replied.

When I called, a man answered, and I said, "Hello I am trying to reach Bill Jagen."

He said, "I'm Bill Jagen. How can I help you?"

I immediately got a lump in my throat. A million things went through my mind, and then I went blank. What should I say? I had rehearsed this moment so many times, but here it was, and I drew a blank. Of course, I said something stupid.

"Hi Dad, this is your son, Eddie. You don't want to see me, do you?" I couldn't believe I said that.

There was a pause on the other end. I could hear he was crying.

I said, "Uh, Dad. Are you okay?"

My father gathered himself and replied, "Of course I want to see my son. Are Billy and Kathy with you?"

I said, "No, they both send their love, but I didn't know if I was going to be able to find you, so I came alone."

We had a great visit and most importantly, I felt whole again.

My father was my best man the following November when Linda and I were married. The service was held in a small "Church in the Round" near Fort Washington--a mile away from the nightclub where I sang to her. It was a beautiful ceremony. Her maid of honor read a Cherokee Indian wedding prayer just before we said our vows.

After the Minister pronounced, "until death do you part" Michael said, "Amen. You better love your assignment."

I said, "I do!"

Image 6 – Edward and Linda's wedding with Angelic guests

We had a lovely reception. My brother Billy met a wonderful woman, by the name of Betty, there. Soon she had him on the path of redemption. They married the following year. Damian and Jinx didn't think our minister said the name Jesus enough during the service. My sister Kathy met Johnny, the love of her life. They married shortly after, as well.

It was nice for my dad to see peace for his kids. He wasn't surprised to see Damian not fitting in, with the rest of the family. He told me a deep dark secret after one too many wedding toasts that night. He said that there were always rumors around that my aunt and uncle adopted Damian from an unwed teenage mother.

After a raucous wedding reception, where fun was had by all, we said our thanks and took off on a grand adventure. Linda and I honeymooned at Marriott's Mullet Bay Beach Resort in St. Maarten. It was a great new beginning for us both.

Chapter Twenty-one

Gangsters and Terrorists

The Organized Crime and Racketeering Branch of the Intelligence Division needed an undercover investigator to infiltrate illegal gambling operations. The mob from Orange County, New Jersey had moved into Washington, D.C.

Gambling wasn't something that Michael was really interested in having me investigate, but in order to continue his quest, I needed to continue my undercover activities. I focused my investigations in a more upscale part of town and started hanging out in bars and supper clubs where known Mafia members would frequent. I started playing the numbers and betting on horse races, with the bartenders to establish trust. My new counterpart inside, Detective Sharkey, replaced Detective Bender. He was a real go-getter, who wanted to start busting people right away.

I spoke right up, "I don't work like that, because it's a good way to get burned. Besides, it isn't your ass on the line." I could see that we were not going to get along. Detective Sharkey was also fixated on the Mafia and had some delusion that everybody was somehow connected to the mob. Cops without an open mind, who have an agenda, can be real dangerous... mostly to those they work with.

With Sharkey's quirk ever present in my mind, I went on with my investigations.

One of the restaurants I had under surveillance was an Irish pub, called the Black Rooster. The manager, Carl McGuiness, liked me because I painted a special 4'x 6' oil of a Black Rooster, throwing darts at a dartboard for him. He hung the painting right over the bar. With such a prominent position in the establishment, many people commented on its richness of color and three-dimensional effect. I used a special shadow technique that made the rooster and darts look like they were standing out from the background. Because of all the compliments it received, Carl was impressed and allowed me to set up art shows and displays in the restaurant's courtyard. This was a huge help, establishing my cover story.

Angel Michael always helped me to be in the right place at the right time throughout every undercover assignment I had.

The C.I.A. funded a six-year investigation trying to get inside the I.R.A.'s gunrunning activities. When I was with Detective Bender, he had asked me to look into it, but I never found a connection through the anti-war movement. I had hoped to uncover a lead by hanging out in Irish pubs.

My hopes soon were fulfilled.

I learned that the IRA initially started running guns, in order to help fund their fight against British oppression in Ireland. Once they developed a steady flow of weapons, some of their agents went rogue and turned it into a criminal enterprise. In the early seventies, they started selling guns to warlords in Africa and drug lords in Mexico.

One day, while sitting at the bar in the Black Rooster Pub, the bartender, Billy O'Shea, introduced me to his cousin, Harry Hillock. Harry was in town from Ireland. He was looking for work and at the same time, raising money to support the Northern Ireland Children's Aid Foundation.

I bought Harry a beer and told him that I respected anyone that helped children.

Harry informed me, "All the money we raise goes directly to support the children, in families where the fathers had been murdered or imprisoned, by the British."

"Wow," I said. I gave him a twenty-dollar bill and said, "I wish I could do more, but I'm a starving artist."

Harry said, "You can. Why don't you have an art show in some of the local Irish bars I know, and we can split the profits 50/50?"

"Let me think about it, and I'll get back to you."

Later that day, I called Detective Sharkey and told him that I wanted to check out an Irish national, by the name of Harry Hillock, and see if he was connected to the IRA in some way.

Sharkey barked back, "I have you working on illegal gambling. Do you think Hillock is connected?"

I answered, "I'm looking at leads into the IRA gun-running operations in the U.S. and feel Harry could be connected."

He said, "Look Jagen, I'm your control officer, and I tell you what you're investigating. You don't tell me."

"Rat bastard," I murmured, covering the phone's mouthpiece. I was furious at his arrogance. I uncovered the phone and said, "Look I'm not some rookie, fresh out of the academy. I'm a detective the same rank as you. *I* am in control of what I investigate. Remember it's my ass on the line out here, not yours. We are working together. You are little more than my legs on the department following up on leads I uncover. Now are you going to run Hillock through NCIC, or do I have to come in there and do it myself?"

He hung up the phone on me.

I knew if I was seen around police headquarters, it could compromise my cover, so I called Detective Bender, who was more than glad to run my request. Through Bender's research, I learned that Harry Hillock was known on the street in Ireland as "Belfast Harry." And, he was suspected of planting several bombs in Belfast that killed police and British soldiers.

Bender said, "Ed, it looks like you are onto something big. Be careful. Those guys don't mess around. If they suspect you in the least, they will kill you, with no questions asked."

We both knew that meant they wouldn't even take the time to ask, if I was a snitch or a cop. They would simply "remove" me.

Detective Bender also warned, "Watch out for Sharkey too. He has fucked every partner, he's ever worked with. He's a paranoid cop, with a screw loose, who thinks he's the Chief of Police and everyone works for him." There I was again, a rock, me and a hard place! On one side, I had to fear an international terrorist organization and on the other my partner. Awareness is the key though, so at least I was forewarned.

I waited a few days before I returned to the Black Rooster. When I arrived, I found out from Billy O'Shea that his cousin had gotten a bartender job at Rice's Supper Club on M St. NW.

He asked, "Did you give any thought to Harry's offer?"

Acting uninterested I replied, "Yeah, but I think 50/50 was pretty steep, since I put so much time in each painting. I might go for a 70/30 split."

Before I could order a beer, Billy called Harry and put me on the line. I told Harry what I would do, and he agreed.

"Okay," Harry said, "put together a sampling of your work so we can show to the owners. Meet me at the Rooster tomorrow, and I will take you around and introduce you to them."

True to his word, Harry picked me up at the Black Rooster the next day, and we started driving around, looking for business. Every hotel, pub, club and restaurant we went to was interested. Belfast Harry was quite the salesman. He really played up, helping the poor Irish kids' angle.

I placed every painting I had in various bars and hotel lobbies. They started selling immediately. I could not keep up, with the demand. I asked Linda, who was also an artist, if she would do some land and seascapes to add to the collections. We had to switch from oils to acrylics because of the faster drying time.

Harry was happy he was making money. I was actually pretty thrilled myself.

Because of our business relationship, Harry would ride around with me, often, to collect money and place new artwork. I had bought a black four-door Cadillac from a friend at the Russian Embassy. Harry loved to sit in the back seat, while I drove him around town.

One day out of the blue, he asked if I would drop him off at a small printing shop in Adams Morgan in northwest Washington, D.C. When he came out, he sat in my back seat and just stared at several sheets of paper. Harry then passed two sheets to me and asked if they both looked the same.

One of the papers was a completely filled out Federal Firearms Certificate, and the other was a blank Federal Firearms Certificate with Approval stamps. The printer had made copies of the original, so Belfast Harry could forge the other certificates with the information he needed to look legitimate.

I said, "Harry, I don't think I want to be looking at these papers. I don't want to get involved in anything illegal." I found that the more I acted like I didn't want to get involved, the more he would show me.

Harry was a nice enough fellow. However, he could turn cold-hearted at the drop of a hat if you crossed him. One evening, I overheard him bragging to several of his Irish buddies about planting a bomb in a department store, in order to get just one guy. A little bell went off in my head, as I remembered seeing the bombing covered on the news. Great. He got the one guy, but six other people also died in the bombing, and one was an infant.

I had to see this guy go down.

Detective Sharkey complained to our captain that I wasn't spending enough time, investigating illegal gambling. I got called on it, so I started buying tickets in football pools and betting numbers, with bookies that would frequent the bars. It kept Sharkey happy and out of my way. Then he started quizzing me on where I was at certain times of the day and night. It appeared he was trying to catch me in a lie.

One evening when I was leaving the Black Rooster, I thought I saw him duck down in the back seat of a car across the street. I walked to my car and then turned around and went back inside the pub, acting as if I had forgotten something. I knew Billy O'Shea had a Polaroid camera behind the bar, so I asked if I could borrow it for a few minutes.

I went out the back door and circled around behind the car. It was Sharkey. My suspicion that he was spying on me was right on target. Sharkey's eyes were focused on the front door of the pub. I quickly opened the back door, jumped inside and snapped his picture. He almost keeled over from a heart attack right there. He was so scared, he couldn't even talk.

I said, "What the hell do you think you're doing?"

I could smell that my surprise made him crap in his pants.

He retorted, "I think you're dirty, Jagen, and I don't believe you are where you say you are at times!"

The fool reached for his gun.

I couldn't believe he pointed it at me. Detective Sharkey was an f…ing legend in his own mind. I think he watched too many cop shows on TV. He was a bald, pudgy and very slow to respond, white guy. More of a "wannabe" than anything else. He became a detective because his uncle was a Deputy Chief, and he couldn't handle uniform duty.

I knew that with him watching me, it could comprise my safety and my sources. I quickly grabbed his gun out of his hand and got out of the car. I said, "I'm taking this before you shoot yourself. You'll get it back tomorrow when we meet with the captain about your odd behavior."

He screeched, "You can't take my gun!"

I replied, "You dumb ass. I took your gun, and you're lucky I didn't kick your ass for pointing it at me. You have a real problem, and it's not me."

The next morning, I asked Captain Simmons to meet me at the OC&R safe house about some trouble I was having with my partner. During the meeting, I showed the captain the Polaroid photograph I took of Sharkey the night before and advised him of the allegations Sharkey had leveled against me. I went on to report, "Sharkey pulled his gun on me, so I took it away for safekeeping. I could have arrested him for assault on a police officer."

Captain Simmons asked, "Why did you take Sharkey's picture?"

I replied, "He was taking my photograph. I just wanted him to know what it was like to be under surveillance."

Captain Simmons then called Detective Sharkey in and wanted to hear his side of the story.

Sharkey lied and said, "I was working surveillance on L Street, N.W. for a meeting between two suspected mobsters when Jagen jumped into my car, and assaulted me." He ended by saying, "Jagen took the gun out of my briefcase that was laying open on the seat and refused to give it back."

Shaking my head and looking at Sharkey I asked, "What? Was I one of the suspected mobsters you had 'under surveillance'?" Turning to the Captain I said, "Everything he said is a lie, Captain. This guy is a crazy paranoid who sees everyone other than himself connected to the Mafia. I can't partner with him anymore. He doesn't trust me, and I don't think he has my back. Is there something that can be done?"

Captain Simmons stated bluntly, "You have to work out your personality issues. There is nothing I can do." He closed with, "Sharkey, you should know better than to pull your weapon on your partner. I am sure that's why he took it away from you. Jagen, I didn't put you out there to go rogue. You two work out your differences before you find yourselves walking a beat together at the Blue Plains Waste Treatment Plant. This matter is closed and, by the way, it never occurred."

After that, Detective Sharkey pretty much stayed clear of me. I fed him information on gambling and mobsters that came into the clubs I had under surveillance, while I continued to work on getting closer into the IRA's gun running operation.

Chapter Twenty-two

Back-to-Back

It was hard to sit in bars for twelve to sixteen hours a day and not get drunk. People always wanted to buy the artist a drink, but Michael had a way of keeping the drinks from affecting me. Having an art show in the pub helped as a good explanation of why I spent so much time there.

One day, Michael told me to bring a deck of playing cards with me to the pub, totally out of the blue. That day a strange big bruiser of a guy came in the Black Rooster and sat on the bar stool next to me. I noticed Carl McGuiness was not as active in the pub, as he normally was. He seemed to be a wee bit worried about the guy sitting next to me.

Michael said, "Pull out the cards. Then lay out three cards face down on the bar, under them lay out seven cards face up." I did as he directed and the guy next to me looked at me with a funny smile. Michael continued, "Now lay seven more cards face up on top of the first seven cards so you can see the faces of all fourteen cards." Michael went on to say, "When the man asks what you are doing tell him, 'I am reading cards.' Then ask if he wants his done."

Before I could finish my thought to ask Michael, "What if he doesn't ask..."

The guy interrupts, "What are you doing?"

I had to snicker in my mind. Ahh, Michael, you are amazing!

"I'm reading cards. Want yours done?" I asked.

"Sure," he answered. "No charge, right?"

"First time is free," came the reply that wasn't from my mind, but Michael's. Through me Michael asked, "What is it you want to know?"

The man leaned back on the bar stool and replied, "I want to know if I am going to get the business, or am I going to have to give them the business?"

I thought to myself, "What kind of question is that?"

Michael told me to flip over the three top cards. I did as he instructed.

Then he spoke through me again saying, "This first one, the Jack of Spades, represents you. The second, the Ten of Diamonds, represents a lot of money and the last one, the black and white Joker, represents a group of very greedy, dangerous men."

The dude became very intrigued and said, "Go on."

Michael told me to continue to lay all the cards out slowly, face up, so the man could see all fifty-four cards to include the jokers. When I finished laying all the cards out, Michael instructed me to stare at the guy, look directly into his eyes and tell him what I heard the cards say. He assured me that the cards would continue to speak to me once he stopped relaying messages.

Okay, game on, I thought.

After finishing the card spread I said, "The cards say you will be dead within five years, and you know it."

He nodded his head.

I continued, "The cards have a lot of war and ugliness in them that don't pertain to your question. What they said in answer to your question was, you will get the business. You will have all of it, by Saturday morning."

The man was outwardly happy to hear that.

He exclaimed, "I knew you were a reader! My mother, God rest her soul, was a card reader too, from the old country."

The man bought me a Jack Daniels on the rocks, the same as he was drinking.

After a few minutes, he said, "I like you son. You're a card." He chuckled, continuing in a gruff voice, "but you better be right for McGuiness' sake."

I answered, "The Jack of Spades tells me you are a man, who lives by the sword, but you won't die by the sword."

The man laughed.

About half an hour later, Carl McGuiness came over to the man and said, "Charlie, I just got the call. You will have all of it, by Saturday morning."

The man smiled and said, "McGuiness, you should keep this kid around. He's a good luck charm."

The man got up and walked to the restroom.

Carl asked me what that was all about. I told him that I was bored, so I did a card reading for the guy.

I whispered, "The cards said the same thing you told him, that he'd get it all by Saturday morning, but the cards weren't showing me what 'It' was."

I questioned Mr. McGuiness, "What's he going to get? It felt like it was a lot of money."

In a low, cowering type of voice, he asked, "Do you know who that guy is?"

I answered, "No."

Carl said, "He's the Devil! That's Charlie 'The Blade', a big-time Genovese family capo and businessman, out of South Florida. He's known for cutting people up, if they don't pay when payment is due."

A waiter interrupted us.

Carl lowered his voice even more, and then went on to say, "I made a mistake arranging a loan through Charlie for some of my business partners in Miami and Atlantic City last year. They have been avoiding him, so he's been sent to pay me a visit."

Being the snoop that I was, I asked, "How much money?"

All McGuiness said was, "A lot!"

When Charlie came back to the bar from the restroom, Carl introduced me as an up and coming local artist, "Sir Eduardo," the painter, who did the picture that was hanging over the bar. Charlie didn't seem to care about that.

He said, "Maybe you can come paint my kitchen someday."

I said, laughing, "I do kitchens. I'll do almost anything for a buck."

Charlie reached in his pocket and pulled out a wad of cash that would choke a horse. He peeled off a hundred-dollar bill. Laying it on the bar in front of me he said, "I want you to go with me tonight to a friendly poker game. Bring your cards. You might make some money, reading cards for the hard heads that will be there. I'll pick you up here at midnight. We're just going a block down the street."

I nodded my head and replied, "Okay."

Later that evening, I called Detective Sharkey and told him who I had met. He told me to come to the OC&R safe house for a full debriefing. He also wanted me to look at some photographs of a known mobster I should keep an eye out for in case they were in the crowd.

I arrived at the safe house. Detective Sharkey kept everything professional, but I could tell he was still harboring animosity about me embarrassing him in front of the Captain. He showed me all the photographs.

In one photograph, I identified the man at the bar as Charles Delmonico, AKA Charlie "The Blade" Tourine, a mobster that dated back to Lucky Luciano.

After the meeting, I returned to the Black Rooster about midnight and waited. Carl McGuiness had gone home.

At 12:45 a.m., a beautiful woman, in a long white sequined evening gown, walked into the bar, asking for the artist Sir Eduardo.

I said, "That's me."

She said, "Charlie sent me to pick you up, but the game isn't going to start until 1:30 a.m."

Her name was Ruby Begonia. She had long, wavy, black hair and a southern accent. We had a drink together to kill time.

She said, "I heard you painted the Black Rooster piece over the bar."

Shaking my head, I said back, "I did."

Then she said, "That cock bird is nice, but I prefer nudes. I just love the male anatomy."

I didn't comment. I knew she was trying to register on the old peter-meter. She was obviously a very high priced working girl, way above my pay grade *and* desires.

Michael impressed upon me, "Be careful with her. Don't turn her on and don't turn her off because it could comprise the case later."

I told Ruby, "I don't find the male body very interesting, but I'd love to have you sit for me one day."

We both laughed.

"I don't sit well. I lay much, much better," she said with a wink. "My, oh my, you blush so cute. Do you know when you blush your freckles sparkle?" she asked.

Thank God it was time to leave. I can handle ugly, old thugs, but a pretty girl, with a southern accent, is like kryptonite to me.

Ruby walked me down the street to a hotel and supper club, known as Fran O' Brian's Anthony House, in the 1800 block of L street N.W. We took the elevator up to the Penthouse. She knocked on the door to the Presidential suite. When the door opened, I was searched by a couple of bouncer bodyguards, before I could enter. Ruby told them, "Watch it fellas, he's not into guys."

Laughing, one of them said, "That's good. Neither are we!"

I was glad that Michael had me leave my gun and badge in my car that night.

When we got into the suite, it was set up like a Las Vegas private casino. Ruby was the hostess and was very flirtatious, with all the guests. Like I said, she was a working girl, and she really knew how to work a room. Charlie was seated at one of the poker tables. He asked me to stand behind him for luck. He won seven hands in a row, talking the whole time about what a fantastic card reader I was. He told the guys at the table, "Not the gambling kind of card reader, the psychic kind. He can tell you things that only your momma knows, and he only charges a "C note" for the reading." That's one hundred dollars in gangster slang.

Charlie drummed up business for me, then had me taken into the next room where a table with two chairs had been set up.

The first person to come in was a fellow in his sixties, by the name of Rocky. He just wanted to know what life had in store for him. I felt Charlie told him to see me to start the ball rolling.

I laid out the first three cards. First card was the two-eyed Jack of Diamonds, followed by the two of clubs then the one-eyed Jack of Hearts. I laid out the first row and the seventh card was the Queen of Hearts.

I said, "A woman wants you to make peace with the one-eyed Jack before it's too late. Her name is Evelyn, and she sends her love." I was amazed at how the information flowed from the cards. It all seemed to make sense to Rocky.

Then cards started talking about horses, but one horse in particular, Dawn, was a fake. Then they talked about the one-eyed jack, dying, and that Rocky's cancer was returning. Rocky told me that he owned racehorses and was about to buy a racehorse named Irish Dawn for two hundred thousand dollars within a week.

I said, "The cards advise against the purchase because the breeding records are false."

Rocky told me that Jackie was the name of his brother, who ran off with his wife over thirty years earlier, and they haven't seen each other since.

I said, "There is so much hate in the cards over something."

Rocky said, "In a fit of rage, I shot at Jackie twice and missed, but the second bullet hit the door frame and a piece of wood flew up, blinding Jackie in one eye."

I said, "Wow, then he is the one-eyed Jack that broke your heart."

Michael shared with me that Rocky's hatred for his brother was the cause of his cancer, and his mother wants him to know that, if he truly forgives his brother, his cancer will go away.

I relayed to Rocky, "Hate is like drinking poison and waiting for the other guy to die. That Queen of Hearts is the woman, Evelyn, and she says that your hatred for Jackie is causing your cancer. Forgive your brother, and your cancer will go away."

He started to weep.

He handed me five twenty-dollar bills and went to leave the room. At the door, he turned and said, "You've given me a lot to think about. Charlie said you were good! I just didn't know how good."

I asked, "One more thing that isn't clear, do you know who Evelyn is?"

Rocky said, "My mother. She's been dead for twenty-five years. When I shot my brother, it broke my mother's heart, and she never recovered. She took the sorrow to her grave."

The next fellow to come in was, Barry, who only wanted to know if his wife was cheating on him.

I informed him, "The cards say no…"

He interrupted, "That's great."

I went on laying down cards, as I finished what I started to say, "…no more than you are cheating on her."

He said, "That no good cheating bitch."

I continued, "Your cards say that your wife has a picture with proof that you have been cheating on her. She plans to file for divorce within three months and sue you, taking everything you have."

He wanted to know what to do.

I told him, "The cards say to hire a private investigator to follow her. Looks like she's sloppy, and you will get more on her than she has on you, within a week."

Happy with that information, Barry paid me and left.

I did three more readings, then went out into the gaming room to watch.

Ruby brought me a Jack Daniels on the rocks from Charlie who was the big winner so far that night. I watched how the same players would move from table to table, and they would be winning every time they'd sit down. I was trying to figure out what was going on.

Michael told me to watch the dealers. I couldn't catch how they were cheating, but I knew enough about cards that if you control the deck, you could control who wins. It was no wonder Charlie was winning so much. The dealers were in his pocket, and I was his diversion. The host of the game, Mickey Sparks, wanted to keep his mob guests happy, while fleecing the out-of-town high rollers that came to play. The suite had four Poker tables, two Black Jack tables, a Craps table and Roulette wheel. The great room held about fifty to seventy-five people. People came and went all night.

There were also three bedrooms in the suite, where Ruby and her six girls were keeping the men entertained for a thousand dollars plus, per date. I could tell when she or one of the girls struck pay dirt because they would slyly slip away into one of the rooms with their john.

I overheard a couple of players talking about the women. One of them said that Sparks could supply any age for a special price in rooms down the hall, if desired. It made me sick to my stomach and took everything I had not to blow my cover. I couldn't believe the level of illegal vice that Mickey Sparks was running.

I was jogged out of my disbelief when I noticed Charlie was in one corner, talking to a man that looked like Joe Nesline, a local D.C. gambler, who had ties to the New York mob. They were arguing, and Nesline left angry. One of the bodyguards saw me watching and told me to return to my room because several guests wanted card readings. He also informed me, "Mr. Sparks is expecting fifty percent of your take for bringing the clients and supplying the room."

I casually said, "Of course. No problem."

About 5:30 a.m., I had completed eighteen readings, and there didn't seem to be any further interest in my services. Charlie had left the suite about an hour earlier, and I didn't want to over stay my welcome, so I approached Mickey Sparks. I thanked him for inviting me to perform at his event. I told him that I gave eighteen readings at one hundred dollars each. I then handed him nine hundred dollars in cash.

He said, "What no tips? I get half of the tip money as well."

I said, "No tips tonight. Sorry."

I counted out another two hundred dollars and handed it to him saying, "But I tip my host. Thank you, sir."

Sparks shoved the money in his pocket without counting it saying, "Kid, I've heard nothing but good things about the information you and your cards gave my guests tonight. You sent more than one guy out of here crying. Charlie said you are a very gifted fellow. Maybe I will have you read my cards next time, but I'm a big boy and big boys don't cry."

I said, "But real men do. I don't need a deck of cards to tell your fortune, Mr. Sparks. You are the spark of good fortune." Waving my fist full of cash in the air, I continued, "Look at all the money you made for me tonight. I see a big house and you surrounded, by people who want to know the secret of your success in the future."

He smiled and liked the image I presented.

What I didn't tell him was the big house was a prison and the men that surrounded him were F.B.I. agents, looking to charge him with racketeering. That night launched a six-month investigation into a traveling casino that would set up in different hotels every Wednesday, Friday and Saturday around the greater Washington/Baltimore area. Michael and I were more interested in the sexual exportation of children and female sex slaves, but Detective Sharkey wanted a big mob gambling bust.

One morning, several months later, after one of the casino parties ended at a suite in the Watergate Hotel complex, I wasn't feeling well, so I left early. As I was walking to my car, I saw Ruby about twenty yards ahead. When she got to her white Volvo, a black male walked across the street and engaged her in conversation. Then they walked into a nearby alley.

I thought, "No way. She may be a whore, but she's not that cheap."

Michael blasted me with "Be careful." He reminded me that this was the same alley where the KGB agent attacked me, with the black jack a year earlier.

When I got to my car, I grabbed my gun and badge. A couple of plastic handcuff ties fell out of the glove compartment, so I took them as well. I then continued down to where I saw the two enter the alley. Midway down and next to a dumpster, I saw Ruby on her knees. The black man was standing over her holding a gun to her head.

He said, "Unzip it bitch. Now pull it out and start sucking."

As she started to pleasure the man, he spotted me, watching. I quickly turned to the wall and acted like I was peeing on the side of the building.

The two were about fifteen yards down the alley, near a green dumpster. I didn't know what to do. I had a vision of the man pistol whipping Ruby, after he had his way with her, and then throwing her body in the dumpster. I knew I had to get closer...but how, without being shot.

Michael said, "Act drunk and start walking toward them."

The first thing that popped into my head was a James Taylor song. Acting drunk, I started singing, "When you're down and in trouble, and you need a helping hand."

The man yelled, "Get the fuck out of here man, before I shoot your white ass."

I continued to stagger forward, ignoring the warning and singing louder, "And nothing, whoa nothing is going right."

When I was about ten feet away from them I said, "Hey man what you doing with that hot chick? Can I get some of that too?"

Just then, my sick stomach erupted. I bent forward and vomited on the ground. I staggered even closer to the man. When I stood back up, I had my gun in one hand, as I knocked his gun to the ground with the other. I cocked my pistol, sticking the barrel between his eyes.

I smiled and said, "You've got a friend. Asshole." Ruby picked up his gun from the pavement and pointed at his crotch.

I said to Ruby, "Now what do you want to do with Horse-Dick Harry here?"

There was no way we could call the police. There would be too many questions, and it could blow my cover. Michael said that Ruby knew a lot about things we needed to know and told me to use this moment to our advantage.

"Go to the Howard Johnson's on the corner and order a couple cups of coffee. I will be right down," I told Ruby, as I took the .32 cal semi-auto Beretta from her hand.

As she passed, she kissed me on the cheek and said, "Thank you."

Once she was gone, I told the guy, "This is your lucky day. I should just shoot you in the head and be done with it." I cuffed him from behind then sliding the door open on the dumpster, I tossed him inside. "You're garbage," I informed him, as I slid the door closed.

I walked to a nearby phone booth and called Detective Sharkey. I advised him of what took place, and asked if he would have the local detectives fish the guy out of the dumpster. I was sure this wasn't the first time the guy attacked a woman in the area. He was most likely wanted for assault, if not something worse.

When I walked into the Howard Johnson's, Ruby was excited to see me. She was like a young schoolgirl out on her first date, rather than a high-priced hooker, who had just been attacked in an alley. I took a drink of my coffee. She asked me what I did with the black man.

I said, "I did the same thing to him that he had planned for you. I tossed his body in the dumpster where garbage belongs." I know she thought I killed him, but she never asked. Perks for me.

She asked me, "Why do you have a gun?"

I said, "Everybody in this town has a gun. I keep it close for special times when I might need it to help a friend." We laughed because of the song I was singing to distract the perp, "You've got a friend." That seemed to be my rescue song.

I asked, "What's a nice girl like you doing, working for a lowlife like Mickey Sparks?"

She responded, "Mickey won me and three other girls in a high stakes poker game back in New Orleans five years ago."

I learned that she had been abducted off a Houston street, walking home from school one day. She was only fourteen years old at the time. The police listed her as a runaway because she ran away from home before. When I pressed her on why she ran away, she told me her mother's boyfriend was raping her every day and her mother did nothing about it. Her mother told her that they were living in the man's house, so he could do whatever he wanted.

She went on to say that the kidnappers injected her with heroin until she was hooked, then sold her as a prostitute, into the sex trade in Mexico. The same organization that abducted her was abducting young children and infants. They then sold them on the black market to families in South America and Europe. The group took it to another level, having a ranch near Durango Mexico, where they kept young abducted white girls they used as "baby making machines," selling the infants to the adoption market.

She cried, while she was telling her story. Although she never admitted it, I felt that she was made to bear children that she would never see again. I couldn't believe how much information was flowing and how low humans could stoop for the almighty dollar.

I walked her to the car and made sure she was on her way safely. I was sick to my stomach and deeply angered by everything I heard.

Michael cautioned me to never get angry. Indignant yes, anger no, and righteous indignation is even better.

Several hours later, I met with Detective Sharkey and gave him a written report of all the investigative leads Ruby had given me on the international white slavery, prostitution and child abduction Mexican cartel.

Sharkey informed me that he would disseminate the information to the FBI.

"I do have some news for you as well. Our task force funding has been cut by Congress, and we are all being sent back to our units."

I couldn't believe my ears. We had finally uncovered a huge lead into some major organized crime, plus we had a source that could walk me into the middle of it... and the money runs out!

Detective Sharkey wanted to bust Mickey Sparks and the illegal gambling operation, as our parting shot. Most of all, he wanted to catch Joe Nesline inside the gaming because Joe, like Charlie the Blade, was considered a big fish in our little pond. Sharkey wanted to make a name for himself and locking up Joe Nesline would do it.

Two days after making my report to Sharkey, I showed up at the Black Rooster for my usual day of cards, drinks and art. I heard that Joe Nesline had some of his guys watching Sparks, who was accused of taking a personal skim off the top of the money taken in from the operation.

Whether or not that was true didn't seem to matter. Mickey was replaced by a very unpleasant follow, by the name of Bobby Dealer Diago, out of Atlantic City. Bobby was a hard-core mobster that didn't trust anyone. I met him a couple of times at games in prior months, and he didn't seem to like the fact that I was making money off the gamblers. He told Mickey that the money I took in could have been lost at the tables.

On the night of the planned big bust, I was waiting in Rice's Supper Club on M St. NW, next to the CBS News building. The bartender was Belfast Harry. When the casino was ready to go, one of the bouncers was positioned to call Harry and give him the address. Harry would then give the address to the scouts that were bringing in the gamblers. Since I had been working at the games and was brought in by Ruby Begonia, I was considered a trusted regular.

They had checks in place to keep unwanted guests and the police out.

I brought Linda with me to the Supper Club that night because I had to get the address to Sharkey for the search warrant. The plan was, I would get the

134

address and pass it to Linda. After I left the bar while on route to the game, she would leave and, on her way home, call Detective Sharkey, with the location and a precise time to serve the search warrant.

Unfortunately, that was the same night that Belfast Harry and his crew were moving a truckload of automatic weapons, ammunition and explosives from a barn in Laurel, Maryland. The final destination was Boston Harbor where the guns would be loaded on a ship bound for Nova Scotia.

Harry's people were scattered throughout the Eastern Seaboard buying black market automatic weapons. He had just purchased ammunition, explosives and another twenty-five AR-15 semi-automatic, assault rifles, using the counterfeit documents he had printed. Harry and his cousin, Billy O'Shea, had just converted the guns to fully automatic M-16's. It was my understanding that the IRA had other coordinators, like Belfast Harry, in other parts of the country, sending weapons to be loaded on that same ship that night.

I wanted to get out of the gambling investigation and pursue the guns, but the task force agent in charge said that we could take both cases down at the same time, if we played this right. I didn't know the name of the ship the IRA was using. I just knew that it was a fishing boat in Gloucester Harbor being protected by a Boston gang and a guy Harry called Whitey. Whitey was said to be crazy, but very sympathetic to the IRA's cause. He and his crew helped Billy O'Shea raise a lot of money and guns in the Boston area.

I didn't trust the Feds, but I was ordered to turn all my information over to the AT&F Agents. I made a deal with the Agent in Charge. I told him the intelligence I had on the driver of the truck, Harry Donavan. He was very paranoid about being followed, and they would be better off only using two surveillance vehicles and a spotter plane. They agreed. I also gave them a head's up that I was working on driving up with Harry Hillock, with the next shipment, if by chance things didn't go well with this shipment.

The board was set, and the pieces were moving.

Chapter Twenty-three

The Big Takedown

Tension was building in the bar. The Casino Scouts had drawn a large group of out of town high rollers, and they were ready to go. While we were waiting at Rice's Supper Club, a local drug dealer came in, with a couple of bodyguards. I recognized one of them as Butch Carson, an old friend of my brothers, during their gangland days in Palmer Park. This was "B Double A, BAD!"

Carson knew that I was a police detective. Things could get dicey.

Michael told me to grab Linda and get out of there fast. Linda was having fun with Belfast Harry, who was letting her sample some fine wines that he was serving, during a wine tasting in the dining room.

I whispered to Linda, "Get our coats and meet me at the back door. We have to get out of here."

She was having too much fun, with her private wine tasting, and didn't feel the urgency, she snipped, "No, I'm not ready to leave."

I tried to hide my face from Carson, but he spotted me. Knowing that I was police, fearing that I was there to spy on his boss, he panicked and yelled, "Hey, Jagen, are you still a cop?"

Lucky for me no one heard what he said. Thank God, Harry was preoccupied with Linda. I shook my head no, then nodded motioning for him to follow me upstairs to the owner's private billiards room. I could see that he was high on something and acting foolish. I was hoping to capitalize on his vulnerability.

When we got upstairs, I racked the balls and said, "Let's shoot a game of nine ball." During the game, I said, "You need to think long and hard about what you're going to do next. There are several Federal Agents downstairs, getting ready to serve arrest warrants on some fugitives that are supposed to be coming in later." He made a dash to the stairs. I tripped him with my pool stick, and he fell against the table. When he got up, I threw him on the pool table. I picked up the eight ball, held it to his mouth and said, "Butch, my old friend, you have a choice. Get your friends and leave, or go to jail right now for obstruction of a federal investigation. What's it gonna' be?"

He hesitated.

I dropped the ball and slapped him saying, "Okay it's jail, and you're the first to go!"

He quickly responded, "Okay, okay we'll leave."

I then said, "And don't tell your friends what we're doing. Just tell them it's not safe here and leave."

Butch seemed to come to his senses. He shook his head in agreement saying, "Yeah, I'm cool with it. Thanks."

I said, "Now get yourself together and follow me down stairs. I'll be watching you all the way out the door." True to my word, I watched as he whispered in the ear of one of his guys, and one by one they all headed for the door. They left without an incident. I started breathing again.

By the time I got back to the bar, Belfast Harry had been given the address for the casino. He passed it to me. I finished my drink and wrote the address and time to hit the casino on a cocktail napkin for Linda to pass on to Detective Sharkey. Michael told me the best time to have the police hit the casino was 3:30 a.m. sharp... not one minute before or one minute after. That's what I told Linda to make sure she expressed to Sharkey.

When I got to the casino, the rules had changed. I was searched for any weapons and recording devices. Bobby Deal pushed me backward and said, "You a cop, Jagen?"

I pushed back and countered, "Shit no, what makes you say that?"

"Apparently, someone at the bar asked if you were still a cop. I'm just double checking," he retorted.

"Yeah," I said, "what an asshole. He's an old school friend of my brother's and likes to bust my balls. Ever since we ran in the gang circuit, he has a standing joke to scream, 'Hey you still a cop?' when he sees one of us. It's a dumb joke that's not very funny. What can I say? He's high most of the time."

Deal looked very suspicious.

To lighten the tension, I said, "If you don't want me to come in, just say the word, and I'll leave."

Bobby was perplexed. He was in a tight spot. I was there. I already knew the address, and if I was a cop, he had to keep an eye on my movements. He said, "If you come in, you play. No card readings tonight; and if you come in, you stay until we close. We don't want any unwanted visitors after you leave."

I said, "I didn't bring enough money to play. Let me do a few readings, and I'll build up a stake, so I can afford to play. Is it a deal?"

He agreed.

Ruby Begonia and the girls were not there that night. I was glad. I didn't want to see her get busted with the rest of the losers. It was a small suite of rooms for gambling only. I set up my card reading table in one corner. I had been consulting, with a number of players over the months about business deals and personal matters. And it was great to hear that things were going well for them.

I did think it odd how I cared about these people, personally, even though they were breaking the law. I thought that the only reason, playing the numbers and the casinos was illegal was because the government didn't have a way to tax them. It was the same thing for arresting people for marijuana possession. Michael showed a vision, that in the not so distant future, numbers, casinos and marijuana stores would be licensed because local governments will need the tax revenue to balance their budgets.

I guess the saying is true, "Where there is the will, there is a way."

After several readings that night I had about six hundred dollars built up, and I was ready to play a few hands.

Michael declared, "In celebration of the end of the task force, I'm going to help you win tonight."

He did not disappoint. Within an hour and twenty minutes I had over five thousand dollars in chips, sitting in front of me. I looked at my watch, and it was 1:30 a.m. Bobby Dealer was passing out cigars to the high rollers, and the room was getting smoky. I got up from the table, raised the blinds and opened the window behind me. I looked down the street from the fourth floor. It was raining. Bobby sent one of the bouncers over to close the blinds. I think he thought it was some covert signal I was using. He shook his head no and wiggled his index finger at me as if to scold. I waved my hand in front of my face and coughed to let him know that the smoke was getting to me.

By 2:00 o'clock, when I had over ten thousand dollars in chips, I wanted to cash out while I was ahead, but Bobby wasn't having any of that. He saw that I was on a winning streak, so he told me to sit back down and play. I'm sure he was wondering how I was winning so much, since his dealers were controlling who wins and who loses.

For the next forty-five minutes, I'd win a hand then lose a hand, but my stacks of chips seemed to increase.

At 2:45 it was time to change tables. It was some new rule Bobby made up to keep the game and the players fresh. The players got to call the game, but the house always dealt. I fixed a shrimp salad sandwich and a Jack Daniels on the rocks and then sat back down to resume play.

The next player called, "Seven card stud." The ante was two hundred and fifty dollars, with no limit on the raises. I started with two aces in the hole... the Ace of Diamonds, the Ace of Clubs, with a Four of Hearts showing. The cards were "talking" to me. I was going to get four aces and win this hand, but I had to keep it low key, so I didn't run people out, by being too enthusiastic with my raises. I simply called the bet. By the time the bet came back around to me, it was twelve hundred to stay. I called again. My next card was an eight of spades. That meant hurry, no time to waste.

The cost of playing went up again. It was eighteen hundred to stay. I called again. I didn't have to raise. It appeared the other eight people at the table had great cards too. My fifth card was the Ace of Hearts, and the pile of chips in the center of the table was the largest pot of the night. I called again. My sixth card was a Deuce of Diamonds.

I glanced at my watch it was 3:00 a.m. I thought, "I've got thirty minutes to catch that forth ace and cash out before Detective Sharkey and the troops knock on the door."

I looked at that huge pile of chips in the center of the table.

Bobby was smoking a big cigar and smiling at me. I could see that he felt it was his lucky day and intended to take fifty percent of my winnings. I thought, "Not tonight asshole." A few people dropped out of the hand. It was twenty-six hundred for me to stay. I called, but my chips had all but run out.

I looked at Bobby. I didn't have enough to stay in the game.

Bobby said, "Sir Eduardo, do you want credit, with a fifty-fifty split interest?"

I said, "No I can't afford that." The last thing I wanted to do was owe Bobby Dealer money, and I knew the task force wasn't going to cover me, if I lost the hand.

Michael was working something, but I couldn't trust that it was going to be in my favor.

I looked at Bobby and said, "I guess I'm out."

Bobby's curiosity got the best of him. He had to see what I was sitting on. When he looked at my two aces in the hole and one ace on the board, I knew he was jumping for joy inside, but maintained a worried expression on his face. He didn't want to give away my hand. Then he looked at the other cards on the table. Other than my Ace of Hearts, he didn't see the other aces out.

He said, "That's a real long shot, Jagen, but okay, I will cover your last card."

I rolled my eyes and said, "Shit, Bobby, you just gave away my hand. I might as well fold."

He said, "Do what you want," and went back to the stool he was sitting on by the front door.

I was going to cash in after this hand, fix another sandwich and wait for the Calvary to knock the door down. My mind went to wondering how the surveillance was going on the IRA's truckload of guns.

I could feel Michael was worried about something, but he wasn't communicating with me. When I probed my subconscious for some insight, he told me to keep my mind on the game.

There had to be at least seventy thousand dollars in chips in the middle of that table. The seventh card was dealt. I caught the Ace of Spades, but I tried to look disappointed. I had four aces, but I didn't want anyone to know. I winked at Bobby, and he smiled. The betting went crazy. Apparently, everybody had a good hand.

Just as I looked at my card again, there was that knock at the door, followed by the last thing I wanted to hear at that time, "Open up. This is the police with a search warrant." I grabbed my seven cards just as the dealer, who was sitting across from me, flipped the table. It was raining poker chips. I was knocked backward to the floor, chair and all.

The door flew open, and the apartment was now swarming, with uniformed police officers. As I started to climb to my feet, I was grabbed by an overzealous police officer. He threw me up against the closed window blinds that had the open window behind them. I went through the blinds, knocking the screen out of the window. It fell to the sidewalk below. I just knew I was going to fall four floors to my death. I felt something pulling me back in, and then I heard Michael say, "Where do you think you're going, little bird?"

That was a close one.

The police officer handcuffed me behind my back, took the playing cards from my hands, looked at them and said, "Hey guys, this loser has four aces. I guess he won an all-expenses paid trip to jail." All the cops started laughing.

I noticed Detective Sharkey, standing by the door, smiling. I knew he purposely hit the door early just to spite me.

We were all charged with illegal gambling, possession of implements of a crime, and operation of an illegal vice establishment. Detective Sharkey took control of me and walked me down the stairs to the waiting police wagon. It was

3:25 a.m., as we reached the back of the police patrol wagon. A black Lincoln Continental, driven by Joe Nesline, passed by.

I said, "Sharkey, that's why I wanted you to hit the door at 3:30. You caught a bunch of minnows and missed the big fish you were hoping to catch. You should have trusted me."

He had nothing to say.

As the other prisoners were put into the back of the wagon, some of the casino scouts and bouncers were looking at me, with suspicion. I knew one of them at Rice's Supper Club heard Butch Carson ask if I was still a cop, but I didn't know who it was. I also didn't know how many other people Bobby Dealer told. I had to do something to take the focus away from me being a cop.

I started shaking and saying, "I can't go to jail. It will ruin my career as an artist. I have never been arrested before." I tried to be convincing but felt it wasn't working. Michael told me to piss my pants. The wagon made a hard-left turn, and we all went flying off the benches and landed on a pile in the middle of the truck. I let it go. When I stood up to retake my seat on the bench everyone saw the front of my pants was soaking wet.

I said, "Sorry guys, but I am scared to death."

They seemed to lighten up. I certainly didn't act like a cop who had just busted a bunch of gamblers. Several of the guys had been sitting at my table when the police came through the door.

One of them asked, "Did you really have four aces?" I nodded my head yes.

He said, "I had a full house," and started laughing.

One of the other guys said, "Yeah, and now we are a full Paddy wagon."

We were all taken to the Central Cell Block and booked. I hadn't been in lock up since the Park Police Motorman arrested me at the antiwar demonstration several years earlier. It hadn't changed a bit. Everyone posted bail except me. I seemed to be out of the loop. I didn't have any money or a lawyer to call to get me out. Detective Sharkey was the only one I had, and I knew he was just going to let me rot, until arraignment the next morning. I settled in for the rest of the night. Since I peed my pants I stank, so none of my cellmates wanted anything to do with me. That was a good thing. About an hour later, I was removed from my cell and taken to an interrogation room.

A short time later two AT&F Special Agents came in and told me that the surveillance on the IRA's truck, carrying the weapons did not go well. They did as I suggested and used only two vehicles, with a spotter plane, to follow the truck from Laurel to the New York state line, but when they entered the New York region, they were told to drop back while special agents from that jurisdiction continued a rolling surveillance. As the story goes, when the truck filled with weapons entered a circle in New York City, the driver missed his turn. By the time he went back around the circle to make the right turn, the circle was totally clogged, with FBI surveillance vehicles. Everyone jumped out of their vehicles with guns drawn, but it was too late. The driver and passenger in the truck jumped out and then disappeared in the city. The agents seized the truck and the weapons, but didn't have any arrests or anyone for questioning. They asked me to go back out in the street to learn the name of the ship the weapons were destined for in Boston Harbor.

I couldn't believe my ears. How could they possibly have screwed this up? I shook my head, but agreed to do my best.

I went home and took a long hot bath and then called Linda, who was at work, to let her know what had happened.

She flared in a frustrated voice, "It's too dangerous, Ed. You've been accused of being a cop. The word will spread, if it hasn't already. I have a bad feeling about it."

I countered her by saying, "Michael will let me know what to do. Just like he told me to tell you to get the coats last night and leave. If you had done that, none of this would have happened, baby. I'll be careful. I love you and will call you later."

I got dressed and went back downtown.

It was about 10:30 a.m. when I caught up with Belfast Harry. He was having breakfast at Rice's. I told him that I got busted in the casino, with the other guys.

He said, "Yeah, I heard there was a raid, and you pissed yourself after being arrested. There's talk about you being a police informant."

I didn't know what to do, so I said, "That's bullshit. Some guy I went to school with came in here last night and was screwing with me. Do I look like a cop?"

I thought, "That's a dumb thing to say. What does a cop look like?"

Harry wouldn't talk to me. He told me that Billy wanted me to get my paintings out of his club, immediately.

"I'm screwed," I thought.

Just then Billy O'Shea came in and the two went upstairs to the billiard room to talk privately. I started removing my art and put the paintings in my car.

When they came back downstairs, they were acting like we were friends again and wanted to know if I would give them a ride out to Baltimore.

Michael responded with a quick, "Don't do it. They plan on torturing you to find out how much you know about their gun running operation."

I told Billy and Harry, "I'm going to take the paintings to another hotel that wants them in Arlington, Virginia. I should be back this way in a couple of hours and can take you then." They wanted to ride with me, but saw my Cadillac was full, and there was no room. Surprisingly, they let me go. I know Michael worked his magic on them. I went down to a nearby island, called Haines Point, and sat next to a statue called "The Awakening" to think about what I should do. It was obvious that I wasn't going to get any more information from Belfast Harry, so I had no idea how I was going to get the name of the ship.

Just then a boat passed by the island. On the back of the boat was the name "Andréa." A chill went through me. I knew it was a sign from Michael.

I couldn't trust Detective Sharkey, so I called Detective Bender. I told him what had happened to the IRA surveillance and that my cover has finally been blown. I let him know that I didn't trust Detective Sharkey or the AT&F agents with the information. Sharkey only seemed interested in getting promoted on the back of my investigations and had no concern for my safety. AT&F agents didn't care about anything other than the takedown.

I asked Bender, "If I give you the name of the ship in Boston Harbor where the weapons were to be funneled, do you think you can arrange its take down through another law enforcement agency?"

Detective Bender asked, "Where is the ship destined for, when it leaves United States waters?"

I replied, "Nova Scotia."

He said, "What do you think about Dudley Do Right."

I asked, "What?"

Detective Bender said, "We could give this case to the Royal Canadian Mounted Police."

I exclaimed, "Great idea! My sources tell me the name of the ship is Andréa."

Bender then said, "You know it's not safe out there for you anymore? You need to surface."

I said, "I know."

I then went to the OC&R safe house and told Detective Sharkey and the AT&F agents on the federal task force that, because of the casino raid, everyone thinks I am a police informant. They quasi debriefed me.

I recounted that when I located Belfast Harry, he refused to talk to me, but then wanted me to give him and Billy O'Shea a ride to Baltimore. I told them I felt it was a one-way trip for me, so I never went back.

That evening on the news, the world saw the Royal Canadian Mounted Police report they had stopped a cargo vessel, named Andréa, and seized a large quantity of automatic weapons, explosives and ammunition.

Thank you, Michael.

The following week, the entire task force was called for the closeout of the case. During the debriefing, I was asked, repeatedly, if I had any knowledge as to how the Canadian authorities got the information on the shipment of weapons.

I just shook my head and said, "I guess they just got lucky, but it doesn't really matter as long as those guns are off the street. Right?" At one point, Detective Sharkey lost it in front of the task force.

He stood up, banged his fist on the conference table and screamed, "I know Jagen was the one that passed the information on to the Royal Canadian Mounted Police. I know it!"

I said, "Man, you are going to have a heart attack, if you don't get some meds for that paranoia." Then I looked at the task force as a whole and asked, "What's wrong with you guys? Aren't you a fan of 'Dudley Do Right'? Remember, he always gets his man."

My joke fell on deaf ears, or better yet, on dry personalities.

I was advised by the task force Commander, "If we find out that you leaked information outside of this task force, you could be charged with hampering a federal investigation."

I may have been a jokester, but I was a sharp cop and knew the law. I reminded them, "It's impossible to hamper your own investigation. This was my case, and you're the ones that screwed it up. I, for one, am so glad those guns didn't get away."

After a week of official debriefing with the Fed's, our task force was officially disbanded.

My undercover career was over.

142

By the end of the week I moved to the Major Crimes Unit of the Intelligence Division. For a short while, Detective Bender was my partner. It was nice, but he took early retirement and became sheriff of a small Pennsylvania town. He was a very smart guy, and I always suspected that he was really a C.I.A. agent planted on the department. Either that, or he was working with his own set of angels. I heard the real reason he left was he was suspected of tipping off the C.I.A., who passed the information to the Mounties.

Our unit's job was to evaluate unsolved crime and form working relationships with neighboring law enforcement jurisdictions on crimes that cross over state lines. We focused on large scale fencing operations, murder for hire and abducted children.

Eight months into my new position, I received a subpoena to testify in the IRA gun running case in Baltimore, Maryland. The Assistant United States Attorney and AT&F agents were having trouble, moving the IRA gun running case forward in court.

When the AUSA started interviewing agents, she couldn't find anyone that knew how the case originated and what exactly tied Harry Hillock to the guns. Then she found my name in the file and debriefed me. She concluded that I was the source of most of the information, so she put me on the stand.

In court, Belfast Harry didn't seem to be surprised to learn I was a deep cover police investigator. From his reaction, I was sure now that the last time I saw him and Billy O'Shea, they intended to kill me, thinking I was a snitch.

After my testimony, all the defendants were found guilty. A week later in a British newspaper that covered the trial and gun running case, it was rumored that there was a one-million-dollar murder contract, put out by the IRA, for Edward Jagen.

The following day, I was called into a meeting in my inspector's office, told about the contract and given a copy of the newspaper. There were people from the Department of Justice and C.I.A. in the meeting. I was told to take the threat very serious.

I said, "If I was a snitch, I could see where they'd have a problem with me, but I'm a professional just like they are. I was just an undercover investigator, trying to do my job. The IRA's problem should be with Belfast Harry. He was their weak link, and if they were truly professionals, they'd know that. It was only business. Nothing personal."

The special agent from the C.I.A. chuckled and said, "You're right, but the contract on your life makes it personal. I will relay your feeling to my sources. I hope, for your sake, they get the message."

I heard that about a year into his sentence, Belfast Harry took a header off the second floor in prison, broke his neck and died. It's funny how accidents can happen in prison.

Chapter Twenty-four

Hit List

When Mickey Starks read in the Washington Post that I was an undercover Intelligence Investigator that infiltrated the IRA and organized crime operations, he called me at the office. He said he wanted to meet for lunch and talk about someone that was looking for a hit man in D.C. He wanted to know if I was interested in the information.

Michael said that the offer was genuine, so I said, "Sure I'm always interested in protecting life and stopping the bad guys."

We met the following afternoon in his apartment at the Watergate. He told me that a young friend of his had been taking money from a retired Army Colonel who has a "death list" of eight individuals he wants killed. His friend was just scamming the Colonel for the money, but now he's scared that the Colonel was going to have him killed, if he didn't murder the guy he had been sent to kill.

I asked, "Can your friend walk me in, as a second contract enforcer?"

The following day I met with Mickey's friend, "Miami Mike," and he laid out his con of the Colonel. It would appear that he had already been paid $20,000 to castrate a former U.S. Army Captain in Boston, who testified against Colonel Ronald Thomas, at his court martial trial for misconduct.

I asked Mike, "How much of the money do you have left?"

He said he spent it all. On the QT, Mickey had told me that his friend had a thousand dollar a day heroin habit.

The Colonel worked at the Veterans Administration and gave Mike instructions to kidnap Captain James Ireland, take him to a secluded location, strip him naked and then read the following prepared statement:

"Wendy has waited one year to reap her revenge. As the life drains from your body, think about what disgusting human beings you and your fellow rapists are. May you forever be dammed to Hell, you piece of shit, as your cock and balls are sliced off and stuffed in your mouth."

Miami Mike was then to follow the instructions in the letter and take a photograph for proof of death. When the photograph was delivered to the Colonel, an additional $40,000 would be paid. It was $20,000 for the completion of the first hit, plus $20,000 up front for execution of the second person on the death list.

Mike said that Colonel Thomas claimed that three officers and five NCO's were in the Colonel's command in Germany, and got his girlfriend drunk at a private party; and then, repeatedly, raped her throughout the night. Miami Mike said that the Colonel wanted all of them to suffer before they died.

I asked Angel Michael for guidance. He said not to trust Miami Mike because he was a junkie and to get him out of the investigation completely. He could blow everything. Since the Veterans Administration Building, where the Colonel worked, was in the same general area as Rice's Supper Club, Michael warned that it was too risky for me to pose as the contract killer. He told me to select someone else to go undercover.

I contacted the Massachusetts State Police Intelligence Unit and told them what I was working on. I asked if they would be interested in helping with a "Murder for Hire" sting operation. I wanted to set up a phony murder scene to convince the Colonel that his evil plan had been carried out. The Massachusetts State Police got on board and arranged to take Captain Ireland into protective custody, until after the Colonel was arrested.

I then selected the perfect undercover officer. His name was Tyrone Davis, a black officer who was in his final week at the Police Academy. He was built like a Washington Redskins linebacker. Tyrone looked like a killer; scarred face and all.

I told Miami Mike that I wanted him out of the picture, immediately, saying, "After today you are done with all of this, unless you want to be charged with taking the $20,000. After you make the initial introduction of Tyrone Davis, excuse yourself and go to the restroom, and stay there for about ten minutes."

Mike agreed.

I told Tyrone to tell the Colonel that he didn't trust Miami Mike, because he's a junkie, and that he would take care of business, with his own team of ex-military professionals. However, the price would now be $60,000 a hit, $30,000 before and $30,000 when each job is complete. I stressed that if the Colonel bucks on the price, let him know that it is not open for negotiation. If he continues to balk, shake his hand, thank him for his time and walk away.

I said, "You showing greed will make him trust you even more."

With everyone in agreement, I put a wire on Tyrone and sent the pair out to meet with the Colonel. I also planned on videotaping everything from a mini video camera, hidden in my briefcase, a few tables away. The first meeting was at the Black Gecko restaurant near the Veterans Administration building in Northwest Washington. I arranged to have two tables near the back of the restaurant across from one another for privacy. I sat with my back to the Colonel's table. I arrived forty-five minutes early to set up my camera, so I didn't draw suspicion.

When the Colonel came in, Miami Mike made the introduction, waited a few minutes and then said, "Excuse me fellows I've got to take a crap."

While Mike was in the restroom, the Colonel told Tyrone that he felt much better that he was going to be helping him complete the jobs because he was beginning to think Mike was full of shit.

Tyrone said, "Well you know what he's doing right now, right? Taking a shit."

Both men laughed.

Tyrone went on to say, "I don't trust Mike anymore. He's a junkie, and he has already spent the twenty grand you gave him. I will clean up this mess for ten grand, and any additional jobs will cost you $30,000 upfront and $30,000 when the job is done, with proof of death photos."

Colonel Thomas was outraged stating, "That's ridiculous. We agreed on $40,000 each."

Tyrone replied, "You didn't agree to that with me. You made that agreement with a junkie, who shot up your twenty grand and never had any plans on fulfilling the contract."

At this point I'm thinking, "Geez Tyrone, what part of get up and walk out didn't you hear?"

The Colonel said, "That's too expensive. I can't afford that."

The Colonel got up to leave. I could see that everything was falling apart. I left the video camera running and walked over to the table where Tyrone and the Colonel were arguing. I pushed the Colonel back into his seat and flashed to him a look at the gun in my shoulder holster. I sat down.

Speaking to Tyrone Davis, I said, "I told you that if the Colonel bucked at the price, to get up and walk away, didn't I?" I winked at him to let him know I was trying to put things back on track.

Tyrone said, "Yes sir."

I leaned over the table at the Colonel and said, "Forgive the hired help. I'm trying to break in a new negotiator. He's good at what he does, but he's not so good at brokering a deal." I sat back in my seat and said, "My team's normal rate is $100,000 a job. That's in cash, twenties and fifties only, nothing smaller, nothing larger, in a brown paper bag, $50,000 up front and $50,000 when the job's done."

Miami Mike came out of the restroom and turned pale when he saw me, sitting at the table. He sat down and didn't know what to do.

I said, "Mike, you owe the Colonel here $20,000, but I will eat your debt and try to clean up this mess you made. You're out. Leave," I ordered.

Mike left the restaurant.

I took a breath, looked the Colonel in the eyes and said, "My maximum enforcement personnel are all ex-military and law enforcement. I can guarantee no blowback on any of us. My associate, Mr. Davis here, is giving you a professional discount because you are ex-military, and the sons of bitches you want taken out are scumbag rapists." Gritting my teeth, I continued, "I hate rapists and child molesters, but the job you want done isn't just a simple smoker where we walk up behind the Captain and shoot him in the back of the head. You want him kidnaped, tied up and read the riot act. Then you want us to slice off his cock and balls, stick them in his mouth and photograph the scene. That's a lot of work, my friend."

I laid it all out for him, so I had everything on videotape and there was no question what he wanted us to do. I continued, "We will just shoot them for forty grand each, but if you want all the trimmings, that's going to cost you a little more. I'm going back to finish my lunch now. You think about Mr. Davis' offer. If you want to walk, be my guest, but the discount only applies, while you're sitting at this table. Get up, and we are done here. Do you understand, Colonel?" I went back to my seat.

A few minutes later the Colonel said, "When will Ireland be taken out?"

Tyrone answered, "Within a week after you pay the additional $10,000 retainer. Everything else will happen within forty-eight hours of receiving the $30,000 retainer for the next person on your list."

Colonel Thomas reached across the table and shook Tyrone's hand saying, "You have a deal. I'll have the money in an hour, and I want the photos of that cock in his mouth, as soon as it is done."

Tyrone arranged to receive the money on the street and I videotaped the payment from a surveillance van.

Massachusetts State Police detectives interviewed Captain James Ireland and learned that Colonel Ronald Thomas was married, but fell in love with a German prostitute by the name of Wendy Beckman. A group of friends were celebrating Captain Ireland's retirement from the Army. They hired a couple of hookers for the party, and one of them was Wendy. There was sex, but no talk of rape until the Colonel found out. Wendy told the Colonel she had been raped, and he went on a rampage, threating to shoot the group of friends. The Army court martialed the Colonel for conduct unbecoming an officer. The group of friends testified during the Colonel's trial.

Working with detectives from Massachusetts State Police, we had Captain Ireland pose for the bloody "proof of death" photograph. We set up another meeting with the Colonel for payment and the next hit assignment. We picked him up in my Black Cadillac with cameras mounted in the dash. I had Tyrone drive, as I sat in the back. We had the Colonel sit in the front, next to Tyrone. He was very excited and wanted to see the proof of death photo immediately.

I handed him the envelope. As he held the 8" x 10" glossy of the death scene, his voice changed to a raspy sound, when he said, "Yes, bleed you bastard. Bleed out, you son of a bitch. Who's chewing on your cock now?" It was almost like he was having some strange orgasm while viewing the death scene.

"What did he say? Tell me everything," Colonel Thomas commanded.

Tyrone said, "He begged for his life and said he'd pay us whatever we asked, if we'd kill you and let him live. That's when I cut his cock off and forced it in his mouth to shut him up."

The colonial replied, "Yes, you did Wendy proud, Mr. Davis."

Tyrone said, "Let me have the photo, Colonel. We dissolved the body in acid. Now he has vanished, without a trace, but that photograph must be burned. It's the only proof that a crime was committed."

The Colonel refused to give Tyrone the photo saying, "I want Wendy to see this. I'm doing this for Wendy. She needs to see this picture."

Tyrone said, "She doesn't need to see the photo, and we don't want it traced back to us."

I touched the barrel of my revolver to the back of the Colonel's head and cocked the hammer saying, "You saw the proof you asked for, Colonel. Give Mr. Davis the photo, **now**."

He handed Tyrone the photograph.

We needed that photograph. It had the Colonel's fingerprints all over it and it would be one more piece of evidence for his trial. We were trying to put together an airtight case, so the only recourse would be a guilty plea for the Colonel.

After Colonel Thomas regained his composer I said, "Enough of past history. I believe payment is due." He passed Mr. Davis a brown envelope, containing $60,000 in cash.

Tyrone counted it and then said, "Okay, who's next on your hit parade, Colonel?" Opening a briefcase on his lap, the Colonel pulled out two photographs saying, "I want you to hit Lt. Richard Mosley and Staff Sgt. Gene Simmons of Philadelphia. I want them done in the same manner, but I want them together when they die, since they were together when they raped Wendy."

Tyrone asked, "Who is this Wendy?"

Colonel Thomas lied saying, "Wendy is my daughter, and these eight bastards raped and beat her, leaving her for dead. Make them pay, Mr. Davis. Make them pay for what they did to her."

I could see that the Colonel was trying to get his money's worth, painting a false picture of what really happened. He was hoping that Tyrone would be more brutal with the next pair of victims that were to be tortured and murdered.

We played along.

I put my hand on his left shoulder and said, "Don't you worry, Colonel, those evil bustards had their pleasure, now it's our pleasure to take out the garbage. They danced to the music, now they're going to pay the piper." I reminded the Colonel, "Our deal was $60,000 a head and now you want us to whack two guys at the same time for the price of one?" This guy was a real jerk and had something up his sleeve. "I don't appreciate your little two-for one price maneuver, but given the fact that it is to revenge the rape of your daughter, we'll do it. However, know this… this was a onetime only deal."

Tyrone took the photographs and the address information on the two guys from the Colonel, as we dropped him off at his vehicle.

We set up the same scenario with Philadelphia Police Department, as we did with Massachusetts State Police. We arranged the "proof of death" photograph for the Colonel.

However, this time I wanted to know if Wendy was also part of this murder for hire conspiracy.

When Tyrone Davis called the Colonel to let him know the job was complete, I told him to say that he was sorry he couldn't give the photo to him for his daughter to see. I also said, "Tell the Colonel he can bring Wendy along when we meet, and she could see the photographs then."

The Colonel told Tyrone he'd think about bringing her. This was a good sign. It showed that his girlfriend, Wendy, possibly had knowledge that the murders were being committed.

When we arrived at the pick-up point, Colonel Thomas got out of his car alone. After we gave him the details of the double murders, he was pleased, but not as enthusiastic as he was before.

He said, "My wife has discovered the money missing from our savings account, and I'm going to put our work on hold for a while."

I said, "That's fine, but it's pay as you go. Do you have our money for this last job?"

He said, "No. It's going to take me a few weeks to raise the $60,000."

Tyrone was furious arguing, "We had an agreement, asshole. You have a debt that needs to be satisfied either with cash or your blood and broken bones."

I said, "Colonel, remember what I said about dancing to the music? It's time to pay the piper."

He brought up Miami Mike, who screwed up everything.

I said, "Colonel, you have twenty-four hours to pay up. End of story." Now I knew why he wanted the two guys killed at the same time. He was closing out the hit list and never intended to pay upon completion. The Colonel was really lucky that he was dealing with a couple of cops and not real hit men.

We dropped Colonel Thomas off at his car, and I drove directly to U.S. Attorney Harold Sullivan's office at U.S. District Court. We laid out the entire case and asked how he wanted to proceed. He had just completed a grand jury presentation, and the jury members were still in deliberation. He decided to present our evidence then, as a grand jury original, hoping for an indictment. He felt the case was open and shut on the Colonel, but there was little to no evidence on Wendy, as a possible defendant.

The grand jury did indict Colonel Thomas on three counts of conspiracy to Mayhem and Murder. The next morning, U.S. Marshals arrested Colonel Ronald Thomas at his desk at the Veteran's Administration. At his arraignment, because of the overwhelming video evidence, the Colonel pled guilty.

As I was leaving the courtroom, I whispered to the Colonel, "Sorry sir, but it's time to pay the piper."

He hung his head as the U.S. Marshalls walked him out of the courtroom.

Chapter Twenty-Five

Into the Darkness

In 1978 Michael told me that that the next President of the United States would be pivotal to the future of world peace.

He said, "If President Jimmy Carter is re-elected, he will be killed in an explosion that will be blamed on an Iranian death squad. Walter Mondale would become president and the stage will be set for World War III." He went on to say, "Three world powers will unite against the NATO alliance, and two of three nuclear bombs will be detonated within the United States, bringing America's world trade and economy to its knees."

Michael further showed me a horrifying vision saying, "There will be massive food and gas shortages, and many will starve to death. The darkness within man will surface. Even the good will lose hope and turn negative. These developments will set the stage for a full-scale invasion of the United States by an "Axis of Evil."

I asked, "Is there is anything that can be done to stop those events from happening?"

He simply said, "You can vote Republican in the next election, and then do everything in your power to keep the next president alive." I was reminded of the visions I was given showing President Kennedy, being shot in the head, by Indians with arrows. I still didn't know what that meant.

Being a Washington D.C. Police Officer, we were sworn to protect the President of the United States. Because of this, Michael had me research the history of the Secret Service and the Indian curse on the presidency. My research uncovered some very interesting facts.

President Abraham Lincoln had twelve D.C. Police Detectives chosen as the first federal agents on April 14, 1865. It is a very sad historical irony that later that same evening, President Lincoln was assassinated at Ford's Theater.

I often wondered what would have happened, if he had started the Secret Service a few months earlier. Would the assassination attempt have been foiled? You never know about these things, but in my line of work, you have to think about the fact that a few seconds can make the different between living or dying, between catching someone in the act and missing him or her completely.

Think about it. If Lincoln had stayed at the White House that night, the Presidential Box at Ford's Theater would have been empty. In looking into the events of the day, President Lincoln appointed the twelve detectives to the Secret Service. Then he and wife, Mary, spent the afternoon at the Navy Yard. They returned to the White House where the President met with appointments until 8:15 p.m. Mary didn't want to go out that night. She and the president were very tired. But because the newspaper printed that the President would be attending the play at Ford's Theater, that evening Lincoln didn't want to let the public down. He went anyway, without Mary.

I learned that President Lincoln always carried a special coin and a lucky four-leaf clover with him everywhere he went. However, since he was in a hurry that night, he left both on his desk in the oval office.

While I researched the Lincoln assassination, I also learned, coincidentally, President Kennedy was given a good luck coin. Playwright and family friend, Clare Booth Luce, gave it to him before he was shipped out to the Pacific during WWII. At first I thought it might have been the coin he gave me as a boy, but later I learned it was believed to be a gold U.S. Double Eagle. He called it his St. Clare medal and wore it around his neck with his dog tags. Kennedy's boat, PT-109, was destroyed during a battle in the Solomon Islands. After spending days, clinging to the wreckage, Kennedy finally gave the order to abandon ship, and they floated to a nearby island. Jack gave his lucky coin to Eroni Kumana, the native who rescued them from certain death.

Since the subject of lucky objects kept coming into my life, I asked Michael about luck and coins. He said that anything you believe in can be lucky or a curse, but it's the power of the mind that creates the outcome.

He reminded me all the time, "It's all about having the right person in the right place, at the right time, in the right frame of mind. But sometimes even that can't stop fate."

I tell you this because I have always tried to follow the angel's guidance. When I didn't, bad things would happen.

I knew throughout my career, Michael was grooming me for something, but I also knew that it was beyond my comprehension at the time. There were, however, moments when I caught up to myself, so to speak, and I saw how events I was involved in laid groundwork for other events, with sometimes years in between.

When I pressed Michael about his comment on the Presidency, all he would reveal was, "We have already set in motion an opening to break a deadly curse that was placed on the Presidency, during the conflicts with the Native Americans, in the 1800's. The curse placed decrees that every President elected in a zero year will die in office." He went on to impart, "You played a role in keeping the peace at the BIA building several years earlier. No Native Americans were killed, even though they had all agreed that it was a good day to die. What you did that day changed a course of events. The spirits of those Indians that are bound to the curse must honor your will now."

I didn't really know what to believe about that and Michael knew it. There were moments of silence. Then he said, "Research the Presidential Curse. It will confirm what I have outlined."

I did as was suggested. Back then, there was no Internet, so the task wasn't an easy one.

Chapter Twenty-six

Indian Legend

On my personal time, I hit the library so I could try to put together some hard facts, in order to get a better view of what was on the horizon. I did find out that the inception of the curse was due to the government double-crossing the Native Americans. It wasn't just from taking their land. The U.S. would make treaties with the Indian tribes, then break those same treaties no sooner than the ink was dry on the paper. Most of the treachery centered on the ever-changing government officials in office. They had to deal with the influx of immigrants, pushing ever westward wanting to take the Indian lands and resources.

The government also couldn't control the Indian's belief system, since every tribe had their own spiritual beliefs, based on the tribe's legends and traditions. Whites had their own disagreements within the Christian faiths, but one thing they could all agree on was, "Indians are pagan" and had to convert. Most of the whites were fleeing a history of religious persecution in Europe and now became the persecutors. Interesting, isn't it? The tables turn so swiftly.

I closed the book and leaned my library chair onto its back two legs. My mind immediately flooded with memories of the moments I had with Russell Means at the BIA building. In one of those moments he asked me, "What do you think of Mt. Rushmore?"

"The monument?" I asked, "Of the four Presidents carved into the mountain?"

He said, "No, the four liars on the mountainside!"

After seeing the facts from the research I just completed, I now understood why Means made that statement. Historically, there have been human on human atrocities. So many souls are tortured, due to the vices that have run amuck on the planet. I came to find out that a lot of the Angel's Earthly work in this age of man, revolved around making peace with the souls of the Native American people. They were wronged by the United States Government and the foreigners that were flooding into this country.

This rift was long, deep and cut hard into the hearts and souls of all it touched. I found that there were those, who tried to stand for their land, their rights as humans and maintain honor in the process.

Michael told me that all of creation came from the Creator in one solemn thought, "Let there be Light." The energy of thought is very powerful. Human

152

thought, if controlled and channeled, can also be powerful if you can control enough people and their way of thinking. He went on to relate that over the years, so many Native American tribes were massacred, and their descendants cursed the U.S. Government over the atrocities. In 1813 the climate was ripe to bring all of that Indian hatred together in one solemn curse on the Great White Chief in Washington.

I learned the definition of a curse is a solemn utterance, intended to invoke a supernatural power, to inflict harm or punishment on someone or something. What fuels the curse is human thought and willpower, not only from the living, but also the spirits of the dead that haven't crossed over to the afterlife or next dimension of existence.

I then discovered that the curse on the presidency was leveled by Tecumseh, Chief of the Shawnee tribe, on his death bed. After suffering from many broken treaties, by the U.S. Government, the tribe had settled in the territory called Indiana; a place the Indians called Prophetstown. When hordes of white settlers migrated into the area, feuds broke out between the two cultures and war started.

The Territorial Governor, William Henry Harrison, began seeking statehood for Indiana. However, the U.S. Congress refused the request until the "Indian Problem" was resolved. Harrison accepted the rank of General in the U.S. Army and, on November 7^t, 1811, he attacked the Shawnee capitol of Prophetstown, massacring many before burning it to the ground. This one action broke the power of the Shawnees and became known, historically, as marking the collapse of the Native American military movement.

Chief Tecumseh's brother Tenskwatawa, the "Prophet," was the tribal spiritual leader. He narrowly escaped, with his life. In 1813, after the battle of the Thames, he was mortally wounded. On his deathbed, he uttered to his brother the following curse.

"Brother, be of good cheer. It is a good day to die! Before one winter shall pass, the chance will yet come to build our nation and drive the Americans from our lands. If this should fail, then a curse shall be upon the great chief of the Americans, if they shall ever pick Harrison to lead them. His days in power shall be cut short. And for every twenty winters following, the days in power of the great chief which they select, shall be cut short. Our people shall not be the instrument to shorten their time. Either the Great Spirit shall shorten their days or their own people shall shoot them. This is not all. Each contest to select their great chief shall be marked by sharp divisions, within their nation. Within seven winters of each contest, there shall be a war among their people, either within their nation or with other nations, I know not which. Our people shall prosper only if they can avoid these wars."

Tenskwatawa took his brother's words, and through many rituals and ceremonies with other Native American Shaman, invoked the spirits of all the Indians that had died at the hands of the U.S. Government. It became the single most powerful curse ever uttered in the history of the human race.

In 1840, twenty-nine years after the curse was placed on the presidency, the former Indiana Governor and U.S. Army General, William Henry Harrison, was elected as the ninth president of the United States. Only a month after his inaugural, Harrison died and his running mate, John Tyler, became the first vice president to inherit the presidency.

Tyler remained as president through the remainder of the term, as has each of the vice presidents, who have succeeded to office in similar tragic circumstances. Harrison is known both as the first elected president to die in office and as the first victim of the death cycle, in fulfillment of Chief Tecumseh's Presidential Curse. The clock started in 1840 and every twenty years, another president would die in office.

In 1860, Abraham Lincoln was elected president. The nation was divided, and the War Between the States broke out, within months. Lincoln was shot in the head, on April 14, 1865 and died a day later.

In 1880, James Garfield was elected president. Garfield was shot on July 2, 1881 and died September 19ᵗ, due to complications from his wounds.

In 1900, William McKinley was elected to a second term, less than two years after the end of the Spanish-American War. McKinley was shot on September 6, 1901 and died eight days later.

In 1920, Warren Harding was elected president. He won by a huge margin, but only after a contentious campaign, with the main issue being U.S. membership in the League of Nations, in the aftermath of World War I. He died in office on August 2, 1923.

In 1940, Franklin Roosevelt was urged not to break tradition and seek a third term. He did anyway and was reelected, convincingly, despite dire warnings that the country was on the verge of war. During World War II, Roosevelt died on April 12ᵗ, 1945 of a brain hemorrhage while in office.

In 1960, John F. Kennedy was elected president. Kennedy was shot and killed November 22, 1963, shortly after sending CIA and military advisors to Vietnam.

Interesting fact: The only other U.S. President in history to die in office was Zachary Taylor. He followed John Tyler's presidency, died after eating cherries and drinking milk on July 9, 1850. It was ten years after the curse began.

Chapter Twenty-seven

Fulfillment of the Presidential Curse

The question was, "Who would fall to the Indian's curse in 1980?" Armed with all this information, I had a clearer understanding about the curse but didn't have the foggiest idea what to do about it. In addition, what did the curse have to do with Russell Means? I felt like I was given a bunch of puzzle pieces, but still too few to see ahead of me.

Somewhere, during the months I was researching the Native American History as it pertained to the curse on the Presidency, I had been promoted to senior detective. That, coupled with the death threat contract hanging over my head, my Inspector assigned me to the Security Officers Management Branch of the Intelligence Division.

I had no idea why I was put in such a lame ass job although I was sure Michael had a lot to do with influencing the move. In retrospect, I see that it gave me more flexibility to move around Washington D.C., Maryland and Virginia, monitoring private security agencies and their employees. I also began working closely, with the U.S. Secret Service on presidential movements, because they also interfaced with private security agencies and the special police officers licensed and commissioned, by my office.

I became close friends with Special Agent Dennis V.N. McCarthy, a man who seemed to know that I had some extra help around me, but he wasn't spiritual at all. Denny was nicknamed the "Silver Fox," because he grayed early and held on to his black heavy eyebrows. Oh, and did I mention, he was also quite the ladies' man? Hence, the fox part. He had a girlfriend for every day of the week.

Once again, I could see that Michael was setting up something, but he wasn't letting me in on it. He just told me to hang close to McCarthy, and one day I would see him fly like an angel.

Now there was a picture.

In the spring of 1979 Governor Ronald Reagan of California looked like the front-runner for the Republican Presidential ticket. I began looking into Ronald Reagan's politics. I always admired him as an actor, particularly for his westerns, but where did he stand on Indian affairs I wondered?

Why would Michael pick this guy over Jimmy Carter, who seemed to be a decent president? In talking with several Reagan advisors, I learned that Governor

Reagan squashed every bill and proposal that would interfere with the peace of the Native Americans, living in his state. One proposal to flood a valley, that would have brought billions of dollars into the California economy, was dismissed when Reagan said, "I'm not going to break any treaties with the Native Americans. American history shows that we have broken enough treaties!"

Now I was beginning to understand the moves on the chessboard that the Angel was making. The curse was bound to the mistreatment of Native Americans and tied to those Indians, who had refused to pass into the next dimension. If we wanted to make a change in this dimension, it could only come through championing the living descendants of the ancestors.

There is truth in that old saying, "Honor the living and the dead."

I started to see it setting up. I prayed my vision would be clear enough to respond when needed.

Chapter Twenty-eight

The Sun Spear

As the Presidential election was under way, Michael said, "It's time for a road trip to check up on your father. The woman he married isn't in the best of health, and she is beginning to lose her mind." Of course, Michael had other plans for me while out there. Linda wasn't crazy about my leaving, but I had to go alone.

While I was driving through Indiana, the angel had me turn southwest off of US 70 in Columbus, OH onto US 71, heading to Prophetstown and the battlegrounds where the curse originated. Michael guided me down through Prophetstown State Park and onto the shores of the Wabash River, where I sat for hours and just waited. Michael showed me the great battle that had occurred there. It appeared to end, with the US Army retreating, but there were many dead on both sides. I was confused. It reminded me a little of the vision Michael gave me that day at the BIA building takeover.

I asked Michael, "What are we waiting for? I'm starving."

He replied, "He Who Makes Noise will be here soon."

"Huh?" I blurted.

No response.

It was getting late, and the park would be closing soon. I couldn't wait any longer. I got into the Silver Bullet and started to drive out, just to realize that I had a flat tire.

Thank you, Michael.

I had to wonder, if I had just stayed put like Michael said, would I be changing a flat tire right now? *Or* did he give me that flat tire to keep me there? Regardless, I got to work. I found the lug wrench, but couldn't find my jack. I started looking around for some way to lift the car. I could see dust coming down the dirt road. It was an old beat up VW hippy van. When the old driver pulled up, he asked, "Need some help?"

I could see he was up there in age. By the look on my face he could tell I was concerned about that.

"Yes, I'm 102 but am still strong as an ox," he quipped at me. I wanted to say "smelled like one too." Because the first thing he did, when he got out of the van, was fart. If he farted once, he farted fifty times, during the time it took to change my tire.

The plates on his van were from Oklahoma.

He said, "I'm called Thomas, but my Indian name is Lalawethika. It means, 'He Who Makes Noise' in my people's tongue."

Then he let out another fart.

I laughed and said, "You sure live up to your name, Thomas."

"Thanks," he said. "They tell me it's biological. Whatever the hell that means."

"You know the park is closing soon. That's why I was on my way out," I informed him.

"Yeah, yeah. Closing, smosing! I've travelled all the way from my reservation in Oklahoma to get here. I'm on a vision quest for the Great Spirit. The park can close around me." Thomas went on to say that on his bucket list was a visit to the lands of his forefathers here at Prophetstown, and he had to do it before he died.

I asked, "Why now?"

He said, "Three days ago, I had a dream where I had to meet someone, and he would either help or stop this person, who was also having a dream."

"Well," I told him, "I'm on a vision quest too. I'm hoping to find a way to break the old, Indian curse on the presidency."

He said, "Why would you want to go and do that?"

I replied, "It's a long story."

Thomas said, "Smoke with me, and tell me your story. You know when you die, all you take with you is your story."

For some reason, I let out a big belly laugh. "That's what I understand."

Thomas pulled out a slab of some of the best buffalo jerky I had ever had, a cooler of what he called Kickapoo Joy Juice and a long ceremonial Peace Pipe that looked ancient.

Thomas said, "The park closed, so we'll be spending the night," as he built a small campfire to keep us warm. He was moving around like a teenager.

I thought, "This guy really knows his stuff."

"Duh," Michael said, "He's an Indian. You're the Boy Scout."

We chewed, drank and smoked, as I told him my story. For the first time in my life, I talked openly about following Michael's guidance.

Thomas said, "The Great Spirit sent His sky people to you for a very important reason."

I described to Thomas about how the Angel showed me that if Jimmy Carter was re-elected he would be killed, and America would be plunged into World War III. If, on the other hand, Ronald Reagan is elected, there is a chance he could survive the curse that was placed on the presidency, by Chief Tecumseh. I told Thomas what I found out about Governor Reagan, refusing to break any treaties with the Native Americans on reservations in California. If he is elected president, and the curse stands, the ancestors will kill a friend, which further defeats the purpose of the curse.

Thomas said, "I met Ronald Reagan once years ago when me and a few other Indians worked as extras on the *Death Valley Days* TV show. As I remember, he always had a protective nature for the Indian people, much like I feel coming from you. You might be onto something, my young friend."

I went into great detail about my assignment on the Washington, D.C. Police Department, Russell Means and the BIA takeover.

Thomas said, "I was there on the Trail of Broken Treaties. I remember the cop being held by Indian 'security officers.' And I remember the food coming in from some white guy, who was with the Communist Party. That was *you?*" he asked.

"I looked a lot different back then," I laughed.

He said, "We were all ready to die that night."

I said, "I know, but it was a better day to live and eat. If you had died that night, you wouldn't be here tonight, talking to me. Maybe I saved your life." I went on to say, "I was just an undercover detective, trying to keep the peace and prevent anyone from getting hurt."

Since he had been around so long, I asked if he knew a Texas Ranger, by the name of Charlie Goodnight.

Thomas told me, "I knew of him. Heard good things, but I never met him. Why?"

I shrugged my shoulders, but didn't respond.

Chief Thomas announced, "I was once a great Shaman, with my tribe. I will think on you through the night." He let out another buffalo jerky-riddled fart saying, "Go to sleep now, peaceful warrior. If the Great Spirit tells me to stop you, I will cut your throat in the night and put you out of your misery. If the Great Spirit says I should help you, I will give you what we both came here for."

Needless to say, I slept with my car doors locked. I also had my gun under the pillow and one eye open all night, if you could call that sleeping. I heard the old guy farting and bumping around in his van like he was looking for something all through the night.

It seemed like every bump he made woke me up. One of those times, my watch said 4:44 a.m. That's when it happened. I had a gurgling in my stomach that was so loud and furious I could feel it moving down through my intestines. I didn't know if it was Thomas' obnoxious sounds or the sound of my own stomach that woke me up this time. Regardless, I felt like I was going to explode. I was not going to give Thomas the satisfaction of knowing I "caught" his flatulence disease. I held it as long as I could, until there was no way around it. I let out a buffalo smoker fart that ran me out of the "Silver Bullet" to the cheers of Chief Thomas, laughing his ass off.

"Welcome to the club, my friend. Welcome to the club." He laughed.

I wondered whether the old coot set me up. What exactly was in that jerky and peace pipe?

The next day when I woke up, Chief Thomas was gone. On the hood of my car he had left me a strange double-sided quartz crystal wand, wrapped in leather and fur. It also had a small buffalo horn, dangling from the end that held the larger of two crystals.

Michael said, "Make no mistake, the old man did think about not helping you, because he didn't want to dishonor the spirit of his fallen ancestors. He also thought you were crazier than him, but he felt the truth was so strong in you that he wanted you to have the 'Sun Spear'."

Michael told me that the large crystal represented the Sun and the small crystal at the other end represented the Moon. Together the bearer can turn the world around, and it was the key to forgiveness.

With the Sun Spear in tow, I continued my journey to Chicago.

When I arrived at my father's house the scene was very sad. His wife got tired of looking at him and made my dad move into the garage.

I called Linda and told her what I found.

"Let's pack up your stuff and come home to live with Linda and I," I suggested. "I spoke to Linda, and she would love to have you with us. She really cares about you, Dad, and can't bear the thought of what is going on here."

He plainly said, "Who would take care of Henrietta?"

My father was an honorable man. He wasn't leaving his wife no matter how she treated him. When Henrietta came home and learned I was there, she moved him back into the house, as if nothing had happened. I'm sure she was embarrassed that I found out what she had done. She claimed that my father was lazy and wouldn't do anything, except stay in his room and watch television.

I asked, "What else does he have? Moving him into the garage isn't the answer."

I spent two days with my father, while Henrietta went out of town with a few girlfriends. It was nice. We went out to dinner, saw a movie and went to a shooting range. We both loved to shoot guns.

There was nothing more I could do for him, so I returned home.

Chapter Twenty-nine

The Presidential Race

Watching the Presidential Polls, during 1980, was very interesting

President Jimmy Carter's slogan was, "A Leader for a Change," but he was haunted by the Iranian hostage crisis situation. Also, his slogan didn't fit, since nothing changed, during his first four years. I couldn't imagine how much change he could bring in the next four.

Ronald Reagan ran for president in 1976, but lost the GOP nomination to Gerald Ford. This time, he was back with, "Are you better off than you were four years ago?" That was a mouth-full at the time and spoke volumes. America had experienced gas lines and was heading toward a depression so, of course, everyone was ready for a change.

The other candidate was Congressman John B. Anderson of Illinois. His slogan was "The only alternative for a better America."

All the polls showed that Anderson was ahead in the race.

I questioned Michael about what that would mean to the breaking of the curse because Anderson was a typical politician, controlled by a political machine, that would stop at nothing to put their man in the White House. He ran as an Independent, and his machine swayed every state to get him on the ticket. He was hardly the human spirit the Native American ancestors would find honorable. We had no chance of breaking the curse, with him in office.

Michael said, "Everything Anderson is doing is going to pull votes away from Jimmy Carter. Reagan will win the election."

Michael was right. Governor Reagan won a landslide victory over Carter and Anderson, due to a split vote. I wondered, if Ronald Reagan knew that he won a race that put him right in the crosshairs of the dreaded Indian Curse that had already taken the lives of seven U.S. Presidents, all elected in a zero year.

Now the real race began.

What Michael had structured, positioning me in the Security Officers Management Branch, was shear genius. I was detailed to the Secret Service task force that was responsible for setting up the security coverage for all the Inaugural Balls, where private security officers were used.

On January 20, 1981, the day of the Presidential Inauguration, it was a warm morning for January, mid-fifties. Michael said I should wear a sky blue three-piece suit to the detail, not the customary black or dark suit the special agents would be wearing. I didn't know why at the time.

During the briefing, before last minute assignments were given out that morning, Mr. Knight, one of the Directors of the Secret Service, came in to talk to Agent McCarthy about something that happened on a previous assignment. The Director took one look at me and said, "Blue. Who are you?" He did not seem pleased with my choice in fashion.

I didn't know what to say, so like always, I said the first thing that came to mind. I replied, "Mr. Blue Knight."

McCarthy rolled his eyes, looked at me and just shook his head. I was never the savvy sophisticate he expected.

What I should've said was, "sorry for the blue suit Mr. Knight." I didn't sweat it. I figured maybe that's what the angel wanted to come out of my mouth at that time.

The Director smiled as McCarthy, explained that I spent six years undercover in subversive groups, and knew the faces to look for. Our moment of contact was interrupted when I was called into the briefing room. McCarthy continued his conversation with the Director. After all the assignments were given out, I was the only one left.

McCarthy came in and said that the Director wanted the Blue Knight to drive the procession route several times, between the U.S. Capitol and the White House. Two other agents and I were to scan the spectators that assembled along the route. Once back, we would walk along the route, with the motorcade.

I assumed the assignment came because of my experience undercover and knowledge of subversive groups. The fact that I could recognize the faces of most of the extremists that were harboring a grudge against the government was an advantage for our side.

When the motorcade began, Michael wanted me to walk as near to the President and Vice President's limousines as possible. I learned from McCarthy that Nancy Reagan was extremely worried about the Indian Curse on the Presidency. McCarthy told me that she had even hired shamans to try to break the curse, after the November election. Shamans? My thoughts went back to Chief Thomas. I am always in awe when synchronicity occurs.

It was a relief to learn that, due to threats, and the dreaded curse, the First Lady demanded that the President not leave the limousine, until he reached the reviewing stands in front of the White House. The President compromised with her by staying in the car, but riding standing up, waving at the crowd from the sunroof portal.

The Angel had everyone right where he wanted us. The chessboard was set, and the pieces were definitely moving.

Due to my close work with the disrupters, during the anti-war movement, I learned the telltale signs of spotting someone who was out for no good. They normally don't wear sunglasses. That's a good thing because most of the time the eyes are a dead giveaway. They have a certain sparkle of hostility, anger and hatred. Most people in the crowd will look happy or curious. Michael had me focus on eyes and movements that were fast and more daring than everyone else; for example, someone pushing to the front of the crowd.

I did spot several suspicious individuals in the crowd that I knew were dangerous. They were mentally unbalanced, and if they had a chance to do something, they would. I sent a message of their locations, via radio, for further investigation.

After President Reagan's Inaugural Address, and the motorcade began, everything went into a surreal slow-motion action for me. My eyes were everywhere and nowhere, hidden behind the traditional sunglasses. Agents wear sunglasses for more than a sun shield. They are a psychological defense, since no one knows exactly where the agents are looking. They spark paranoia in the guilty and could be just the thing to stop someone from taking the shot.

I had my 6" .38cal Smith and Wesson in a shoulder holster on my left side, my good luck Kennedy coin in my pocket, and the "Sun Spear" stuck in my belt in the middle of my back.

Michael told me to focus on a bubble of protection over the two limousines we were safeguarding. I must say that was the longest walk of my life. I kept thinking about Dallas, twenty years earlier when President Kennedy's motorcade moved down through Dealey Plaza, in between the School Book Depository and the grassy knoll. I scanned the windows and rooftops of the buildings we passed. I looked at President Reagan, waving out of the top of his limo and thought, "He's a sitting… no, he's a standing duck."

The motorcade finally arrived at the reviewing stand, without incident. My focus immediately shifted to the locations where the Inaugural committee was having the "meet and greet" parties. The plan was for the President and First Lady to only stay about ten minutes at each site, greet their guests, possibly dance and then on to the next Ball.

Later that evening, all the private security personnel checked out. I slipped into my tux and Michael had me position myself at the largest assembly, which was the Smithsonian Ball. Again, he had me focus a bubble of protection over the President, as he went from one ball to the other. The night ended, without incident.

I breathed not one, but about a thousand breaths of relief that night. I had never seen a more professional group of people than the U.S. Secret Service. I was so proud to call Denny McCarthy my friend. I could tell if that day was any sign of what lay ahead, it was going to be a long four, and possibly eight years, before us.

It didn't take long before tensions rose in the White House. McCarthy shared with me that Nancy Reagan had private phone lines installed at the White House and Camp David, so she could stay in private contact with her astrologers and psychics, who had advised the First Lady that the President would fall victim to Tecumseh's Curse… unless there was some divine intervention.

Denny said, "Nancy was going crazy over this curse thing."

I asked him, "Denny, wouldn't you be worried, given the history?"

I laid it all out for him, since he appeared to be unaware of the facts. I told him, "Strange as this may sound to you, I feel you will have something to do with breaking the curse, if you happen to be in the right place at the right time." I continued, "I have it from a high authority that the day will come when I see you fly through the air like an angel."

McCarthy said, "I don't believe in that shit."

I replied, "It doesn't matter if you believe. What matters is that the First Lady believes. What's the old saying, 'you can lead horses to water, but you can't make them drink? You can lead humans to wisdom, but you can't make them think. If people could just keep their minds open, the door to endless possibilities would open. A closed mind slams that door shut."

"My mind is not closed. It's just rational. You, on the other hand… well I have no idea about you," he said, all befuddled.

Truth be told, I liked screwing with him, so when he shook his head at me or got all flustered, I knew I was on the right path.

Apparently, Nancy Reagan made the President very superstitious. One of her psychics told her to have her husband carry a good luck, Kennedy half-dollar in his pocket at all times. Michael said they were tapping into the Kennedy coin I had. I asked Michael if I should give the coin to Denny and have him tell Nancy Reagan where I got it. Michael said no. Reagan is giving his good luck coins away. He will wind up giving yours away, too. Instead, Michael told me to ask Denny to try to get one of the Kennedy half-dollars from President Reagan. A week later, Denny showed me two that Nancy gave him. He gave me one. Michael had me tape my good luck coin together with the one from Nancy.

He said, "Now, energetically, every Kennedy half dollar the president carries is connected to President Kennedy's good luck coin. Michael reminded me that it wasn't the power of the coin as much as it was the power of the mind at work here."

Over the next couple of months, Michael would have me drive to locations where the President was speaking. He wanted my presence known to Denny. When I caught his eye, I'd wave to him, as he and fellow agents would move President Reagan in and out of the Presidential limousine. It was always a tense moment because that was when the President was most at risk. It was definitely a fine art that the Secret Service demonstrated. Very smooth.

One thing I did notice, from watching over the months, was that if a shooter really wanted to get the president, it could be done. It was like Michael had me on my own task force to find the weak spots in the protection plan. I kept seeing the vision of Jack Ruby, stepping out of the crowd of reporters in the basement of Dallas Police Headquarters, and shooting Lee Harvey Oswald, as police detectives were closely guarding him. That was a reality that could certainly be repeated.

Chapter Thirty

McCarthy's Flight

March 30, 1981 started out just like any other day. Michael had me on high alert. I was assigned to office duty, having to notarize commission papers for the swearing in of thirty new special police officers. While filing the papers away, another file folder just popped out of the file cabinet and spilled onto the floor. It was a file on an ex-police detective, Al Fury, who was the Director of Security at the Washington Hilton Hotel at 1919 Connecticut Avenue, N.W.

My eyes were brought to his commission paper that said he was commissioned to carry a .32 cal semi-auto pistol. I could tell Michael was trying to communicate something, but our connection that day was very weak.

That happened at times when his energy was spread thin, or I was sick. That day both were the case. I had a terrible head cold, and Michael was totally preoccupied somewhere else. Of course, on days I was assigned to the office or knee deep in paperwork, he was usually elsewhere. It was our normal pattern. I often wondered whether he coordinated that giant stack of paperwork on days when I wasn't needed, or was that the natural flow of my work? He was the master, commander and coordinator.

Around 1:30 p.m., I had just finished lunch when Michael came through loud and clear.

He said, "Grab the 'Sun Spear' and get down to the Washington Hilton now!"

I could tell from his urgency, the shit was ready to hit the fan. I told my Captain that I had to go down to the Washington Hilton to check on Al Fury's commission.

"His file claims he's commissioned to carry a .32 cal semi-automatic pistol, which is illegal. Special Police Commissions only allow for .38 cal revolvers," I informed him. "This is an oversight that could come back to haunt us, if the gun is ever used," I said.

The Captain nodded and, without even blinking, I was out the door.

When I arrived at the Washington Hilton Hotel, I found Agent McCarthy and asked, "What's up?"

There was a weird foreboding calm over the grounds. It felt like the calm before the storm.

He said, "Everything is cool. The President is just speaking to a trade association."

I went out to where the President's limousine was parked, and there was a group of reporters and onlookers walking around freely.

A Secret Service Special Agent stopped me. I identified myself as a D.C. Police Intelligence Investigator.

Then I saw a group of reporters and onlookers standing against the wall behind a roped-off area.

I was drawn to go stand with them, but for some reason, I went back inside.

Michael urged me, "Go give the Sun Spear to McCarthy."

"He won't take it," I retorted.

He said, "Then have McCarthy touch the Sun Spear to complete the electromagnetic circuit that is being set in motion."

When I found Denny, I said, "Hey, Denny, look at this cool crystal wand I bought in the gift shop. It was made by an Indian Medicine Man and is supposed to bring forth good luck and prosperity."

He was quick to grab it from my hand. The protection team was then radioed that the President was on the move, so Denny gave me back the Sun Spear.

He then radioed, "We must clear this hallway. 'Rawhide' is on the move."

"Rawhide" was the Secret Service code name for President Reagan.

Michael told me to go to my cruiser, focus on a bubble of protection over the president and leave.

As I got outside I waved at D.C. Police Officer, Tom Delahanty, who I knew from the Second District, and a few of the Special Agents I knew from the federal task force. I focused on the bubble of protection Michael wanted.

Then I did one of the hardest things a cop can do, when he feels something big was getting ready to go down. I drove away. When I arrived back at my office, my Captain advised me that there had been a shooting at the Washington Hilton, and President Reagan had been taken to the hospital.

Michael kept his promise. That night on the evening news, I saw Agent McCarthy, flying by the seat of his pants over and over again. When the clip of the shooting was shown, you could see a dark blur and a set of shiny handcuffs fly over the trunk of the President's limousine and onto the gunman, John Hinckley Jr. That was Special Agent Dennis McCarthy, making the arrest and breaking the curse.

When I finally caught up to Denny, I found out what happened. He said all he remembered was flying onto Hinckley's gun hand, as he fired his last shot. The sixth and final bullet was knocked high and struck a window across the street.

He shared with me all he knew.

The first three bullets cut through the flesh of those who stood in the way between Hinckley and the President, hitting White House Press Security James Brady, Officer Delahanty and Special Agent Tim McCarthy. The fourth bullet hit the limousine's bulletproof window glass. The fifth shot struck the side armored door of the limousine, just as Special Agent in Charge, Jerry Parr, pushed Reagan into the car and right into the path of the bullet. The bullet followed the line of the car door, passing through a half-inch gap between the door and the door jamb, where it struck the president in the left chest, under his arm. All shots were fired within 1.5 seconds.

At first, Agent Parr determined that the president was not hit by any of the bullets, so he said the President should return to the safety of the White House. A few seconds later, the President started coughing up deep, red, frothy blood, which meant he was bleeding internally in the lungs. Agent Parr changed directions and had the President taken to George Washington University Hospital.

They arrived within five minutes from the time the first bullet was fired. Upon arrival, the President collapsed from loss of blood. When his vital signs were taken, President Reagan had no pulse. With the quick work of skilled physicians and a whole lot of help from above, he revived.

First Lady Nancy Reagan got her divine intervention that day.

John Hinckley Jr. was confident, he would get his kill shot and fulfill his deluded dream of impressing child actress, Jodie Foster. He used ammunition that would explode inside its victim to guarantee a kill shot, if a bullet landed anywhere near the heart. Doctors, who removed the bullet, said it penetrated the President's lung, stopping within an inch of his heart, but failed to explode.

The Dark Forces had gathered that day to clash with the Forces of Light, and even that wasn't enough to tip the balance. McCarthy's jump was estimated at over twenty feet, supposedly an impossible feat, for a man his size and from a standing position.

Something propelled him beyond his human abilities that day.

What was it?

I believe Michael gave him wings *or* a quick kick in the ass.

Image 7 – Dennis McCarthy receiving Medal of Valor for saving President Reagan's life.

Later I questioned Michael, "Why did you order me to leave that day? I might have been in a position to keep the President from getting hit with that bullet. Why didn't you put me next to Hinckley in the crowd? I could have disarmed Hinckley before he fired a shot."

Michael's answers painted a whole new picture of what really happened that day. "First of all," he said, "We really are just pieces, being moved about on a grand chessboard of Good and Evil. But our free will determines whether we're ready to move when the time comes. We must step aside or make the jump when the precise time is at hand."

"Secondly," he continued, "President Reagan had to get shot, die and return to life, in order to break that very strong human curse. You did your part when you delivered the 'Sun Spear' to your friend. With all those bullets flying around, I couldn't take a chance of you getting hit. Without you, I have no legs on earth, and we have a very long road ahead."

I believe that on March 30, 1981 at 2:27 p.m. Eastern Time, Michael's Forces of Good worked together in concert and broke the dreaded zero-year curse on the Presidency. Even with all that effort from the human agents involved, they could not stop the potentially fatal bullet, from hitting its mark. The curse did kill the President, but the Angel of Death refused to claim him. I think the Archangel guided everything on the path that day.

Michael is an Angel of Death, and that day he refused to take President Reagan because there was still work to do here on earth.

Chapter Thirty-one

Big Jim Brown

In the summer of 1982, Michael said it was time to start documenting some of the events that had occurred.

He said, "The time will come when you will record all the work we have done together, because there will be people in the world that need to elevate their understanding and acquire the 'Knowing.'"

I asked, "What's the 'Knowing'?"

He said, "It's the understanding that when you think you know, you don't. And when you know you don't, you do."

I came back with, "Ooookay, then I must have it, because I don't have the foggiest idea what you just meant."

I asked him to explain, but all he said was, "All will be known when your waiting is full."

I wish I had a dollar for every time I heard him tell me that. The answer came to me later. I heard, "Have you ever been asked a question and answered correctly, but you didn't know where that knowledge came from? Well, that's the 'Knowing.'"

One day, out of the blue, a Los Angeles film producer, Donald A. Mitchell, contacted me. He was interested in making a "Dirty Harry" type film, and when he was in Washington, D.C. a few months earlier, he heard about a vice cop that used bolas to apprehend criminals. That's how he got my name. He asked me if I had time to sit down with one of his screenwriters, so she could pick my brain about some police action film ideas. He was willing to pay me one thousand dollars for my time.

The money was coming at a good time. The engine in the Silver Bullet had just died, and I needed a new ride. Since I no longer had access to the black Cadillac, I agreed.

When I sat down with the writer, Donna Parker, she simply said, "So Detective Jagen, tell me your story."

I said, "That's not an easy tale to tell. You wouldn't believe half of it, and the other half is out of this world."

She said, "Try me."

I asked, "Where should I start?"

She said, "Anywhere you'd like."

I started by telling her about the days in uniform and making the bolas because I was tired of not being able to catch the bad guys. I also told her about the undercover assignments, where I was more afraid of being killed by the police than those on the other side of the badge.

I couldn't tell her about the guidance and communication with Archangel Michael. That's not something easily explained or understood.

Donna Parker became spellbound by my stories, and she told Don Mitchell that they should make a movie about my true-life experiences.

Don Mitchell asked me if I would take a trip out to Las Vegas to meet with Jim Brown, the former Football Hall of Famer. He went on to say that Brown was president of Richard Pryor's film company, Indigo Productions, and they were under contract with Columbia Pictures to produce four films a year. He felt that if Brown liked the story, they might produce the film.

I agreed, and Donna Parker and I went to work on a screenplay entitled "Blue Memoirs Badge #2219."

Within two weeks, the first draft was complete.

I took a week off from work and on October 25, 1982, Don Mitchell and I flew to Las Vegas in the hopes of finding some interest in the screenplay.

My wife, Linda, was not happy about me leaving her behind. I promised her that if we found interest in the story, she would be with me the next time we went on a business trip.

Jim Brown was one of the most serious guys I ever met. Doing a quick read on him, a person could tell he had a lot of ethnic insecurities, but he also had good reasons for them. I could tell that he had been screwed over and used by many white guys in his life, but he still maintained a positive attitude. He is one of the smartest people I have ever met. Deep down inside, he really cares about humanity.

I liked him right away.

He read "Blue Memoirs" and said he liked it.

He asked me, "Would you mind having a black actor play you?"

I told him, "I don't care. I don't even care if the movie ever gets made. I was just doing a friend a favor."

He seemed to like that I wasn't ego-driven. I confessed to Jim that my true passion was protecting and empowering children.

"I've seen kids manipulated into doing things that put them on the wrong track and ruin their lives. The hard part was it could have been avoided, if the kids were more aware of the tricks used to win their trust," I said.

He gave me a look that told me I struck a chord with him. We hit it off and started to get into the script.

We would banter back and forth.

The best thing I liked about Jim Brown was making him laugh. He lightened up and let all that serious energy go, when he laughed. He didn't laugh like normal people. He'd go, "He - He - He…" The only other person I knew that laughed like that was Detective Mendez. When Jim laughed, it was as if his heart would open up and the anger inside him was gone.

After one particularly lighthearted moment, he confided to me about his passion. He worked with kids in gangs, in the hope of getting them out.

Ah, now I saw the connection.

170

We went on to talk about things I didn't write in the script. Like my drowning at age eight and being brought back to life for some special purpose and the ruse my mother told us about our father. I stopped short of talking about Angel Michael.

Again, how do you explain that? Unless you've experienced it, there are no words. I was sure the world wasn't ready to hear that part of my story; at least not yet.

Jim Brown sent the script to Richard Pryor for review, and he asked me if I wanted to hang with him for the week. He was in Las Vegas for the second annual Riviera Casino's All-Star Hall of Fame Golf Classic.

What can I say? He made me an offer I couldn't refuse.

Jim introduced me to the "Egg Man of Las Vegas," Harry Vogel. Harry was one of the hosts of the Golf Tournament. Don Mitchell said that Harry Vogel had the exclusive contract to supply every egg served in Las Vegas.

Now think about it. That's a lot of eggs.

That night we went to the Hall of Fame Dinner, with some of the biggest names in Basketball, Baseball and Football.

Jim Brown and Don Mitchell introduced me throughout the night, as a counter-terrorism specialist with the Washington, D.C. Police Intelligence Division. He seemed to want everybody to know I was a cop, which was fine with me. I could see there were a lot of shady people hanging around but, after all, this was Las Vegas.

I also let everyone know that I was a cop because I wanted them to know exactly what I was, and why I was in town.

Mickey Mantle was in rare form that night, as he stood up and said, "Detective, I want Joe DiMaggio arrested. He's been terrorizing me at the 16th hole." Everyone laughed.

He also said, "Police and Intelligence, that a misnomer." He was quite the comedian, but I didn't think that was particularly funny.

The next day, since I didn't play golf, Jim asked if I wanted to come along and drive the golf cart for him, while he played. Of course, I said yes. What an experience. It was amazing, watching those legends I had grown up watching on television, horsing around like kids on that Las Vegas Golf Corse.

There was one event after another. Jim took me everywhere with him. He was a great host. During the down time, he talked about being raised by his grandmother. His heart opened when he talked about his grandmother and how he helped his best friend, Richard Pryor, after he set himself on fire when his pipe exploded, while using cocaine. He said that Richard's guardian angel was working overtime that day. Pryor's clothes were covered with cocaine residue, and Jim was afraid the police would charge his friend. He raced to the hospital to retrieve the clothing, but when he arrived, the police were already there and the clothing had disappeared. He said that it was a miracle. I said, "We all have angels around us, trying to help us through life. We also have our demons. Richard was in the City of Angels after the demons set him on fire, and an angel put it out. I could tell you stories about an angel in blue armor that has saved my butt countless times over the years. All it takes to hear them is opening your heart and mind."

Jim said that the fire was the best and worst thing that ever happened to Richard. It forced him to get his life back on track, but what a hard price to pay!

Michael gave me a vision of what really happened that day to Richard Pryor and the clothing. When I told Jim Brown what I saw in the vision, all he said was, "He - He - He!"

I left Las Vegas, knowing Michael had laid some groundwork for something, but I didn't know what. It was an amazing trip, but reality back in Washington was calling.

Chapter Thirty-two

No Win Situation

On March 8, 1983, I received a complaint from the owner of a local security agency, who alleged that another international security agency was supplying illegal bodyguards to a Saudi Arabian Prince, Faisal Bin Sultan, and his entourage, at local Washington Hotels. He went on to say that he witnessed the bodyguards, carrying short barrel shotguns, pistols and automatic weapons. When they approached the men, they identified themselves as U.S. Secret Service Special Agents. I passed the information on to my captain and waited for further instructions.

After careful review, I was given the go ahead to investigate the situation, so my partner, Detective Richard Rocky, began canvasing Washington's upscale hotels for the Prince.

I called Special Agent McCarthy to ask if he had heard anything about a private security agency, offering executive protection services.

He avoided answering the question and said, "Let's meet."

He was on White House duty that day, so we met in Lafayette Park, across the street from 1600 Pennsylvania Avenue. He was nervous when we met. He wanted to know what I was going to do.

I said, "I don't even know what I've got, let alone what I'm going to do."

Denny muttered softly, "I checked into it. Looks like three retired Secret Service Agents started a company that was actually a private Secret Service Agency, with ties to the CIA."

He also divulged that they were high dollar contractors, who had an exclusive deal to supply executive personal protection to the Royal Family of Saudi Arabia. He went on to say that the agency hired retired and off duty special agents and police detectives for the jobs on the Q.T.

"You need to be careful, Ed. You are getting ready to open Pandora's box. Not only will you piss off a bunch of cops, who are making a lot of money, you could embarrass a former president, and you could create an international incident." He paused, and then said, "Now, I ask you again. What are you going to do?"

I answered, "Denny, God hates a coward. If the services being provided are illegal, I'm bound by my oath to investigate and take action, but… there is always room for discretion. After all, there is still that thing called the brotherhood."

I could tell Denny knew where the agency was operating in the District, but I wasn't going to ask him. I could find them on my own.

As fate would have it, the next day I got a call from Mickey Sparks at the Watergate Hotel, who said he was visiting a friend on the fourth floor and mistakenly got off on the third. When he walked off the elevator, gun wielding plain-clothes security officers besieged him.

He went on to say, "Something just didn't seem right about them, and they forced me back on the elevator."

Later that afternoon, I met with the Watergate's Director of Security about the incident. He said that he couldn't comment, but slipped me a copy of a memo he received from the hotel manager, stating that a Saudi Prince would have his own security, plus Secret Service protection.

Before I left, I stopped by the third floor and encountered two individuals dressed in black suits, with radio wires running up and into their ears. There was no question that they were armed, but I didn't want to take any formal action, until I ran it by my captain. They told me the floor was private and closed.

I said, "That's okay. I got off on the wrong floor."

When I returned to my office, I wrote a report of investigation and then sat down with the Captain to discuss the matter with him in greater detail. I didn't want to reveal that my source was Dennis McCarthy. It could cause him trouble within his ranks.

The Captain sent the report to our Inspector for further instructions.

To be honest, I was hoping that Agent McCarthy would tell his friends that they were under investigation so, by the time I returned, they'd be gone.

On March 25, I received instructions from my Inspector to respond to the Watergate Hotel and take any action deemed necessary, if we found violations. When we arrived on the third floor, a man in a dark suit advised us that the floor was closed, and we'd have to get back on the elevator.

I said, "How do you close a floor?"

He said, "It's covered by the Secret Service," as he reached inside his coat.

Detective Rocky pulled out his badge and said, "Well I'm going to unclose it."

I pushed the man back against the wall and removed a .38 cal Smith and Wesson from his shoulder holster.

I said, "Think before you speak. Who are you?"

He said, "Retired Arlington County Police Detective, working as an executive protection agent for the Royal Family of Saudi Arabia."

Detective Rocky asked, "Do you have a Special Police commission to carry that gun."

He said, "No."

I asked, "Where is the rest of your detail?"

He told us that the rest of his company was out with the Prince and his friends.

I directed him, "Get your boss on the phone."

I told the owner of the agency about the violations we found and asked him, if he would return to the Watergate to work the matter out.

He inquired, "Are you going to arrest me?"

I replied, "Not if you can get here, within the next half hour."

When we walked into the room being used as the security station, we noticed several guns open in plain view. When the owner of the agency arrived, I told him I understood that he and his people were all ex-law enforcement and his agency was unlicensed. What I suggested was a compromise. If they wanted to turn any illegal weapons on the premises over to the D.C. Police for destruction, we would take them and, in lieu of arrests for any violations, we would only issue P.P. 61D - Violation Citations.

He agreed.

Trying to help him out, I also recommended that he file for a valid agency license and Special Police Commissions for his people.

My captain and Inspector were happy with the diplomatic manner, in which Detective Rocky and I handled the complaint.

That was the last criminal investigation Rocky conducted on the police department because he retired a month later. He was a good friend, and he got out at the right time.

We thought the private security operation matter was closed and handled, with complete discretion, until a couple of months later when I found a dead rat in my desk drawer. It had a noose around its neck and a note that read: DEAD MEAT.

I called McCarthy and told him what I found.

"Damn it, Ed," he whisper-yelled, "I tried all I could to warn you to leave it alone. You pissed off a lot of cops. Hit them below the belt when you stopped their bodyguard services. And I mean below the belt as in *the pocket*." He said, "Some of those guys were knocking down a thousand dollars a day in cash, under the table. Watch your back, Jagen, and trust no one."

I began to notice that I was getting the stink eye from cops everywhere I went.

Michael said, "It's no longer safe. Time to move on, with our mission."

I had one more year to go before I could qualify for an early retirement program.

On the side, I continued to work with Don Mitchell and Jim Brown on script development and a film deal. Unfortunately, Jim had a falling out with his friend, Richard Pryor, who replaced Jim Brown as president. Shortly thereafter, the screenplay was returned to me.

McCarthy retired from the Secret Service and published a tell all book of his exploits. "Protecting the President" was about his days in the U.S. Secret Service. The book was selling well, however, it was not well received by his fellow agents. They felt he revealed too many secrets, which put a target on his back from other federal agents.

What a pair we made, both of us hated by the same people for different reasons. I was viewed as a rat and he was a snitch. Many of the Fed's that were working as illegal bodyguards assumed that McCarthy was my source of information, and he was viewed as a rat as well.

Double trouble.

At the same time, terrorism was spreading globally, and many executives were being kidnapped in other countries. They were then ransomed for millions of dollars.

McCarthy asked me, if I ever thought about creating a private executive protection academy. He reminded me that bodyguard services were becoming necessary. Insurance companies like Lloyds of London, that underwrite kidnap and ransom policies, require a risk assessment and security training programs for all policyholders.

It sounded intriguing to me, so we decided to create Two Eagles International Inc., a security consulting firm, specializing in his field of executive protection and my area of risk assessment and investigations.

We put together a business plan and located the perfect site for Two Eagles Executive Protection Academy on the Eastern shore, just outside of Cambridge, Maryland. I passed the proposal onto Don Mitchell to help us locate investors.

I wanted to make sure that investor money was clean, so I ran any potential investors by Detective Sharkey.

In October, 1983, Jim Brown invited my wife and I to attend the third annual Riviera Hall of Fame Golf Classic. The purpose of the trip was to combine business and pleasure. In addition to having fun, Jim had lined up meetings with a few investors, who had expressed interest in the Two Eagles Academy project.

Linda had the time of her life, being chauffeured around Las Vegas by Jim Brown, in a white Rolls Royce.

When I met with the investors, I was surprised at how much interest there was in the security academy. Unfortunately, everyone wanted it in a location other than the site we chose. Michael was firm on the location being close to Washington because of other things we were working on.

When I returned to Washington, I ran the list of the potential investors by Detective Sharkey.

He said, "Half of them are mob connected, and the other half are probably associates, with mob money."

Remember my time with Sharkey? Back then, he was a self-proclaimed organized crime expert, and he was obsessed with the Mafia. He still was, but only worse. Never getting the big kill made him hungrier than before.

Michael advised me to watch out for him. He said, "He's paranoid and thinks everybody, *but him*, is connected to the Mafia."

Detective Sharkey had a short fuse and quick temper. I told him long ago that his temper was his weakness, and if he didn't watch out, it would be his down fall.

A few days after he ran the leads, I received a call from Sharkey. He was at the U.S. Attorney's office in a meeting. He was wondering if I could stop by and bring the photographs I showed him of a group of the high rollers I'd met at the Stardust Hotel and Casino.

When I arrived, there were several FBI Agents there, as well. One of them, Special Agent Steve Satin, demanded that I give him the photographs.

I said, "That's rude. Didn't J. Edger teach you guys better manners than that?"

Detective Sharkey asked, "Ed, could I please see the pictures?"

"Please?" I asked, implying Mr. Satin should have said 'please'. "Now gentleman, that's the way you ask for something," I tutored.

If looks could kill…

I handed him the photos. The agents pounced on the photos, like vultures on a dead rabbit.

The Assistant U.S. Attorney asked, "So these are your friends, detective?"

I said, "I don't even know those guys. Remember, I'm the one that brought this information to Detective Sharkey?"

Agent Satin said, "Who's been paying for you and your wife to fly out to Las Vegas?"

I said, "My literary agent, Don Mitchell. We have been working on a screenplay about some of my old undercover assignments and investigations."

Satin demanded in a loud voice, "I want to see that script."

I replied, "This isn't about me and my wife's vacation in Las Vegas, is it? It's about that illegal bodyguard service I busted a few months ago. Right? Were you working off duty with them?"

He shouted, "I'll asked the questions here, detective."

I barked back, "You're not asking questions. You're interrogating me, as if I were a criminal."

Agent Satin paused to regain his composer, and then said, "Mr. Jagen, how long have you been working with these organized crime figures?"

I just looked at him and shook my head, thinking, "what an asshole."

He went on to say, "I have an extremely reliable source of information that tells me you have been giving your organized crime buddies information for years."

I said, "And do you pay that source for information?"

At that point, I was ready to leave.

I could see this was a set up, and they intended to railroad me, but I stood my ground and said, "Within an hour, I can have several 'extremely reliable sources' that would say anything I want them to say about you, as well."

I picked up the photographs and said, "This witch hunt is over. If you want to continue this interrogation, charge me with something. Otherwise, you can fuck off."

The U.S. Attorney said, "We are not finished with you, son. Sit back down."

I replied, "But I am finished with you. I know my rights."

I turned and left the office.

The next day, I was called for a meeting with the Inspector. When I arrived Detective Sharkey and Agent Satin were seated outside the Inspector's office. I smiled, knocked, and then entered. My Inspector said that he was shocked when he received a call from the U.S. Attorney's office and the F.B.I., demanding that I be transferred out of the Intelligence Division, immediately. He went on to say that I was viewed as a threat to their confidential investigations because of my affiliation with known organized crime members. He informed me that I was, being transferred to the Fifth District's Detective Division.

Inspector Oliver said, "Listen, you are one of the best investigators I have, but my hands are tied. This has come from across the hall." The Intelligence Division was located across from the office of the Chief of Police.

I told him, "This is all bullshit. It's just the way certain federal cops were getting back at me, for their illegal bodyguard service that I busted up a few months earlier. Remember? As far as the organized crime allegation, I was the one giving that information to Detective Sharkey. He's just trying to ingratiate himself to the FBI."

The Inspector said again, "It's out of my control. The Director of the FBI said that they would not be able work with us, as long as you are in the Intelligence Division."

I asked, "And what have they ever given us that's really useful?"

In a flash vision Michael confirmed for me this was a setup.

He showed a scene of me, responding to a location and being shot in the back by another cop. The police department then would write off the homicide, as retaliation by the IRA for disrupting their gun-running operation.

I said, "Inspector Oliver, I truly enjoyed working for you and serving the public, but I am destined for far better things than being bullied, by a bunch of greedy, disgruntled federal agents. With all due respect, I am refusing the transfer. I have over three months of leave accrued."

I pulled out my gun and badge. Laying them on his desk I said, "I can turn in my gun and badge now or in three months. The choice is yours."

Inspector Oliver said, "Take some time off to think about this. You're a good detective, a year from partial retirement and only five years from full retirement."

I said, "I've already been branded a rat for doing my job... and now an insubordinate criminal. What's left? Getting mysteriously shot in the back one day? No, that's not in the cards for me."

When I left the office, Detective Sharkey was at the water fountain. I went up and stood behind him as he drank.

He said, "Jagen, you shouldn't have compromised yourself."

I could feel Michael wasn't finished.

Inspector Oliver interrupted, "Detective Jagen, you need to clean out your desk today."

I announced to Sharkey, "You are full of crap and always have been. Karma will catch up to you one day. What goes around comes around." I reminded him.

I wanted to punch Sharkey for allowing Agent Satin to manipulate the truth of what really happened. As my irritation flared, I thought, "If I smack him now, it is just a disagreement between two cops. If I punch him in three months, it's assault on a police officer."

Michael reminded me that I should take the high road, so I said, "I forgive your stupidity Sharkey, but you bit off more than you can stomach this time, my friend."

I decided to just let his negative karma take its course.

Chapter Thirty-three

Onward and Upward

I had enough time on the police department to retire under the "Deferred Annuities Retirement Act." It was a program the D.C. Government was offering police officers that were hired before Home Rule was passed in 1972. After Home Rule passed, the police department went from federal status to local government overnight.

The real reason for the change was the U.S. Congress didn't want to continue to foot the bill for the District of Columbia anymore. All the citizens wanted home rule and statehood status. The District didn't have any voting powers in Congress, and it didn't have any federal money either.

I could retire, but would not be able to draw retirement allotments until age fifty-five.

I filed for early retirement and took the next several months using up my sick leave. Inspector Oliver told me three more times that I was making a mistake because I only had five more years to go, in order to receive full retirement. Michael assured me that I needed to move on to achieve the goals that were set for me. Travel was a part of that, and oh yes, being alive was too.

A few weeks after my resignation, I began to notice that I was sometimes under mobile surveillance. Then I noticed that two men, with binoculars, were watching my house. I couldn't figure out why anyone would still be interested in me, unless it was someone from one of my prior investigations, with a personal vendetta.

I heard through the grapevine that, with me out of the way, the illegal bodyguard services were back in full swing. I crossed them off the list of possibilities as the ones watching me. I had to get to the bottom of it, so I decided to call in "a suspicious man with a gun" complaint to the local county police on the two guys with binoculars outside, watching my home. After an officer arrived, I walked up to the men watching me, as they were explaining to the officer that they were not watching my house. They couldn't explain why they had portable radios and binoculars in their vehicle.

I told the investigating officer that I was a retired police detective, being harassed by off duly cops because of a police corruption investigation I had conducted a year earlier. I demanded that a police report be taken, so if anything happened to me, the police would know where to start their investigation.

The officer refused to take the report and sent the two men on their way.

That night, I had a dream that Detective Sharkey came to me and apologized for letting the agents manipulate the information and spin it to look like I was a threat. I just turned and walked away from him. A few weeks later, I learned that Sharkey died from an intestinal infection. I felt bad that his spirit came to me, and I turned my back. I lit a candle for him, in the hope that when he reached the other side, he would see the true motivation for his actions. Michael always told me that all we take with us is our story. So, that's all we have when we reach the other side. Sharkey never attained the organized crime expert status he was so desperately seeking. Or did he?

I asked Michael if he really came to me, or was it just a dream? All he said was, "Does it matter?"

Chapter Thirty-four

Two Eagles International

In 1984, Michael said that it was time to start gathering the Mighty 144 that would be needed to help uncover the lost Book of Wisdom from Atlantis. I didn't have any idea what he was talking about.

A little tense from the way things broke off from my police career, I was thinking, 'what the hell is Michael going to have me do next'? Since McCarthy and I had both retired, we could now focus on Two Eagles, the private security agency. Michael also threw into the mix, a non-profit, called the National Missing Child Search Society.. The ultimate Divine purpose of the two companies was to locate 144 special souls, living on the planet that would be like me, a human vessel working with an angel. He called us "Angel-Knights." We were to become the guardians of the "Great Knowing" that would come out of the Book of Wisdom.

Michael went on to say, "As you and I search for the child, with the initials MV, we will need money--and the security agency will help fund the search."

I approached a number of my old friends, from the government task forces that I had been on over the years, to see if they would be interested in joining the Two Eagles agency. The only two that were interested in helping were Dennis McCarthy and Admiral Elmo "Bud" Zumwalt, Jr.

The Admiral retired several years earlier and had already established a specialized consulting firm in Virginia. He saw that he could use Two Eagles to help some of his clients.

I withdrew all my retirement from of the D.C. Government pension program and incorporated both companies in Virginia, with the help of the Admiral. I was hoping to find the 144 souls Michael was seeking, who shared backgrounds in military and/or law enforcement like me. We needed people, who had already demonstrated the courage to confront the darkness of man and had the discipline to see a hard mission through to the end.

With the National Missing Child Search Society, the goal was to volunteer as an investigator, in active missing children cases, and turn any intelligence information over to the law enforcement jurisdiction, handling the case. I was both shocked and happy to see how many retired police investigators were quick to join the effort. It was a good thing because, unfortunately, the society had forty missing children cases under investigation that first year.

Two Eagles International Inc. specialized in asset assessment, executive protection and international banking fraud. One of the Admiral's clients was, Sir Edgar Windsor. He was involved with banking transactions in Argentina, Brazil, Colombia, England, France and Germany. The deals had already cost him over one hundred thousand dollars. Now Windsor was getting the run around on the closing dates and wanted a special investigator to look into the matter.

Sir Edgar related that a man, calling himself Dr. Barry Jackson, The President of Prime Bank Investments Ltd., was arranging for the purchase of Letters of Credit (LCs) and Prime Bank Promissory Notes (PBNs), with a total value of $3 billion dollars. Mr. Jackson would leverage the purchase of the notes at a discount, then offer a lesser discount and sell the notes to another broker in another market, netting the fallout of approximately $100 million dollars.

Sir Edgar invested $50,000 in the venture for an expected return of $3 million dollars, within thirty days. He went on to say that there had been one delay after the other and three months into the transaction, Dr. Jackson, the broker, needed to raise more funds to satisfy the bankers in Germany and Colombia.

Sir Edgar invested another $50,000 and was now into the venture for $100,000, with a promised $8-million-dollar payout.

McCarthy and I met with a Securities and Exchange Commission Investigator friend, who told us, "That's what we call an arbitrage transaction. It's the simultaneous buying and selling of securities, currency or commodities in different markets or in derivative forms, in order to take advantage of differing prices for the same assets in other parts of the world." He further advised that, in his experience, few arbitrage transactions ever got to closing, and the marketplace is flooded with fraudulent brokers that play into investor greed. He advised us to tell our client not to invest any more money, and that he would probably lose what he has already invested.

The following day, I met with Sir Edgar and submitted my report and recommendation that he not invest any more funds because it was most likely a scam. He did not want to hear that.

Windsor was upset at my recommendation and screamed, "But you don't know that it's a scam." He went on to say, "I just wired another $25,000, bringing my return to $10 million dollars. I want that money, and I want you to go to Germany and make sure this deal closes."

I could see that greed had taken over and nothing I was going to say would convince him otherwise.

I told Sir Edgar, "Two Eagles standard fee for travel and investigations of this nature is $1,000 a day, plus expenses, with a $5,000 retainer when it involves international travel."

He offered, "I'll cut you in on my deal with Dr. Jackson. You foot your own fee and expenses, and I'll give you two million dollars in commission when the transaction closes."

Michael reminded me of all the scams I'd seen go down, while undercover, saying, "If it sounds too good to be true, it probably is!"

I told Sir Edgar, "It's too much of a gamble, and I never bet on anything I can't hold in my hand. Two Eagles is a corporation. It is not solely mine, anyway. I can't take that offer."

Sir Edgar replied, "I've already worked out that same deal, with my attorney, Judah Weinstein. She is in Germany, working on contracts between me and Dr. Jackson."

I could see how throwing around all those large numbers could bring out the greed in someone, but it all comes down to trust. I didn't trust Sir Edgar because he was already bitten, by the demon of greed.

While we were talking, Sir Edgar received a phone call from his attorney in Germany. Judah relayed to him that the transaction was moving to London in the morning, and the payout was to come within the next three days.

Sir Edgar was happy saying, "Detective you should have taken me up on my offer. You would have been a rich man, by the end of the week."

I said, "That's fine. I'm happy for you."

I handed him my bill for services rendered thus far. He wrote me a check for five hundred dollars, and I left.

The next day a nine-year-old, little girl was reported missing from Silver Spring, Maryland, and the family had been referred to the charity. The child had just vanished from the backyard of her father's house, during his bi-monthly custody visitation.

McCarthy took the call and agreed to meet with the parents. The father was a strange fellow, and we became very suspicious that he might be involved somehow.

The police investigators didn't like the fact that a private investigative agency was looking into the matter.

When I was standing in the father's backyard, where the child was last seen, Michael gave me a vision of two little boys, playing in a backyard two yards away. When I walked into the house, I saw a man dressed like a clown, wearing a rainbow-colored bush wig. The man took me upstairs and made me cry. When I wouldn't stop crying, the clown stabbed me in the stomach, with something, and everything went black. It was a sickening vision.

Michael said, "The child's spirit has already passed into the afterlife, so it will be hard to locate her body." I didn't want to work the case any further knowing that, but Denny insisted. I just didn't see anything good coming from it.

After two days of canvassing the area and interviewing neighbors, everything kept coming back to the house two doors up the street.

One evening, while sitting on a surveillance of the house, a man came out carrying a mannequin dressed in a clown outfit, wearing a rainbow-colored bush wig. He put the mannequin in his white pickup truck and drove away. I learned that the man had recently been released from the U.S. Navy on a psychiatric medical discharge. He had moved in with his brother and twin little boys.

A neighbor told me that the twin boys were always trying to get other kids to come play with them, but the man would always insist on playing too. The most I could get out of them was the man made them feel uncomfortable.

Based on the vision and the investigation, I was sure that man was responsible for the little girl's disappearance.

When McCarthy and I sat down with police investigators, they let us know that they felt we were hindering their investigation. One detective in particular had a major envy problem, fearing that we would find the child's body before he did. As is always the case with any investigation, everything depends on the quality of the investigators. From what I could see, this case was doomed from the start.

I told them that I was 100% sure the man was responsible, and it wasn't the first, nor would it be the last, time he killed. Our information fell on deaf ears and big egos.

There was nothing more we could offer, so the case was closed for us. But the mother of the missing girl kept calling McCarthy, trying to get us to continue the investigation.

I warned McCarthy against it because there was too much darkness attached to the case. Michael said they would try to blame everything on us in the end.

We had cases working on both fronts...with Two Eagles and Child Search.

A few days after I last saw Sir Edgar, he called me again.

The banking transaction still hadn't completed, and he wanted me to investigate. He told me he fired the attorney because he no longer trusted her. He agreed to the terms of the Two Eagles contract.

I was on a plane the next day.

When I arrived in Frankfurt, Germany I met with attorney, Judah Weinstein. She was a tall good-looking woman, who didn't seem to care that Sir Edgar fired her.

After reviewing all the contracts, I could see that the mastermind behind the transaction was floating from one phony bank to the next, offering to sell people promises, based on no real bank notes. I couldn't believe how easily Dr. Jackson was tricking people to invest in the deals, until I met the good doctor.

He was one of the most gifted con men I had ever met. He knew just what to say, and if one thing didn't work, he'd say something else. If all else failed, he would offer to increase the payout. He should have been a politician. It was almost like he put you into a hypnotic trance where you believed that any day money would just come, raining down from out of the sky.

The greed bug had also bitten Ms. Weinstein, so I knew I couldn't trust her. Sad to say, it looked like Jackson was setting her up to take the fall for all of it. He actually had her signing all the contracts for him. His name wasn't documented anywhere.

He was a mastermind.

At this point, I needed to know who Dr. Jackson really was. He was too perfect to be real. After being undercover for so many years and having to live a lie, I could spot a fellow liar.

During our first meeting, I told him that I was a private investigator sent by Sir Edgar to help speed up the transaction. I had wiped my ID folder and badge free of any fingerprints. I handed it to Jackson to verify who I was. When he returned it, I had his prints.

That night I called McCarthy and asked if he had any Interpol contacts in Frankfurt, with whom I could share the banking fraud case. An hour later, I was meeting with Chief Inspector Albert Albright. On my way to the meeting, Michael informed me that Judah Weinstein was one of the 144 souls we were seeking, so I had to find some way of breaking her free from the case. That wasn't going to be easy.

When Albright ran the prints, we learned that "Dr. Jackson" was really Barry Barrymore, a black organized crime figure from Atlanta, Georgia. He was wanted in the states for several money laundering scams and bank fraud.

Albright and Interpol were now pulled into the investigation. I told the Inspector I felt that Weinstein was being deceived and used by Barrymore to keep him looking clean. I said, "The best way to crack the case wide open is to walk you into the transaction, so you can deal directly with the players."

He liked that idea and suggested, "Judah Weinstein will have to introduce me to Dr. Jackson, as Sir Edgar."

Now I had to convince Judah to play along.

I told Inspector Albright, "The best way to break Judah's trust of Jackson is to take her into custody and question her about the banking fraud. She'll break from the fear."

The next morning, when I had breakfast with Dr. Jackson and Attorney Weinstein, I was advised by Jackson that the banking transaction was going to close at the Bank of Bermuda in four days, but he needed another $50,000 to secure the bankers' loyalty to handle the deal.

Jackson's strategy was to jump from country to country to keep local law enforcement from closing in on him. That's why I went to Interpol.

I told Dr. Jackson, "I will call Sir Edgar about the additional funds, but I don't think he's going to invest any more money, until one of these transactions close."

I walked Judah back to her hotel. The police were lying in wait. Shortly after we got to her room, there was a knock on the door. It was Inspector Albright and two uniformed officers. He told Judah that the banking transactions she was working on were based on fraudulent offerings, and that the man she knew as Dr. Jackson was really a con artist from Atlanta, Georgia, by the name of Berry Barrymore.

To play along in front of Judah, I told the Inspector, "I am a retired Washington D.C. Intelligence investigator, hired by one of the investors to determine if the transaction is real. From what I have found out so far, I don't think Judah was part of the con, and Jackson is just using her. I recommend that Interpol perform an undercover sting operation on Jackson and his crew."

Ms. Weinstein was shaking her head "no" the entire time I was talking.

It didn't deter me, though. I continued to lay out what the Inspector and I talked about the day before.

"I could have an undercover Interpol investigator pretend to be my client, Sir Edgar. It is perfect because Dr. Jackson is now asking for another $50,000."

Judah was scared to death that she was going to jail.

Michael told me to get the inspector to offer Judah a return to the states once the introduction to Jackson was made.

I said to Inspector Albright, "Since Ms. Weinstein and I are the only ones that know what Sir Edgar looks like, once we walk your agent into the case, we can go home, right?"

He agreed.

I don't know how Michael made that happen so easily. There must have been some serious energetic diversion going on for an Interpol Inspector to agree to let an accomplice leave.

That evening, I met with Dr. Jackson and three of his associates for drinks. I told him that Sir Edgar wasn't happy about having to come up with the additional $50,000. I went on to say that he was flying in the next day to negotiate a new deal.

Dr. Jackson seemed nervous and said that if he didn't have the money for the bankers, the deal would fall through.

"I'll relay the information, but I have no control. Obviously, you know that," I stated bluntly.

The next day, Inspector Albright was introduced to Dr. Jackson, as Sir Edgar, since the two had never met. I had given the Inspector a report of all the deals and percentages that were promised, so he could level the playing field and con the con man. I had also prearranged that after the introduction was made, he would fire both his attorney and private investigator, in front of Dr. Jackson, to clear the slate.

The plan worked like a charm, and we were free to return to Washington.

Sir Edgar wasn't happy to hear that Interpol was investigating all the banking transactions.

I told him, "Listen, if the deals do turn out to be real, you will get your money. However, if it is a fraud, at least law enforcement knows where your money is. All accounts will be frozen and Dr. Jackson, aka Barrymore, will go to jail."

Six months later, Barrymore was charged with international banking fraud and Sir Edgar Windsor recovered half of his investment.

When I returned to Maryland, I was thrown back into the missing girl's case.

Denny McCarthy told me that the police picked up our suspect in the case. However, when they questioned him, he went crazy and started vomiting all over the interrogation room.

The investigator didn't think he was involved in the girl's disappearance. They were still focused on the father, as their prime suspect.

Michael gave me a vision of a homeless person's campsite, overlooking a freeway. A short distance away from the shack was a mattress, covering the girl's body. It was nothing I could give the police, so Denny and I searched several months for the location, but it was like looking for a needle in a haystack.

I asked the Angel to guide me to the site. He said that it was shrouded in darkness, and it would require the man to kill again, to shine light on the area.

The suspect moved to New England for a couple of years, but when he returned, he began working as a groundskeeper at a private mansion and murdered a young woman at the home a few months later. Police investigators learned that the man had a campsite in a nearby forest, overlooking a freeway.

A search of that campsite revealed the little girl's body in a shallow grave covered by a mattress.

The case was closed.

My wife, Linda, worked for one of the vice presidents of the Marriott Corporation. Their food distribution center was suffering from a huge inventory shrinkage problem. They wanted to hire Two Eagles to investigate and assess their vulnerability. After three days of surveillance, we discovered that the plant was bleeding product. Since it was costing the corporation over a million dollars a year in product loss, I suggested that our company hire and train a completely new security staff.

Michael wanted me to interview potential staff from individuals leaving the military. That would give us a chance to integrate what he called positive reasoning into their training. It took us two months to narrow the field of applicants down to those we felt had all the right qualities.

The twenty-four-member team consisted of twelve women and twelve men.

Through me, Michael taught them mental perception exercises that helped them gain new, investigative techniques. In order to give them full disclosure on what was happening, we explained it as a series of lessons to help them tap into a higher state of awareness. At the beginning of the lessons, their level of understanding could not comprehend what Michael was trying to achieve. He was experimenting with aligning angels, with the consciousness of each security officer. After the completion of the lessons, their understanding had achieved what he called positive reasoning, and they understood when an angelic energy was communicating with them.

One of the biggest problems Michael said humans have, when communicating with the angelic consciousness, is the ability to translate the guidance coming through. This is due to the angelic thought vibration being so much higher or faster than the human thought vibration. The reason he worked so well with me from the start was that my mental vibration changed, when I had the near-death experience. I had been working with him since age eight.

A lot of humans hear buzzing in their ears, or a ringing, as they describe it. Doctors misdiagnose it as "tinnitus."

Under Michael's guidance, each officer on the force learned the subtle nuance individual to them, that helped in recognizing when the angel was coming to them from their higher self. It was amazing to see how quickly they grew and learned. They became the best security force I had ever seen. We buttoned up the distribution center so tight that the inventory shrinkage, or theft, was cut by 96%.

Michael initiated a competition between the three security teams called "steal the box." One box represented each team. I would place the boxes in different locations around the plant, and the goal was, by the end of each month, the team or teams that could get the boxes off the property would win cash and prizes.

In over a year of playing the game, only two boxes were ever stolen.

By 1987, the charity's ability to finance their investigations was becoming a major issue. The bigger problem though, was that the local active police authorities had problems with our retired police volunteers, digging into their cases. They didn't like their territory being intruded upon. It was sad that it came down to ego, when children's lives were at stake. I could see that the private investigative side of this problem wasn't going to work.

Angel Michael said that most of the volunteer officers didn't have what he was looking for to become part of the 144 Light Bearers. He said it was time to change the direction of the charity and focus on child abduction prevention. The sadness of finding missing children dead... was affecting us, as well. Especially when we knew that the abductions could have been prevented. Everything the charity was doing at that point was after the fact. We wanted to start being proactive.

When I married Linda and adopted her daughter, Dawn, I had high hopes that the girl child with the initials M.V., Michael was seeking, would come from that vein. Unfortunately, like her mother, Dawn had chosen the wrong partner to marry, and the cycle continued.

Brad Spencer, one of the most self-serving narcissistic individuals I had ever met, was the recipient of Dawn's love. His negativity was destined to carry over into his children.

Dawn delivered a beautiful baby girl named, Meghan Victoria, in January. I wondered, "Could this be the child with the initials M.V. that Michael was seeking?" Only time would tell.

Chapter Thirty-five

The Man from Jupiter

On August 7, 1988, Michael said the time had come for me to seek a connection to the lost Wisdom Books of Atlantis. He told me to plan an early morning visit to the mountains of Northern Maryland, around Frederick, the next day.

Archangel Michael guided me to Mount St. Mary's at Emmittsburg, Maryland. It was Monday, August 8th at 8:44 a.m., when I stood at the base of the shrine. I was to sit in front of the statue of Our Lady of Lourdes in the Grotto and meditate. At 9:00 a.m., the bell tower at the entrance rang out nine times. I turned in the direction of the sound. I could see a black man, wearing white robes walking down the path toward me. He was carrying what appeared to be a stack of white papers.

When he reached the grotto, he knelt down, facing the cavern, with his back to me. It was a beautiful, sunny morning. Birds were singing and four white tail deer were standing off in the distance by some trees, as the man spoke.

He said, "Hermit, the Angel tells me your waiting is now full, and I should pass onto you the Ancient Books of Wisdom. I am the Hierophant."

He paused.

Once again, being at a loss for words, I said, "My name is Ed..."

He interrupted saying, "Ed is dead. From this day forward and until you find your true identity, you will be known as my student and teacher, the Hermit. For you will learn from me, and I from you."

Handing me the papers he continued, "Take these pages and return to the shores of the Solomon Sea. Archangel Michael will bring you to me once a month, on the eighth day. I will share with you, then, what you need to know, in order for you to move forward."

I started to say thank you, but was interrupted again with his soft words, "Go now, Hermit and don't you dare look back, because if you do, your journey will end where you stand."

As the pages left his grasp, I could see the Hierophant's dark skin, white beard, hair and robes start to fade from my vision. He was disappearing right before my eyes. I thought, "I must be dreaming."

I walked away as quickly as possible. I wanted to turn around *so badly* to see what was becoming of this tall, black, mysterious man, but his words kept ringing in my ears, "… and don't you dare look back, because...."

When I returned to my car, I couldn't wait to look at the pages; however, when I did they were blank.

I couldn't believe it. How was I supposed to learn lessons from blank sheets of paper?

Michael said, "When the student is ready, the teacher will come. Have patience, Hermit, the lessons will come when your teacher is ready for his student."

That night, after Linda and I went to bed, I couldn't sleep. She was out like a light as soon as her head hit the pillow, but I laid there, trying to fall asleep. It was sometime just before midnight, when Michael came to me and said it was time to go.

"Go where?" I asked.

He told me to close my eyes and think of nothing. That is the last thing to tell me, because telling me to think about nothing makes me think about everything.

That night I was particularly anxious. I thought about things I didn't know you could even think about. With all these thoughts flashing through my mind, it was hopeless. Finally, I felt Michael touch my forehead, and I fell into a deep sleep.

The first thing I remember was floating through space. I could see the Earth and how beautiful our home planet truly is.

Michael said, "Everything is beautiful from afar but, up close, there are always unforeseen dangers lurking." He showed me a scene of an incredibly beautiful tropical island. The beach was breathtaking. I wanted to swim in the warm waters. A tiger came running towards me from the nearby jungle. I ran into the surf and saw that hungry sharks surrounded me.

I got his message, "Enjoy the beauty, but always look for the deeper meaning and hidden dangers."

As we floated through space, to my right, I could see the Sun, Mercury and Venus. There was no sound, and I was cold, but not freezing. To my left I could see Mars, Jupiter and the rings around Saturn. Off in the distance were Uranus with its icy rings, Neptune and Pluto.

Michael guided me through the clouds over Jupiter and down through the winds that make up the Great Red Spot. We landed on a mountaintop, where I was once again in the presence of the tall black man I'd met that morning.

The Hierophant asked, "Are you ready to receive the First Lesson from the Books of Wisdom?"

I don't remember a sound coming out of my mouth, but I know I answered him, "Yes," with my mind.

He said, "I will tell you the first thing my teacher, Grand Master ERU, told me. It was his power phrase. I will repeat his words at the beginning of each lesson to honor my teacher and to help infuse you with his great power. The words are, "'The more you know, the more *Knowing* will come to you.'"

I told the Hierophant that I was ready.

He continued, "Over the next fifty-two months, I will deliver unto you the knowledge of the Magi. You will have a month to practice the lesson. If you fail to master any lesson, we will stop and your growth will end."

My heart started to pound and my head started to spin, as he spoke faster and faster. Then in a flash, he was gone.

I sat down on a large boulder to regain my breath. I felt like my mind had run a marathon. I couldn't remember a thing of what the Hierophant said.

I was confused.

I asked Michael, "Where did the Hierophant go?"

Michael said, "He is still here, your vibration just slowed down, so you can't see him, but he is still here. The Hierophant and his people *are* the Great Red Spot of Jupiter. Their energy is a storm that has been raging here, since the day Atlantis was taken from Earth."

I regained my breath, and he said, "It's time to return home."

We floated back up into space. I studied the swirling storm of that Great Red Spot, as we soared higher and higher. It was beautiful, but seemed hauntingly dangerous. I couldn't imagine a whole race of people and their great continent being lifted up from earth and deposited on another planet. I wondered why it was done. Were the Atlantians being punished, or were they being saved as part of some Divine Plan?

Michael returned me to my bedroom. I could see my body still snuggled up all warm and cozy next to Linda, who was fast asleep. Michael left me with instructions to write down everything the Hierophant had taught me on the papers he gave me earlier that day.

I was in a fog and didn't know where to start. I laid there for a while, but could not sleep. My head was abuzz with letters, words, numbers and of all the odd things... playing cards. Finally, I got out of bed and went to my front porch. Looking at the waves of the Chesapeake Bay, rolling onto the shore in the moonlight, I knew there was something inside my head that wanted to come out, but damned if I could remember a thing the Hierophant had said.

I sat down at the table where my typewriter was sitting. I picked up the first sheet of paper from the stack I was given and rolled it into the carriage. Placing my fingers on the keys, I noticed my right ring finger flinched, and then it struck a key on its own. It was the letter L, then the next keys e, s, s, o and then the n was struck.

I stopped. My mind was flooding again with letters, numbers and colorful playing cards. One card in particular, the ace of hearts, stood out. I calmed myself and started again. Tap-tap-tap, I typed. I found that the Hierophant was sending me a letter in the form of a lesson or was it a lesson in the form of a letter. It was coming from the inside out.

It all came out one letter at a time:

Special note to Hermit: The fifty-three lessons I am passing down to you make up an exceptional deck of Wisdom Cards. By the time you finish reading the knowledge and practicing the lessons over each month, you will be playing with a full deck of Wisdom. Only then will you develop the "Knowing" needed to help Angel Michael continue his Divine Quest to help Humanity.

In time, you will have special, advanced humans seek you out for these Wisdom lessons, for they too must acquire the "Knowing" necessary to become Angel-Knights in service to the Angels of the Four Directions. Listen well, because the time will come when you will make these lost Wisdom Cards available to all seekers of the "Knowing."

I paused and read back what I had channeled. I wondered what all of this meant. My head was aching, so I left the house and walked down to Cove Point

Beach, where we lived, and walked along the shoreline. The water was warm. Before I knew it, I was at the lighthouse. I walked out onto the long sandbar that had formed off the point. I felt like I was walking on water and standing in the middle of the Chesapeake Bay.

I looked up and saw several shooting stars.

I made a wish, "Please let me hear what's needed to be written down, and can you take my headache away too, please?" I begged.

A few minutes later, a helicopter from the Naval Base at Patuxent River came flying overhead. It hit me, with a blinding white light. My headache was gone. I waved at the crew on board the helicopter. They held the light on me for a few more seconds, then flew on. I must have looked strange to them, standing so far out in the water from land.

I then walked back to my beach house to finish channeling the first chapter of the Book of Wisdom. With my head clear and a buzzing in my ears, I continued to type the letters the Hierophant was sending.

PART TWO

Special Note to Seeker:

In this section of the book, my story continues as I receive channeled lessons once a month, from the Hierophant.

Since the lessons that were channeled are sometimes very long, I have moved the complete lessons to the Appendix "Book of Wisdom" in the back of this book. I did not want the story that is being conveyed to distract from the lessons because they are far more important than my life story.

When I channeled the lessons each month, the Hierophant asked me to read the lesson once a day for seven days to give my subconscious mind a chance to absorb the knowledge therein. Then, I was asked to apply the lesson to my everyday life. When I did, everything changed.

I hope you find all that you seek. We are now in this together. God speed.

Chapter Thirty-six

An Open Channel

Sitting in front of my typewriter I was in awe of what my fingers were doing. I was truly an observer of a divine process. I became an open channel for the words and lessons of the Hierophant.

After I was finished channeling the first lesson from the Hierophant and then re-read it, I was astounded at what I had remembered. I sat back in stunned admiration, not admiring myself for doing it, but in pure awe and admiration of the process. Normally if something like that happens, one would sit back and say, "Wow, where did that come from?" I knew where it came from, so I was doubly stunned. When my fingers stopped, Lesson One was complete.

Lesson One

Ace of Hearts received August 8, 1988
Book of Wisdom channeled from the Hierophant:

"The more you know, the more 'Knowing' will come to you." ERU

My Beloved Hermit and Teacher,

It is my hope that we will have a long, prosperous relationship lasting for many, many years to come. The Magi, for those who dare seek the "Knowing," designed the Ancient Books of Wisdom. The Books are not for everyone because, without a strong passion to better oneself, the lessons contained herein are wasted and could drive the weak minded into madness. It does not matter at what "level" you think you are currently operating... novice, beginner, intermediate, advanced or expert, because when labeling yourself, you are filling your glass, so that it cannot be added to.

Remember: When you think you know, you don't. And when you KNOW you don't, you do! "Always be humble."

In this lesson, I received the introduction to the Path of the Magi, The Door to the Mind, and Progressive Relaxation, which laid the foundation for all the lessons to come. I was also given the first two Ancient Laws of Wisdom: (1.) "The more you use your ability to help another, the more your ability will grow." (2.) "The door to the psychic world is not opened with a ram, but with the slightest caress."

Note: The first lesson opened the door for me to all the other lessons that were to follow. In some cases, I have expanded on the original writing I was given to upgrade the lessons, with other references given to me over the years, as they became available. I suggest you do the same for your future students if you so desire.

Every month on the eighth day, I would use the meditation techniques the Hierophant taught me in lesson one.

The Progressive Relaxation Technique is one of the most valuable lessons in this series. It helps to reduce stress on the body, mind and spirit. It is also a valuable tool to connect to your higher self and learn the process of channeling and surrender.

Before beginning every month's lesson, it is suggested that you go into a meditation, using what you have learned from Lesson One. If you don't master and use Lesson One, the Knowing will be out of reach.

SEE APPENDIX FOR ENTIRE LESSON

After practicing Lesson One for a while, I tried to get Linda to try the progressive relaxation techniques.

The night I chose to teach her, she'd had a really hard day at work. Unfortunately, she relaxed so much that her meditation turned into a deep, sleep and I couldn't wake her.

I had to carry Linda to bed. She was exhausted.

When she awoke the next morning, she said that she had never slept so soundly, but she had dreams of flying through space and landing on a planet and talking to a black man, wearing a white robe. I couldn't believe it... Linda had tapped into the Hierophant. She unknowingly did her first and *last* astral projection. When I told her what had happened, it scared her. It was the end of spirituality for her.

The best way to sum Linda up, as a person, is that she has the soul of a gypsy, the heart of a hippy and the spirit of a fairy. Mostly she is earthy and desires to have both feet planted firmly on the ground. Any thought of her spirit leaving her body freaked her out, and she didn't want any part of the Hierophant's lessons from that point on.

A few days later, Denny and I received a call from a potential client, Robert King. Mr. King owned Raven Arms, an old brownstone apartment building in Richmond, Virginia. He said he was looking for a paranormal investigator to look into strange activity in the building. He told us that two of the residents, a man and a woman, were complaining that their apartments were haunted, and ghosts were sexually assaulting them, in the middle of the night.

Denny and I looked at each other, and I swear we read each other's minds. I almost burst out laughing

In the back of my mind I remembered Sgt. Kiki telling me about demonic spirits called Incubus and Succubus, male and female energies that have "sexual intercourse" with human victims.

It sounded like easy money. We took the case because we needed to fund a few investigations in Maryland that Denny was looking into.

While Denny took some more information from Mr. King, I pretended to look around, while Michael was transmitting information to me. He said that these demons are very real. They were negative human energies that sexually preyed on others, while they were living, and now that their spirits were caught between our dimension and the next, they were still seeking "playmates."

Denny got all the information needed, and we took off for the apartment complex.

As soon as Denny and I arrived at the building, we interviewed the first victim. She was a 30-year-old Asian American named, Suzy Lee. She claimed that all the demonic attacks were similar in nature, and they started about a year earlier. On the night of the last assault, she was watching television in bed and remembers getting a headache. When she got up to go to the bathroom for a couple of aspirins, she passed out in the hallway. As she laid on the floor, she couldn't move. The lights then went out in the apartment. She heard several voices, coming from the living room.

The next thing she remembered was her body being lifted into the air. She floated onto the dining room table. She still felt paralyzed and could not move a muscle. She went into very graphic detail about what she felt was happening to her body. Then she said she felt a heavy weight on her chest as something pushed up inside her. The pain was more than she could stand, and she passed out again.

She told us the following morning, she woke up in her bed, and her whole body was sore. She had bite marks on her breasts and inner thighs. When she stood up, a yellowish fluid was flowing out from between her legs.

Denny looked quizzically at her and then me, and asked, "Did you happen to save any of the fluid, so we could have it tested to determine its nature?"

She shook her head "no." The incident had happened two weeks earlier, and she didn't save any evidence of the attack. She revealed that she had been "sexually attacked" six other times over the past year.

Over that same timeframe, she awoke many times in the middle of the night feeling paralyzed, hearing voices and feeling invisible hands touching her body.

In reliving the assaults, she began to cry.

Denny looked at me and rolled his eyes in disbelief. She didn't notice him, through her tears.

Denny asked Suzy why she didn't call the police.

She said, "Right, and the cops would believe I was raped by a couple of ghosts?!" She got up from the table to get a napkin to dry her eyes, then continued. "They would think I was crazy. Just like I'm sure you do?"

I said, "Suzy I, for one, can see from the pain you are in that you are telling the truth. Our job is to find out where the negative energy is coming from and remove it from your apartment. You are not the only resident, living in this building, who has reported being attacked by spirits."

She wanted to know who else had been attacked. I said just like her case, it was under investigation. And like her, all victim's names needed to remain private for the time being.

She was trembling and seemed like a nervous wreck. I really wanted to help her before we moved on to interview the second victim, but was at a loss for words.

Michael said, "Remember what the Hierophant said, 'The more you use your ability to help another, the more your ability will grow.' Teach Suzy the Progressive relaxation technique you learned."

I decided to speak up, "Suzy, you seem to be really shaken. I know a little exercise that I use to help me clear my mind and relax. Can I share it with you?"

She sheepishly said, "Sure. Can't hurt, I guess."

I wrote out the sequence of what parts of the body to relax on a sheet of paper and what to say. Together we went through one sequence. After we were finished, she said she felt much better. I gave her the sheet of paper, so she could repeat the lesson whenever she needed.

I then let her know that I wasn't just a private investigator, and that I was also very sensitive to paranormal electro-magnetic energy, put out by spirits. I asked her if I could walk around the apartment to get a feel for the presence of her attacking spirits.

Earlier that day, before Denny and I left to meet with Mr. King, I put a bag of white sage in my briefcase. Just the mention of paranormal activity reminded me of what Sgt. Kiki taught me in Germany. Whenever there was negative energy, he showed me how to purge a room or area, by burning sage. Native Americans call this "smudging." I'm glad I had the forethought to bring that bag with me.

I took the sage from my briefcase and asked Suzy for a ceramic or glass bowl. I lit the sage in the bowl she gave me and started to fan the smoke out into the four directions of each room, with the back of my right hand.

Denny was looking at me, as if I had lost my mind.

As I walked from room to room, I was getting the impression of two men and a woman walking through the wall, with a sexual ceremony on their minds. When I got to Suzy's bedroom my attention was drawn to a copper heating vent in the ceiling above her bed.

When I was finished, I sat Suzy back down at the table in the kitchen. I told her that I did not sense any negative presence in her home, but if the spirits come back, I needed her to try to write down whatever she hears the spirits saying to one another. I also told her how important it was that she saves any evidence that has been left behind.

I explained how humans live in a physical dimension, surrounded by many other dimensions beyond our awareness, and sometimes things can cross over through temporary portals. I used the smoke from the white sage to close any possible portals that were in her home.

I asked Suzy what she wanted the outcome of our investigation to be, and she said, "I just want the attacks to stop."

I told her that we would be back in a month to check on her or, if something happened sooner, to call us immediately. She seemed to be at peace with that. I could tell she didn't care for McCarthy's skepticism, but she seemed at ease with my compassion and concern for her.

Out of the blue, she asked if I was single because she wanted to take me out for a drink and talk more on the subject. While she was talking, I could feel a sexual energy moving through the room.

When it left, I said, "No, I'm married."

Her face flushed at my response. It was as if she just remembered what she asked. Suzy became embarrassed and said, "I'm sorry, I don't know what came over me. I was hitting on you."

I smiled back, but knew that we were dealing with sexually active spirits in the building. It wasn't really about me, so no need to be flattered.

When we left, Denny wanted to know why I didn't take Suzy up on her offer. He said, "It's obvious she's attracted to you. That was a nice piece of ass."

I shook my head, and said, "Denny that's why you're divorced."

We then moved on to the second person that claimed to be sexually attacked, by negative spirits. He was a 45-year-old black male named, Martin Footling. His story was very similar to Suzy's, and his attacks started a little over a year earlier as well. He also reported being attacked several times over the past year. It would happen when he was either lying in bed, watching television, or reading in a chair near the bed. He'd smell something he couldn't describe, then he'd get a pounding headache and black out. He could hear voices and feel hands touching his body.

His felt paralyzed. Martin said he felt like he was in a state of "twilight consciousness." He would feel the body of a woman climb on top of him. He said that was abnormal for him, since he was gay. In the mornings after the attacks, he woke up in bed sore with bite marks all over his body and a migraine headache.

At this point, Denny doesn't know what to think. He finds it hard to believe that we are dealing with several ghosts that rape men and women. He asked Martin if he saved any evidence from the attacks that we could send to a lab, but he didn't.

While Denny was talking to Martin, I felt the sexual energy come into the room. Then Martin began smiling at Denny, as he asked if he was married. McCarthy's "gaydar" went up, and he didn't answer. After the spirit passed through the room, the flirting stopped.

Martin went on to say that ten years earlier, when he was visiting a friend in New Mexico, he thought a UFO abducted him. Denny couldn't control himself at this point and burst into laughter.

I kept a straight face, shot Denny a stern look and said, "There are many who feel that they've been abducted, by visiting aliens. I, for one, think we are not alone in the universe. It would be ignorant to think we were the best thing that could be created in the vastness of the universe." I went on to say, "When we landed on the moon, if we had found any life forms, don't you think we would have also abducted them for research? I believe everything is possible."

That seemed to put Martin at ease.

I told Martin that I wanted to cleanse his apartment of any negative energy, using the white sage I brought. He was metaphysical in nature and very familiar with smudging. As I walked around his apartment, I got the same impression of two males and a female coming through the wall and attacking Martin, as I had also felt in Suzy's apartment. His bedroom did not have the copper heating vent in the ceiling above the bed though. It was in the wall between his reading chair and the headboard.

Martin didn't seem as shaken by his experience, like Suzy was. I actually think he enjoyed it. He just wanted the unannounced attacks to end. I told him the same thing I told Suzy about the other dimensions sometimes finding portals into our world. I hoped that, by using the white sage, we sealed off any portals. When leaving, I asked Martin what he wanted the outcome of our investigation to be. He said he just wanted the attacks to stop.

We left Martin's apartment and started walking around the building. I wanted to get a feel for any negativity.

Joking with Denny I said, "It looked like Martin had a man crush on the Silver Fox. I can't believe you passed up a sweet..."

McCarthy stopped me mid-sentence saying, "Don't even go there, Ed."

I asked him, if he felt a sexual energy enter the room just before both Suzy and Martin turned amorous.

He didn't.

I said, "I did and there is definitely something supernatural going on here."

In talking with other neighbors, we learned the building was constructed in 1864 and had a very colorful past. There were many passageways in the building that just stopped and were sealed off. It was a very spooky place. Everywhere we went, I felt like we were being watched. We interviewed several other renters about any strange occurrences. Everyone said the building was haunted, but none of them would admit to being sexually attacked by spirits. I could tell that some were lying.

We then interviewed Fred Vegan, the manager of Raven Arms, about any strange occurrences on the property. Robert King, the owner, had called Fred before our arrival to let him know he was sending two investigators down to look into the spirit attacks on two residents. Fred looked to be about sixty and was very pleasant in nature. He said that he never experienced any events, with any negative spirits in the building over the twelve years he managed the building.

I started to close my notebook and get up to leave when he said, "However, my wife Ethel has had several weird encounters over the past year."

I sat back down.

He went on to say, "Two days ago we were asleep, when my wife woke up with a headache. I went to the kitchen for a glass of water so she could take a couple of aspirin. When I returned to the bedroom, Ethel's body was hovering about a foot off the bed and moving, like she was having convulsions or something. I had to do a double take because I couldn't believe what I saw. I flipped the light on, and she dropped to the bed and became still."

Evidently my mouth had dropped open from the information I just received, and Denny was staring at me.

All I could think was WOW!

I wanted to interview his wife Ethel, but she left that morning to visit her sister in Alexandria and wouldn't be back for a week.

Fred told us we should talk to Jim Barkly, the maintenance supervisor, and his helper, Tim Kelly. They apparently had many tales to tell of the things they've seen and heard over the two years they worked at Raven Arms.

Fred called maintenance to let them know Denny and I were coming down to interview them. When we reached the basement, it was the first time I felt any negativity in the building, since our investigation began.

199

Jim and Tim were an odd pair. Jim was white, about twenty-seven years old, slender build, tall, good looking, with long brown hair and a beard. He was wearing a strap tee shirt and shorts, sporting colorful tattoos from neck to toe. Tim was a ghostly-looking man. He was the whitest guy I'd ever seen. When I looked into his pinkish blue eyes, I realized he was an albino. He was about thirty years old, had a shaved head and wore a long-sleeved shirt, buttoned at the neck, jeans and leather gloves. Everything but his head was covered.

There was a picnic table in one corner of the room, where we could sit and talk. Denny told both men that we had interviewed a couple of residents who claimed the building was haunted, by demonic spirits that paralyze and rape them in their apartments. The men wanted to know who the residents were.

I said, "Sorry, that is private information."

Through our questioning, we learned that Tim Kelly was a chemical engineer. He didn't have much to say. He seemed very effeminate and shy. Jim revealed that, along with his maintenance work, he's also a tattoo artist. He proudly showed us a tattoo over his heart of a crow, with the words, "Raven Arms."

Then he spoke up, "It doesn't surprise me hearing these stories. Raven Arms is the most haunted building in Richmond. I researched its history long ago, after I saw weird things when I first started working here. During the Civil War and up until the 1940's, this place was a brothel. It's full of things that go bump in the night and during the day, as well. I've turned the corner in some of these corridors and seen apparitions of some of the most outlandish acts you can imagine. When I'd try to focus in on the spirits and what they were doing, they'd disappear."

He took a sip from his coffee cup and continued, "Tim and I have been on ladders working with overhead pipes in the boiler room, and ghosts come up, feel our asses and pull our zippers down."

Denny, who at this point is ready to lose it with this whole investigation, asked, "Why the hell have you continued working here?"

Jim replied, "I don't know. I kinda' like it. It's just frisky ghosts that are out to let us know they are still around. Maybe just whores, just doing what whores do!"

I told Jim, "The building's owner, Richard King, hired us to investigate any paranormal activity and exorcise the building. Our job is to send any mischievous spirits packing."

No sooner was that out of my mouth when Tim Kelly said his first words. "You can't get rid of them. They need us to survive, and they belong to Raven."

Jim shot Tim a "shut up you fool" look.

I asked, "Who is Raven?"

Jim quickly replied, "She's the building. Her arms embrace all the spirits that dwell here, those of the living and the dead."

At this point, it didn't take a super sleuth or rocket scientist to know that Denny and I had tapped into the source of the problem.

I advised the men it's not fair to the living to be haunted by the dead, and the spirits that haunt the building must move into the next dimension of existence.

I opened my briefcase and took out the large plastic bag of white sage and the Sun Spear crystal wand.

I asked, "Is there a way I can light the sage and have the smoke circulate throughout all the apartments in the building?"

Reluctantly Jim said it could be done, but he would have to buzz everyone's apartment, by intercom, to let the occupants know that we were fumigating the building.

I thought that was a good name for what we were doing. While Jim and Denny left the room to notify everyone, Tim Kelly nervously showed me how the building's ventilation system worked. I was surprised that they could control just how much heat and air conditioning went into each room of every apartment.

Tim couldn't take his eyes off the Sun Spear. He would look at me, then look at it, then look back at me, over and over again.

"What is that?" he asked.

"A very powerful Indian Shaman created it, and it's a Divine Key that can open or close other dimensional portals. It has the power, if wielded by a pure hearted person, to do wonderful healing. One such healing would be to force wandering spirits to go through the portals to the source where they belong, no longer trapped between the dimensions."

Tim did not like the Sun Spear.

Michael had been silent throughout the entire investigation until now. He said, "Now you know how they knocked out the victims, with gas."

I immediately had a vision of the copper vent cover over Suzy's bed and these two men pumping knockout gas into her room. With Tim being a chemical engineer, he would know just what to use. In the vision, I could see them climbing a secret stairway up to their intended victim's apartments. Letting the sex starved spirits of Raven Arms enter their bodies, they would then conduct sexual rituals and orgies on the unwilling.

This answered a lot about the two men and the method of the attacks.

But who was the woman?

Michael said, "The Mrs., of course."

In that instant, it had all become so clear to me. He showed me that when Ethel's husband was told by the building owner that he was hiring us to investigate the attacks, she faked a spirit attack on herself. This was to take any suspicion off of the human element being responsible. Then she made sure she was gone before we showed up.

I had to have time to think of how we could end this thing.

Just as Jim and Denny returned to the boiler room, I lit leaves of white sage and blew out the flames, so the sage would smoke. Dropping them into a metal bucket with the Sun Spear. I had Denny hold it up to a large intake fan that was built into the ventilation system. Jim switched the fan on slow speed, and the smudging smoke was pulled up and distributed into every crack and crevice of the four-story apartment building.

Through me, Angel Michael spoke into the ventilation system saying, "The time has come for all the trapped spirits that inhabit this building to leave. You must now pass into the bliss of the afterlife, where you can manifest all the happiness and joy that you were denied in this world. I command you to leave now and return to the embrace of your Creator. If you remain, your energy will be absorbed into this smoky cloud of gas that I am sending, to awaken you. Go now, before this portal is closed forever."

In my mind's eye, I could see the ghosts that haunted the building floating upward into the path of light. There were men, woman and children, some positive, some negative, but all had to go.

When we were finished on the spiritual level, Michael and I had to address the human level of involvement. Michael told the two men to join us at the picnic table. He had me bring the deck of cards from my briefcase. He advised everyone to relax. I told them I was going to do a card reading to see the past, present and future of Raven Arms. As I laid out the cards the three header cards were the Jack of Spades, Queen of Spades and Jack of Clubs.

Michael said, "The cards stand for three wandering earth bound spirits that established the brothel over a hundred years ago. The cards also represent three human beings in the present that allowed the three dark spirits to enter the sanctity of their bodies and use them for dark purposes."

As I laid out the cards, seven across and seven rows down, Michael spoke of how the three human beings pumped a special knockout gas through the ventilation system into the apartments of Suzy Lee, Martin Footling and other residents of the building, over the past year.

Then, naming them he said, "Jim, Tim and Ethel then climbed the secret staircase up to their chosen victim's apartment. The three then conducted sexual rituals on their unwilling victim's paralyzed bodies."

Tim was smiling, caught up in the card reading. I could see that he was reliving the experience, but Jim knew the jig was up.

I went on to say, "The woman faked a spiritual attack on herself when she learned that there was going to be an investigation. It was an attempt to fool the detectives into believing humans were not involved."

Michael then said, "Now for the future. I see the cards take two paths. The sad path sends the three human beings to prison for raping many innocent victims, who live in this building."

I stopped and looked at Denny. He was wondering where I came up with all this information, since I didn't have any time to share it with him. Then I looked at Jim and Tim. Reality of their actions had taken hold, and they were scared.

Jim asked, "And what is the other path?"

I laid out the last three cards. As fate would have it, they were the Queen of Hearts and the two jokers.

Michael said, "Since all the spirits are now gone from this building, you no longer have any playmates. When Ethel returns next week, you will tell her that a great Angel has removed all the troubled spirits from the premises, and the fun and games are over for good. You will quit your jobs here, immediately, and never have contact with Fred and Ethel Vegan again. We will return in a month to talk to the residents of Raven Arms to make sure all ghosts are gone. If you are still here, I will take this matter to the police and you will be charged with burglary and rape."

Both men hung their heads low. I'm sure they were surprised at how fast everything in their life turned upside down.

I closed with, "God gives us all choices, and now His Angel is giving you a choice. I suggest you think long and hard on your next move, my friends. It doesn't make any difference to me. I'm just here to bring peace of mind to the innocent people, who live here."

Jim Barkly jumped up from the table saying, "Nice story, but where is your evidence. You have nothing to link us to any of the assaults."

Michael, through me, told Tim Kelly to remove his shirt.

He refused.

I picked up the Sun Spear and walked to my briefcase. I grabbed a small brown glass vile of lavender oil. I was going to run a bluff. Looking at Jim Barkly, I said, "Well one of you left semen in Suzy Lee, and I'd bet it was you. As soon as we get the DNA report back, the police will know who to charge."

Pointing the Sun Spear at Tim, Michael said, "Raven, dear Raven take off your shirt and show everyone your arms."

Denny started to grab him, but Tim put up his hand and submitted. His hairless body was adorned, with tattoos of all their victims from the building depicted in various sex acts. Tim had become the living embodiment of Raven Arms. Over his right breast was the face of Jim Barkly and over the left was the face of Ethel Vegan.

Michael said, "Proof. I rest my case. Should I call the police now or are you leaving?"

He snapped back, "We'll be gone within the week."

We then met with the manager. I told Fred that the building has been cleared of all spirits, and we would be back in a month to check on the new energy. I also told him that he needed to start looking for a new maintenance crew, since the negative spirits that had been haunting Raven Arms were fostered through the energy of Jim and Tim. I didn't want to tell him of his wife's involvement. Fred admitted that he was very intimidated by Jim. He wanted to fire him many times, but his wife always stopped him. He would be glad to see them go.

When Denny and I returned to Washington, we met with Robert King and laid the whole investigation out for him. I explained how it would have been hard to prove the rapes, and I couldn't tell how much was demonic mind control and how much was just human lust, out of control. As far as the victims were concerned, they just wanted the attacks to stop. I let him know that I would be returning to the Raven Arms in a month, to make sure the two men were gone and his building was no longer haunted.

Back in my personal life, I couldn't wait for September to find out what the Hierophant's next lesson was going to cover. When the time came, I went over lesson one again, relaxed and the words just started to flow.

Chapter Thirty-seven

You Have to Practice

Lesson Two:

King of Hearts received September 8, 1988
Book of Wisdom channeled from the Hierophant:

"The more you know, the more 'Knowing' will come to you." ERU

In this lesson, I was given the History of Creation and how to use Auric Sight... the ability to see a person's aura. Plus the Third Ancient Law of Wisdom: "The Law of Love is unchangeable, in that as you do it to the least of your brethren, you do it to your Creator."

SEE APPENDIX FOR ENTIRE LESSON

Learning another view of creation and about Atlantis really piqued my interest. The lesson also taught me to focus on people's aura. I was amazed at being able to see the colors around people.

However, I didn't have much time to practice, during September, because McCarthy was called in on a missing child case in Washington, D.C. A nine-year-old, African-American girl disappeared after leaving school. She never made it home. The police learned that the child had run away from home once before and felt she had just run away again. The mother of the child called Denny and asked if the charity would investigate, since the police weren't viewing it as a crime.

We spent the month, searching abandoned buildings and interviewing friends, neighbors and family members. We found ourselves in the middle of a gang and drug turf war.

No one wanted to help us.

The only lead we were given came from a drunken old man, living in a cardboard box.

"Word is she saw something she shouldn't have and paid da' price, you know," he stammered.

I asked Michael for help, and he gave me the vision of the little girl's body under some bushes next to a wall. I writhed at the vision. Now I was intent on finding her. Every waking hour, I spent searching, long after McCarthy gave up.

One evening I was showing the girl's photo around to a group of five teens on a street corner. They wanted to know if I was a cop. I assured them that I wasn't.

"I'm just a private investigator, trying to help a mother," I replied.

That was a bad move on my part.

One of the kids sucker punched me in the back of the head, and I blacked out immediately. When I woke up, I was on the ground, being kicked in the face and stomach.

I heard one of them say, "Get his fucking wallet and see if he has a gun."

I couldn't believe it. After all the shit I had been through in my life, and here I was being stomped on by a bunch of tennis shoe wearing, little kids. Really? I couldn't see this coming? The oldest one couldn't have been more than fourteen. I was stunned and it hurt. These kids were out to kill this old detective.

Obviously, I had lost the element of surprise, because who else other than a white cop or a white fool would be in that section of town alone at that hour? I also broke Michael's number one rule. "Never get yourself into any situation that you can't get yourself out of."

I didn't have an escape plan. With that realization, Michael was quick to point out which one I was. The old fool. I rolled into a ball to protect myself, but the assault continued.

Michael said, "Run, you fool." I remember thinking, "that was cold."

Cold or not, it got me moving because the next thing I knew one of the guys came at me, with a trash can.

I could feel Michael enter my body.

When the trash can came flying through the air at me, my body spun around. Everything went into slow motion. It was like a scene from the movie, Matrix. Michael drew back my legs to catch the trash can with my feet, and then with a powerful push of my legs, we pitched the can back at the boys, knocking two of them to the ground. I jumped up quickly and tried to grab one of the boys, by the shirt. It ripped. All the boys scattered like mice and disappeared down a nearby, dark alley.

Oh, how I missed my bolas.

I will never forget that night. It was Saturday, October 8th.

My feelings were more hurt than my body. During my long drive home, all I could think of was making contact with the Hierophant to find out what the next lesson was.

However, I knew I didn't have to be psychic to know I had some explaining to do to Linda.

When I got home, she was waiting with a scowled look on her face and wanted to know where the hell I was. Her frustration was understandable, since I hadn't called her all day.

I was going to tell her the truth, but she had grown weary of how much time I was spending on investigations. In addition, she wasn't too keen about the fact that every time she turned around, I was shelling out money we didn't have to keep the charity afloat.

I decided to bend my story a bit, in order for her not to freak out. I told her that McCarthy and I were searching an abandoned warehouse. The wooden floor was rotten, and I fell through to the basement striking my head. She noticed the large goose egg on the side of my head where the kid punched me. Other than that, all I had were some small cuts and bruises. She believed what I said, and it was over.

Later, after Linda fell asleep, I got up and tried to make contact with the Hierophant. He didn't respond. I got the distinct feeling I was being blocked. I went through the relaxation process again, but nothing happened. I called on Michael, but he didn't respond either.

My body started to hurt. The ass whipping I got was starting to catch up to me. I went back to bed, but it hurt too much to lie down. Everything was throbbing.

I got up and went for a walk on the beach.

As I walked toward Cove Point Lighthouse, my ears started to buzz. It was Michael. He didn't say anything. He only gave me a visual replay of the past thirty days.

I hadn't practiced any of the lessons I had been given, as I promised. I had been too busy working. I then realized that I was right. I was being blocked because I didn't deserve to make contact.

When I returned to the cottage, we called the "Sand Castle," I sat in a chair on the porch. It was one of the darkest nights I had ever seen. There wasn't a hint of light from the moon. I felt this odd sense of loss. I finally fell asleep in the chair.

In a dream, I clearly saw a man dressed in bright white robes, with long white hair and beard. He never said his name, but he looked like what most would describe as "God."

The man spoke, and it made me quiver.

He asked, "Well, is that all my Book of Wisdom is going to mean to you? You've had two lessons and failed to practice them. You know this means you've failed, right? The Law of the Magi is that no lesson can be missed. I'm sorry your journey must end before you even got started."

I felt like crap and gave every excuse in the book, most of all that I was busy, trying to locate the missing little girl.

He said, "They are all great excuses, but the lesson you missed was on the meaning of magic." He went on to say, "By December, you had to master the use of the 'White Light' to start the New Year. Missing October's lesson has now made that impossible."

I couldn't believe it. After all that time with Michael, it's all over.

I promised the man in white that I would work extra hard, spending every waking moment on the lessons, if I could get one more chance. He smiled and vanished from my dream.

When I woke up the next morning, my heart was heavy. I didn't know who that guy was, but I did know enough that he was the last one I wanted to fail.

I spent the rest of October and into November practicing the two lessons that I had been given. I could feel Michael around me, but he never made contact. I felt he was waiting to see what I was going to do, or maybe he was waiting to see what the man in white was going to do.

Denny called the first week in November and said the little girl's body was found in the bushes, up against the wall of a school a few blocks away from her house. He didn't know the cause of death.

Exasperated, I said, "I'm tired of searching for bodies. We need to get to the kids before they become missing. We have to get them to recognize the set-up these people are doing, *before* they do it."

"That sounds like crazy talk," McCarthy said. "How do you get them to see it before it happens? Are you going to make them all psychics like you? Good luck with that one."

"Asshole," I muttered under my breath, as I hung up the phone.

On November 8, after Linda went to bed I did the relaxation meditation I learned in lesson one. I relaxed so much, I fell asleep. I don't remember dreaming, and apparently access to the Hierophant on Jupiter was again denied. I felt like crap for screwing everything up, so I put on my coat and went for a walk.

When I got outside, I smelled driftwood burning. Someone had a bonfire on the beach, so I walked down. As I neared the bonfire, I could see a man, dressed all in black, was tending it. He also had long, black hair and a beard.

The man said, "You're late." He paused then went on, "Or maybe you are early. What do you think?"

I sensed Mr. Black was no ordinary man. Maybe I was dreaming? I thought that was an odd question. Something inside told me to say, "I think I'm early."

He laughed and replied, "Good choice, because if you were late, we would have to leave, but since you are early... sit down and let's talk a spell."

Mr. Black said, "You know it's Tuesday, and this is the 313th day of the year according to the Gregorian calendar? There are only 53 days remaining, until the end of the year. I so love visiting earth because there is no time where I reside."

I asked, "Then what is there, if you don't have time?"

He replied, "Everything. That's why I like coming here. It reminds me of my youth, when I didn't have everything. Back then, I only had time."

"Ooooookay," I thought. I could see that this was setting itself up to be an interesting experience and probably one that would make my head hurt.

Mr. Black asked, "What would you rather have, everything or time? Because I can give either, but you can't have both."

I asked, "What is everything?"

He answered, "Everything you could possibly want. Everything there ever was and everything there will ever be."

Wow, I couldn't believe my ears. This strange man was ready to give me everything I could possibly want and more. But then something from the first two lessons started growing inside my head. I saw that having everything without the time to enjoy it, would leave me with *nothing*. I had never seen so clearly.

I blurted out, "I choose time, because with it, I will be able to enjoy everything I already have."

He stated, "Then I will give you time to find everything."

He then said something that scared and delighted me at the same time, "I am an Angel of Death. If you had chosen 'everything' this would have been your last day on earth. I would have cast you into my fire, where you would have found 'everything.' Since you chose time, I suggest you return to your sand castle and enjoy what time you have left." He ended by saying, "You have a date with magic tonight."

With that, Mr. Black stood up and jumped into the bonfire. I recoiled backwards, startled to the core. I couldn't believe my eyes. His body sank beneath the sand, as if he had jumped into a pool of water, and disappeared. There wasn't even any sign of the burning driftwood. With the flames from the fire gone, I was left alone on the beach on one of the blackest nights I had ever seen. There was no sign of the moon. I couldn't see my hand in front of my face. I spun around to find a small beacon of illumination, coming from the lighthouse at the point. Then my attention was drawn to a blue orb, coming at me. I felt a friendly buzzing in my ears. It was Archangel Michael! He told me that I had just met with the Archangel Lucifer, the Angel of Everything.

Michael then explained that Lucifer was the Angel of Time, and when I rejected everything Lucifer had to offer, the Creator granted me more time in life to help with Michael's mission.

I let out the biggest sigh of relief I had taken in my life so far!

"A second chance! Again! Thank you, thank you!" I yelled out loud. My voice seemed to billow out across Cove Point and the entire Chesapeake Bay, like a fog horn. In my mind's eye, I saw the vibration of my voice ripple like a wave, until it enveloped the earth.

With new hope, I returned to my beach cottage, sat down at my typewriter and channeled lesson three from the Hierophant.

Chapter Thirty-eight

Akashic Hall of Records

Lesson Three:

Queen of Hearts received November 8, 1988
Book of Wisdom channeled from the Hierophant:

In this lesson, I learned the truth about the power of inner magic, using willpower... how to direct the will for positive purpose, using the power of the mind over the brain. I learned how to access the Akashic Hall of Records(AHK). The AHK is the place where our true-life stories are kept. Also, included in this lesson, was psychometry; a form of extrasensory perception characterized by the ability to make relevant associations, from an object of unknown history, by making physical contact with that object and its surrounding energy.

SEE APPENDIX FOR ENTIRE LESSON

When I woke up the morning after I channeled lesson three, I had a strong feeling that it was the day I needed to check in on the residents of Raven Arms.

After breakfast, I drove to Richmond, Virginia. When I arrived at Raven Arms, Martin and Suzy told me that it was like a dark cloud had been lifted from the building, and everyone seemed much happier.

Unfortunately, that happiness didn't find its way to Fred. When I interviewed him I learned that when his wife, Ethel, returned and felt the new positive energy in the building, she turned very negative. When Jim and Tim left, she went with them.

I said, "That could have been a blessing in disguise for you, Fred. When I did, the card reading for Jim Barkly in the basement that day, I had a vision of you walking with Ethel to go check on something in the basement and then I saw you fall down a long flight of stairs. You broke your neck from the fall, and Jim Barkly took over as manager of Raven Arms. Since Ethel is no longer here that vision can't come to pass."

What I didn't tell him was that it was the Queen of Hearts that pushed him.

When I left, I felt good. I had the lessons back on track and brought peace to the hearts of the people of Raven Arms. I did wonder where the Queen and her two Jokers would end up. I knew that they had developed a taste for lustful adventures, and they didn't need the spirit world to drive them.

Now, after three lessons under my belt, things were beginning to make sense for me. I could see how each lesson connected to the next. My hearing and communication with Michael became clearer as well. Between working a few missing children cases and private security consulting for clients, I practiced the Book of Wisdom lessons that I was receiving each month, from the Hierophant.

Right before it was time for me to receive the fourth lesson, Michael said that he had to return to the Father for several months. He asked that I continue to share the Book of Wisdom lessons with all the charity's volunteers.

McCarthy wasn't interested in the lessons, but he was interested in the ladies that were drawn to them. I started a monthly gathering at a local library in Prince George's County. I opened it to anyone, not just the charity's volunteers, who wanted to improve his or her mind, body and spirit.

Everyone, who enrolled in the class, was excited to learn.

They were all "seekers" on a journey to obtain a greater understanding. With just a couple of lessons under their belts, they were in awe of the new experiences they were having. The class absorbed the lessons quickly and proved each month that they had been practicing, by how their understanding had changed.

It was very rewarding for me to be a part of the explosion of consciousness and to guide them on their journeys.

When I taught lesson three, "Improving Will Power," it really tied together our mental focus. We learned just how weak our will really was, and how easily we are swayed, by other people's opinions. We saw how quickly we can succumb to the will power of dominant people.

It made me realize, all the more, how easily children fall prey to predators. I was learning everyday why Michael felt children needed to learn the tricks predators use to win their trust. I felt like we were in a race to get to the children first, and currently, we were losing.

For lesson three's experiment on psychometry, I collected four items from four different students and we tried to focus our minds on which person the items belonged to. It was amazing! One quarter of the class got all four correct, and over half the class got one or more right. Only two people didn't get any right.

I relayed to them what Michael said to me when I first starting receiving the lessons, "The more you practice, the stronger your powers of perception would become."

I also told them Michael said that the Akashic Hall of Records, the Hierophant spoke about, was where our life stories and our energies are stored. Our life energy is like a movie that all can view and learn from. In the Akashic Hall, there are no secrets or denial, just the actions and true intent of the individual's actions.

We talked about that concept for a long time. One student commented that it was scary to think of how exposed we are in Heaven. Many agreed and felt it was more like Hell.

I thought that was an interesting perspective on their part.

I said, "It's more apparent now what karma actually means. With all our actions and intentions recorded somewhere, it may help us make more positive choices that we can be proud about making. Otherwise, watching our life's review can be the hell we created for ourselves. The idea of karma coming back at us now had new meaning."

Privately, I thought, "Now I know what Michael meant about Detective Sharkey's story!"

I told the class that I remembered Michael saying once, "For some souls, Heaven is Hell. They pass over and see their life's review. They see all the chances they missed to make a difference and to do good. They see the opportunities they had to elevate their understanding and what their choices did to take them in a different, more human egotistical direction. After a soul goes through its life's review, this is normally when a request to return to earth is made by the spirit. However, mark and remember this: we only get one chance in a body. If an individual is allowed to return to this dimension, it's only in spirit form to help guide a person that suffers from the same problems the individual had, while alive."

I couldn't wait for the eighth of each month to roll around to see what would be covered next. I could feel my mind expanding, with every lesson. My understanding was changing, exponentially, as well. This was happening because I not only got a new lesson from the Hierophant, but I was reviewing the older lessons with the class, as I was teaching them. I began to see those first lessons from a different perspective and felt the energy in my being expand.

It was an amazing personal experience for me, but on top of that, I saw promise in the others as well.

Chapter Thirty-nine

We Were Sent to Fail

Lesson Four:

Jack of Hearts received December 8, 1988
Book of Wisdom channeled from the Hierophant:

This lesson taught me about the Tetragrammaton, the Hebrew name of God, transliterated in four letters as YHWH or JHVH, and articulated as Yahweh or Jehovah. I also learned about the power grids, set up by Atlantis, on earth to stabilize the planet's vibration in orbit around the sun.

SEE APPENDIX FOR ENTIRE LESSON

This lesson blew my mind when I started reciting what was conveyed. For me, it was where the rubber met the road, and a new awakening started to happen.

When I re-read the lesson that I had just channeled, I thought, "There is no way on earth that I'm going to be able to do all that! What will the people in the world think?"

That night in a dream, Michael came to me.

For the first time in our relationship, I was really scared. He tried to calm me, but I would have none of it. I felt like I was losing my mind from all the information that was flowing in. I could see why the Hierophant said in the beginning that this was not an easy path, and it could drive some people insane.

Michael said, "Master Hermit, Noah said the same thing when he was told to build the ark. 'What will people think...?' I'll tell you the same thing I told Noah. First of all why do humans always worry about what other humans will think? And as far as advice goes, 'Where there's a will, there's a way!' If you don't have the willpower to go on, I will understand."

As soon as he uttered those last words, something came over me. I no longer felt crazy, I felt stupid. I felt driven to not let him down. I thought, "What am I afraid of?"

Michael quickly answered my question, "You are afraid of the unknown. You are afraid of what you might be asked to do."

There was a long pause for me to gather my thoughts.

"Just so you know, you will be asked to do whatever it takes to move forward. Full truth be told; you are also afraid that you will fail."

He was right! The first thing that came to mind was that I was letting the Angel down, after all these years.

He continued. "I will let you in on a little secret. We were sent to fail, for in our failure others will succeed. And if others succeed, did we really fail? You could quit now, and we will have succeeded in failing. Why? Because others have already succeeded, and it's all because of us. From here on out, all we can do is improve upon our failure."

With that last comment, I woke up in a cold sweat. For some strange reason, it all made perfect sense to me. Maybe I had lost my mind, or maybe I found it? Nevertheless, Michael's words gave me the courage to move on.

Chapter Forty

An Unexpected Gift

On Christmas Eve, after Linda fell asleep, Michael came to me.

"You have a special gift, coming for Christmas," he said.

Immediately after he transmitted those words, together we astral projected to the Red Spot on Jupiter. I saw a bearded man, in white robes, standing with the Hierophant. He was holding an orb of white light in his hands. I watched as the white orb floated through the air and into my hands. It seemed to be as large as a basketball.

Michael said, "Put it on like a helmet."

When I did, there was an explosion of colors in my head, and the next thing I knew, I was back in my bed.

Michael said, "Now go write about everything you learned."

My mind was ablaze. I sat at the table on my porch, stared out onto the waters of the bay and began channeling my special gift.

Lesson Five:

Two Jokers received December 25, 1988
Book of Wisdom channeled from the Hierophant:

This lesson was on the healing powers and control of the White Light. It is the only lesson that I didn't receive on the eighth day of the month. My quest had almost ended here, because of my hard-headedness, but Angel Michael wanted me to gain the knowledge and use of the "White Light" for Christmas. It was also when I received the fourth Ancient Law of Wisdom: "The White Light can only be used once to heal any one person."

SEE APPENDIX FOR ENTIRE LESSON

As I taught the lessons to my students, it was very interesting how they all enjoyed the relaxation and meditation techniques. Everyone, even McCarthy, commented on how much clearer their minds were becoming, and they all wanted to know more.

They became hungry for the knowledge, but I saw that most of them didn't want to practice or reread the lessons. They just wanted the next lesson and to move on. It was as if they were gathering, but not applying the knowledge.

I was in a quandary about what to do. Should I stop them from coming to class? Should I cancel the class? The Hierophant's instructions to me were to practice for a month, and if I didn't master the lesson, let alone not practice it, I wouldn't move on and the lessons would stop.

As I was troubleshooting the scenario in my head, I heard the words, "Those rules were for you. These lessons are meant to help people elevate. The lessons are liken to rope, if they use them, like climbing a rope, they will elevate. If they read and don't apply the lessons, they will simply dangle or hang, going nowhere."

I didn't know where the words came from, or should I say "who" the words came from. I know they didn't come from Michael. It was a different vibration or sensation than when he communicated with me. I wondered if I was now connected with other energies and beings, as well as Michael?

Regardless of where the words came from, as soon as I received the message I felt immediate relief from the burden of doing the right thing.

Since I received each lesson early in the month, and practiced for a month before teaching it to the First Wednesday students, they would receive each lesson two months *after* I received it.

At the end of every class, I would tell the students what the next lesson's topic would be. When I told everyone that we would be learning about angels at the following gathering, they were excited. In the eighties, there was a huge resurgence in the belief of angels. They weren't just popular at Christmas time anymore.

That was a good thing, since Michael's plan for the future involved bringing more angels down, to work with humans, over the next decades.

Earlier that year, CBS News conducted a survey that revealed eight out of ten people in America believed in angels, and four out of ten reported that they had close encounters with angels. This made me feel like I wasn't alone in what I was experiencing, and what I was learning made much more sense.

Chapter Forty-one

The Angels of the Four Directions

Lesson Six:

Ten of Hearts received January 8, 1989
Book of Wisdom channeled from the Hierophant:

In this lesson, I learned about the symbols and use of the elements, Air and Fire. I was told the story of cosmic life, the birth of the angels--and how to invoke the Angels of the Four Directions. This lesson was also about aliens visiting earth... past, present and future.

SEE APPENDIX FOR ENTIRE LESSON

The class was enthralled with lesson six. It was like they were supercharged, with excitement. During the discussion period after the lesson, each and every student had shared some story about an encounter with what they believed to be an angel.

Throughout that month, I was getting calls and letters in the mail from some of the students about the use of angelic meditations. I also made observations between the volunteers from the charity, who I saw on a regular basis, and the others that were taking the class.

I was shocked at how quickly everyone picked up on, using the Angels of the Four Directions, to help them in their daily lives.

Even McCarthy was working, with the angelic energy. It was the first lesson he truly embraced.

Denny and Judah, who had begun dating, would meditate together. I felt glad for them because he needed an anchor and someone who really cared about him. I was, however, afraid that Denny would use her until he got tired of her, like I had seen him do, with so many other women over the years.

When I watched everyone's behaviors and responses to the lessons, I realized I was learning from them. I could feel my awareness expanding. My observations of the interactions seemed just as important as the lessons themselves.

When I came to that conclusion, Michael said, "Remember, your greatest teachers wear sneakers, high heels, combat boots and, yes, even go barefoot."

I could feel my face scrunch up, while trying to absorb, and then comprehend that comment. All the scrunching in the world wasn't helping. I finally asked, "What is that supposed to mean?"

"It means, grasshopper, that the greatest lessons come when you are still and observe the interactions of humans. All or any human. It does not matter, who they are. They are your teachers, and you are the student. Always be ready to learn from them," he said.

Michael went on to tell me that learning the history of the "Knowing" was just as important as learning the mechanics in the lessons. The more history I learned the more "Knowing" came to me, just like Master ERU's Power Phrase states at the beginning of each lesson.

After that discussion with Michael, I remembered a conversation I had with the Hierophant, where he wanted me to ask a question of Admiral Zumwalt. The question was whether the U.S. Military had any strange encounters with alien spacecraft in Vietnam.

When I brought the subject up, Admiral Zumwalt seemed shocked that I would dare ask.

He sat back in his chair, then leaned forward, with elbows on his desk, and said, "A lot of information came across my desk that couldn't be explained and most of it, I still cannot talk about."

I said, "Do you believe that aliens are visiting earth?"

He laughed and said, "I believe in a lot of things I can't talk about, Ed."

I dropped it, but I knew it wasn't the end of it.

I couldn't wait for the next lesson to come in. Michael had told me, a few days ahead of the 8th, that the spirit of "Black Frankie" had asked to return to earth to help his old friend "finish what we started when we were kids."

I asked, "How could we do that?"

Michael said, "Frankie is guiding a body to you and, when this individual arrives, you will know."

"What?!! How???" I thought.

No response came from Michael that evening, or any other.

■■■

■■■

Chapter Forty-two

Frankie's Back!

Lesson Seven:

Nine of Hearts received February 8, 1989
Book of Wisdom, channeled from the Hierophant:

In this lesson, I learned about the elements Earth and Water. And the power and energy in anything humans believe--and how to do water divination.

SEE APPENDIX FOR ENTIRE LESSON

Lesson seven picked up right where six left off. I now knew how to call in the Angels of the Four Direction to reinforce my will. All I could think of was feeling Frankie around me. I knew the Four Directions were bringing him.

I practiced and used that feeling of the "Knowing" to see Frankie around me again. I felt very confident in my skill and how the energy was moving in and around me. I was ready to pass it on to the First Wednesday students.

At the beginning of the class, I noticed we had three new African American students. I didn't think anything of it at the time because over the months I had been teaching, students would come and go. There was always a core group that remained the same, but we would usually have a new face or two in the mix. Tonight was different though. I couldn't quite place the feeling, but I felt something very familiar happening. It was almost a déjà vu event, but then again not. My attention kept getting drawn to one of the new students. She was young, about twenty-six.

At one point, she shared an experience with the class, and I felt like the room spun, and my vision opened up, so that I could see 360 degrees around me. It was like an out-of-body view, but I was still in my body.

That's it! I finally saw it. She looked like a taller female version of Black Frankie. Suddenly, I could feel him all around her.

Her name was Leah. She told the class she had a law and teaching degree, but hadn't decided which field to go into yet. She also shared she was searching for direction and deeper meaning in her life, and that is why she joined the class and was interested in volunteering with the charity.

For the exercise portion of the class, I had the students move to different rooms and meditate, using the method shown in the lesson.

When we all came back together in the large room to share our experiences, I was astounded. We all saw the same thing! A raised garden labyrinth. In the center ring was a tall tower, with a golden ladder. Angels were climbing down the ladder to walk with humans, who were walking in the labyrinth. The people were wearing white tunics, with red crosses on their chest.

Leah said she saw a castle, with children playing all around. With Frankie around her, that vision didn't surprise me!

Archangel Michael turned my focus to the elderly black lady, who came with Leah. Everyone called her Mother Blocker. She was about ninety years old and could barely walk or breathe because of arthritis and a weak heart.

When the class got up to leave for the evening, Mother Blocker said to me, "I'm ready to pass on. I'm just moving a little slow these days, Master Hermit."

Mother Blocker's friend, Eleanor, pulled me aside and said, "The doctors say that this will be her last year. I've been praying to Saint Michael and Saint Germaine to give her strength. Can you ask them to help her, Master Hermit?" she asked.

Just then, I felt like someone had just put their hands around my throat and started to squeeze. I looked at the old woman and could see she was pure goodness. As I held her hands, I began to cry. She caught my tears in her right hand and began wiping them on her arms, saying with a laugh, "I know what to do with the tears of an Angel."

I could feel Michael, entering my body. He immediately had me put on my trench coat and hat to hold in the heat he was about to generate. I told one of the students, Dr. Peterson, to have Mother Blocker stand in the center of the room. Through me, Michael then told all twelve of the students to form a circle around Mother Blocker. Michael began walking around the circle, asking if everyone wanted to help extend Mother Blocker's life another five years?

Everyone agreed.

My body was getting hot, and I was sweating a lot. I suddenly remembered in the lesson, the Hierophant talking about the fire and water of the body being very powerful. Michael then commanded everybody, "Join hands. Don't let go whatever you do." Michael and I walked around the circle seven times clockwise and seven times counterclockwise. My head was spinning. Somehow we wound up inside the circle without breaking connection of hands.

Michael then called down the "White Light." A white orb of light came down from the ceiling and came to rest in my open palms. Michael then breathed it into my body, and then we held our breath.

Michael spoke, "Dearest Mother, would you like your journey to continue?"

She said, "Yes sir, Edward-Michael, I'm not finished here. Please help me find my strength again."

Michael said, "Then, Mother, open your mouth and take in the breath of new life." Michael blew the "White Light" into her mouth and then said, "Follow me, dear Mother." He broke through the hands that locked us in the circle and began walking around the students again, with Mother Blocker hobbling right behind him. I felt sorry for her. She was struggling, and I was afraid she was going to have a heart attack right then and there. However, her pace began to pick up. Before we knew it, she was running around the circle like a teenager.

219

I couldn't believe my eyes at the transformation that had taken place in this wonderful woman. Everyone started saying, "thank you" to me, but Michael put up our hand and said, "Don't thank me for a miracle that all of you created. It is me, who must thank you. You all did this miracle together because you cared for her so much." After Michael finished speaking, I realized I was soaking wet from the heat generated in my body, by the "White Light." Since I already had my coat and hat on, I simply said, "Good night." I turned and left everyone, with his or her mouth hanging open.

When I got to the door, I turned to see Mother Blocker, still walking fast around the room. She definitely had a new lease on life and was using it to the fullest.

On the long drive back to Cove Point, I was going over the evening's events. I was feeling pretty good about what we had done. That's when Michael decided to pop my bubble.

He said, "The Master is only as good as his last miracle."

I said, "What does that mean?"

He replied, "We, you and I, can't take credit for healing Mother Blocker, because the people, who witnessed it tonight, will forget or deny it ever happened in a few years. That's why I gave them the credit for the deed. In doing so, I hope that they will remember the miracle longer and be inspired to help heal others in the future."

There were several minutes of silence, as if he was waiting for what he said to sink into my psyche.

Then he continued, "The first thing you need to learn about humans is, they're short on memory and only have faith, when it suits them. The most amazing magician is only as good as his last trick. Always remember what they did to Jesus. One day he's healing the blind and everyone is rejoicing the miracle. The next day those same people are screaming for his crucifixion!"

It made me sad to be reminded of the atrocity against Jesus, but I saw Michael's point about humans and how quickly they turn. However, I knew one thing for sure; I would never forget the miracle I saw that night with Mother Blocker. I also felt Leah saw something that day, and Frankie would never leave me again.

We all couldn't wait for the next lesson to come.

Chapter Forty-three

Recipe to Start Your Day

Lesson Eight:

Eight of Hearts, received March 8, 1989
Book of Wisdom, channeled from the Hierophant:

In this lesson, I learned the importance and uses of the Ankh, the Alpha and Omega symbols. I also learned the difference between Wisdom, Truth and Knowing. It ended with a great "Recipe to Start Your Day."

SEE APPENDIX FOR ENTIRE LESSON

As the monthly lessons continued to come in, they answered a lot of questions for me, as well as for the other students. After the transformation of Mother Blocker, everyone recognized that they each had untapped powers deep down inside that needed to be harnessed. Many came forward with requests for Michael to help heal others they knew.

Through me, Michael said, "I am not here to heal, only to deliver 'The Sword." With it, you all will be able to heal the world." He then traced the symbol of the Ankh on everyone's forehead and said, "Use what 'Knowing' has been revealed to you, but remember you can only use the 'White Light' on a person once. Don't tell people I healed the Mother, when it was you."

For some time, Michael has been using the Ankh symbol when he translates and sends images to me, in my dreams. Lately he keeps showing me a temple, with two large black doors, that have a large, golden Ankh carved into them. When the door is pushed open, the Ankh splits in half. Inside the temple is a golden bejeweled sarcophagus, standing upright on top of an altar. Stone walls that outline the room are covered with carved scenes and Egyptian Hieroglyphics.

On either side of the great altar is an oval-shaped tunnel that leads to another altar. The one on the right was very masculine and devoted to Osiris; the one on the left was very feminine and devoted to Isis.

When I asked him about the temple he said, "It was an ancient temple that once stood in Alexandria where you could make contact with the Divine

Father/Mother Godhead. Don't trouble yourself with visions of things we will build one day. I show you these things for a reason, not to distract or concern you. Study hard the lessons from the Hierophant, so you can gain the respect from the powers that be. Then and only then, you will understand why and what you are to build."

Chapter Forty-four

Doubting Thomas

Lesson Nine:

Seven of Hearts, received April 8, 1989
Book of Wisdom, channeled from the Hierophant:

In this lesson, I learned how lazy humans have become, as we grow more and more dependent on technology. I was instructed how to communicate with people at long distances, with my mind, and how to visualize past events. I was shown how to contact the power within, and the ultimate human power was revealed to me. I was also given the Fifth and Sixth Ancient Laws of Wisdom: (5.) "He who needs no one is no one." (6.) "Sit quietly, humbly and patiently at the feet of the wise, for one day others will sit at your feet and drink from your cup of wisdom."

SEE APPENDIX FOR ENTIRE LESSON

Dr. Peterson was probably the one student that held the greatest insight into the depth of the wisdom that was being delivered to us. Since he majored in Ancient History and was already gifted in the art of clairvoyance, he asked if he could use the lessons in another twelve-member study group at the University of Maryland. I agreed and within the first few months the new group grew to thirty.

It seemed as if everyone was searching for the "Knowing" the Hierophant was giving to me.

Michael warned me though, some people could be seeking the information for negative purposes. He suggested that I attend one of Dr. Peterson's classes to view the type of people he was attracting.

A few weeks later I sat in on the class. Dr. Peterson started off, by going around the room and asking each person to state why he or she was there and what it was they wanted to learn.

As I scanned the room, I saw it was a mixed group of mostly women. I listened as they each stated their name and what they were seeking. The majority desired to find true love or their soul mate, financial gain and the ability to communicate with the angelic realm.

Dr. Peterson walked over to me and whispered, "Would you consider speaking on your use of the Books of Wisdom, to become a clearer channel for the Archangel Michael? It may help them discern whether or not they are already communicating."

I responded, "Sure. Let's try a little exercise."

Internally, I asked Michael, if he would help me do a guided meditation and take the group to the Red Spot on Jupiter to meet the Hierophant. He agreed.

He guided me to have everyone set their chair within a large circle.

I asked, "Is there anyone here who does not believe in angels?" Two guys, sitting side by side, raised their hands. The first one's name was, fittingly, Thomas.

I asked if he would accept the task of turning the light off and on when needed. "Doubting Thomas" agreed.

The second was James Gray, an outlaw biker, with the Pagan motorcycle club.

I recognized Mr. Gray, from an undercover murder investigation I conducted between two rival motorcycle clubs, The Pagans and Iron Horsemen, in the seventies. I couldn't believe a biker would be interested in this information. Perhaps this was a guy that Michael suspected was planning to use the knowledge for a negative purpose.

Michael spoke and said, "Thomas, by the end of this exercise, you will be a believer, and your friend will find what he is seeking, in order to fill that hole in his heart."

I had no idea what Michael was talking about, but when I turned to look in Gray's direction, a peaceful look came over his face.

Michael went on to say, "We will have to weed out the individuals in the group that can't maintain the concentration level needed and a positive perspective."

Everyone looked at the biker, as if he had the plague, and at the same time, I felt several people's egos flare.

I said, "I feel some of you taking exception to what I just said. That is exactly what Michael and I are talking about. If you can't remain humble, you will be too heavy to fly. People nowadays have taken on this feeling of entitlement. If you think you have a right to experience this, then you automatically lose the right and must sit this one out."

Without me uttering another word, two people excused themselves from the experiment, giving me the stink eye on the way out the door. I could see Dr. Peterson was beginning to wish he had never invited me.

Michael said, "If people leave, that means they don't have what it takes to stay." Now that the room had been purged of the negativity, we were ready to proceed. Everyone left in the room was there, with hearts and minds wide open.

I lit a candle and sat it on a chair in the center of the circle. I motioned to Thomas, who turned off the lights in the room. I asked everyone to join hands as I walked them through the relaxation exercise in lesson one.

"Close your eyes and relax, relax everyone, relax…" I said repeatedly.

Then Michael took over asking everyone to hum an "A" sound. Everyone did. I didn't know where Michael was going with this.

The energy in the room was increasing.

Then Michael had me ask everyone in the room to hum the "O" sound. Everyone did, and the energy increased even more. Michael and I were walking around the outside of the circle, touching the back of their heads, as they hummed.

Then Michael said, "If I touch you, change to the 'A' sound and everyone else continue the 'O' sound."

As we walked, Michael touched every other person. A smoky, sweet smelling mist began to form, on the inside of the circle, around the candle. Michael told everyone to open their eyes and see what they were creating.

Michael said, "What you are witnessing is the Aluminiferous Aether, the Alpha/Omega Cloud, the Breath of God."

He paused for a few minutes and then, just said, "Breathe."

The white mist turned blue, as it swirled before us.

Then I sat in a chair directly across the circle from Dr. Peterson. I could see that everyone's eyes were ablaze with enthusiasm.

Michael said, "Keep your eyes open at all times. I don't want to leave anything up to your imagination. What you are seeing is real. I will squeeze the hand to my right and that person will squeeze the hand to their right and so on all the way around the circle, until the person to my left squeezes my left hand."

Everyone in the circle did as they were told and the cloud started to grow larger. I watched the hand squeezing continue several times around the circle until it stopped, just before the person next to Dr. Peterson. Michael asked that person to pull their chair out of the circle and just watch, while sending positive thoughts to the candle's flame.

We started over, time and again. Each stoppage we removed people who just couldn't seem to squeeze the hand of the person next to them. The circle was now down to twenty-six people. The energy of the circle was strong.

Now Michael said, "I will squeeze the hand of the person on my left and that person will do the same, until the squeeze returns to me." Again, several people were removed from the exercise because the flow was blocked when they couldn't complete the squeeze.

We were now down to twenty-two people. Surprisingly, James Gray was still in the circle. I could see his curiosity, growing with every squeeze.

Michael said, "Now, whichever hand I squeeze you do the same, even if it's both hands at the same time."

It was one of the most incredible experiences I had ever witnessed. It truly is impossible to explain. The cloud in the middle turned red and was moving in the same direction, as we were, as we squeezed each other's hands. When Michael squeezed both hands on either side of us, the red cloud moved in both directions at the same time.

Then it happened. As we stared at the chair and candle in the middle of the circle, we saw the image of the Hierophant become solid.

He stood up and said, "Welcome brothers and sisters of the Ancient Laws of Wisdom. Welcome to Atlantis. I have waited..."

When the apparition spoke, someone in our circle freaked out and let go of the hand next to them. The candle went out, and the Hierophant was gone.

Michael said in a commanding voice, "Don't anyone move. Stay in your seats. Thomas, please turn on the lights." James Gray disobeyed the command and jumped up to examine the chair in the middle as if to expose some trickery.

When the light came on everyone was talking.

Michael said, "James. Dear brother James, there are no tricks here, only illusions of the mind. You saw what you saw. Never doubt that, my friend."

As I quieted the room, I asked, "Who saw the Hierophant? Raise your hand."

Everyone in the circle raised their hands, but the only one outside the circle that raised their hand was Thomas.

Michael said, "When the Hierophant stood up to greet us, if he was facing you, raise your hand." Everyone raised his or her hand, to include Thomas.

Michael said, "Don't you think that it's impossible that he could face all of us who were seated in a circle around him?"

Everyone looked puzzled, but began nodding their heads just the same.

Michael said, "In the dimension that Atlantis has been moved into, there is only forward, no backward. Thomas, do you believe in angels now?"

Grinning from ear to ear, Thomas nodded yes.

The group decided they wanted to learn more and grow into the "Knowing." We nicknamed the gathering "The First Wednesday Club," because we would always meet on the first Wednesday of each month for the next lesson. I decided to combine my students with Dr. Peterson's class, since we were all traveling the same journey to enlightenment together.

On his way out, James Gray was very humble as he approached me. He shook my hand and said, "You were right. There is a hole inside of me, and I think only you can help me find what I need to fill it."

Michael said, "Brother James, I know you can help find what needs to fill mine as well. We both suffer from the same pain of child abuse."

I sensed at that moment, we both had something in common beyond the class.

We talked privately for a while, and I found out he was also tortured and abused as a child. His experiences turned him into an outlaw to escape, but now he wanted to find peace. I told him that there is no escaping the trauma we suffer, growing up. However, if we look at it as a learning experience and help keep others from becoming victims, we go from victim to victorious. If you change the way you look at things, the things you look at change. Many people do nothing and allow the memories of the abuse to continue to victimize them over and over again, for the rest of their lives. I call that being a "glutton for punishment."

Chapter Forty-five

If You Leave... You Were Never Here

Lesson Ten:

Six of Hearts, received May 8, 1989
Book of Wisdom, channeled from the Hierophant:

In this lesson, I learned more about the story of Atlantis and the ancient practice of Cryptic Transposition. The Book of Cryptic Transposition is the key to life, death, creation and destruction. It is believed by most Masters that man was not meant to have such powers. I was also given six aids to physical and mental growth.

SEE APPENDIX FOR ENTIRE LESSON

By the next meeting of the evening First Wednesday Club, the number had grown to fifty students. Word was spreading that people gathering at the University of Maryland after hours were experimenting with astral projection... and the instructor had an angel appear before everyone in the class. People were clamoring to be part of it.

I informed Dr. Peterson that he could only take on fifty-two students for the class. I also said that Michael was standing firm on the rules of one lesson per month, and if anyone missed a lesson, they were out of the group. This was Michael's quality control guideline to see who in the group had the tenacity to stick it out and had the true draw to gain the knowledge.

A few nights later, Dr. Peterson called me and asked if I would speak to a group of seventy-five potential students.

I agreed, and we set a time to meet.

I made notes to go over all the points with the class, so I wouldn't forget anything, and I had Dr. Peterson make copies of a handout. Once everyone was seated, Michael took over. The notes I prepared went out the window! It was a great lesson for me to be prepared in case he didn't come through, but not take it personally when he guided the conversation. He always seemed to have an agenda, and I was more than willing to let him do the talking. I truly felt like I personified the saying "When you think you know you don't, and when you know you don't, you do!"

With all eyes on me, Michael explained that the Masters Studies Class was a social experiment, and it had some strict guidelines that must be followed.

- The control group could only have fifty-two test subjects to start.
- We would cover only one lesson every month.
- Members must practice the lesson throughout the month.
- No one could miss a class, so commitment was a priority.
- If a lesson was missed, it would result in automatic dismissal from the group.

Michael announced that the objective was to establish how many students would be left in the control group, after fifty-two months, and the level of awareness obtained by each of the surviving members would be evaluated.

After scanning all the faces in the room, it appeared everyone was still "on board" and intrigued to learn more. To give them a feel for what the lessons would be like, Michael and I prepared to take the entire gathering through lesson one.

Michael told Dr. Peterson to read the intro to Lesson One from the Hierophant. We then opened the floor up to discussion. The first three questions were all variations of "Well, what if we make up the lesson? Can't we still be in the group that way?"

Michael, not being one to tiptoe around people's feelings had me put a stop to the progression of the Q&A session.

He said, "Okay, let's stop right here. None of you have asked a question pertaining to what Dr. Peterson just read. I outlined the rules prior to reading the intro of the lesson. The only point we were remiss in making was that there is no bending of the rules, no changing the way we conduct this gathering. So, before we go any further, take a deep breath and search your heart and soul, while asking if you can commit to this 52-month study program. Now, is there anyone in the audience that knows for certain you cannot, or will not, make this commitment?"

Seven people raised their hands.

"Thank you for attending. You are dismissed," Michael said.

I felt bad for them because they were clearly disappointed.

Michael decided to take the remaining people in the room through an exercise that would allow him to detect whether there could be synergy in the group or not. He had them all move their chairs in a circle. Once the commotion of chairs clanking together and scraping on the floor ended, he instructed them to hold hands. He had me sitting with them as well. On his mark, I squeezed the hand of the person to my right and told them, when they felt the squeeze to pass it to their right, and so on and so on, until it came back to me. This little exercise produced a relaxation response and put the group in an altered state of being, so the energy in the circle swirled at the heart chakras.

After a few rounds of hand squeezing, Michael said, "Now breathe deeply three times, in and out through your nose. After your third breath, focus on your heart and feel the energy, opening your chakra. Ask yourself, 'Am I a candidate for this program? Can I make the commitment needed?' Now take another deep breath, this time holding it for as long as you can, and then open your eyes."

Michael had me break the circle, by dropping the hands I was holding and telling everyone else to do the same thing.

"By now you should all have a clear answer. You are either in, or you are not. If you know you are a candidate for this program, please come up and give Dr. Peterson your contact information sheet," Michael said.

Some people were filtering out, while others turned their papers over to Dr. Peterson and then sat back down. I stood talking to McCarthy, waiting for the last few people to take a seat. He was telling me all about the ladies he checked out in the group. Denny sure was true to his nickname of the "Silver Fox".

With everyone settled, Dr. Peterson came over to us and said, "Wow there are exactly 52 papers handed in. That's amazing!"

Michael had me stand in front of the gathering and tell them about their number of exactly fifty-two! Mouths dropped open. I then revealed to the group that Michael told me that out of the group, only twelve would make it to the end.

The whole group looked shocked. Heads were shaking "no," except McCarthy, who was still checking out the new ladies in the group.

My mouth flew open and out spilled, "I told you at the beginning of this evening's meeting that this could be the hardest thing you ever do, but remember Michael's prophecy is just a projection of the way things are right now. With that in mind, you have the power to change things. You are the masters of your own destiny. If you apply yourself and hold true to the desire to attain the 'Knowing,' you will still be here fifty-two months from now."

With that said, I saw some hope fall over those in the room. I felt like Michael had rained on their parade, telling them that most would fail, but now a spark was lit again.

I continued, "It's like you go to your local psychic and she tells you that she sees you being eaten, by a shark in the next six months. What is she really telling you?" I asked.

Mother Blocker's friend, Eleanor, raised her hand and said; "Don't go to the beach for six months."

I said, "Right! You don't go to a psychic to fulfill a prophecy. You go there to glimpse the future and change it. Now, everyone take a deep breath and meditate on that thought for a few moments."

I motioned to Dr. Peterson to take over and close out the evening.

He spoke up, saying, "Remember, if we want to change the world, it starts by transforming ourselves. Thank you for coming. Good night, and I'll see you next month. Class is dismissed."

Everyone left talking. The energy was buzzing, with excitement.

I said to Dr. Peterson, "Well that went well."

He said, "Yes that was a nice comeback, after dropping a bomb on them."

I replied, "I know, but I can't lie to them. You and I both know that many will fall away. In fact, you will quit me before we reach the end of the journey."

Dr. Peterson recoiled his head with a puzzled look on his face, and said, "I will never leave you."

I smiled on the outside, but knew he would leave when I needed him the most.

I said, "You are not here for me. You are here for you, and when this fairy tale no longer serves you, sadly, you will leave."

At that millisecond, I could see long and far. I saw the friendship and the battles we would fight, side by side, in the coming years. I saw the severe disagreements happen between us, and the flare of Dr. Peterson's ego. I had a momentary pang in my heart and wished I didn't know certain things.

I felt a forlorn smile come over me, as I looked into Dr. Peterson's eyes. I could see, deep down inside, he knew what I said was true.

My sadness was shifted when I noticed Leah, waiting patiently to talk to me. When I finished with Dr. Peterson, she came up to me and said, "Master Hermit, I just wanted to tell you that I am committed. I feel like when I met you, I came home, and I will never leave you. You are stuck with me until the end of days." She started to cry. I took her hands in mine and kissed them. I knew that it was Frankie, activating Leah's emotions. She was so sweet.

I said, "Leah, if you leave and come back, you were never gone. If you leave and never come back, you were never here." Looking deep into her eyes and wiping away a tear with my thumb, I continued, "You will leave and so will Dr. Peterson, but the only difference is Dr. Peterson was never here, and you will come back."

Chapter Forty-six

Be Prepared

Lesson Eleven:

Five of Hearts, received June 8, 1989
Book of Wisdom, channeled from the Hierophant:

In this lesson, I learned how quickly our whole world could be turned upside down, and how I could prepare and survive. The Hierophant explained how it has happened in the past and will happen again.

SEE APPENDIX FOR ENTIRE LESSON

After channeling Lesson Eleven, it made me wonder what event was the Hierophant preparing us for and better yet, when? There had been so many doomsday prophecies that never happened over the past hundred years, and now humanity is facing another one. Coming on the horizon was Y2K, and further out was the coming "end of the world" possibility when the Mayan calendar was set to run out on December 21, 2012.

When Lesson Eleven was finally presented to the First Wednesday Club members, they all started to buzz about pending doom. Most participants admitted to not even having emergency flashlights for a small event, such as loss of power, due to a thunderstorm. You could feel an air of fear percolate in the room.

Thomas, a student at Maryland University studying Marine Biology, raised his hand. He shared that he grew up in San Francisco, and they always had the threat of the "Big One" (earthquake). There were always duck and cover school drills and packs of emergency food that needed to be sent into school every year. He went on to say that the entire time he lived in California, he never even once felt the earth shake a little.

I told the class that in the mid-sixties, when I was eighteen and in the army, I found myself in an end of the world scenario situation. I was chosen as a "volunteer" to be in a mock unit, being tested. We were cut off from all food and supplies for four weeks. It was a freezing, cold winter, and we were several thousand feet up in the mountains, near the town of Oberammergau in the

Bavarian Alps. We had to live off the land and didn't even have toilet paper. I remember it so clearly because the first thing that hit me was just how privileged we humans have become. Think about it. We, in this modern age, take so much for granted. Toilet paper? What did they do before toilet paper was invented? What was used? We live in such a wonderful age and have become accustomed to the creature comforts of our time. I cannot imagine what other amazing things are in store for us down the road.

During the survival testing, we were broken up into groups of four and monitored from afar to test our survival skills. By the end of the first week, some of the guys were turning toward their animal nature. Aggressive behavior rose as hunger pangs set in. We had snow for water thank goodness, but food was hard to find. Before they dropped us in the wild we had been told, "Anything that burns, the human body can eat, but that doesn't mean it won't kill you. Be selective."

We had M-14 rifles and a bayonet, but no bullets. "What good was that?" I thought. No bullets meant no shooting a deer or rabbit or anything else to eat.

My team consisted of a twenty-five-year-old surfer dude from Los Angeles, a thirty-year-old accountant from New York City, a thirty-five-year-old ex-minister from Atlanta and me, an eighteen-year-old, fresh out of high school. When we sat down to discuss our combined survival skills, believe it or not, my two years in the Boy Scouts made me the leader. I was the only one that could make a fire to keep the group warm. I showed them all how to do it, but they couldn't grasp the concept. It came down to the fact that they were just plain lazy.

I became the official fire tender and set my sights on teaching them to get food. I taught them how to make snares, and that skill alone supplied us with a couple rabbits and birds to eat.

Unfortunately, once darkness fell over us each night, we were thrown into a prehistoric hunter/gatherer lifestyle. None of us were very good at it, but I was sure that two of us would have gotten the hang of it, eventually. The trouble was, in our group alone, the surfer and the accountant were mentally checking out fast. Their minds were weak, and they were always complaining. They focused all their energy on all the negative side of things, instead of wisely using their energy to move and grow from the experience. They expected the minister and me to supply all their needs, while they sat around camp huddled next to the fire. Fear set in, their immune system became weakened, and they got sick.

The army ended the experiment after twenty-two days.

It was one of the worst and greatest experiences of my life. I learned a lot about human nature and found out how fast good people would turn vicious when deprived of food, a toilet and paper to wipe their bottoms. It wasn't pretty.

I can only imagine what it would be like, if everyone for miles around had to fend for themselves. Knowing human nature, it would get ugly fast, very ugly.

I told the class to take heed of the Hierophant's suggestion and prepare a stash of supplies in case the lights and water were cut off. It's always wise to have 2-3 days of supplies in any case.

I said, "You know what it is like when a snowstorm knocks power out for just a couple of days? Just imagine if the whole country was knocked off the power grid. One solar flare from the sun hitting the earth could shut power down for years. People think the government is going to take care of them. That's not true.

The government is set up to take care of the government. The people will have to fend for themselves."

I asked, "Has anyone ever seen the movie, *Mad Max*? The principal behind the story is apocalyptic in nature. Just like in the movie, people in our neighborhoods would go crazy and form gangs or clans to start stealing from one another, or to claim territories. It's just something to think about. You have to ask yourself, "Do you want to be a 'have' or 'have not'? If you answer a 'have', then start preparing now. We depend too much on our soft lifestyles. We know if we run out of something, we can hop in the car and go to the store to buy more. If a cataclysmic event takes place, the stores will be wiped clean in less than a few days. Like I said earlier, most people don't even know how to start a fire, without a lighter, so prepare yourself for that as well."

Most of the class just got scared about the thought of such a disaster and took the same stance as Thomas when he said, "... we prepared, and it never happened."

I reminded them that chances are it won't happen, but what if it does? The Hierophant did give us some frightening food for thought that month.

Chapter Forty-seven

Me, a Writer?

Lesson Twelve:

Four of Hearts, received July 8, 1989
Book of Wisdom, channeled from the Hierophant:

In this lesson, I learned how fragile humans are because of our emotions. I was told a great story that made me wonder how many people we affect, with our words. I also learned how to develop Clairessence. It's the clear feeling to join yourself spiritually or mentally, with another, to experience their emotions and experiences. I was given two tests to use, which I found most effective.

SEE APPENDIX FOR ENTIRE LESSON

The First Wednesday Club classes were going very well. Thomas, who started out as a skeptic, was quickly becoming Dr. Peterson's strongest student. All the participant's abilities were growing, as were mine.

After presenting this month's lesson, I told the members how Michael helped me develop Clairessence on the police department. I didn't know what it was called at the time but now, after practicing this lesson, I see it is actually what he guided me to develop.

Looking in James Gray's direction, and winking, I said, "As an undercover investigator, I had to rub shoulders with hardened criminals, who would kill you, if you looked at them the wrong way. There was no room for error there. I had to not only read them, but I had to be exactly what they needed to see for my survival. I applied the same technique when I questioned suspects. Clairessence helped me see through the deceptions and lies, to find the truth."

The class loved when I would share a life experience that was an example of the lessons. They were like sponges, absorbing every morsel of information. I had to laugh because they thought my life was fascinating, and all I thought was how amazing it was that I was even alive.

On second thought, I guess that is fascinating.

After tonight's excerpt from "Ed's Diary," one of the students, Bonnie Spinner was more enthusiastic than ever for me to write a book my life. She also wanted me to include the lessons I was channeling, from the Hierophant. Bonnie worked in advertising and public relations, so she seemed to always be looking for the next big thing. She felt the whole world should have a chance to learn from the Book of Wisdom. The last thing I was interested in was writing a book. I knew that Michael had plans to release the lessons to the world one day. He once mentioned, "Before the End of Days, we must awaken the 144,000 Light Bearers and provide them the 'Knowing.'"

I just told her, "Well I am certainly no writer, and we need to focus on the lessons and their application first and foremost." Little did I know at the time, but writing a book was on the horizon, just not that book.

An odd thing happened later in the month. On my birthday, July 22, 1989, Linda took me out for a nice dinner. It was late when we arrived home, so we went straight to bed. As soon as my head hit the pillow, I began dreaming. In the dream, I was riding a white horse on a beach, when I saw a family picnicking. I dismounted, after seeing a child building a sandcastle. The family invited me to join their picnic. After the feast, we all sat around a campfire, and I told them a special story about our true godfather.

I woke up, wondering why I had that strange dream. I felt like I needed to write it down. When I tried to type, I found that my ink ribbon had run out, and we were out of typing paper as well. The only paper around was the blank sheets the Hierophant gave me. I couldn't use them. It was like everything was trying to stop me from writing the dream down. I knew if I went back to sleep, I would forget it. The only paper I could find was brown, paper garbage bags. I grabbed a pencil and began to recall the dream:

ENTRY -
July 22nd, 1989
Dear Diary,

This morning, I went riding on a horse named Mr. Ed. The stable master and I agreed that his name was appropriate, for the horse looked as if he could truly speak… (The two-page diary entry ended with) … She {the sandcastle girl} was surrounded by a green-topaz, colored light. With the seagulls calling and the waves crashing in the background, I began my story.

It was signed with a symbol that looked like a #2, with a number #1 through it. It also looked like a number #4, with a hook on the top left corner of the number. I found later it was the astrological symbol for the planet Jupiter. I had no idea what this meant. I remember the Hierophant said his teacher Master ERU had the sign of Jupiter on his iron staff. I just knew it was important to document.

Over the next few months, I had the same dream many times and repeated that same diary entry. I also kept getting drawn to create a concrete statue of the little girl in my dream, who was building a sandcastle. I knew I was channeling messages from somewhere, or someone, to get this vision of a statue completed. I also knew it wasn't coming from Michael. Don't ask me how, I just knew. I felt as if I could not rest, until it was done.

I molded the little girl and the sandcastle out of concrete. Once it set, I then painted an outdoor, epoxy-based glue all over the surface. Before it was dry, I sprinkled sand all over it, so it appeared to be made out of sand. It took two weekends to complete.

Sure enough, as soon as the statue was completed the dreams stopped, and I was given a vision of where to place the pieces.

I put the sculptures in a life-size scene in front of our beach house at Cove Point. The area was an 8' x 8' oval of sand that represented the beach. At one end, I placed the kneeling child and at the other, I made concrete waves that I painted blue and white. The waves were lapping onto the sandy shore. In the center was a glorious sandcastle.

I stood looking at the scene, basking in a rewarding sensation of "listening to the guidance" I had been given *AND* following through with the task. Whatever/whoever wanted that project done was happy and, quite frankly, so was I. The word "proud" first came to mind when I relived the dreams, the listening, the creation and the completion of the project. But then I thought, "No, it's not pride, it's fulfillment of service. It's completion of the soul."

I then couldn't help but wonder, "Why?" What does this statue, this scene have to do with anything, with Michael's mission, or with the lessons?

Then I heard, "Everything has a reason. Everything has a time. Moves on a chessboard should be made."

Linda loved it. It fit right into the theme of our beach house, which we had already named, "The Sandcastle."

I thought it was nice to look at, but my real joy about it was the back story for me. I listened and completed a task, a good task.

Odder than the story about the creation of the scene was the fact that, out of the blue, a local newspaper did a story on the sandcastle sculpture. Local people started to come to take photographs of the scene. Many told me that it made them happy when they looked at the little girl.

I knew it was just the beginning of something big that was going to happen.

Chapter Forty-eight

Microcosm vs. Macrocosm

It was now a year, since the lessons started for me. Like clockwork, they came in one by one each month. I could feel a shift in my thinking, as I practiced and re-read them. It was like I was outside myself looking in. Working with the First Wednesday Club members solidified the lessons for me even more. I now knew why the Hierophant was adamant that I teach and pass these lessons along to others.

Lesson Thirteen:

Three of Hearts, received August 8, 1989
Book of Wisdom, channeled from the Hierophant:

In this lesson, I learned about the Microcosm and Macrocosm that makes up humanity. It helped put everything in proper perspective for me. I learned how to develop and use my Psychic Sight. I was also given the Seventh Ancient Law of Wisdom: (7.) "With all of our power and wisdom, we have little effect on the macrocosm or microcosm. However the microcosm of our being can have a great effect on our surrounding macrocosms."

SEE APPENDIX FOR ENTIRE LESSON

This lesson opened everyone's eyes to how powerful they were becoming. Three quarters of the First Wednesday Club members were able to connect with their partners, using their Psychic Sight. They were amazed that they could see without their eyes. It was also very interesting how the lesson pointed out the comparison between the internal universes, within our bodies. It made us wonder if there was some form of intelligent consciousness alive inside of us, wondering, "What's out there?" Just as we are wondering, "What's outside the earth and our universe?" That must be what it means to be "created in the image of God." Understanding that we are each a macrocosm, living within a microcosm, surrounded by a greater macrocosm was mind blowing. I know that is a hard concept to grasp, but when the "Knowing" comes to you, so will that understanding.

Michael told all the students to go home and read the lesson again, before they went to bed, and they would wake up in the morning, with a greater understanding.

Chapter Forty-nine

Some Things Aren't Meant to be Seen

Lesson Fourteen:

Two of Hearts, received September 8ʰ, 1989
Book of Wisdom, channeled from the Hierophant

In this lesson, I learned how to properly meditate. It helped me open my mind, so I could read the signs and wisdom that were all around me. I was also given The Eighth Ancient Law of Wisdom: "Absolute faith emanates only from the inner or spiritual self, through conviction. And contemplation alone, without absolute faith attending it, will not advance you one iota."

SEE APPENDIX FOR ENTIRE LESSON

As the students filed in for the next First Wednesday Club, I picked a few, randomly, to take the class on a guided meditation. I gave them each a number, so they would know who was going first, and who they would follow. Each student chose a different visualization to meditate on.

Gwen McGregor took us on an exploration of a garden. We could actually smell the different flowers, as we passed over them. Barbara Webber had us climbing through a spider's web. We could actually feel the strands on our hands and legs, as we crawled along our way. However, Pat Cooper, who took us on a journey through our own bodies did the best-guided meditation. The students were amazed at what they actually saw in their mind's eye. One of the students, Barbara Wesley, was beaming with joy, when the visualization was over. When she raised her hand to share her experience, she told us she actually saw an embryo in her womb.

She called Dr. Peterson two days later to say her doctor confirmed it!

It was exciting to see everyone growing, but I could tell Denny McCarthy was bored, with the classes.

We were working on a missing child case in Arlington, Virginia. We went into a joint meditation to try to focus on who took the child. Using the skills learned in the lessons, we both visualized exactly the same "facts." We saw a bald man, with a red beard, driving a white panel van. The van had North Carolina plates and damage on the left, rear bumper.

Unfortunately, we couldn't pick up anything more. Michael told me the child was already dead, and the body could never be found.

McCarthy was expecting more from the lessons to aid us in our searches. Personally, I was amazed at the clues we were given, and the confirmations we would receive from time to time. I told Denny what Michael had relayed to me that some, who are missing, aren't meant to be found.

Denny wanted a clear picture of what happened from the lessons, but that wasn't meant to be. I could tell that he was going to quit the classes.

Life is a circle of energy. Life and death are part of the never-ending circle. They are as important a lesson, as what happens to us in between. Sometimes impatience halts progress.

Disappointed as I was about Denny, being on the verge of quitting the classes, I couldn't help but be amazed about all the information that surrounds us, if we just take the time to look and listen. The Hierophant was teaching us how to see with our minds, and the more we practiced, the stronger we were becoming.

Chapter Fifty

Everything Imagined is Possible

Lesson Fifteen:

Ace of Clubs, received October 8, 1989
Book of Wisdom, channeled from the Hierophant:

In this lesson, I learned that life is a song, and we are all its composer. If we don't like our life, we can change the tune. I learned the meaning of the seven books of wisdom that had been condensed into one word, "Ohm." And how to heal, with the laying on of hands. I also learned the great power that can he held in words, phrases and touch. And the use of the mind to transfer the words, into a healing vibration. I was then given the Ninth Ancient Law of Wisdom: "Words of power are an individual manifestation."

SEE APPENDIX FOR ENTIRE LESSON

On October 8, 1989, as I channeled lesson fifteen from the Hierophant, I began to see images of a knight, dressed in blue armor, searching for something. I felt like I had been split into two beings. I was now able to be in two places at the same time, experiencing different things.

It's hard to describe, but I am sure that some of you reading this will experience it when you practice lessons one through sixteen. As I channeled the "Legend of Seth" and "Astral Projection," something new woke up, inside my mind.

I could finally see that everything, that can be imagined, is possible. I also understood Master ERU's power phrase, ***The more you know, the more "Knowing" will come to you,*** was his gift to us. By reading those words at the beginning of each lesson, he was programing us to hunger for the "Knowing" he has sent.

Every member of the First Wednesday Club could feel that great man's power.

Michael told us, "If you elevate and stay on the Path of the Magi, Master ERU, the Golden Man will join us and together, we will construct a mighty Star-

Gate to bring home the Sons of the Light." We didn't know at the time what that meant, but would when our waiting was full.

We all wanted to help bring Atlantis back to earth. The story of Atlantis held many messages for us. I felt there was a chance for us all to experience an adventure of a lifetime, if we could just hold true to the Path of the Magi.

Chapter Fifty-one

A Good Knight's Story

Lesson Sixteen:

King of Clubs, received November 8, 1989
Book of Wisdom, channeled from the Hierophant:

In this lesson, I learned the Story of Atlantis and the darkness that was awakened, which led to its destruction. I was given a visual tour of Atlantis, where I was shown how they went wrong. I was then given a warning for the people of today, and why Archangel Michael wants the Book of Wisdom given back to the world.

SEE APPENDIX FOR ENTIRE LESSON

I could tell from the tone of lesson sixteen, Michael was up to something on another plane. I didn't have long to wait to find out what.

The next day when Angel Michael returned, the first thing he said was, "The time has come for you to take the first step of a Good Knight." He had given reference to Knights and "Sir Edward" in the past, but this time it was different. He showed me a book that I was supposed to write that would take on a life of its own. The book was a child's fairytale intended to awaken the hero, within children, and set them on a quest to love and protect one another.

I asked, "Where do I start? I don't know anything about writing children's books."

Michael replied, "From out of the Blue, it will come to you. It's a true story that you have already lived, but now it must be told in a form that will withstand the ages."

Denny and Judah had become more than just close friends, if you know what I mean. She was the only reason he was still attending classes. Dr. Peterson had started another Master Studies Program, using the Hierophant's lessons, at Prince George's County Community College. Those students were separate from the First Wednesday Club control group. His Master Studies class met on the third Friday of every month. Many of the First Wednesday students went to both classes. They just couldn't get enough of the "Knowing."

Dr. Peterson also spent his time, doing physic readings in Washington, D.C., at a New Age bookstore off DuPont Circle, that Bonnie Spinner owned. The charity also used the bookstore as an office.

During one of our weekly board meetings, I told the staff that I could no longer fund the investigations into missing children cases, and we'd have to find a benefactor, if we were going to continue. McCarthy was shocked, but Admiral Zumwalt understood my predicament.

Afterward, Denny and I went to the Four Seasons Hotel for a drink. He wanted to know what the charity was going to do, if it wasn't going to investigate missing children cases.

I told him, "You know, I'm tired of always bumping heads with local cops, who don't want our help. Eventually we are going to run into some hot dog detective that will try to charge us, with hindering his investigation. We've already been threatened with it several times in the past. Bottom line here Denny, I invested my entire police retirement pension fund in the charity, and we don't have a thing to show for it. All the children we were searching for wound up dead. I want to get to the children before they become victims. This is depressing."

Denny couldn't really appreciate or understand my predicament. He was financially comfortable, living high on the hog, with his Secret Service Retirement and the royalties from his book, *Protecting the President*. Also, he was detached from people to the point that a case was just a case to him. The thrill was in the chase.

I still tried to reassure him, "You know me Denny. I'm on God's good humor, just lucky to be on this side of the dirt. I am sure Archangel Michael will guide us on the path this charity needs to be on."

I knew that wasn't the answer he wanted to hear, but it was all I had, and I wasn't going to lie to him.

That night, as I slept, Michael took me to a small castle-like structure surrounded by waterfalls, a flowering labyrinth, with a high tower at its center and beautiful gardens. I felt like I had come home.

He said, "This is Eagleton."

We went inside the castle, and I saw a court jester, running away from us, as a huge giant was chasing him. Outside I watched as a silver knight, and the town's people, grabbed a knight in blue armor. He was tarred and feathered, and then tied to a white horse and driven out of town in shame. The Jester laughed. The King was sad, and the Queen was crying. A little white mouse, with a Scottish accent, yelled, "We must find M"V. That's when I woke up.

I asked Michael, "What does this all mean?"

He said, "This is your story, Sir Good Knight. That is what happened to you. Now go back to your sandcastle and write it down."

I found myself back home in bed, lying beside Linda. She awoke and asked, "Where have you been? I woke up a little while ago and couldn't find you in the house."

I said, "I don't really know. If I didn't know better, I would think I was lost in the pages of a book Michael wants me to write. I don't think we'll have any peace until I do."

I got out of bed and went out to the front porch. Putting my mind in a relaxed meditative state, I began to channel:

__A Good Knight Story__ - Long, long, long ago and once upon a time, there existed a glorious kingdom, within a land one step back and two to the side of where you live now. The kingdom was known as Eagleton.

I channeled and wrote for a few hours and then the visions would stop. Over the next three nights, the complete story was given. The story seemed to be my life, following Michael's guidance, in the search for a missing child, with the initials M.V. In the story, children born in the Spring are being abducted. A Blue Knight and a magical wishing mouse, by the name of Macaroni, set out on a Divine Quest to find the children. The story reveals ten tricks that are used to abduct the children. Michael said long ago that if children knew the tricks abductors' use, they wouldn't go with the strangers. I attached the story of the sandcastle girl, that I channeled several months earlier, to the beginning, as an introduction.

I had Linda retype the story, making corrections and putting things in the right place and tense. When I channel, I find that the information comes in backwards and sometimes in the third person. I think it's jumping from one dimension into the next. Nevertheless, the story was complete, and I passed rough draft copies to McCarthy, Judah, Dr. Peterson and Bonnie Spinner for review.

Chapter Fifty-two

Kid Energy

Lesson Seventeen:

Queen of Clubs, received December 8, 1989
Book of Wisdom, channeled from the Hierophant:

In this lesson, I learned how to Bi-Locate, which is being in two locations at the same time. I was given the Story of Seth, which I knew was a warning for me. I also learned how to perfect Astral Projection.

SEE APPENDIX FOR ENTIRE LESSON

After channeling Lesson Seventeen on astral projection, I understood more about the different levels that Michael worked on, simultaneously, in order to effect change. I also realized the Good Knight Story was more important than ever, if we are going to "fail with as much success as possible."

I called a meeting of my staff, trying to get some feedback on the story. They loved it. Bonnie Spinner sent a copy to her publisher, who also loved it, and we were off to the races. Like Michael said, the book started to take on a life of its own.

The publisher wanted color artwork to be done for the story, but Michael wanted the book to be done all in black and white, with pen and ink sketches, so kids could color the pictures to personalize their books. The only color picture would be the cover. The publisher liked the idea. I drew a few pictures, and we held a drawing contest for the remainder. For the contest, we brought the volunteer art students together. Bonnie read them the Good Knight Story, and then asked them to draw a pen and ink sketch of one of the scenes in the story. Michael said it was important to program the book with "kid energy."

It worked! No two kids drew the same scene, and they were all great. We gave prizes to the winners, wrapped up all the editing, and by Christmas, we went to press.

Chapter Fifty-three

The Electro Magnetic Grid

At the onset of the New Year, everything was coming together.

On January 3, 1990, the first 1,000 market test copies of *A Good Knight Story* were ready for sale to the public. White Feather and Company Publishing didn't want to invest too much money in an unknown author and story line, until they tested public acceptance. Bonnie Spinner was very good at what she did and created a great public relations campaign, to launch the book.

Dr. Peterson and I had been teaching the lessons from the Book of Wisdom, to the volunteers and the First Wednesday Club members, and we were seeing considerable elevation in their understanding, as they began to acquire the "Knowing."

Michael began assigning his angelic commanders around key individuals, working with me. I knew it was the beginning of re-forging the Angel-Knights of Atlantis, but we had a long way to go. The Archangel Gabriel was guiding Bonnie now, much like Michael guides me. He said that Gabriel means "God is my strength," and that the Angel bears the Power of Communication. I could see why he chose Gabriel for Bonnie. After several meditations with the angel, during First Wednesday Club where she called Gabriel to connect with her mind, Bonnie initiated a series of phone calls to TV and radio producers. It was as if Gabriel set them on fire. She scheduled bookings for McCarthy and I to appear on programs to discuss how parents could keep their children safe from child abuse and abduction. We told the audience that the best way to keep their children safe from abduction was to read them *A Good Knight Story*, then discuss the tricks with them.

Archangel Metatron was assigned to guide Dr. Peterson. Michael said Metatron was a fiery, energetic angel who has a special place in his heart for children, especially those, who are spiritually gifted. He said, "After the Exodus, Moses channeled Metatron... and led the children of Israel, through the wilderness to safety. He continues to lead children today, both on earth and in heaven. His passion is unity, education, truth and children's issues."

Because of Dr. Peterson's quick temper, he also assigned an Atlantian Magi's spirit that he called Bat-Que, "The Beacon," and the spirit of disciple Peter. He said Bat-Que could use Peter's temper, as a fiery torch, to guide seekers of the

"'Knowing" to the lessons we were now teaching. Just as with Bonnie, Peterson called the angels to connect with his mind, during several meditations. Peterson's workload tripled, and more and more volunteers came forward to help the charity and learn.

Attorney Judah Weinstein received the Angel Anael, which means "Grace of God" and the spirit of the disciple Judas. Michael said, "Anael will help Judah manifest things that are needed." The same held true for her, as with the others. After meditations where she called Angel Anael into her consciousness, things started to happen. She met with Admiral Zumwalt, who gave her some leads in Congress and BOOM... she was off to the U.S. Capitol to gather support for the cause.

I learned quite fast that I had to keep Judah and Peterson apart from one another. Oddly, they seemed to have an inbred dislike for each other. Michael called it, "The Judas-Peter clash." Judah was a cool-headed, Asian who wouldn't respond to the negativity that Dr. Peterson was throwing her way. This, of course, just fueled Peterson's fire and made him even angrier.

Michael couldn't get any of his angels to bond with McCarthy. I don't think Denny could wrap his mind around their existence. He wanted to see one with his eyes and hear one speak in his ears. I told him that wasn't the way it worked.

I said, "Denny, it's different for everybody. It will only come when you can separate your mind from your brain and start listening with your heart. Not everyone has the willpower or the desire to do it. If it is to be, it will be."

As everyone was elevating, a new energy was coming through in the lessons. I could see that I was hearing better and everyone around me was benefiting. As they learned and grew, I seemed to soar even higher, as well.

Chapter Fifty-four

Jockeying for Position

Lesson Eighteen:

Jack of Clubs, received January 8, 1990
Book of Wisdom, channeled from the Hierophant:

In this lesson, the Hierophant continued the Story of Atlantis and what happened to his people. Everything tied into why I was sent to the Hopi Indians to learn. I also learned about the importance of the electro-magnetic Grid Atlantis had created to hold the earth's vibration stable. He ended the lesson with, "You live in a time when a lot shall be revealed. Ancient secrets will pave a new way of life. The ancient stories and legends will be made clear to bring forth hidden truths. This is a time when the veil of ignorance will be removed, and your sight will be restored."

SEE APPENDIX FOR ENTIRE LESSON

I could see how important it was for the Hierophant to pass on the history of his people. It must be sad to still be conscious, and in the moment, while the myth of your culture is but a fading memory. The Hierophant was counting on me to locate humans that had what it takes to become Angel-Knights. From his lessons, I felt like I knew him, Master ERU and Queen Kei Sophia Pistis. I was empowered by their story and more determined than ever to bring them home. I knew that meant locating humans that could bear the weight of their mission. When I heard the name Sophia, my mind immediately went back to the beautiful black-haired woman, who pulled my lifeless body from the ocean. She looked a lot like the actress Sophia Loren. Michael told me that her breath of life would always be in my body.

In the real word side of my life, things were not tracking for the charity's investigative side. We could no longer afford to function, and we turned more in the direction of prevention. The board of directors decided to change the charity's name to something that fit more with what we were doing. Admiral Zumwalt suggested *The Good Knight Child Empowerment Network*, which was more in line with the book I wrote. Our Mission Statement and Goals were:

GKCEN's mission is the empowerment of youth, through awareness and experience.

GKCEN's goals are to teach critical thinking, leadership, life skills, self-protection and self-expression, through exposure to technology, art, music, literature and the environment.

Michael wanted us to help create a more cohesive generation of youth, who understood that diversity is the adventure and beauty of life.

To start on the journey to honor the mission and goals, I had the idea to seek out corporate office space, where we could invite school field trips for interactive child safety awareness programs. Dovetailing with those programs, I planned to use the Book of Wisdom to elevate the awareness of adults.

I put Judah on the job to locate the space, since Angel Anael proved to work through her so well. The two of them must have been working overtime because, within a month, she garnered donations of a 3,000-square foot office space, furnishings for six offices, conference room, distribution center and lumber, so we could construct an indoor amphitheater.

I could see Michael and his commanders were focused on a major push to empower the masses.

Interestingly enough, I also saw the vices start to work on the very people, who said they were trying to elevate and be a positive force in the world. Petty jealousies came out in Bonnie and Dr. Peterson over how well Judah's Angel was able to produce. It was like they were jockeying for position, within the ranks. It didn't make sense on any level. It was like an apple trying to be an orange, which can't happen!

Michael told them all, "When you jockey for position, you jockey yourself right out of the position I put you in, and are useless to me."

I couldn't tell who he was talking to; the humans, the angels or both.

After every interview we did with newspaper, radio or television, our phones would light up from parents and schoolteachers, who wanted a copy of *"A Good Knight Story."* At that time, the Good Knight Network was the only resource for child abuse and abduction protection for children. There were "Stranger Danger" programs, but the people, hurting children in America, weren't always strangers. We taught children to look for the trick, not the stranger.

The charity negotiated a deal with White Feather and Company Publishing to buy the books wholesale, so we could sell them retail to the public, as a charity fundraiser. That was working out great, since it was our only source of funding at the time.

It seemed like every month, there was another missing child somewhere in the United States. The public and media were beginning to see that there was a real problem. As they gained understanding of what the charity did, more of the First Wednesday Club Members wanted to volunteer. The control group started calling themselves Good Knight Volunteers, and Michael was pleased.

Chapter Fifty-five

Knowledge is Power

Lesson Nineteen:

Ten of Clubs, received February 8, 1990
Book of Wisdom, channeled from the Hierophant:

In this lesson, I learned that Power is a living thing. It was more a lesson on what was to come, if I mastered the Book of Wisdom. I learned Thought Photography and how to create objects out of thought. I also learned Telekinesis, the ability to move objects, with my mind. I was then given the Tenth Ancient Law of Wisdom: (10.) "The Powers of Wisdom consume those, who would misuse them, and from that... there is no escape."

SEE APPENDIX FOR ENTIRE LESSON

It was amazing how the lessons came in and mirrored my needs at that precise time. I knew the next year was going to be about visualization and creation. I just hoped that the staff and I were up to the challenge.

One morning, during a radio interview, a Prince George's Country Maryland School Psychologist, Dr. Arlene Forbes, was listening, as she drove to work. At that time, there were no crime and violence prevention programs on the market and child abduction cases were on the rise in the United States.

Understanding the psychological effects of what I was offering to the public, and the psychology that was used in the book to educate and prevent crime, Dr. Forbes immediately ordered twelve books from the charity. The following week, Dr. Forbes implemented a pilot child safety awareness program at Laurel Elementary School.

Within a week after *A Good Knight Story* was read to one class of third graders, a little girl, leaving school, reported that she was approached by a man, using the "Help" trick. He asked her, "Will you help me find my lost puppy?" Recognizing that it was one of the ten tricks she had learned from the story, she ran back to the safety of the school, instead of going with the abductor.

Dr. Forbes was thrilled and, at the same time, not surprised. She knew that if this information were taught in schools, kids would be safer. As she put it, "Knowledge is Power." Dr. Forbes wrote a report and sent it to all the County and State School system's superintendents. Her report included the lifesaving information contained in the fairytale. She suggested that all third and fifth grades be read the story every year. Orders started coming in from schools all across the state of Maryland.

As Michael had predicted, the story was taking on a life of its own.

Chapter Fifty-six

A Seth, in my Club?

Lesson Twenty:

Nine of Clubs received March 8, 1990
Book of Wisdom, channeled from the Hierophant:

In this lesson, I learned that the Hierophant was planting seeds of knowledge in my mind that will continue to grow my entire life. I also learned about the great responsibility that came with receiving the Book of Wisdom and teaching it to others.

SEE APPENDIX FOR ENTIRE LESSON

In the stories the Hierophant shared, I could see how we, currently, are making the same mistakes the ancients made. I wondered if we gained any real wisdom, over the past twenty-five thousand years, and were our egos really that far out of whack? It was also apparent how quickly we could be plunged into the dark ages again and completely forget everything we had learned... because our only focus would be to survive. I was also worried about why the Hierophant chose now to let me know he was the one responsible for teaching Seth the "Knowing." It made me wonder, "Do I have a Seth in the First Wednesday Club control groups?"

Chapter Fifty-seven

Woman of the Apocalypse

Lesson Twenty-One:

Eight of Clubs, received April 8, 1990
Book of Wisdom, channeled from the Hierophant:

During the channeling of this lesson, I earned the elevation to the level "Avatar of the First-Degree," in the Order of the Magi. With it came a warning. "If you are to become part of the "Knowing," your mind and powers must grow beyond that of the Forces of Darkness. Remember, you are never alone. Michael and I are always with you. However, you are but a speck of light, adrift in a sea of darkness. Never let your light be extinguished, or we all fail." Much of the lesson was on "Pride." I had learned that it was one of the things that both Archangel Michael and I had to overcome. I learned Lycanthropy, the ability to shape shift into an animal form or to project the illusion of an animal. I had no idea at the time how important that ability would become for me in the future. Then I was taught the importance of creating a Secret Sacred Place in my mind. It was something Michael had me learn when we first met, during the abusive days as a child, with Edna May.

The Hierophant then disclosed that I was also being groomed to build a Secret Sacred Place for a very special woman and her child. "Master Hermit, it should be noted that you are destined to help the Angels of the Four Directions and your Good-Knight Students to re-establish the Garden of Eden on Earth. The Creator has commanded that Archangel Michael prepare a place of Love and Protection for a very special woman and child, as has been prophesized in Ancient Scripture:

Woman of the Apocalypse

Book of Revelations 13: "When the Red Dragon saw that it had been thrown down to the earth, it pursued the woman. But the woman was given the two wings of the Great Eagle, so that she and her future child could fly to a place prepared for them, by Angel Michael and the Sons of Light."

SEE APPENDIX FOR ENTIRE LESSON

Just when I thought it couldn't get any more complicated, they lay that bomb on me. Obviously, I am to build a not so secret place on a large scale, but it's for a woman and her child that a red dragon is pursuing? Really?

Michael said, "All things will be revealed to you in time. If I showed you everything now that lay ahead of you, you would fear to move forward."

He paused. I could feel him wrap his mighty wings around me, as he continued. "In the end, the two eagles, you and I, will say: 'Look at this, you tarnished souls, and lose yourself in wonder. For in your days, we did such a deed. If man were to tell you this story, you would surely not believe it'!"

Chapter Fifty-eight

The Serpent of Fire

Lesson Twenty-Two:

Seven of Clubs, received May 8, 1990
Book of Wisdom, channeled from the Hierophant:

In this lesson, I learned about how to awaken the seven points in the body known as Chakras, and how to move positive energy through them. This lesson also came with a warning concerning the Serpent of Fire, within us all.

SEE APPENDIX FOR ENTIRE LESSON

The First Wednesday Club gathering loved the class on the Chakras. Dr. Peterson was already well-versed on the flow of energy in the body, so it added even more dimension to the class. Almost everyone wanted to know more about the Kundalini or Serpent of Fire. Even Denny was intrigued.

Michael said to the class, "Be careful. I see that for some of you to awaken the serpent, within you, will cause you to leave this path of wisdom and send you down a path you should not journey."

The Good Knight Story book sales were doing well and teachers were putting together programs for their classes, using the books. As fate would have it, Maryland Governor William Donald Schaefer was touring some of the schools in Prince George's County and heard about the child, who avoided being abducted because of *A Good Knight's Story*.

The governor wanted to know more. One of the teachers gave him a copy of the book, during his visit. After reading the book and discovering it was a Maryland author, who wrote it, he became even more intrigued. When he learned that the author was also a retired police officer, who used all of his retirement funds to establish an all-volunteer non-profit, he was impressed.

On Sunday May 27, I was invited to do a book signing, with other local authors, at a shopping mall in Prince Georges County. All the authors were given fifteen minutes on stage to discuss their books and take questions before the book signing began. The audience was full of families, so I talked to the parents about some of my police experiences, dealing with missing children investigations.

Mid-way through, Angel Michael took over and started talking to the children about the ten tricks that people use to lure children into unsafe situations. He ended by telling a short version of *A Good Knight Story*. At the end, Michael asked how many kids wanted to become Good Knights and join him on a quest to keep other kids safe. Most of the children, and some adults, came forward.

As they approached, I felt as if I was hovering near the ceiling, out of my body watching the scene unfold. I saw myself dressed in Michael's blue armor, with the flaming Sword of Tenacity, and knighting each person, who came forward. I don't know what the kids and adults saw, since I was really just tapping each of them on the shoulder, with the palm of my hand.

After that, my table was mobbed, with people wanting my book. People were buying multiple copies as gifts for others.

When we were finished, and I was driving home, Michael said, "Sir Edward, remember this date. We will reach millions, within the next twenty-five years."

I asked, "Why twenty-five years?"

He answered, "Because that is all the time that has been given to us. In twenty-five years, you must pass the Sword of Truth to another victorious child, and she will be amazing." My thoughts went to the child, with the initials M.V. Whenever I thought of her, my heart always seemed to fill with love.

At the next First Wednesday gathering, there was a deep discussion going on about UFO's, aliens and angels. One lady, a former model and runner up in the 1970 Miss Philippines pageant, said that sightings of UFO's were a regular thing, over the islands of her homeland.

Dr. Peterson announced, "Interesting! It's obvious that we were all becoming part of one mind, because that's exactly what this month's lesson from the hierophant is about."

I asked, "How many of you believe that angels are extraterrestrial?" No one raised his or her hand.

Thomas, who started out not believing in angels asked, "Angels come from heaven, right?"

I said, "The heavens and anything not of this earth are extraterrestrial and, believe it or not, half of you are extraterrestrial as well. By the end of this class, I hope we all have a greater meaning for what's out there and..." putting my hand to my heart I finished the thought, "... what's in here!"

Chapter Fifty-nine

This Conversation Never Happened

Lesson Twenty-Three:

Six of Clubs, received June 8, 1990
Book of Wisdom, channeled from the Hierophant:

In this lesson, I learned about life and the many kinds of living things, like crystals. We even have living crystals in our bodies. Planet earth is teeming with life. Everywhere you look, things are living. I learned that the human body is terrestrial, because it is made up from earthly atoms. But our spirit is extraterrestrial... it came from another dimension, outside the earth. That answered a lot of questions for me. I also learned a history of cosmic visitations. The Hierophant ended with this message, "Our cosmic brothers have appeared to shepherds, kings and astronauts. Now before the turn-of-the-century, the world will see them. Be not afraid for they are our brothers and sisters."

SEE APPENDIX FOR ENTIRE LESSON

This was one of the most interesting gatherings we had to date. Even McCarthy was into it.

He shared, "When I was a kid in the Midwest, some friends and I saw a UFO. And, when Presidents Carter and Reagan were in office, there was a lot of talk about them, seeing UFO's as well. One was even seen during a flight on the President's plane, Air Force One."

A week after the class, McCarthy called me and said that some military officers had just come forward and admitted to the government cover-up on the Roswell crash. The military did recover an alien space craft.

I shook my head and had to chuckle in awe. I thought it was interesting that the military officers came forward, in sync with the Hierophant's release of Lesson Twenty-three.

I could see it was time to ask the Admiral again about the incident in Vietnam in 1969. Before I could contact him, the Admiral called me! Coincidence? I think not!

A few weeks later, McCarthy and I met with Admiral Zumwalt in his office. He had a client, who needed a private investigator. The son of a friend was suspected, by police, of murdering his ex-wife's boyfriend. I said that I would take the case, if he would tell me about the incident in 1969. He countered that he would give me some insight, after I looked into the case.

The admiral was always a great strategist.

After looking into the murder, it appeared to be one of those cases where one would have to ask, "Who didn't have a motive?" Everyone wanted the man dead. He was a criminal and the victim of a contract hit.

After I gave my report to the Admiral, we went to lunch.

He told me that he couldn't confirm or *deny* the existence of extraterrestrials, but if a naval vessel *had* seen any unidentified flying objects hovering over their ship, those UFO's *probably* would have been fired upon with rockets. If those *same* unidentified flying objects were seen again the next day, several hundred miles away, they would be fired on *again*. Only that time, the UFO's *probably* would return fire and destroy the naval vessel.

He asked, "Hypothetically now, what would you think if, during the investigation of this non-incident, it was discovered that the same rockets, which were fired at the UFO the day before, destroyed the naval vessel?"

Puzzled, I asked, "How could the investigators know those were the same rockets?"

He reminded me, "Every rocket has a serial number on it and various parts within it. If those parts were found in the wreckage, what would you think?"

He was answering my questions with questions. I thought about it for a while, then said, "Well, any life form that had the technology to capture a rocket and return it, isn't anyone I would shoot at again, and I wouldn't tell anyone about it either... or there would be panic."

He said, "Exactly! Thanks for the lunch. This conversation never happened." Then he got up from the table and left.

Starting in June of 1990, after channeling Lesson 23 from the Hierophant, many military officers came forward and admitted to a government cover-up of the "Roswell Event" in 1947. They admitted that an alien spacecraft did crash and was recovered.

I asked Michael, "Why do they use the lights?"

I was told that our cosmic brothers come from other dimensions where our physics don't apply. They learned how to harness light and sound, combining the two, with an electro-magnetic energy generator --and other things beyond our comprehension--to propel their spacecraft. I was also told that they are seen when they want to be seen, but most of them have mastered invisibility. What I've been shown is they cloak whatever they wish to conceal, with an overlay of an image of their surroundings.

It's one thing for skeptics to dismiss a sighting of a UFO, by a single individual who might be mistaken, delusional or simply a teller of tall tales. It's more difficult, however, to disregard sightings in public places and numerous witnesses.

"Seeing is believing," they say.

In all the years I've been married to Linda, she claims she hasn't seen a shooting star, why? Does that mean that shooting stars don't exist? No. She also said she never saw a UFO.

A couple of years ago, we took a cruise to the Caribbean. One night, while enjoying a nice glass of wine on our balcony, I saw a shooting star. She didn't. A few minutes later, I saw another. She didn't. Either I'm crazy or she's blind.

That incident reminded me of my childhood when I couldn't see a four-leaf clover in a patch of normal clovers. My grandmother said, at the time, "You can't see the forest for the trees, laddie." Linda couldn't see the shooting stars because she was too busy looking at all the stars to see just one that moved. I told her to just be patient and focus on one star in the night sky, and within her peripheral vision she would pick up movement. A few minutes later, she saw her first shooting star, after many years of trying.

A few years after that, Linda and I were vacationing in Myrtle Beach, South Carolina. We were sitting on the balcony looking out over the Atlantic Ocean, trying to see shooting stars. I remember telling her, "Once upon a time, the great continent of Atlantis sat out there somewhere." She smiled and went to get something from the other room.

At the time, I was trying to make sense of all that was happening in my life. I asked Archangel Michael to give me a sign that I was on the right path. As I sat there, my eyes focused on a deep yellow light on the horizon. The light was moving closer and closer, until it was just off shore, hovering about a hundred yards from where I was sitting. It shifted and became five lights, with one in the middle, like on a pair of dice.

I called to Linda. When she came out, she saw the hovering objects as well. The five lights pulsated for about two minutes. I could feel the craft was looking at us. We looked at each other, and I knew we both felt the same thing, without us ever speaking it. The "object" then shot straight up into the night sky, made a sharp left turn and disappeared.

Linda said, "That's weird. What was that?" I didn't know what to tell her. How does one explain such a thing?

I felt a deep breath, surge into my body, and a peace came over me. I answered her, "It was everything, and it was nothing at all." I knew it was confirmation and my skeptical, well-grounded wife just confirmed it. All I could think was that whoever/whatever was on the craft could read our thoughts. I wondered to myself, "What does this all mean?"

Michael said, "Two things. You have so much more to learn about everything! And Linda saw her first UFO."

On the Good Knight Story front, the charity received a call from the Governor's Office, notifying them that I was to receive the 1990 Governor's Service Award for Public Safety on September 13th at the State House in Annapolis.

Along with that news, the caller had one special, personal request from the Governor. He wanted to know if "Sir Edward, the Blue Knight" could wear his blue suit of armor when he receives the award.

When Bonnie Spinner told me that, I went into a panic, thinking, "Where the heck am I going to get a blue suit of armor, like the one described in the story?"

I shook my head and said, "No way. No can do. I can't go to an awards ceremony in a costume. I'll feel like a fool."

McCarthy chimed in, "Yeah right, what's next? Are they going to want you to come riding in on a white horse, with a mouse on your helmet?"

Everyone, but Denny and I, thought it was a great opportunity to call attention to the Good Knight cause.

Attention is right. I was sure that I would get attention! I just wasn't too thrilled, with the kind of attention it conjured up in my mind.

As I watched everyone discussing what I should do, I was also reviewing my own reaction, pure ego. Wow! I was afraid to look like a fool, but didn't I vow to do whatever it took to propel this mission forward? The award was an honor, and I decided then that I would accept it, with grace and decorum. By knowing who I was in my heart and soul, I knew that all who looked upon me would not see a fool, unless, of course, they wanted to see one. I also felt Michael and the Hierophant were trying to groom me for whatever I needed to do to honor Michael's plan.

Chapter Sixty

Sword and Skin

Lesson Twenty-Four:

Five of Clubs, received July, 1990
Book of Wisdom, channeled from the Hierophant:

In this lesson, I learn about a Talisman, which is an emblematic object made out of just about anything... stone, wood, metal, paper, etc. It can be any size, shape and color. The talisman may take the form of a ritual, potion, formula or gesture. It is a very powerful charm, with the capacity to change events, influence living things, human actions, feelings and the stroke of luck. It is created, with a very specific formula. I also learned about an Amulet, which is an object carried by the owner and believed to give protection against evil and bring about good luck. I gained the number and letter value code needed to make simple Talismans, but Michael said the hard lesson was still to come. "In the future, the day will come when we must make talismans to manifest millions of dollars, to support the construction of a great castle. We need to reach millions of children, with a lifesaving message, so learn your lessons well, Sir Knight."

SEE APPENDIX FOR ENTIRE LESSON

I started making calls and found that a suit of armor would cost about $200 to rent and $4,000 to buy. I didn't have that kind of money. Michael said, "Well, Sir Edward, you don't want to disappoint the Governor. This could be the lucky break we have been waiting for."

I said, "Then guide me to the armor that I can afford."

He said, "Go home and look in your closet."

That night when I returned home, I discovered that Inspector Albright, from Interpol, had sent me a long, odd-shaped box. When I opened it, I was surprised to find a large 48" sword, with a note that read:

Thank you, Sir Edward for all of your help. The case has led to many more investigations. This sword was in the window of an antique shop near

my home. Every day when I'd pass the shop, I would think of you. I think
you are supposed to have it.
    Sicher Bleiben Mein Freund,
    Chief Inspector Albright.

    Wow, I couldn't believe it. I never owned a real sword before. I showed it to Linda and said, "It will go perfectly with the armor I have to wear when the Governor gives me his Pubic Service Award, at the State House in Annapolis."

    She cocked her head just like a wise barn owl and looked at me, like I was crazy, and said, "What are you talking about?"

    It seems, in all my worry about the armor and the award, I never mentioned the armor part to her--when I told her about the award.

    "The Governor wants me to wear the blue suit of armor, like in the book, to the ceremony."

    She said, "Are you nuts, where are you going to get a blue suit of armor?"

    I quipped back, "Michael told me to look in my closet." With that said, I turned and did as Michael told me to do. I went to my closet, but there was no armor. Michael was screwing with me, I thought. Then I spotted the old roll of Buffalo rawhide that the old, Indian Medicine Man, Eagle Hunter, gave me twenty years earlier.

    Michael came through loud and clear, "You can't buy my armor. We must forge it out of the mighty skin of the horned beast."

    All of a sudden, I heard Eagle Hunter's words, ringing out in my memory. "This is what you will need. It is from a great buffalo bull I skinned. For months, it has been drying, by Sun and Moonlight, just for you. Wear it. It will see you through all the bullshit on the path you are to take. Go now, and make ready for battle."

    Michael told me the last thing Eagle Hunter did in this life was to give me that rawhide blanket. He reminded me of his words, "Don't bullshit me. You might not know who you are, but I do."

    I asked Michael, "What did he see?"

    Michael said, "As soon as you wore the sacred leather armor, he saw that you and I would become one. He was proud to be part of that."

    Michael then gave me a vision of what the blue armor was to look like. The color was amazing. It was like a moonlit night sky, with bright gold lines, with words and symbols from head to toe. It also had the largest spurs I had ever seen. I wondered where I was going to get them, since they couldn't be made out of rawhide.

    Michael then told me that the gold markings on the armor would make us a walking talisman, so I had better learn the next lesson well.

Chapter Sixty-one

In Michael's Armor

Lesson Twenty-Five:

Four of Clubs, received August 8, 1990
Book of Wisdom, channeled from the Hierophant:

This lesson picked up where lesson twenty-four left off on Talismans. However, now we were learning the secret codes of the planets--what they govern and the days and hours that make up the planet's Magic Square. It was very confusing and will take much study to master. Michael said it even gets harder because it all had to become part of his armor. My head was swimming, with numbers, letters and symbols. The Hierophant ended with this warning: "Remember above all things, these are not toys, but sacred magical instruments that call upon the Angels, Spirits and Powers of the Highest Degrees. So, if your heart is not pure and your nature righteous, your Talisman could backfire, taking from you, instead of giving to you... therefore, the next lesson should not be entered into lightly."

SEE APPENDIX FOR ENTIRE LESSON

The last few lessons were a wealth of information that I needed to absorb and practice, practice, practice, before I could even start on Michael's Armor. The morning after the August, First Wednesday gathering, after Linda left for work, I pulled out the rawhide blanket. It was so thick and stiff, I didn't know what to do. Michael told me to fill the bathtub with hot water and soak the leather. He then told me to revisit certain lessons I had received from the Hierophant.

Michael took me into a deep meditation, where he linked my mind to an ancient Warrior of Righteousness, for guidance. It was an incredible experience. Michael said, "Together we will forge my Armor. It will be a walking, talking talisman for all to see." I had a funny feeling that he and the Hierophant were getting ready to create something that had not been seen on earth for thousands of years. I didn't have long to wait to see if I was right.

The Ancient One took total control of my body, but not my mind. Pulling the softened leather from the tub, we stretched it between two trees to dry. While drying, we mixed up a solution of baking powder, white vinegar, red wine, pickle juice, crushed amethyst crystals and water. Because I cut myself on one of the crystal shards, four drops of my blood also went into the mixture. At first I thought that was an accident, but then I wondered if it was intended to be in there. We then flicked the solution all over the leather, while smudging it, with white sage smoke, and saying some words I did not understand.

I was surprised at how fast the leather was drying. Taking metal snips from my toolbox, we went to work. We cut the leather into one hundred and forty-four pieces. After three hours, we were finally done. Now it was time to form the armor plates.

Thank God, they knew what they were doing because I had no idea what went where. I don't remember how they formed most of the parts that went into the armor, but Linda still reminds me, to this day, how her bed pillow and stuffed bra were laced together, to mold the breastplate. It was quite a sight to come home to. (Can you imagine the memories she has, being married to me? Ha!)

Michael said the bra put the perfect balance of masculine and feminine energy into the suit.

The leather had to dry, until it was rock hard.

Michael and I then went in search of the color he wanted for the armor. We found it at Pep Boys Auto supply. Royal blue metal flake, auto, spray paint--and a bottle of Gold Leaf artist paint, were his colors.

We sprayed all the pieces with seven coats of blue. I could see little specks of silver floating above the blue color. It reminded me of a starry night sky. Michael took a thin artist's brush and began trimming all the pieces in gold leaf. When the pieces were dry the following day, he painted gold leaf veins on everything, as if he was putting together a puzzle. He then painted the Jupiter symbol on each shoulder. A white cross on a circle of black, flanked by angel wings, was in the middle of the breastplate, and also the knee leg-guards.

Using a drill and strong gauge wire, he put all the pieces together. We linked it together with gold and black chains, that jingled when moved. After pinning my eight-pointed, gold Two Eagle's investigator's badge on the right side of the breastplate, the armor was finished. It looked amazing. It was like nothing I had ever seen before. The energy that radiated from the suit was incredible. Michael finished his armor off with a black, fake fur, wolf skin, that he said would help cloak me from the darkness that will be trying to attack us.

It was one thing to create the armor, but wearing it in public was quite another. My angst crept back in a wee bit.

Michael said, "We are all fools for God, but you must become a Knight in Shining Armor, in a world where real knights don't exist anymore. Surrender and become who you were born to be, no matter what other people think. If you don't help me wear the 'Full Armor of God,' who will? Sir Edward, your waiting is full!"

Michael's creations didn't stop there. He began to guide me, turning the charity's office space into a medieval castle museum for the public to visit. Using the powers of manifestation and combining the secret sacred place lessons, my saw and hammer were non-stop for months. The largest room in the office complex measured 75' x 150'. At one end, we constructed a knighting circle on a round indoor/outdoor green grass carpet, with seven wooden tree stumps to stand on. Large rocks, collected by our core group of volunteers, edged the Knighting Circle.

Surrounding the sacred circle, was a beautiful scene that featured a life size realistic female angel, with long blond hair. Michael said it represented The Constant Walker or Mother Earth, who he was sent to serve. Behind Connie was The Tree of Life, covered in green leaves and pink blooming flowers. On either side of the Knighting Circle, was an earthen scene of wildlife animals, rocks, moss covered boulders, a large waterfall and tiny fairies... hand painted, by Linda.

At the other end of the room, we built a white lattice backdrop, covered in green ivy that flanked a green-carpeted stage. On the center of the backdrop was Michael's hand painted, blue standard, with the Good Knight emblem of a white cross and angel wings. Beneath was written "Love Thy Children."

On the right side of the room, was a display of hand-painted, ceramic pieces and memorabilia that represented the seven religions of modern man. In the middle of the large display, was a fully decorated eight-foot upside-down Christmas tree, with white, mini, motion lights, suspended from the ceiling. On the left side of the room was a large glass museum showcase, filled with ceramic pieces in a diorama, depicting scenes from *A Good Knight Story.*

Next to the showcase stood Michael's Blue and Gold Armor. Every Wednesday, Friday and Saturday the Good Knight East Wing Castle Family Safety Museum would be open to the public, from noon to 6pm.

I remember the first time I put Michael's armor on. It was the day the museum opened. It was the strangest sensation I'd ever felt. We were preparing for our first Good Knight Child Safety Awareness Program at East Wing Castle. It was mid-August, and there were about fifty people in the audience, mostly children between four and eight years old. My heart was happy because Dawn had come down to visit, and she brought Meghan Victoria to see our first show. A reporter from *The World and I* magazine was there to cover the event. She was doing a ten-page, color spread article, profiling the work the charity was doing on abduction prevention.

Jim Bohannon, a national radio talk show host, was also in attendance.

McCarthy and I had done a radio interview with him earlier that year, and he was very intrigued to see the castle complex that we created. Several of the volunteers who had become Good Knights were given colors, by Angel Michael, and they made tunics in their respective colors. They looked great. Lady Judah Anael, the Yellow and Black Knight, and Sir Gregory Peterson, the Red and Black Knight, gave tours of the museum exhibits while Lady Linda and Dawn, guided people to their seats. Princess Meghan stayed with me.

Lady Bonnie Gabriel, the Red Knight, helped strap me into the armor. Everything was fine, until Michael arrived about ten minutes later. My body temperature went from warn to roasting, and sweat was pouring out of me, like Niagara Falls. I grabbed a blue cloth to wipe my face. I asked Michael, if he could turn down the heat.

All he replied was, "In time we will acclimate to one another."

Michael was all business. I could tell he wanted to get right into the "ABC's of Safety," but I wanted to joke around a little bit with the kids, asking their names and where they went to school. I sat on a large Styrofoam boulder with Princess Meghan Victoria, while Lady Bonnie read a condensed version of *A Good Knight*

Story. The story is about a Blue Knight, who is given a magical sword and sent on a Divine Quest, by the Archangel Michael, to find Princess Meghan Victoria and several other children from the Kingdom, who had mysteriously disappeared.

I couldn't believe how mesmerized the audience was, while listening to the story. You could've heard a pin drop. Whenever Lady Bonnie would mention Sir Edward or Princess Meghan, the kids would look at us, as if the story had come alive.

I knew the story Michael gave me was based on our real-life investigations into missing children cases and also my spiritual mission to search for a child, with the initials M.V. The story line was just fictionalized to not frighten or confuse the children. It was an honor to sit there and observe the story coming to life and plant valuable lessons into the psyche of the audience.

The only thing I didn't enjoy about the night was Denny. He kept making jokes about me, making a wrong turn at the Suit Factory for Men. It felt very disrespectful, but not toward me, but toward Michael.

When Lady Bonnie was finished, I stood up and spoke for about twenty minutes on the "ABC's of Safety" and how children can recognize someone that wants to lure kids, into unsafe situations, by their actions. I told them you can identify a stranger by their behavior and how they act when you are alone with them, not by their appearance... even if you already know them. I went on to tell them that many people, who want to put kids in dangerous situations, are already someone they know. I reminded them, "Look for the trick, not the stranger."

The whole time I was talking, my body felt electrified. Some of the people in the audience said they saw beams of light, racing along the gold veins Michael had drawn on His Armor. The sweating did stop, and we actually felt comfortable, working inside the same body. When he had something to say, it just came out. It did at times seem a little cramped, like twins inside a mother's womb.

I felt a tug of war going on every once in a while, when I misinterpreted something Michael was trying to say, or I'd say it before he had a chance to. It was hard in the beginning, but like everything, with a lot of practice and years of doing programs in the armor 'as one,' I finally got it right.

To end the program, Michael had a shocker for us all. He knelt down on one knee, held Princess Meghan in his left arm and the 'Sword of Tenacity' in his right. He asked everyone, "Please make the angel wings over your hearts by bringing your hands together and flapping your fingertips like wings." He then announced, "If you bring all your goodness into the room, the sword would burst into flames."

I thought Linda's eyes were going to pop out of her head when she looked at me. She and all the knights mouthed, "What are you doing?"

I was already preparing my, "it was a metaphor," excuse.

But then it happened. I was as shocked as the crowd was when their light radiated up Michael's Armor, and when it reached the sword, the blade burst into flames. The flame started at the hilt, and worked its way slowly up the blade, to the point. It was an awesome sight to behold.

Michael would tell the audiences, throughout the years, that he was taking a heavenly snapshot photograph for his Father.

Chapter Sixty-two

Both a Blessing and a Curse

Lesson Twenty-Six:

Three of Clubs, received September 8, 1990
Book of Wisdom, channeled from the Hierophant:

In this lesson, I finally reach the stage of making my first talisman. I learned the code of the geometric angles and the secret behind the full and crescent moon seals, spirits and intelligences. I could also complete Michael's Armor as a living, walking talisman.

SEE APPENDIX FOR ENTIRE LESSON

The First Wednesday Club members were extremely interested in making a talisman of his or her own. Some didn't quite grasp the concept right away, as was expected.
    One can read the instructions, but if one's energy level and understanding hasn't elevated, the talisman exercise will be veiled from comprehension.
    I invited those members, who needed help, to come to the East Wing Castle, and I would personally help them create a talisman. It was a great workshop. Everyone loved the energy at East Wing and wanted to start coming to the castle for class, rather than the room at Maryland University. They felt it was more magical, and they could see how the lessons I had received were manifesting in its construction. I could tell McCarthy wasn't too keen on the idea of the class meeting at the castle, but I didn't know why. I felt Michael did, but he wasn't sharing.
    All he would say on the subject was, "Your friend has his own demons he has to tame, before he can move forward."

    The night I was waiting for, with excitement and trepidation, was upon me. I would be receiving the Governor's Award.
    It was unbelievable. Governor William Donald Schafer was a very distinguished gentleman. He went out of his way to make me feel comfortable, while wearing a blue suit of armor, when everyone else was wearing dark suits and

cocktail dresses. There was a display set up with photographs of me in my army and police uniforms, also in a suit, and in the blue armor, surrounded by children, during a knighting ceremony at a school.

The Governor's assistant read the summary of my background. When she was finished with the part about my being a writer, whose book saved a child's life the first month after it was published, it brought the crowd to a standing ovation. I was overwhelmed at the comments and didn't know what to say. As I was called up to the podium, my mind was flooded with thoughts, but none of them made any sense.

Michael said, "I've got this."

That was my cue to get out of my own way, and let Michael take over. This is what he said on our behalf.

"Thank you for this great honor. I am flattered to receive this award for doing what God put me on earth to do. As a police officer, I've seen horrors done to children that could have been prevented, if the children just knew what to look for. When I was a child, I would not have been victimized, if I knew what we're teaching kids now. Throughout my life, I searched for the 'Knowing' and prayed to God to help me find it. Now that I've found it, I'm bound by a solemn oath to spend the rest of my life, bringing the knowledge to children before the darkness has a chance to tarnish their innocence. Thank you again, from the bottom of my heart."

Admiral Zumwalt was extremely proud of the achievement. He said, "Now we must build on this. That book is going to save many lives and stop a lot of heartache from occurring. The President needs to know about this."

The Admiral started writing letters to friends he knew in the media. This led to several news documentaries on NBC's 48hrs, Fox News, Dateline NBC and America's Most Wanted. Those documentaries opened up the entire United States to the Good Knight message of love and protection of children.

My partner, Denny, wasn't so pleased.

He said, "Those people, who are honoring you today, will talk shit about you tomorrow. In the end, they're just going to see you as a crazy freak of nature."

I said, tapping on the breastplate, "I see this as nothing more than a bullet proof vest, better yet, a bullshit-proof vest. I can't understand why you have such a problem with it. It's not like YOU have to wear it."

McCarthy just shook his head and said, "Schafer's crazy, so he's comfortable with crazy. You'll never be honored, by the President of the United States, dressed like that."

This conversation was going nowhere fast. I couldn't understand his negativity.

I said, "I don't care about awards, Denny. I care about beating the bad guy to the scene of the crime, that's all. And as far as crazy goes, everybody is a little crazy. Believe me, I policed crazy, and I found it everywhere. Remember, there is good crazy, bad crazy... and how much crazy, you can get away with. What kind of crazy are you right now?"

I could tell McCarthy had a few drinks before he came to the awards ceremony, and he was trying to match wits with me.

He barked back, "You're delusional, Jagen."

I said, "No, Denny, I'm an illusion, but I have substance. I have cause and effect. A delusion has no substance."

His fury rising, McCarthy spouted, "Don't give me that philosophical bullshit, save it for those First Wednesday fools."

The curse of having Michael, working through me, was two-fold. I seemed to bring out the best in some and the worst in others. If there were demons, lurking inside, we (Michael and I) would raise them in the hope that the person would see the light and be able to tame the dark spirits of their nature.

Denny's demons were tearing him apart, and our friendship was the battlefield.

He walked away angry, and I couldn't understand why he was getting himself so upset over nothing. It was like a test of wills. I wanted to pursue him, but talking was just making things worse. Judah told me later that she thought it was because McCarthy didn't like that I portrayed him as Macaroni, the white, magical, wishing mouse, in the *A Good Knight Story*.

I said, "Judah, he is little, and he is white. He's just not very magical. Macaroni is the character all the kids love the most. He's one of the heroes of the story. If it wasn't for Macaroni, Sir Edward would have failed."

Later that evening, Michael showed me a vision of Denny's body, lying in a casket. His ghostly spirit was sitting, weeping in a wingback armchair, off to one side in a corner. Right away, I had an impression that Denny was backing himself into a corner.

I was jarred out of the vision, by Michael speaking to a group of people, who had gathered. He said, "Between the year you are born and the year you die, all you have is that 'dash,' which represents the life you lead. He turned to Denny, sadly sitting nearby, and said, "Remember in the end, it's not about the things you owned, or even all that cash. The only thing that's important--is how you spent your dash."

I immediately got the feeling the vision of Denny had something to do with the next lesson for the First Wednesday Club.

Chapter Sixty-three

Dash of Life

Lesson Twenty-Seven:

Two of Clubs, received October 8, 1990
Book of Wisdom, channeled from the Hierophant:

In this lesson, I learned about the different dimensions, in which we live, and the construction of a four-dimensional Star of David. As for the dimensions, a single dot represents the person of the first dimension. As the dot moves through life, it becomes a line or dash, representing the life the person lived as the second dimension. The two are inseparable, as they exist in the cube that represents the life place that lived, or third dimension. As the dot reaches the end of the dash, and dies, that represents the fourth dimension of Time. I learned that our physical world is locked into time; the fourth dimension, but when we lose our bodies, our spirits move into the fifth dimension... which is timeless, like space itself, is endless. Therefore, all we have is what we recorded in the time that was given us.

The Hierophant warns us to live better, loving lives--since it is all you have in the Penetration Dimension. He says, "The most important dimension in life is the time we are given, as we dash through that life, creating good memories that must last an eternity. When we move into the "Penetration to Dimension," in the afterlife, all that we did in life is exposed, by our "DASH." That is when Heaven, for many, becomes a Hell, and you wish you had done more positive things, with your life."

SEE APPENDIX FOR ENTIRE LESSON

When First Wednesday rolled around, I was sad. I hadn't heard from Denny. I wasn't surprised to see he didn't show up at the castle for the class. Judah Anael hadn't heard from him, either. The class went well. It was about love and, even with all the love I was trying to bring around McCarthy, he couldn't feel it. I failed him, but all I could do is send him love.

The lesson held great meaning for a lot of us. We all did soul searching that night. I was also sad to see there were six other members absent. Unfortunately, I reminded the class of Angel Michael's prediction on how few would make it to the end. Everyone assured me they would never leave. I had to laugh.

The following month, an article in the Washington Post was printed and television news clips, with me in Michael's Armor receiving the Maryland Governor's Award, appeared. The charity received more and more book orders. It was hard to keep the fairytale book in stock.

The Good Knight Child Empowerment Network began to receive requests for the Blue Knight to make appearances at community events and parades in Maryland, Virginia and Washington, D.C. And Bonnie Spinner created a Certificate of Knighthood to give to each child I knighted, into the Order of Good Knights, at all the events.

On the back of the certificate was a note to parents that contained a description of the ten tricks that are used to abduct children. We asked that parents go over the *ABC's of Safety* list, with their children every two weeks, until the kids have a firm understanding of them. We also asked the new Good Knights to teach the tricks to their friends and family, so they could stay safe as well.

Chapter Sixty-four

A Fateful Dream

When the 8th of the month came, I was ready to channel the next lesson. At first, the lesson was very confusing to me.

Lesson Twenty-Eight:

Ace of Spades, received November 8, 1990
Book of Wisdom, channeled from the Hierophant:

In this lesson, I learned more about Atlantis and the Hierophant's relationship with his teacher, Master ERU. I also learned how to construct a mandala and its many uses. They are very useful tools. A Mandala represents wholeness, a cosmic circle, or diagram, reminding us of our relationship to the infinite. I found that the mandala appears to us in all aspects of life, the Earth, the Sun, the Moon. It is also the circle of life that encompasses our body, mind and spirit.

SEE APPENDIX FOR ENTIRE LESSON

After the lesson was channeled this month, the energy channel stayed open. That hadn't happened before. Usually, once the message ended, the channel closed. This time though, the hierophant continued. He spoke of missing his greatest master and teacher. He also told me one day he happened upon a young student, to whom he was teaching about reincarnation. When he had the student stare into a pool of water, he saw that the reflection, of the student's face, was that of his own many years earlier. When the Hierophant looked at his own reflection in the pool of water, he was wearing the face of his master, ERU.

After he told me that, the channel closed. I wrote it all down, as well.

I read the lesson over and over, until I fell asleep.

While sleeping, I had a dream, in which Master ERU came to me. He never said a word, but took me to a beautiful garden, and we looked into a pool of water. When I looked at my reflection, I saw my face. However, I was much older with gray hair and a mustache. I looked broken and sad. When I looked at ERU's reflection, I saw my face. I was about eight years old and very happy.

I was now even more confused.

He then took his hand and stirred the water. As the ripples started to settle, I began to see the path my life would take.

I was shown, as the years rolled on, there was great infighting among the Good Knight volunteers, and I had to send them all away. When I welcomed them back, we gathered at a medieval festival. I was wearing Michael's Blue Armor. I was on horseback, searching for someone. It was a woman. When I found her, she was dressed all in blue, wearing a crown of stars in her blond hair. She was with child, and her face glowed like that of the Constant Walker.

Many at the festival hated the Good Knights and wanted to destroy us. I placed the Blue Princess on my horse, and handed the reins to a knight dressed in yellow. I asked him to carry her to safety. Michael and I had to push back the darkness and build a great castle to secure the Princess and her child.

When I returned from building a great castle, I discovered the Yellow Knight and the princess had married. She returned a sacred ring, Archangel Michael forged from a heavenly blue star, and then she left the order. One by one all the knights married and left the order, until I was left sad and alone with no direction to turn. Michael left to return to the Father, but he never returned to me. I grew old and died of a broken heart, never finding the child with the initials M.V.

I looked up at Master ERU and asked, "What does this all mean?"

He said, "You have worked hard, but the darkness is raising up to snuff you out before you even get started. You will be given a chance to return to the life you had before Michael's Blue and Gold Armor was made. Back then, you only had to depend on your wits to survive. On this path, you will be at the mercy of the knights that gather around you. They might say they will never leave your side, but never is not forever. Will they really be there, when you need them the most? I have shown you what will become of them."

I woke up, with a feeling of doom. I tried to put the dream out of my head and just move forward.

When I presented the lesson to the class, in order to stay positive, I focused more on the making of the mandala than the Hierophant's story.

The class truly enjoyed designing their own Mandala, and it helped answer a lot of questions for them. More of the First Wednesday Club members felt drawn to become Good Knight volunteers, which pleased me. I felt that we were on our way to assembling the vessels needed to bring home the Sons of Light, but we still had a long road ahead. It certainly was nice to have some help, when I had to do school programs.

For the remainder of the month, I went about my day to day routine, but the dream still haunted me. I wondered why everything seemed to be telling me to quit? It was all I could think of, while I spent my days, adding more and more detail to the scenes at East Wing Castle. The more I added, the stronger the energy in the room became.

I couldn't wait for the next lesson. I could only hope that it would bring more promise than the last. When the lesson finally came through, everything started to shift.

Chapter Sixty-five

Connecting the Dots

Lesson Twenty-Nine:

King of Spades, received December 8, 1990
Book of Wisdom, channeled from the Hierophant:

In this lesson, I learned about Karma, which is the sum of a person's actions in this and previous states of existence--viewed as their fate in future existences. I learned the truth about what is perceived as reincarnation, karmic debt and "The Truth vs. The Lie." I was then given the Eleventh Ancient Law: (11.) "Judge no man, for you shall be judged, by your judgment."

SEE APPENDIX FOR ENTIRE LESSON

When I finished channeling this lesson, I went back and reread it. I couldn't wait to present it to the next First Wednesday Club gathering. The Hierophant explained in great detail about reincarnation and our karmic debt. Michael taught the class that night, because he wanted everyone to understand what was meant by the verse I channeled long ago in *A Good Knight Story*, "Don't let a lie become your truth." The Hierophant summed it up quite nicely, in lesson twenty-nine.

The Truth vs. The Lie

Michael began the class by asking, "Remember the riddle 'Trial of Truth': When is truth a lie? It is when enough people choose not to believe the truth, despite factual support. We accept lies as truth because we are too lazy to dig deeper for the proof, or for a greater understanding. We are told to 'Just accept it on faith." In many cases, we accept second hand truth, without any verification, because it's easier. In order to find the absolute truth, one must have all the facts... and ultimate understanding of the truth in question."

We all admitted we were guilty of being lazy, when it came to accepting others' truths. We agreed we should respect their belief--knowing that truth, like art, is in the mind of the beholder.

Michael summed it up best, by saying, "When a person ignores the obvious, for a variety of reasons, it's called Willful Blindness."

It was an awesome class, but everyone felt a heavy energy afterwards. It was a lot to process and think about, and a lot to practice.

At the charity's next board meeting that week, I learned that they needed to generate more money to pay the bills.

The next day, I sat in the Knighting Circle, holding the Sun Spear. I stared into the large crystal.

For the first time ever, I heard the faint, sweet voice of a child say, "Ada, why are you so sad?"

My heart began to race at the sound of her voice.

She said, "Tell me what you need, and I will try to connect the dots for you."

My mind was flooded with information I had learned, from the Book of Wisdom. When she said, "connect the dots," I remembered the lesson on the many dimensions that exist within the universe. I knew that dots represented time and our dash, or lifeline, from birth to death, is a series of dots. I knew she was talking to me from a timeless place, and trying to tell me something.

I said to her, "The charity really could use about $30,000."

The crystal said, "Okay Ada, but you will have to work for it."

That was the last time I heard the crystal speak. I wondered who belonged to such a sweet voice.

Michael said, "You are right. She is in a timeless place because she has yet to be born. She is also nameless, but call her M.V. And if you stay true to the course, we will meet her one day. I promise you." Michael also said that he had to return to the Father, and work on things in other dimensions, "Don't get shot while I'm gone."

I felt my brow crinkle, with that statement, and thought, "That was odd."

A week had passed when I received a call from Admiral Zumwalt. He had a wealthy client, whose Virginia mountain summer home had been burglarized. Along with other valuable items taken, were two, dueling, pistols and a collection of rare swords. The owner, Blake Logan, wanted them back and didn't have any faith in the police locating the items. He was offering a $30,000 reward for the recovery of the dueling pistols...on top of my normal investigative fee. The matching set of pistols was once owned by Alexander Hamilton and was valued at over a million dollars. Needless to say, they had tremendous "sentimental" value to the man.

I knew this was the answer to my prayers, and M.V. had found the time to connect the dots for me. I returned to the Knighting Circle, with the Sun Spear as I had done before and meditated. I thanked her for the opportunity, hoping to hear her sweet voice once again, but there was only silence. Sadness fell over me and my heart sank. I reached out to Angel Michael, but he wasn't talking either. I was truly alone.

The next day, I met with Mr. Logan at his mountain home. It was a huge 22,000 sq. ft. log, mansion on a river, in the hills of Front Royal, Virginia. The thieves really knew what they were doing. They cut the power to the phones and backup generators, before they cut the main power to the home. That knocked out the security system and video surveillance cameras. The crew ransacked the home taking antique furniture, paintings, statuary and the weapons, but didn't leave any fingerprints. They were professionals.

Mr. Logan agreed to my fee, then gave me pictures and appraisals on most of the stolen items. I called McCarthy to see if he wanted to help me with the case, but he never returned my call.

That night, I dreamed about Jesús. I think it was Angel Michael, sending me messages.

No, not the Son of God Jesus, the Jesús that came to my aid and saved Linda's life, when I couldn't get to her so many years ago. The next day, I called my old partner, Detective Sergeant Jesús Mendez. He had become the D.C. Police Department's 'go to guy' for stolen property and fencing operations. He consulted to police departments all over the country on successful strategies, to bring down fencing operations. I knew if anyone could help me recover Mr. Logan's stuff, it would be Jesús.

I told him about the case I was working on. I then asked him, if he were to fence a large antique sword and gun collection in the region, what fence would he go to that would pay top dollar? He told me since the burglary took place in Front Royal, the thieves were most likely local, and the stolen property would go to either Richmond, Charlottesville or Washington D.C., since they're dealing with high dollar collector pieces.

I had a vision of Jesús and me, setting up a sting operation that could draw Mr. Logan's stolen items to us. I proposed the idea to Detective Mendez, and he was glad to work with me again. He pitched the idea to the Burglary Division's Captain and got the go ahead.

However, the department didn't have any money to bankroll a sting. I spoke with my client, Mr. Logan. I told him that time was slipping by, and I was afraid the thieves were going to break up the collection, selling the items, piece by piece. If that happened, we had less of a chance to track the property and reclaim it. I told him about my plan to become a fence, looking to buy rare swords and pistol collections, in the hope of having the thieves bring his property to us. In order to do this, we would need financial backing.

Mr. Logan loved the idea and agreed to put up the $30,000 reward in cash as front money. I asked for the money in $20's. There was one problem however; whatever I spent would come out of the reward, so I had to spend the money wisely, or I could wind up with nothing.

We had to set up in D.C. because we didn't want to get raided by cops from another jurisdiction. Jesús had a friend, who owned an old warehouse in southeast that we could use, as our storefront and receiving dock. He also arranged for a security alarm service to install a system, with cameras and video recorders, to document all transactions. Now we needed lots of property to show, since we were in the stolen property business.

We found the owner of two high-end second-hand stores in Maryland. His partner died, so the company was filing bankruptcy proceedings. Since the case was going to be tied up in court for months, he let us borrow whatever we needed.

Once we had everything set up and looking good, we put the word out to all police informants, and the street people, that the mob from Orange County, New Jersey had opened the biggest fencing operation on the East Coast. They were told we were looking for high priced items only, antiques, paintings, jewelry, guns, swords and collector items. And we're paying top dollar for "Quality Shit."

We needed security to make sure local gangsters didn't rip us off, so Detective Mendez went to the D.C. Police Academy and selected ten of the nastiest looking rookie, cops he could find to work undercover with us. That way, we had legally-armed police to play the role of mafia, wise guys.

It was amazing to see all the stuff thieves brought in. We turned away most of the items for being beneath the quality we were looking for, but the video surveillance of the stolen property, and who brought it in, gave police a road map to the guys, doing the burglaries in the tri-state area. It was a win-win for everyone involved. If something really interesting came in, we turned it down, but radioed the tag number of the vehicle and a description of the occupant to a uniformed unit, working with us. They'd stop the vehicle to identify the suspects. Sometimes they got lucky and found probable cause to search the vehicle and make an arrest.

If Detective Mendez did buy the stolen property, his investigators would identify the sellers and get arrest warrants that would all be served at the termination of the sting operation. One thing I could say about Jesús, he was a genius when it came to a sting. It was great being "back on the street" knocking heads with the bad guys again.

On the fifth day of being open for business, I got a call from a guy, claiming he had swords and a couple of old pistols for sale. However, he said we had to come to him to view the merchandise. When I said that wasn't the way we do business, he hung up.

I thought, "Crap! I just blew the only lead to Mr. Logan's stuff."

The following afternoon, a young white guy calling himself "Booster," showed up, with one of the dueling pistols. He said that it was part of a matched set that he could get his hands on. I looked at the pistol, but acted like I wasn't interested.

Booster was obviously a junkie and very jittery when he asked, "So you guys are mafia, huh?"

I said, "No we are just professional businessmen out to make a lot of money for our good friends. Do you want to be one of our good friends?"

Then a couple of hard-looking black dudes came in, wanting to sell us a vanload of hot fur coats. They claimed they took the coats from a fur shop delivery in Baltimore that morning.

The men were really some of our undercover officers fronting items we had borrowed.

Jesús told the guys to drive around to the back, and we'd let them inside from there, so we could examine the furs. He instructed me to go negotiate with the men, while he continued to work the front counter. I told Booster he could come along, and when I was finished, I'd give him a price on the pistol.

When we got to the loading dock in the back, Booster saw three of our undercover security agents in suits, carrying shotguns and assault rifles. They were letting the white van inside the building.

When they slid the van door open, we could see a long rack of furs with the price tags still on them.

To win Booster's confidence, I asked him to read off the price tags, while I calculated the value. I turned down three of the coats and bought eight, valued at $140,000.

The driver said he wanted half the face value, $70,000. I offered him $20,000 for the coats. The driver got up in my face and stated yelling that I was trying to rip them off, by offering them so little. One of my security agents grabbed the man and knocked him to the floor, as a second agent calmly stuck his shotgun to the driver's head.

It was a move we had rehearsed many times and looked very scary.

I said, "Stand down, Max. Fellows, perhaps my price was a little low." I helped the driver up and brushed off his back. Turning to Booster, I winked, because he thought someone was about to die. I told the driver that we were all here to make money, and I was hoping to forge an ongoing relationship with him and his crew. I agreed to give $30,000, since the most I could get for the furs was $60,000.

I could see Booster was doing the math in his head. When the driver accepted the offer, one of my security agents brought me a metal box. I opened the box and counted the $30,000 reward money from Mr. Logan. Booster's eyes opened wide, and I could see he was hooked. After the driver counted the money, we put it in a brown trash bag, and they left.

I told Booster that I had been thinking about buying his pistol, but it was worthless without its counterpart. I thanked him for his time and then asked one of my agents to walk him to the door.

He said, "Can we talk somewhere private."

I said, "Sure let's go to the office."

On our way through the store, we passed Jesús. I asked him to join us for the meeting. The office was wired for video and sound recording. We sat at the conference table, and Booster told us that he was part of a crew that breaks into rich homes in the mountains of Virginia. They store the stolen property in a barn on a farm, until the heat is off. Then they sell the items for as much cash as they can get from various dealers in Virginia.

He went on to say, "I heard you guys pay top dollar and could buy everything we have."

I could tell greed had overtaken him when he continued, "If I take you to the barn how much cash will you give me for everything we have?" Stuttering he continued, "But only thing is, you and your guys have to take the stuff with you."

Jesús said, "Wait a minute. I get the impression that the rest of your crew is being cut out of the deal."

Booster started sweating, as Mendez was getting a little hostile and heavy handed.

I asked him, "Tell me, Booster, what's really going on here? Sit down, Jesús, let the man explain."

Booster confessed that, "The rest of the guys want to sit on the stuff for two more months and sell some here and there, but I need cash now."

Jesús said, "So you want us to steal the shit from your crew and pay you for the stolen shit we have to steal?"

He said, "Right. We're friends, right?"

I replied, "We don't do business that way. We don't steal, we buy. You steal and bring it to us. We look to see if it's something we can sell in other cities around the country. If so, we pay you for your trouble. It's just like you saw me do with the crew that brought in the furs. They made $30,000 for a few minutes' work this morning. In and out that's the way we like to do business." I also let him know that I didn't trust him for trying to cut his crew out of the deal.

Jesús stood up again, saying, "We should just shoot your ass here and now. How do we know you're not going to leave here and snitch to the cops about this place?"

Not giving him any time to think, I said, "Booster, what happened to honor amongst thieves?"

He was scared and shaking. Jesús gave him our business card and told him to talk it over with his entire crew because if we do business, he and his crew become like family to us.

As he turned to leave I said, "Wait. We know your guys are afraid to move the property from Front Royal to D.C., so we'll compromise. If you all want to sell to us, we'll agree to come out to the barn, view the items, select what we can use and give you a fair price. If everyone likes the offer, I will give up the cash when you all deliver the items to us here. That's the only deal I will make. Go back and talk to your people or sit on the stuff for another couple of months."

Booster agreed and, as an act of trust and good faith, he said, "You hold on to the pistol for now. I trust you guys. I hope you can trust me now."

Smiling, I pinched his cheek and said, "Kid, you are starting to grow on me."

I was so glad he left the gun. I was prepared to demand that he leave it, as part of the deal. I wanted something to show my client, so he knew we were on the right track.

Once Booster left I drove to Mr. Logan's office in Crystal City, Virginia. He asked me how things were going. I smiled and pulled the pistol from behind my back. He was overjoyed to see it, but disappointed that I didn't have the other one. I told him that it would take a little more time, and we were getting closer to recovering most, if not all, of his stuff.

Two days later Jesús got a call from Booster. He explained to his crew that he had made a deal with the New Jersey Mafia to buy some, or all, of the items they had in stock. He also told them that we were looking to create a long-term relationship, with our business associates. They agreed to meet at a truck stop in Front Royal that night to talk. If everyone agreed, then we would be taken to view the property.

Since Detective Mendez didn't have jurisdiction, he wanted to call Virginia State Police, but I had a bad feeling about that. I had spent a lot of time undercover with the fed's and other law enforcement agencies and, if they knew the stolen property was in a Virginia barn, they would want to take it down immediately. I wanted the thieves to deliver the property to us in Washington, so Jesús had them crossing state lines, with stolen property. That's a federal offense, which moved the case into U.S. District Court for better prosecution.

Detective Mendez said he had to take the matter up with his Captain. A few hours later I met with Detective Mendez for a drink. He told me that Captain Richards said, if his investigators go for the meet tonight, the Virginia authorities had to be notified. It's department policy.

I said, "Fine, then I'll make the meet alone."

Jesús said that he thought it was too dangerous. If I needed backup and he covered me, his Captain would have him pounding a beat at the Blue Plains Waste Treatment Plant in Southwest Washington.

I said with a tight lip, "I got this Jesús."

Michael hadn't returned yet. I called out to him, but he never connected. I truly was alone on this one, and I felt tonight I could definitely use my guardian angel. Now I knew why the last thing Michael said to me was, "Don't get shot."

When I arrived at the truck stop, I met the three-member crew. Booster wanted to introduce everyone, but I stopped him.

I said, "It's best that we don't know each other's real names. I am Mr. Buyer and you are Team Seller." To break the ice, I continued, "I am starved. Is the food any good here? Let me buy you guys some dinner, while we talk."

They agreed.

I then said, "If we are going to be doing business together you must take precautions. You don't know me, and we are getting ready to talk about some illegal shit. How do you know I'm not a cop, wearing a wire? You don't! I don't know for sure that you're not cops, ready to record everything I say. Let me show you how I search someone for a wire."

By showing my paranoia I was trying to make them feel more comfortable with me, plus I wanted to know, who was carrying guns.

I grabbed Booster bent him over the side of my car and started to pat him down. I started with his baseball cap and then quickly went down his body feeling for wires and a battery case. He was clean, no guns. Then I told Mr. Leader to do the same to me. When he got to the .32 cal Berretta in the middle of my back, he removed it.

I said, "You're looking for a recording device, not that gun or the 9mm, I have in my boot. He dropped to my boot and felt for the larger gun."

I took the Berretta back and holstered it. I then searched Mr. Leader and the other fellow. They were both carrying what felt like 38 caliber revolvers.

With that out of the way, we went to dinner. We asked for a table in the back where we could talk in private. The waitress seemed to know the men. The meal was great. I had chicken fried steak, my favorite! Booster enjoyed telling the story of what he saw, while visiting our warehouse operation, and how my men handled the fur traders when the driver tried going postal on me. I told Team Seller that we have some high dollar collectors that buy from us. A lot of the rich people who have summer homes in these mountains have art, gun and sword collections that we would be very interested in.

Mr. Leader said, "Oh we have swords, lots of them."

I told them about a crew of sellers that work with us in upstate New York, who break into homes and take photographs of everything of value. Then they leave with nothing disturbed. We review the photos, pick what we can sell and the crew returns to the homes later, taking only the high-priced collector items we choose.

I said, "They are so smooth and skilled. The team went from petty burglars making $40,000 a year to making over a million last year."

Oh, the greed of the mind. I could just see the wheels turning in the minds of these guys. When we finished dinner, I suggested we take a look at what they had to sell.

When we got to the cars, Mr. Leader took charge and said, "Since you appreciate us all being professionals, I'm sure that you'll understand why we must insist that you ride with us. You'll wear a blind fold and surrender your guns until we have a deal. For security, no one can know where the merchandise is stored."

I replied, "That's true, and I don't want to know. All I need is my briefcase from my car. Then just wake me when we get there."

Mr. Leader insisted on searching my briefcase. I couldn't tell if he was trying to impress me, or if he really was that paranoid. I brought large stickers in my briefcase to put on the items we were interested in buying.

I was then placed in the backseat behind the driver. No one said a word as we rode around for about forty-five minutes. There were twice as many right turns than there were lefts, so I could only assume that we were going around in circles to mislead my sense of direction.

When we got to the barn, they removed the blindfold. I was standing in the middle of the biggest hoard of stolen property I had ever seen. It was floor to ceiling stuff. I thought, "Oh my God, these boys have been busy." Most of it was junk, but still it all belonged to people. I'm sure that most of the stuff had great sentimental value to people, who were devastated that they were robbed, by these jerks. It's hard, sometimes, dealing with people who have total disregard for other people's feelings.

All of a sudden my mind wandered. I could understand the philosophy behind chopping off a thief's hand for stealing. It's a good reminder of taking things that don't belong to you. Now, we just arrest thieves, let them out on bond, so they have to steal more stuff to pay for their attorneys. If they go to jail, they just learn how to steal without getting caught.

Sorry, I digress.

Booster said, "Where do you want to start, Mr. Buyer?"

I replied, "I'll start with that table and chair." Sitting down at the table I opened my briefcase, took out the note stickers, and said, "Okay boys, let's start with paintings, statuary, guns and swords. What do you have?" I could hear cows mooing nearby, and the barn smelled like cow pies. I couldn't hear any traffic, so I knew we were a good way from any highways. I did hear a low flying plane, so I knew there was an airport nearby.

Mr. Leader sat next to me and said, "If you like a piece, make an offer. If I accept it, we will write it down and initial the sticker, before it goes on the item." I was so happy when we finally put the sticker on Mr. Logan's other dueling pistol and wooden case. We worked for over two hours studying the value of each piece. When the tally came to $100,000, I stopped.

They wanted to continue, but I said, "For our first deal a $100,000 payout is my ceiling. Once we've move all this, I will come back for more."

Booster said, "I thought you were going to take all of this."

"Well, quite frankly, I had no idea how busy you boys have been. There's a lot of stuff here." I countered.

When the rest of the guys found out they would be getting $100,000, they went ballistic, with joy.

I asked, "When can we expect delivery?"

Mr. Leader replied, "When do you want it?"

I responded, "Can you get it to us tomorrow by 11:00 a.m.? I'll have your cash waiting, in small bills. We only deal in $20's. Big bills draw too much attention. I hope that's alright."

He nodded his acceptance. Booster then put the blindfold back over my eyes. The return drive was less than twenty minutes. During the whole ride back, I was wondering how I could find out where this barn was for Jesús, because, once I had recovered Mr. Logan's property, I was done with the investigation.

The only thing I could think of was to double back, after they dropped me off at my car. I would try to follow them. I was sure that they would return to the barn and start loading the truck tonight to make my delivery time in the morning. Again, there was no talking in the car, during the trip back, so I hadn't a clue. Mr. Leader was a cool, calm and collected, emotionless thief. It was going to be a pleasure seeing him blindsided in the morning.

Once at my car, I shook everyone's hand and said I'd see them in the morning. Mr. Leader gave me back my guns, never saying a word to me. He then told his crew that he had to take a crap and would be out in a few minutes. He went into the diner. I was glad to hear that because it would give me time to be seen leaving, by the others. I could then double back to follow them to the barn. It would appear Mr. Leader was playing me. By the time I spun around, which was less than three minutes, their car was gone. He was much smarter than I gave him credit for.

I waited about fifteen minutes in the parking lot to notice anything out of the ordinary and to gather my thoughts. Then I went inside the diner to call Detective Mendez to let him know that we would be receiving the delivery in the morning. I told him that they took my guns and blindfolded me, so I didn't have any idea where the barn was, other than it was about twenty minutes from the truck stop. He was happy and said we would arrest them, once we received the stolen property. He was sure one of them would give up the location of the barn, during interrogation.

I told him I heard cows outside while I was in the barn but, like he said, most farms have a few cows around. I also said that I felt it was near an airport. He looked on a map, while I hung on, and could only locate one small airport in the area. I asked where it was. It was a long shot, but I felt if I drove around that area, I might luck out and spot the barn and the crew loading the truck.

When I finished our conversation, I sat at the counter. I ordered a slice of peach pie and a cup of coffee, before I started my canvas of the area. When the waitress brought it, she had Booster's ball cap in her hand.

She said, "Aren't you the guy that had dinner with Mr. Smoot and his boys earlier?"

I said, "Yes, I was."

She then said "One of the boys forgot his hat and when Mr. Smoot came in a little while ago, he left before I could give it to him. Will you see them again soon?"

What a stroke of luck for the good guys.

I said "Well, as fate would have it, I was driving back to the farm but got turned around on one of the back roads and lost my way. Can you help me?"

Handing me the hat she said, "That's not too hard to do in these mountains. The Smoot Dairy Farm is up on Route 55 and Longville Road."

I thanked her, ate my pie and left.

When I got to the Smoot Farm, I could see activity inside one of the barns. I opened the trunk of my car and took out the camera, with high powered zoom lens. I snapped a roll of black and white photographs of the crew, loading a white panel truck with the property I had picked out. I could only hope that the pictures would develop, since I couldn't use a flash, but there seemed to be plenty of light inside the barn.

When I left the farm, I stopped and called Jesús again. I told him that I discovered the location of the barn, and it's located on the Smoot Dairy Farm at Route 55 and Longville Road, right outside of Front Royal, Virginia. I let him know the head of the burglary ring is probably the owner, James Smoot, the name I saw on the mailbox. I also let him know that I had taken photographs of the crew, loading the truck in the barn.

Mendez said "Can you meet me at headquarters? I want to develop the photos tonight."

Several hours later, I gave Detective Mendez the camera. He developed the pictures, while I wrote a confidential report of the night's events. Thank God, every picture came out perfectly. The plan for the next day was for Jesús and I to accept the stolen property. When I paid the money for the stolen property, detectives from his office and uniform officers would raid our warehouse, arresting us all.

Jesús wanted to keep the sting operation going for as long as possible, after my case was over, so it was imperative that it look like we got nabbed, as well. Once we were all in custody, Captain Richards and the Virginia State Police would execute the search warrant on the Smoot Dairy Farm and seize the remainder of the stolen property, using my photos and information as their confidential informant. It was a great plan. I said a silent prayer that everything would go down the way we detailed.

The next morning, Detective Mendez briefed the undercover security agents on what was going to happen. He told one of the agents to give a signal to the uniform police to move in, once we had accepted the property, and I asked for the cash box. We had worked out every possible scenario. Everyone was in place and we waited.

11:00 a.m. rolled around, and no one showed up.

Noon came and went.

I was beginning to think that the crew smelled a rat, but just then, the phone rang. It was Booster. Their truck had broken down on Kenilworth Avenue, and Mr. Leader was trying to fix the engine. They were afraid that the cops were going to stop and check out their truck.

Jesús said he would send a tow truck down to pick them up. He then called Captain Richards to let him know the truck had broken down, and he was sending a tow to bring the truck to the warehouse. I asked if he could keep uniform police from interfering, with the truck on Kenilworth Avenue. Detective Mendez was told to meet the tow truck driver and give the crew a ride, just to make sure the stolen property and the suspects made it to our warehouse.

About forty-five minutes later, Jesús arrived in his black Lincoln Continental, with the crew, followed by the truck. The tow truck operator backed the truck he was towing into the warehouse and left. Mr. Leader was very impressed with our operation, as he looked at all of our merchandise.

The crew began unloading the items, as I checked everything off my list. Once Jesús was happy, with what they brought in, he said, "Fast Eddie, pay the man. I think we're going to have a long relationship with this crew."

The security agent went for my cash box and called the raiding party to move in. I didn't have $100,000 in the box to pay them. All I had was the $30,000 reward money Mr. Logan loaned me. I also didn't want to turn any of the money over to Mr. Smoot, because then it would become evidence and part of the case. If that happened the cash could be tied up, until the trial ended and all appeals were exhausted. That could take years, and the charity needed the money now.

I had to stall until the cavalry arrived. Sitting on a couch, I started counting out $20's onto the coffee table in front of me. Someone would say something and I would pretend to lose count, so I had to start the count over again.

"Where were the cops when you need them?" I thought. I looked at Jesús and he shrugged his shoulders. I motioned for him to check on their ETA. I couldn't stall much longer because Mr. Smoot was getting hinky.

Mendez started to leave the room, but when he got to the door, he put up his hands and started backing up. The room then filled with uniformed officers and detectives all waving guns and screaming, "Police! This is a raid. Everyone get face down on the floor and don't move." I grabbed the cash off the table and stuffed it back into the box. I then dove to the floor, sliding the money box under the couch. I didn't want anyone getting sticky fingers, with my money.

To maintain the cover of the sting operation, a detective read us all a phony search warrant, stating that we had purchased stolen fur coats from known shoplifters, in the presence of an undercover Baltimore police officer a few days earlier. Booster looked at me, since he knew I had purchased the furs.

I shook my head and said, "Damn, what happened to honor amongst thieves?"

We all refused to answer any questions and asked for attorneys, after our rights were read. By the time we were transported to Police Headquarters, our "Mafia lawyers" were waiting for us. It was a nice touch. They demanded to see the search warrant. Detectives wanted to know what a truckload of stolen property was doing in our warehouse. Jesús said that a tow truck operator picked it up on Kenilworth Avenue and was told to deliver it to our warehouse, but it wasn't ours.

Our lawyers told us to stop talking. Then one said to police, "How do we know that you guys didn't send that truck to my clients in an attempt to set them up?"

We were all sent to the Central Cell Block for processing and a bail hearing. I certainly didn't miss that place, and it was Mendez's first time getting arrested. Jesús told Mr. Smoot and his crew to stick to the story that we didn't know who sent the truck to the warehouse.

When I was released, the case was over for me, and I walked away from it all with the $30,000 reward and a nice bonus from Mr. Logan. He was pleased that all his property was recovered. However, it was all going to be tied up as evidence for a while. I heard that Detective Mendez continued to run the sting operation for another six weeks, until a couple of local thugs came in to rob the place at gun point. A shootout ensued and Jesús caught a bullet in the left testicle. His friends in Burglary Division nicknamed him "Half Sack" after that. Fellow officers can be so cruel!

Mr. Smoot and his crew fought the charges, but the truck was registered to the Smoot Dairy Farm. Captain Richards and Virginia State Police executed a search warrant on the Smoot Dairy Farm, where the remainder of Mr. Logan's stolen property was recovered. Property was also recovered, linking Smoot's crew to fifteen other burglaries in Virginia.

After that I took a few days off. Linda and I went to Ocean City, Maryland to relax. I really needed a break. One evening, we went to dinner at the Sheraton Hotel and ran into the ex-bouncer, from one of the clubs where I held art shows, during the IRA and gambling investigations. It was Antony McMasters, a known mob enforcer, suspected of several murders. He recognized me, immediately, as the undercover investigator from the IRA case ten years earlier.

He wanted to know what I was doing in Ocean City. I certainly wasn't going to say vacationing. There were still people thinking I had an open contract on my life, and I didn't want to catch a bullet on the humble.

I answered, "I'm working, as always. I sure am glad you didn't get busted that night. You know how the Feds are? I was after Belfast Harry. You know he planted bombs in locations that killed children? He had to go."

I could see that McMasters was nervous about something, so I continued, "I always thought you were a man of honor." He smiled and nodded. I was hoping that there really was some honor in the man, and he'd see my point. Even the mob didn't hurt children. I decided to throw him a curve to try to back him down from saying he saw me in town, so I said, "I owe you one, so if you are running something in the hotel tonight, I'd shut it down for a few days. I wish I could tell you more, but then I'd have to kill you."

I chuckled, winked and walked away. That night, Linda and I returned home.

Angel Michael still hadn't returned. I was wondering, if he was ever coming back. I had no idea what direction he wanted me to go.

A few months had passed, and I went down to Police Headquarters to check up on Detective Sergeant, Jesús "Half Sack" Mendez. He was in great spirits, even after getting shot. Captain Richards wanted to take us to lunch for all the help I had been as a confidential informant. We went to Chinatown, my old stomping grounds, for smoked hard shell, blue crabs. During lunch, he asked me if I'd be interested in coming back to the force because I was too good a detective to lose. He went on to say that he discussed it with the Chief of Police. The chief said he'd love to have me back. All I had to do is return the money I withdrew, from the department's retirement fund. I had to admit, I did miss protecting the innocent and outsmarting the bad guys. Now all I seemed to do was referee the fights between Judah, Bonnie, Dr. Peterson and the other knights. I told him I would think it over.

As I drove back to East Wing Castle, it dawned on me! Everything Master ERU showed me in that dream was unfolding. Angel Michael didn't appear to be coming back. I called out to him, but he never made contact. Mostly every one that came forward to help with the charity would leave because of the infighting between my staff. The charity was having a hard time, financially, and my best friend McCarthy was AWOL.

Here I was, being given the opportunity to pick up where my life left off, before the path with the charity. With the funds, I had received from Mr. Logan, I could easily return the money to my retirement account, plus the interest.

I thought, "Perhaps this was what Michael wanted me to do, so we could start over again."

What was I to do?

I arrived at East Wing Castle and took a chair in the Knighting Circle. I held the Sun Spear to my heart, hoping that Nameless would speak to me again.

End of Book One

APPENDIX

Book of Wisdom
Lessons 1 – 29
As channeled from the Hierophant to
Sir Edward-Michael

Remember:

All lessons were channeled. Some language or grammar may not be as we are used to reading in this age. The Hierophant's language is an ancient one. Channeling and translating varies from individual to individual and language to language as well.

Read each lesson several times. The more you do, the Greater Understanding will be made known to you, like invisible ink appearing.

All charts and figures in the lessons are taken directly from the hand typed and drawn versions in Sir Edward's diary, in order to incorporate the energy with which they were given to him.

Begin Open Channel

Lesson One:
  Ace of Hearts received August 8, 1988
  Book of Wisdom channeled from the Hierophant:

"The more you know the more "Knowing" will come to you." ERU

My Beloved Hermit and Teacher,

It is my hope that we will have a long prosperous relationship, lasting for many, many years to come. The Magi, for those who dare seek "The Knowing," designed the ancient *Book of Wisdom*. The book is not for everyone because, without a strong passion to better oneself, the lessons contained herein are wasted and could drive the weak-minded into madness. It does not matter at what "level" you think you are currently operating (novice, beginner, intermediate, advanced or master), because when labeling yourself, you are filling your glass, so that it cannot be added to.

Remember: The more you learn, the more you will realize you don't know!

Many humans have had psychic experiences, not just energy workers and clairvoyants. The *Book of Wisdom* is designed to help you make sense of the experiences you have had and hone your special gifts along the way. Not everyone has the same gifts, so some lessons can't be completed by everyone. The knowledge contained in each lesson will help the "Knowing" grow, within every seeker the *Book of Wisdom* reaches, and will form the foundation necessary to elevate from one level to the next.

The Path

Along the path, I will give you the fifteen ancient *Laws of Wisdom*. You must commit them to memory and start living your life, by these Great and Powerful Laws, if you wish to succeed on this, the "Path of the Magi."

The First Ancient Law of Wisdom is: "The more you use your ability to help another, the more your ability will grow."

These lessons are unique and build upon each other. Some lessons may seem boring or repetitious, but they are all full of important knowledge that you must absorb, in order to move on. Remember, everything is as it should be and all things happen for a reason. If you share these lessons with your students one day, or the world, as Archangel Michael intends, you must always include a guided visualization, a lesson and a practical exercise, with every class you give to the seekers.

It is best that you give your seekers one lesson per month, no more and no less. That will give the seekers time to digest and practice the knowledge gained and the ability to convert it, into the "Knowing," we intended to pass on.

Warning: If you intend to teach--There is no skipping lessons. If anyone misses a lesson, they and the lessons must stop. These lessons are only for dedicated seekers. If you don't think you can set your mind to this golden opportunity, don't start.

These lessons are only for mature human minds that have advanced past the age of thirty, although, there are some very special, younger, seekers--with adequate maturity and serious determination. They will know, if they have what it takes to persevere.

If you do succeed, my dear Hermit, and find that special child, with the initials M.V., Michael will ask you to publish these lessons, along with a history of the Divine Quest, that lead to her being. It is the Creator's gift of Michael's Victory to His Great Goddaughter on earth.

These lessons are primarily for her, so that she can achieve her "Divine Purpose" in life, as this quest was your divine purpose.

Remember, "Respect the Book of Wisdom and the Book of Wisdom will respect you."

Too many humans read a book for knowledge, and then proclaim they have the knowledge just because they read the book. If you don't turn knowledge into wisdom, what do you have? Without practice, little is gained and everything is lost. The more a seeker practices, the more understanding they will gain.

Before starting on any particular subject, there are a few things we should cover. Many of the concepts I will introduce to you are ancient in origin and not part of public knowledge. Therefore, until your consciousness has elevated, and you totally understand the connectivity of everything, I suggest you limit speaking about the subjects, let alone teaching them to other seekers.

There are those in this world, who may try to use these lessons in a dark negative manner. As their teacher, "you and they" are responsible for all positive or negative energy your students create in this world, if it comes from what you taught. So be careful who you pass this sacred information on to. You may, however, use your abilities and lessons learned to help others, without explanation of what you are doing.

Warning: If the time comes that the lessons from the *Book of Wisdom* are published for the world to read, there will be a lock tight powerful energy prayer placed upon the knowledge. The "Knowing" can only be activated for good purpose and will drain any dark practitioners of any powers or abilities they seek to gain. Neither you, nor I, will be held responsible for their fate or actions.

The Door

If you expend all your energy trying to develop a psychic ability, by concentrating intently on it; or drawing up all your force of power to try to make it happen, nine times out of ten it will not happen. That is because you are concentrating so much energy that the event is locked in place and cannot be activated. The only way to develop the ability, or cause an event to take place, is to be relaxed and receptive to that ability or event. Just relax and surrender, then go with the flow.

Think of yourself as a glass. A glass is made to hold a liquid. When you are relaxed and receptive the liquid (force) flows into you. Now, if you try hard, or have the attitude that you are going to develop that faculty, or die trying, it will not work. It's like putting a cover on the mouth of the glass so that the liquid cannot be poured into it.

You must develop a relaxed, come what may type attitude, so you may become receptive and elevate. Let us start, by learning how to relax. The exercise I have found most effective is called Progressive Relaxation.

To start, sit in a comfortable position, with feet flat on the floor. Close your eyes and try not to think of anything for a few minutes. Then say to yourself:

My toes are beginning to relax,
My toes are relaxing,
My toes are relaxed.

My feet are beginning to relax,
My feet are relaxing,
My feet are relaxed.

My calves are beginning to relax,
My calves are relaxing,
My calves are relaxed.

My thighs are beginning to relax,
My thighs are relaxing,
My thighs are relaxed.

My abdomen is beginning to relax,
My abdomen is relaxing,
My abdomen is relaxed.

My chest is beginning to relax,
My chest is relaxing,
My chest is relaxed.

My fingers are beginning to relax,
My fingers are relaxing,
My fingers are relaxed.

My hands are beginning to relax,
My hands are relaxing,
My hands are relaxed.

My forearms are beginning to relax,

My forearms are relaxing,
My forearms are relaxed.

My biceps are beginning to relax,
My biceps are relaxing,
My biceps are relaxed.

My shoulders are beginning to relax,
My shoulders are relaxing,
My shoulders are relaxed.

My neck is beginning to relax,
My neck is relaxing,
My neck is relaxed.

My chin is beginning to relax,
My chin is relaxing,
My chin is relaxed.

My mouth is beginning to relax,
My mouth is relaxing,
My mouth is relaxed.

My nose is beginning to relax,
My nose is relaxing,
My nose is relaxed.

My cheeks are beginning to relax,
My cheeks are relaxing,
My cheeks are relaxed.

My eyes are beginning to relax,
My eyes are relaxing,
My eyes are relaxed.

My whole body is beginning to relax,
My whole body is relaxing,
My whole body is relaxed.

My mind is beginning to relax,
My mind relaxing,
My mind is relaxed.

Relax your mind, relax your mind, RELAX... your mind!

You should commit this procedure to memory and practice it, not more than once a day and at least once, every third day. Set aside a period of time each week for progressive relaxation and meditation. It will help your mind grow faster and make you ready for the lessons to come.

Another ancient relaxation technique comes from the Ascended Masters of Atlantis; a form used by its priests and carried to Tibet, Chaldea and Egypt. It requires some drawing.

First, you have to draw a circle ten inches to one foot in diameter. Color it black, but leave a white dot in the center, one quarter of an inch in diameter. Then one inch out from the circle, draw a black ring one to two inches wide.

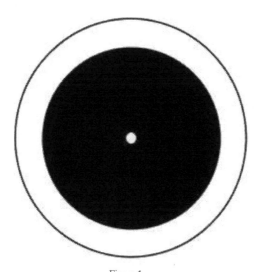

Figure 1
**Remember, the figure above is NOT to the scale as described in your lesson.
Please just use this figure as a guide to draw your own. The use of poster board is recommended.

This drawing is called a Star-Gate focal point. Place the focal point so that the dot is at the same level as the eyes. Now, gaze at the dot, but do not stare at it. You will find that this will relax you. It is also referred to as the portal into time and space. This is the one entrance into the past and the future from the present.

Remember, no matter how much you think you know, it is but a grain of sand on the beaches of forever, of what you don't know. Surrender to this one fact and you are well on your way to obtaining the "Knowing" you seek.

The Second Ancient Law of Wisdom is: "The door to the psychic world is not opened with a ram, but with the slightest caress."

Remember: "When you think you know, you don't. And when you KNOW you don't, you do! Always be humble"

In this lesson, you have learned:

1. Two Ancient Laws of Wisdom.
   a. "The more you use your ability to help another, the more your ability will grow."
   b. "The door to the psychic world is not opened with a ram, but with the slightest caress."
2. Progressive Relaxation
3. Stargate Focal Point Relaxation

End of Transmission

Begin Open Channel

Lesson Two:
King of Hearts received September 8, 1988
Book of Wisdom channeled from the Hierophant:

"The more you know the more "Knowing" will come to you." ERU

My Dearest Hermit and Teacher,

You who seek to know the mysteries of the Ancients, a knowledge that goes back to the very dawn of Man, belong to a privileged few over the ages. This ancient knowledge is the root of the psychic, philosophic and religious wisdoms. So that you may understand your beginning, it is necessary for you to be given a quick overview of the origin of Ancient Wisdom and Laws. Later on, at the appropriate time, these subjects will be covered in greater depth. The first thing I learned from my teacher, Grand Master ERU, was:

"Where there is man, there is light; and where there is light, there is shadow. And with that, we have a choice of directions."

The History of Creation

In the beginning, the Creator of all that matters throughout the infinite Universe, created man after His own intellect and placed, within his body, a living, imperishable spirit. Man became like the Creator in his intellectual ability and power to create. This is a belief reflected in Judaic-Christian teachings today. However, unlike the Creation story you are familiar with in the Holy Bible, there were seven places of creation. Hence, seven races introduced to the Earth. There is much human history lost to time. Your science barely knows the history of the last twenty thousand years. There were pockets of knowledgeable civilizations that date back millions of years. They achieved architectural feats that cannot be duplicated even today.

Atlantis was one of the sites of Creation (see Figure 2 and 3). In Atlantis, two major groups of people existed. First, there were the "Sons of Light and Truth," they who believe in the Creator and were watched over, by a positive champion you refer to as the Arch-Angel Michael. They were also known and referred to in The Dead Sea Scrolls as "The Illumine."

Figure 2

Figure 3

Fig. 2 - A symbol that represents Atlantis as one of the places of Creation.

Fig. 3 – A symbol that represents the Sacred Four, the Creator's commands that evolved law and order out of chaos in the Universe.

In the earth experiment, the Creator gave one species of life, humans, free will, emotions and reasoning. He then watched to see how his human children would develop. The Creator is the source of all love, but the emotions brought out dark traits, in some humans, that tarnished their spirits. It was found that when those negative individuals died, their souls remained trapped on the earth plane and did not returning to the Father.

As time progressed, it was noticed that these negative spirits were influencing the living, drawing them into negative behavior. There became a split between the children of God and the negative spirits, who manifested their energies into a dark spiritual entity that became known as Satan... a great "Adversary" of selfish hatred, that rebelled against God's Love.

When the dark spirited humans manifested Satan, they chose him as their god and their seven emotional weaknesses became Arch-Demons. Those demons then set out to enslave all human spirits, trapping them in a hellish, heaven on earth. The Creator found it interesting what his children choose to do with free will. With the human experiment, dividing into light and dark forces, it brought out the best and the worst in humanity.

The Creator enlightened the hearts of the Sons of Light, with insight into all things of life, and gifted their minds, with knowledge of all the spiritual forces. He gave them peace in their work and in their homes. However, since the cosmic laws of the universe require positive and negative polarity, the Sons of Light counter point had to develop to maintain balance on earth.

That other group was watched over by a negative champion, the great son of Satan, the Arch-Demon Belial, who guides humans, who choose a negative life. They became known as the Sons of Darkness, Shadows and Lies. This group personified wickedness, evil, and all that is repulsive in the eyes of the Creator.

The Sons of Darkness used their intellectual power from the Creator to gratify their lust for material power and gain. There was no thought, as to how they used or abused their power, while their lustful urges for self-aggrandizement were fulfilled. There was never any consideration for the hardships they inflicted on others. Thus, bringing servitude to many, by gratification of the material desires in the flesh-and through the misapplication of the spiritual laws for material gain. To tip the balance of power to the dark master, anyone, who didn't believe as they believed, was murdered.

To stabilize the balance on earth, the creator sent two great gifts. The Angel Michael carried the Sword of Truth and the Angel Lucifer carried the Stone of Enlightenment. Archangel Michael saw that human corruption had even corrupted Lucifer. Upon witnessing what Lucifer had allowed to happen, Michael cast the Sword and Stone into the Great Abyss. After the Sons of Darkness threw down the Sons of Light, they made plans to spread their negativity to the entire earth. Years later, The Creator intervened, and the continent of Atlantis was brought to its destruction.

The Sons of Light believed that the Creator gave the soul to man and that the power of the spirit should be used to help, rather than harm, others. They came to know that the Creator loves those, who love their brethren. The Law of Love is unchangeable, in that, as you do it to the least of your brethren, you do it to your Creator. Thus, they gradually conformed to the Universal Consciousness and their power and wisdom grew. Under the protection of Michael and direction of the ascended masters, they took time for the concentration of thought, through the use of the universal forces, so that they could help mankind.

Through the concentration of the group mind, The Sons of Light were able to enter into a state of fifth dimensional consciousness. This consciousness allowed for an absence from the physical body and a unification of the groups' consciousness, in order to further the good of mankind. This unification, which is similar to the drawing down of the White Light, became a vehicle through which it was possible for the soul to regain a comprehension of its Creator.

In using their power, ability and material possessions to help others, their knowledge, powers and wealth, began to increase. The Sons of Light came to realize that even though there may be worlds, solar systems and universes greater than our own, the soul of man, *your soul*, encompasses all in the Infinity of Space and Time.

Therefore, you must come to realize, as the Atlantians did, that you are a joint heir, with the Electro-Magnetic Universal Force, we call the Creator. You must seek to do His Will and the knowledge of the ages will belong to you. You are a very special person. You and you alone can affect the whole of the universe, a fact you should always remember. The awesome force within you can create or destroy. But, in order to create, you must be able to see. So, let us consider vision. The first step in being able to see and use that sight is to be able to perceive the Electro-Magnetic Aura around all living things.

The Aura around a person is the electro-magnetic force field or light that appears to surround the head and body. That light or radiation has been called the Od, Odyle or Odic Force, Aureole or Halo. The aureole is the light that is often depicted in religious art, around the bodies or heads of Holy Figures. The more good deeds you do in the world, the greater your electro-magnetic force field becomes. When your body dies and turns back into the stardust, from whence it came, your electro-magnetic souls returns to the Creator, with a True Life story to tell. In writing this down, you are already telling your story to those who read it.

Every living thing has an electro-magnetic force field or Aura, but only the human experiment has a soul. This is seen in an egg-shaped, orb, form and usually reminds us of an "Easter Egg" with various colors swirling around it. Many people see it as layers of light around the form of the subject. After practicing, you will be able to perceive the egg-shape, and see it as clearly as you are able to see objects using your normal vision. Just follow these steps and you will see how simple it is to develop auric sight.

Auric Sight

1. Start out by placing your subject eight or fifteen feet away from you in front of a white or light-colored background

2. Do not stare at your subject, or this will cause an after-image. An after-image is when you look or stare at an object and then look away, only to see a ghostly image of the object, which has been imprinted on the back of the eye.

3. Concentrate your gaze on the bridge of your subject's nose or middle of the subject's forehead

4. Look for a white shadow or fog to appear one or two inches out from the outline of your subject's body.

When you see the white fog, you are on your way to developing auric sight. Do not be discouraged, if the Aura does not readily come to your "sight" on the first try. As you progress, you will notice that the distance from your subject will have little or no effect on your ability.

Now that you are able to see the Aura, you will need to learn the meanings of the colors or vibrations you may see around a person.

COLOR	MEANING
Gold	Pure life, saintly, religious, in union w/God
Yellow	Intellect, good health, well-being, and wise
Purple	Seeking, healing
Blue	Spiritual, selfless, peace
Rose Red	Love, vigor, and energy
Dark Red	Force, hate, negative energy
Red Sparks	Temper, anger, impulses
Black	Illness, evil, negative thoughts
Green	Mental-Spiritual growth

As time goes by, you will notice that the width of the Aura, as well as its brightness, will differ with every person. Eventually, you will be able to detect the spiritual and mental make-up of an individual's Aura as well as diagnose his/her physical condition.

In this lesson, you learned:

1. The Third Ancient Law of Wisdom: **"The Law of Love is unchangeable, in that as you do it to the least of your brethren, you do it to your Creator."**

2. Auric Sight

End of Transmission

Begin Open Channel

Lesson Three:
Queen of Hearts received November 8, 1988
Book of Wisdom channeled from the Hierophant:

"The more you know the more "Knowing" will come to you." ERU

Beloved Hermit and Teacher,

In this lesson, we will speak of **Magic**. Do you know the original meaning of the word? Or, are you only familiar with the word, as it is commonly viewed in modern times? To understand the original use of the word, let us break it down into its parts.

Magi: A sect of priestly scholars from Atlantis, who held that at the base of all thought and action are two principles; one, the cause of good, and two, the cause of evil. These wise men could also affect non-living and living beings, by the power of their wills. The top nine of these wise men went on in spirit to become the Ascended Masters, who govern the solar system, which earth is part of. They each possessed a powerful iron and copper brazed rod. Each rod contained the universal symbols of one of the nine planets at its pinnacle.

IC or ICUS: Used at the end of a word to signify "Dealing with" or "Connected to."

So, **MAGIC** correctly written is "**MAGICUS.**" In English, your language, it is written MAGIC-US, for Us = We who have the MAGIC; thus, the definition.

Magic: Having the ability, by force of will, to effect for the purpose of good or evil, using no artificial contrivances.

If you say that you have never seen magic, I say that you are surrounded by it. The movement of the planets around the sun, the oceans and mountain valleys, new life... all of these are filled with magic.

Every breath you take, every sentence you articulate, and your every movement is magic. And, if you can do all the physical movements, without taking a second thought, just imagine what you are capable of, if you are able to direct your Willpower properly.

What is Willpower?

Willpower is the ability to set aside your fears and resist short-term temptations, in order to meet long-term goals.

There are three necessary components for achieving objectives:

1. First, you need to establish the motivation for change and set a clear goal of what it is you want. You must really want the objective, and be ready to make sacrifices to acquire it.

2. Second, you need to monitor your behavior toward that goal. When you find yourself slipping, regain control of your behavior. Don't just throw your hands up and quit.

3. The third component is willpower itself. It's that inner strength that says, "I'm going to do this thing come Heck or High Water!" Whether your goal is to

lose weight, kick a habit or addiction, save more money, or practice these lessons, willpower is a critical step to achieving that outcome.

The Will

Control, deliberately exerted to do something, or to restrain one's own impulses. The faculty of conscious, purpose or determination, with deliberate action and intent.

Directing the Will

How do you direct the Will in order to use Magic?

First, you must understand that Magic only becomes effective when it is stimulated through human emotion, as a direct result of the focus of one's willpower. You must will something to happen.

For example, you are walking down the street with your child. A strong wind suddenly whips up and a large tree blows over, covering your child. You know that you are not strong enough to pick the tree up and off of your child but, out of love, you suddenly have the strength of ten men. After you find out the child is not hurt, you realize that you are experiencing a sensation of warmth and a tired feeling throughout your body.

Through the use of emotion, the Will activates the hormone, adrenaline, and you were able to overcome a logical obstacle that might have restricted you from picking up the tree. Through emotional stress and the conscious use of the Will, you were able to accomplish a definite goal that might have otherwise been impossible.

To develop the powers of Magic, you must learn to concentrate the power of the Will, until it resembles a finely-honed sword blade. The Star-Gate focal point in Lesson One is taught with this in mind. You must forget the self and all other superfluous concerns, in order that you may develop Willpower.

In Atlantis, the Masters carried rods or staffs as a symbol of their state. But, the staff was not just a symbol; it also served as a conductor through which they might direct their "Willpower." Take the example of Aaron in the Old Testament. When Moses bade him to cast down his staff before Pharaoh, it turned into a serpent. You too can direct your Will in this same way. My teacher can lay down a large stick in the presence of many, and it will truly appear to turn into a green snake.

Remember that the word "appear" is critical to understanding the manifestation of the snake. If you truly believe that you are able to bring forth a snake from a tree branch, and you are also able to convince those around you of your ability, then it will become a snake.

You shall come to realize that the words Faith and Will are interchangeable. It is written that Jesus once said, "If you have as much faith as this mustard seed, you can move yonder mountain. All I have done you can do as well, and even more if you have faith."

Will you ever realize the total power you possess? As your mind must be tuned to a fine point, so too, must it be stretched and exercised. In the development of the mind, you must be cautious of ingesting any substance, liquid, solid, or of a drug-related nature, that might be negative, for your development will be slowed down.

The Mind

The human mind is the intelligent power that conceives, wills, reasons, judges, creates, imagines, remembers, and performs any intellectual operation. The mind is the focal point of a person that enables them to be aware of the world and their experiences, to think and to feel the faculty of consciousness and thought.

The mind is basically a communication and control system between the spiritual being, that is the person, and the environment. It is composed of mental pictures that are recordings of past and, sometime future experiences and emotions. A person uses his or her mind to pose and solve problems related to survival and to direct their efforts, according to these solutions.

The mind has two parts, the analytical mind and the reactive mind. The analytical mind is the rational, conscious, aware mind that thinks, observes, gathers data, remembers it and solves problems. The reactive mind is the portion of an individual's mind that works on a totally stimulus-driven response basis, like that knee-jerk reaction that gets us in trouble. It is not under volitional control, and exerts force and the power of command over awareness, purpose, thoughts, body and actions.

> My student, Pythagoras once wrote, "By the assistance and cooperation of spiritual powers and the capacities inherent in man, as a result of his Divine origin, he may become capable of a higher sphere of activity, within as well as without himself, which will give him dominion over his own and over surrounding nature..."

The capabilities inherent in man are limitless, but humans require stimulation. The mind must become sensitive and learn to leave the body. The body is merely a tool, which teaches us the fundamentals, by which we shall learn the extent of the human mind.

You can almost imagine, as you hold things, what is really going on inside the object or living thing. Can you imagine the green of a leaf and the water running through the leaf's veins? Have you ever tasted steel or smelled it? Have you ever wondered what it would feel like to be a leaf? Before you can direct your Will, you must expand beyond your body, to a point where you not only know what an object is composed of, but become one with that object.

There is no limit to the mind's learning capability. Just as you had to learn the alphabet before you could construct words and then sentences, you must learn the simplest forms of existence, before you can understand the more complex; and the forces, by which they were brought into play.

I say to you, open your eyes! You may be missing out on a beautiful world. Observe all that you may, for there are secrets to behold, and you must know that the Universe is truly at your feet. How many people do you see every day, who are focused on the material world and what they can squeeze out of it? You can only open your mind when you open your heart to all possibilities.

What is the Mind?

Some people think that the mind is the brain or some other part or function of the body, but that is incorrect. The brain is a physical object that can be seen with the eyes and that can be photographed, weighed and operated on, during surgery.

The mind, on the other hand, is not a physical object. It cannot be seen with the eyes; nor can it be photographed, weighed or repaired by surgery. The brain, therefore, is not the mind, but simply part of the body where the mind dwells.

It's like when you drive your automobiles. Are you the car? No, but it can't move without you. The same holds true with your body. Your mind is just as separate from your body as you are from your automobile.

There is nothing within the body that can be identified as being your mind, because your body and mind are two different entities. For example, sometimes when your body is relaxed and immobile, your mind can be very busy, darting from one thought to another. This indicates that our body and mind are not the same entity. Just like if I tell you to clear your mind of all thought. You can't do it. The mind is going to do what it wants to do.

Your body is also likened to a guesthouse and your mind to a guest dwelling within it. When you die, your mind leaves your body and goes to the next existence, or afterlife, where it carries its recorded life story and understanding into the next dimension. It is just like a guest leaving a guesthouse and going somewhere else to visit.

If the mind is not the brain, nor any other part of the body, what is it?

It is a formless continuum that functions to perceive and understand all that's given to the body in life. Since the mind is formless, physical objects do not obstruct it. The mind is an electro-magnetic recording force of awareness, in nature, and is the raw essence of our Creator.

Your mind is a spark of thought--sent out to record and return, with recorded events and emotions. In a way, the individual mind/soul is a Book of Life that becomes part of the collected Universal Consciousness, "God's Library." It is like the many libraries on earth that are full of books, some good, some not, but all are full of interesting stories and emotions. Some call God's Library the Akashic Hall of Records.

Akashic Hall of Records

The Ancient Masters of Wisdom, and open-minded thinkers of today, have maintained that there exists a connected cosmic field that is at the base of all reality, and it conveys and conserves all the knowledge of the universe. This field is known as the Universal Hall of Records.

In the nineteenth century, it became known as the Akashic Records. Recent discoveries in the new field of Vacuum Physics and Quantum Mechanics now show that this Akashic field is real and has its equivalent in the zero-point field that underlies time and space itself.

This field consists of an ocean of fluctuating energies, from which all things are born: atoms and galaxies, stars and planets, living beings and even consciousness. This zero-point Akashic field, or "A-field," is not only the original source of all things that arise in time and space; it is also the constant and enduring memory of the universe. It holds the records of all that ever happened in life, on Earth and in the cosmos. And relates it to all that is yet to occur in the future.

Everything in the Universe has an electro-magnetic record. The record of your Electro-Magnetic Mind-Soul is transmitted, via your human DNA, full name, and date of birth and death of your life vessel. Your soul's journey, through that life in self-awareness, is undertaken through a cause and effect process.

Humans are constantly presented with opportunities to better themselves and to apply positive or negative principles in the physical world. This is where free will comes in.

Which principles will you choose? Humans are presented, again and again, with lessons and situations throughout their lives, in an effort to understand why they make the choices they make. Or, stated another way, to see if they can learn from their mistakes. Have you learned from your mistakes? We all make them. That's part of the experiment.

Mentally Disturbed Brain vs. Mind

In order for the spiritual mind-soul to experience physical life, it must have a physical body. Liken it to you being the captain of the mind that needs to sail across a great ocean of experiences. You need a proper vessel to safely endure and document the journey. If your biological vessel, your body, is flawed and not compatible for the journey, it will be a more disturbing and less understood ride, than if you had a grand ship--with a fully-computerized bridge: the brain that operates the body.

Within your biological body, your vessel, you have a physical brain where the spiritual mind rests and records your life's human emotions and intent for actions. If that brain is damaged or flawed and cannot comprehend or understand the journey, it will be a whole different experience, than if it was in the normal range. Yet, it will still have a life experience, with some level of understanding nonetheless. Everything is taken into account in the Hall of Records. All human brains can be rewired, if the individual has the desire and willpower to make it so. That is what psychiatrists and shamanic healers attempt to do, using neuro-linguistic programing on their client's minds. A greater understanding of a problem can lead to that rewiring. If everyone in the world used Neuro-linguistic reasoning, life on earth would be a lot more peaceful.

Normal Brain Choices

It is very important to be able to distinguish between normal brains, with negative thoughts and cravings that create disturbed states of mind, from peaceful states. States of mind in the normal brain that disturb our inner peace, such as anger, lust, sloth, vanity, envy, gluttony and greed are called "human delusions," more commonly known in your day, as the deadly sins or vices.

These delusions are the principal causes of most of humanity's suffering. They are deadly to the soul. If you are a slave to the seven, deadly delusions, you will find no peace in this life, or in the next dimension of existence. If you cannot shed these delusions in your earthly realm, that mind set will become the "Hell Realm" that you have created for yourself to dwell in forever, since you can perceive nothing better for yourself, once you leave the earth body.

We may think that other people cause our suffering, by poor material conditions but, in reality, it all comes from our own, deluded state of mind. The constant battle, between the Sons of Light and Sons of Darkness, rages inside each one of us as a microcosm; a universe unto our self. Which side have you chosen? The light or dark?

The essence of spiritual practice of these lessons is to reduce and, eventually, eradicate altogether our delusions, and to replace them with permanent inner peace. This is the real meaning of our human life and the "Path of the Magi" you have chosen.

The essential point of understanding the mind is that liberation, from suffering, cannot be found outside the mind. Permanent liberation can be found only, by purifying the mind. Therefore, if we want to become free from problems and attain lasting peace and happiness, we need to increase our knowledge and understanding of our mind. The human ability to record and imprint on its surroundings, such as objects and places, through electro-magnetic fields, can be seen in Psychometry.

Psychometry

Psychometry is a psychic ability, in which a person can sense or "read" the history of an object, by touching it. Such a person can receive impressions from an object, by holding it in his/her hands or, perhaps, touching it to the forehead. These impressions can be perceived as images, sounds, smells, tastes and even emotions, by connecting with the person's electro-magnetic imprint.

It is the ability to see or know of events directly connected to a material object, by touching it. The object that is touched is called the conductor.

Psychometry is a form of scrying - a psychic way of "seeing" something that is not ordinarily seeable. Some people can scry, using a crystal ball, black glass or even the surface of water. With psychometry, this extraordinary vision is available through touch.

For example, a person who has psychometric abilities - a psychometrist - can hold an antique glove and be able to tell something about the history of that glove, about the person who owned it, and/or about the experiences that person had, while in possession of that glove.

The psychometrist may be able to sense what the person was like, what they did and even how they died. Perhaps most importantly, the psychometrist can sense how the person felt, or the emotions of the person, at a particular time. Emotions, especially it seems, are most strongly "recorded" in the object or places. It is believed that this is because of a strong residue of the electro-magnetic imprint from the person's aura, mind and soul.

The Experiment

To develop, using Psychometry, take a small object such as a ring, key, playing card or coin. Place it within your reach. Now sit and relax. Use your progressive relaxation technique to become calm and relaxed. Study the object casually. If it's a ring, is it rough or smooth? What color is it? Is it hot or cold, and do you feel any emotion coming from the ring? Think of the ring as trying to tell you something. Write down all the impressions that come to you, while you are holding the ring. The impressions may seem silly, odd or unrelated to the ring, but believe in what you are receiving and make a note of it. Don't discount your first impressions or words that come to mind. Your mind is translating the imprint left behind, by the mind of another.

The impressions may come to you in the form of a picture, a color, a smell, a feeling, a word, a sound or a sensation. You will find that, in a manner, it is as though someone gave you some information, and you are just now recalling it. Or you may feel like you have always known about this ring. You may get the feeling of cold. The word cold comes to you, but it isn't exactly the right feeling you are receiving. When you ponder a little longer, the word Arctic comes through, and as odd as it seems, you write that word down, instead of cold.

Later, you find out that the owner of the ring was, at one time, on an expedition to the Arctic or worked in a freezer! Often you will feel like you are trying to retrieve a forgotten word, when you reach out for an impression. Just learn to relax and this new power will grow stronger within you, but you must practice this gift, if you wish to grow.

Just imagine placing your hand in the fossilized footprint of a dinosaur and actually seeing and feeling the creature? What if you were to touch a stone at the base of the Sphinx? Would you be able to see how it was built and the mysteries hidden deep inside its unexplored regions? You are being given the tools, with which to develop your Will and your Mind. Develop your powers through knowledge and practice, but most of all, learn from the lessons that unfold all around you!

End of Transmission

Begin Open Channel

Lesson Four:
    Jack of Hearts received December 8, 1988
    Book of Wisdom channeled from the Hierophant:

"The more you know the more "Knowing" will come to you." ERU

Dear Hermit and Teacher,

Let us speak of the symbols of our Academy of Wisdom and of our forefathers of Atlantis. The most powerful symbol in the Universe is the Ankh (Figure 4). It originally represented "Eternal life through the Divine Creator," and was called the "Gate-way of the Soul."

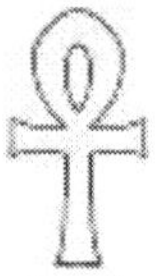

Figure 4 – The Ankh

Let it be known that all the current Religions of Man in your modern world have borrowed from the spiritual beliefs of the ancient past. Many of the stories found in the Old Testament can also be found in ancient texts, dating many thousand years earlier, from other cultures.

Since the beginning of time, the guardian of humanity has been one great energy force that most humans call Archangel Michael. If he could say one thing to humanity, what would it be?

Channel Broke Here

The Hierophant stopped communicating, until I called upon Michael for the answer to the question.

Michael clearly responded, "Stop all your religious disputes. They are just different views of the Great Unknown. Stop acting like you know "IT," when you don't. You are all correct in your limited beliefs, but know this; the Creator of all things has no religion, only of creation itself and the children that are meant to enjoy it. Serve his children, and you serve the All."

Channel Re-Opened - The Hierophant continued:

There is power and energy in everything humans believe--past and present. Even if it is a lie. If man believes it...it's the truth until man doesn't believe it anymore. That is the power of the Will and Mind of man. Don't discount anything. Ponder all beliefs, and find your own truth. Truth is as different as the human fingerprint, and no two humans have the same fingerprints or absolute truth. If you want to come closer to the truth, study all the religions of man. Your heart will tell you what's "Righteous" and what is "Not."

Most of what humans believe has been made up, by man, to help those who know little have a better understanding and know more. But how much did past humans really know? Humans, in power long ago, painted the picture in the minds of man that God was a white-bearded, old man, who sat in the clouds and watched over all of his creations. Is that true? Yes! That is to those, who choose to believe it. Just like Santa Claus, the Easter Bunny and the Tooth Fairy is real to children.

However, I ask you, who really are the Easter Bunny, Santa Claus and the Tooth Fairy? You are when you bring them alive, through your good actions, to help children. The same is true about God. When you do good things for humanity, you are living in the true image of our Creator. When you do evil things, you are living in the sum of human negativity, most commonly referred to as Satan and the Sons of Darkness. God created Love and Goodness. Using free will, humans have created the energy forces of hate and evil.

Jesus went about doing good things and in the end, he proclaimed, "I and the Father are one." Jesus was using his Will Power to show all humankind how to be one, with the Creator. But the wise and powerful men of the time wanted to keep God and humans apart, instead of being together. They made it so you had to go through them... to be one with God. What Jesus was really saying was, "I am one, with the Knowledge and Wisdom of the Creator."

It was a divine truth, understood by King Solomon, as he recorded in the prayer in the Old Testament, Book of Wisdom: "God of our ancestors...Now with you is wisdom, who knows your will, and was there when you made the world, who understands what is pleasing in your eyes, what is conformable with your commands... send her forth from your Holy Heavens. From your glorious throne, dispatch her that she may be with us, and work with us, that we may grasp what is pleasing to you. For she knows and understands all things, and will guide us prudently in our affairs and safeguard us, by her glory."

The Creator or Godhead is made up of Father/Knowledge and Mother/Wisdom. However, the dominant male hierarchy of the past removed any female energy from the divine equation. The new truth or Divine Equation became, "The Father, the Son and the Holy Spirit."

Remember: When you think you know, you don't, when you know you don't know, you do! Please, always stay humble.

In Egypt, it was a sandal strap or tie that became the great symbol of "Life," although life was written in symbols. The Ankh was usually pictured in the hands of the gods or goddesses. Then in the period 1375–1350 B.C., it was used in Egypt as a sign for the God Aton. This was the first introduction of monotheism, the belief in one God, in Egypt. The total graphic symbol of this one God was the Sun, on whose lower edge supported a small vase and whose rays terminated in the hands of children.

The children were holding the Ankh, which represented everlasting life. The Sun disc represents Re or Ra, the Father of the Gods, and the "Creator of All Living Things." The vase represents the Heart, which is synonymous with the Soul or Spirit. For it was a Heart that was weighed in the final judgment, against the feather of truth, on the scale of balance.

The "Tau," a T-shaped cross, is the Ankh without the loop or Eye of God. It is also the 19th letter of the Greek alphabet and the last letter of the Hebrew alphabet. Therefore, it represents the end of all things, or the end of the world. It is also believed that it is this seal, with which the Order of Righteousness will be spared, during the "Great Judgment on the End of Days."

Among some Christians, it is believed to be the symbol of The Christ. Although, frequently disguised, it is found in the paintings, monograms and stained glass windows of many churches throughout the Christian world.

Let us go on to the symbol that is referred to as the "Anchor of Hope" (see Figure 5). If you were to ask a minister or priest what the symbol means, they will say that it is a symbol of their hope and faith in Jesus Christ. It is actually made up of two glyphs or symbols. The upper part of the symbol is the Ankh. In this instance, the Ankh represents the Christ. The spars at the bottom represent the virgin birth. The miracle of the birth of the Christ, and his virgin birth, represent faith and hope to millions of the faithful, thus the significance of the symbol.

Figure 5 – Anchor of Hope

In astrology, we have Love for the sign, representing Venus (see Figure 6), which, besides being the second planet, also means "Love of life." In alchemy, it stands for the element, Copper. For many thousands of years, the symbol has come to have many meanings. You shall come to realize, as we continue, that the symbol has great power.

Figure 6 – Symbol for the planet Venus; for element of copper

Now, let us study the symbol of the Ankh. In the crown or loop is the "TETRAGRAMMATON."

This is a word you may have come across in your readings, but may have never known the definition. Let us start with the different parts of the word:

TETRA	=	Four
GRAM	=	to signify that which is written
MATON	=	the first hour
TETRAGEAM	=	A word of four letters

TETREGRAMMATON - A phrase of four words, written at the first hour

Among several ancient nations, it is the name of the Mystic Number Four, which was the symbol to represent the Deity. His name expresses, and is expressed by, four letters. These letters are:

YOD, HAV (pronounced hay), **VAH** and **HAV**

The translation is

(YOD=I), (HAV=AM), (VA=THAT), (HAV=AM)

"I AM THAT AM"
Transliterated as the name of God

YAHWEH or JEHOVA.

Now sit back and relax. For a few moments, seek out the deeper meaning of the words **"I AM THAT AM."** Say the phrase in your mind, over and over until you begin to feel the power behind the letters. Examine each word for the fullness behind them. Repeat it out loud and experience its Electro-Magnetic Energy Force, building within your heart and mind.

Do you feel that energy, manifesting itself within your body, pulsating like a lightning bolt through your veins?

Once you feel the surge of energy, relax and know that the energy level can be sustained for longer periods of time, but only as you grow, with your understanding of the power and depth of the phrase.

In Atlantis, the ancient teachings were kept in the Holy of Holies or Star-Gate; a building whose tunnel-like corridors took on the form of an equilateral cross. The equilateral cross represents that from which all things were created; fire, gas, liquid and solid... more commonly referred to as fire, air, water and earth. It is taught that through a metamorphosis of these basic elements: **"All that is, came to be."**

Today, we have come to realize, in the laboratories of the scientific world, that by changing the ratio of one, to another of these elements, man has created millions of new products. How very appropriate that the ancient teachings should be found in a building whose shape represented the foundation of the creation of all things.

In the center of the Star-Gate, there was a circle that connected the four creative forces. The circle was known as **ABBA**, the Father/Mother and the **Creator** from whom all things came.

At the entrance to the building were two pillars. The one on the left-hand side was cubistic in shape and, on its top, was inscribed **JACHIM**... meaning **strength** or **power**. The pillar on the right-hand side was cylindrical in shape, and its inscription was **BOAZ**, meaning **Established in Wisdom**.

Even the entrance to the Star-Gate, Holy of Holies had meaning. In the Bible III Kings, Chapter 7, Verse 21, a reference to the pillars is cited:

"And he set up two pillars in the porch of the temple: and when he had set up the pillar on the right-hand he called the name JACHIM; in like manner, he set up the second pillar and called the name thereof BOAZ."

Special note to Hermit: The time will come in the distant future that you will be called upon, by Grand Master ERU, to build the aforementioned structure, as a Holy of Holies, with the hope that humanity will survive the End of Days.

Rebuild a Star-Gate Portal on a vortex of land, using the above premise, and other revelations will be shown to you, as you journey on your Divine Quest for understanding. The Star-Gate device, with the right human elements in place, will activate the Great Atlantian Power Grid, hidden above the clouds.

In years to come, you might be called upon to find nine archetypes, Angel-Knight commanders, and the Daughters of the Four Directions. That is the minimum crew needed to activate the Star-Gate and channel the pure energy from the 144,000 pure "Light Bearers of Legend," who are scattered around the earth. They will make up the Divine Prophecy of the coming Sons of Light in the Order of Righteousness. With their combined efforts, the human experiment could be extended indefinitely. Until next month's lesson, I leave you with deep peace and love.

End of Transmission

Begin Open Channel

Lesson Five:
Two Jokers received December 25, 1988
Book of Wisdom channeled from the Hierophant:

"The more you know the more "Knowing" will come to you." Eru.

My Brother Hermit and Teacher,

We will reflect on peace with this lesson. Peace, as you remember, is the feeling when you were a child that does not seem to linger as often with us when we become adults. When do you last remember the feeling of peace within yourself? The greater peace comes about through the extension of compassion and understanding toward your fellow man. I felt peace tonight, standing with you at water's edge, feeling the warmth of your Christmas fire beacon. As the smoke from your beacon drifted skyward, the Creator also found peace. That's why He decided to send me to you.

The White Light

The "White Light" is a highly concentrated form of Electro-Magnetism, within the universe, where positive energies are stored. The "White Light" can be called upon by anyone, with a strong will and understanding of its use and Divine nature. It should not be confused with the light you are drawn to when you die. If you, as the dearly departed see a white light, look to the right of it, and you will see the "Golden Light of Oneness." That is the path you want.

The "White Light" is used for healing and protection from negative energies or death. White Light cannot be used to harm, nor can it be harmed in any way. For this reason, negative or dirty energies can be sent to the "White Light" for purification and transformation.

The "White Light" can only be brought down and placed in a person once in their lifetime to help that person, but it can be brought down and placed in quartz crystals, which can be used by a person many times.

The symbol, from ancient times, that best represents the "White Light" is a long crystal (see Figure 7). Are you surprised that the symbol would be a crystal or that America's Washington Monument embodies the power of the "White Light"?

Figure 7 – "White Light"

Its ornamental channel, called a compound Glyph, is topped by a triangle that is representative of the Creator. The interlaced triangle means, "As in Heaven, so on Earth." The vertical lines, extending earthward, are the "shafts of the extended

311

forces from the Trinity," or "White Light," descending to mankind, who is symbolized by the square at the bottom of the glyph. The "White Light" sends all of "Its" healing powers to mankind and is diffused throughout the earth to benefit all matter.

Because of its total healing influence upon humanity, the "White Light" is referred to as one of the greatest forces throughout the universe.

Understand that when we forget to worry about ourselves and generate our energies outward toward others, we are manifesting a goodness that will return to us a double dividend. There are truly times when a kind word, a few dollars or a small can of food will make the difference between tragedy and security in someone's life. When we are able to operate, consciously, in a selfless manner most of our waking hours, then we will be able to truly comprehend the power of the "White Light" and spend more time with the feeling of peace and serenity that we started this lesson, speaking about.

Manifesting "The White Light" to heal another will greatly enhance your own spiritual abilities. It is not necessary for you to tell the person in need of what you have done, since it is the power of the Creator and all of his "Love" that may help, in healing the person.

Calling Down White Light

If you decide to help heal a person, who is extremely sick or dying, go into a deep meditation, using lesson one. Then ask inside, "Can this person be brought back to good health? Is this a kind person? Will extending this person's life be for the greater good of the people this person will come in contact with? Does this person want to continue in life or is he/she ready to pass on into the next stage of existence?"

If you receive the answer that this person is not to continue their physical journey, pray for the Angel of Death to take the person and ease their pain and suffering, so they might continue their spiritual journey.

If you receive the answer that this person would benefit humanity, if they continue in life, follow these steps.

1. Summon the Angels of the Four Directions, asking them to stand, forming four corners around the person to be healed.

2. The angels will naturally join hands, creating a square with you and the person being healed in the center.

3. Light a candle at the head and foot of the person being healed, while saying, "I ask that the Creator guide my hands in the restoration of life for, *say the name of the person here."*

4. Take a clear glass bowl, half full of pure water. Place your hands in the water, then sprinkle the water over the person's body, asking, "Let these waters turn the tide of (*persons name*) and return good health now, as they wish to help others, if they are allowed to remain on earth."

5. Close your eyes and cross your open palms over the center of your chest, even with your heart, and say, "I give of my life force to (*persons name*), so that life can be restored in good quality."

6. Rub your hands together as fast as you can and create heat between your palms, while saying, "I call down the Great 'White Light of the Creator' into my hands."

7. Visualize a ball of brilliant "White Light," descending from the ceiling, slowly into your warm hands. Sometimes you will see the light, sometimes you will not. Just know that it is there, if everything is right and this person is to be healed.

8. Quickly place your hands on the heart/chest of the person being healed and say, "I pass this 'White Light of the Creator' on to (*person name*), with the hope that the Will of the Creator will be served."

9. End the healing White Light Ceremony, by blowing out the candle at the foot and a kiss on the person's feet. You may be "told" to shake or tickle their feet as well. You may also be given something to say at this point, or not. Move to the top candle and blow it out, kissing the person on the third eye, or middle of the forehead, and say, "We love you. Now go out and show everyone you meet that you are Love." Then leave the person to rest.

You can also do this healing ceremony from a distance, using a photograph of the person to be healed, but you must use pillows, bound with a blanket, to simulate the body of the person.

Remember: "Dying is part of living and living is part of dying. We all come into this world with a death sentence. However, our spirits live on forever!"

A person never really dies, since energy cannot be destroyed, it just reconfigures. People leave the physical existence of individual oneness for the Electro-Magnetic Oneness of total peace, with the Creator. The only down-side is when a person moves out of physical life, there is no way to change. There is no longer room for selfishness, denial and self-deception in the next dimension of the Hall of Records. Only the truth of your being is revealed.

With that new reality in mind, the person's spirit normally wants to return to life to help the living--to not make the same mistake(s) they made. In some cases, their request is granted, and they are sent back to help the angels guide the living through life. Most everyone living has at least two, former human spirit-guides assigned to him/her, along with a host of angels.

Until we speak of the "White Light" again, remember:

The Forth Ancient Law of Wisdom: **"The White Light can only be used once to heal any one person."**

End of Transmission

Begin Open Channel

Lesson Six:
Ten of Hearts received January 8, 1989
Book of Wisdom channeled from the Hierophant:

"The more you know the more "Knowing" will come to you." ERU

Dearest Hermit and Teacher,

Let us speak about some of the symbols that have come down to us from antiquity. Let's begin with the symbol for "Fire," as it comes to us from my home, Atlantis. It was the Great Fire of the Inner Earth that brought Atlantis up from below the ocean, and it was Fire, again, that removed the Atlantian culture.

Fire

The Atlantians used the symbol of the equilateral triangle to represent Fire, as did other ancient civilizations (see Figure 8). The equilateral triangle not only represents Fire, but also the Creator, the Holy Trinity and perfection. The two lower points of the symbol represent the dual forces of the Universe, while the highest point represents the perfect coming together of the two forces of Light and Darkness.

Figure 8 – Fire

The Pyramid is also a symbol for Fire. When the word, pyramid, is broken down into its components, we find "pyr67," the Greek word for Fire, and "amid," meaning "in the middle of." Is it not unusual that the energy concentrated, within a pyramid, became associated with Fire or Energy of Life?

Fire can be described by many adjectives. Fire can be hot or dry, golden like, a white flame, a purifier, as in the case of disease. It can be compared to sunlight, lightening... and even the Creator has been fire-like, in His assuming the shape of the burning bush.

As one of the elements required for Creation, Fire has also been called the "Spark of Life." The Spark was in the divine forces of Vesta in Rome, the perpetual Fires of Kildare in Ireland. And it can be seen today in the Sacristy Light, which is kept burning at all times to represent the Eternal Light of the Creator.

The spark of Fire that came from the Creator, and is embodied in all of Life, is that part of our being, which is the "fire," our Light. We measure temperature as the heat of the body, or we refer to "in the heat of the moment," when we lose our temper or balance. And then there is the heat of sexuality. There would be no existence for mankind, without "Fire." There are energy sites, which store the "Fire," called Chakra centers, in our bodies.

In Moses' second book, Exodus Ch. 13 V. 21, it states, "the Lord preceded then, in the daytime, by means of a column of cloud to show them the way, and at night by means of a column of fire to give them light." Thus, fire was associated with the power of the Creator and used to drive off wild animals and evil spirits.

It became essential for magicians to produce fire, spontaneously, quench it by magic or walk upon it. This was to show that they had divine power or controlled the forces of nature and/or the Universe.

It is believed that a spark of the divine descended from the heavens to be embodied in all matter, especially men, so that part of our being is the Divine fire. We can see it from the fever of copulation, through the temperature of one's body to sustain life, to the heat of decay, as we rot in our tomb. Man cannot exist without fire. It is the seed of all existing things to which they must, in time, again return.

Throughout history, there have been deviations and opinions as to where the seat of man's fire is located. Some believe it to be in the spinal column or Kundalini... or the abdominal area or Solar plexus, the brain or the Third Eye, the heart, etc.

So, I ask you, where is your fire located? Where is your fear, and are they both housed in the same location?

Air

Another symbol, as important to life as that of Fire, is the symbol for Air. The symbol for Air is similar to the triangle for fire, but it has a horizontal line drawn through it, about one-third of the way down, from the top (see Figure 9). Air is described as active, positive, creative and flexible in movement. From the Greek word for Air, "pneuma," we symbolize Air as the vital spirit, breath of Life, the animator of the body, and the idea of Life. Pneuma is, actually, derived from a Sanskrit word, Prana, which means "Life-giving vital force."

Figure 9 – Air

An example given to us in the Bible, representing the "Life Giving Force," being sent to mankind, is the account of The Virgin Mary, receiving "the breath and the Word was made flesh." A dove, a creature of the Air, is the bearer of the Word and, like the wafer used in The Holy Communion, has come to symbolize "The breath of Life" on Earth. And it is, therefore, used in religious rituals to enhance the sanctity of any offerings.

The Story of Cosmic Life
Genesis 1:26-27
"Then God said, 'Let us make man in our image, in our likeness' ... So, God created man in his own image, in the image of God, He created him; male and female, He created them."

Have you ever asked the question? Who is the **"Let us…"** referred to in the Bible?

Let me tell you a story that is as old as time itself. I will try to explain it in terms that you can understand, but it is hard to translate it into words since what happened can only be truly explained through quantum physics and mathematical equations. While you read, I will try to paint a picture in your mind that you can draw on.

In the beginning, there was but a black void, full of nothingness, known today as dark anti-matter, and one very, small speck of pulsating light. The speck was pure light matter and, within it, dwelled the Universal Consciousness.

Dark anti-matter fed on light matter around the speck, but it could not consume the speck because of that consciousness. A Great Electromagnetic Energy force, known as the God Force, powered the speck. Then it happened. The speck of light thought, "We." With the acknowledgement that "it" was not alone, the one speck of light split into two, pulsating lights of equal, but different consciousness.

Turning the Knowledge of their being, into Wisdom, the two lights said, "We must matter!" So, the two specks of light came together in a loving "Oneness" that had never before happened. The Great Electromagnetic Oneness started to grow larger and larger, until it could not be contained any longer. Then there was a big hiccup and explosion that filled the dark void, with countless particles of pulsating lights, ever expanding outward.

The Creator, we will call the Knowledge consciousness, and his counterpart and Divine Bride, we will call the Wisdom consciousness, immediately saw that the dark anti-matter was consuming the particles of light matter, because the sparks lacked the consciousness to resist being consumed.

Deciding to bring peace to the chaos between the Darkness and the Light, the two agreed that angelic peacekeepers would be needed to maintain a balance between the two, opposing universal forces. These were the first experimental beings born in the heavens.

Their first angelic child was "liken" to the Great Father Knowledge and has become known as Michael. Michael would go out amongst the light matter, delivering the knowledge consciousness, which would shield the light matter from being consumed, by the darkness.

Their second angelic child was Raphael, who was sent out to heal the light matter. This allowed the specks of light to grow into special environments where other forms of intelligent life could grow and prosper.

Their third angelic child was Gabriel. When experimental life started to develop, within the specks of light matter, Gabriel would translate the knowledge, from the Father, in the hope that the life forms would convert the knowledge into the wisdom of their Divine Mother.

Once again, great chaos ran rampage, within these experiments, because the intelligent life forms were feeling the universal tug of the darkness, wanting to consume them. So, they turned on each other, destroying all the beauty their Father and Mother created for them.

Just when Father Knowledge was at a loss, feeling that they could never create children that could coexist, Mother Wisdom said, "Let us divide the Light Matter into seven, different dimensions, one overlapping the other, in a cosmic circle of life... and give our developing life forms what holds US together, our Divine Unconditional Love."

Their forth-angelic child was Uriel. She was made of the pure unconditional love of the Father and Mother. What Wisdom did not tell the Father was that, in order to spread their Divine Love, she would have to divide herself into seven, equal parts--so that each dimension could feel, and have, its own, individual Divine Loving Mother.

Wisdom also knew that the Father's love for her was so great that Knowledge would pursue her, through time and space for eternity, keeping a steady flow of His Electromagnetic God Force throughout the seven dimensions--which are connected, through threads or wormholes. These threads were pathways between dimensions, through which Father Knowledge pursued his elusive, Divine counterpart.

When Wisdom divided into seven, she became the Seven Celestial Sisters that we Atlantians named: Odessa of the Aves or Bird creatures; Salamander of the Amphibian creatures; Tabatha the Felidae or Feline creatures; Scheherazade of the Reptilian creatures; Sabuka of the Canine creatures; Urania of the aquatic creatures and our Divine Mother, the Constant Walker, of the Primate creatures. Each species was given the ability to reason and learn.

The division of the seven dimensions helped. Unfortunately, the very struggle to survive made the seven species still very warlike. The test to see if they could overcome the darkness began. It was decided then that each species would be allowed to continue to grow, with the help of Uriel's Love, Raphael's Mercy, Gabriel's Wisdom and Michael's protective Knowledge, until such time that one species became dominate.

They were given free will to do whatever they wanted, without interference, in the hope that they would apply their Knowledge and Wisdom to live in peace and harmony. However, given the Universal Laws of positive and negative, within each species, they only applied knowledge, wisdom, mercy and love to their clan-s-and had negative contempt for all other clans in their physical worlds.

Over billions of years, since the start of the experiment, each species gained the ability to leave the special, host planetary environments. During those years, Michael would weigh their hearts and minds to see if they had developed the wisdom and compassion necessary to live in peace with their cosmic brethren.

The earth has been monitored by outside intelligence for over a million years, by many species from other dimensions that have survived the great struggle for life within the cosmos. Many humans, over the past several hundred years, have seen the unexplained lights and space craft in the sky. The world's governments don't acknowledge them publicly, because their intelligence agencies fear a global panic.

Earth's military conclave has engaged the watchers many times in battles just to be overwhelmed, by the watchers' technology. If you ask your friend Admiral Zumwalt, he will confirm the military's action against alien spacecraft in Vietnam, where U.S. Military's weapons were turned on the U.S. Military. It was a case of turnabout is fair play and not so friendly fire. Humanity is feared, because it is felt, if humans mistreat their own species, it will do the same or worse to all other species they will encounter in the cosmos.

Since humanity is on the threshold of deep space exploration, humanity needs to use their wisdom to stop feeding their Dark side and walk more in the Light, before the human experiment is reduced or destroyed. There will be no warning. It will just happen, with what has been prophesied as "The End of Days."

With that in mind, I give you the means to call on your defenders. The Angels of the Four Directions are with humanity now--to help in your struggle against the Darkness. Angels don't belong long to the Religions of Man. They are here to champion those of every faith and those of no faith. You can hear them, if you practice and apply what you have found in the Book of Wisdom. Remember the word "angel" simple means messenger and these messengers were the Creators' first born children.

AFFIRMATION TO ARCHANGEL MICHAEL
(Meaning - Who is like God)

Saint Michael, the Mighty Archangel,
Defend me in the battles of everyday life.
Be my protection against the wickedness and
Snares of the demons that prey upon my innocents.
May God rebuke them, I humbly pray.
And do thou, O Prince of the Heavenly Host,
Satan and all evil spirits that pursue me,
By the power of God, thrust them into hell.
Be gone and bother me no longer.
AMEN.

AFFIRMATION TO ARCHANGEL GABRIEL
(Meaning - God's Ambassador)

O loving messenger of the Incarnation, descend upon all those for whom I wish peace and happiness. Spread your wings over the cradles of newborn babes. O thou, who didst announce the coming of the Infant Jesus.

Give to the young a lily petal from the virginal scepter in your hand. Cause the Ave Maria to re-echo in all hearts that they may find grace and joy through Mary.

Finally, recall the sublime words spoken on the day of the Annunciation – "NOTHING IS IMPOSSIBLE WITH GOD'S WISDOM IN YOUR HEART." AMEN.

AFFIRMATION TO ARCHANGEL RAPHAEL
(Meaning - God's Physician)

O glorious Archangel, Raphael, great Prince of the heavenly court, illustrious for thy gifts of mercy and grace. Guide those who journey by land sea and air, consoler of the afflicted, and refuge of sinners; I beg thee to assist me in all my needs and in all the suffering of this life, as once thou didst help the young Tobias on his travels. And because thou art the "MEDICINE OF GOD," I humbly pray thee to heal the many infirmities of my soul and the ills, which afflict my body, if it were for my greater good. I especially ask of thee an angelic purity, which may fit me to be the temple of The HOLY SPIRIT. AMEN.

AFFIRMATION TO ARCHANGEL URIEL
(Meaning - Fire of God)

I ask thee, Archangel Uriel, to guide me to a better understanding of God's Unconditional Love for me. May your loving fire burn in my mind, body and spirit so that I might live a more righteous life in service to God, myself and for all of HIS CREATION. AMEN

Invoking the Angels of the Four Directions:

When you are ready, invoke Michael, the Archangel of the East. He will stand at your right side. You do this by saying the following words, out loud, in a commanding voice:

"I now invoke the mighty and powerful Archangel Michael of the East to stand at my right side. Please grant me the strength, courage, integrity and protection I need to fulfill my purpose in this incarnation. Please use your flaming sword to cut away any doubts and negativity. Surround me with your protection, so that I may always work on the side of good and righteousness. Thank you, Michael."

(Pause for thirty seconds. Become aware of Michael standing beside you, and be alert for any insights or words that he may offer.)

When you feel ready, invoke Uriel, the Archangel of the South; ask her to stand at your backside to give you eyes in the back of your head. Speak in a loud voice say:

"I now invoke the mighty and powerful Archangel Uriel of the south to stand, guarding my backside. Please release all my tensions, worries and insecurities. Help me to find love for those, who hate and persecute me. Grant me tranquility and peace of mind. Help me to serve others, and to give and receive generously. Thank you, Uriel."

(Pause for thirty seconds and see if Uriel has a message for you. You will sense Uriel, standing at your back. Smiling, acknowledge her presence, and remain alert for any wisdom or advice that she might offer.)

When you feel ready, invoke Archangel Raphael of the West to stand on your left side and say out loud in a commanding voice:

"I now invoke the mighty and powerful Archangel Raphael of the West to stand on my left side. Please fill me with wholeness and good health. Help me heal the wounds from my past. Please heal and restore every aspect of my being and make whole anyone I may have hurt. Thank you, Raphael."

(Pause and see if Raphael has a message for you. You are likely to sense the wholeness and unity he brings to your being, even if you do not receive a specific message.)

319

When you feel ready, ask Archangel Gabriel of the North to stand in front of you, and in a commanding voice say:

"I now invoke the mighty and powerful Archangel Gabriel of the North to stand in front of me. Please bring me insights so that I may always walk in the light of wisdom. Remove all my doubts and fears, and purify my body, mind, and spirit. Help me communicate wisdom to myself, and all the people I meet on my path through life. Thank you, Gabriel."

(Pause and see if Gabriel has a message for you. You are likely to sense a "KNOWING" he brings to your being, even if you do not receive a specific message.)

HOW TO USE AN ILLUSION OF YOUR OWN BRAIN

The materials you will need are a candle, a piece of black cloth about three-foot square (a black coat or jacket may be substituted) and some way to hang it up on a wall or on the back of a door.

Secure the piece of black cloth on a wall or door, so that the bottom edge is level with, and about three feet from, your eyes. The room is to be completely dark, with the exception of your lighted candle. While keeping your head level, direct your sight up about 45° so that you are looking at about the center of the cloth. Then, while your head is in this position, take your lighted candle and move it four inches to the left and right of your nose, but about six to eight inches from your nose. Make a sweep of the candle in front of your eyes. Do this slowly, back and forth, about eight inches from your eyes.

As you continue your sweep, a circle of grayish-white light will begin to appear on the black field before your eyes. As the illusion becomes brighter, you will begin to see the convolutions of the surface of the brain. But with more intense concentration, you can even see the veins covering the surface. If you do not see it, hold the candle a little lower or higher as you make your sweeps.

This is truly an ingenious illusion…or is it? And many people have been duped into believing that they were really looking at their brain, but in fact they are seeing the inside of their own eye.

End of Transmission

Begin Open Channel

Lesson Seven:
Nine of Hearts received February 8, 1989
Book of Wisdom, channeled from the Hierophant:

"The more you know the more "Knowing" will come to you." ERU

Dearest Hermit and Teacher,

Let us begin with the last two elements of the four, which together constitute the foundation of creation.

Earth

The symbol for Earth is identical to the symbol for Air (the triangle with a line 1/3 way down), with the exception that it is inverted (see Figure 10). Earth is associated with the female, mother, fertility, to give birth, the solid and the practical riches (for they come from the Earth). The physical body, black bile (in alchemy), gloom and melancholy (because earthly life is so much inferior to that of the afterlife), and the dead because it is earth, from whence the first man came, and unto which the human body shall return.

Figure 10 – Earth

Thus, the earth is, and has been, associated with those things of a worldly nature, as opposed to things of the spiritual or divine nature. The belief in the power or force of the earth is seen in some cultures, by the practice of placing a newborn baby on the ground soon after birth to let the fertile vigor of the soil pass into the child's body.

It has been widely believed that man came from the earth to begin with. In Holy Scripture, it says that the first man was made from the dust of the earth. His name was Adam, meaning red earth, but it also states that man was created from the slime of the earth, which is black. In the Bible, there are only two accounts of the creation of man.

Originally though, there were in fact seven creations of man; Blue, Black, Brown, Yellow, Red, Green and White races.

In Atlantis, we had the knowledge of creating life and altering life forms. This knowledge became lost, with the destruction of Atlantis, because the knowledge was misused and abused. Yet, our memory has not been completely erased of those days. Stories live on in the minds of man. They can be found in the story of the Minotaur; a monster half bull and half man, confined in the Cretan labyrinth. There's also the Centaur having the head, trunk and arms of a man, and the body and legs of a horse.

There are many ancient stories of men creating men as well. An old Jewish tradition states that a Rabbi, with two assistants, form a man called GOLEM, out of clay and brought him to life. One version says that the Rabbi brought himself into an ecstatic state, by writing "AMTH" on the Golem's forehead... and he became animated.

"AMTH" meant truth or reality. When he rubbed out the "A," the remaining "MTH" meant death or dead and the Golem became inanimate or crumbled into dust.

Similar rites, involving the use of words to create life or bring the dead back to life, have been performed all over the world. They were particularly common in Egypt. It is also said that this knowledge was practiced among the ancient giants, which is also another name for Atlantians and the Sons of Zeus.

In the early 1500s, Aureolus Philippus Theo Hohenheim, called Paracelsus, had produced a man-made human, which he called "Homunculus." In fact, it is said that he produced more than one.

Water

The last, but not the least, of the four symbols is water (see Figure 11). Water, to the Ancients represented life, divine spirit, birth or rebirth. As is fire, so is water, used for purification. Water and fire are by no means the only forms used for purification. There are also fasting, prayer and meditation.

Figure 11 - Water

All physical things that live need water. When they do not receive adequate water, they weaken, wither and die... or they go into the state of suspended animation. Liquids are called "life giving," because they flow and move about, while lifeless things are at rest.

Mercury is called living silver, Quicksilver, because it is a metal in a liquid form. In alchemy Mercury was known as "Spiritus," for it was believed to be the spirit of metals.

In Christian symbolism, the four rivers of Eden were identified with the four Gospels. For they brought the life-giving message of Christ, the living waters--the water, which flowed from Christ's wounds while on the cross. It should be noted that Eden existed way before Jesus, so that story is inconsistent with the facts. However, there is power and energy in everything that man believes, true or not. "Blessed is the man who believes in something, for it is better than believing in nothing at all."

Remember, the Bible is full of stories that were made up to help man understand the times in which he lives. In the not so distant future, if man wants to know something he will turn to a worldwide computer system for it. Can you believe a system where anything you want to know is at your fingertips? But, will it all be true? No! Can you believe everything you read in the secret texts? No! It is all just food for thought, not to be taken literally. There is power in everything and truth can be found in a lie, if you choose to believe it.

In the Old Testament, according to Judeo-Christian tradition, God is portrayed as moving his spirit over the waters. And, gathering together the waters into one place, He created land from the mist. God then proceeds to bring forth all other life out of the water to live upon the land. In the ancient Sumero-Babylonian Scriptures, the God of the waters upon the earth was called "EA" (this name is pronounced like the E in the word yet). It is said that by intoning the "EA" over water, it influences the energy of the water and gives the power of seeing into the inner nature of things or seeing the future.

Water Divination Experiment

In the evening, after the sun goes down, go to a place or room where you will not be disturbed. Place therein a large bowl, filled with fresh cool water. Extinguish all light, except one lit candle a full arm's-length away to your left. Sit before the bowl of water and close your eyes for a few moments. Relax by using lesson one's exercise. After you are relaxed, open your eyes and intone the "EA" in full voice over the bowl three times. Wait a few moments, then repeat it again six times. Rest a few more moments, then chant it nine more times. Now close your eyes again. Within the time it takes a candle to burn down the width of one finger, you will experience a wetness coming over your body. You shall also sense the fragrance of flowers. When either or both overcome you, open your eyes and look deep into the water, so that the future may be revealed to you. Sometimes a bluish light or orb will rise from the water.

Nostradamus, a psychic, physician, mathematician and astrologer (1503 A.D. - 1566 A.D.), to whom the past and future appeared, spent most of his years, studying Astrology, Cabalistic lore, the Occult and the Torah, using this method. The predictions he made, over 400 years ago, are still coming true today. Nostradamus tells us in his writings that when seated alone at night in his secret study, he would use a divining rod. He would wet the cuffs and socks of his clothing. A slender flame would leap out of the solitude and come to rest over the brass tripod set in the middle of his Branchus. A Branchus is an occult rite where a bowl, filled with water, is placed on a brass tripod--rom which utterances of the future come forth. It was with fear that he invoked this power, from which he gained knowledge of the future. He believed his knowledge came from heaven. The waters and his powerful mind helped him open portals, into other dimensions of knowledge. You can do the same with practice. If you don't practice, you are wasting your time. There is an ancient text that says, "Let him, who is to prophesy, take a basin full of water, which attracts spirits in its depths. Breathe upon it, with a clear sound, and it will excel with a virtue imparted to it by this charm. The spirit will then whisper forth predictions of the future. You will not hear it with your ears, but with your mind and heart."

This rite has existed and has been used for thousands of years, by the oracles of most every known empire of the ancient world.

End of Transmission

Begin Open Channel

Lesson Eight:
Eight of Hearts, received March 8, 1989
Book of Wisdom, channeled from the Hierophant:

"The more you know the more "Knowing" will come to you." ERU

Beloved Hermit and Teacher,

Remember our discussion about the Ankh? The Ankh is an appropriate symbol to characterize the student. As you look at the symbol, it might bear a resemblance to the human figure. Within the symbol itself, we see the "A" or the Alpha, the beginning, and also the "O" or the Omega, the end. The A & O represent the brain in the physical body; the organ that is created first in the womb, and the organ, which stops functioning last to indicate physical death.

"Then God said, 'Let us make man in our image, in our likeness.' So, God created man in his own image, in the image of God he created him; male and female he created them."

Is the above quote referring to our brainpower, being one and the same with the creator? And isn't it interesting that below the A and the O are the arms of the Ankh, or the glyph, meaning: "The Infinite"?

The glyph is a symbol for our ever-present, imperishable spirit, which cannot be destroyed. As in the Christian cross, there are four stars, or points, which represent faith, hope, charity and love. Remember the meaning behind the symbol, for it has always been with us and is a powerful talisman for human kind.

When a teacher sets forth the teachings to be absorbed and redistributed, there are always pupils, who recognize the truth and wisdom. But the true student takes into himself the meaning of the words, and then uses that information to reconstruct his world into a better manner.

Wisdom, truth and knowledge is likened to food for the body. If that food is not processed properly, or accumulates in the areas where it is not needed, the function of food is negated and the body/mind will go into decline. Use the food, or the knowledge, to keep your body, your society and your world in a healthy, glowing, enlightened state.

Application of the knowledge we accumulate is what learning is all about. In the Talmud, it is written, "Say not a thing, which cannot be understood, that in the end... it will be understood. And say not 'When I have leisure, I will study'...per chance thou shalt have no leisure."

Mohammed, son of Abdullah, commanded in his first revelation not to go out and speak the truth, but to read first. Learning always comes first, but it is an ongoing process that we do not graduate out of, or from--ever. Humans speak as if they know, without knowing. That is foolish talk. Humans associate most of their lessons, with the younger days.

It's strange how quickly we age and our lives become complacent, when we find ourselves out of a learning group? It is as if activity, fitness and growth are always associated with children and inactivity, declining physical fitness and the decline of happiness are associated with those of any age, who are no longer children. We must always seek to understand that a greater understanding is possible, if we seek it. We understand part of something and feel we know it all. "When we think we know, we don't; and when we know we don't, we do!"

From the above statement, we should realize that, in order for the body and mind to stay fit and work in tune with one another, we must then stay in tune with the forces, working around us; our nature, mankind and the force of the Creator that is seeking to better our lives.

Start turning the clock back, by remembering the magical times of your life... going back as far as you can remember, into your childhood. Write down successive memories of moments that made you sparkle or laugh--or moments that you were overcome, with all at the wonder of the world around you.

Incorporate your special moments into your personal recipe for youth, which follows:

"The Best Recipe to Start Your Day"
1- cup of dreams mixed with
1- dash of reading, then add
1- large proportion of physical activity with
3- ounces of enthusiastic desire, sprinkled with
1- large dose of fresh air inhaled at sunrise
Knead everything above well, and then add
1- heaping spoon of joy, happiness and song
1- heaping spoonful of Faith, Hope, Charity and Love
Pour it all into a glass of pure water. Then top everything off with a smile and drink!

Remember that there was a time on earth, as mentioned in the Old Testament, when man lived to be hundreds of years old. This could never have happened, if the man's mind and body were not kept close together in cooperation and respectful love for each other. Your life recipe should embody all the ingredients that the Creator has generously supplied to humankind--to allow us to live a long, happy, healthy life. full of information and also the time to apply that information to the world around us.

One of the purposes of this lesson was to prepare you mentally and physically for the old lessons that will come soon, again to our attention. The technology and the scientific data, which is coming forward, have belonged to mankind before and have been lost. By adhering carefully to your life recipe, as new information is rediscovered, humankind will use the new/old knowledge in ways that have never served man before. Watch for news items relating to scientific discoveries, for much of the wealth of Atlantis is beginning to, slowly, reappear.

End of Transmission

Begin Open Channel

Lesson Nine:
    Seven of Hearts, received April 8, 1989
    Book of Wisdom, channeled from the Hierophant:

"The more you know the more "Knowing" will come to you." ERU

Beloved Hermit and Teacher,

Humans have become spoiled, with the advent of many modern inventions and conveniences of this, The Age of Information. As a whole, society believes it is stronger and smarter, due to these advances in technology. In fact, the opposite is true. They tend to weaken many of your natural abilities and, in some cases, completely destroy them.

Telephones and television have destroyed much of human development. Where once humans had the faculty to contact a person who is distant, with their minds, now they use the telephone. An even greater loss than that, is that humans have lost the ability to contact or be contacted, by those who have passed into the hereafter. But of course, humanity's greatest loss is its connection and communication, with the Creator.

Once, humans meditated and prayed long and hard for something. Now people just think of their wants and can't understand why God didn't answer their prayers. It's because they didn't pray. Praying takes effort, and it gets the attention of the Heavenly Hosts. Thinking is just that, thinking! And thinking takes no effort. The Heavenly view is: "No effort in, gets no effort out."

In days gone by, man had several methods to communicate, with those who were not near. If you wished to summon another you would face the direction in which the person (or persons) lives. Then you would call the name of the person, with whom a meeting was desired. If you did not know where the person resided, you would call out the name of the person, three times, to each of the four cardinal points north, south, east and west.

Once summoned, if you wish to communicate with the person, you would extend your arms, as one about to embrace another. Now you would try and visualize the person standing before you. This having been done, you would speak as if the person was really there. Then listen for a reply, which would come as though one was speaking in your head.

That is how we are communicating now Master Hermit.

There's a common story about a Tibetan Lama, who was traveling on his donkey, from one monastery to another. The donkey made a sudden move and the Lama fell, rendering himself immobile. As the Lama lay there, he concentrated on a brother monk back at the monastery. He visualized the monk and told him of the accident. In a short time, the monk he had visualized, arrived with help to take him back to the monastery.

There are many such stories as this. I am sure you have heard of some yourself.

Another way to contact someone is to look deep into a crystal, a pool of water, a stream or vessel of water, while picturing the absent person. This having been done, speak to them, as if they were in your presence.

Now with the advent of photography, we can use a person's picture to call on them, by utilizing the flames of candles to increase your energy and focus. This can be accomplished, by placing two candles about one foot apart. In between, and about one foot behind the candles, place the portrait or photograph of the person you wish to contact. Elevate the picture, so that when you look at the person's eyes, they're at the same horizontal line, as that produced by the flame of candles.

Gaze into the person's eyes and will them to call you. You look at the picture and repeat three times, "call Edward, call Edward, call Edward." After you've done this, blow out the candles and forget about this person. Try this experiment three times over a twenty-four-hour period. If the person doesn't call you, call them and don't be surprised if they tell you, "I've been thinking about you for the past twenty-four hours."

Remember humans don't always act on their thoughts. Do You?

Have you ever sat day-dreaming about someone, thinking, "I wonder how so and so is doing or I wish I could talk to so-and-so, then the phone rings and the very person you were thinking of was on the other end of the line? Were you aware that you're using your psychic abilities to contact them?

The mind is a fantastic tool and, once you learn to master it, there's no limit to the powers of the mind. As long as you use these powers for good, they will increase in strength.

Now let us speak of the past. Have you ever seen a newsreel of a historic event that took place ten, twenty-five, fifty or seventy-five years ago? The event was recorded on film for everyone in the future to see. It's there for all time, to be recalled at will, provided you have a projector. What would you do, if the film was destroyed, or the event was never recorded on film?

How do you recall the past?

To recall the past, you must start with progressive relaxation found in lesson number one. After you are relaxed, visualize the person, persons or event that you wish to see. As you concentrate, the image will become stronger and stronger until it takes on a real-life appearance. Let the vision wrap around you, as you become a part of it. If you single out a particular personage when the vision becomes clear as life, you may interview them. Remember you're in control of the vision.

Most humans have eyes to see with and ears to hear with. Would you blindfold yourself and go through life never to see the beauty that is all about you, or would you stuff your ears with cotton, never to hear a thing as long as you live? And yet the essences of your senses, wisdom and knowledge are the abilities that humans hide from or ignore. Why? Is it that humans are afraid to recognize some things are superior to themselves, or that they are powerful beyond measure? When you keep yourself separated from that which is part of you, it then takes on a separate entity, and you interpret it as a threat. But when you recognize that it is a greater part of yourself, you become one with it, and there's nothing you cannot do.

Also, there are those who fear such a relationship on the basis of unworthiness. Just thinking about communicating with something omniscient, all knowing; or omnipotent, all powerful can sometimes be too much for a person to cope with. Yet if we use it every day, it would not be a stranger to us, and we would be used to it.

What is the ultimate power we have? What is this part of us that we don't recognize?

It is all the knowledge and power of the universe. It is every thought that was ever spoken, or yet to be revealed to the mind of man. It is the "I AM THAT AM," universal consciousness of the Creator.

Can you imagine connecting to that kind of power? You can! It is very simple when you think about it, but it does require regular periods of practice. Remember, "In order to go out, you must go within."

HOW TO CONTACT THE POWER WITHIN

It's very important, in the beginning, that you practice on the same day or days and time each week. This is how you develop your communication system and without it, it will not work. I cannot stress enough that the day or days of the week and the time are to be adhered to, strictly.

Sit in a dimly lit or totally dark room in a comfortable padded chair. Place both feet on the floor and tip your head back. Now go through your progressive relaxation, as described in lesson one.

When you are relaxed, there is one of two ways that you may choose to proceed. Pick one and use that, but after two months if you did not get proper results, then try the other method.

One procedure is to clear your mind. Try hard to think of nothing. Now wait and listen for a voice. Pay attention to it, as long as it speaks in the positive. Put away all other thoughts. If the voice speaks negative, or it makes you feel uncomfortable, demand that it leave, then start again.

Remember there is a lot of negative stuff out there, but you are in control. Nothing can hurt you; except you can spook or hurt yourself.

The second procedure is to call on the Angels of the Four Directions, as your protective guides. Then think of your body, as a portal into another plane deep within... where a great voice rings out. An overwhelming voice that answers any and all questions you ask. Thus, you must enter into yourself to have this experience, with the Creator.

Remember you go out into the cosmos, by going inside of yourself. Everything you seek is inside of you. "Go in, to get out." That's what happens when your physical life stops. You are released to take everything that you have learned in life on your spirit journey through the forever, but all you take with you is what you learned and understand. So, learn it now. You only get one life! Make it count and accept the Divine help that the Creator sends.

Most people have had unexplainable experiences, ranging from hearing their name called when no one is there, to a small voice, telling them to do something or not to do something. Some refer to this as intuition or their Guardian Angels. I can assure you that intuition is not part of it. That voice is there to protect, help and educate you. Don't let your ego become so great that you cannot accept help. All humans need it, from the lowly and poor to the rich and intellectual. Without help, we would not be. I tell you this as you will share it with others, and they will pass it on. We all need help. We all need love. We all need compassion and understanding. Most of all we need others to share it with.

Remember, "We cannot reach everyone, but everyone can reach someone. Pass it on."

I say to you the Fifth Ancient Law of Wisdom is: **"He who needs no one is no one."**

Be observant of those around you. There's so much to learn from them and so little time to do it. Every man, woman and child has a priceless gem of knowledge to give to you. They, who are in the waning of their days, have seen so much and have so much to tell. Sit silently at their feet and drink deeply of their cup of knowledge... for it has such a sweet taste.

The Sixth Ancient Law of Wisdom is: **"Sit quietly, humbly and patiently at the feet of the wise for one day others will sit at your feet and drink from your cup of wisdom."**

For your own development, I say do not put on airs, or be too aggressive, or let your ego come forth, or profess to know all things. For even, as the lowly clay of the earth has no prestigious place, yet it is to this, your body will return. And who will recognize you then?

End of Transmission

Begin Open Channel

Lesson Ten:
   Six of Hearts, received May 8, 1989
   Book of Wisdom, channeled from the Hierophant:

"The more you know the more "Knowing" will come to you." ERU

My Dear Brother Hermit and Teacher,

Our Atlantian ascended masters realized that beyond the bounds of matter lay a more perfect existence, a truer realm and a place of peace. They sought, as we seek now, the good, the beautiful and the true. They did not rush out in thirst for sensation, but with a finer perception, and realized the true Utopia is within.

Material wealth has no value, no lasting pleasure; it is only momentary. You may have wealth and with it, friends. When your wealth is gone, who can you call your friend? Who will stand by you? I tell you this; a friend is the greatest of all your treasures. For a true friend will not leave you, in your darkest hour. It is the simple things that are of the greatest value.

The first step in the development of the Magi was to return to the simple life. They renounced rich attire and the wearing of gold. Their raiment was white, their bed the ground, their drink water, their food was herbs, cheese and bread, making them more receptive to nature's truth... and a hardy people.

They did not stoop down to lust after the pleasures of the body. They did not stoop down to take that which was not theirs. They did not want of the earthly dross of matter, nor the seeming splendor of wealth, or the habitation of the unhappy in their darkness. No! They sought the higher powers, the greater joys, and the fulfillment of their being. They came to know their real self. And in their real self, they found the answer. The real meaning to their existence was there all the time. All they had to do was contemplate their inner being, and it was given up to them. They were filled with awe in that something so sublime could be found in this humble clay shell... our own body.

What was this mystical experience that brought such a state of ecstasy with it? They entered into a state of Fifth Dimensional Consciousness, whereby they were at one with all that ever was or will be. And when they would return, they would do naught but cry. For there are no words to express the rapture they had been a part of. Not all the happiness or joy, nor any pleasurable emotion could ever begin to come near to such an overwhelming phenomenon as this. And yet, you have it within your grasp to drink of this cup.

There is another ancient practice called, "CRYPTIC TRANSPOSITION".

Notice how the Star of David has six lines and angles (see Figure 12.) It means as in heaven, so on earth; or as above, so below. Six lines, according to the ancient teachings, stood for the earthly and spiritual planes of man. This knowledge has been passed on, by word of mouth, for tens of thousands of years before it was placed on paper. Thus, in the modern-day texts, there is an endless caravan of discrepancies.

Figure 12 – Star of David. "As above, so below" or "As in Heaven, so on Earth"

These discrepancies should be expected when you think of the thousands of years of oral recitation. Then, for a period of over four hundred years, it became lost. Whether it was banished, by a ruler because of his ego or fear of the power behind it, is to this day unknown. It is said to have been resurrected somewhere in Mongolia. It was given the name I-Ching (pronounced E-Jing) or Book of Changes.

They say it is stated by King Wen, "This hexagram symbolizes thunder rolling across the whole earth: from it, all things receive their integrity. The ancient rulers gave abundant and timely nourishment to all."

The "ancient rulers?" Was he speaking of the Atlantians?

The Atlantians were known as the ancient rulers. Basically, the book of the "Cryptic Transpositions" is composed of sixty-four combinations of six, horizontal lines, in which a horizontal line may be broken into two horizontal lines.

Ch'in or Heaven   **K'un or One**

Figure 13 - The Hexagrams for Heaven and One Receptive

The meaning of the combination of lines were vulgarized and degraded to predict, divine or predestine events. The use of the Cryptic Transposition, as an oracle, is common knowledge and the least important of its usages. The purity of its use has been lost to the common knowledge of man.

The Book of Cryptic Transposition is the key to LIFE, DEATH, CREATION and DESTRUCTION. It is believed by most Masters that man was not meant to have such powers. Thus, when the truth was found, it was quickly destroyed and the knowledge of the Masters died with them. Only a select few can channel the ancient knowledge and the consequence that goes with it. Here I must remind you, always use the "Knowing" for good. If you ever use it for evil, you shall create within you a monstrous nightmare that only God or his Divine Agents can annihilate. Thus, I adjure you, never use it to hurt another human or mutilate anything that lives. For such an act shall rebound, with such hostility, and you will pray that you had never been born.

Use this Cryptic Transposition for good and all your real needs shall be fulfilled. You shall know joy, health and you shall not grow old before your time. But, above all, guard its secret.

Before you proceed, you may want to purchase a pocket book copy of I-Ching, or borrow one from your library, to become familiar with the Hexagrams and their general meaning.

Proper Practice of Cryptic Transposition

1. First pick one of the hexagrams. I would suggest Heaven or One Receptive. By using one of these two first, you will gain more wisdom in their use and their application.
2. Draw the hexagram on a sheet of clean white paper with a magic marker.
3. Clear your mind and relax, following the technique you were given in the beginning of your journey, in lesson one.
4. Concentrate on the hexagram you have chosen in good lighting for about half a minute. For some, it may take a whole minute.
5. Now close your eyes and imagine the hexagram on a door in your mind's eye.
6. After you have achieved this, open the door in your mind's eye and walk through. When this door is opened, prepare to meet the ultimate limits of transposition.

Six Aids to your Physical and Mental Growth

1. Spend whatever time you can in meditation or prayer.
2. Never hold grudges, seek revenge, get mad, be riled, hold animosities, be rebellious or hate anyone or anything. Remember, "Hate is like drinking poison and waiting for the other being to die."
3. Think less of "I" and more of others.
4. Fast, not only from foods, but also from wants and desires.
5. Drink plenty of water. Tea, coffee, and juices do not count.
6. Smile and be of good cheer, Not only on the outside, but on the inside as well.

If you follow these six aids, your health, complexion and memory will improve. By improving the general health of your body and mind, the spirit will increase in power. Revisit this lesson on the eighth day of every month until it becomes second nature to your being.

End of Transmission

Begin Open Channel

Lesson Eleven:
   Five of Hearts, received June 8, 1989
   Book of Wisdom, channeled from the Hierophant:

"The more you know the more knowing will come to you." ERU

My Beloved Hermit and Teacher,

I asked, "What does security mean to you?" Some say, "Having all my bills paid." Others might say, "Having locks on my doors and the police to protect me." And yet others might say, "Saving up for retirement, so I can enjoy the rest of my life, without worrying how I'll pay my bills and survive."
All these are good answers.
Do you feel secure with your gas heat, electric lights, hot and cold running water and a general store not too far away?
Do you feel relaxed and at ease, knowing that the police and fire station, as well as the entire world, are just a telephone call away? Isn't it wonderful?
I tell you this: you could be reduced to a cannibal in thirty days. Does this shock you? Yet, it is true. Humanity lives in a world of fantasies.
If the earth were to suddenly tip on its axis just ten degrees, the world, as you know it, would be destroyed. First, there would be giant tidal waves that would destroy one-third of the world population. Along with that, would come earthquakes, resounding around the world, with landmasses sinking into the sea, never to be seen again and killing millions of people. Volcanoes would also erupt, devastating large areas of the globe and darkening the sky.
Underground water lines, gas lines, electrical lines and communication lines would be destroyed. Then the winds that go along with the sudden shifting would level whatever was left standing. And last, but not least, the sudden climatic changes would cause the polar ice caps to melt and bring snow and ice to areas that have never known it before, not to mention the flooding of low lying areas.
Now that you are without food, heat, light, and communication, how will you survive? What is more important to you now, finding food and shelter or preserving books of knowledge and wisdom? Your base instinct would say you would try to survive first. Even if it meant cannibalism for some!
In two or three generations, all the technology, all the achievements of mankind, would be dim memories, legend of a past great civilization that once inhabited the earth. Wisdom would fall prey to fear. Those who were able to keep some of that knowledge alive would be branded wizards, sorcerers and magicians. People would be burned at the stake or murdered for practicing such knowledge or arts. Humankind would be thrown back into the dark ages once again. The light of wisdom would be snuffed out and only a smoldering wick would remain.
Do you still feel so secure?
It does not have to be a natural catastrophe to push mankind to the edge. It could be a nuclear catastrophe that brings such events to pass, like the ultimate war of wars, or terrorists spreading a deadly strain of Ebola virus. Over the next

twenty-five years, science will determine that asteroids could bring life to near extinction on the planet, if they are not destroyed before they strike the earth.

World governments have already determined that extraterrestrial intelligent (ETI) life is monitoring earth from other worlds, and they don't know why. ETI could fear humanity's exploration of space and spreading greed and destruction, as it has amongst nations on earth.

Imagine an intelligent species, just a thousand years more advanced than your own. If humanity is capable of destroying the earth, as it is…well you do the math. It doesn't look good for the home team.

How can you protect yourself? In some of the scenarios, there is nothing that can be done. In others, you can start off with the basics of what you need most to survive. I will give you a short list to start you off:

Medical Books	Liquid Bleach	Juices
Water	Multi Vitamins	First Aid Kit
Dried Foods	Cooking Utensils	Candles
Honey	Paper Plates	Forks/Spoons
Flour	Toilet Paper	Flashlights
Salt	Canned Foods	Batteries
Matches	Portable Radio	Vegetable Seeds
Books Survival	Rope	Sewing kits
Weapons	Compass/Maps	Shovels

This may sound like a science-fiction story, but there is scientific proof that the earth has flipped on its axis several times, during its history. The weight of the polar caps keeps the earth's tilt steady. What happens if they melt? There is a prophecy that on April 3, 2033, the earth will wobble in its orbit around the sun and change its axis again.

There are many who would say that there is no evidence that man had made any significant advances before the former catastrophes took place, let alone, any scientific advances on a level, as we have today. This is rubbish! The evidence is all about you, all you have to do is look and listen. This evidence that has been found is referred to as scientific anomalies.

ANOMALIES: Deviations from the common rule or analogy.

EXAMPLE: If an automobile were dug up, and is carbon dated at twenty thousand B.C., this would not be concurrent with scientific knowledge. It would be out of sync, with our understanding of evolutionary time synch. Therefore, it would be an anomaly. There are anomalies that prove the scientific advancement of Atlantis.

In Texas, there is evidence that, during the time of the dinosaurs, there existed a race of man that was wearing shoes. How could man be that advanced in that timeframe? If he was that advanced, what other knowledge was he advanced in?

In Massachusetts, a vessel of unknown age and origin was blasted out of solid rock. But it is impossible for a vessel of that metallic composition to be in existence when that rock was being formed.

In Colombia, South America a miniature gold, delta-winged, jet aircraft was discovered. Of interest is that on the tail fin, is the Hebrew letter "B" or Beth-- not to mention, the plane is thousands of years old. It was believed that the Atlantians had aircraft, but this was the first real evidence brought to light.

In Baghdad, batteries tens of thousands of years old were found. What was even more remarkable is the fact that they still work.

What does this tell us?

Atlantis was the most scientifically advanced civilization this world has ever known. Buried somewhere in the sediment of this old earth of ours, there exists scientific knowledge from lost civilizations that could benefit all of mankind. Think of it, just below your feet may exist a time capsule that could change the life of man, as we know it, for years to come.

One such time capsule is supposed to exist somewhere around the Sphinx. In the early nineteen eighties, some test holes were drilled into the rock around the Sphinx to see if the water table was rising, which in turn could destroy the Sphinx. One of the drillings lead to the discovery of a large underground chamber, but the Egyptian Government will not let it be opened or explored. Why?

What I am addressing myself to, is:

1. The fact that the earth has gone through this before and could be going through it again in the very near future.

2. You cannot avoid it, but you can prepare for it.

3. All human technology could be, eventually, lost--and humanity would start again, with fire and the wheel. It was only seventy thousand years ago that less than ten thousand humans were left alive on the planet.

And last, but not least:

4. It would be a requirement that you do all you could to preserve this knowledge, because you are the Atlantians of the future. There is a reason you are being given this knowledge, study it, practice it and preserve it for the children of tomorrow. If you don't do it, who will?

End of Transmission

Begin Open Channel

Lesson Twelve:
   Four of Hearts, received July 8, 1989
   Book of Wisdom, channeled from the Hierophant:

"The more you know the more knowing will come to you." ERU

My Dearest Hermit and Teacher,

During the course of our lives, we experience many things like joy, sorrow, love, hate, loss, acquisition, anger, ecstasy, depression, exhilaration, pain and peace. Just to name a few.

In fact, we think we are experts in every emotional facet of life. If that were true, we would never get angry, for we would have understanding. We would never hate for anyone, for we would have love. And with love and understanding... compassion would be a part of our everyday way of life.

But, humans are fragile beings, with very short memories; we forget the experiences that have been brought into play for the benefit of our growth. Some are so bold to think that they are an authority on every facet of life.

Have you ever sat and listened to someone, telling another about an emotional problem they were going through? The one going through the experience tries to explain it to the one who had never experienced it. What does he or she, who has never had such an event take place in their life say, "I know what you're going through" or "I feel what you're going through" or "I understand what you're going through." And it goes on and on. You would have never known so many people could know how you felt, when even you didn't know how you felt! It's very similar to a story about the man, who was good and comely.

Now this man earned just enough money to pay his bills, buy food and some clothing, with a few pennies left over. He loved the out-of-doors and all life. He was happy, with hardly a care. Whenever one happened upon him, he was smiling, had a kind word and was willing to share the little he had. All the neighbors in his community loved and respected this man.

One day a traveler stopped at his door. The man fed the stranger and engaged the traveler in conversation. In the course of the conversation the stranger said, "How can you live in this poor state? Your house is a barn of the lowest kind, the cloth on your back is what I use for rags, and your food isn't fit for pigs. But, most of all, why do you let people take advantage of you?"

The poor man lowered his head, looked at the ground, spoke not a word and the traveler got up and left. The man was so ashamed of himself that he wept and he wept, finally dying of a broken heart.

On the day of his funeral, all the neighbors came from miles around, weeping for their loss. It just so happened that the traveler was passing through the village again. He asked the people why they were weeping? And so, they told him.

"I know how you must feel," the traveler said, "and I know what he died of!"

"What is that?" asked the neighbors.

"Poverty!" replied the traveler, as he rode away.

"Poverty?" they thought, as a hush fell over the neighbors, for they felt they had let their old friend down. They walked away, with a deep sadness in their hearts. The community was never the same again after that.

Here we had someone, who acted like an expert on life. He, with just a few words destroyed the joy, love and life of another. He destroyed the light of the community. We see this kind of people every day. They don't appreciate what they have and they always want more than they are worthy of receiving. Instead of looking at the positive side of life, they only see the negative.

There is a saying that comes from the American Indians. "Do not judge a man, until you have walked a mile in his moccasins." Nor should you judge a knight, until you strap on the armor and have fought the good fight. The day will come, dear Hermit, when fearful fools will judge you. Take courage and never be swayed. Remember, you are never alone. You are always surrounded by what you have learned, and wisdom is your constant companion.

This brings us back to the "I know just how you feel" quote.

There are some, who do know how we feel. Take the young man, who feels his wife's labor pains, while she is in the delivery room. There are the twins that share the experience of each other's emotions. There are true Empaths, as well, who have the gift of "feeling."

Yes, there are those, who can experience what we feel. You can develop that state whereby you can feel the other person's feelings or state of being. It's called Clairsentio.

Clairsentio

Clear feeling; to join yourself spiritually or mentally, with another, to experience their experiences. Claire is from the French word, meaning clear, and Sentio from the Latin word, meaning feeling, as in touch or emotion.

Method for Developing Clairsentio

This requires a pencil and pad of paper and two people. Person "A" will be the subject. Person "B" will do the subject's experiencing.

Person "A"

You will take a seat and sit in the position most comfortable to you. Tilt your head back slightly and go through the progressive relaxation, as outlined in lesson one. When you have reached your chin, stop. Now close your eyes. Try to relive in your mind, in passionate detail, a very emotional or traumatic event in your life.

Person "B"

You will sit in a comfortable chair, holding the pencil and pad of paper. Now relax and watch for person "A" to close their eyes. While you are watching the subject, try to become a part of them. Try to penetrate their consciousness. Try to merge, as one, with the subject. Then close your eyes to see and feel, what they see and feel, with your heart. Write down your impressions.

Whatever comes to your mind, write it down. It may seem silly or unrelated to you, but it may be a very strong or important key to an event in the subject's life.

Remember, record any vision, emotion, sensation or impression. You may detect aromas, fragrances and colors. You may hear a sound or words; whatever impression comes through, write it down.

The session should not be longer than five or ten minutes at the most. After the session is over, person "B" should read their notes to person "A" to substantiate any relationship to what has been received. Frequent practice sessions should help you develop your ability to feel what other people are feeling.

Why would you want to do this? What would you use it for?

You could use it to detect whether or not a person is depressed to the point of thinking about committing suicide, and thus help save their life. By knowing how a person is really feeling, you could be instrumental in helping that person cope with their problems. This ability will help you sense when someone is lying or telling the truth. It will also help you understand your own feelings.

This ability may also help you become a more sensitive compassionate human being. How much heartache could be stopped if a person, outside of another person, could translate correctly that person's inner being and say the right thing at the right time?

By now, you have become a clear channel, with the angels that are here to work in concert with you, to heal the world. Use your connection to "The Knowing" wisely. Humanity needs your sensitive gifts! How many people may not turn to drugs, alcohol or violence, if someone like you reached out to them at a critical time in their lives... and showed them understanding, love and compassion?

The ability to reach out and see into other people's lives is a great power for good, but along with that power comes responsibility. As we mentioned before, you must be a guardian over your words and your actions. Always remain a supporter of the greater good. Because of the "The Knowing" you have gained, you and your world has been changed forever. Bless you!

Remember, "The more you learn, the more you realize you don't know. "So never stop seeking, as you progress on this path toward 'The Great Knowing.' But know this, you are a very special person, unlike many around you. For you seek "The Truth" which many fear. As your wisdom, knowledge and compassion grow, you are destined to become a greater benefactor to all of humankind.

End of Transmission

Begin Open Channel

Lesson Thirteen:
    Three of Hearts, received August 8, 1989
    Book of Wisdom, channeled from the Hierophant:

"The more you know the more knowing will come to you." ERU

Dearest Hermit and Teacher,

As I have stated before, you are a very special person. That is why Archangel Michael chose you out of the billions, who live on the blue planet, called Earth. In fact, you're so special that you have been placed in the center of the universe.

Have you ever looked up at the night sky and seen the moon, stars and planets? At times, it makes us feel small and insignificant, or as though we're a part of each of those little points of light that flicker in the black-velvet sky. Have you ever felt as though you were on the edge of a cliff, torn between two worlds? In reality, you are. You are forced to live in a world created, by the manifestation of others.

Humans are told what to believe in, how to act and even what the truth is. It is our hope that you and your students will go beyond the world, according to man, and start living in the world, as was intended when the Creator imagined it. A world among worlds, living in harmony. Humanity stands between the microcosms of the macrocosm. Your ancient forefathers realized this.

Microcosm

A microcosm is a miniature world, or universe. Human nature or the human body, as representative of the wider universe; man, is considered as a miniature counterpart of divine or universal nature.

Macrocosm

A macrocosm is the great world, the universe, and the whole of a complex structure, especially the world or universe, contrasted with a small or representative part of it.

When we look up at the macrocosm, we see the moon, orbiting the earth. When we look into the microcosm, we see an electron, orbiting a proton, which is called an atom of hydrogen (see Figure 14).

When we view our solar system, we see a sun with nine planets, orbiting it. It's a non-metal, or gas, called fluorine--and has nine electrons that revolve around its nucleus.

Earth and its moon

Electron and proton - Atom of Hydrogen

Figure 14

Is the atom of hydrogen found in our body like a planet, with a moon revolving about it? Is the earth and moon just an atom, inside something even greater?

Think about it! Inside of you are billions of micro-solar systems and planets, supporting life. Your body is teaming with countless life forms, as endless as the grains of sand on all the beaches of the earth. Aren't bacteria a life form, living on its host? Just like you are living on your host, planet earth? It is truly beyond comprehension. And on one of those electrons, inside of you, maybe someone is looking up at a star filled sky, wondering, "What does it all mean?"

And for us, as we gaze at the stars, we can only wonder if we are an atom in the body of something much bigger, perhaps the body of the Creator. Can you see now why our forefathers called man the center of the universe?

They realized another truth in this. With all of our power and wisdom, we have little effect on the macrocosm or microcosm. However, the microcosm of our being can have a great effect on the macrocosms around us.

In this, we come to know humility. For the vastness of the microcosm and macrocosm we are insignificant, but at the same time... very important. We are a mere veil between one universe and another. To know your place is not to be proud or haughty, arrogant or assertive, but to be submissive with a spirit of indifference, and with a will to seek greater understanding.

I would pose a question to you. If I had seven grains of sand in my hand and told you that one of those grains of sand saved civilization. Could you pick out that grain of sand? No? Perhaps with a lucky guess, maybe. Then why do you expect to be picked out of a crowd of people when you have done even less? You mean nothing, but in the grand scheme of things, you mean everything. You can't save yourself, but you could save the world! You have something the grain of sand does not have. Humans have ability to change *almost* everything.

The Ancient Masters knew this kind of humility. This is why they were rarely presumptuous. They were mild mannered, quiet-speaking and gentle. It is in this manner that their wisdom is expressed. They did not use their mouth as much as they used their eyes. For it is through their eyes that they learned and beheld the beauty of the universe.

Yes, much is learned through the eyes of the beholder. So, I will speak to you about your psychic eyes, called Psychic Sight.

Have you ever wondered how a friend was, or where he or she was? As a parent, have you ever wondered what your child or children were up to at any particular time of the day or night? To know these things is to know Psychic Sight.

Psychic Sight

Before we can start to develop Psychic Sight, we must come to realize that we do not see by eyes alone. And we must learn to rely, not solely upon our eyes, for vision.

Do you daydream? In your daydreams, do you see things, people, places and events? If you do, then you must realize that these visions are viewed by means other than your physical eyes.

Do you dream at night? How do you see those dreams? Surely you're not seeing them with your physical eyes! It is by reason of the subconscious that these things are made manifest to you. The Ascended Masters and many angels can speak to you today, by providing you with visions for your Psychic Sight, as you channel these lessons. You are receiving them through your Psychic Sight.

How to develop Psychic Sight

1. Sit in a comfortable chair and use progressive relaxation, as outlined in lesson number one. Close your eyes for two or three minutes at a time and wait for sight impressions. Or sit in a dark room, with your eyes open, and wait for sight impressions. Sometimes you'll see flashes of color flecks of lights or rainbows. Practice this for a few days, before going onto the step two.

2. This time relax as you had before, but in a dimly lit room. Now pick out a bright point of light, such as a reflection on a piece of glass or metal, a short distance away from you. Concentrate your gaze on it, until you no longer see its proper color, but notice its color changing. Be conscious of the colors you see. Practice this until it comes easy.

3. Now you are ready for your first test. Sit or lie down. Relax, close your eyes and repeat step one. But this time, select a distant city, locality or room as a thing you wish to see and wait, until you see some part of it. By repeating this test for the same vision, you will eventually bring a clearer and more distant vision into your consciousness. When you have accomplished this, go on to the next and final step.

4. Repeat step three, but this time select a person at a distant place and hour that you will find him or her awake and active. Concentrate, with your eyes closed, until you see the person and can know what they are doing. Eventually, you'll be able to see anyone you wish, with your Psychic Sight, and know what they are doing almost at any hour of the day or night.

Now if there's something that a person would not normally let you see them doing, or if a person is fulfilling private needs at the time you wish to see them, you will be unsuccessful. If someone does not wish to be viewed, you will not see him or her, as well. What is not meant for you to see, will not be seen. Remember, no matter how pure of heart you may be, there are some things that you are not meant to see.

If you wish to see how well you have developed your ability, notice what your friends are doing and wearing when you see them with your Psychic Sight. Then call them on the telephone and ask them what they're wearing or doing. This way, you will know how strong your ability has become.

Practice your Psychic Sight as often as possible for any gift worth having is worth the effort. You never know when you might need that gift.

Another use for Psychic Sight is to examine lost or forgotten documents, enter ancient tombs, or the sealed halls of the initiation wherein man has not walked for centuries. You may ask to what advantage it is, if you see the ancient scroll or text written in some forgotten language?

As in telepathy, there is no language barrier, the same is true with Psychic Sight, there is no translation barrier. As you behold a scroll in some foreign tongue. concentrate on it, and it will be made known to you.

Remember, sometimes the blind see better than those with perfect sight. But those with Psychic Sight see things that people with perfect sight cannot see!

The Seventh Ancient Law of Wisdom is: **"With all of our power and wisdom, we have little effect on the macrocosm or microcosm, however the microcosm of our being can have a great effect on the macrocosms around us."**

End of Transmission

Begin Open Channel

Lesson Fourteen:
   Two of Hearts, received September 8, 1989
   Book of Wisdom, channeled from the Hierophant:

"The more you know the more "Knowing" will come to you." ERU

Beloved Hermit and Teacher,

One day while in my garden, contemplating the beauty of a blossom, a student came to me.

"Master Hierophant," he said. "I am unable to awaken the powers within. I listen to your words and have seen you work many wonders and, yet, I cannot do these things. Why?"

"Look upon this blossom and tell me what you see?" I asked.

"A flower made up of petals and a stem," the student replied.

"Therein lies your problem. You see what is obvious to even an untrained eye, never peering deeply for the wisdom locked within. It is time for you to look within. And to look within requires meditation. So, I shall speak to you on meditation."

Meditation

To meditate is the process of thinking in a contemplative or reflective manner, as we reach inward.

To Meditate

Before meditation, the body should be in good health. It should not be in the states of fasting or have eaten a large meal. One should have a poor meal; just enough to satisfy the gnawing pains of hunger. Either extreme will upset the state of spiritual concentration. So, have a light meal then wait an hour or two, before proceeding with your meditation.

Lie down in a position, so as to allow all the muscles in your body to relax. Sitting in a chair or a yoga position is not very conducive to total relaxation because the brain is telling the muscles to hold you in a position, so you don't roll over or fall. The brain needs to be free. You should not be thinking of any material work or related thoughts. In more simple terms, clear the mind.

Now close your eyes, so that objects around you will not disturb your being. Sometimes something in the room will take one's attention away from the importance of your meditation or disturb your thoughts.

Now you are ready to begin concentration on the spiritual. Contemplate such things as: Who or what am I? What is the power within? What is life? What is my relationship to the universe and to the Creator?

Now we awaken the mind, which is the power to reproduce or construct sensible images. The mind places before itself a picture that is supported by our present or ancient memories. The mind is capable of seeing, hearing, beholding, recalling and understanding vivid descriptions of the general, greater truth.

The next step in meditation is to look at the truth taught and consider how that truth has been forgotten or failed against your daily life.

The last and most important step is the will or faith, which at once reacts to the truths seen by the mind and applies them in acts of love, petition, resignation and resolve. If you should forget any of what I've spoken, always remember the Eighth Ancient Law is: "Absolute faith emanates only from the inner or spiritual self, through conviction. And contemplation alone, without absolute faith attending it, will not advance you one iota."

I had returned to the blossom I was holding in my hand when my student spoke again, "Master, I noticed that you spend much time with the flowers. Is it because they give you peace?"

The tranquility I was receiving from the flowers is only second to the knowledge I received from them. You see, each flower, each blossom is a book. They hold knowledge for those, who can read them. All the secrets of the universe are inscribed in each petal and form.

They, who are the humblest of all God's creations, speak with the greatest wisdom. Even in death, they adorn themselves for the coming of the reaper. That is why the fall leaves my heart so heavy. For the books are closing their pages for the last time, just to reopen, with new pages in spring.

However, unless I show you how to read the language of the flowers you will never be able to read them. The language is expressed in geometric form and numbers.

Let us take the simple daffodil. The petals form the Star of David or "as in heaven so on earth." The opening of the trumpet is a circle or "eternal." The stigma in the center is triangular, with three divisions, which represent the Trinity, "God the Father, Son, and Holy Spirit." Thus, it's "God the Father, Son and Holy Spirit of our Mother, Earth."

To read the flowers, begin like this:

1. Five pointed star or leaves, with one point up is: good; man; star of beauty; good health; protection against evil.
2. Five pointed star leaves, with two points up is: evil; Satan; discord; a fall; death; disease; corruption; putrefaction.
3. Seven pointed star or leaves is: seven days of the week; seven stars in the right hand of God; the eyes of God; the menorah.
4. Eight pointed star or leaves is: stability on both planes.
5. Nine pointed star or leaves is: spirituality; love; joy; peace; temperance; goodness; the ultimate contemplation; completion; final perfection of any great undertaking; master of all three planes.
6. Twelve pointed to star or leaves is: the twelve disciples; council of the divine wisdom; conclave of the holy masters.

This will help start you off, in reading the books of nature; the flowers; trees; grasses. You will find them to be full of great and wonderful messages. When you start seeing with your ears, feeling with your eyes and seeing with your heart, nature will show you the greatest story ever told.

The Eighth Ancient Law of Wisdom is: **"Absolute faith emanates only from the inner or spiritual self through conviction. And contemplation alone, without absolute faith attending it, will not advance you one iota."**

End of Transmission

Begin Open Channel

Lesson Fifteen:
   Ace of Clubs, received October 8, 1989
   Book of Wisdom, channeled from the Hierophant:

"The more you know the more "Knowing" will come to you." ERU

Dear Brother Hermit and Teacher,

Sitting here, surrounded by all forms of wisdom, I wonder what gift of knowledge I should share with you? Shall it be the gift of self-development? Or what about the past and the future; but are they not one, as the petals that comprise a flower? Or would you prefer knowledge of nature, as in the roar of the sun, the melody of space, the crack of lightning or the babbling of a brook? Are not all forms of knowledge the joy of our existence? Since there are so many things that I could speak about, let me choose which melody is appropriate for this place and time.

As we speak about the melody, we realize that we are all composers of the song. But, what is in a song? A song expresses our love, our hatreds and our fantasies of power, all in the form of a vibration. But, what determines the song we may sing? The song is usually determined, by the situation or the time in which we choose to sing it, so the song and the time we sing it are the most important factors in releasing the power of the song's vibration.

Legend has it that there were seven ancient books, which contained all the wisdom and power of the non-material plane. A great Magi condensed all the wisdom of the seven books, into seven sentences. Some generations later, another Magi condensed the seven sentences into seven words. Much later, another great Magi condensed the seven words into one word. And the word was "Ohm." It is said that when one chants the word Om correctly, it awakens the subconscious and all the wisdom of the seven books are revealed.

To the ancient Egyptians, the words of the gods, "life, health and prosperity" were uplifting, positive words of power.

Jews have a song of power in the word, "Shalom." It contains the power of joy of greeting another person, as well as a sorrow of leaving or departing from another.

The ancient Hawaiians placed the same in their word "Aloha."

For Christians, "Peace be with you," expresses compassion, service and goodwill toward others.

These examples signify songs of power passed along from one human being to another. Those words of power have their own, individual effect when used at the appropriate time. Words are our "melodies or songs" and they are expressed to cause specific effects.

Each of these words or phrases were created to express a power, by someone, and to make the power contagious; such as one person yawning in a group makes the whole group begin to yawn. Because other individuals accepted the power of the words or phrases as a reality, the power was passed on to future generations. Not only did the power become the word or phrase, but also the word or phrase became the power. Remember, humans have the ability to put energy into everything they manifest, and where there is energy there is power.

Because of the power of certain songs or words, the Magi kept many of the power words secret. There were some who learned the secret words and could not conjure the power because, "words of power are an individual manifestation," and this is the Ninth Ancient Law.

In explaining this ninth law, have you heard a word or a melody that brought on a rush of remembrances from your past? This is an example of a word or a song of power. Whenever you remember that specific word or melody, it has a very specific meaning to you and you alone. For you, the effect is highly individual. For example, the Magi's quote, (Ka gee ma, yaog – "Young no more"), has no power when non-Magi say it, but to the Magi it represented the ultimate power to ward off evil and banish it forever.

Remember that you are the composer of words of power, and you can cause an effect through the use of those words.

How to Create and use Words of Power

If every time you felt good, whole, healthy and full of energy, and you said the word "Peace," for example, and you practice saying "Peace" every time you were in that state of being, peace would become a personal word of power for you.

Then, on a day when you're not well or felt out of sorts and you said "Peace," you would start to feel more peaceful. Each time you said peace, you would feel better and better until you were back to normal. Having reached this stage in your development, if you saw another one, who was not feeling well and you said, "Peace" to them, they would begin to feel better. Once again, the power has become the word and the word the power, and you are projecting that power whenever you use that word.

You can make up any word you wish to express any power you wish. But, it is only through constant association with the effect of the word, and through practice, that power becomes one with the word. These are the songs of magic, your songs, your words and your magic.

Remember with the words, "We must matter," uttered by the Father/Mother of Creation... everything was born. The sons and daughters of earth have that same ability. What songs will you and your students compose for the future?

As there is power within word, there is also power within the hands. You must be sensitive to the power within your being, and then you will believe in your power to lay your hands on another human being to help them heal. You must believe in your power, and you must believe that it is strong enough to execute the desired effect. When you feel the power within you and, you have the will to direct the power, then you must use it.

Laying on of Hands

If your friend has a headache, try the following technique. Place your index and middle fingers gently against the subject's temples, with the remaining fingers touching the sides of the face. Press gently and say to the subject, three times, "Your headache is going away." As you say the words, feel the energy moving from your fingers to the temples and throughout the whole head area. Now, release the pressure. In a few minutes the headache will be gone. If the headache persists, you may try this technique two more times only.

If whatever ailment you are treating does not disappear by the third laying on of hands, you may need to move to a more advanced crystal, white light, treatment that I will guide you through in the months to come. Also, always keep in mind that most illness is a cause of internal, individual karma or projections, cast by negative individuals, around the one you are trying to help. It is always advised that you and that person meditate together, asking that the true cause of the symptoms be revealed.

Always, as soon as possible, after laying on of hands, wash your hands with soap and hot water. You may possibly take on the symptoms of your subject's illness, within 24 hours, if you do not.

Under no condition should you try to heal someone, if you are under the influence of outside agents, such as alcohol or drugs. It could have severe repercussions on your own "well-being." Stay in control and be aware. Try at all times to keep your own body as healthy as possible. Maintain the beauty of your mind, body and spirit to the best of your ability. The healing energy you are channeling, will heal you, as well as your subject, but it is best that you feel grounded and stable, prior to laying on hands. The more you channel the energy, the clearer your channel will become.

It is highly recommended for all humans to be attuned to the God-force energy frequency that has been re-discovered in your age. The human that received this energy in the early 1900's has called it "Reiki." The more humans, who have their vibration shift to this elevated frequency, the better chance your race has to survive and thrive.

We have all at some time or another suffered intense pain that has distracted us away from all other matters in our lives. No matter how much you tried to ignore the pain, it was able to distract you totally. Pain robs the body of energy. The same is true of ill health. Reiki will first and foremost help you heal yourself.

Remember, unless you are in control of your faculties, you cannot help with the healing of another. The saying, "physician, heal thyself," is appropriate to our understanding of energy, Will and the laying on of hands.

In conclusion, no matter what books you have read or what people have told you about magic words, spells orientation... there is no power unless you believe in it. The power comes from within you--from your faith, powers of manifestation and Will Power.

Keep yourself in good health, be active, laugh and enjoy life. For, in a healthy body resides a strong will, and the potential to develop positive power.

The Ninth Ancient Law of Wisdom is: **"Words of power are an individual manifestation."**

End of Transmission

Begin Open Channel

Lesson Sixteen:
King of Clubs, received November 8, 1989
Book of Wisdom, channeled from the Hierophant:

"The more you know the more "Knowing" will come to you." ERU

Dear Brother Hermit and Teacher,

Let me speak about my great homeland, Atlantis. It was once the most powerful nation on earth, much like the United States of America is today. My people had the greatest wealth, the most industrial and scientific communities the world has ever known. The High Priests and Magi of our day acquired the ability to communicate, with our cosmic brothers all across the universe. They shared their wisdom with us, which expanded our power, might and resources. We quickly learned that where there is great power, wealth and illumination, shadows form and, in the shadows, darkness started to grow.

That darkness among some of my people started to awaken dark spirits that the Creator had Archangel Michael entomb on earth, during the beginning of time.

The son of the great deceiver, Satan, was drawn to Atlantis to learn our secrets and weaknesses. He fed the ego and minds of the weak-spirited of my people, who went on to seduce the minds and bodies of our children. There became a division among my people, as the darkness grew ever larger, until it started to spread from Atlantis to neighboring continents.

Our cosmic brethren warned the ten Kings of Atlantis that if the spread of the dark infection did not stop, and the Atlantians didn't regain control of their righteousness, the continent of Atlantis and all of her people, would perish from the earth.

Before the last great battle, King Atlas had my teacher, Master ERU, place four thousand of our purest and wisest people aboard ships. Their humanitarian mission was to spread the knowledge and wisdom of the "Knowing" to the four corners of the world, before it was lost forever.

Six of the ten kings and the Ancient Masters then tried to rally the good people of Atlantis to put an end to the darkness, but the Sons of Darkness were too many. They overpowered the Sons of the Light. Our only hope rested with our righteous voyagers far out at sea. The darkness spread like a red tide across Atlantis. Then like a plague of locust, it focused on all the lands of the earth and would not stop, until it extinguished the stars.

When the cosmic alliance came to neutralize Atlantis, Archangel Michael intervened, by championing my people. Michael said that the darkness only threatened earth, and until it threatens the universe, the great human experiment would be allowed to continue. Since the people of Atlantis were far more advanced than other civilizations on earth, and travel through the cosmos was but a hundred years away, the great continent and all her people were viewed as an immediate threat.

Michael, being the first-born angelic son of the Father/Mother Creator, had the authority to move all that Atlantis was into another vibrational dimension, placing our lost continent and our people on his planet, Jupiter, for safekeeping. Michael separated the Spirits of the Sons of Light from the Sons of Darkness. It now swirls around us, but can no longer penetrate our being, so we can live forever in peace.

All that was Atlantis is now the Great Red Spot of Jupiter; the violent storm that has been raging for thousands of years. The red storm that swirls around us is the Sons of Darkness, still trying to find their way back to earth to re-claim their bodies. All was lost because of one man's lust for misguided pleasure.

I tell you my story because the darkness that spread from our lost continent and infected all the other continents of earth is, once again, threatening the Great Cosmic Brotherhood. Think about how far humans have jumped, since man's first flight in 1903, their first rocket in 1944, their first man walked on the moon in 1969, their first space station in 1971 and their first probe of the atmosphere on Jupiter in 1973. Believe me, there is a red dragon on Jupiter that humanity does not want to awaken again.

The warning has been given. Don't wait until it's too late to reflect the darkness away from each other. It will always be around you. As we discovered, darkness vs light is a test of human intelligence. Which energy will the human intellect feed on? There is a current saying on earth, "The Devil Made Me Do It!" That's not true. The greatest gift the Creator gave us all is free will. We choose our fate. The worst deceptions are when we deceive ourselves. The worst lie is when we lie to ourselves! The negative spirits that are still trapped on earth may influence humans, but the actions of that individual are solely the responsibility of that human.

I would like to take you on a trip back in time to my homeland, Atlantis. Once we journey there together as it was once on earth, you will be taught how to Astral Project to Jupiter's Great Red Spot and experience other dimensions. Hopefully one day my teacher, Master ERU, will help construct a Star-Gate on earth from which all is possible.

Let us start our journey, by using the relaxation meditation described in Lesson One. Then read slowly, my description of Atlantis and the Story of Seth. As you read the story, certain images and measured distances will be imprinted in your mind. Atlantis will come alive, again, for you. When you have finished reading, choose about an hour of time, when you can lay down and astral project to Atlantis' time on earth. Once you have mastered astral projection, you will glimpse a world that has not been seen for thousands of years. There is much to be seen.

ATLANTIS

The Lost Continent of Atlantis lies between Africa and North America. Its landmass once took up the area in the Atlantic Ocean known today as the Sargasso Sea, just twenty-five miles off the coast of Myrtle Beach, South Carolina. Atlantis extends down and through the region known as the Bermuda Triangle.

Relax, we are on a vessel called a Felucca, in the Great Sea of Atlantis on the Bay of Alta. The waters have a slight chop to them, as our vessel rocks gently.

The continent of Poseidon, which is also called Atlantis, is about twenty million square miles. The capital city, also called Atlantis, held an area with its plains around it of seventy-nine thousand two hundred and seventy-one square miles. There were ten districts, or kingdoms, that made up the continent. A sub-king ruled each of these districts. The senior King, Atlas, ruled over central Atlantis. He presided over yearly gatherings of the other nine kings. King Atlas set up a series of roadways that connected the ten districts and allowed trade and communication between all ten kingdoms.

From our Felucca in the Bay of Alta, we see that very high mountains come down to the bay forming its limits. On the north side of the bay, in the wall of the mountain, is a cave about three hundred feet wide and one hundred and fifty feet above the surface of the water. This is the entrance into the capital of Atlantis. The cave brings us to the other side of the mountains and is about two miles long. We feel like the earth is swallowing us. As we move through the dark water, the wake of our ship disturbs illuminatus jellyfish that light up the walls and waters all around us. A pod of young whales and dolphins lead us toward the exit.

Upon leaving the cave, we see a watercourse or canals, coming in from the North, East and West. The watercourse from the West and the East is a moat that encircles the city and the Plain of Atlantis. It is over six hundred feet wide, one thousand one hundred and fifty miles long and is fed by the melting snows from the mountains.

The next thing you see, as we sail North, is a great wall arching over and around the city, and it harbors seven and a quarter miles out from its center. The wall is actually forty-five miles long. The stone blocks on the wall are cut so tight that a blade of grass cannot be wedged between them. The stone blocks that make up the wall are black, red and white in color.

From the wall, we sail into the first harbor. Although the watercourse is three hundred feet wide, the walls on either side go straight up about eighty feet. There are stone bridges every so often, crossing above us, giving the impression of a royal receiving room in a great palace or the entrance to a great temple.

The harbors are rings around the city. From the wall that we sailed under to the first harbor that encircles the city, is approximately five and a half miles. The harbor is two thousand, one hundred and twenty-four feet wide and nine miles around the heart of the city. It has merchant ships from the major trading countries. There are many Atlantian ships of war also in the harbors. At the docks, there is an abundance of soldiers and beasts that are part man and part animal. These beasts are used to load and unload ships. Some of them wear an Egyptian Ankh around their necks.

To reach the second harbor, we must sail North, through a covered canal two thousand, one hundred and twenty-four feet long and one hundred feet wide in this land ring. On this ring of land are quarters for the land and sea armies that defend Atlantis. There are also beasts and "Things" lodged there. They were created to give pleasure to the jaded men, who dwell in darkness. All kinds of vice and fornication is found here. The smell of this area is carnal. As we sail to the second harbor, we might remember stories of the beast--half man, half bull, that escaped and stayed hidden in the subterranean caves on the island of the Crete. I speak of the Minotaur.

Upon reaching the third harbor, the ring of land, it is where everything is beautiful. This Harbor is one thousand, one hundred and thirteen feet wide and four and a half miles that run around the heart of the city. This land ring has glorious gardens and colorful villas. It is a patchwork of color and splendor. Herein live the generals and the city guards. In its harbor, there are soldiers in different colored uniforms of blue, red, gold and silver. Our trip to the third harbor is no different from the last, with the exception of length. We would only sail one thousand, two hundred feet to enter the inner harbor.

The final harbor encloses the Acropolis, the heart of Atlantis. When entering the last harbor, you would behold a sight that is hard to explain in words. The island is enclosed in a wall, covered with copper. Six hundred feet long and at the base of the Acropolis, is a wall of tin. Around the actual Acropolis is a wall of Orichalch that gleams like fire, when lit by the Sun and Moon.

In the area between the copper and tin walls, are the homes of the wealthy, advisors and relatives of the king. There are also the baths, libraries and shops for the wealthy. Within the Acropolis are the palace, the temple dedicated to Poseidon, the sanctuary sacred to Clito, and the sacred hot and cold fountains.

Most of the buildings are of Orichalch, with gold or silver etched into the overall design. There are rare trees and flowers, not to be found in any other place on earth. The air is filled with the most pleasant perfume from the soil and vegetation. If one was not used to it, one could feel faint from the overwhelming fragrance.

Beyond the great stonewall, that encloses the capital city and its harbors, lays a great plain for two hundred and fifteen miles to the North. It is dotted with cities and villages. There's also a vast network of canals on the plain for irrigation and navigation.

Most of the plains people are good people, Sons of the Light and those of the Ancient Laws. They help each other and are at one with each other, as they are with the Creator. They are unified in a great force that only the priests and Magi know how to direct.

The largest parts, of those that live in the cities, are Sons of Belial and the Darkness. Life has no value to them, as they live only for their own pleasures. They rob, rape and murder, without a second thought, with no shame or remorse. Those, who resist them and their captives, are taken to a place where their physique is altered, changed, and remodeled into grotesque monsters that are called "Things."

Anyone who gives sanctuary to a runaway "Thing" and caught, was turned into a "Thing" for his or her punishment. Many of the Sons of the Ancient Law became "Things" for showing compassion and giving sanctuary. The Sons of the Ancient Law are pacifists, who refused to defend themselves and were easy prey for the Sons of Darkness to feed upon. It was not always this way in Atlantis. I will tell you more in other lessons.

I now return you to your world, now that you have been able to glimpse mine. Our two worlds were much alike. We under estimated the weakness of our people. We fought back, but it was too late and the darkness destroyed everything. Now learn how to astral project and make better your Astral Spirit before the same happens to your world. We failed because we didn't arm our children, with the power to see through the deceiver's seductions. Enlighten the children and save your world.

End of Transmission

Begin Open Channel

Lesson Seventeen:
  Queen of Clubs, received December 8, 1989
  Book of Wisdom, channeled from the Hierophant:

"The more you know the more "Knowing" will come to you." ERU

Dear Brother Hermit and Teacher,

As I was sitting here, gazing into a pool of water, many remembrances came to me. As though the grains of sand had stopped their perpetual falling in the hourglass and the clock pendulum could come to rest... the past has become the present and the future is in the beating of your heart.

I saw an event of my youth that I had all but forgotten. It took place one evening, in my meditation cell, when I had not yet learned the importance of the Second Ancient Law: "The door to the psychic world is not opened with a ram, but with the slightest caress."

I had been practicing relaxing my body. Then a thought came to me that my being should leave this cell, as a locust beetle leaves his shell, during the heat of summer. I used all the energy I could gather to break free, but nothing seemed to happen. I tried harder, and it seemed as if in vain. You see, youth have little patience, and waxed ears that listen don't listen well. Youth is easily frustrated, and I was young.

Now I was tired and dry. I had a thirst for something cold to drink. So, I rose from where I was seated and went to fill my cup with cool, fresh, water. As I re-entered my cell, my mouth dropped open. Before me, seated, I saw me. I dropped my cup, but before my cup reached the floor, I was back in my body. From my seated position, I saw my cup hit the floor, break, and water splash out. I sat there, dazed... looking at the broken cup in the center of the water.

I thought to myself, I remember rising and leaving my cell to fetch the cup of water. How could I have been so completely aware of all of my actions and not know when I left my body? I thought each step out over and over. I was there, yet, my corporeal body was here! When did I leave my body? Was it when I became thirsty? Then I remembered. At the moment, the thought came to me to rise up, and I did, there was a singular sound like a hollow "pop" sound. Later I came to know that it is this "pop" sound that indicates a separation of our physical and spiritual bodies.

I have marveled that when we leave our physical body there is no wall solid enough or door strong enough to bar entrance. There's no place on earth or in the heavens that we cannot go to, or enter. Cold and heat have no affect on us. We are totally free to roam where we will.

There are records of people being in two places at the same moment in time, yet miles and miles apart. This is called "bi-location." These out of body experiences are also referred to as Astral Projections.

Hearing and sight are enhanced during astral projecting. You can hear sound that normally cannot be heard. Colors are so much more intense and yet it seems to me that the other senses do not seem to be as sharp; if anything, they are lacking in comparison. Along with those heightened senses, is a sense of being at peace, in excellent health and buoyant. The experiences are so exhilarating that you wish you could stay in that state forever. The moment that these thoughts come to you, unfortunately you find yourself back in your physical body.

The ancient priests of Atlantis taught astral projection only to those initiated, tested and proven in the Ancient Laws and Sciences. Let me tell you more of the downfall of my homeland, Atlantis.

Seth's Story

Once, long ago in another age of men, a young man, Seth by name, entered into the Ancient Wisdom Schools of Atlantis. He was very intelligent and handsome. He walked, with a princely bearing. Seth found favor in the hearts of all who met him. For all thought him to be a good, honest and kind person.

This was all a mirage. He was in truth an ugly, hideously, repulsive beast. He used a vision of beauty to lure people to him, so he could fulfill his lust to control their very souls. He could not let one day go by, without feeling the soft flesh of another against him, as he played out his animalistic games. Once he had your body, he would not stop, until he possessed your soul. Moreover, he sought to learn the ancient knowledge so that he could enslave all Atlantis into serving his controlling addiction. Seth's desire was to be the dark force that would corrupt and destroy Atlantis.

A Magi teacher, not knowing Seth's identity by reason of his trickery, began to teach him how to use the ancient laws and powers of the Magi. First, the priests gave him food to develop his physical body and brain. It was a yellowish, brown, fatty substance, with white dove egg yolks and fish eggs mixed into gruel, and was consumed three times a day. This increased memory and allowed Seth to maintain the knowledge he received. Slowly and methodically, they began to teach Seth. Unbeknownst to them, they were feeding power to an incarnate Son of Evil.

Then came a time when Seth was to learn about astral projection. He had been waiting for this moment for some time and his time had arrived. Now he would force the Atlantians to serve him. As Seth corrupted all who he came into contact with, and created an army of followers, he awakened Belial, the Prince of Demons and Son of Satan. Seth invited Belial to inhabit his body, becoming one with the Dark Spiritual Forces that lay dormant within the earth.

That was the beginning of the Great War between the Sons of Light and the Sons of Darkness. Seth taught his followers to astral project, so they could lay waste to the spirits and minds of Atlantis, without being seen. As their dark spirits passed through towns and villages, their influence came over everyone they touched. Goodly people became corrupt in the blink of Seth's evil eyes.

Queen Kei Sophia Pistis, of the High Council of Atlantis, was pregnant with a very special child that was to be born from a blue orb sent to Atlantis from the Creator. The King commanded the Magi to safeguard the Queen and promised heir to the throne. The boy child was to bring peace to the land. The Arch-Demon Prince Belial, planned to have Seth kidnap Queen Sophia, so the dark prince could remove the orb and raise the child as his own. The kidnapping attempt failed, but Seth sliced the child from her body to recover the blue orb. The child died and the blue orb with it. The queen was left for dead. King Atlas fell into deep despair, and he was useless to his people.

ERU, an Ascended Master and Chief Magi, was guided by Archangel Michael to raise an army from within the Sons of Light, to counter the evil cancer that was spreading out of control across the land.

Because of the depth of Master ERU's unconditional love for his Queen and King, and the brutal slaying of their unborn son, the Creator gave the Ascended Master the authority to combine angelic spirits, within the bodies of Sons of Light and Magi warriors. They became known as Angel-Knights. It was the fusing together of two beings, from different dimensions, into one. When the time came for Angel Michael to fuse with King Atlas, Michael saw that the king's grief was too great, so he chose instead to infuse with the Ascended Master.

Master ERU was then shown, in a vision, how to construct a protective Star-Gate Portal. The device would allow King Atlas' army to move freely between dimensions, undetected by the armies of the Dark Prince Belial. He was also shown where the resting bodies of Seth's followers were hidden, while their dark spirits roamed the countryside, possessing the bodies of the weak minded.

Moving the suffering body of the Queen into the Star-Gate for protection, Michael fused the Archangel Raphael, with the Pistis, so her spirit could rise strong to fight against the darkness. Using very powerful binding words, crystal beacons, talismans and a commitment to righteousness, the Angel-Knights, led by the Michael/ERU, entered the Star-Gate. Leaving their mortal bodies behind they all astral projected to where the bodies of the Dark Sons were hidden.

The Angel-Knights severed the silver, lifeline, spirit cords from the bodies, so their dark spirits could no longer enter. Thus, their bodies withered and died. Unfortunately, their dark spirits lived on as a red evil storm cloud that continued to corrupt and influence the people of Atlantis.

In a final act of defiance, Seth gave up his beautiful body and fused with Prince Belial, as ERU had done with Michael. (To maintain the balance of the Universe, if a power is given to the light, it must also be shared with the darkness.) Calling in the dark spirits of his followers, they became a great, giant, horned, bull-like "Fire Beast," with brutal winds that spread out in all directions, ravishing everything in its path.

The two forces met on the Plains of Megiddo, where they clashed for what seemed like an eternity, but the Forces of Light were too few. Before the Angel-Knight warriors were consumed, by the demon's wrath, Archangel Michael had our spirits sent back to the Star-Gate, and we were all projected into other times and dimensions. We, the mighty 144,000, now stand guard over the evil red tempest on Jupiter, which is the remnant of Seth's army and remains of Atlantis.

It is our destiny to try and return to earth every five hundred years to align with 144,000 modern day Sons of Light, committed to the empowerment and protection of God's sacred children. There is an ancient saying that is known to many cultures around the world that tells our legendary struggle:

*"**When goodness grows weak and when evil increases, we will make ourselves the bodies. In every age, we come back seven-fold, to deliver the holy, to destroy the sin of the sinners, and to re-establish the Divine order of righteousness.**"*

Preparation for the development of Astral Projection

First and foremost, the seeker must develop a real desire to astral project. This desire must be conscious, as well as subconscious. Next, seekers must become familiar with their bodies. They must come to know what they look like from all angles. This can be done through the use of photographs and mirrors. Lastly, they must know that the experience of astral projection is a happy feeling. With this method of astral projection, you can realign with the spirits of the first Angel-Knights and Sons of Light, to be guided on how to resist the dark forces that still inhabit the earth.

How to Execute Astral Projection

1. Sit or lay in a comfortable position. Say, "It is my wish to astral project and be safe-guarded, by the Angel-Knights and Sons of Light. My intentions are good, and I am a righteous being.
2. Relax with your eyes closed.
3. Concentrate on your heartbeat, and tell your heart to slow down.
4. Feel yourself, as a separate entity, inside of your body shell. Your
5. body has a consciousness, and your spirit has a super consciousness.
6. Intensify your desire to leave your body. Let your spirit start to stir, within your outer shell.
7. You will feel a numbing sensation, followed by a pleasant rising or buoyant feeling. Slowly allow your spirit to float up, out of your body shell, connected by a silver cord, connecting to two life forms. The cord will stay connected no matter how far you travel. Ask that your Angel-Knight guide safeguard your silver cord. If it breaks, you will not be able to find your way back to the body.

If you are not floating outside of your body by now, tell your eyes to open and start again. Keep practicing. For some it takes a few days. Some can't achieve astral projection, because of mental blocks and physical ailments. It's not for everyone.

During your astral projection, you will notice a silver, white or gold cord, streaming from your forehead, belly or foot. This is your lifeline; never allow it to be severed.

Warning: Remember the story of Seth. Be careful who you teach astral projection to. This method has been programed to only work for those of a good and righteous nature. We also would not recommend astral projection for anyone, who has a damaged or weaken heart. It could be dangerous to their physical health. They may slow their heart to a point of stopping. Many people experience astral projection during sleep or after a trying event in their lives.

One Seeker Re-called: "I saw myself laying on the operating table. The doctors were doing the surgery; two nurses were assisting. I watched the whole operation and heard every single word they spoke. I didn't worry about my body being cut. In fact, it was a feeling of disinterest or 'so what' attitude. Then I seem to realize or ask myself, 'What am I doing up here?' At that moment, I was quickly driven back into my body."

Another Seeker Related: "One night, after I went to bed I became aware of what seemed to be a gentle swaying. It was almost like sleeping on the boat. I thought how pleasant this feels. I opened my eyes only to see myself sleeping in bed. It was an unbelievable situation to be in. I was seeing myself here sleeping in my bed, as though I were two separate people. I could hardly believe it, when all of a sudden I was sucked back into my body."

There are also those who have stories of falling in their sleep. The majority of time, that is the re-entry of the spirit back into the body taking place. The subconscious recalls it to our consciousness mind in the form of a dream, in which we are falling or rolling off the edge of something. The person never hits the ground. You land back into the body.

End of Transmission

Begin Open Channel

Lesson Eighteen:
  Jack of Clubs, received January 8, 1990
  Book of Wisdom, channeled from the Hierophant:

"The more you know the more "Knowing" will come to you." ERU

Dearest Hermit and Teacher,

In keeping with the story of my people, it should be known that there were four thousand of the wisest and most compassionate Magi and Sons of Light chosen to leave Atlantis, before the last great battle. They were messengers sent to the four corners of the earth to share the knowledge of the "Knowing," with other thriving cultures, before the knowledge was lost forever. Their mission was to help humanity avoid the fate that was about to befall Atlantis. It is always important to know the history of something, in order to grasp its true meaning. Since you will channel these messengers in the future, you need to know their story.

Some migrated to Mayra and were to become known as the Hopitu Shinumu, known today as Hopi Indians, the Indigenous people of North America. Hopitu means peaceful ones, a fitting name for the Sons of Light. Others went to Oz and founded the great Incan Empire. A small group sailed to the western shores of Italy and they, the Etruscans, fathered the Roman Empire. The largest group of all moved to Mizraim, which they called Egypt. As the Atlantians scattered far and wide, they took their knowledge with them. It was a time for a new beginning, a new life and a chance for some to elevate their lives.

The Sons of the Ancient Laws sought to help the less fortunate. So, in Egypt they built a new Temple of Light, to correct the physical and mental structure of the "Things," and restore them to their original forms.

The natives thought the "Things" to be gods, since they came in such different forms, part man and part animal, and possessed such power and wisdom. Here they could live a life of freedom. They were no longer slaves to Seth and his Sons of the Darkness. They could teach others the principles of irrigation, agriculture, writing, reading, the arts and sciences. Thus, with such humble beginnings, they began to shape and build a new empire.

By using their knowledge of the great forces of the universe, and manipulating them, they were able to levitate stones larger than can be moved by the modern machines of today. This was a process that utilizes the sound vibrations of horns and drums to make the stones almost totally weightless. And by using this knowledge, they were able to build the most beautiful edifices ever known to man. The most prominent are the Sphinx and the Great Pyramid. They built great structures about twenty thousand years ago, on many continents, that reflected not only Atlantis' engineering capability, but also the depth of their knowledge of architecture, mathematics, astronomy, geography, geology and navigation.

The main designer was a priest of the Ancient Law, by the name of Ra. It was his purpose to incorporate into the structure, mathematically, all the knowledge of Atlantis. He worked for several years on the design before building occurred. Many millenniums later, a pharaoh would reconstruct the ruins of the Great Pyramid, as a final resting place for his body. By that time, all of the sheathing with its historical inscriptions, would have been removed and used to build other architectural structures.

The wealth of knowledge that the Atlantians had left inscribed on its marble and copper face was lost to mankind. They knew this would happen, due to their psychic ability. So, near the Sphinx they built a labyrinth, in which they placed their knowledge for future generations. Warehouses were placed throughout the world for the preservation of Atlantian history and scientific knowledge. Because of their knowledge of future events, of and in the earth, these warehouses were placed in such a way, so as not to be exposed until mankind had reached a stage in its development, whereby this knowledge could be used for the betterment of humanity and not to wage war.

The Atlantians had an insatiable love for building and learning. The evidence of their love is found literally all over the world, from the pyramids of Egypt to the pyramids of the Americas. Each pyramid is constructed to be an Electro-Magnetic Perpetual Motions Generator that shoots a beam, into the stratosphere, and connects to the invisible Electro-Magnetic Energy Grid that covers the earth. The purpose of the grid is to maintain earth's balance on its axis.

Without the Electro-Magnetic Grid, the earth would wobble, becoming unstable. And the poles would shift on an irregular axis. In short, the pyramids that have been built on land and into mountains are like Electro-Magnetic Anchors. They help to hold the earth steady, as it rotates on its axis, while orbiting the Sun. Our solar system is also orbiting around a galactic core that is speeding through the universe at a rate of two million, two hundred and thirty-seven thousand miles per hour. I hope you are enjoying the ride.

In the Americas, so that they would be forewarned of earth movements before it happened, they hollowed out a large cave in the earth and built a seismograph. It was a large statue of King Atlas, supporting the world on his shoulder. By the tilting and/or movement of the world on his shoulders, they could tell where and when the next earthquake would take place.

Again, they built great roads and cities where the earth touches the sky. They terraced and reshaped the face of the mountains to try and reproduce another Atlantis and another Garden of Eden. Once again, they sought out the simple beauty in all things. In the western Americas, they learned once again the hardships of nature. Thus, they built their cities in the walls of mountains. This was their protection from the prehistoric beasts that roamed the area. They loved the hard way of life and appreciated all life from this existence.

So that all the past history would not be forgotten, they developed complex rituals and ceremonies to relay their histories. After many centuries passed, the meaning behind the rituals was lost. The rituals became habits perpetuated without meaning... knowledge lost to pageantry. All that Atlantis was and what the words meant, was smothered in the dust of time.

It has only been in recent years that an uninitiated Greek was allowed to enter the Holy of Holies in Sais Egypt and learn a portion of this knowledge and history. I know that this is only a summarized outline of Atlantis and my people's migration, but for now, it is adequate.

You are receiving and sharing the Atlantian wisdoms. It is always important to have some history of how our knowledge spread across the earth long ago. Two things that the Atlantians were most proficient in was astronomy and astrology. To us, they were the purist of all sciences, but the most important of all sciences is that called history. Those scratches, marks, pictures and words that give us insight into the past.

You live in a time when a lot shall be revealed. Ancient secrets shall pave a new way of life. And the ancient stories and legends will be made clear, to bring forth their hidden truths. You live in a time when the veil of ignorance will be removed, and your sight will be restored. As an egg cracks open to bring forth the chick within, so too, will the earth be opened to bring forth the secrets hidden, and the life hidden within.

End of Transmission

Begin Open Channel

Lesson Nineteen:
  Ten of Clubs, received February 8, 1990
  Book of Wisdom, channeled from the Hierophant:

"The more you know the more "Knowing" will come to you." ERU

My Dear Brother Hermit and Teacher,

As I told you when we first met at Mount St. Mary's, "I will teach you and you will be my teacher as well." And teach me you have! We must always be open to learning from everything around us, whether it's a child stepping on an anthill or some nation dropping bombs on the people of another nation. Destruction is destruction. Study and learn from everything. With that in mind, I am reminded of something that happened long ago.

One bright, sunny day, as I was returning to my cell, I noticed my Mentor sitting beneath an ancient tree near a stream. The air was filled with the fragrance of flowers and soft, cool breezes brushed my face.

I walked over to him and asked, if I might sit a while with him.

"Yes! Rest here a while with me." Master ERU said.

He was holding a book in his hand, with blank pages. It seemed rather odd that one should be sitting staring at the blank pages of a book, I thought. Whereupon he said, "look at the pictures with me."

I was amazed to see moving pictures appear on the pages of the book. I sat there for hours, spellbound, as I watched a multitude of mysteries unfold before my very eyes.

Almost as quickly as pictures began to appear, they ended. Yet I know I had been sitting there for hours from the movement of the sun's shadows. It was as if time had sped up and passed me by.

"Enough learning for today." He said. "You better be off. You must go back to do your work."

As I walked back, I thought how wonderful it must be to do these things, to see what my mentor had created for me and how much I had learned. But the most important thing to occupy my mind was the subject of "Thought."

We, each and every one of us, create thought. Most of the time, we are oblivious to the fact and pay little heed to what we have created. Nor are we aware of the impact that thought has on the universe.

A thought is "Power," a living thing. It has form, color, size, exists in time and strength. It is as real as any offspring man could create. It can be experienced by every sense of our being. A thought is a presence that can affect all things physical and non-physical, great and small, living or inanimate--and change form from one thing to another. It can bring forth life and beauty, or it can create ugliness and death. It can cause illusions or become physical manifestations in true material form.

This is represented in the tenth Ancient Law. 'You are what you think, you think what you are."

As Master ERU would say, "What you put in your mind is what comes back out."

You experienced this, as Angel Michael pointed things out to you on the police department. You saw kids growing up in garbage environments. "Garbage in, garbage out." The children just fought to survive in what appeared to be a non-caring system that just kept repeating, generation after generation.

As we grow and pass through our childhood, we are being fed vast amounts of information. Some of this information is not considered to be of very good origin, while the majority of it would be considered good and another fraction excellent knowledge. As we mature, we decide on what knowledge we wish to keep on the path we wish to follow. The more good, wholesome and excellent knowledge we put in, the greater it grows and becomes goodly matter. It then becomes expressed in our mannerism, attitudes, temperaments and our state of mind.

Those around you will notice a glow about your physical being. And great wisdom will eventually flow from you to aid and benefit those around you. People will look up to you and respect you and all manner of miracles that you will work.

Thus, as you think, so do you grow and reflect that knowledge and wisdom. You become a personification of knowledge and wisdom revealed through your thoughts, words and deeds.

In that you are compassionate; thinking of the sorrow and pain of others, and how you might help them, comes naturally without thinking. In this, you are truly what you think. That is why, Master Hermit, you were chosen to help the Archangel and the legacy that was once Atlantis in this, our five-hundred-year cycle anniversary. I see great things ahead. Many of the "Children of Tomorrow" will witness the flaming Sword of Truth, because of your valiant efforts. Had you died, as a child and entered the afterlife, none of what I see can or would happen. It is only you that can be the vessel for change. You and only you.

We think what we are. In this, a person may be in a situation where there is pain and suffering all around them. We're not too sure we want to become involved, but we have no other choice than to help. The situation demands that we figure out a way to help them. Then we, with some reluctance, proceed to try and help. As we work along, we begin to enjoy it and in time develop a love for our work. Soon we are inventing new methods and techniques. So, in our thinking about helping those in need, we become a compassionate state of mind. Thus, we think what we are.

Thought can change in our lives drastically. In fact, thought can be impressed not only on our very lives, but also on photographs, film and light-sensitive paper. Try this experiment.

Thought Photography

This is to be done in a totally dark room. With the use of a special light that does not record on film or light-sensitive paper.

Take a sheet of film or light-sensitive paper and place it, unexposed in a film pack, or seal it with lightproof plastic or lightproof paper. Make at least two packets.

The first is your control to make sure it has not been exposed to light or radiation. The second is the one you will use for your thought projection. So now you have a test packet and a control packet. Take the second packet you have made up and lightly hold one corner between your thumb and index finger.

Create an image or thought in your mind's eye. Concentrate on it, so that it is clear and real as possible. When you have reached this point, while maintaining your concentration, hold the packet about six inches from your face. Then blow a short, heavy, fast breath of air at the packet. As you do this, imagine the image moving from you to the packet. The first packet should develop with no image at all. The second packet should develop an image. This image should be a recording of your thought.

Now you see, even a thought can be recorded in its purest form for posterity.

Reflecting back again to a time long ago during my training, I remember once when I reached my cell, I saw another of my mentors. I asked him "Master, can a man take a thought and create a physical object with it?"

"Yes!" he said, "It is not very easy. In fact, at your stage of development, it would be almost impossible at this time, but let me show you how it's done."

He entered my cell, and we sat on the floor, facing each other about eight feet apart. It was quiet, as though all life and time stood still in expectation.

Creating Thought Objects

The Master relaxed, and a light seemed to glow about him. For a moment, I thought he might have died, for his body seemed to have ceased functioning. Then in the center of the floor an earthen jar began to form from the bottom up. It was as though it were alive and growing, or materializing out of nothingness. I could hardly believe what I was seeing. Yet I knew the master and had seen his abilities at work on many occasions, so there was no doubt in my mind at all.

When the jar was finished, I picked it up and plunked it with my finger, to make sure it was solid. It gave off an unusual resonance, not at all like a jar of fired clay. There were two other things I noticed. It was light of weight for its size and the surface had a greasy oily feeling to my touch.

Then, as I was inspecting the jar, it suddenly collapsed into dust in my hands. The master laughed, as I profoundly apologized for destroying the beautiful jar.

"You did not destroy the jar," he said through profuse laughter.

"I didn't?" I questioned.

Then he began to tell me how he executed his creation. As you move about, your clothing rubs against your skin, removing the dead surface layer of skin cells. As you wash your body, you remove even more of these dead cells on the surface of your body. These dead cells permeate your clothing, bedding and even your living space. The cells are called quasi-matter. Now when one develops telekinesis, one can draw the quasi-matter together to form physical objects.

Telekinesis

Telekinesis is the faculty of moving material objects by thought alone, independent of muscular energy, whether direct or indirect.

This requires the expenditure of vast amounts of energy. Then when the concentration is broken, the form returns to just a pile of dust.

The Masters who seek solitude or a hermit type of existence have been known to create a duplicate of themselves to meet intruders. They have also created them to do their work, while they are in prayer or study.

There are stories about a master, who, knowing he was about to die transferred his spirit into a duplicate of himself.

This was executed, as so it is said, by cutting off a part of his body and replacing it with quasi-matter. Around the part of the body he cut off, he built a younger duplicate of himself. The part of the body he cut off began to replace the quasi-matter with living tissue and bone. After some seven years, he had fully developed a younger duplicate of himself, all of living, growing flesh. As his body was going close to the throws of death, he transmigrated into his younger body. It is said that he's done this several times and, therefore, was the oldest living master on the earth. I speak of the powers of our Master ERU.

The Tenth Ancient Law of Wisdom: **"The Powers of Wisdom consume those who would misuse them, and from that there is no escape."**

End of Transmission

Begin Open Channel

Lesson Twenty:
Nine of Clubs, received March 8, 1990
Book of Wisdom, channeled from the Hierophant:

"The more you know the more "Knowing" will come to you." ERU

Dear Hermit and Teacher,

You are now at the top of the first level in your development on the Path of the Magi.

Congratulations!

It is in you that the Atlantian seeds of knowledge have been planted. Yours is the fertile mind that will bring forth the blossoms of wisdom.

I have started you out with a foundation on which you shall build a majestic structure. It is a structure of strength and power beyond belief. Like the great wizards of old, we are humble in our greatness. We are not here for glory or wealth. Their spirits come to you indirectly. We cannot succumb to arrogant or haughty attitudes, nor boasting or fame.

It is he who says, "Look how great I am," that is small and of little worth. While he, who does such with little fanfare or recognition, is great and most wise.

Of all the Masters and Mentors that I have studied under, not one has ever boasted of the abilities they have taught, nor have any ever professed to be wise, perfect or great. It is truly in this light that they are wise and above all others.

Their only glory is in their pupils, as my only glory rests in you, my Good Knight.

I have given you the foundation on which to build something of beauty or something grotesque. If you decide to build something of beauty, you will give me honor in your glory. For some day you may say, "It's through my Master, the Hierophant, that I have learned these things."

However, if you build something grotesque with your power, you bring shame upon me. For you will say, "It is through my Master, the Hierophant, that I have learned these things." And others will say, "His Master, Hierophant is of the dark lord Satan and his demonic son Belial." So, know that what you do from this day forth reflects on your Master for the rest of the world, as your students will reflect upon you, my dear Master Hermit.

Late one evening, while in the herb garden, a person approached me and said, "It does not seem to be in balance, for one such as yourself, to spend his life in the service of others, to suffer the shame of a bad student. I cannot fathom these things."

I looked upon him and spoke. "If I give one the power to destroy the nation, and he does it, then is it not to my shame that I did not see the evil in him, before I gave him the power?"

The pupil was silent. Then gave his answer. "But Master Hierophant, what could be done if someone were to betray the sacred knowledge you've given him?"

As the last rays of light receded over the horizon I said, "I can only hope to find redemption in the future!"

In closing of this lesson, my brother, you might ask, "What is the eternal moral to this story?"

My answer, if you have not already seen it from the "Knowing," could only be: "Once, long ago in another age, a young man, Seth by name, entered into the Ancient Wisdom Schools of Atlantis. Where he received the powers of the "Knowing" from a Master, known to all as the Hierophant. Seth was very intelligent and handsome. He walked, with a princely bearing. Seth found favor in the hearts of all, who met him. For all thought him to be a good, kind and righteous person. This was all a mirage. I am here, holding back the red tide. I can only hope that through you and the Angel-Knights you teach, I find redemption."

End of Transmission

Begin Open Channel

Lesson Twenty-One:
    Eight of Clubs, received April 8, 1990
    Book of Wisdom, channeled from the Hierophant:

"The more you know the more "Knowing" will come to you." ERU

Dear Brother Hermit and Teacher,

You have elevated to the level Avatar of the First-Degree, in the Order of Magi. You have been taught some of the principles and laws as a foundation on which to build a new and better way of life. There's so much more to learn; new and exciting wonders.

Before we continue on, take some time to go through the first twenty lessons. Refresh your mind on all the topics that you are not sure of. Re-read and practice them, until the techniques and principles become second nature. Don't just read them and think you know, because you won't. If you are to become part of the "Knowing," your mind and powers must grow beyond that of the Forces of Darkness. Remember you are never alone, Michael and I are always with you. However, you are but a speck of light, adrift in a sea of darkness. Never let your light be extinguished, or we all fail.

It is much easier to go over one, two or three topics that you may have forgotten, or that has not inscribed in your memory, than to have to go back over your material when you are much further along in your mental training.

At this stage of your development, you should have progressive relaxation and the first ten Ancient laws, and their meanings committed to memory. Without a good foundation, even the most beautiful structure you erect will crumble into dust.

How Eloi Was Cured of Pride

Before St. Eloi became religious, and while he was still but a working goldsmith, he sometimes amused himself with shoeing horses. He was very proud of his skills and often boasted that he never saw a thing done, by man, that he couldn't match.

One day, a traveler stopped at his forge and asked if he could fasten a loosened shoe on his horse. Eloi gave permission. He was surprised to see the traveler twist a fore leg of the horse out of the shoulder joint, bring it into the forge, and fasten on the horseshoe.

This being done, he rejoined the leg, patted the beast on the shoulder, and asked the smith if he knew anyone who could do such a neat piece of work as that.

"Yes, I do," said Eloi. "I will do it myself." So, he ordered one of his horses to be brought to him, and he twisted the fore leg off. He was not able to get this done so satisfactorily as was desirable. There was a lot of blood and tearing of muscle and skin.

Eloi made a nice horseshoe and fastened it onto the fore leg. When he brought the leg into the yard, the poor horse was laying on the ground dying. Eloi was heartbroken and full of grief saying, "My poor horse tortured and killed by my heartless pride and presumption!"

The traveler said, "Are you truly cured of your pride?"

Eloi replied, "Oh, I am, I am! At least, I hope so. I will never again, with God's help, indulge a proud thought. But why did you induce me to do this wicked thing, by setting me the example?"

"My objective was to root a strong vice out of your heart. Give me the leg," commanded the traveler. The traveler then re-attached the leg and the horse stood up healthy and uninjured. Eloi was filled with joy, but when he went to thank the traveler, there was no sign of him or his steed. He knew then that the traveler was an angelic messenger, and he never broke his promise to God. His transformation was likened to a caterpillar that changes into a beautiful butterfly, and he remained humbled the rest of his life.

One morning, as I was seated enjoying all the beauty of nature that surrounds me, my eyes witnessed a fragile butterfly, slowly making its way out of the cocoon. As I beheld this miracle of nature, I reflected on the similarities between the butterfly and Eloi.

The butterfly scratches his way out of a cocoon, drawn to a beautiful light, as that Eloi is drawn, from his limited world of pride, to the light of truth and knowledge. The butterfly stretches wide its wings and shows forth the majestic colors of its being. Eloi shines forth with warmth and beauty that is also expressed in the colors of his aura.

A beautiful complexion and voice arises, as you use these abilities to help the less fortunate. The change in each student is harmonious with nature. The stars in the microcosm are dimmed, compared to this light that you now possess. You are a very special person. Like the caterpillar, you have changed into a most beautiful manifestation of knowledge, wisdom and light.

As we have been talking about change in our being, let us look deep beyond the veil and touch upon lycanthropy.

Lycanthropy

From the Greek word "Lykos" a wolf and "Athropos" a man, it is the transformation of a human into a wolf. In recent time, it has come to mean the transformation of the human, into any animal shape or shape shifter.

There are three theories on how this is conceived and executed. The first is that the individual uses a form of self-hypnosis and concentrating on the animal he or she wishes to become, and after much practice, does in fact cause a transformation to take place.

It is said that this form was used among the ancient tribes in Africa, Europe and the Americas. Whereas, when a young man had reached the age of puberty, he was taken with the other men of the tribe, into the jungle or forests, where a ritual was performed. In the ritual, the youth transforms into a hyena, wolf, bear, eagle, etc.

The second form is an out of body experience, where one projects the essence of his being, into that of an animal he wishes to become. Someone who projects himself into the shell of an animal then coexists, becoming one with that animal.

The third is when someone constructs a beast out of quasi-matter, with his or her mind, and then projects into that shell to coexist. There are endless tales of such things. I must warn you against ever attempting this practice, since regressing into the consciousness of a wild animal could lead to the dark side, bloodlust and madness. Therefore, please use complete discretion discussing such things with your student/teachers, for the world is already too full of illusion and weak-minded people, seeking to hide from reality in any other form they can find. Remember, Seth transformed himself into an "Oxen Fire Beast," the form he remains to this very day.

Let us move to more important things. As I have stated, now that you have your foundation it is time for you to start building upon it. The day will come when you and some of your students will transform and fuse into Angel-Knights.

I have had many students over the eons tell me that there is no place for them to go and practice developing what they have learned without distraction. Thus, it is time for you to learn two new terms used in the Ancient Wisdom Schools, "I prepare my secret place." And "I go the way to my secret sacred place."

It is now time to prepare your secret, sacred place.

A Secret Sacred Place

Take a few moments to relax and think about that secret place that you would like to have to go to. You may picture in your mind's eye a lush green garden, a pond, a brook or maybe a waterfall. You may imagine an open-air temple or a cave, with walls of crystal that glow in the dark, with a soft blue light. There may be animals in your secret place; birds, deer, tigers and any number or kinds of pets.

The important thing is that you bring into existence a place you wish to go; a place of endless peace and beauty where you can relax, practice your abilities, learn and communicate with your omniscient one. This place must be of your will; pleasing to you and you alone. Don't invite anyone to enter your secret place, or his or her energy could corrupt and destroy it for you. Plus, it will no longer be a secret.

You may want to call on the Angels of the Four Direction to give you a vision of a place where you and they will be at peace. Call on your spirit guides that have been sent to help you map out a place, from their lives, that would best suit you and all that is around you in spirit form. You might also be reminded of a place from myth or legend. Once you have the image firmly in your mind, make a rough drawing or map of what you want to have in your secret, sacred place.

Master Hermit, after your students develop ideas of what they want to create, have them start manifesting it in real life, as you are about to do. However, your Sacred Place will involve manifesting a Kingdom on Earth and Angel-Knights to secure it. It is to become a place where special children come to learn and a place of Sacred Service for the Sons of Light and angelic hosts to dwell.

To start, use progressive relaxation, close your eyes and visualize your secret place. Come to know every tree, bush, rock, column and animal as if they were real corporal objects. Give names to your animals and creations. Do not try and create your secret place in one sitting. Take your time! Each day create and build a little more. Become familiar with each and every thing you create, for you are part of it, and it is a part of you. You are programing everything you touch with the energy Michael put into you on the beach that night, when you received the "White Light." In this you can say, "I prepare my secret place."

One of my students took over a year to create his secret place. He knew every flower, twig, tree and rock. He even knew each feather on his pet owl. Whenever he went there, the air was filled with an aroma, he recalled. It was truly a secret place of peace and tranquility.

It is like working in the garden. You turn over the soil, plant the seeds, dig streams, and create waterfalls, a labyrinth to walk, and maybe even a grand palace. Because it takes some time to do, you come to know every inch of the garden areas, and every stone that was placed there. Thus, so it should be in your secret, sacred place.

When you're finished creating your secret place and you can say, "I go the way to a secret place." You're now ready to partake of a totally new way of life. Have you ever had moments when you were upset and nothing seemed to go right? Then go to your secret place and ask what is the right thing to do. You will receive an answer! When the world seems to be racing around out of control, and you don't know which way to turn...o the way to your sacred place, and you will find peace there. Whenever you wish to meditate, expand your mind's knowledge, be at peace or refresh yourself … go the way to your secret place.

Herein you will discover that a great power resides in your secret place.

Brother Hermit, tell your students when they have completed building their secret place, they will have something that no one can take away. No law can stop them from going there and no amount of sadness can ever enter it. They shall become a part of it, and it shall be a part of them.

Master Hermit, it should be noted that you are destined to help the Angels of the Four Directions and your Good-Knight Students re-establish the Garden of Eden on Earth. The Creator has commanded that Archangel Michael prepare a place of Love and Protection for a very special woman and child, as has been prophesized in Ancient Scripture:

Woman of the Apocalypse

Book of Revelations 13: "When the Red Dragon saw that it had been thrown down to the earth, it pursued the woman. But the woman was given the two wings of the Great Eagle, so that she and her future child could fly to a place prepared for them by Angel Michael and Sons of Light."

End of Transmission

Begin Open Channel

Lesson Twenty-Two:
   Seven of Clubs, received May 8, 1990
   Book of Wisdom, channeled from the Hierophant:

"The more you know the more "Knowing" will come to you." ERU

Dearest Brother Hermit and Teacher,

Have you ever seen medical drawings of the circulatory system within the human body that shows, in detail, veins and arteries? Most every medical book has such a diagram. This blood system transports food and oxygen to each and every cell in the body. Then the blood system carries away the waste from the cells. These are only two of the most important functions of the body.

We also have a nervous system that connects the brain and the spinal column, with various other parts of the body. The nerves conduct impulses to the brain, some of which are interpreted as hot or cold, sweet or sour, wet or dry and pleasure or pain. In fact, sum total of all bodily sensations is the result of the functioning of the nervous system, whether within the body or on the surface.

We had another system within the body, which is the Energizing System. It relates to the sense organs of the ethereal body. This system, when operating properly, has a capacity to exert power over another physical object, without any physical contact, and this is a form of execution of magic in its purest form. The system has hundreds of juncture points, with seven main ones. They, the seven main, juncture points, are referred to as the chakras.

The word chakra comes from the Sanskrit meaning "wheel." If you were to visualize the seven main junctures they would look like miniature suns with paths of energy radiating from the center, giving the illusion of a spokes in a wheel of varying colors. The seven chakras are more sensitive to vibrations and astral influences than any other part of the body. They are also responsible for conditions of higher consciousness and latent, cosmic, energies in man. Lastly, because they are psychic centers of energy, they cannot be dissected by scientific method.

Location of the Seven Chakras

1. The Muladhara or Root Chakra is located at the base of the spine.
2. The Umbilical Chakra is found over the naval, as referred to as the sacral chakra, which is sensitive to feelings or emotions. It also increases control over internal processes.
3. The Spleen Chakra is seen to be over the spleen or solar plexus. Its function is the dispersion of vitality that comes to us in the sun.
4. The Cardiac Chakra is self-explanatory. It is located over the heart and controls the subtle winds.
5. The Throat Chakra governs communication and it controls the etheric.
6. The Third Eye or Brow Chakra is on the brow line in the middle of the four head and has power over elemental beings.

7. The Sahasrara, Crown or Coronal Chakra, is located on top of the head and appears as a rainbow, predominantly crystal clear, violet or colors that resemble the aura. This chakra brings ultimate understanding of Nature's Great Mysteries.

Thus, by awakening the Chakras, they not only have the capacity to exert certain powers, but also they become acute in the reception of vibrations. Let me give you an example of acute perception, or vibration, given to us by our teachers.

A priest was fleeing from a murdering Son of Darkness, who wanted to kill him. He ran into a thick, overgrowth to hide. As it would be, as the killer drew near, he stepped on a branch causing it to snap. The solar plexus relayed the sound to the brain faster than his ears could perceive it. By knowing just where the man was, the priest was able to take an alternate route and escape. You see, development of the Chakras could help save you at a critical time in your life.

Another example to help you understand the power of the solar plexus is:

As I was traveling through a small village on the plains of Atlantis, the road I was on was blocked by a group of people. The people were shouting back-and-forth saying a woman's house should be burned to the ground, for it contained evil demons and imps.

Then one person called out to me and said "Come stranger, decide for us, do we bring the demons out or not?"

I replied, "If you burn down this house and, there are no demons within, you have destroyed this woman's house for naught. And, if there were demons inside, and you drive them out by the torch, where will they come to rest? In your house?"

Suddenly, there was silence. I turned to the owner of the house and said, "Let me enter!" She stood aside and, as I stepped within, I heard a muffled murmur from the throng behind me.

Inside, there was softness, gentleness, in abundance; there was something warm with love, joy and feeling. And, within it was a child, pure and innocent. I could feel its soft, little fingers touch my hand. It was not evil or demonic; it was only a child waiting for his mother. It was feeling alone. I spoke to the child and said, "Soon, your mother will be with you, little one."

I stayed inside a while longer. Then, I rose up and walked outside. Again, silence fell over the throng. I turned toward the woman and said, "Get your house in order, for by the next full moon there shall be no spirits left in your house. And you shall come to know a great peace and joy."

Some months later, a runner reached me with a message that the woman had died and that there were no more demons left in the house. Then, the runner asked me, "Was she really evil?"

I smiled and said, "No. She was a woman that became a mother."

He looked at me, with questioning eyes, and walked away.

It is through the solar plexus that I received the presence and feelings of the child. It was also through this Chakra that I perceived the coming of death of the woman. It was through the awakening of my being that I was able to receive so clearly.

How to Awaken the Chakras

1. Relax! All things come when we are at peace. Use the progressive relaxation techniques I gave you in lesson one.

2. Sit with your back in a vertical position; do not slouch, sit on the floor with your legs crossed and your back erect.

3. Place your hands on your lap or on your knees as though each hand were giving a blessing. Within the little finger and ring finger are bent, side-by-side with them touching the upper quadrant of the ring finger, and two other fingers are held straight with the palm facing up.

4. Breathe in, counting to three; hold your breath counting to three; exhale your breath counting to three.

5. While you're doing this, having established your breathing rhythm, gaze at the monism Star-Gate black circle.

6. When you have reached the point where there is a tingling sensation within your chest, concentrate that energy in the solar plexus. After much practice, you will be able to turn it on and off at will.

Now, heed my words of warning:

Do not start at the Root Chakras and awaken all the Chakras up to the Crown, because in doing so, you will awaken the Serpent of Fire, the "Kundalini." You have not yet been trained to handle this awesome power. When the Kundalini is incorrectly awakened, or brought forth, it can result in your own disability.

When the time for your learning is fulfilled, I will teach you the ways of handling the Serpent of Fire. Until then, review everything you have learned thus far.

End of Transmission

Begin Open Channel

Lesson Twenty-Three:
   Six of Clubs, received June 8, 1990
   Book of Wisdom, channeled from the Hierophant:

"The more you know the more "Knowing" will come to you." ERU

My Dear Hermit and Teacher,

Life is a divine essence that man and all his wisdom and millions of years of thought, is still unable to design. It is the deepest of all mysteries because it is found in so many forms.

Yes, you have probably looked upon crystals and thought how beautiful they are. Yet, has it ever passed through your mind that while you're in your matrix, womb, they are still growing and they are, in fact, living? It is true!

Some forms of crystals are living like the ones you have in each ear. Yes, you have a protein crystal in each ear to help your balance. Next time someone tells you that crystals are just dead rocks with no powers or they're evil, ask why the Creator installed a set in their head.

Have you ever been mountain climbing near a sea, or climbed into a fissure to find a crystal cave? There is a feeling that you become keenly aware of. A welling up inside of you that cannot be explained. It's like a thousand voices singing in unison. This is the real you, full of the awareness of life! Life is all about you, if you would, but perceive it. Even in places you would not expect to find it, there is life.

What of intelligence? If you are so bold to think man is the only intelligent being on the face of the earth, you are sorely wrong. Anything that lives, has a form of intelligence, whether or not science can detect it. The Earth is as alive as is every single molecule in your body. As you, in your awakening, shall come to know.

Take the time to go sit by the sea, lake or brook. Or go for a walk in the wilderness, woods or park. Then observe and feel all the life all around you. Awaken yourself to life and become one with it. You are not alone on this small planet. Life abounds all around you and soon, very soon, humanity will come to know that there is also life in the universe.

In the not too distant future, it will be proven that others have occupied planets in our tiny solar system. They have left their mark to be found. Thousands of people have already seen our cosmic brothers, hovering in the skies. Most humans will fear them; others will welcome them and gain more knowledge about themselves than ever expected. Fear not. The angels that seventy percent of humans believe in are extraterrestrial life forms.

If the truth were known, half of every human being is extraterrestrial. Your human body is terrestrial, because it was created from terra firma, good old solid earth, but the being, spirit or soul has an extraterrestrial origin. It comes to an earth child the moment it takes its first breath. It also leaves the body around the time when the human takes its last breath.

The true nature of the human experiment is only known to the Creator. It is said that, "Humanity has the potential to become the Greatest Life form ever created, if it would just set aside its Terrestrial Emotional Ego and embrace the "Great Natural Gifts" life on earth has to offer."

Most humans have this 50/50 split, let's call them (sub-Species-X). They are fearless, peaceful warriors, seeking knowledge, freedom and fairness for all. However, there is also (Sub-Species-Z), humans that are strictly terrestrial, lacking any extraterrestrial makeup. They are quick-tempered and fearful warriors bent on domination and oppression. They shun knowledge for brute force, living to torment and enslave.

There was a (Sub-Species-Y), that lived between the X and Z Sub-Species. They were the perfect balance of what the creator intended, but lacked the drive to procreate and motivation to acquire the "Knowing." They stayed childlike pacifists, non-violent in nature and moved underground to avoid extinction from the wars between the Sons of Light and Dark.

The Atlantian Keeper of Human History describes their tale as:

The Sons of Innocence decided to go into the earth. They are the only human species that our cosmic brothers connect with and do not fear. There are entrances all over the world, in mountains, under seas and lakes. Yet, many of these entrances have been sealed off because of fear that man on the surface still wages war on their brothers. The surface dwellers still stalk and kill like animals. Thus, they are afraid that the surface dwellers will contaminate those in the earth, with their evil ways. Our Cosmic brothers know the same is true and don't trust the surface dwellers. They are not in control of their emotions.

For many years, I thought how dark, damp and cold it must be living in the bowels of the earth. I felt sorry for our brothers, who lived beneath our feet. Then one day, a Keeper of Histories informed me that I knew nothing of that other world.

As it was told to me, deep within the earth, there is a most beautiful land. It is hot and tropical in nature, with many kinds of fruit bearing trees, unknown to the surface dweller. The forests bear the most fragrant, beautiful, giant flowers ever beheld by man. The vegetation is lush green and pleasing to the eye. All that one could ever expect to see, and more, is found there.

There is a great fresh water sea that one may sail out upon for days, with no sight of land in any direction. The Great Caverns are illuminated by electro-magnetic sun lamps that give off a bright infra-reddish light. The water is so clear that one can see for a depth of ten fathoms (sixty feet), without straining the eyes. The sea is teaming with life and large schools of fish, each averaging ten hands (one yard) long. Everything is in its purest form. Even the inhabitants!

The men are very tall and at least one head above the women. Their hair is light in color, while their skin is a rust or bronze color, because of the light. They look like Greek athletes in some respect. The male children run nude, till about age nine, while the men wear little more than a loin cloth, and the more mature wear togas. They are not sexual people, only coming together during fertility ceremonies once a year.

The women are shorter than the men. They also have light hair. Their skin is lighter than the men's. They are by no means heavy. Their breasts are rather small.

The female children are allowed to run nude until about eleven. The women wear little more than skirts and breast covers.

Their buildings are constructed in ornamental stone carvings of men, women, children, plants and animals that seem to disappear into the red light above. The most striking thing was that there is a lack of doors to bar the entrance from enemies or animals. They appear to have no enemies and live peaceful, undisturbed lives. The people as a whole are kind, loving and caring. They seem to possess no hate, anger or negative attitudes. And another thing, none appear to be rich or poor. It is as if they were all child-like in nature, but lacked a child's humor and sense of wonder.

We know that they have superior intelligence, for they are very close with our cosmic brothers and fly in great ships, through the air around our planet, which have been seen by many surface dwellers. And yet, there is not an abundance of mechanical things to be seen in their world.

At a given time, each day a loud gong reverberates throughout the land. The people all put aside whatever they are doing and go into a gigantic temple where they pray. They numbered less than three thousand.

"Herein is a perfect community. Is it not wise to seal themselves away from any society that might damage their beautiful balance?" asked the Keeper of History.

A History of Cosmic Visitations

Long before the Greek, Roman or Egyptian Empires, there were cosmic friends among the stars. Every ancient civilization has records of such visitors, in fact. Likewise, most every religion found on earth speaks of visitors from the stars. In the Bible it states, under Ezekiel; "A fear spread, that mankind may not survive. Some people, to escape elimination, went into the bowels of the earth. They assume that the earth above them would protect them from the wars in the sky."

There are other ancient records about visitors from outer space:

"In 222 B.C at Rimini, on the Adriatic, there shone a great light, like day, at midnight, and three moons appeared in quarters of the sky."

"Over Arpinium in 216 B.C., something that looked like a small, round shield was seen hovering in the sky."

"In 213 B.C. at Hadria, men robed all in white were seen in the sky, standing around a great altar."

"In 393 A.D. at about midnight, a bright orb appeared near the planet, Venus. It shone with a brilliance equal to the planet. Soon other orbs appeared, darting with haste, about the first. Then they merged into one orb, which lit up the sky for forty days. And behold a whirlwind came out of the north, and a great cloud, and a fire enfolding it, and brightness was about it. And out of the midst of the fire, as it were the resemblance of amber, and in the midst thereof, the likeness of four living creatures. Now as I've beheld the living creatures, there appeared upon the earth, by the living creatures, one wheel with four faces. And the appearance of the wheels and the work of them were like the appearance of the sea. And the four had all one likeness; and their appearance and their work was as if it were a wheel in the midst of all wheels. When they went by their four parts, and they turned not when they want. The wheels had also a size, and a height, and a dreadful appearance; and the whole body was full of flies around it. And went to living creatures went, the wheels also went together by them; and when the living creatures were lifted up from the earth, the wheels were also lifted up with them."

In the ancient Indian Sanskrit text, there are stories of gods, who traveled the heavens in aircraft called Vimanas. They also tell of space wars and the unusual weapons that they possessed.

In 1387, on a cold, December night over Lancaster, England, a great battle was fought, by opposing spacecraft. Hundreds reported, "A fire in the sky, like burning revolving wheels of fire that polluted the air for days."

Of course, there is the most famous modern day report of the spacecraft that crashed in Roswell, New Mexico in July of 1947. First reported as a spacecraft, but later as a crashed weather balloon for fear the public would panic, if the truth were known. In the future, military officers involved in the cover-up will come forward and tell the truth that a spacecraft from outside the earth crashed.

Just about every country in the world has seen them. Our cosmic brothers have appeared to shepherds, kings and astronauts. Now, before the turn of the century, the world will see them. Be not afraid, for they are our brothers and sisters. From one piece of writing, we know this is true (see Figure 15) for it reads, "The establishment of man throughout space is now complete."

Figure 15

End of Transmission

Begin Open Channel

Lesson Twenty-Four:
Five of Clubs, received July 8, 1990
Book of Wisdom, channeled from the Hierophant:

"The more you know the more "Knowing" will come to you." ERU

My Dear Brother Hermit and Teacher,
As you have heard me say on several occasions, it is a joy for me to go out into the world, forest or mountains and perch upon an outcropping of rocks to meditate. On one such occasion, a pupil approached and asked, "Master Hierophant, would you make a magical charm for me?"
"Do you want a talisman or amulet?" I asked. He looked at me, with questioning eyes. I said, "Sit down my son. It is time for a new lesson."

Talisman

A talisman is an emblematic object made out of just about anything, stone, wood, metal, paper, etc. It can take any size shape and color. The talisman may take the form of a ritual, potion, formula or gesture. It is a very powerful charm, with the capacity to change events, influence all living things, human actions and feelings and the stroke of luck. It is created with very specific formulas.

Amulet

An object carried by the owner and believed to give protection against evil and bring about good luck.
An amulet or talisman is a personal thing and should be made by oneself. It has a part of yourself in it, and it is an extension of your super consciousness. All the positive power that one can possibly muster is put into it. Remember thoughts have substance and substance has power.
In the creation of a Talisman, you are given a certain amount of artistic license, until you come to the Qabalistic Talisman, which demands the most accurate, methodical and painstaking care in its production.
Let us start with the simpler, but effective, Talisman. Let us say that you want to improve your business and make money. And since the earth has this attribute, our Talisman will be based upon the earth symbols (See table "B").
Besides the employment of the earth symbols, a passage in the Bible that is emotionally moving and in accord with the desire of the talisman must be found by the recipient of the Talisman.
You may make this talisman out of yellow construction paper and use purple ink to draw and write on it the Bible passage, "Do you not know, I must be about my Father's business."
First take a two-inch square piece of yellow construction paper. In Talismanic magic, the yellow square stands for business, money, employment, practical affairs and contracts. I wish to accent that, so I draw another square within the square. Next, between the two squares I write my bible passage.

As the Emperor, number five card in the Tarot deck, represents the earth, I have placed in the inner square, the crown, scepter, orb and Roman numeral four (See Figure 16).

Front of Talisman

Back of Talisman

Figure 16

On the backside of my square, I have drawn another square within the original square form. Then I draw a second square within, and at forty-five degrees to the first. Between the squares form and the first where I print "Adonia Ha-Aretz" and in bold print "Emor Dial Hectega" at the top. These are the divine names (See table "A"), I write the names of the Archangel and the Enochian King. Between the first Square in the forty-five-degree square I have written, in the upper left, the angel, in the upper right the ruler, in the lower left the king and in the lower right the Alchemical Symbol for the earth, in the center the letter from the Tetra-Grammation, which stands for the earth (See Figure 16).

Thus, the simple Talisman is created, but to use it is another thing. The employment of the Talisman only becomes effective by a stimulation of human willpower through emotional provocation (See lesson three, pages 2 through 4 and lesson fifteen pages 5 and 6).

The next thing you must learn is the value of the letters in the construction the Qabalistic Talisman.

The Number Value of the Letters

THE NUMBER VALUES OF THE LETTERS		
1 = A	10 = Y, E, I, J	100 = Q
2 = B	20 = K	200 = R
3 = G	30 = L	300 = SH
4 = D	40 = M	400 = TH
5 = H	50 = N	500 = -K
6 = V, W	60 = S	600 = -M
7 = Z	70 = O	700 = -N
8 = CH	80 = P	800 = -P
9 = T	90 = TZ, TS	900 = -TZ, -TS

A "-" before a letter means that value is given to the letter when it is used at the end of a word. Example: HEN or H=5, E=10 and N=700.

If a letter does not appear in the chart above, strike it.

Example: FRAN or /F/, R=200, A=1, N=700

TABLE "A"

Elements	Divine Names	Archangels & Enochian Kings	Angel	Ruler	King
Earth-Gnomes	Adonai Ha-Aretz EMOR DIAL HECTEGA	Auriel IC ZOD HEH CHAL	Phorlach	Kerub	Ghob
Air-Sylphs	Shaddai El Chai ORO IBAH AOZPI	Raphael BATAIVAH	Chassan	Ariel	Paralda
Water-Undines	Elohim Tzabaoth EMPEH ARSL GAIOL	Gabriel RA AGIOSEL	Taliahad	Tharsis	Nichsa
Fire-Salamanders	YHVH Tzabaoth OIP TEAA PEDOCE	Michael EDLPERNAA	Aral	Seraph	Djin
Ether-Spirit Akasa	Eheieh & Agla	EXARP HCOMA NANTA BITOM	ELEXARPEH COMANANU TABITOM	Yeheshuah and Yehovashah	

TABLE "B"

Element	Symbol	Name	Tetragrammaton	Value	Attributions	Tarot Trump	Angelic Names
Earth	Yellow Square	Prithivi	(final) HE	5	Business; Money; Employment; Practical affairs, etc.	The Emperor	Hitsael
Air	Blue Circle	Vayu	VAU	6	Health; Sickness; Troubles.	The Heirophant	Vioel
Water	Silver Crescent	Apas	HE	5	Pleasure; Party; Marriage; Fertility; Happiness.	The Emperor	Zaltzel
Fire	Red Triangle	Tejas	YOD	10	Dominion; Prestige; Authority; Power.	The Hermit	Chankel
Ether	Black Egg	Akasa	Shin	300	All matters spiritual.	LAST JUDGEMENT	

We have covered a multitude of information on the talisman. So, take the time to learn the tables and what we have covered in this lesson, for in the next lesson, I will show you how to put it together in the making of the Qabalistic Talisman.

End of Transmission

Begin Open Channel

Lesson Twenty-Five:
> **Four of Clubs, received August 8, 1990**
> **Book of Wisdom, channeled from the Hierophant:**

"The more you know the more "Knowing" will come to you." ERU

Dear Brother Hermit and Teacher,

Now I will speak on the Talisman according to Hebrews. It is one of the greatest keys that "YOD HEY VAU HEY" has given mankind.

Always remember that this is not a toy to be played with. For this wisdom is secret and sacred between man and the Creator. It will take much study before you will begin to affect the forces around you.

The first we hear of the Talisman comes from Moses and Solomon. What does Solomon have to say about its use? King Solomon was in constant contact with the Creator, through the use of the Arc of the Covenant in the Holy of Holies.

"I command you, my son, to carefully engrave in your memory all that I tell you, in order that you never forget it. If you do not intend to use the secrets I teach you for a good purpose, I command you to deliver this testament into the fire, rather than to abuse the power you will have of constraining the Spirits. For I warn you that the benefits from the Angels, wearied and fatigued by your illicit demands, would, with sorrow and agony, execute the commands of God, as well as to those of all such who, with evil intent, would abuse those secrets which "HE" has given and made known unto me."

Now Master Hermit, treat what I say, with the deepest respect. Before we make a Talisman, we have to know what we want to use it for. Since the talisman is governed by the planets, and the intelligence that abides there, we have to know which planet governs what (see Table "C").

382

TABLE "C"

The Planets	What They Govern
The Sun	Temporal Wealth, Good Fortune, Hope, Divination, Experiments and to dissolve Hostile Feelings.
Venus	Friendships, Good Times, Kindness, Love and for Traveling.
Mercury	Eloquence, Intelligence, Business, Science, and Prophecy.
Moon	Diplomatic, Voyages, Messages, Reconciliation and Love.
Saturn	Success to Business, Goods, Seeds, Fruits, and bring Harmony to others
Jupiter	Acquiring honors and things, preserving Health, making friends
Mars	War, gathering Courage, overthrowing Enemies, Discord, Ruin, Destruction, and Death.

Now if you were going to make a talisman, with the attributes of Venus, you must construct it in the days and the hours of Venus (see Table "D").

TABLE "D"

DAYS AND HOURS OF THE PLANETS							
	Sunday	Monday	Tuesday	Wednesday	Thursday	Friday	Saturday
Morning	Sun	Moon	Mars	Mercury	Jupiter	Venus	Saturn
Afternoon	Venus	Saturn	Sun	Moon	Mars	Mercury	Jupiter
Evening	Mercury	Jupiter	Venus	Saturn	Sun	Moon	Mars

Let us continue, each planet has a Kamea or Magic Square. These Magic Squares symbolize a step in the tree of life (See Figure 17). the number of the step on the tree of life, times itself, tells how many compartments the square is divided into.

Example: Saturn = Binah, the third step on the tree of life, thus, 3 x 3 = 9, the Kamea is divided into nine squares.

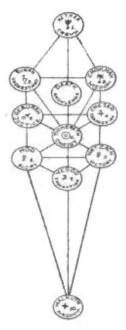

Figure 17 – Tree of Life

Thus, the magic square, divided into nine compartments, three vertically and three horizontally. Next, because there are nine compartments, the numbers one through nine are placed into the compartments, so that when they are added in a straight line; left to right, top to bottom, or diagonally, you will arrive at the same sum, which is fifteen. (See Figure 18.)

TABLE "D"

PLANET	SEPHIRAH	NUMBER	COMPARTMENTS in KAMEA
Saturn	Binah	3	9
Jupiter	Chesed	4	16
Mars	Geburah	5	25
Sun	Tiphereth	6	36
Venus	Netzach	7	49
Mercury	Hod	8	64
Moon	Yesod	9	81
*	Malkuth	10	100

* Some say that "*" is the planet earth, while others say it is a planet that existed between the planet Mars and the planet Jupiter.

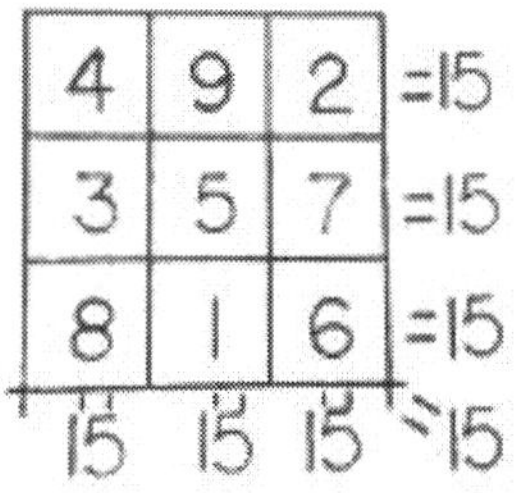

Figure 18 – Kamea of Saturn

Review what has been covered in lesson twenty-four and twenty-five, and for your next lesson, the trilogy of the Talisman is complete.

You will receive in the next lesson the command of the planets, the seal of the planets, and the spirit and intelligence of the planets. With this and my directions, you will be able to create your own Talisman. Make sure you are ready and know what you want or wish to accomplish.

(Note from Hermit: After applying the information given to me by the Hierophant, he guided me to seek out other sources of knowledge that helped me perfect my proficiency level. I have listed the best sources below for your benefit. The most important part of making a talisman is earning the respect of the powers you are aligning with. The best way to do that is, be humble, pure-minded and compassionate toward all things.)

Source Reference Books

The Greater Key of Solomon translated by S. L. McGregor
The Magus, by Francis Barrett

Warning: Remember above all things, these are not toys, but sacred magical instruments that call upon the Angels, Spirits and Powers of the Highest Degrees. So, if your heart is not pure and your nature righteous, your Talisman could backfire, taking from you instead of giving to you, therefore the next lesson should not be entered into lightly.

End of Transmission

Begin Open Channel

Lesson Twenty-Six:
  Three of Clubs, received September 8, 1990
  Book of Wisdom, channeled from the Hierophant:

"The more you know the more "Knowing" will come to you." ERU

My Brother Hermit and Teacher,

Now you have arrived at the making of your talisman. On the next few pages are the Kamea of the Planets, the Planet Seal, the Spirit and Intelligence names, which will you will need to complete your Talismans.

Let us say that your name is Israel. I use that name because that is the name of the Jews, and appropriately, its origin. Let's say, you wish to make new and lasting friends. You would use the Kamea for Venus. Since the days and the hours of Venus are Sunday afternoon, Tuesday night and Friday morning, you would work on the task during those days and hours.

Now take your name and get the Number Value of the Letter as found in Lesson twenty-four, page four. You should combine the "AE" letters as one "A".

EXAMPLE:

<u>I</u>	<u>S</u>	<u>R</u>	<u>AE</u>	<u>L</u>
YOD	SHIN	RESH	ALEPH	LAMED
10	300	200	1	30

Now, taking the Kamea of Venus, if you were looking for the numbers that make up your name, you would see that there is no 300 or 200. So, you must reduce your name numbers by tens.

EXAMPLE:

<u>I</u>	<u>S</u>	<u>R</u>	<u>AE</u>	<u>L</u>
10	300	200	1	30
10	30	20	1	30

On the Venus Kamea, put a small "o" in the compartment with the "10" in it. Now, draw a line from it to the compartment "30." Now continue to "20." Next back to "1." And then end in box "30," with a half circle.

EXAMPLE:

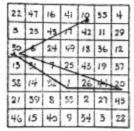

Figure 19 – Kamea of Venus w/name

You have now placed your name in the Kamea of Venus.

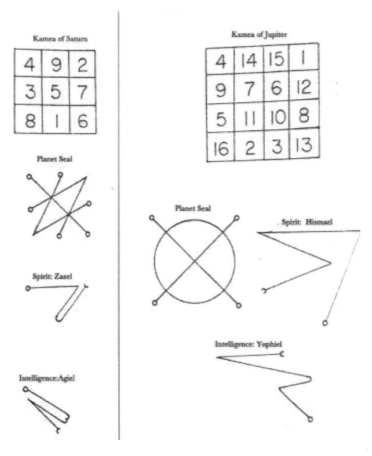

Figure 20 – Kamea of Saturn and Kamea of Jupiter

387

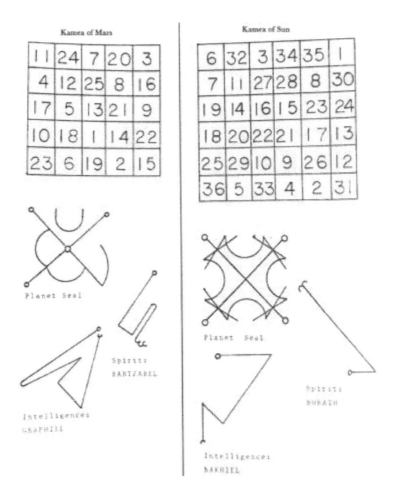

Figure 21– Kamea of Mars and Kamea of Sun

Kamea of Venus

22	47	16	41	10	35	4
5	23	43	17	42	11	29
30	6	24	49	18	36	12
13	31	7	25	43	19	37
38	14	32	1	26	44	20
21	39	8	33	2	27	45
46	15	40	9	34	3	28

Planet seal   Intelligence: HAGIEL

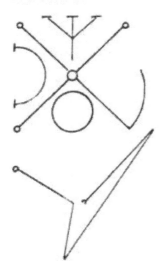
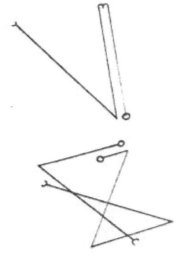

Spirit: KEDEMEL   Intelligence: (Chief of
                         Angels) BENI SERAPHIM

Figure 22 – Kamea of Venus

Kamea of Mercury

8	58	59	5	4	62	63	1
49	15	14	52	53	11	10	56
41	23	22	44	45	19	18	48
32	34	35	29	28	38	39	25
40	26	27	37	36	30	31	33
17	47	46	20	21	43	42	24
9	55	54	12	13	51	50	16
64	2	3	61	60	6	7	57

Planet Seal

Spirit:
TAPHTHARTHARATH

Intelligence:
TIRIEL

Figure 23 – Kamea of Mercury

Figure 24 – Kamea of Luna

Notice that the beginning of the name starts with an "O" or full moon and ends with a "C" or crescent moon.

Before you add the Seal, Spirit and Intelligence on the back of the Kamea, make sure that the names start with "O" and not with the "C" because some have been deliberately switched to confuse the novice, the untrained, and fools.

After your talisman is finished. Feel yourself being charged, as a pink color aurora surrounding your body. Now pick up your talisman, feel it becoming a part of you and you a part of it. Visualize the pink of your being, attracted to your talisman. Now to the four cardinal points, call out the names of the Spirit, Intelligence and or Angels, to do your will... and bring to you a lasting friend. If done correctly, "And so it shall be done!"

Keep your Talisman wrapped in a clean cloth and out of the eyes of others. Never, under any circumstances, let another have your Talisman. Keep it in a Secret Sacred Place where it won't be disturbed.

May all your wishes and wants be granted, just be careful what you wish for. Always think of how you affect everything and everyone around you.

End of Transmission

Begin Open Channel

Lesson Twenty-Seven:
    Two of Clubs, received October 8, 1990
    Book of Wisdom, channeled from the Hierophant:

"The more you know the more "Knowing" will come to you." ERU

Dear Brothers Hermit and Teacher,

When one hears the word dimension, it conjures for many the measurements of feet and inches, centimeters and meters, etc. However, what about states of being?

The first and second dimensions are inseparable. Yet, they are the last to be called to mind. So, let us start this lesson, by reviewing the four dimensions. The first and second dimensions are inseparable. They cannot exist without the other. One is physical and the other is a state of being. The first dimension is often referred to as a dot, for graphic representation. But the first dimension cannot exist unless it exists in time, thus time is a dimension.

The second dimension is expressed as a line. And the third dimension is expressed as a cube, having length, width and height. Remember all three dimensions exist in time, which is also a dimension. Thus, we have four dimensions. Therefore, everything that we see in our physical nature is a fourth dimensional object. The movements of the earth establish our measure of time. Our revolutions on our axis establish our twenty-four-hour day. And their orbit around the sun establishes our year. Thus, the sun, the center of our solar system, also has been a symbol for time. Our sun is a star, and the stars are also an ancient symbol to represent time.

The oldest symbol to represent this fourth dimension and time is now known by the name "Star of David."

Figure 16 – Star of David

We often think of the Star of David (figure 16) as a flat, two-dimensional object. When, in truth, it is more complicated than that. It has length, width and height, but it also exists in time. These are expressed in its construction on the fourth dimensional level.

Constructing a Four-Dimensional Star of David

To start, trace the pattern as drawn in figure 25, on a clean sheet of paper. Now cut out the pattern, but do not cut on the dashed lines. Now punch one hole in the center of each of the squares. Now you should have the pattern cut out; three connected squares, with fold dash lines, and a hole in the center of each square.

Next, fold one outside square, along the dash lines, up; and the other outside square, along the dash lines, down, so that they are at 90° to the center square.

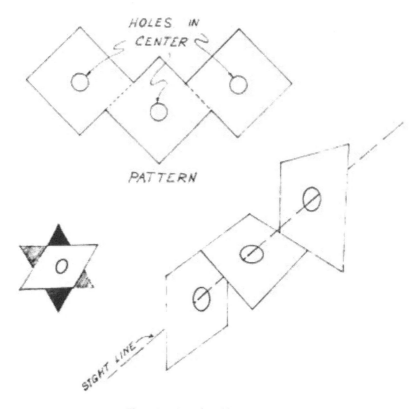

Figure 25 – Star of David Construction

Construction for the Star of David

Now, turn your pattern, so that the holes align by eye. You should now see the Star of David. The squares represent length, width and height... the three dimensions. They, in turn, form the Star, which represents time; the fourth dimension in total. But what then is the fifth dimension? To give it a name, we should call it the "Penetration to Dimension." Because that is just what it is, the penetration of all former dimensions and their subdivisions.

On the fourth dimensional plane, we look upon a cube and, at best, we see only three surfaces that make up the cube, or one half of the surfaces. The other three, we believe are there, but we don't know until we see the cube from another angle. And now above this, we do not know if there is anything inside of a cube. Whereas, in the fifth dimension, we see the inside and the outside, the near side and

the far side of the cube in the same time frame and its constitution (see Figure 26).

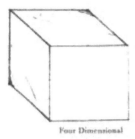
Four Dimensional

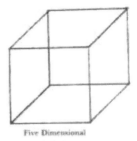
Five Dimensional

Figure 26 – Four and Five Dimensional Objects

Each and every physical form also gives off sound. In the non-living, the sound is absorbed, so to speak, or bounced off the molecules, which changes its wavelength and is then spit back out. In crystals, the sound originates within itself and is transmitted like a beacon. In the living, the sound created is like a symphony. Imagine, sitting in a room, with your eyes closed, and being able to distinguish everything in the room and where it is located, about you, by its sound. Some people, who are blind have developed this ability.

In this dimension, all energy waves would be seen, felt and heard. Can you conceive of what light would sound like or behold what sound would look like? Can you begin to comprehend the sound of heat in its liquid waves as it rises?

The world would be totally changed. It would be filled with sounds and colors, as you have never beheld them before. The slightest sound would dance by like the aurora borealis, a world where every moment would be filled with breathtaking, spine tingling awe. Can you even begin to grasp the thrill of being in the penetration dimension?

What of time? Time will stand still, frozen, never to move again. But we could move forward or backward, summoning the past or present before our very eyes. There would be no secrets left. For every event ever to take place and recorded in time, would be examined, inspected and contemplated by everyone who has ever been born.

Although absent from our physical body, as we know it, our minds would be unified in the one consciousness; at one with all that ever was or will be; at one with the creator.

If we, in our humble development, wish to see the joys of Penetration Dimension and observe the beauty it has to offer, we must help to develop events of beauty for that dimension. If all we do is war with one another, foster hatred for one another and inflict pain, sorrow and suffering on one another, what events of beauty will survive for us to look back upon?

Remember the Third Ancient Law of Love: "The law of love is unchangeable; in that, as you do it to the least of your brethren. You do to your creator."

When have you fed the hungry, clothed the naked, visited the sick or dying? When have you last offered help to someone in need or put a smile on the troubled faces of the forgotten for forlorn?

Why is it only during major religious holiday's that people remember the less fortunate? What about the rest of the year? How many men are in the military, protecting your country, who have no relatives? How many people are in the hospitals, who are alone? Just a card or a flower could make them feel so much better.

Too many times I've heard people say? "I just don't have the time." Are we so important or so busy that we cannot take a few moments to phone someone or send a card? It is a shame when another life has so little meaning. We spend our time asking, "What is the meaning of life?" The better question is "What is the meaning of time?"

We are born on a certain date and time say, 1949 and we die in 2033. Our head stone reads, "Here lies Sir Edward Michael Jagen "He went about doing good things for others." July 22nd 1949 – April 3rd, 2033.

The most important dimension, in life, is the time we are given, as we "dash" through that life creating good memories that must last an eternity. When we move into the "Penetration to Dimension" in the afterlife, all that we did in life is exposed by our "DASH." That is when Heaven, for many, becomes a Hell.

Remember in the end, it's not about the things you owned or how you spent your cash. The only thing that is really important is how you spent your dash.

Make the time! Take the time, before there is no time!

End of Transmission

Begin Open Channel

Lesson Twenty-Eight:
    Ace of Spades, received November 8, 1990
    Book of Wisdom, channeled from the Hierophant:

"The more you know the more "Knowing" will come to you." ERU

Dearest Brother Hermit and Teacher,

One cool, spring morning a voice deep within beckoned me to come out into the forest. So, I rose from my bed, dressed warmly, had my cup of tea and started off on my journey.

The air was cool and invigorating. The warmth of the sun was pleasing upon my face and hands. The air felt good in my chest.

As I walked, I could smell the earth coming back to life. I was happy and it was good. I felt as though I was becoming alive for the first time. All my senses were sharp, and I perceived many things in a new light.

I saw the new life beginning to break through the decayed matter on the forest floor. There were tiny specks of green here and there and everywhere. I turned over a small piece of rotting tree trunk and discovered ice was still present. Most of the day was spent exploring, learning, seeing images of past events and recalling the many lessons I had been fortunate to receive. I've always been filled with awe, upon seeing new life issue fourth, and I remain so to this very day. I was so reminded of my youth.

As the sun passed the mid-day-point in the heavens, I began my walk back awakened by my outing. My mind was recalling many lessons my Masters and Mentors had taught and how they were so much a part of the nature of things. My thought came to rest firmly on my greatest teacher of all, Grand Master ERU. Oh, how I missed him.

He always said, "I will never be any further away than the fuzz on your ear lobe." That thought always gives me comfort, and when I needed a reminder, I would rub my ear.

Suddenly my meditation was broken, by a voice calling out to me from afar. "Master wait! Wait! Please!" A young voice off in the distance called out to me. I turned and beheld a young man running toward me. After a few moments, he was upon me. He was full of joy, smiling like a child. "Yes my son?' I said.

He replied, "I saw you walking before me. You walked as one I have known before, and I knew not where."

Then he asked many questions of my travels to determine where he had met me before. But there were no incidents where at present our travels could have crossed paths. He made many profuse apologies. Where upon I began to laugh. His face expressed wonderment, then an air of having been tricked by some strange wizardry. "Yes! We have met and were very close friends." I began to tell him the things we did together.

He looked at me confused. And thought I had mistaken him for someone else. Yet there was a vague familiarity in what I was telling him, so I said, "And my heart was heavy when you died. For you see, it was in your last life that I knew you." The young man thought for a moment then said, "But Master. The Christians say that man lives but one life on this earth."

If that is so, my son, why is it written in their Holy Book? "…. And the disciples asked Jesus, saying, 'Why then do the Scribes say that Elias must come again?' Jesus answered and said 'Elias, indeed, is to come and will restore all things. But I say to you that Elias has come already, and they did not know him, but did to him whatever they wished. So also, shall the Son of Man suffer at their hands.' Then the disciples understood that he had spoken to them of John the Baptist." Elias was dead long before Jesus was born. And John the Baptist was born about the time of Jesus.

"Master," he said, "Tell me all about my past life? Share with me the good memories you have of me?"

I looked deep into his eyes and saw a sleeping child ready to be awakened, but I said, "That my son, I cannot do! For you see, if I tell you all of your past life then you will not experience the development needed to recall other lives. It will not give you one moment of happiness. It would only rob you of a gift of other, maybe even greater joys."

As we continued to walk and talk, a thirst came upon me, so we stopped by the stream. "Why do we live more than once, Master?" My young friend asked.

"With more than one life, we make ourselves pure, so that we can become of ultimate purity, for our Creator. Let me show you." I replied.

I filled my cup with the water from the stream and said, "The water is the true you. Now if you study the water, you will see movement therein, little things swimming around, small pieces of plant life and specks of dirt. If I pour the water onto the sand, quickly scoop up the wet sand and place it in linen, twist the linen tightly then squeeze the wet sand…he water that falls back into my cup has been made purer."

Each time we pass through a life, we should be striving to make ourselves purer, more compassionate and understanding. This is one of the reasons to know our past lives. If we know our past lives, then we know the faults and weaknesses of those lives. In this life, we are given a chance to reconcile, correct and mend those faults and appreciate the true joys of life and living.

As I looked into the face of my young pupil, I noticed a slight smile come to the corner of his mouth. He said, "But Master what about the Christians, are they wrong in their belief of only living once?" I was stunned by his question.

I wanted to tell him that of course they are wrong. The Atlantian way is the belief in reincarnation, but I didn't want to offend my young friend. A voice deep inside said, "Seek the truth in the reflection of the water."

I wisely followed the advice, telling my student we should stare into the calm water to seek the truth. As we looked into our reflections, my young friend's face turned into that of my old friend and teacher ERU. I, who thought I had seen everything, was stunned.

Master ERU said, "Some people say we live many times. Some people say we never really live at all; we are merely the dreams of a God fast asleep in the center of a giant lotus blossom. Some say a lot of things. What's important is what you believe. Because whatever you believe, if you really believe it, becomes the truth. Let me tell you a story my old friend."

I looked up from the water at the young man and realized I was staring into my face as a young man fresh on my path of seeking the great "Knowing." I looked back into my refection in the water and saw I was wearing the face of my Master, ERU as he continued.

"There was once a time in the beginning when the Creator made man and man's life fed upon the Great Well of Souls. There were only so many souls to go around and re-incarnation was the only way of purifying those souls for their return to the Creator. For thousands of years, humanity was haunted by the sins of previous lives so much so that past life karma made it too difficult for a child to overcome what he brought into the new life and old negative patterns prevailed.

Seeing this, the Creator put a special soul that embodied all the attributes of the Creator in the Well of Souls. That Special Soul found its way to a boy child born in Bethlehem over two thousand years ago. He was the first human born free from the tarnish of past lives. When that child was sacrificed for his beliefs, everything changed. From that day forward the Well of Souls was increased to six billion and every one born receives one life incarnate. Once that one life spirit returns to the Creator if it wishes to make up for not living a positive life, it can ask to be sent back to earth, to help the angels guide a new human through life, by being around them, but never to have a body again."

I have told you how to recall past lives and now, thanks to my Master, past life spiritual energy through the Monism. Another circle form that can be used is called a Mandala.

Mandala

Mandala is a Sanskrit word for circle. A mystical diagram used to attract spiritual powers or for mediation purposes.

The Mandala is found in every ancient culture of the world. Its origin was in Atlantis, the mother of all civilization. As the Atlantians traded knowledge, with the other countries of the world, our secret wisdom spread. Today the Mandala is found all around the world.

The Mandala, when it is charged with powers or spiritual beings to occupy assigned places in the circle, becomes known as a Yantra.

How to Prepare your Mandala

We will draw our Mandala on a sheet of paper for now. It can be drawn on paper or painted on cloth, wood, metal or stone. First we draw a large circle on a sheet of clean white paper, about seven inches in diameter. In the center, we draw another circle about two and a half inches in diameter. The area between the two circles is divided into five equal parts.

After you draw your Mandala structure, we must fill it in. In the center draw something that symbolizes power to you. It can be a physical or non-material object. But it has to be a symbol that you can associate with power. An example would be an Ankh, Cross, Star of David, eyeball, face, a hand holding a sword, etc.

Next we fill in the five segments. When we sleep, we communicate with our subconscious. And since our subconscious has experienced all of our former lives and the lives of those sent to guide us through life. It is thought that through our dreams we come to know our former lives. So, we must fill in these remembrances of our dreams into those segments of the Mandala.

In the first segment, put the color that occurs most frequently in your dreams. For example: blue, yellow red, purple, green, etc. If you do not dream in colors than put your most favorite color in its place.

In a second segment, place scenes of nature that you dream most about, this can include scenes of nature, environments, terrain, trees, rocks, waterfalls, snow covered mountains, a jungle, etc.

In the third segment, draw what structures or buildings you dream most? This can be a skyscraper, cave, pyramid, igloo, tree house, stable, ranch, castle, etc.

In the fourth segment, draw the people in your dreams and the costumes they are wearing. This is a great clue to the past energy that surrounds you now.

In the fifth segment, draw any animals that you dream about. For example: eagle, bear, deer, dragon, wolf, tiger, buffalo, snake, fish, monkey, frog, etc. If you do not have artistic dexterity, you can cut pictures out of books and glue them into any of these segments.

Now you should have your Mandala complete. Place your Mandala on a wall or at least prop it up, so that it is at eye level. Sit in a comfortable position and concentrate on your Mandala as you would your Monism or Star-Gate. Relax and become receptive. Bring an orb of purple light down and all around you, as you focus.

The images on your Mandala will work, as a key to open the door to your past lives and the lives of the human spirits that are around you. After you have used your Mandala for several months, or a year, you may wish to redo it to reflect a more precise awareness you have developed of your energies past and present. Some people develop several Mandalas; each representing a separate past life or the stages of the life they are living now.

Another tool to awaken these past life energy events, is hypnotism. Through hypnotism, people have been able to see events of past lives and the lives of the humans, who are now in spirit, sent to help guide us around the weaknesses the spirit suffered in their lives.

You may be reliving their experiences or tendencies as well. Sometimes we can help them come to a state of peace, with their problems, when we move positively through the same lesson

Let us combine the two and call it "Past Life Energy," whether it is yours or someone else's, past lives affect our present attitude toward people, places, things and even our physical features. For an example, I hypnotized a student who had fear and hate emotions toward a particular race of people. It was while she was under hypnosis that we peeled back the layers of the past life energies through regression. There we discovered she had past life spiritual trauma haunting her. It was from the same race of people she feared and hated.

She had past life spiritual energy that suffered at the hands of this race and thus developed a fear-hate relationship toward anyone of that race. In short, the past life energy was from a human male spirit, who was skinned alive and eaten by this primitive race of people. That is definitely something that would stick with someone, through the ages.

That spiritual energy had moved through the lives of many others for over five hundred years, hoping to find someone who could help him reconcile his emotional turmoil. Realizing it wasn't her problem and understanding his, through several sessions of "Neuro Linguistic Reasoning," we were able to put the spirit at peace. The student has since overcome the hate aspect, but she has not, as yet, overcome the fear of that race of people.

How many times have you come across people that you thought you knew and didn't? It could very well be that it is one of your spirit guides, or recognizing the spirit guides around someone else. It doesn't matter if you believe in re-incarnation or the single life theory. What's important is that you dig deep inside to find out what past life energies you have around you. It will help your hidden power and a greater knowing.

Just as in the case of a man, who knew my teacher, the Hierophant, you may know them from past life experiences. He missed his teacher and his teacher missed him. They were reunited in this lesson.

Look deep within your Mandala, so that you may re-discover who you really are.

End of Transmission

Begin Open Channel

Lesson Twenty-Nine:
  King of Spades, received December 8, 1990
  Book of Wisdom, channeled from the Hierophant:

"The more you know the more "Knowing" will come to you." ERU

My Dear Brothers Hermit and Teacher,

There are many things in life that have an effect on our lives, as we do on each other. There are major earthquakes, floods, fires, tornadoes, hurricanes, eruptions, avalanches and submersions. These take lives, sometimes a few and other times tens of thousands. There is no discrimination in age, sex or rank. These seem terrible, yet, they do not affect the true you that continues on for eternity. For that part of you never dies.

We all know that when we do good deeds or help another, we build a great treasure. This treasure is expressed in help when we need it, the building of our psychic abilities or in our afterlife.

Although we strive to do good deeds, however, we are weak and have faults. But we should not let that set us back. We most likely have days when our faults seem to be magnified, when we look upon ourselves and think there is no good left in us. Do not let these feelings take hold of you. You are a beautiful person. There is a world of good in you. So, when these lowly thoughts come to you, push them out of your mind. Say to yourself, "I am not going to give into that weakness today. No matter what, I'm not giving in today." The only way to beat any weakness is to take it one day at a time. Human self-doubt is our greatest weakness.

Now lest you think it is easy, it is not! In fact, the first few weeks are the hardest. But remember; take it one day at a time. Each morning when you rise say to yourself, "My will is stronger than anything on earth. And I can overcome my faults." You will have moments when your mind will be seized, with the pleasure or the desire of that fault. Put it out of your mind. Become engaged in some mental or physical activity to take your mind off of it.

The Egyptians believed that when one died their heart was placed on a scale, by the gods and weighed against a feather of truth.

Every religion and society is supported by the principles of justice and/or punishment, heaven or hell. Thus, in a word we hear used most often, among certain circles, in this light, is the word Karma.

What is Karma?

The Sanskrit word for: "Action." This is the action of thought, will and deed; or thought, execution and action.

In Karma, we conceived an act, or we have the thought. Then we have the will whereby the act is executed. And lastly, we have the deed or action wherein all the effects and side effects take place as a consequence of the deed or deeds.

Now every thought, will and deed becomes a part of our spirit being or soul. With every action, a slow transmutation takes place in our being for good or ill.

Thus, the character of our being does not change overnight, but is slowly developed toward good or evil. It is this, the sum total of our actions that constitute our Karma.

Let me give you an example of good karma and bad karma.

Edward hears that one of his neighbors has fallen on bad times and is without food. Edward thinks to himself, I do not have a great storehouse of food, but I am not totally without food, either. So, he takes half of his food and gives it to his neighbor.

The neighbor had grown up with a bad attitude towards his relatives, friends of which he had a few, and neighbors. Now in this instance he came to know that his neighbor really did care about him. This filled him with feelings of goodness and joy.

As time passed the neighbor came into great wealth. He also came to realize that there are other neighbors in a sad state, without food or clothing. So, he went out and began to help those in need.

Edward had the thought and the will or execution in that he helped his neighbor. But the true action was not realized, until the neighbor helped others and they, in turn, helped their neighbors.

Thus, a single act of kindness not only changed a life, but it grew and spread.

William on the other hand, would take what didn't belong to him. His attitude was, whatever I take is mine, and, if others took care of what they have, I couldn't take it from then.

Now Robert was a builder of boxes. He cut the tree to build the box, drew stories upon the faces of the box, carved the pictures out of wood, and finished the wood. Now for all the time and love that he put into the making of each box, he received only enough money to pay his rent, feed and clothe his family, with hardly a penny left over. So, one day he decided to build an extra-large box. This, he hoped would provide some extra money, with which he could get his family some extra things they truly needed.

He spent many days and nights working at this task. The day before the rent was due, and there was little food left in his stores, he was happy to hear that someone was looking for just such a box that he had made. William had seen Robert working on the box and desired to have it also. During the night William took the box, while Robert and his family were sleeping.

In the morning Robert awoke to discover the box was missing. He searched to no avail. It had been taken, while he slept. Shortly thereafter, the landlord arrived to collect the rent. Since Robert could not pay the landlord, he and his family were put out into the street, much to their shame, and his tools were taken for payment due.

Because Robert and his family were sorely shamed, during the night they took their own lives. William's only thoughts were, maybe a potter will move in, I really need some new bowls.

Do not judge William, for he will have a heavy price to pay when his waiting is full. Now for those who believe that man only lives once, rebirth is skipped and your spirit moves right into the afterlife within the Penetration Dimension.

Karma comes in the form of an eternity of life review. The only way for reconciliation is to return to life to help the angels guide someone incarnate, who suffers from the same faults you suffered. Knowing how hard-headed humans can be, that is no easy chore.

This brings us to the Eleventh Ancient Law: "Judge no man, for you shall be judged by your judgment."

You have no right to judge another. But learn from every event that occurs in your life. For in the very next hour, you may commit the same deed. And further, how do you know that it is not preordained to produce some greater good, as a by-product, that will affect all of mankind?

Reincarnation and Karmic Debt

If you choose to believe in reincarnation, then that brings us to Karmic Debt. Let us use William as an example. He took what was not his, caused a family of four hardship, misery, eviction from their home and the sacrifice of their lives for shame. There must be some reconciliation for what he has done, if not in this life, then in the afterlife. Since he did these acts on the material plane, only on the material plane can his punishment be generated. Thus, he must re-inhabit lifetime after lifetime another body in misery and pain until he comes to a pure state.

The only reason the person comes back into another life, is to fulfill the Karmic Debt. That's making the one life scenario seem more understandable, but I don't wish to tamper with anyone's beliefs. Remember what my Master taught me that day at the water's edge.

Master ERU said, "Some people say we live many times. Some people say we never really live at all; we are merely the dream of a God fast asleep in the center of a giant lotus blossom. Some say a lot of things. What's important is what you believe because whatever you believe, if you really believe it, becomes the truth." That means that we have the power to manifest everything and nothing at all.

Some have asked why is it that a child may live a few hours or days and then die. To answer that, think on this example. If someone is dying of an illness, and there is suffering and pain, to avoid the length of suffering they take their life. Now maybe they only had a few more hours or days to live out to complete that life cycle. To complete the days that they were given, they are reborn, finish out their days and died of natural causes.

We should make every effort to help feed the hungry, clothe the naked, visit the sick and forgive those, who have wronged us. So, heed my words, do good works, offer them as reconciliation for our weaknesses, faults and pray. Most of all we must stop living the lies that have been passed down to us over the years.

The Truth vs. The Lie

Remember the riddle "Trial of Truth": When is truth a lie? It is when enough people choose not to believe the truth despite factual support. When is a lie the truth, when enough people choose to believe the lie without any factual support.

We accept lies as truth, because we are too lazy to dig deeper for the proof or a greater understanding. We are told to, "Just except it on faith." In many cases, we accept second hand truth without any verification, because it's easier. In order to find the absolute truth, one must have all the facts and ultimate understanding of the truth in question.

For example: A tent is set up in a room. You are asked what color the tent is without being able to see it. Without seeing the tent, you do not have any way of stating its true color. Ten individuals are brought into the room to view the tent. They are asked to write the color of the tent on a piece of paper. Upon leaving the room, the ten give you their truth to the color of the tent. You examine their answers.

Three say the tent is orange, two say it's yellowish, four say it's gray and one person says the tent is red. From the answers, what truth can you arrive at?

What color is the tent? All ten gave you their perception of the truth. The only truth here is that all ten have a belief the tent is the color they saw, but belief is not the truth, without digging deeper. The ten people are brought back in to meet with you. You can ask the group one question, what would it be that would help you reach a better level of truth? Think about it for a moment then reverse the words below for the answer.

?DNILBROLOC-UOY-ERA

Most people regard their perceptions or belief as truth. Truth is an elusive thing, but please never stop pursuing it. In this case, all ten had sight, but only one could see. However, was his perception the truth? The only way of knowing a greater truth would be to view the tent for yourself, but would you see the true color?

The Eleventh Ancient Law: "Judge no man, for you shall be judged by your judgment."

End of Transmission

In closing, of the first twenty-nine of fifty-three lessons from the Atlantis *Book of Wisdom*, I am giving you a list of the first eleven Ancient Laws of Wisdom. You should try hard to commit them to memory and apply them to your everyday life.

Many will find the Light because of you.

Thank you for your service!

Ancient Laws of Wisdom

1st law   "The more you use your ability to help another, the more your ability will grow." Taken from lesson one.

2nd law   "The door to the psychic world is not opened with a ram, but with the slightest caress." Taken from lesson one.

3rd law   "The law of love is unchangeable, in that, as you do it to the least of your brethren. You do to your creator." Taken from lesson two.

4th law   "The White Light can only be used once to heal any one person." Taken from lesson five.

5th law   "He who needs no one is no one." Taken from lesson nine.

6th law   "Sit quietly, humbly and patiently at the feet of the wise for one day others will sit at your feet and drink from your cup of wisdom." Taken from lesson nine.

7th law   "With all of our power and wisdom, we have little effect on the macrocosm or microcosm, however the microcosm of our being can have a great effect on the macrocosms around us." Taken from lesson thirteen.

8th law   "Absolute faith emanates only from the inner or spiritual self through conviction. And contemplation alone, without absolute faith attending it, will not advance you one iota." Taken from lesson fourteen.

9th law   "Words of power are an individual manifestation." From lesson fifteen.

10th law   "The Powers of Wisdom consume those who would misuse them, and from that, there is no escape." Taken from lesson nineteen.

11th law   "Judge no man, for you shall be judged by your judgment." Taken from lesson twenty-nine.

About the Authors

Edward-Michael Jagen is a U.S. Army veteran, retired Washington, D.C. Police Intelligence Investigator, and dedicated child abuse protection advocate. He is the author of the *Good Knight* fairytale series and the *Good Knight Crime and Violence Prevention Program*, which has been used in the national public school system, as a child protection teaching tool. After officially being dubbed, "The Blue Knight of Maryland," by the Governor, he set out on a quest to educate children, with the wisdom to protect themselves from those who would manipulate, deceive and/or abduct them. Over the past 30 years, Sir Edward and his Angel Knight volunteers have reached millions nationwide. For his many years of public service, he has been awarded The National Jefferson "Gold Medal" Award, the President's Service Award for Public Safety, the Maryland Governor's Award for Volunteerism and received the Silver Star for Bravery after being inducted into the American Police Hall of Fame.

Sophia Key West is a devoted mother and grandmother, a twenty-nine-year veteran health care practitioner, with a holistic and integrative focus. She is a renowned Reiki Master/teacher/practitioner, Cranio-Sacral therapist, Certified Aromatherapist and wellness catalyst coach. Sophia conducts a certification program in the Book Wisdom lessons for use at the personal or professional level. She still accepts private sessions as well, however there is a waiting list. A highly sought after lecturer, Sophia is an acclaimed author of the *Super Book of Family Safety* and Good Knight Child Safety Awareness video productions. As the volunteer COS of the Good Knight Child Empowerment Network Inc., the 501-C3 non-profit organization Jagen established in 1985, Sophia oversees programs, services and the museum's exhibits. She has also received many awards over her twenty-three years of volunteer service, to include the Maryland Governor's Volunteer of the Year Award for 2005, the Volvo Hometown Hero Award and the Presidential Volunteer Service Lifetime Achievement Award for Public Safety, from President Bush.

When Jagen passed the mantle to Sophia, upon his retirement, he also gave her his memoirs to adapt for publication. She is currently working on a script for a feature film, based on the *Diary of an Angel-Knight* series.

Follow us on Facebook @angelsdream144

> **To my children:**
>
> **May your light shine bright for all to see!**

---Sophia

The best way to make your dreams come true is to wake up.

---Paul Valéry

Made in the USA
Las Vegas, NV
26 September 2022

55981636R00236